BREAKING FAITH

Also by Graham E. Fuller

Turkey and the Arab Spring: Leadership in the Middle East
Bozorg Press, May 2014

Three Truths and a Lie: a Memoir
September 2012

A World Without Islam
Little Brown, August 2010

The New Turkish Republic: Turkey's Pivotal Role in the Middle East
US Institute of Peace, 2008

The Future of Political Islam
Palgrave, May 2003

The Arab Shi'a: The Forgotten Muslims (with Rend Francke)
St. Martin's, 1999

Turkey's Kurdish Question (with Henri Barkey)
Rowman and Littlefield, 1997

A Sense of Siege:
The Geopolitics of Islam and the West (with Ian Lesser)
Westview, 1994

The New Foreign Policy of Turkey:
From the Balkans to Western China (with Ian Lesser)
Westview, 1993

The Democracy Trap: Perils of the Post-Cold War World
Dutton, 1992

The Center of the Universe: The Geopolitics of Iran
Westview, 1991

How to Learn a Foreign Language
Storm King Press, 1987

BREAKING FAITH

A NOVEL OF ESPIONAGE AND AN AMERICAN'S CRISIS OF

CONSCIENCE IN PAKISTAN

GRAHAM E. FULLER

Bozorg Press

Published by Bozorg Press
www.grahamefuller.com

Library and Archives Canada Cataloguing in Publication

Fuller, Graham E., 1937-, author
     Breaking faith : a novel / Graham E. Fuller.

Issued in print and electronic formats.
ISBN 978-0-9937514-1-7 (pbk.).--ISBN 978-0-9937514-3-1 (pdf)

          I. Title.

PS8611.U445B74 2015   C813'.6   C2015-900656-2
                                               C2015-900657-0

Cover image by Maryam Mughal: the Badshahi Mosque in Lahore, Pakistan. License for use of front cover image painting issued to author of the book. Copyrights reserved by Corporate Art Task Force. E-Gallery: 1-catf.artistwebsites.com

Author photo by Ana Santos

Contents

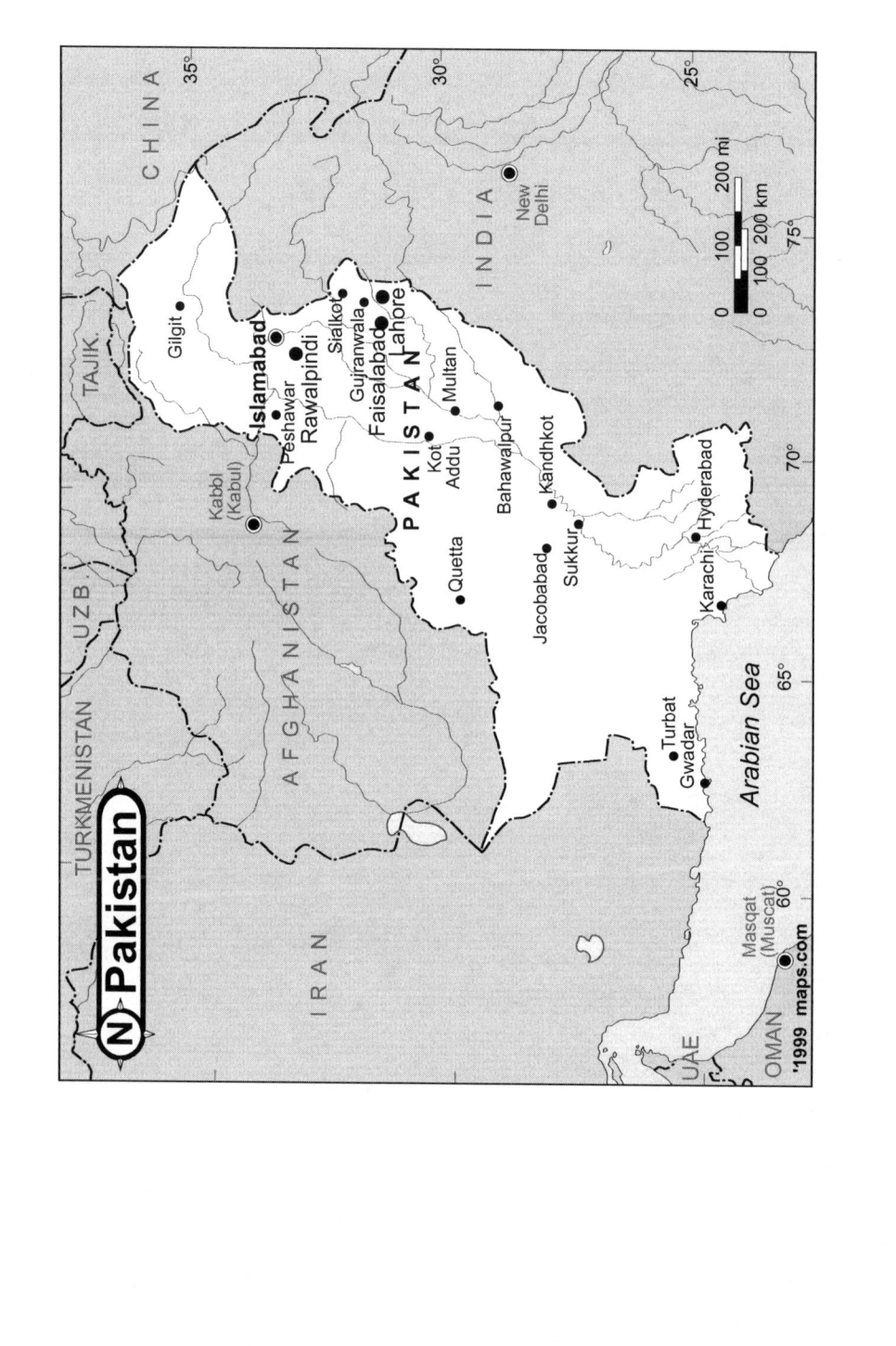

Prologue

Treason—it's an ugly word. I can see that thought crossing your mind as you listen to me. It's been gnawing away at me for some time now. What does it actually mean? Is it a thought? A state of mind? An act? And what is called treasonous today, might it not be acceptable tomorrow?

It's on my mind because it's now clearer to me than I ever would have expected in my life. It's been a long time brewing. I look around and feel out of step: the system, the people, their thinking and assumptions, their jargon and in-jokes—these people live in a different world. It's like they're living inside some huge compound with a high wall around it—but they don't know it.

OK, it's a wall that wasn't fully evident to me for a very long time either. But now it is. What's more, I've been up to the top of that wall, looked out, and seen that there's a whole different world and way of perceiving things out there.

That's the hell of it. Once you've peered over, you can't just forget and go back down the ladder again like nothing's happened. You've changed. You've lost your virginity, your innocence, or your ignorance—whatever you choose to call it. But what do you do then, if other people don't see that wall, much less anything beyond it? The only way to survive is to pretend you don't see it either. But that eats away at your sanity in the end.

Chapter One

Mission

You do not become a "dissident" just because you decide one day to take up this most unusual career. You are thrown into it by your personal sense of responsibility, combined with a complex set of external circumstances. You are cast out of the existing structures and placed in a position of conflict with them. It begins as an attempt to do your work well, and ends with being branded an enemy of society.

- Vaclav Havel

Today would be Jonah's last day on earth. He would never make it to his brick-making job again—in these weeks as the feast of Christmas receded behind. His mother had been sick all night in their run-down house that was unblessed even by running water. Unable to drink or eat, she lay on her thick cotton mattress with its cover of crude and exaggerated floral design, rolling and moaning in the little alcove off the common family room, clutching her stomach. The smell of kerosene cooking stoves and the contents of their day's curries drifted in through the window, barred but without glass, affording an intimate exposure to the sounds and activities of surrounding tightly-packed dwellings. Her stomach pains, which had been growing worse for months, reacted poorly to the pungency of food smells in the air.

Jonah was the last of seven sons and three daughters in a Pakistani Christian family in Lahore; their father had died seven years ago in a construction accident, his two oldest sisters were married and came by every few days to help out. Jonah and his youngest sister, who had already gone out to her morning work as a seamstress, were the last children in the home to keep an eye on their mother. Jonah fetched a rickshaw to take his mother to the hospital. Their social status did not command rapid attention and she was left on a gurney waiting for hours. Only much later did Jonah get a few minutes with a doctor where he obtained some medicine for her. He brought her home again by rickshaw, laid her down to rest among her pillows and then immediately set out on his bicycle, many hours late for work. Then, at the edge of the crowded road he was greeted by the telltale hiss of air from his tire. His workplace was still several miles away and he had no spare tube. Cursing his luck he ran his bicycle to the nearest repair shop.

Jonah knew his foreman disliked him. He claimed Jonah was slow at his job, not sharp enough to pick up on the new machine technology or to remember the right combination and sequence for the mixing of materials for the bricks. When he got angry he called Jonah a dirty Christian, and never missed an opportunity to severely penalize him. Jonah urged the tire repairman to hurry up, but he seemed to be taking his time, gabbing with other customers, smirking at Jonah. Jonah finally grabbed him by his shirt and told him he might lose his job. The repairman cursed Jonah as a Christian, as a simpleton. "And you're a dirty Muslim," Jonah hurled back.

The die was cast. The fateful words had been uttered. Events could now only flow along a predestined course. Bystanders said they had heard Jonah curse the Prophet Muhammad. Several people grabbed Jonah, threw him to the ground, and someone called the police to report him. But Jonah managed to elude them, ran out, grabbed another bicycle leaning against the shop, and took off towards the Christian community center for refuge. Six men jumped in a car, others followed on foot and bicycles through the crowded and dusty streets. Jonah, in his panic, collided with an elderly woman carrying a huge basket of onions. She fell heavily, onions scattering. Jonah was not about to stop. He sped on, then jumped off the bike, dashed into the Christian center and locked the door behind him, panting in fear. A dozen pursuers came up only half a minute later and banged on the door, demanding that he come out as a fugitive from the police. Three other Christians in the center grew terrified at the growing mob outside. Voices yelled that Jonah had struck the onion-woman, leaving her unconscious and bleeding in the street. The other Christians at the center told Jonah he was creating danger and must leave. Meanwhile word went through the crowd that Jonah had cursed Islam and the Prophet and then had fled from the police and killed a woman.

After banging on the door, the crowd grew unruly. A man broke a window with a metal rod and attempted to climb in. The Christians in the center rushed to push him back out. A second window was breached and a man forced his way in and opened the door to the crowd. Dozens rushed in and grabbed all four Christians, not knowing which was Jonah. They proceeded to beat them with sticks. Someone claimed they had found a torn Quran in the building, sullied; did it not smell of urine? Another said that several Christians had been rubbing a Quran in mud while cursing the Prophet. Others said Jonah had killed a Muslim and was in flight from the law. The four Christians were beaten to near unconsciousness and lay inert on the concrete floor. As the crowd bellowed with excitement, a heavy man with glassy eyes in a grey *shalwar-kameez* dragged a canister of gasoline into the building and sloshed the contents out around the floor. He lit a match, tossed it onto the ground and retreated to watch the flames fuse into a rising inferno. The center was soon burning furiously, beyond salvage by the time the fire truck arrived. The firemen were able to save only two of the men from the flames. Jonah was not one of them.

Confusion reigned as more people gathered in a crowd, lurid accounts escalating. The violence stimulated the blood lust, inciting the crowd to further mayhem. A bearded man in their midst emerged, shouting "The Nasrani eye clinic! The missionary eye clinic! That is where these infidels preach corruption! They blaspheme Islam in the Christian clinic!" And he led a jeering crowd down the street to the well-known "Christian" clinic, only a few blocks away. By this time several in the crowd appeared well-prepared for the task, lugging a heavy beam of wood from a nearby construction site to break down the door of the clinic.

As the mob advanced on the clinic, a boy from the community ran to the house of the missionary, Harley Anders. Harley, who had been taking a nap, struggled to grasp the excited and incoherent account of the boy but knew he had to protect his clinic. Just as he arrived, the crowd had succeeded in smashing down the clinic door and swept inside. Harley could hear the shattering of his optical equipment and the breaking of bottles. Enraged, he pushed his way inside, screaming at the mob in Punjabi, "How dare you destroy this clinic! This is for the community! Get out, get out!" Harley was hit over the head with a bottle and dragged outside. A Molotov cocktail appeared out of nowhere, was lit and hurled through the broken window where in seconds flames began leaping up. Harley, in his fury, lost all fear and stood up again against the mob, gray hair and face streaming with blood, cursing them. Someone struck him in the face with a tire iron and he fell heavily. As Harley lay on the ground, he was kicked in the face and torso, beyond the grasp of those who recognized him. Some in the crowd yelled, "Don't kill him! He is a doctor!" "Leave him alone, he is a good person!"

The remains of Harley's clinic went up in flames behind him. The large sign proclaiming "Clinic" that had hung out over the street, its big symbol of a blue eye visible from a block away, was soon within reach of the flames. The sign—and its watchful eye—gradually turned brown and then black, vision extinguished, as it fell to the street. The crowd—some sated, some by now ashamed—dispersed with a range of different accounts to propagate. Some Muslims saw it as an act to defend the Faith of the Prophet in the neighborhood. But many others felt a disturbance in their hearts; most knew the act had been dishonorable and against the teachings of their Faith. Some realized ignorant mob passions had devastated a man who served the community.

The local news that evening repeated various embroidered stories, including one by a mullah who claimed that Harley Anders had long been preaching against Islam in his center. Security forces announced that the entire neighborhood where the incidents had occurred had been closed off, including the area where many of the Christians lived. Terrified at the presence of explosive emotions around them, the community gathered together to desperately collect weapons for self-defense. When a police guard arrived, one of the community attacked a policeman with a knife, fearing they would be arrested. More police were called out. Senior security officials denounced the incident and imposed a curfew until sectarian passions cooled. Another senior official announced that mob rule and mob justice would not be tolerated; a full investigation would take place. Further violence from any quarter would be severely punished.

The turmoil of the torrid and volatile afternoon and evening slowly subsided but emotions had been stoked high. Harley Anders, whose mission it had long been to operate the clinic, lay between life and death. And nothing is ever forgotten.

*   *   *

Alex Anders forced open an eye in the darkened cabin—thirty minutes to go, and one hour behind schedule. Two back-to-back red-eyes—Minneapolis-London and London-Karachi—had intensified the misery of traveling half way around the globe. This last short hop—Karachi-Lahore—would complete the journey, back to his former world, to visit his parents for Christmas.

His stomach was back in the last airport and grew more unsettled with other recurring anxieties about his arrival. He already could see his father, early at the airport for sure, muttering, checking his watch, fretting, deprived of absolute control.

Coming home. And under lousy circumstances. The letter from his mother had confirmed part of what he had feared. How much could he even call it home anymore? The excitement of returning, now in his senior year at university, combined with his new and evolving sense of self-autonomy—who he was becoming. It hadn't been just two years away—it was a tectonic shift in the order of his own mind. Would his parents be even meeting the same person anymore? Filled with the sophomoric wisdom of a university education, would he still view his parents in the same light as before?

He had been warned by his older brother Jack, who made the trip back at Christmas last year. "It's not a good scene, little brother. Lucky you weren't here. Dad's little Christian community is shrinking, less and less people showing up on Sunday, and he's getting more pissed and more paranoid. Attendance at his clinic is dropping off. He sometimes takes it out on mom. He yells at her, over nothing. She's withdrawing, doesn't have much to say and just tries to stay out of his way. Where have you been? You should get your ass out there with me this Christmas." Alex was used to Jack's jaundiced views of things, even if he was half right. They might have to take firm action to open his father's eyes to a possibly deteriorating environment.

This was not a task he had wanted to come back to, but he felt an overdue obligation. And his mother had begged him to come back for Christmas this year. Alex had initially hesitated, preferring to stay away from a messy situation. And then the letter from Majeed, who tried to tactfully warn him—"Alex, you should know, missionaries are not very welcome here these days… not a good situation for your parents. The mood of the country is shifting."

While he was worried, Alex wasn't really surprised. He'd always felt his father's mission—seeking to convert Muslims to Christianity—was a bit of a fool's errand. And every misgiving Alex had ever felt about religion had only been reinforced through his courses at university; things had never been so clear to him before. Trying to convert Muslims, even if it was partly through the means of medical service to the community through his father's eye clinic, was one thing. But now courting potential violence was something else. Alex knew his father wouldn't take kindly to a long-absent college-age son returning as a newly-minted oracle of wisdom, freely assessing the validity of his father's life enterprise.

The fading lights of Lahore stretched out before him against the pink of the dawn. Allama Iqbal Airport. Steps rolled up against the newly opened aircraft door that admitted the damp and acrid outside air—the smell of cooking fires, some undoubtedly still fueled by dried cow dung in the countryside, the signature odor of the Indian subcontinent. It combined with the whiff of jet fuel on the tarmac. The December morning air still retained a bit of coolness, a welcome respite before the searing temperatures of late spring when all creation would sit gasping and parched in anticipation of monsoon relief. Alex felt a twinge of guilt. This should be an exciting moment, a return home, but in some ways he wished he didn't have to be here.

He advanced half asleep in the glacial passport line, surrounded by other bleary eyes, some Pakistanis in traditional dress, other Pakistanis in Western clothes, some Europeans. An impassive immigration officer idly flipped through the pages of passports scanning for nothing in particular. He stamped it as if annoyed at his life's calling and tossed the American passport back at Alex. At the baggage pickup, a porter seized the opportunity to grab Alex's bag as Alex reached for it; Alex reluctantly yielded. He knew the game: these weren't services rendered by porters to travelers, they were often services by travelers rendered to porters—God knows they needed to keep body and soul together.

As they exited the terminal Alex began the search for familiar faces in the sea of humanity around the seething gate. His mother spotted him first; waving, she worked her way through the crowd to give him a hungry hug. His father chose not to negotiate the crowd or hasten the emotional awkwardnesses of greeting, but when Alex finally broke free, his father advanced and embraced him stiffly. "You're late."

"Sorry, but I wasn't piloting the plane, Dad." And did he catch a whiff of sweet cloying odor on his father's breath?

His father tried to assert control over the bag but the porter held on to his sinecure—each extra minute was money in the pocket. His mother lubricated the encounter with a series of neutral inquiries about the details of his flight as they negotiated their way to the parking lot.

"Same old Landrover, I see," Alex remarked. "Would you like me to drive, Dad?"

"I'm perfectly capable of driving, young man. Take a seat in the front."

"Oh, son, I've missed you so," his mother hugged him again, surveying him. "And you look well. You've gotten taller than your father now. Though I see you've let your hair grow. You'll have to educate people here about that, they'll think you're a hippy."

"Nah, Mom, I'm just up with the times. You haven't been back to the States for a while."

"The Beatles never made their way to Pakistan," his father observed.

"Well, anyway, people in this community may need a little shaking up, they're kind of out of touch."

"No, not out of touch," his father asserted. "Just living in a more timeless world."

Alex tossed his luggage into the back and reluctantly took his seat up front with his father, who appeared in good enough shape to drive.

"So how are you feeling, Dad? The clinic still doing well?"

"I'm OK, still plenty to do."

"How're things going with the whole community?"

"Coming along, coming along. Rome wasn't built in a day."

"No, I guess not in Pakistan either."

The car negotiated an entry into the outlying orbit of the turbulent traffic like an asteroid entering a solar system, chaos theory on full display: drivers constantly seizing a few meters advantage over another when opportunity presented itself, rewriting the traffic rules on the run. Alex had lost his sea legs for Lahore traffic. He slammed his foot onto an imaginary brake pedal several times as they jockeyed for position in the sea of vehicles, his father leaning on the horn—a driver's most essential piece of equipment here.

"Mom, you've been keeping well? Are you finding enough to keep you occupied in the empty nest?"

"Oh yes, son, I'm fine. But I think about you both so often, I'm just glad that you're safe back at home in the States."

"Yeah, college is pretty safe—except for rowdy hallway parties."

"Well, I'm sure you're not a rowdy…We're happy you have a chance at last to experience a good life back in the States. Life is more than just Lahore and its problems."

"You're right, it is a different world there. It's been strange getting used to things actually working, and other conveniences—but the food is still better back here at home in Lahore."

Beams from the back seat.

As they waited at a long intersection, Alex tested the waters further. "Majeed wrote to me about the situation here, more religious fanatics. He says the atmosphere for foreigners here these days isn't so great. He's afraid it's deteriorating, maybe some Westerners thinking about leaving. I hope you guys are being careful."

"Don't take Majeed's opinion as gospel," his father growled. "He's still wet behind the ears. But yes, it's more awkward now."

"Awkward?"

"A lot of radical ideas creeping in from outside. The war in Afghanistan against the Soviet occupation there—it whipped up fundamentalists everywhere."

"But aren't we helping in the war against the Soviets there?"

"Yes, but there's still suspicion about US motives, imperial power and all that. Besides, the US isn't seen as really all that friendly to Pakistan—more pro-Indian. And lots of Pakistanis are angry the US is helping prop up the military regime here—keeping President Zia in power."

"I don't understand. I thought it was Zia who put through all these new Islamic laws, why would the US support all that?"

"Well, Zia seems to think he can gain more legitimacy with the people that way. Anyway, we've got a whole lot more Islamic fervor here than we've ever seen before."

The familiar crowds thickened around them in the clamorous downtown streets; people on bikes pushed up against the edge of the car waiting for the traffic policeman on the box to wave them on through the intersection according to some system known only to himself. Alex had forgotten how claustrophobic the enveloping mass of humanity could be. Faces peered into the car, and Alex suddenly became aware of feeling white again.

The passage of time and changing circumstances had imposed changes on his parents. His mother had gained weight, her skin hung more loosely around her neck and she seemed to have acquired a slight stoop; his father looked thinner, his beard whitening, liver spots more prominent on his hands, face and neck. A certain overall stiffness of movement, maybe reflecting a state of mind. He seemed less alert to all the pedestrian conditions while driving through the crowds and Alex a few times inadvertently hissed out, "Watch it!"

"I've been driving in these conditions most of my life, thank you very much. Looks like you're the one who's lost touch with traffic in the subcontinent."

And they drove for a while in silence, down past the crowded sidewalks—a cultural slide show in themselves: garish movie billboards advertising lurid action figures with slashing vines of Urdu writing descending angularly across them, the brilliantly colored material hanging from the sari shops, smells of kebabs from sidewalk grills, rickshaw putt-putts spewing dark exhaust and jostling for position, people everywhere, pedestrians darting out at random. He'd forgotten the intensity of the scene.

"And how's Jack? When is he arriving?"

His mother glanced away. "I'm afraid your brother's not going to be here in time for Christmas day. He's arriving a few days later."

"How come?"

"He says he's too busy at business school. He said there was too much going on, exams. I guess he couldn't get away in time."

"I can't believe that he couldn't make it back in time for Christmas day, since I did."

His father interjected. "Well, it's nice that you could grace us after two years. But let's call a spade a spade. This is mostly about that girlfriend of his, her influence."

"Who's his girlfriend?"

"We don't know much about her, and of course we haven't met her," his mother offered. "But we're unhappy about the arrangement."

"Arrangement?"

His father broke in. "She's moved in with him, that's what. We've had some words with Jack over this, it's entirely inappropriate and we've told him we don't accept this—living together like that...in sin."

Living in sin. Alex felt a twinge of sexual envy.

"I'm afraid our communications have broken down," his mother offered. "He knows we're unhappy. But we can't stop him."

"If I had had my way we'd tell him we don't want him back here—as long as this relationship persists. It's a violation of our deepest beliefs. But your mother, typically, has begged to let him come back."

"OK Dad, but you do know that this isn't all that unusual any more. I mean, lots of young people are living together these days."

"That doesn't make it right. It's very clear it's a sin, it's fornication."

"Things have changed since when you were young, Dad. You've got to roll with the times. Surely you don't want to destroy your ties with your son just because you don't approve of new values."

"You see, Harley, that's what I've said," said his mother. "Family is more important than moral positions, we can't break family bonds."

"New values? It's no values! We can't abandon our beliefs just to keep the family happy. But, no, your mother has prevailed, I won't lock the door against him. Still, I can't say I will welcome him with any warmth under the circumstances."

It's going to be a great Christmas.

*   *   *

The soft medicinal smell of eucalyptus trees confirmed his return. They drove up to the dun gates. Even before Alex had gotten out of the car to open the way into the compound, Nazir the cook and Aftab the bearer came running out, faces beaming. Alex didn't recognize a new gardener, who nodded his head from a distance, placing his hand upon his heart in greeting. A long ritual of greeting phrases in Urdu and Punjabi from Nazir and Aftab ensued, inquiring after his welfare in every possible variation. Alex at first responded in Urdu but quickly found that, although he understood everything said, he was stumbling around beyond the old set phrases, groping for words. He was embarrassed to have to start answering in English. Still, the language would come back soon enough, and home wasn't home without the servants he had grown up with, the pillars of his daily existence.

Alex stepped back to look over the long bungalow built in single storey brick, vines crawling up the side, the spacious veranda, the manicured garden, flowers and trees. Mixed emotions swept through him, evoking his whole childhood. The garden where he used to climb the trees. A flash of old anger about how his father had failed to notice his infected eye until Alex had largely lost his vision in it. Loss of the eye had never prevented him from doing things like playing soccer, and he had learned how to compensate in judging distance with his good eye.

He walked down the cool tiled hallways to the back and found his room. Except for an abnormal degree of tidiness and a musty smell, it was unchanged: shelves of books, his sports trophies, a few posters and pictures of soccer champions on the wall. It was his room, but another him, a step back in time. Back home, yes, but it was really his parents' house now and he was still their child. He sensed his newly-acquired independence and sovereignty becoming subtly eroded in the parental presence, making it harder to deliver the message. It was really their house, and it resonated with their rhythms to which he would have to conform, now almost as a guest. His life was still open to their review, scrutiny and measure, even as he was about to take their measure too, maybe more severely. He worried about having to grapple with these issues of his parents' welfare. But he would yield up neither his autonomy nor his concerns.

"Why don't you lie down and take a nice nap, son, and we'll make it a late noon meal, it's been a long trip." His mother placed her hand on his shoulder. "I'm so glad you've come. And I hope you can talk to your father." *Yes, it has been a long journey.*

*   *   *

At one o'clock dinner, the main meal of the day, Aftab the bearer was still presiding maestro over the symphony of the grand British Raj-style table: its impeccably white tablecloth, rigorously replaced after receiving each meal's spattered offerings of curry-stains; series of plates in graduated sizes, one on top of the other, a daunting battery of cutlery on each side. On top of the plate perched a mammoth fresh napkin rendered into an extravagant origami of folded linen: large and elaborately wrapped at the base, suggestive of a turban with a crinkled fan-shape of linen extending upwards from the middle like a flower nearly eight inches high. It always seemed a sacrilege to dismantle such a creation and place it on your lap. Indeed, his parents' earlier life in Ohio could never have prepared them for all this dinner-table pomp either, but Raj traditions were integral to any well-to-do house where self-respecting local servants presided. To slack on protocol was not informality, it was a slight to the servants themselves, a suggestion they were no longer masters of the tradition. And Aftab himself still wore his own fine white turban with its fan-like flourish at the top—comfortably conforming to an earlier era of Victorian colonial functionaries. Aftab relished the role; he had been with Alex's parents since their arrival, working his way up to his position of trust and authority as chief bearer in the house.

His mother reached out to take Alex's hand as they offered grace. His father gave thanks for Alex's return and asked that his children be guided by wisdom. Alex hesitated, then opted not to interpret the remark as personally directed at him.

Nazir had remembered one of his favorite lamb curries, *roghan josh;* Alex spooned its glistening perfumed sauce over his basmati rice, cooked to perfection so that each grain was distinct—so aromatic the rice alone could be eaten all by itself with pleasure.

An unwritten truce to stay off contentious subjects was duly observed for everyone's comfort: they chatted about unseasonably warm weather, the servants' lives, their comings and goings, changes in the household, neighbors; harsher issues remained lurking in the antechamber.

"Alex, we haven't heard much from you while you've been away, except for a few notes from you, and your aunt. How are your studies coming along? How are you doing in Arabic?"

"Actually, I wanted to tell you, Dad. I finally decided not to major in Middle East studies and Arabic after all. It was just too close to home. I wanted to try something new."

"But I thought you were really keen on this—to be a specialist on this part of the world. You have a good foundation in Urdu, it's all been part of your life here—our lives."

"I know Dad, but I just wanted a break from it all, to do something different."

"So what have you opted for?"

"Actually I'm in Russian language and lit. I just got fascinated by the Russian writers in a comparative lit course I took. I really love it, it's a real change."

"Russian! But why? Of course I know—Tolstoy and all that. But the Soviet Union is a mess, it's… a threat to civilization. The whole communist system is a curse to the world. They trumpet atheism, kill their own citizens, invade Afghanistan. I mean, what's the appeal? What's the use?"

"I can't explain it, Dad, it just fascinates me. And if the Soviets are the enemy then it's important to understand them. I like the Russian language, it's an interesting culture. It's such a change of pace from all this life here."

His father fell silent. He seemed to take Alex's decision as a personal slight to him, to the family's life and its work in Pakistan. Alex decided to hold off on discussing his parents' future in Pakistan for now.

His mother anxiously took up the slack, passing along news to Alex about family friends and acquaintances—oil on the waters. His father seemed irritable, had little to say for the rest of the meal and retired to his study thereafter. The hours lost in travel halfway around the world suddenly unloaded upon Alex and after a short walk around the neighborhood he went back to his childhood room early to overcome his exhaustion and to face the new day afresh.

*   *   *

Breakfast the next morning was of course also a Pakistani affair. His parents had bent to the environment—at least in respect to food. American-style breakfasts were an abomination in the hands of Pakistani cooks anyway. And his father had wanted to enter into the rhythm of Pakistani life so he could develop the sensitivities to convey the gospel most effectively. Alex could not remember a time when he had eaten fried eggs, hash browns, or pancakes at home. And bacon was of course strictly out of the question.

The smell of the dishes continued to flood memories back to him. Nazir brought out a tray with *halwa puri cholay,* the center of a Pakistani breakfast: chickpeas and potato cooked with ginger, chilies and spices, then a sweet *halwa* made of semolina, dried fruits, almonds, cashews and ghee; and, his favorite, the irresistible *puris*, crispy feather-light little balloons of wheat flour that puffed up into small hollow pillow shapes when deep fried. He had missed puris and only occasionally got them in a cheap Indian restaurant in Minneapolis where they were amateurish, thick and greasy. And he had begged Nazir to make for him one of his other favorite dishes, *Aloo Paratha*, potatoes blended with garlic, onion, chilies, and spices, all stuffed inside a delicious buttery whole-wheat flat bread. He had tried to describe these breakfast dishes to his friends in the US, but received blank looks from most of them, prisoners of the anemic Yankee cooking that was only slowly giving way to the impact of Asians, Mediterraneans and Latinos who were jump-starting American popular food. In the States, Alex often found himself going to small ethnic groceries to buy more interesting and spicy food. He did have a good Indian friend who occasionally invited him home for the authentic taste he so missed.

Breakfast had barely been served when Alex decided to open to his main concern.

"Dad, I know we didn't really have a chance to talk about it yet, but I'm worried about how you guys are doing here. I wonder if you have any plans for the future, if things should change here for the worse."

"Worse? It's never been easy, and there are always ups and downs. But if you are asking if we're ready to quit, the answer is no. We're not quitters."

"No, not quitting. But frankly, Dad, I sometimes feel like you're up against a stone wall here…with all this missionary effort."

"Look, let's not get into that again. It's not easy, but it's the Lord's work. It's what we were meant to be doing." Alex exchanged glances with his mother across the table.

"I'm just thinking about common sense, your own welfare here."

"Well, thank you for your concern, but this is where we've chosen to live and serve, in good times and bad. That's not about to change."

"Do you think things could come to physical violence here?"

"Against us? No. It can be a rough society in some ways. Maybe periodic violence among some local groups. But we've never felt any threat against us personally. Nothing to change anything." His father's answers came terse, clipped, canned, deflecting, unrevealing. Conversation designed to disengage, rather than engage.

"What's different then?"

"More bully boys around, trying to enforce strict Islamic norms. More fundamentalist prejudice against Christians. A lot of this is Saudi-inspired thinking—and Saudi money. And I'm afraid there's a lot of anger against the US right now, American policies toward Pakistan and the like. That rubs off sometimes."

"But against you, no change?"

"No, not really."

"But, I mean, you wouldn't be planning to stay here forever in any case, right? You'd plan on retiring at some point."

"That is too far down the road for us to consider now. It's unhealthy to be thinking about giving up."

"OK, fine, I don't mean giving up. I just hope you guys are going to be realistic about things here… I mean, as you get older."

"We're not ready to be put out to pasture yet, young man. You'd be better served to think about arranging your own future instead of meddling in ours."

"It's not meddling, it's just that…" he glanced at his mother again, "times change and you have to adapt. Jack and I are concerned about you both staying on here."

"Thank you for your concern. I'm sure your mother has put you up to this conversation as well. Now let's give that subject a rest."

*   *   *

Alex's gaze drifted out the windows, out onto the lawn with its flame trees, jacarandas, and hibiscus. Yes, it was still in his blood, this place whose palette of colors, sounds and daily human rhythms constituted the sole reality of his youth. Whatever he was becoming, wherever he was going, this had been the starting point.

But he had to speak out. His father seemed increasingly cut off from reality while his mother just fretted, tried to accommodate him, and was occasionally the butt of his father's irritation for all of that. His parents had believed their mission of saving souls here could make a difference, but now new religious fervor was beginning to shape the Pakistani identity more intensely. Alex felt rising impatience to bring his message of clarity and direction to his parents' drifting ship. Their attitudes seemed still rooted in the values of small town mid-western American life. Alex hadn't grown up in Ohio—his own life's roots were here.

But how to persuade them? Alex saw things more clearly now. His courses at university had talked about the psychological and cultural elements of identity and religious belief. He could understand much better how his parents' own background and experiences had pushed them in this obsessive direction. What they had been nourishing, practicing—it was the Truth to them, so why shouldn't it be offered to the heathen? Or were they perhaps blinder than the people whose eyes they were trying to open?

*   *   *

His mind wandered back to his earliest memories. Wrapped figures move through the chill of the winter morning mist, men with earth-hued blankets around their shoulders covering long tunics and ballooning baggy pants; women carrying baskets perched above long shapeless robes. The smell of diesel hangs in the air as extravagantly decorated trucks, dangerously overladen, their drivers fueled by little more than tea, cigarettes and faith, move out early on their runs. All around the sounds of the day opening in the bazaar, periodic arguments breaking out in the distinct rhythms and intonations of Punjabi, Urdu, and Pashto.

A small white child with blond hair wearing Western short pants in the bustle of a Pakistani market, lost but for the cook grasping his small hand as they negotiate the bazaar on the regular shopping expeditions. His impressionable young mind absorbs the colors, smells, textures and sounds of a pulsing market place, not yet sanitized into the cellophaned efficiencies of a Western supermarket. Pieces of meat remain nakedly associated with the original animal: whole skinned sheep, their eyes more prominent in death; goat, and even buffalo, carcasses hung from hooks, freshly killed that morning, waiting for customers to point out the cut they want to be sliced off and rolled up in a sheet of newspaper for the midday meal before the butcher runs out of fresh meat and closes down till next morning.

The cook and his small charge navigate their way around the maze of wooden bins, the pungency of turmeric in mounds of brilliant distilled yellow, whole coriander seeds awaiting roasting and grinding in the home, cumin and fenugreek seeds, the staple of any kitchen; fiery hot dark-red chilies dried and flaking, fresh green curry leaves waiting for hot ghee to release their elusive aromatic essences into the day's curry-stew; heaps of ginger, fresh or dried into twisted shapes, lentils of every color and shape: pink masoor dal, yellow channa, black sabut, hard brown chickpeas, yellow urad and green mung dals;

the mounds of sticky dates, bin after bin of other spices whose names, if he knows them at all, he knows only in Punjabi as the cook makes the rounds.

The exotic is strictly relative. For the little missionaries' son this is commonplace, the colorful spectacle characterizes home. He doesn't yet realize that the exotic in the bazaar is not the riot of spices but the blond-haired child, who evokes kindly smiles, fingers that rumple his hair and affectionately pinch his cheeks—sometimes pinched till they burn. And his mouth is regaled with free samples of various goodies—including crinkly pretzel shapes of fried dough dripping with thick orange-colored syrup and rose water—redefining the very meaning of the word sweet. His parents don't want him eating it, but what they don't know won't hurt them.

This was the only life Alex had known, except for the periodic visits back to a truly exotic place called "the States," for about a month every few years. His parents somehow called that place "home," even though it wasn't. Maybe for them it was. It was where they had grown up, where his uncle and aunt and cousins lived. It was fun to go to the States, to see bright city lights and freeways, to watch television and play with the fancy toys of his cousins. Where meat came in a package and you couldn't tell what it was unless you read the label. America was a Disneyland, a special treat, a short faraway vacation in a place strangely called "home."

Alex did note while in America that he no longer stood apart, he looked just like every other boy, nothing special. It was only when they returned to Lahore again that he felt he was truly home, back to the familiar, the routine, the servants who spoiled him with furtive morsels in the kitchen. To where he belonged—even if he didn't really. His cousins back in the States could never imagine his life here. He found how quickly their interest in the details of his daily life in Pakistan vanished after a few cursory questions—like whether they had McDonald's or Spiderman in Lahore.

He had grown up with the call to prayer echoing across the roofs at pre-dawn, "*God is great. I testify that Muhammad is the Messenger of God. Come to prayer. Prayer is more worthy than sleep.*" He knew the noon prayer time and the afternoon prayer time, and the long Friday noon prayers where Aftab the bearer sometimes took him and where he had to sit still through the entire sermon. Islam was all around him. He knew he wasn't Muslim because his parents had told him so. He participated with his family in that defining act every Sunday, going to a small makeshift church discreetly maintained inside a normal residential house. A few people of the neighborhood who visited his parents weren't Muslims either, they were part of a small minority of local Christians. Nazir was Christian. Nazir sometimes quarreled with Aftab as to who was boss. Aftab and the garden boy were Muslims, and on the big religious holidays like the Feast of the Sacrifice Aftab sometimes took Alex to his own home where he saw firsthand the rituals and celebrations of Muslims. His father disapproved of his participation, his exposures to these Muslim ceremonies. "I don't want Alex confused about who he is—we don't want to lose our son to the Muslims in the process of our saving Muslims in the True Faith." Alex wasn't quite sure what his father was saving these people from, other than fixing their eyes at the eye clinic. Bringing them sight had multiple meanings in his father's eyes. Eyes seeing eyes. Except his own son's eye, irony of ironies.

Many of the visitors and patients at his father's clinic were from among the local Christians too, although Muslims sometimes came, and his parents had a few Muslim friends and neighbors. Akmal, the father of Alex's good friend Majeed, was a Muslim judge who had studied several years in England and enjoyed coming over for friendly debates over theology. Harley had experienced unexpected delight in finding how many educated Muslims found relish in friendly sparring over the details of their respective faiths.

"These conversations remind me of the spirit of Muslim India," Akmal told Harley. "Many of the Muslim Mughal rulers used to sit around court and debate theories of religion, just like we are doing. Did you know that one of our greatest Mughal emperors, Akbar, invented his own religion, a fusion of all known religions at the time? He called it the Divine Religion. To be honest, not all mullahs were so enthusiastic about the idea," he winked at Harley, "but who has the courage to tell an emperor he is a blasphemer."

"Well, that is encouraging. It shows you Muslims are more open to appreciating Jesus, Akmal."

"But explain something to me, my dear friend Harley. How can you talk about One God, when you talk about Jesus as a second person to be worshipped, alongside God? And then this strange idea of the Holy Ghost—also to be worshipped?"

"Well," Harley sighed, "yes, a difficult concept, the Holy Ghost. It just really means the Spirit of God."

"But are you saying the Spirit of God is different from God? God's spirit is not part of God? What is God anyway if he doesn't have his Holy Spirit? And Harley, enlighten me, I am confused," Akmal said with a coy smile, "yes, confused...with God, Jesus, Mary, the Holy Ghost, it all sounds like God is being divided up. A whole family in one. That's what confuses us poor simple Muslims who are stuck with the idea that God is strictly One."

"You're welcome to that idea, Akmal. And God knows I don't want to confuse you—although I'm not sure I really believe you are quite the poor simple Muslim." Akmal laughed, slapped Harley's knee and poured more tea.

Alex himself already encountered disputes with some of his Muslim playmates on these topics. "Is it true what Daddy says," he asked his mother one night while getting into bed, "that Muslims will go to hell?"

"Nobody knows the way of the Lord," his mother answered. "If they are good people the Lord will probably recognize the truth in their hearts and they probably won't go to hell. Your father just wants to bring them into the fold of the Lord's community, that's all."

And when Alex went to play with Majeed down the block, his friend asked him why Alex didn't go to the neighborhood mosque. Alex told him he wasn't Muslim, but a Christian. "Why are you Christians?"

"Because we are. My father says that if you aren't Christian you will go to hell."

"That's not true, *you* are the ones who will go to hell, you are *kaffir*, non-believers."

"But we do believe, we believe in Jesus Christ."

"You mean you don't believe in God?"

"Yes, we do, but we believe in Jesus, his son, too."

"My father says that God is One, you can't worship Jesus, he was just a man, a holy Prophet, not God."

"No, Jesus was the son of God!"

"Come on, God doesn't have children!"

*   *   *

Aftab rang the lunch bell. Round two.

Alex came in from the garden where he had been napping under the trees, listening to the bustle of life outside the walls, the calls of itinerant peddlers hawking the virtues of their luscious wares. The air was hot, and he felt a film of sweat across his face; Minnesota had stolen his longtime tolerance for the Lahore climate.

Aftab beamed and bowed again to Alex, delighted to have him back. The dining room was a comforting place with its earthen tiles on the floor, white walls that showed off the carved rosewood furniture that made up the sideboard with its many curlicues, for all the world looking like a miniature Moghul fortress. The chairs were high-backed, the dark rosewood polished and glowing with their own wooden balls decorating the top. Exuberance of style here stood in eternal resistance to the lean egalitarian Ikean esthetics he associated with contemporary furnishings back in the States.

"So Dad, how is the community itself doing?" Alex pulled out his chair, sat down, and began to dismantle the complicated artistic foldings of his napkin. "Are things more difficult for Christians now too?"

He saw his father stiffen. "Times are not so good now, no, the community is keeping a lower profile. I'm focusing more on the clinic myself, it's the best way to reach people, to show them that we care."

"But there's been a small Christian community here for a long time. Why is there be so much anti-missionary feeling now?"

"It's just the hard-liners, stirring up trouble. That's the trouble with Islam, it can turn out these zealots."

"Well, it sounds like it's a tricky time to be operating a clinic. They're probably suspicious you're still trying to convert them."

"We *have* changed them. Our eye clinic has brought sight to a lot of people in this area. It's an example of our faith—the power of the love of Jesus Christ in action. But these wretched fanatic mullahs— they're even trying to discourage simple people from coming in to the clinic."

"But in a way, can you blame them? I mean you are after all trying to convert them." Code yellow.

"And what's wrong with that? Trying to bring them to the Word, to save their souls in the end, should I be ashamed of that?"

"No, I don't mean ashamed. But this isn't just about religion. After all, Islam is part of the culture. Look at the few families that you have converted. Has it been completely good for them?"

"Good for them?" His father's voice rose. "How can you question bringing them to accept the Word of Jesus Christ? Opening the door to the path to salvation? I'm proud we've helped open their eyes, enrich their lives and souls."

Aftab brought around the platter to each person with second helpings of rice and a bowl of chicken curry accompanied by a bowl of vegetable curry. Alex wasn't sure he could handle this quantity of food. He hesitantly pressed on in response to his father. "But isn't this risky for them? Some of these fundamentalists even accuse them of apostasy."

"Pioneers always have to pay a price."

"Come on, Dad, that's a bit glib. Who's to say that they're pioneers? They're poor people, they may be making a big mistake. I don't mean about Christianity, but at least about taking steps that puts them at odds with their community, their culture."

Harley slammed down his fist. "Alex, what has come over you? Who do you think we are? Your mother and I, we wouldn't be here, we wouldn't have devoted half of our lives to being here if we didn't believe in our mission, in the clinic and the enlightenment it can bring to people. You think I should have stayed in Ohio and sold insurance?"

"Dad, you know that's not what I mean. I'm just saying it's hard to say your belief is better or more correct than someone else's." Code orange.

His father plunked down his spoon and stared in silence for a moment. "Is that the half-baked stuff they teach you in college? Equating everything, one idea is just as good as another? Post-modern thinking, is that what they call it? No wonder nobody knows what to believe, or even has the power to act on their convictions. Gutless wonders…that's what you'll all become."

"Dammit, Dad, I'm not gutless. I'm not saying that one idea is as good as another. But who are we to tell a major culture that they're wrong and we're right? Isn't that sort of arrogant?"

"You're the one that's a little arrogant, young man. I don't find this very pleasant, having you come home to challenge everything in this house, everything you've grown up with. Telling us that we've wasted our lives in everything we've done."

"I'm not saying you wasted your lives, I'm just concerned about tampering too much with others' ways of life. Maybe there's more than one way to be religious is all I'm saying."

"There certainly are! And some of us believe there's been some progress in the world over human history in learning about the ways of God. We have to work from convictions, something you don't seem to know much about."

"That's not fair, Dad."

"Fair! You call all these challenges and insults to me in my own home fair? Maybe you better wait another two years before you come back for another visit."

His mother broke in, with a tremor in her voice. "Let's not get into this anymore, Harley. It only leads to bad feeling."

"It's your son creating bad feelings, Abby. You can sit here if you like and listen all you want to his sophomoric drivel."

Harley crumpled his napkin, threw it onto the table. Abby grabbed his arm. "Please Harley, let's eat our meal together in peace."

"Some peace! You can go on, I'm tired." Harley threw off her hand and walked out.

Abby's eyes filled with tears and she looked down, wiping her eyes. "Did you have to raise all these issues during our first days together, Alex? Don't you know what a sore point this is? It's hard enough living with him these days."

"I'm sorry, Mom. He's just so stubborn."

"So are you! You're both stubborn! And you're going to make my life a hell if you keep this up!"

Alex knew he should reach out and touch his mother's hand. Instead, he sought to recover the situation.

"Mom, I'm sorry, I didn't mean to disrupt things. It's just..."

"It's just that you don't know what this is like now. Preaching theories isn't going to help him change his mind. He needs encouragement to start rethinking things."

They ate in silence for a few minutes.

"Look Mom, I'm just concerned. I know *you're* concerned too. I think it is time for Dad to pull out of this kind of work, maybe for you guys to think about moving back to the US."

"Attacking missionary work isn't the right way to go about it."

"I'm sorry, he's just so damn self-righteous about all of this."

"You're not going to change his ways at this point in his life. We just need to think practically about the problems involved, especially as we get older."

Alex finally went over and put his arm around his mother's shoulder. "I'm sorry. I'll try to be more tactful. And thanks for the great lunch, my favorite dishes. It's great having them again."

"I'm glad you liked it. I thought you might find it nice to come back to a few of your old favorites."

"I wonder if maybe Nazir could make a few vegetable dishes next time too? I've kind of gone off eating so much meat."

"Certainly, I'll ask him." Her eyes remained fixed on the table.

"Not just for me. It's not good for you or Dad to be eating tons of *ghee* either. All that butter and stuff, it's bad for the arteries."

* * *

Alex's parents had met in the course of working in a Methodist missionary organization in Ohio. Neither had ever left the state before they married. Harley was an early refugee from a parental home locked into the perpetual masochism of ugly quarrel; worse, his parents had willfully chosen to sustain the battleground rather than accept the surgical release of divorce. Harley had tried to maintain a scarce presence at home during his rocky teenage years, honing his skills early on in putting away a six-pack nightly, courtesy of an older brother of a friend; in later teens his life alternated between low-paying service jobs and lost hours in a rented room above a garage increasingly given over to alcohol. His older sister Rachel had more successfully walled off the corrosion of their parents' agonies and maintained her sanity and stability; she dragged Harley to his first AA meeting. The experience proved a revelation, offering him the first credible prospect of exit from the paralysis of a loser's syndrome. He indeed came to feel that his life had gravitated into the hands of a higher power. His uncle then came on the scene; an optometrist, he took on a sober Harley for odd jobs until he persuaded him to go back to school, to take up optometry, even offering to help pay his way.

Harley needed no further persuasion: an active Christian member at the meetings helped Harley understand that Jesus could bring light into his bleak life. And indeed it happened; Harley's newfound belief saved him and provided him the courage to break with the bottle, to learn a profession and turn his life around. This wasn't about faith—this was plain facts on the ground to be seen. Not some promise of the next world but miraculous salvation in this. It created a powerful obligation—an urge—to bear the message to others. Firmness to the program and its set of beliefs did bring salvation—Harley's own new life was evidence. During his final year of studies in optometry Harley had heard about the existence of overseas missions and the chance to bring the power and efficacy of the Lord to those who were poor and who had not yet been blessed to receive the power of Christ into their blighted lives. Harley did not condemn the religious beliefs of others, but he did know the proven efficacy and power of his own. And what better way to serve the bereft, to transform lives and bring the gift of the message of the Lord than through his skills in ministering to the eyes of others? In opening the eyes.

Alex's mother Abby had come from the opposite direction. Her father had been a minister of the Baptist Church, and she had grown up in its bosom. The church and its demands were strict, the world was a corrupt and sinful place and one needed a spiritual refuge to maintain human decency. Drawn to social work, she met Harley who was already working with a charitable eye clinic. As colleagues in charity, they gradually fell into a comfortable daily routine and came to speak of the possibilities of serving the Church's mission overseas. And it was the call and practical planning for such an overseas mission, rather than any immediate passion, that had hastened the logic of their matrimony. In the end they both recognized the parched and sterile roots of their childhoods, those sullied memories of place and people that had failed to bond them to the area. Life did not lie in where they were, but in where they would go. For Abby, to throw in her lot with Harley was the path of least resistance, for an overseas life whose contours were utterly unknowable, in a remote country she had scarcely even heard of. But religion had never been her instrument of personal salvation as it had for him.

Abby was convinced that the most Christian act was charitable action, good works, faith as living example. Hadn't Mother Teresa said how much more valuable it was to take a broom and sweep someone's house than to preach to them? But there were worries too. Life overseas represented a true calling but also a huge personal sacrifice in leaving behind life in the best country in the world. She feared possible violence, especially in the Indian subcontinent. She had read about the great Partition, when under the British Pakistan was divided off from India in 1947, and about the British-engineered population exchange—all Muslims to go to Pakistan, all Hindus to India. The British Raj had played off Hindus, Muslims and Sikh against each other, culminating in vicious ethnic cleansing. Out of the twelve million souls that had migrated either east into India or west into Pakistan to a new home, maybe one in ten had died in confused communal butchery on all sides: Hindu, Sikh and Muslim all outdoing each other in fear-crazed murder.

And she was aware that women had been routinely raped in the course of civil conflict. She shuddered but believed Harley could protect her and their future family. She believed she should not pass judgment on the lives of others. After their arrival in Pakistan she soon met many Pakistani women whom she quickly perceived to be good people in spite of their religion. God moved in mysterious ways and she did not try to reconcile these two conflicting thoughts.

Comfort, reassurance and consolation—that was what Abby sought. She had felt alone in the world growing up. Her only other relative she had felt close to was a barely older uncle whom she had adored. And yet Uncle Alex had been taken from her, victim of his own idealism when he volunteered at age twenty-one to go to Spain to fight for the Republican cause against Franco and Fascism. For his troubles he took a bullet in the head on the front lines outside Barcelona. His death had been devastating to Abby, a shattering introduction to the concept that no good deed goes unpunished.

What business had her uncle being there? Could he—could anybody—have really made a difference? Cultures moved along grooves scoured out by thousands of years of history; how could outside do-gooders deflect that trajectory?

*   *   *

"Majeed, it's me, Alex! Yes, I'm just back… Just great! … It has been a long time… Jihaan's for tea at 3pm? … Terrific."

Alex left the compound and walked down to the main street and approached a three-wheeled motor rickshaw under a tree. "*Rickshah khali hai?*" The driver was dozing inside. Clearly it was available but you never knew if the driver felt like taking you. The driver flicked his head toward the back seat and Alex clambered in. He always loved the experience of the rickshaw trip, their brightly colored enclosed awning coverings covered with designs and Koranic phrases, scenes of paradise with lakes, trees and snow mountains, the name of God or various Sufi saints, the inside decorated with more religious symbols, personal photos—no two alike, each one singularly embellished to reflect the personality of the *rickshah wallah*. The driver had naturally asked too high a fare, and Alex relented—that was the price of being a Westerner, even if you knew the language and the correct fare; he didn't feel like scoring the point on this trip. The engine putt-putted its way into action and down the street as the driver wove in and out through the traffic emitting its signature black trail behind.

Majeed embraced Alex as soon as he stepped out of the rickshaw in front of the café. Alex noticed Majeed was dressed in his *shalwar-kameez*, the long tunic with an embroidered vest over it, and traditional baggy pants. Alex now had an inch height over Majeed, but Majeed's face showed the same lively intelligence, dark eyebrows highlighting his piercing eyes, sometimes bemused, slightly mocking, confident smile. He was clean shaven, shorter hair than Alex. He had added a few pounds.

"*Assalamu alaikum*, Alex, it's been a long time. *Kya haal hai?* It's great to see you here again," he added in Urdu.

"*Thik hun*. Praise God, I'm fine. How have you been, Majeed? I've missed you."

"What, no more Urdu?"

"It's a bit slow at the moment I'm afraid, but it's coming back. But what are you up to? How are your parents? You were at London University for two years I heard?

"Yes, I was, but alas my family couldn't afford it any more. It was fun in the big city while it lasted."

"So you're back at university here now?"

"Yes, in Islamabad, finishing in poli-sci. It's not a bad place, and I need to be back here anyway, it's useful for contacts for later on."

They entered the café, quiet with only a few customers at this hour, and found a table at the back. A refrigerated glass counter purveyed a swirling array of colorful sweets. The smells brought back memories. "Wow, Majeed, I've got to have the *ras malai*, I used to love that desert as a kid, haven't had it for years and my Mom would never have it made at home for me... So tell me, your parents, how are they?"

"Praise God, they are fine."

"And Zubayda? I haven't seen her for years, how is she?"

"Ah, Zubayda, yes, she often speaks of you. I think she's always had some crush on you. You must come over another day and see her, see all of us. She's back from a training course right now. But we're all a little more conservative now after the Islamization campaign. And you're back with your parents?"

"Right, it's been two years or so since I was here, I was at university back in the States and then staying with my aunt and uncle on vacations or working a summer job in Ohio. I needed to earn money for school."

The waiter brought them two sweet chai and two bowls of *ras malai*. Alex couldn't wait to dip his spoon into the creamy cardamom-laced textures.

They caught up on gossip about friends from the old soccer team. "And no girlfriend, Alex?"

"Well, no real girlfriend yet, but I do go out a good bit on dates."

Majeed nodded, was silent a moment and then lowered his voice. "You got my message."

"Yes, I did, thank you for it."

"When I wrote to you I just wanted you to know, for your parents' sake— I'm sure you've heard—about all these problems—suspicion of Westerners, less tolerance."

Alex sipped his chai—tea boiled with milk, sugar and spices, cooked thick almost like a dessert, one of the staffs of daily life in Pakistan and India.

"Yeah, I have heard about problems... And you're right, I am worried about them, especially my father's missionary work."

"Things are a bit tighter now, I'm afraid. There's more anger, bad stuff going on."

"But the neighborhood knows he's done a lot for the poor, helping people with their eyes and all. He tries to keep a low profile."

"There's just distrust now, Alex, including about America. And missionaries—some people see them as stealing our culture. Many people think your father is just using the eye clinic to lure Muslims away from Islam."

"Well, yes, in a way, I mean, he does want to show how Christians can work to serve the poor, you know, model of Christian love and such. He's always been open about that. But beyond that…"

"Look, Alex, there's a general rise in violence in the country now. It's sad to say—more Sunnis killing Shi'a and vice versa. And a lot of it is new, outsiders helping foment some of this sectarianism—Saudi Arabia, the Gulf, Iran, Iraq, India—all involved in supporting sides. And now it's all gotten more intense since the war against the Soviets in Afghanistan. And then there's always worry that India wants another war, to destroy us. America is seen as a friend of India. And America is trying to stop us from developing a bomb."

"Come on, Majeed, that much is understandable. I mean, it's not good if Pakistan gets a nuclear bomb, that could lead to nuclear war."

"Nuclear war?" Majeed darkened, looked around and lowered his voice again. "Are you telling me you've forgotten how the bloody Hindus exploded a nuclear device over a decade ago? God knows what radiation coming over the borders? You don't think we have a right to defend ourselves against that? It's OK for the US to use the bomb to kill thousands of civilians in Hiroshima, but it's not OK for us Pakistanis to defend ourselves against Indian nukes? Do you think we should just let the Americans tell us what's OK to do? Because they've done everything to try to stop us getting our own bomb! That's the type of thing that's making a lot of people angry. And I don't blame them." He sat back in his chair.

Alex was disturbed at how fast the temperature of the conversation had risen. This wasn't the way meeting with old friends should go. He felt he had blundered into a confrontation.

"Look, Majeed, I'm sorry, I'm not here to defend the policies of my country. Let's not talk about that."

"Ahh, it's 'my country' now? When you were growing up here you felt like you belonged here, and America was far away."

"Well, I've been there for some years now, and I see things a little more from their perspective. But I didn't come to argue with you."

"*Achha*, that's fine. I don't want to argue either. And it really is good to see you again, Alex." He clapped him on the shoulder. "My father has often asked after you."

"Give Akmal Sahib my regards. I will come over soon to give my greetings. How is he?"

"He's fine, praise God. He feels pressures himself now, the struggle between Western laws and Sharia-based laws. Lot of politics involved."

"That's really too bad. I know he's tried to stay out of politics. Does he still spend a lot of time studying religion?

"Yes, well, you know my father, almost too much. He goes to various shrines, cultivating various *pirs,* holy men and Sufi leaders. I've had arguments over that with him. He's angry about the way religion is exploited in politics here.

"And your cousin Salman, is he still staying with you?"

"Salman wants to go off to California to study engineering. You'll see him, Alex, he's become an American wannabe, smitten with Western pop culture. Earphones on all day listening to rock music. My father doesn't feel he's very serious."

Alex didn't know Salman very well, as the boy had kept to himself at Majeed's house where he had lived since his parents and sister were killed. Alex had heard the story. When Salman was eight years old, he, his sister and his parents were returning home from a trip to town in Waziristan in the Frontier area. Their vehicle was overtaken by two SUVs that forced them off the dirt road. His father was dragged out of the driver's seat and shot in the chest, but lurched back to the car, reached for a pistol and tried to return fire. The assailants had pulled out an AK-47 and sprayed them with bullets. Salman had ducked down behind the front seats. After the SUVs departed, Salman crawled up and found his sister's lifeless body on the back seat, as well as his father and mother slouched in the front. He had hidden crouched in the back of the vehicle with the bodies reeking of blood for hours in the darkness, until finally another vehicle came along and found him. Majeed's parents had adopted their orphaned nephew. Alex was glad to hear Salman seemed to be coming out his shell.

"So how does all this religion business affect your life at university? You know, social life."

Majeed smiled. "You mean do I get laid? No, not any more. When I was in London... well, that's a long story. But you know, it's never been exactly a nest of free love here like you have in the West. There's just not much dating going on. We sometimes go to parties in wealthy homes and see some girls, and we can call each other for a lot of private talk, but we can't go on real dates here."

"No girlfriend?"

"No, that's not really possible. Anyway, my parents want me to get more serious, they'd like me to get married, maybe next year after I graduate."

"Anybody in mind?"

"Not especially, but they are looking around."

"Surely, Majeed, you wouldn't let your parents choose your bride in this day and age?"

"No, not choose exactly. But they are in contact with lots of good families to find out about eligible girls. They will probably start inviting some of these families over for tea—so I can meet some of their daughters, see what I think about them."

"Boy, things haven't changed here that much then, have they? I'm surprised you're willing to go along with that old system."

"Alex, it may be the old system, but it works fairly well. I can't just go out and meet eligible girls anywhere. This way I can meet a lot of them from decent families, compatible families, and make up my mind. I'm not forced to marry anyone I don't want."

Alex shook his head in disbelief.

"Come on, Alex. The system here seems to work a lot better than the one you have in the States. You've got the highest percent of divorce in the world—over fifty percent. That's from your so-called love marriages."

"You're not going to have less divorce when the couple isn't even in love."

"The love usually comes with time. And why do you think we look at the families the girls come from? If the backgrounds of the couple are too different then they're going to find stresses as they get older. They don't communicate as well."

"So the parents know what is best?"

"No, they don't know what is best, but they do know the other families. They know if there's a problem they can all come together and try to help solve it. They have a stake. You don't have that system with so-called love marriages."

"Yeah, but how much freedom do they have?" Alex looked Majeed in the eyes.

Majeed looked around. They were attracting the attention of a young couple with a small child at a nearby table. Majeed lowered his voice again.

"Don't give me that old crap about freedom. You know my mother, she's a tough woman. She may not argue in public with my father, but let me tell you, she makes most of the basic decisions about the family and our finances. She basically runs my father. That's true in a lot of families I know. And my sister? Zubayda's a demon. Nobody will accuse her of being down-trodden."

"But what about education…"

Majeed waved his hand impatiently. "Have you come here to score points or something? Do you think women here would be happier having to go to work every day and leave their kids to strangers to take care of them and then have to do all the housework alone at night because their husband won't, and the family can't afford not to work? Come on! Don't give me all that shit about all the liberation of the Western woman. I've seen it."

Alex too was growing uncomfortable as the conversation seemed to get out of hand again, falling into well-trodden, senseless exchanges of counter-charges. This wasn't what he came to see Majeed for. He'd hoped to find the old spark, laugh over old times. He hadn't expected to find Majeed so defensive.

Both of them felt the need to move on to other things, more reminiscences. But the conversation now seemed slightly more pro forma, a touch more cautious. Each seemed to retreat a little bit more into his respective culture. "So what are your plans now, Majeed?"

"I don't know, I think I'd like to become a lawyer and maybe go into politics later. What about you?"

"I'd like to do something related to international relations. It's in the blood, growing up here and all. I'm thinking about becoming an academic, but I'm not sure what that kind of life might be like. I'm studying Russian now too."

"Russian! That is different." Majeed looked at his watch. "Alex, look, I have to go somewhere with my mother shortly, but let's follow up soon." Alex reached for the bill, but Majeed grabbed it from his hand. "You've forgotten the customs, Alex. My turf, my treat."

As they stood outside about to part, Majeed drew Alex over. "I really think you need to encourage your parents to consider giving up the clinic and going back to the States, Alex. My father heard a few mullahs specifically mention the clinic as a Christian conversion center. That's not a good sign. Things can get hot here quickly."

"I'll definitely be talking to them. But you know how stubborn Dad can be, he's not going to give in easily… I'll stay in touch with you on this, we need to talk about it more."

They embraced warmly again but Alex felt a touch of regret that something had shifted slightly, the old warmth, the instant rapport of a shared adolescent life had given way to a more adult kind of relationship as each moved into his own circle. Majeed was truly an old friend, they had been together in school in Lahore, lived in each other's homes, and had gone on trips together. Now they were arguing as American and Pakistani. It was as if he had ceased to be just Alex and had morphed into some kind of representative of his own country. Or was it Majeed who had changed? Majeed seemed to have bought into the Pakistani way of life more than Alex had expected. He seemed to *belong* more.

In the States Alex sometimes felt like he was a visitor. Sure, he talked like an American, but his classmates somehow viewed him as just a little different, not out of the exact same mold, not quite a regular guy as others were in his dorm—the kid who had grown up abroad. But in Pakistan it was different for Alex. If he distanced himself from Majeed here, he would be cutting himself off from his own past. This differed too from his parents' situation, who lived in a world of their own making. They still felt America was home even if they had little to do with it anymore. Just long-term visitors in Pakistan—that's what they really were. But Alex had never been just a visitor.

*   *   *

Alex was ten and the fasting month of Ramazan was again near. Nearly all his friends were Muslim, including Majeed and Soheil whose homes he spent a lot of time in. Alex's family held Christmas celebrations at home each year—the centerpiece of the family's year—but Christmas seemed to contain nothing quite like the sustained warmth, allure and drama of the month of Ramazan when in Pakistan normal daily life came to a halt: all Pakistanis would refrain from eating or drinking anything during daylight hours for the whole month.

"Mom, Dad, Majeed has invited me to come and stay with him at his house this Ramazan for the ceremonies of breaking the fast each day. I'd like to go. And I'd like to try keeping the fast like all my other friends do," he added. Alex's mother glanced nervously over at his father; he remained silent for a few moments, then sighed. "Alex, you can attend some of their *iftaar* dinners in the evening during Ramazan, but you cannot go and live with them for a month."

"Please, Dad, they're my friends and Majeed's mother and father invited me especially. You know what a great celebration it is. All my friends are together and it's a lot of fun."

"Religion isn't 'fun,' Alex, first of all. Second, we're Christians. I have no objection to your witnessing Muslim celebrations here and there, but you are not to turn Muslim for a whole month, fasting. That is not your tradition."

"But Dad, it's not going to hurt anything. My friends all want me there with them. I'll learn a lot. Besides, Majeed's Dad says it's good for the health to fast sometimes."

"Well, I don't see you eager to observe any Christian fasts. This isn't a game and I won't have it. Answer is no."

Alex turned tearfully to his mother who put her arm around his shoulder and led him out of the living room.

"I'll try to speak to him, son. You know he's stubborn on religious matters."

"How can it hurt, Mom? I'm not going to become a Muslim or something. I'd just like to see if I could do it, me and my friends."

Late that evening, Abby quietly raised the issue. "I don't see why we can't let the boy go to his friend's house for Ramazan, Harley. It means a lot to him. Besides, maybe he will learn something about self-discipline from the fast."

"Abby, it's the principle. It means he's becoming more Muslim than Christian—with all that degree of focus on Ramazan fasting. It's not good for him, it will confuse him about religion, where he belongs."

"But you've often said that there's a lot of Christian ideas in Islam. Ramazan is especially a social thing for children, you've seen that. It's about the excitement of breaking the fast at night, and all the festivities—that's what he wants to share. I can't see it will hurt him."

"We must maintain boundaries, Abby, he's probably absorbing too much of this country as it is!"

"Well, didn't you know that when you brought us here in the first place? Her voice rose. "This isn't home, it's a foreign land. If you don't want him to be influenced then we should have stayed home in the US."

Harley glowered.

"And most of all, you don't want to make Islam seem like some forbidden fruit to him."

Harley turned back to his book. The next morning a cold silence reigned over breakfast, crystallized into an unspoken test of wills. That afternoon, Majeed's father Akmal came over to pay a call on Harley.

"You know, my friend, we have often had our friendly debates about religion. Our families are both religious. My family would love to invite Alex as a guest at our home for Ramazan. You know how much we respect Christianity. It is part of our Islamic teachings as well, Jesus is one of our great prophets, Mary is the most important woman in Islam. We certainly are not trying to convert your son, but Majeed would love to have his friend with him and we would enjoy his company. I just wanted you to know that the invitation was sincere and honest and he will be among respectful friends."

*   *   *

"Guess what, Majeed! My Dad says I can stay with you!"

"Wow, Alex, that's great, we'll have a great time! Can you bring your stuff over before Ramazan starts tomorrow?"

Jack made fun of his little brother for submitting to the rigors of the fast. "What would you want to do that for?" he asked. "You're not even Muslim, shrimp, you'll just dry up and blow away." But Alex sensed some grudging respect behind Jack's cool. And Nazir, the Christian cook thought the whole idea of fasting for a month was crazy, whispered to Alex that he would save some food for him in the refrigerator every day if he got too hungry—an offer Alex rejected with indignation.

After school Alex packed up his small bag of clothes and went over to Majeed's house, thrilled at the adventure and his first long stay away from home. So, on this night before the scheduled start of Ramazan, Alex and his friends waited to hear the cannon shot that would signal the official sighting of the first tiny sliver of the crescent moon and the beginning of the month of Ramazan.

Around 9pm the shot went off—Ramazan had begun! They would all now get up before dawn for the *sehri*, or big breakfast—the last food and liquid of the day until sunset. He had brought his own alarm clock, but Majeed said everyone would be getting up together. The next morning Alex ate as much food and drank as much water as he could comfortably hold before the cannon shot announcing daybreak and the start of the fast. He headed off with Majeed and other friends to school, happy with a warm insider-sense of belonging.

The first day of fasting took its toll. By noon, all Alex could think about was how he missed his lunch. But as the day drew on into the hot afternoon it was the sense of thirst that dominated, he could feel his throat parch. Some of the older boys, copying the religiosity of the truly pious, spat with bravado out on the soccer field in the afternoon rather than swallow their saliva. Towards sunset they headed off to Majeed's home for *iftaar*, the first breaking of the fast.

The neighborhood kitchens of all households had been stoked up, busy baking and frying various Ramazan treats—whose aromas further whet anticipation of the coming feast. "It's not a real feast tonight, like at the end of Ramazan," Majeed said, "but the iftaar on the first day of Ramazan feels very special."

The sun sank with excruciating slowness toward the horizon; as they watched from their balcony, its last golden rays flickering over the hills, they listened intently for the cannon to signal sundown. As the last centimeter of the red ball disappeared, it was as if the whole world was watching. The cannon shot immediately echoed over the city and the neighborhood mosques picked up the cue, broadcasting the call to prayer over loudspeakers from their minarets. Alex sat down with Majeed's family on rugs and pillows on the living room floor with a cloth spread in the middle where the food was placed. The circle on the floor created a special atmosphere of family closeness and solidarity compared to sitting at their usual, more formal dining room table. Prayers were offered and then the iftaar began.

"We are gentle to our stomachs, and do not wish to show signs of greed, as if we were desperate. So we don't jump in straightaway to the food, we go slowly and with thanks," Akmal told Alex. "We take something light first to start the evening."

"My father's always reading religious books in the study," Majeed whispered to Alex. "But I like it during Ramazan because he comes out of his room a lot more and spends more time with us." They helped themselves to *lassi*—fruit juices mixed with yogurt—and then some dates and fried *pakora*, crusty little triangular pies stuffed with spicy meat or vegetables that melted in the mouth. How good it all tasted! But they were not to eat too much now, this was just to break the fast, the main meal would come later.

Formal prayers were next. Alex followed the family to the mosque for the *Maghreb*, the sundown prayers. He had been in a mosque many times before, but never when it was so crowded. He followed some of the prostrations as best he could. "It's not the prostrations that matter," Majeed's father said. "Ramazan means you must try to have a pure heart, to think of the wellbeing of others, and of your own weaknesses. It is a wonderful time to reflect about your own life. And we need to remember the mercies and blessings that God gives us." Majeed's uncle visiting from the Frontier area even gave up his beloved cigarettes for the entire month. "Fasting is good for the body as well as the soul," he said.

Majeed's uncle sometimes spoke a different language with Majeed and Majeed's mother. "It's Pashto," Majeed explained, "my mother's from the North-West Frontier, near the Afghan border." His uncle loved to talk about the politics of the Frontier, but his father said it wasn't appropriate to discuss politics over food during the beginning of Ramazan.

After the Maghreb prayers, the family returned home for a more extensive meal: lamb curries and pilaf, stuffed vegetables, chickpeas and chicken; creamy smooth *baingan bharta*—a spicy whipped eggplant, salty yogurt drinks and all kinds of other colorful dishes, ending with several kinds of rich dessert. Alex's favorite was *gajar ka halva*, a thick and rich orange pudding made of cooked carrots ground up with butter, raisins, cardamom, sugar and almonds. He also loved the *firnee* or baked rice pudding with a delicious thick skin on top where the milk and sugar had congealed and browned into caramel; he broke the caramel skin with a spoon to reveal the sweet and aromatic creamy milk mixed with rice, sugar and cardamom within. And there were other deserts of fried dough in a pretzel shape drowning in thick orange syrup, and *gulab jamun*— round balls, squeaky to the teeth, of cottage cheese, flour and spices, drowning in syrup.

And there was Zubayda. She was two years older than Majeed, with flashing black eyes and an impish expression beneath her headscarf. She would smile at Alex, then turn away and ignore him. He felt drawn to her, but rarely had much occasion to talk to her. One time she looked at him as he sat alone in front of the TV before the family came in and reached out and stroked his cheek; he felt the electricity for hours thereafter. And she smiled especially for him when no one else was looking. One time Zubayda had driven away some older boys from a nearby neighborhood who were picking on Alex. He worshiped her. The family liked to complain that Zubayda was too free in her behavior, but she was the apple of her father's eye and he could never rebuke her for anything.

Majeed's family, like every home, had the television playing in the background during the meal, tuned to the special Ramazan programs of brief moral lectures, followed by the wonderful *qawwalis,* religious songs, whose words and music soared into the air backed by a harmonium and drums. Majeed's father was a devotee. "Some people think qawwalis are too emotional and that music is not appropriate in Islam. But God can touch us in so many ways."

The fasting over the month served to bring rich and poor together in a daily interval of shared hunger and temporary deprivation. "We who are well off are reminded that many poor families often don't get enough food throughout the whole year," Majeed's father said. "Ramazan is a time of reflection on ourselves, to learn to live selflessly. As we feel hunger and thirst, we must remember how many people suffer that condition over long periods of time. We try to keep the thought of God's benevolence in our minds during all waking hours, and gratefulness for how much he gives us during the year."

Children were allowed to stay up much later during Ramazan, especially on the first *iftaar*. Tonight the older children went to the mosque again for the last prayer of the day, the *'Isha*, marked by the fading of the last trace of color in the western sky and the fall of true darkness, putting an end to the vibrancy of the day's activities. Soon sleepiness overcame excitement and the boys went off to bed, mindful that in not too many more hours they would be getting up soon enough again for *sehri*.

And so Alex was awakened in the hour before dawn again for the last bit of food and water before beginning that day's long fast. Out in the street, the Ramazan drummer man came around in a brilliant orange outfit and a red vest swathed with floral designs and little inset mirrors, beating his big barrel drum as he walked through the neighborhood waking people for *sehri*. The children ran to the balcony to see the drummer man, and he waved and beat his drum extra loud and quick for a few moments, and then bowed. They all waved and bowed back.

It was a big meal, mostly the plentiful leftovers from the night before, that would have to hold them for the long day, along with a last few swallows of water in the last minutes before the sun peeked over the horizon again, signaling formal daybreak. Some of the Muslim boys at school made fun of Alex and told him Christians couldn't handle fasting. Alex bristled, his confidence intensified, but inside he wondered: "Will I be able to keep it up for the whole month?" He was proud of sharing the common experience with his group. Today again it wasn't the hunger that came to him during the day—it was the thirst; the thought of cool clear water tortured him by late afternoon. But it also made him feel proud and adult that he shared in this communal austerity to become a better, stronger person.

His Muslim friends were impressed; Amin told him his diligence was a good sign, and that shortly Alex would realize how good it was to be a Muslim and he would convert. Alex knew he would not share that remark with his father when he went home after the first few days for a visit. "How is my little Muslim brother doing?" Jack asked, but didn't say it in front of their father, and he didn't tease him as much about it this time. His mother inquired anxiously how Alex was holding up, and seemed pleased with his diligence. "But if you feel too hungry or weak, don't hesitate to give it up," she said. His father offered little comment. "If only he can now learn to be as good a Christian."

The days and nights of Ramazan blended into a long parade, a caravan of lights, colors, smells, activities, hubbub, and endless company. Neighbors came over on some nights for iftaar and Majeed's family went on other nights to their friends for iftaar. One night Alex's own mother and father were invited to Majeed's home for iftaar, as Harley paid his traditional Ramazan calls upon his Muslim neighbors and shared the fast-breaking, as did other Christians as well. And there were special visits with Majeed's family to the bazaar for new clothes for the children. On some nights they went to the mosque late to hear the Koran being recited. Strings of lights strung between the minarets, some of which spelled *Allah* in Arabic, or Blessed Ramazan, and lent the mosque a special magic. "It is great in the eyes of God to recite the entire Koran during Ramazan," Majeed's father said. "But Majeed is not as good at memorizing long passages from the Koran as I was at his age," he chided. They were chanted with a special sonorous intensity, as different reciters displayed their skills at weaving lines of melody into their recitations of the *suras* or verses, emphasizing the dramatic power of Arabic with its many sounds issuing deep from the throat, giving it a mysterious formality, an otherworldly quality. Alex found he could stay still listening to these powerful sounds even though he did not understand the meaning of most of the Arabic phrases. Few in the congregation understood all of the classical Arabic, but most adults were familiar with what the text was supposed to mean in Urdu, having heard it on so many occasions, and some having memorized some *suras* themselves.

As the weeks wore on, lack of sleep and intensity of fasting had begun to weary Alex. But he was determined not to let his parents know. And although a few boys cheated in their fasting and furtively bolted down some handful of nuts or sweets during the day when no one was looking, most of them refrained; cheating never crossed Alex's mind. Their teachers in school, even the Christian ones, gently overlooked their pupils' sleepiness during this season. "Remember as you fast," one of their teachers told them, "only human beings are capable of delaying gratification, by utilizing their gift of the mind and willpower from the Creator. That is the supreme gift."

Excitement arose again as the last days of Ramazan drew close, the *Eid ul Fitr*, or Holiday of the Fast-Breaking was to take place. The last night of Ramazan, *Chand Raat* or Night of the Moon was a very special occasion when the whole family took a motor rickshaw and went downtown to make sure everyone had a new outfit for the Eid. The commercial streets were brightly lit in the festive atmosphere—garish-colored neon lights and signs, crowded streets, families everywhere, food carts hawking all sorts of delicacies, feasts at home and delicious snacks in the street, qawwali music pouring out of the boom boxes of passing rickshaws and from many shops and small street vendors—a tumultuous symphony reaching a crescendo of enthusiasm, happiness and piety at the end of the month.

And then, the next morning, dawn broke quietly. No cannon at sunrise, no one shook Alex awake, no pre-dawn breakfast, everyone could sleep late for the beginning of three days of holiday when there was no school, no business.

People slowly arose, adjusting to the strange new rhythm of the day without the fast. The men and boys went to the mosque in the morning as everyone exchanged greetings, *Eid Mubarak*, "May you have a Blessed Holiday." Each family gave extra alms to the poor, the *zakat al fitr*, to complement the tithes they paid throughout the year in thanks for their own blessings and bounty and to help the less fortunate. Alex noted how Majeed and even his father Akmal sometimes kissed the right hand of the elderly and then raise it to their own forehead as a sign of respect and veneration. When children offered Eid greetings to their elders and grandparents they usually received some coins or candy. Alex accompanied Majeed's family as they visited relatives, neighbors and friends, bringing small gifts or food. The next day the family went to the park for a big picnic on the grass with other friends, followed by dinner at a popular kebab restaurant: delicious spiced, grilled meat cubes pulled off the long spit or *shish* and wrapped in a whole wheat chapatti that absorbed the running juices.

Even Alex's parents were drawn into the festivities as Muslim friends and neighbors came by and his parents wished them a blessed Eid. "I thought you didn't agree with Islam," Alex asked his father. "They worship God, and that's good," he replied, "but unfortunately they cannot receive the full benefits of salvation without Jesus. That's the message I'm trying to get across to them."

As the three-day Eid finally drew to a close and the month of fasting was a past memory, a wistful feeling settled over the community—the very special atmosphere of family, communal and religious celebration had come to an end for the year. And Alex now had to come back home, leaving the excitement of Majeed's home behind. "I'm glad you had a good time, they are good people," Abby said as she kissed him goodnight, "but you have to remember that this is where you belong. They have their culture and we have ours. And don't argue with your father about it."

"I'm not arguing. It's just I don't think it's any better to be a Christian than to be a Muslim. And I think we should get along."

"Shh, just think it in your mind. Don't talk about it." She stroked his hair. "You're my little peace keeper."

"Mom?"

"Son?"

"I know we're not Muslim, but you know, at Majeed's house… It's different. It feels very warm. They tell stories, and joke, and hug each other a lot and do things together."

"You miss that at home here?"

"Sort of. Dad just seems always busy, and he gets angry easily. Sometimes I feel more comfortable over at Majeed's."

"Hush, Alex, don't worry. I know what you mean. It is hard to be Christians here in Pakistan, and I think it makes your father tense."

"But if he is tense, then people maybe won't listen to him as much."

"He does a lot for people, he takes care of their eyes. He cares..." She paused looking at Alex's left eye.

"I just wish we could be part of a bigger community that does stuff together."

"I know. Your father has chosen a difficult path for us, but, God willing, it is a path that pleases the Lord."

Alex wasn't quite sure what that meant. But he hugged his mother.

Alex had accepted the beliefs of his parents, and accepted the centrality of regular church attendance with them on Sunday—in the small discreet building whose rec room served as a church in the community of Christians in this part of the city. Jack, however, had not been as acquiescent to this Sunday ritual and attended only under duress. Perhaps Jack's three-year's seniority gave him earlier insight into the foibles of their parents. But Jack was at heart a skeptic. Though the oldest child, he broke the supposed pattern of greater conscientiousness and did not readily yield to his parents' attitudes. As a result Alex often kept his true feelings to himself in his earlier years.

Alex felt torn between loyalty to his parents and a respect and admiration for the independent-mindedness of Jack who had informed Alex about the facts of life and made little effort to conceal his regular ministrations to himself under the sheets at night by the time he was thirteen. "It's called jerking off, and you'll be doing it one day soon too, little brother." Alex felt that this was perhaps an overt, if private, act of disloyalty to his mother.

Their parents decided to send Jack to high school in the States, where he could live with his aunt and uncle in Ohio. Maybe because it was better for his education, maybe because they felt uncomfortable trying to deal with an adolescent son, maybe because so many expatriates overseas did the same. "They're kicking me out," Jack told Alex. "But I'm happy to go. Mom's just too uptight and Dad is off in his own world with his Pak church. I'll take the freedom of life back in the USA. Good luck, buddy, you're on your own now. You'll be ready to bug out in three years too, take my word for it."

But it was different for Alex. Abby feared for her own purpose in life without children to occupy her; she persuaded Harley to let Alex continue high school at the Lahore American International School. It would help fill her life with him around.

"Why do we really live in Pakistan, Mom?" Alex asked one day. "Don't you and Dad like life back in the States?"

"Of course we like life back in the States, it's the most wonderful country in the world. I miss it every day. But your father wants to do something for the world, and for the Lord, so we have been willing to give up a lot to come out and work here, to save people's eyes, and their souls if we can. Your father may not communicate a lot, but he cares very much for the lives of people in the community here and we want to help them."

"Majeed and Soheil at school say that Americans are rich and spoiled and try to tell Pakistanis what to do."

"They don't know what they are talking about. America is a very generous country. It takes on a lot of burdens and expense to try to make the world a better place. If it wasn't for America being strong and keeping the peace, the Soviet Union would take over the world and destroy the West and Christianity. We would have war all over the world. Americans have sacrificed a great deal for world peace and freedom, but we don't get much credit for it. So don't listen to what those boys say." That answer held the fort, for now.

*   *   *

When Alex was finishing local high school years later, he planned go to a good college back in the US. He was excited about going. America was the land he did not really know, but that he had found exciting when the family went back on trips. His parents always spoke of American ideals and tried to inculcate them in Alex: tolerance, diversity, opportunity, creativity, ambition, freedom, standing up for the less fortunate. His father had hoped Alex might follow in his footsteps as a missionary but knew there was scant chance of that. Failing that, Harley had hoped Alex would pursue studies on Arabic, Pakistan and the Muslim world. Alex agreed he wanted to plumb more deeply the elements of Middle Eastern life. He spoke good Urdu, was learning to read and write it, and he wanted to study Arabic.

*   *   *

With both Jack and Alex in the States, Abby grew increasingly tired of holding her own fort. She could sense the change in atmosphere. Their small Christian community had grown more cautious in displaying their religious affiliation in public, and Muslim friends came by much less, their conversations on the street more perfunctory despite years of acquaintance. On religious occasions the Christian community seemed to dwindle. Abby felt their own mission had perhaps gone as far as it could, that it was time to return home. She would not broach the issue with Harley directly—who had never acknowledged even the possibility of returning to Ohio one day.

But she knew he too was feeling the strain of the shifting environment and could come home depressed, or in a dark mood. He would often sit in silence at dinner, staring fixedly at the plate, offering little response to her efforts at conversation, deflecting her efforts at inquiry. She would remain silent and try to be supportive.

But one day when she went into his study to locate Alex's birth certificate for his college application she found in Harley's drawer a half empty flask of locally brewed whiskey. The thought gnawed at her for days, but she dared not raise it with her husband. Yet one night before bed she clearly smelled his sweet cloying breath. How could he have regressed to that poison that had destroyed his youth, whose evils God had revealed to him, from whose coils God had rescued him? But even then she could not bring herself to speak up, as if denial was her only defense. Yet she couldn't ignore the few slurred words here, a certain unsteadiness on his feet there. The smell more evident. She resolved to wait until her sons came home on vacation when she could share her fears with them. Where else could she turn?

Worse, an inflexible commitment to sobriety had been the cornerstone of Harley's life commitment and belief—his religious belief had once saved him. Even a slight return to the bottle was not only a sign of despair, but a deeper indication that his own pillar of belief and certitude was eroding. Abby sensed that Harley himself knew it, saw a new defensiveness in him.

He bristled if she even strayed toward a theoretical discussion of maybe going back some day. "Abby, what is this talk of Ohio you are purveying now? If you are hankering to visit relatives, then alright, go if you must, but I'm not going. My life is here, my mission is here."

"Harley, don't you think a break might do you good? You've been working hard and the conditions are more difficult. You know you need to get away for a while yourself."

"Abby, I'm not going back. Ohio holds nothing for me except bad memories. This is my mission…what I was chosen to do!"

Abby screwed up her courage. "The mission is hard Harley! You know it! The tide may be going the other way." Her voice trembled. "I'm afraid we're going to be swept away."

His voice rose, "God grant me power in spreading the Word against the false religion of these bearded fanatics. They're all around me now, like hornets!" He retreated to his study and closed the door to her. Abby did not notice him come to bed before she finally fell asleep. But his despondency signaled its presence in the warm night air in the waves of tinctured breath to Abby next to him. And he was late getting up to go to his clinic the next morning.

*   *   *

Alex found his boyhood memories colliding with the realities of the present visit. The scenes, noises, and smells were as alive today as when he had left, but his relationship with his parents had migrated into something else. Yet, despite Alex's considerable irritation with his father, he also felt a sadness for him. Perhaps with age his father had come to the painful perception that his own future was no longer open-ended. He seemed to have lost a spark in carrying out his mission to the country. An imperceptible wall of defensiveness seemed to have crept into his view of his surroundings, a vision of restless opponents prowling the perimeters, sensing the vulnerability within, testing as the clock wound down.

*   *   *

Two days after Christmas Jack flew in, further shifting the balance of forces within the house. His arrival was a subdued affair: his father yielded to a stiff grudging hug, exchanged a few pro forma greetings and details about the trip. The studied silence over the burning central issue on everybody's mind was deafening. Abby had gotten Harley to promise not to spoil the holidays with a showdown; a cool correctness reigned over spontaneity.

"So, little brother, what's it like being back after two years? You were always into this Pak culture a bit more than me."

"It's kind of strange, but it's also, I don't know, comforting. The minute I heard the old Urdu around me and smelled the food, I was right back."

"Yeah, I love the food too, but the place seems like it's more screwed up now."

"How do you mean?"

"From what I hear the country doesn't seem to be able to get its act together, same old military coups, same old crap with border tensions with India, or in Afghanistan, or somewhere. They're so damn touchy about their national feelings, like it's triggered and ready to go. Every time I come back I remember all this shit going on. Like going back to another century."

"Well, India is breathing down their necks next door."

"You're always defending them, Alex, you know?"

"It's not defending them. It's just I can see things the way people here see it as well."

"Well, let me tell you, I've shaken the Third World dust off my feet. Business school is the way to go. Those guys are forward-looking thinkers, not mired in some traditional shit like this part of the world. There are even some very smart Paks there. Believe me, I'm happy to be out of here. And have a chance to make a little money as well. It's a pity—Mom and Dad condemning themselves to this hopeless struggle for their whole lives. What have they got to show for it?"

The brothers closed the door to their bedroom for the night. Jack sat down on the bed and lit a cigarette.

"For chrissake, Jack, at least open the damn window. You know Dad."

"Yeah, I know him, stubborn old man. I almost didn't come. I'm not going to sit around and take a lot of shit over Kathy. He still can't handle it, that we're living together."

Jack threw open the window and stared out into the night air. He then turned. "So what are we going to do about them?"

"I don't know, it's touchy as hell whenever I even mention the issue of plans."

"You can see it plain as me. He's getting older, the mission here is failing, he's depressed about it. The whole environment for this missionary shit is only getting worse. They could end up getting themselves killed."

"Yeah, but he doesn't see it—or can't admit it. Mom senses the situation better. I think she really wants to go back now. Sometimes I wonder if she's ever really been happy here."

"Have you actually talked to them about going back?"

"Yeah, some, but he's really touchy. And then the whole situation starts bugging me, and then I lose it myself and start arguing damn theology with him—total waste of time."

"It is. Anyway, this isn't about theology—we both know he's hard over on that. It's about their situation, even safety."

These were uncharted waters, The balance of power between generations in the family had begun the inexorable shift. Alex still felt a certain obligation of respect and deference toward his parents—but he also experienced eruptions of childish rebelliousness partially driving his arguments with his father. Each encounter challenged the old strategic ground rules in their relationships.

*   *   *

Alex noticed his mother listening quietly from the sides, hiding her emotions as she went about various forms of household activity. She seemed angry and frustrated. Meanwhile, his father displayed various forms of bravado in justifying their life in Lahore. Alex sensed a mutual wariness settling in between his father, and himself and Jack. Harley acted as if they were circling him, like hawks in the sky over prey, looking for an opening. And Alex himself felt unnerved by an awareness that he had already crossed a threshold with his father—had stumbled, intruded his way into his father's inner sanctum and world of beliefs, in deeply threatening ways. His mother's confirmation of his father's return to alcohol was something he dared not broach himself. Having transgressed into his father's private realm, it was hard for Alex to retrace his steps; the sanctuary had been profaned.

Yet Alex couldn't help himself. He felt a moth-like attraction to his father's candle. He could not remain silent. This was not just a war of ideas but equally a desire to demonstrate his independence, his maturity, his ability to think critically about his parents, even to demonstrate the adult nature of his thinking, surpassing his parents. He paused, almost on autopilot, calculating the right time to deliver the *coup de grâce*. And so, the next day, sitting outside towards the end of tea when his father had seemed particularly curt with his mother, he went for the jugular.

"Dad, you know what?" he opened casually. "I had this course on world religions this year, and I've been thinking a lot about things. I'll have to be honest. Don't you think that in some ways Islam is more tolerant than Christianity? Islam accepts Moses and Jesus as great prophets. But Christians reject Muhammad and call him some kind of heretic or devil. Think about it—shouldn't Christians lighten up on this business about the Prophet?"

"Lighten up? You think this is all just a matter of being nice to each other? Ignoring the realities so we just get along? Jesus is the heart of the matter. No! To reduce Jesus to just a great prophet is to undercut our Christian faith entirely, the whole miracle of the Resurrection. It is Muslims who have distorted—rejected—Jesus as the Son of God."

"But Dad, how can God condemn those who were born in the wrong place, far from Christianity, and deprived of hearing the Gospel?"

"Muslim ignorance of the Word of the Lord is their tragedy. It's a tragedy that goes back many, many generations, when their ancestors made a conscious decision to embrace Islam. God will be just, but the sins of the fathers are indeed visited upon the children."

"Dad, look, take Majeed. He and I have been close friends since we were kids. You know him, he's a good kid, he's been in and out of our house for years. Do you really believe that he's going to hell because he's not Christian?"

"If he hasn't discovered Christ who is the only road to salvation, then sadly, yes, he cannot be saved. That is why we have to help bring the word to him, to give him a chance to know God."

Jack rolled his eyes, chiming in to support Alex. "I just can't believe this anymore. You sit there and say God is merciful and loving. Then why wouldn't he love Majeed? And his family? And most of the other people in this country?"

Harley frowned and spoke with pointed deliberation. "He does love them. But they cannot fully find their way to Him, except through Jesus. That is their tragedy."

"You're telling me that God is willing to allow all these people to suffer in hell forever because they never got the word—your word?" Jack charged.

"It's not *my* word. It's the word of God. Look, you can't pussyfoot around these core doctrines. No one can be truly saved except through Christ as intercessor."

"Damn it! I'm tired of this crap!" Jack burst in. "How can God love people and yet create them to be tortured and destroyed? If God knows in advance what people will do in their lives, then why does he create people that he knows will go to Hell and burn? What kind of a loving God is that? That's ignorant, medieval!"

Harley glared, and got up from his chair. "You know what? I'm not even going to rise to that provocation. What kind of juvenile points are you two trying to score?" And he stormed off into the house, the predictable conclusion of such discussions.

His mother glowered at them. "Alex, Jack, do you think that is being helpful? Your father is right—that kind of remark is juvenile and disrespectful—to your father, and to what we are doing. If you want to encourage him to retire from the mission, that is not the way to do it. It's worse, you're just making him more stubborn."

Her words struck home.

"I'm sorry, Mom. I'm just frustrated… I can't seem to get through to him," Alex replied.

Abby left the room to follow Harley who had stumbled down the hall into his study. She reached out to embrace him, her own antennae receiving the same pain as her husband. The words from Alex had been piercing to her as well, not because of the challenge to his theology but because she recognized the pain they were inflicting upon her husband's body and mind. And partly because they resonated with doubts and anxieties growing within her own heart as well. She was convinced their fallout with Jack was in part due to the rigorous set of family rules and values which had caused him to rebel, to reject, to act out against received family values.

Harley stood in his study, looking out the window. Did he really believe what he had said? When challenged peremptorily by his son, what voice was speaking back? Was it the angry voice of a father whose authority was being challenged by his child? Or was it his beliefs that were being challenged? Or was it that the son had found the hole in the argument that had always disquieted him, causing him to instinctively argue back with the old line that he had always preached? God knows he had struggled himself with this teaching. "The heathen" was no abstraction to him as it had been back in Ohio. Out here it was real flesh and blood people, Muslim neighbors, friends and acquaintances. Many really good, caring people. How much was it their fault that they had not heeded the mission of Jesus?

Abby took Harley's hand. "Harley, please, let's not allow religious arguments divide our family. We both believe we are serving God by serving the needs of Christians and Muslims in Pakistan. They all need care of their eyes. That's all that matters." And she was certain of it. Muslims *would* come to Jesus by way of admiring the actions and behavior of Christian missionaries— there was no need to actively preach as such. This was America's generous gift to the world, its willingness to share its ideals and aspirations to bring change, enlightenment, freedom, new moral awareness, the willingness of the individual American to go off to difficult and backward places and personally work to change the lives of others, to introduce new notes of decency and order into the native roughness. It was a long task, but a vital task—one worthy of accepting a life of hardships to bring it about.

In this light she had to acknowledge Harley's growing frustrations in trying to maintain the little Christian community. It erupted in his periodic irritation with her on small issues, that would initially hurt until she realized that these eruptions were aimed not at her but at the situation. For all she knew, his anger might stem from a flash of tormenting clarity about his own life—just as a car's piercing headlights along a bumpy country road could suddenly probe down the darkened contours of the path of remaining life ahead, only to reveal it to be twisting and short.

*   *   *

After the previous day's assault of pain and anguish upon each other, everyone was on their best behavior. In an important gesture, Alex and Jack asked Harley if they could accompany him to his evening clinic three blocks away. The place was just like Alex had remembered: same one-story building, white and blue, a large swinging sign on the outside with a big picture of an eye—with a blue iris—and the word "Clinic" written in Urdu and English. Inside a slight odor of disinfectant, brightly colored wooden chairs in hand-made village-style lining the walls in the waiting room. A floor of large dark-red clay tiles, uneven so that the chairs didn't sit quite flat. Their father didn't want it to be too fancy-looking, it might intimidate people from coming in. Although open to all, it was known locally as the Christian clinic, but Muslims came too when their children had eye problems. Sometimes their problems didn't have to do with eyes at all, but at least he could hear their complaints, answer elementary health questions and suggest what doctor they might see.

Today four people sat inside waiting. The patients all stood up and bowed, almost reverentially, hand on their hearts as "Doktoor Sahib" entered to begin the evening clinic. One was a woman in a sari with a teenage boy accompanying her, and two older bearded men in turbans and rumpled, soiled clothing. One had a pair of glasses that looked like the bottom of a Coke bottle. Inside the inner office was a raised leather seat surrounded by the gangling articulations of an optician's equipment. A large eye chart hung on the wall adorned with simple symbols and shapes, including half circles and M's and W's turned at various angles to accommodate the many illiterate. Frames for glasses were set in the corner on a counter next to a wooden box with felt-lined sliding drawers that held individual glass lenses for testing. Bottles of eye solutions and disinfectants sat on a shelf.

"The picture of Jesus preaching, it's gone," observed Jack.

"Yes," said Harley, "I took it down quite some time ago. I'll have to admit, it wasn't a good idea. I don't need to offer my enemies any more ammunition."

"So who all comes to the clinic now?"

"Not so many people any more. My biggest regret is that I don't get so many Muslims coming in now. They've been warned off by the hardline mullahs. So it's mostly just what's left of our Christian community. Still, it's an important service for them with free eye examinations and glasses."

"Can't they get help at government clinics?"

"Yes, but there aren't enough of them, or they're not nearby. We're able to stop a lot of basic blindness here. At least thirty percent of cases of eye loss that I see could have been easily prevented."

"So what do you do?" Jack asked.

"This is mostly just basic eye health, trying to get their kids in if they have eye infections—they're easy to pick up from the dust and lack of hygiene, and it leads to corneal scarring. And old people with cataracts—it's a joy to be able to give them some treatment via medication and see their sight partially restored."

Alex cringed at his father's insensitive ignoring of his own eye loss, but decided not to raise it here. Both he and Jack were moved by the deep sense of gratitude that the patients showed to their father. Many of them knew him not only as a doctor but also as a community pastor in their private religious services.

It was an hour and a half before the patients had all been examined and had departed. Harley closed down the clinic and was in the process of locking the door when they noticed a mullah in robes standing outside nearby with a scowl on his face. "There's one of them now," their father said under his breath, "he's been coming around every so often just to stare, observe. That's what intimidates Muslims in the community from coming in." The mullah wandered over towards them. His long untrimmed beard, as well as the shorter robes in place of the baggy shalwar pants and tunic worn by most Pakistanis, marked him as a zealot.

"*Assalaamu aleykum.*" Harley nodded preemptively.

"*Wa aleykumu assalam,*" the mullah replied sourly. "Who are you helping here, Doktoor Sahib?" he asked in Urdu.

"I'm helping Pakistanis, to save their eyes," Harley answered in Urdu.

"And who do you help? Just Nasranis?"

"No, not just Christians, I serve anyone who comes, Muslims too."

"Muslims will not come to you because they do not want you to turn them against Islam, to make them Nasranis. That is against our religion."

"I do not turn them against Islam. I serve them. I only tell them about the Prophet Jesus if they are interested."

"We know about the Holy Prophet Jesus, Doktoor Sahib. We honor and respect him. He is part of the way of Islam. We do not need your teachings about him." The mullah paused and stared hard before delivering the real message. "You are not welcome here."

"I am trying to help the people."

"You are harming the people with your beliefs. We know you are a Christian. We do not need you here. People say you are a spy for America. I warn you. If you do not close your clinic some of your followers will have difficulties."

Alex sensed the latent threat and saw red. He rose to defend his father, harassed and humiliated by this primitive presence. He started to speak angrily in halting Urdu but his father waved him off.

"I do not accept threats," Harley told the mullah. "I am here to serve the people, and serve God."

"We know you, Doktoor Sahib. You and your missionaries have already divided our society by bringing outside ideas to our Muslim land, to divide the people. We do not need that. You would be smart to leave Pakistan, Doktoor Sahib. Do not make trouble that you might regret."

Harley turned his back and walked away ahead of his sons who followed, shaken. "Those swine," he muttered. "That's the most blatant threat yet. These fanatics are getting out of hand."

Alex exchanged glances with Jack, but for the first time his heart went out to his father in these circumstances. This arrogant bearded bastard, blatantly trying to intimidate his father. Yes, his father was naïve, but dammit, he cared, he was committed to helping take care of people's eyes. That was well beyond religion or politics. And Alex had a haunting vision of the end of the line his father was facing.

*   *   *

Alex sat with Jack in the darkened living room. They couldn't sleep, too hopped up by events. "You know that we're going to have to take Dad back home now," Jack said.

"I guess, but I still don't know if he's ready for it."

"What kind of a life is this, Alex? Babysitting a bunch of down-trodden Christians who are outcasts in their own society, and besieged by Muslim fanatics all around? Their situation is never going to change. It's a losing gambit."

"Jack, you can't just talk about them that way. You know a lot of these people yourself, we've known their kids."

"I know they're good people. That doesn't mean that they aren't on the wrong end of the system. I think all these damn foreign missionaries are actually making life *harder* for them, associated with foreign powers."

"Dammit, Jack, whatever Dad's weaknesses, he's no tool of Washington politics. You know how critical he is of that!"

"Wake up! It's not about reality, it's about perception. American missionaries here, dedicating their lives to the Christian community? Of course it makes Muslims wonder what the real game is. Sooner or later some nut in a turban is going to take him out!"

The incident with the mullah festered in Alex's mind; he called up Majeed the next day. "Could we meet down in the Old City? I need to talk. And I'd love to revisit some of the old places there."

An hour later Alex alighted from the rickshaw at the base of the Old Fort and spotted Majeed leaning against the wall. Alex quickly recounted the incident with the mullah.

"What's going on here, Majeed? I can't believe these guys are openly trying to intimidate my father into leaving like this."

Majeed shook his head. "Alex, I told you, times are not good. There is general anger against the US. It rubs off on these poor Christians as well."

"So why should they be discriminated against? Just because they left Islam?"

"Alex, most of these Christians here in Pakistan today were never Muslims to start with."

"What do you mean?"

"Lots were Hindus! And Hindus of the lowest caste, the so-called untouchables. They were despised within their own Hindu community. The lowest of the low. Menial laborers. They had every incentive to get out of the Hindu caste system. And British missionaries were happy to convert them. You know about all this. The bloody Brits loved to set us against each other, keep us divided, keep their Empire strong."

Alex felt uneasy as he noticed various people standing around, some seeming to listen in on their conversation. They left the huge open square in front of the Emperor's Fort and walked in through the towering gate of glowing red sandstone, the signature building material of Lahore's Mughal monuments. Atop the gate were four smaller stone towers covered by cupolas. They entered through the massive gate, and into the vast space inside where they were confronted by the gleaming white Alamgiri Gate to the inner fort itself, framed by heavy white stones with fluted towers.

"You know what Alamgiri means? Grasping the world. I remember when I was a kid," Majeed said, "the thrill of coming here. Our imaginations overflowed with the tales of the battles and Mughal heroes associated with these places, all charging out to seize the world. It makes me proud to this day—just to think this is where they all lived, the great Mughal emperors, the height of the glory of Muslim rule in India. Sadly, the British Partition of India ended up giving so many of the great Muslim cities to India, leaving the new state of Pakistan with almost nothing. But thanks be to God, Lahore was able to stay with Pakistan."

Alex wanted to continue discussing the mullah incident but Majeed seemed to want to let it rest. And so they wandered among the waterfalls of the Shalimar gardens that cascaded down along marble channels, surrounded by flowers, shrubs and trees. "When Shah Jahan built all this four hundred years ago," Majeed said, "there used to be seven different levels of the waterfalls. There are only three left. It's a Mughal image of paradise. And now that seems crumbling, shrinking." They sat on a red stone bench, listening to the comforting gurgle of the cascading water.

"Look, Alex, have you ever thought about just what kind of a favor these Christian missionaries have been doing by converting people? They create small groups of Christians who are no longer part of the culture they live in— little social pockets alienated from their own societies. It's tragic. Now, anytime a Christian here gets into some quarrel with a Muslim, he may end up getting accused of uttering some anti-Muslim blasphemy—whatever the reason. I respect your father and all, but that's what he's up against."

Alex felt a desire to defend his father's ideals, yet knew Majeed was right— it was ultimately a naïve project going nowhere.

"So what should he do then, just toss it all in?"

"You want my frank opinion? Yes."

"And just give in to these crazies? You sound like you're on their side now!"

"Listen, Alex. I'm trying to be honest with you. You think I'm extreme? You should meet some of these young fundamentalists if you want to hear how some of our angry young people are talking today... Even within my own family."

Alex looked out across the Shalimar garden, divided by the channel of water running down the middle—and was pained by the unwelcome new tension in this place of his childhood.

*   *   *

Majeed was the child of Pakistan's own complexities. Culture split his family down the middle. His father was Punjabi so Majeed had grown up in Lahore, one of the classic Mughal cities, the heart of Pakistani Punjab—a background marking him as part of Pakistan's elite. Elite, but not always universally admired: Punjabi dominance of the political, social and economic order of the country was often resented—even challenged—by other major ethnic groups in the country, especially by the Pashtuns, or Pathans as they were often called in Pakistan. And that was his mother's side: a querulous, tribal and romantic people capable of both breathtaking generosity and steely-eyed revenge; a people whose legendary warrior prowess and traditions lifted them to high places within the Pakistani military structure.

It was his mother's Pashtun side that captured Majeed's imagination early on. Kashmala came from a prominent family in Mingora in the lush Swat valley near the borders with Afghanistan. While Majeed and his siblings grew up speaking Urdu and English with their father, they had shared the Pashto language with their mother. And when his family would seek escape from the summer heat of the Punjabi plains, they would flee to her family in the hills of the North-West Frontier province near Afghanistan—in Swat or other family branches west into Waziristan.

*   *   *

Harley lay in bed staring straight ahead, as his wife got ready to turn out the lights. She sensed the rigidity of his body lying next to her.

He sighed. "Maybe they're right," he said.

"Right about what?"

"About giving up on all this."

"Harley, it's not about giving up, it's about passing the baton. You have had a great impact here, you've done a lot of good. But we all know at some point there's just... missionary burnout."

"I don't know Abby. I've tried, God knows I've tried. I just don't have the same confidence in the mission anymore."

"You've brought sight to hundreds of people, that's a vital mission in itself."

"No, I mean about the importance of bringing these people over to a Christian faith. I believe in the message, but I'm just not as sure any more that this is the only road to salvation—at least for them."

"Harley, who knows what the road to salvation is for anybody. Maybe there's many roads."

"Yes," he sighed, "Maybe." He was silent for a few moments. "But frankly Alex said what's been on my mind for quite some time. How could a loving God create a billion Muslims all doomed to burn in hell—and another billion Hindus on top of that? And can I make any difference in the face of that?"

She leaned over and kissed his cheek. "I don't know how many souls you may have saved, but we have saved people's eyes so they can see."

"I take solace in that, Abby, I take solace in that."

He reached for her hand. That rock of certitude, that spark of joy—that he knew the truth of the Lord and bore witness to the world—now seemed gone. A door of doubt had been cracked open. How much of the rest of his belief would survive scrutiny?

His lips moved soundlessly. "Oh Lord, help me preserve my faith. Help me preserve my belief and keep me strong on the path of Thy works."

*   *   *

Alex's mind was still aswirl, keeping sleep at bay. By two am he finally gave up and went down to the kitchen to get a snack and drink some hot milk. The kitchen during the daytime was not a place he felt fully at home in–it was Nazir's realm, and although Nazir was happy to welcome people into it as guests, Alex felt he was trespassing into someone else's home uninvited. Tonight he was surprised to note light coming from under the kitchen door. Surely Nazir can't be in the kitchen at this hour, he thought. Alex pushed the swinging door slowly open. As he peered around the cupboard in the dim light from the counter, he noticed a figure seated at the table in the middle of the room: it was his father. He seemed bent over the table, but suddenly looked up, startled as Alex came in from behind. Then Alex saw the bottle on the table, half-filled with a brownish liquid. Harley blanched and grabbed for the bottle, but only succeeded in knocking it to the floor where it shattered, spreading shards of glass across the stone tiles. The smell of whiskey rose up. His father seemed paralyzed, speechless, and simply stared transfixed at Alex. Alex looked at his father, overpowered by uncertainty; he considered turning around and walking quietly out of the kitchen again, pretending nothing had happened and sparing his father further humiliation.

"Son?" he mumbled. "Son?"

"Yes? Dad?"

"Son…don't judge me," he said in a tired voice.

"I'm not judging you, Dad."

"You…you don't know how hard things have been." The words were slurred.

"I know they have been hard."

"Harder than you know." His voice quavered.

"Let me help you clean up the glass, Dad," Alex replied, not knowing what to say, or how to proceed, or how to deal with his father, now exposed, revealed in weakness and dependency, humiliated in front of his son. Turning to the practical matter of sweeping up helped shift embarrassment away from the overall situation. He went to turn on the overhead light but his father waved him off. "Just sit down."

Alex felt awkward sitting at the table in close emotional proximity to his father.

"As you can see…I've been drinking…" he slurred. "I've been drinking for several years now."

Alex was silent, speechless.

"Your mother knows, but she spares me. She doesn't talk about it, but she tries to throw it away whenever she finds it."

"Dad, I'm sorry. I don't know what to say. I can imagine how hard it is for you to try to continue to work, hold up the community in these times."

His father pondered his glass with the few swallows left in it. "It is. It really is. But that's not the hard part," his voice trembled. "I don't know what I believe myself any more. I feel like I…I'm just an empty vessel."

Alex remained paralyzed. Here they were, father and son, encountering each other on unexplored intimate ground. Never before had his father exposed such a crack in his permanent façade of certainty, of control, of patriarchal powers and frequent withering condescension. *The Wizard of Oz* somehow invaded his mind at this moment, the book read to him as a child; he recalled the moment at the end of the story when the Wizard's curtain of magisterial power falls to the floor, revealing the diminutive and weak man behind it manipulating the image.

"I'm sorry, Dad…that things are rough. You've had great courage in facing these challenges."

"Courage? Maybe… Or foolishness… Maybe it's the same thing."

Self-examination had never been a quality he had witnessed in his father. Alex remained caught off guard, embarrassed. He held his silence, not wanting to appear judgmental. "No, I don't think it is foolishness," he said softly. "It's commitment."

His father seemed equally unprepared for hearing acknowledgment of even a dollop of admiration from his son.

"I know I've been hard on all of you… you and your mother, your brother. I just felt I couldn't say what was on my heart, my fears. I would look weak, foolish." These words overwhelmed Alex, words of intimacy and openness that he had longed to hear throughout his life, but for which he was now unprepared. Could he even believe what had happened? Or would this new window of intimacy close down with the new day?

"No, you're not weak, just worried, preoccupied, Dad," Alex said softly, unsurely.

"Worried. Yes, I suppose you could say that. And now I'm back where I started, with a bottle in my hand. My life's cycle… I'm not worried about my community, I'm worried that my own faith is gone. My faith that saved me from the bottle when I was young… spared me to be something, come to this place, create something."

"Dad, you have created something. You have stood up for your community, you've ministered to their eyes and their health." The irony of his encouraging words overwhelmed Alex; he and his father had now reversed roles in their judgments about his father's life work.

"Sure, sure," he waved Alex off. "And I know I was stubborn about your eye, didn't get it treated soon enough… I don't know if I have ever really asked your forgiveness for that."

"You have, Dad, you have."

"And I need to apologize to your mother, for giving her a hard time for so many years. I pray to God her life's not wasted."

"I think she knows, I don't think it's wasted."

They sat in silence for a few moments longer, his father breathing heavily. He then looked up. "Well, Alex, you've all been after me to cut my losses here. Maybe you're right." He offered a weak smile.

"It's not a matter of being right, Dad, it's just about taking care of yourselves here, in harder times." They pondered the question as they gazed at the floor.

"Dad, if there's anything we can do to try to help you, help in any transition, we're here. It pains us to see you in hard times."

"Well, thank you, that's kind…" His voice quavered. "I'll think about it." He began to rise to his feet.

"Let me help clean this up, it's dangerous," Alex said, as he too stood up.

They stood next to each other looking at the glass shards all across the floor. His father looked at him, and then lurched forward into a clumsy embrace. Alex felt frozen. His father heaved a sob.

"I love you, son," he cried. "I have probably never told you that before, but my days may be short, and I want you to know."

His father's unprecedented behavior unnerved him. He had never heard words like this before. Or was it just the liquor talking? Alex patted his father's back in a few fumbled gestures.

"I love you too, Dad… I guess we just haven't had much chance to talk about these things before."

"I'm glad we have now, son, I'm glad we have… And now, if you'll excuse me…" and he moved unsteadily across the kitchen and lurched out the door.

Alex swept up the mess—the mess of so much. And he needed to remove the whiskey smell so that Nazir would not notice it in the morning. As he cleaned, his mind churned. How should he now proceed with his father? Was this a turning point, or merely a brief parting of the clouds, a moment of clarity in a drama that would return to its tortured contours with the harsh light of day?

*　　　　　*　　　　　*

Jack and Alex sat out in the garden, admiring the riot of colors as the young gardener waved greetings to them, placing his hand on his heart. Aftab had brought them out lemonade and spicy fried chickpeas.

"So you're studying Russian now, little brother? I thought you were going to please Dad and be a scholar on Pakistan."

"I decided I wanted something new and different. Russian is kind of neat, a different world."

"Well, why study any foreign language? Haven't you had enough of all this overseas culture and shit? Get on with an American life, land of opportunity."

"Naw, it's kind of in my blood. Besides, nothing else grabs me right now."

"So how're you going to make a living out of this? Teach Russian at some dumpy little provincial college somewhere?"

"I don't know. Maybe some university, maybe the State Department, who knows. I'd like to spend some time in the Soviet Union if I could, just to really learn about the place."

"Jesus, Alex, Russia's a hole."

"What do you know about it, you've never been there."

"I don't have to go there to know. The economy sucks, food is lousy, nothing works, police state all around. Not a fun place."

"Well, it's the focus of US interests right now in the Cold War. Sounds to me like I could make a living at it."

"OK, be my guest. I'd far rather live in Pakistan if it came to that. Not that I plan on that either. I've just had it with all this religion bit. They're both nuts, these Christians and Muslims."

"It doesn't need to be that way, Jack. If people just stopped trying to change everyone, like Dad is doing. And from what Majeed tells me, our embassy here is pressuring the Paks a lot too, on nukes and stuff. I just wonder how much foreigners understand what makes this place tick."

"Could be, but is it worth wasting that much time over? If people spent more time working on getting ahead they wouldn't have time for all this navel-gazing."

"Well, it's not just about money. Yeah, you're right, there's a lot of religion here—but I like the place. I like the people."

"Liking people doesn't pay the bills. Pakistan isn't going anywhere. And it's a losing proposition for Mom and Dad. They need to cut their losses." And their conversation turned to their plans for their two-day trip together to Jhelum early the next morning to visit the huge Rohtas Fort.

*　　　　　*　　　　　*

They clambered into the car with boxes of food prepared for them by Nizar. Jack drove. "Do you remember how Dad took us there one year when

50

we were little?" Alex said. "We ran all around the fort and I remember I got lost in the huge rooms upstairs. And we saw that monster gun and cannon exhibition."

"Yeah, we went camping too. And we had that lightning storm. One of the best family times we ever had. Even the old man loosened up. I remember how he taught us to make a fire without matches."

They spent the day and night in Rohtas, in reverie of a family trip in happier and more innocent times. But when they got back in early afternoon the next day the house was in an uproar. Nazir greeted them with tears in his eyes, and told them that there had been rioting at the community center and that Harley had gone over to help protect the building. Their mother was out in the bazaar. Alex immediately ran for the car.

Roiling black smoke served as a beacon through the maze of streets to guide them towards the community center. As they drove up amidst the confusion of milling people, the fire was still blazing but bystanders said the mob had gone on to their father's clinic. As they drew near, Alex leapt out of the car before Jack had fully stopped as he saw his father surrounded by a small group of people who were attacking him, two of them kicking and beating him, one of them brandishing a tire iron. In a sheer surge of adrenalin Alex ran forward into the fray roaring in rage, pushing aside two of the attackers and positioning himself over his father's prostrate body curled on the ground. Harley's face was covered in blood, his nose was smashed, mouth bloodied and several teeth knocked out.

The horror of the scene wiped away any further hesitation Alex might have had as he threw himself onto the wielder of the weapon, screaming at him and striking with his fists. Taken aback at the arrival of family members to rescue Harley, the rioters backed off, as Jack too tore into several of them blindly. "It's his sons, his sons, don't hurt them!" someone in the crowd shouted. "Don't hurt Doktoor Sahib, he's a good man," another ordered. Together Alex and Jack managed to chase off the receding attackers. Their father was groaning, barely conscious; his left leg was grotesquely twisted and the jagged end of a broken shinbone protruded from the skin dripping blood. They picked him up and carried him to the car.

"Where is the goddam hospital?" Alex shouted. Neither of them could remember. Twenty minutes later they finally found it and orderlies rushed out to carry Harley into the hospital. By then he was unresponsive, appeared lifeless, and was immediately swept into intensive care. Alex gulped back a flow of tears as he registered him into the hospital. "Christ, I don't even think he's going to live!" he cried to Jack. "You stay here, I'll try to go back and see if I can get Mom," Alex instructed. "If he's not going to make it she's got to be here."

"No, you stay, I'll go find Mom," Jack countered. And he took off for the car.

As Alex sat in the waiting room, his own clothes and hands covered in blood. "Are you injured?" an intern asked him, but he shook his head, went into the washroom and tried to wash off some of the blood. He stared at himself in the mirror; blood smears on his face where he had wiped away sweat and tears. *My own father's blood, part of my own make-up, now on my own body.* He suddenly felt a flush of a deeper physical intimacy that had begun after midnight in the kitchen a few days earlier. As Alex came out to sit in the waiting room he found his shoulders heaving in sobs. How had it all come to this?

In what seemed like an eternity his mother came rushing into the waiting room, crying and accompanied by Jack. Alex embraced her. "How is he? Is he alive? Is there any news?" his mother cried.

Alex could only shake his head. "I don't know, Mom, he seemed in terrible shape and unconscious when we brought him into the emergency unit. His head and face was badly hurt as well as his leg—lots of other cuts and bruises. They haven't told us anything yet."

As they sat on the bench, Abby held the hand of each of her sons on either side of her on the bench for some minutes as she quietly wept and prayed. Finally a white-coated Pakistani doctor emerged and said in English, "He's in a coma. He's been badly injured, but the key signs are stable. We have reasonable hope he's going to live. But frankly we have no idea when he will come out of it."

The doctor outlined the details: severe head concussion, the skull broken in several places, a complex fracture of his shin bone, several broken ribs, one of which had perforated the lung. Several bones in his hand, his jaw and arm broken, teeth lost. "I'm sorry to say that recovery will be long and difficult. It may never be complete."

Abby insisted they be allowed to go in and see him. And there Harley lay in bed, a mummy swathed in bandages, tubes penetrating the cocoon in various places. His eyes were closed, still in a coma. Alex went up to his side. "Dad? Jack, Mom and I are here. Maybe you can hear us? We love you and we'll stay close to you. You're going to pull through just fine."

Abby lightly stroked the small unbandaged part of Harley's cheek. "We are praying for you, dear Harley, and the members of the community too have you in their prayers."

They sat quietly with him for hours before they finally went to get some tea and nourishment in the cafeteria.

"What are you going to do now, Mom?" Jack asked. "Surely you won't be able to stay on here now, even if Dad had wanted to."

"Jack, of course we can't stay now. The doctors can't even promise whether he'll ever get his health back. We're tired and your father had already been growing deeply discouraged…" She covered her face with her hands. "God forgive me, but I feel almost like the Lord has abandoned us. This community was something he had helped bring up, nurture, like our own family. I just don't know why the Lord is testing Harley, these poor people—testing all of us—in this way."

"Maybe it isn't testing, Mom, maybe it's just the way the situation is," Jack suggested. "You can't blame yourself for what's happened. It's just been in the cards, everybody knows the local situation has been getting worse."

Abby urged the boys to go back to the house, to reassure the servants. Jack and Alex insisted that she too go back for some rest. "Not tonight, boys. I must stay with your father. I'll try to get back home for some rest tomorrow."

For Abby this was the nightmare she had often imagined, the kind of disaster one heard about as befalling others, but now devastating her own family. One part of her wanted to salvage the family, to depart Pakistan as soon as Harley could travel. Another braver part told her that she and Harley had an obligation at least to see the Christian community through the worst of this crisis, to perhaps get immediate aid and support from church headquarters in the US and to line up a replacement.

And the next day, pale and worn, she rose to the occasion. She gathered as many of the community's women together as possible to urge calm and told them she would seek police protection for them even as the community's leaders were in negotiations with the authorities. But she felt little confidence in this legal road for the community. And she was fearful their own home could be attacked or torched. As the potential dimensions of the situation grew upon her, she took the rare step of contacting the US Consulate to ask for protection. A consular officer came out to her home and visited the charred ruins of the community center and the clinic. Commentators in the local media reported that it was highly irregular for the US mission in Pakistan to be involved in a partisan way in intercommunal relations in Pakistan. Rumors even spread that the US Embassy was backing the Christian community center. A few stories in the sensationalist press claimed that the whole missionary enterprise was part of a grander American Embassy operation to divide Muslims and weaken Islam.

*   *   *

Majeed rushed out as soon as Alex rang from the gate and embraced him. "Alex, my God, your father! I can't tell you how sorry we are, this is truly shocking. To think that they would have attacked him like that. How awful!"

As Alex stepped inside the main drawing room, Akmal got up from his chair and came over to embrace Alex. "Terrible, terrible, my son. May God forgive these people who did this! I am praying that Harley will recover from this vicious attack by such ignorant miscreants. Have you seen him? How is he feeling today?"

"Oh, Akmal Sahib, not well, not well at all. He's still in a coma…" Alex felt his voice tremble. "He's pretty badly injured. But thanks for your good wishes, it means a lot to us."

"I must go and visit him as soon as possible."

"I'm sure he'd appreciate it, but it may be a while before he's ready to see visitors."

"No, no, I insist. It is important that his Muslim friends and neighbors show solidarity with him and come and pray for him."

Kashmala, accompanied by Zubayda and Salman, came out to greet Alex as well, bearing tea and expressing her sorrow. Zubayda took his hand, "Alex, this is so awful. I don't know what to say. Your father always tried to help people here. I'm so sorry."

"Thank you, Zubayda." Alex choked back tears. "I appreciate your concerns, all of you."

There were awkward silences, during which Majeed's father would sometimes shake his head and simply mutter "Allah, Allah… These fanatics. They are getting out of hand. Outsiders drive this as well. We are all caught in the middle."

Akmal insisted he and Majeed go and see Harley the next day. Alex warned them the sight would be disturbing. As they entered the hospital the next morning, they peered in to Harley's hospital room; a nurse was just coming out, carrying bloodied bandages. "Please don't try to make him talk," she said. "You can only stay for a few minutes."

Akmal placed his hand softly on Harley's chest and he and Majeed whispered Arabic invocations as they stood over Harley's battered body. "May God give you comfort and ease. May this ordeal be past."

Majeed paled and turned to Alex. "I just don't understand how they could do such a thing," he murmured. "We'd heard all the threats but this! How can civilized people do such a thing to a man of God?"

"To anybody!" Akmal echoed. "Yes, what kind of Muslims are we?"

*   *   *

Abby looked as if she had aged ten years as she came back from the hospital two days later. "Boys, I'm sorry… the news is not good." Her lip trembled and she pressed back her tears as Alex and Jack came over to hug her. "I just wish it were not so. Your father will be in the hospital for quite a while, at least two months. They're not sure he will ever recover fully. At least, he'll live."

"I'll stay of course," Alex offered. "Yes, me too," Jack said.

"No, there's nothing any of us can do to help him right now, it's just going to take a lot of time. And of course you both have to get back to school. I'll be alright." Her voice was not convincing. "I have some friends here who can stay with me and help out."

"No, we're staying on, Mom," Alex said. "We've got to see you and Dad through this. Akmal and Majeed would really like to help too."

"Alright, I'd be grateful. But we need to start planning the move back—as soon as your father can leave the hospital. We simply can't stay on here any longer." Her eyes watered up again. "That question has at least been taken out of our hands... resolved for us."

∗   ∗   ∗

It was a full seven weeks before Harley was able to come home in a wheelchair, in delicate shape psychologically as well as physically. Alex and Jack had been persuaded to return to their studies in the US after their father's condition stabilized. Akmal, Kashmala, Majeed, Zubayda and Salman all kept in close touch with Abby to assist her.

Harley sat in his wheelchair in the garden with Abby, hunched over the rewarding simplicity of a cup of tea. His shrunken figure melted into the blanket around his shoulders. He remained silent for long periods, eyes fixed on some distant point, his thoughts God knows where. "I don't blame myself, you know, Abby," he ventured during a moment of silence. "But I wonder... what I could have done different."

"Shhh, don't try to talk too much, Harley, you're weak, and your jaw is still delicate."

His mouth worked. "The Church will need a younger man now. To go in and pick up the pieces. The congregation must be wondering why the Lord continues to test them. And what have they done to deserve this persecution?"

Abby arranged for their departure back to Ohio as soon as Harley was finally able to travel. Jack and Alex came back to Lahore to help them pack and prepare for their exit. Against the boys' better judgment, Harley insisted on holding an open house for their Pakistani friends and congregation. But he was hardly fit for the wrenching occasion. He sat, often sobbing, in his wheelchair, feeling compelled to try to rise onto crutches to embrace each member of the community as he bade them farewell, offering a blessing to each. They clung to him in tears, "Don't leave us, Doktoor Sahib, don't leave us!" many implored. He was abandoning them, his own children. Yet everyone could see that he was a broken man.

And, worst of all, worse even than the constant pain throughout his broken body and his crushed spirit, was a yet more haunting thought. Might not this community in fact have been better off, safer and more secure, if they had abandoned their Christian identity and joined mainstream Muslim society? Maybe long long ago?

And in Alex's own mind another thought grew clearer: maybe in the end these things weren't really so much about religion for these poor people at all. Maybe it was more about integration—the need to belong in a community: the simple and universal pressure to conform to the social norms of one's larger surrounding community. The thought was not fully formed, but it was becoming clearer how hard it was to be a minority when the conditions around you pressed for conformity. *Maybe that's the way it's been for minorities throughout history.*

Harley did not live long thereafter. Once back in Ohio he found little point left in life. He had no roots in the community, very few relatives, none of whom shared anything of his long life away in distant lands. He had little to say to anyone and grew listless towards world events. His efforts to write a journal of his experiences kept only swerving back to the bitter conundrum: the roots of failure.

Alex and Jack visited as often as they could. They found some solace in the fact that he reacted more warmly toward them than they could ever remember. It was as if his ordeal had cracked his long-standing defenses and enabled him to tap into some heretofore undiscovered wellsprings of emotional expression and human communication.

For Alex, visits to his parents in Ohio seemed unreal. How distant — physically and culturally—was this modest and plain milieu, suburban house from the parental home in Lahore. Upon reflection, that earlier life sometimes took on the quality of near-fantasy in a distant and bygone world. In one sense his parents simply hadn't belonged in Ohio. He felt a sadness at the schizophrenia of his parents' life—blending in completely neither in Lahore nor in Ohio. He watched helplessly as his father no longer felt urgency to maintain his physical struggle for presence on this plane that had delivered primarily heartbreak and failure.

Nor was he up to the harsh winter. He grew weaker, contracted pneumonia, and just after Alex and Jack had come on another visit to see him in the hospital, Harley suddenly declined rapidly and drew his last breath before they even had a chance to see him for a last farewell. He was buried in a large family plot in which neither he nor those resting around him had much if any experience with each other—except for Harley's parents to whom he had felt scant attachment. Alex watched his mother grieve, yet she almost seemed relieved at the closure. She showed further signs of aging from the trauma of events over the many months, but she instinctively turned to volunteering her time to local charities. After all, her life had been dedicated to mission.

Above all, Alex was touched by the tragedy of a life shaped by a set of rigid beliefs to which his father had clung at great personal cost. And in the end it was these beliefs that had served to blind him to the reality closing in around him, even as he lived in the midst of it.

Chapter Two

Recruitment

Most people are mirrors, reflecting the moods and emotions of the times; few are windows, bringing light to bear on the dark corners where troubles fester.

- Sydney J. Harris

Casual choices have major consequences. After all the ugly events back home in Lahore and his father's death, Alex threw himself into his Russian studies at Macalester College in Minneapolis-Saint Paul, Minnesota. He wanted to put real distance between himself and the hollow intensity of theological arguments. It had all been simply too close to the bone.

Classes like anthropology fascinated Alex with their penetrating glimpses into distinct, discrete worlds. Each culture was like a small circle of oil drifting on the surface of cold water—each droplet an island to itself. They could bump into each other, sit next to each other, but it was not always easy for the walls around the droplet to break open and merge into a larger whole.

Foreign languages had come to capture him the most, the symbols and vehicles of these cultural islands, keys that open the door to whole worlds. Languages were systems of thought, ways to name things, maps to order the world in the mind. Each had its own pedigree, rules, style, personality, history, its own boundaries you can only fully fathom by growing up inside it. But Alex discovered he could still derive immense pleasure from swimming in the linguistic sea even if he couldn't plumb all of its depths.

He loved the sense of exploring new psychological terrain as he learned Russian. How remarkable was this laborious process of language study: learning how to string strange sets of arbitrary meaningless sounds together in ways that had intense meaning to others; it was like gaining access to their private cultural club, creating a special kinship with them, their psychology, the codes to their world that he was slowly absorbing, acquiring, penetrating. Yet even the words were not always enough for a breakthrough. His father had learned Urdu, but he had still remained shackled by other restrictions— mental, religious or ideological—that separated him from the people and culture around him.

What made an outsider? Even Alex's own native English wasn't enough to quite pass himself off as a "true American." Sure, he had made friends at college, he had attended the obligatory dorm beer parties, got throw-up drunk the requisite number of times, cheered the home team at football games, was a participant in numerous all-night bull sessions in the dorm. But he hadn't known the names of the big national stars in football and basketball, or even that much about the games themselves—nor did he have any great desire to. He didn't know the popular TV shows or the current top-of-the-charts songs. His fellow students seemed to like him well enough, included him in their parties, but he was always viewed as a little bit different. When he told people he had grown up in Lahore it always got a laugh. "La whore! Oo la la! Now we know about you, Alex, what you've been doing over there!" And so he came to be known to some of those around him as La Whore, or sometimes just "Whoro" to the preppier crowd; he winced at first, but chose to take it as a sign of gruff male bonding that brought him a little closer to his classmates as a regular guy. He avoided volunteering information about his background unless it was unavoidable; easier just to pass over it so as not to raise questions, an obfuscation of his own life details to others. He knew he could never really break into the psychological inner circle—those who possessed an instinctive and unerring sense of the boundaries of their in-group and who skillfully never strayed outside it, never raising the fatal eyebrow of a peer. As an outsider Alex could see that momentary flicker of hesitation on the part of others when they met him for the first time and pondered just how to place him in their familiar constellation.

Russian studies provided a welcome psychological retreat. He was consciously aware of himself here as the outsider again, knocking at the gates with the credentials of hard study to acquire a foreign culture. His American classmates too represented a kind of foreign culture, but he was unwilling to toil at studying their particular anthropology to gain admission to it, not in the same way that he was determined to do with his world of the Slavs.

These were the two faces of quite strikingly different psychological experiences—one opened his personality, the other narrowed it. With Russian it was an exercise in reaching out to embrace something totally new, to try to absorb it in order to succeed in it—an expansion of his personality into new realms. How different that was from the world of his dorm where he conducted an exercise in hiding aspects of his personality and experiences that were outside the familiarity and comfort zone of his classmates—by pretending he was something *less* than he was.

It was with the foreign students that he felt a more immediate connection. Together they shared an unspoken world not visible to others—an existence beyond the seemingly self-contained world most other American students lived in, comfortably unaware of alternative universes, values, ways of thinking, speaking, eating and romancing. These foreign students might not have fully consciously realized it, but they also shared a common assumption that once the formal ritual of a US education was finished, most of them would slip through the screen that shielded the US from the rest of the world to go back to place of their births; there, blessed and anointed by their American academic rituals and rites, they would go on to lay claim to a role of leadership in their native lands, where knowledge of American ways was both a credential and a weapon; many of them no longer mere grateful children eternally loyal to their American alma mater but rather proudly equipped with US-imparted skills that could, if need be, even be turned back upon the country that had tutored them.

And so, thousands of miles away from Pakistan he was surprised to still find a spontaneous empathy for many of the Muslims in his class—he instinctively felt he knew who they were. There was especially Noura from Syria to whom he was drawn; he used to haunt coffee shops with her, talking about their backgrounds and experiences in college, but a few weeks later when he thought he had earned a chance to become more intimate with her she let it be known that she had acquired a Lebanese boyfriend and the trail ran dry. And Alex ran across a few Pakistanis. Just hearing Urdu tugged on his heart, reminded him that there was indeed still such a place on the other side of the globe; it represented his other identity, his past, tugging him back uncomfortably to a distant world.

That distant world was still intensely real to him, even though others around him didn't know about it, couldn't see it. Like scuba diving. When you drop below the surface of the water a whole new world comes to light. It has its own hills and valleys and rocks, its own geography, its reefs here and its sandy spots there, precipitous drop offs and level sandy fields. You learn the terrain as you swim back and forth over it. All that is above you is a mere shimmering glass ceiling of the surface from where sun filters down. But eventually your emptying air tank creates its own urgent reality, you breach the surface and there it is in front of you again: the sea and the beach and the land that had been out of mind for an indeterminate period while you existed away below the waves. And that world below the waves, whose physical features you had traversed and memorized—it was now all gone, vanished, like it had never existed. And the world on top with all its reference points suddenly became the dominant one in your life again. The twain would never meet. But you still knew that other world was there, waiting beneath the waves. You couldn't see it, but you had faith it was there, and it was different. Pakistan lay under the surface of his mental sea that almost no one else knew existed. And the occasional Pakistani student he met was living evidence of it.

"Stop eating your heart out, kid," Jack told him when they got together one weekend. Jack had graduated from business school and was now an intern in a financial corporation. "They'll never accept you. We're basically weirdos. I know all about it. We're screwed from birth, we're different and there's not a damn thing we can do about it."

"So what did you do about it?"

"Me? I just clammed up about my past. Never mentioned anything about where I grew up, that I knew anything about that rag-head world over there. I can fake it pretty good, you know, I can pass for native here now. Bet you can't. You're too hung up on understanding it all. That's a rough road to hoe, little brother. And anyway, once you get into the financial world, people don't have a lot of interest in where you come from. They're from all over. You just have to be smart, creative, deliver. But you, look at you, it's not bad enough you're from Pakistan, now you're going after some crazy-ass Russian messed-up world. Leave these loser cultures alone, they'll only screw up your life more. You're like some damn chameleon! Be yourself!"

But Russia indeed had snuck into his psyche when he read *The Brothers Karamazov* in his course on Great Books of the Western Tradition. The boy who had grown up in Lahore now found exoticism in the world of Dostoyevsky—these wild people, rushing around trying to find themselves. Their religion was not something that ordered their lives on a daily basis as in the Muslim world, providing a source of certitude and identity; to these Russians it was instead a source of craziness, people running around babbling about sin, begging for forgiveness with tears streaming down their faces, taking up with prostitutes, questioning whether God existed or not, life in constant fury and turmoil, filled with obsessions, no social calm or order. And modern Russia—the Soviet Union—became to him a distant dark star, an incomprehensible, impenetrable, hostile, relentless force. This was the exotic culture that beckoned. Then he was engulfed again, this time by *War and Peace*, a sweep of humanity he had never experienced in any other book.

So there were Muslims. And there were Russians. And there were Americans. America too presented an amazing profile that he now saw up close for the first time. It attracted him with its own set of strong national values, steady democracy, tolerance, exercise of global power, leadership and respect, its openness, its creativity, its hospitality, its vision, its music, its rich layers of folk-culture, its restlessness, its can-do. His mother had always told him about the wonderful things America stood for, and he had come to admire these qualities. How different it all was from Russia! He met local White Russian émigrés who would invite him over for tea and memories, sad musings about what had been, what should have been, what might have been, and what would now never again be in their lost country, hostage now to crude communist commissars. But America was sprawling, vital, a country with a vision broader than its own borders, it had broken free of the narrow self-focus of Pakistan and Russia. This, warts and all, was what made him proud.

The summer after his father's death he drove out on a month-long trip to the Great American West with Claire, an obliging classmate in American literature who had found Alex alluring and different, at least for a fling. Claire was from Bozeman, Montana, and he liked her and liked sharing her bed. He felt a pride lingering in his groin of this first sustained physical relationship that he had ever had. She was bright, sunny and enthusiastic, but there was no mystery to her, nothing that truly intrigued him. The intensity of their sexuality in mountain motels, surrounded by pine forests and the smell of wood smoke combined with the amorous smells of their bed, all imbued his first experience of the Western outdoors world with the special pheromones of sexuality. And Alex was captivated too by the intense, grounded feel of western mountain towns and ranches, the magnificent scenery and Big Sky that took his breath away, the hardiness of it. He ceremoniously bought himself a big silver belt buckle that proclaimed to the world that "Montana is what America was."

After growing up in the intensity of Pakistan's roots, deeply entwisted into the earth of millennial history, the American West felt simple, uncomplicated, fresh, almost virginal. He reflected on what it might mean to grow up in a land without the burden of timeless history lying upon it. There was a sprawling hardy honesty to these mountain states, a hospitable, flinty, individualistic and resourceful tradition that he now understood was what had helped make America what it was. He knew his mother would be thrilled to hear of his recognition of these qualities in her native land that she had so profoundly cherished during her long exiled years in Pakistan.

*   *   *

"So why are you studying all this Russian crap anyway, Alex? What good is it? A lousy communist country, they hate us, what's the attraction?" Jack never relented each time he saw him.

"I don't know, just interesting, that's all. Aren't you ever interested in something that's different, a culture that's different?"

"Noooo, can't say that I am. Anyway, at least choose a language from a nice place to go, like French or Italian. You're already from one shit-hole out there in Asia and now you're out sniffing around in another? What is it about these hostile places that grabs you? Masochism? Kind of weird if you ask me."

"Yeah, maybe weird, but it sure beats business. I'd rather study Russian than learn about calculating dividends, flow charts and business plans."

"Yeah, well, I'll be earning the big bucks. You'll be off somewhere off doing something in frigging Siberia. You're weird, man…"

*   *   *

It had surely been inevitable. As predictable as winter gives way to spring. How long does it take to get sniffed out? There are many watchful eyes in this world. You don't study the enemy's language and hang out with their émigrés for long before you come up on somebody's scope.

There is a black loam of a netherworld out there where secret armies meet secret armies to perpetuate the struggle. They operate in a twilight world beyond the headlines and the superficial media that parades only the trivial and the transient. But beneath the surface the struggle abides, forces are gathered and deployed; high priests are required to serve at the temples where sacred traditions of secret intelligence are kept alive and transmitted from generation to generation, operating entirely within its own world, gripping and utterly consuming within the rarified context of its own special logic.

It was early in Alex's senior year. A Mr. Phillips had called and left a message with Alex's roommate, something about a possible summer job. Could he call back? Alex got only an answering machine, and left his name. Next day a hearty Mr. Phillips returned the call, explaining he worked with a firm that did research on trade and foreign policy in the East Bloc. They were always looking for qualified young interns with some background. Might even have a summer job offer. Was Alex interested? Since Mr. Phillips was going to be in St. Paul for a few days, how about meeting for a beer somewhere to chat about it in more detail? Call me Jonathan.

Two days later they met at Tavern on Grand, a popular St. Paul watering hole with its country log-cabin decor. As Jonathan had said, Alex found him sitting at the bar near the entrance, reading a newspaper. "Hi, I'm Jonathan," he said, sticking out his hand. "You must be Alex, let's have a seat at a table." They walked into the room with dark tables at the back. "It's nice to be back in St. Paul, I miss the old atmosphere. You know, once you leave here you get caught up in daily affairs and it's hard to revisit the old haunts." Turns out Jonathan, too, had studied Russian a number of years ago. He plucked a thick card out of his breast pocket and passed it over to Alex—solid, beige-colored, "Wilmington Research, Integrated Analysis on Eastern Europe and the USSR" embossed across the top in weighty print; below, "Jonathan Phillips, Director of Research," a New York PO Box, and phone.

Alex guessed Jonathan was in his early forties. He had a plump face and pleasant appearance, hearty—not the executive type but slightly rumpled academic clothing, casual yet intelligent manner, affable company over a beer. "Just out of curiosity, how did you get my name?" Alex asked.

"I've still got some ties with professors here, and you're on the list at the Slavic department. Not all that many people major in Russian these days. It's a small enthusiastic band interested in a place you can't readily visit, with a tough language, shitty food, nasty system, and not much tourism. Takes a special kind of person. How did you get interested?"

Alex told him about his fascination with languages, the appeal of this strange culture, a new world distant from any he had known. They chatted about experiences in learning Russian, the peculiar world of Slavic studies. Jonathan seemed fascinated in hearing the details of Alex's childhood experiences in Pakistan. Before Alex realized it nearly an hour had gone by, just casually shooting the breeze on a whole lot of things, all with a guy he barely even knew. Jonathan seemed enormously comfortable ensconced in his chair, in no hurry to go anywhere, drifting from topic to topic, schmoozing on like old friends.

"So, Alex, any plans after graduation?"

"Not positive, but I'll pretty surely go on to graduate work in Slavic studies somewhere."

"Sounds interesting. I sometimes wish I might have gone on to do the same. But I'm sure you want to know why I called you. I have a proposition that might interest you. My firm does specialized research on Eastern Europe and the Soviet Union, and we're always looking for new people who have a solid background in Soviet studies." Suddenly Jonathan threw out a question at Alex in fluent Russian—not just small talk but a substantive one: "How comfortable are you in using your Russian for research purposes?"

After momentarily being taken aback, Alex responded comfortably enough in Russian and the ever-so-casual language probe went on for a few minutes. Jonathan seemed pleased. He was also impressed by Alex's experiences of growing up abroad. "That's a huge asset you have there, Alex. How many Americans do you think are comfortable living in an overseas Third World environment like you are? Or speak Urdu?"

They discussed whether Alex might be free in the coming summer. "Think about it," Jonathan said. "I'm not exactly sure yet what summer projects we'll have going this year, but we always have a few. If you're interested at all, how about just filling out this quick bio form? I'll get back to you with more detail in a few weeks when I'm back in town. I can't promise anything of course. In the meantime, why don't you keep it to yourself since we don't advertise for openings, we like to handpick suitable summer interns."

Alex duly filled out the form and sent it to Wilmington Research, attention Jonathan. A few weeks later the phone rang, and there was Jonathan's affable voice again at the other end. "Hi, Alex, up for another beer? Tavern on Grand?" This time Jonathan, buying again, had a little more info to offer. Wilmington Research was a small firm, specialized in producing information on the USSR, tailored for a variety of clients in different fields, financial, commercial and governmental. Sometimes its researchers traveled to the USSR for interviews and meetings, but mostly it was research based on perusing the Soviet press, and sometimes making contacts with travelers who had been there, who could help assess the business environment and mood of the politics in Moscow. The pay was attractive, much better than most normal summer jobs Alex could expect. Some of Wilmington's clients were confidential—after all doing business in the USSR required discretion.

Alex allowed he could be interested in a summer position. Jonathan seemed to be thinking beyond summer too. "You know, from what I've seen of you, you're a lively, active guy, interesting background. Do you really want to bog yourself down in academia? There's a big world out there. Growing up in Pakistan makes you one in a thousand in having a feel for life overseas. Hell, it's not up to me to judge, but I just wonder if you'd ever be happy teaching in some small college in Iowa for the rest of your days."

Come February, Jonathan explained, they'd like to invite Alex down to their Washington office for a few days—"we maintain offices in various major cities around the US, even in Europe." One of the directors of summer research would like to meet him and further assess his qualifications. "We are a bit competitive you know. I think you're well equipped for our needs, but I'd just like a few other people to get a sense of your abilities." Wilmington Research kept a deliberately low profile, Jonathan explained. "Our success is partly based on our confidentiality. You can't cut a wide swath as a foreign firm working in the USSR and stay afloat in Western business circles."

And shortly into the new year Alex received an envelope in the mail containing a round-trip ticket to DC. And he had a three-night reservation waiting for him at Hotel Harrington at 11th and E St., right downtown. It was convenient, they explained, for Alex to stay in a central location where various people with an interest in talking to him could drop by and meet him. Alex was intrigued and was hard put not to tell his friends about it except to mention a possible summer job.

As the plane circled National Airport, Alex could make out the Washington Monument and the Reflecting Pool below. Yes, Washington, his first time! He felt a thrill; here he was actually making a business trip into the nation's capital to visit people who actually appreciated his skills enough to pay his way. That evening Alex walked around the downtown area past the White House, Washington Monument, Reflecting Pool, Lincoln Memorial, pinching himself to remember that this was all real. Later Jonathan called him at the hotel to make sure he had gotten in safely, they'd meet him in the morning.

They came to his room promptly at nine, Jonathan and two other men. Jonathan, this time in a business suit, introduced George, who, he said, did more of the direct research work. George, it turned out, was a lumbering Russian émigré, slightly gruff but gregarious enough, who spoke good English with a thick accent. He tended to squint at Alex from the side when Alex wasn't looking right at him. George tested out Alex's Russian, and then asked him to do a translation from a newspaper for half an hour on the spot, using a dictionary.

After talking about Alex's experiences in college, his future interests, Jim, the older member of the group, spoke up. "Actually, Alex, we have something of a division of labor. Our New York office handles more of the commercial research, while here in Washington we do a good bit of work for the US government—usually the State Department, Commerce, Pentagon, sometimes of a classified nature. Would you still be interested in a job? I can't give you all the details now but if you are, we'd appreciate your filling out this questionnaire—this one's a bit longer, but it's government regulations for our employees, so we can look into getting you a security clearance if need be. You may eventually have some chances to travel overseas in helping us collect information for our reports, although probably not to the USSR. You still interested?"

"Sure, in principle. But I've got to make some decisions about whether to apply for graduate school for this fall as well."

"Of course you do, but we think you'll find this work will give you a chance to look at the USSR much more closely than you ever would from a university." And Jim told him that they could offer him good pay. "You might want to consider it for a year—at the least you could build up a nest egg for grad school a few years down the road."

By the end of the day, Alex was hooked. These people were serious about him, and offered him a chance to do some interesting work for the next year as he thought about his further options later.

"By the way, Alex, we'd appreciate it if you wouldn't mention any of this to your family or friends for now," Jim said chipperly, "since the job isn't in the bag until we can get some government clearances for you. And two small things. One, your eye. You said you lost most of the use of your left eye as a child. Does that hinder you from normal activities, driving, physical activities, etc? And two, you mentioned your mother had an uncle who died in the Spanish Civil War? Could you give us a few more details on that?"

*   *   *

"Mom, I was thinking about your Uncle Alex who died in the Spanish Civil War, and realized I never knew any of the details. Can you tell me a little more about him? And what happened?"

"There's not a lot more to tell, son. He was an idealist, he believed in fighting for justice. He was an artist. He went off to Spain when he was twenty-one to fight against the fascists there in the late 1930s. It was a terrible thing. He was killed there, in the trenches... I still feel pained about it."

"He went by himself?"

"He was part of something called the Abraham Lincoln Brigade. They were a lot of American idealists. It was tragic, they were just sent in as cannon fodder. He shouldn't have had to die."

"What would he have felt about it now if he had lived?"

Abby sighed. Her health had declined severely since Harley's death. "Who knows. I guess it was easy to be disillusioned with capitalism during the Great Depression, even to become a communist. But I don't think anybody could have remained a communist after they saw what the Soviet Union did." She paused. "I know he would have totally turned against communism if he had lived—it was a lie."

Alex pondered. "That must be tough, see someone believe in something like that, be willing to die for it, and yet have it all fall apart later on."

"Yes, it was, for a lot of people. I know it almost killed my mother to see her brother join the party, and then die for it."

"The party? He was actually a member of the communist party?"

"It was a long time ago. Times were hard. People thought the capitalist system was falling apart."

"OK, but to become a communist?"

"Today it seems hard to believe. But from what my mother told me, communism looked like it had the answer to capitalism, that seemed to be collapsing in the Great Depression. Uncle Alex had been a member of the party for a year before he went off to Spain."

"What did he do in the Party?"

"How come you're interested in this all of a sudden?"

"Just curious, I'd read about the Spanish civil war."

"Well, he was an artist, you've seen some of his sketches. He was gifted. He drew a lot of illustrations for the labor movement."

"How come you named me after him?"

"We wanted to remember him, and my mother was thrilled. And you have a little of his spirit I guess," she said, patting him in the arm, "you're always sticking up for justice."

*   *   *

He explained it all to Jim over the phone, and the whole business of Uncle Alex and Barcelona was over. And he assured Jim that the loss of much of his vision in his left eye did not hinder him in performing any daily activities. Alex was called down again for a further interview in Washington.

"We're impressed with your skills and potential, and we might be able to offer you some interesting possibilities beyond what we've talked about. Feel free to tell people that you're looking into a research job with a consortium that does trade with the USSR."

To be courted, to be the object of special attention by people who appreciated and understood his skills, who laid out interesting future options for him—it was overwhelming, and undeniably flattering. Alex was exhilarated at the step-by-step introduction into an inner sanctum of apparent depth, scope, sophistication, and unrevealed contours. Jonathan and his colleagues seemed so much more purposeful than so many of the professors in the regional studies program. They were highly knowledgeable, had unusual insights into the USSR beyond the stuff in newspapers. They spoke of clear plans and goals, a practical approach to the complex task of understanding the Soviet Union. Above all they were people to whom the facts mattered. Not through some ideological prism but an effort to grasp the reality as it was, whatever it was.

Alex was thrilled to find himself involved in the central issue of American foreign policy—the nature of the threat of the USSR. It was the organizing principle of international politics and its East-West divisions. The Soviet Union was armed, possessed an aggressive ideology of expansion, ran a closed, isolated, failing system under a harsh totalitarian dictatorship, lied to its people, offered an unreal mirror-image of the real world, and oppressed its citizens with a police state. Few would challenge that vision. The superiority of American society, its values and way of life, its freedoms, transparencies, opportunities, and creativity were beyond question when it came to comparison with the Soviet Union. It was a cause Alex could readily embrace.

And there was something more, maybe the single-most important thing for Alex. For perhaps the first time in the States he felt understood for who he was and where he had come from—he was accepted. The perpetual sense of being an outsider in American society seemed lifted from his shoulders in this company. For most Americans the only real world was the US, real things happened only here, not overseas, not outside the country. Even television rarely touched on foreign countries absent some terrible telegenic disaster, or when the US was at war somewhere. Most of Alex's past life was irrelevant to others except for a few passing moments of polite curiosity. "Oh, wow, you really grew up in Pakistan? That sounds cool. I'd like to hear about it some time." But of course they really didn't.

Jonathan and his colleagues were the complete opposite. They intuitively understood Alex's background, even though they'd never been to Pakistan. They valued his experience, understood the additional dimension that it brought to his view of the world. They made Alex feel not only American, but an exceptional American, accepted, valued for who he was.

"What, no grad school?" Jack asked the following weekend when he and Alex got together.

"Well, I might want to take a little time off before then, and I've had a decent job offer."

"Fill me in."

"Not a lot to tell, some research relating to the USSR, I can use my Russian."

"Who's it for?"

"Oh, some trading company in East-West business, not very well known."

"Who wants research on the USSR these days, except the government?"

"Well, it does have a link to the Pentagon."

"You mean government, then."

"Sort of, the details of the job are still not quite clear yet."

"You're being evasive, little brother," Jack said. "Sounds like you're getting into some spook stuff. Better look out."

Jack was on the way to becoming a financial analyst with Merrill Lynch. "That's where the money is, my friend. They love my knowledge of Pakistan, I mean at least I know something about how Pak culture works, some of my old classmates are in business there, useful contacts. That's money in the bank for Merrill Lynch. Why don't you look into the financial world, much more straightforward than doing spooky research for unknown companies in Washington. I can help you out if you want."

"Maybe down the road. I want to check out this angle first."

*   *   *

Before the summer job was to start, Jonathan showed up again in St. Paul and they went out for their ritual beer and dinner.

"We've processed your clearance, Alex, should you need it for some of our work. Do you mind the idea of doing confidential research, requiring some discretion?"

"No, on the contrary, I'm interested. But you've never said exactly what kind of research this is, and whether I'm qualified for it."

"Let me put our cards on the table, Alex. Actually we represent a branch of the CIA. I've had to be cautious with you up to now, pending your getting a clearance. How do you feel about this?"

"Well, I guess I'm not totally surprised. You were beginning to sound a little spooky about some of the details," Alex grinned.

"Do you feel up to that kind of career? It would require you to maintain some cover story about what you really do. Are you ready for that?"

"Sure, I'm frankly intrigued. I assume you were serious about getting involved in research on the USSR and the use of my Russian."

"Absolutely. And you know a lot about Pakistan as well."

"Look, Jonathan, one thing. I grew up in Pakistan and I have a lot of memories and friends there. And you know my father ended up essentially getting killed there. That's my personal life, I don't want to deal with it professionally."

"Your call, Alex. There's plenty to do with the Soviet Union to keep you busy for a long time. And now let's talk about schedules and training programs."

*   *   *

Jack had gotten Kathy pregnant. "Fortunately, I really like her. We probably wouldn't have wanted a kid quite that fast, but in the end it just hastened the wedding," he told Alex. Abby was delighted with her grandson, even if Roger was born a little too quickly after Jack's marriage. And Jack, Kathy and Roger were now back east with Merrill Lynch in New York. "Big bucks, little brother, big bucks. That's what you should be thinking about. Pull yourself out of the mire." Alex was irritated at his constant references to material success, but enjoyed Jack's strong interest in international finance and its impact on global politics. Jack was even interested to talk about Soviet economic issues once he got done ragging Alex.

Alex told his mother and Jack about his new job. Abby was proud that Alex was engaged in interesting and important work. The USSR, after all, was the main threat to the West; it was a ruthless society that persecuted believers, promoted atheism, was armed with nuclear weapons and nourished a desire to take over the world. This was a long-term struggle and she was pleased that Alex was part of it. "Your father would have been very happy as well."

"Spook, Alex, spook, that's what you are," Jack jibed.

"Look, just lay off me, OK?"

And shortly after the thrilling news of her grandson's birth and Alex's new career, Abby suddenly succumbed to an Ohio winter's pneumonia, closing the Lahore chapter of Alex's family life there.

*   *   *

Alex was excited to receive a letter from Majeed. He tore it open.

Dear Alex,

We've been out of touch for too long. I wanted to tell you how saddened my whole family was at the news that your mother passed on recently. I know that life for her became difficult after returning home to Ohio and after your father's passing. Verily we are from God, and to Him we shall return. We all send our belated condolences. I hope that you and Jack draw strength from your parents' courage and dedication to others. It is not easy to commit to living in a foreign land.

I am sad about those terrible incidents from a selfish point of view as well. You are not very likely to be coming back to Lahore anytime soon I fear. And we shall miss you! Well, the world is small, inshallah we will meet again in some other location, who knows when.

It is very worrisome that all this political and religious feeling is still on the rise here, due to many different things. I have to say, the trend is negative, and I fear for Americans still living here in particular. We all respect individual Americans—their honesty, hard work, frankness, friendliness—but what your government is doing here is the source of a great deal of ill-will.

But inshallah this too will pass.

Meanwhile, I do have some big news for you! I have found a wonderful girl here, the daughter of some good family friends. We have met a number of times now and I feel sure she is the one. Her name is Aysha, she is beautiful, intelligent, she has studied English literature, and she plays the piano well. We are excited that we are to be married next month. (You see, my dear Alex? Our system does work, and it came up with a marvelous person and from a family we all like very much.) My mother and Zubayda are especially thrilled. We would love to have you here at the wedding if you could manage it.

So, new wife and hunting for a job—I think my mother's uncle with his military connections can help me find something interesting in Islamabad.

Please give our greetings to Jack, we miss you all.

Your old friend,

Majeed

*   *   *

Dear Majeed,

Thank you for your note about my mother's death. I know how my parents were close to your family for so many years and my father admired your father Akmal and their lively debates over religion. It was really a terrible thing that my father should have seen his life's work collapse all around him in disillusionment, and come to such a sad—almost pointless end. I think he just couldn't bear to have to abandon all his work there.

Mom, at least, was not bitter about the experience, for all the hardship. I think she knew all along the risks and problems of the work they were doing. But she had been lonely after returning to Ohio and of course my father's death. Even though Ohio was where she grew up, she was never quite able to think of it as "home" again. Jack and I meanwhile thank you for your kind words.

I am delighted to get word of your marriage. I would love to come back for the occasion and meet Aysha, she sounds great! But I am too tied up in my plans for graduate school, or maybe some other job next year—and it is a lot of money to travel there. But I will come back to Pakistan sometime, I promise, I hope in the not too distant future. It is my home in so many ways.

When I last saw you in Lahore I told you I was in Russian studies. The language is a lot harder than Urdu! And I can't even go and spend time in the Soviet Union. I'm not sure yet what I will do after graduating—but I definitely want to go overseas. Maybe with some international business, or maybe some diplomatic something, we'll see. Life overseas is in my blood.

Alas, for me no bride on the horizon yet! (And I wouldn't have trusted my Mom to find me one either!)

A job with the government in Islamabad could be great! I hope you will find something rewarding—you're already ahead of the game—and just starting out in life.

Well, back to my studies. Graduation is next week. It's noisy here—too much booze and partying going on in the dorm. (Just what the fundamentalists would expect here in America!)

Please give my warmest salaams to your family, especially Akmal and Zubayda. What will Zubayda be doing? Let's stay in touch. You are a brother to me.

Alex

*   *   *   *

Before Alex knew it, he was up to his eyeballs in being a spook. He was thrilled that he had been accepted, in every sense of the word, into the inner sanctum of US power and policy making. He had only known about CIA from adventure flicks, so experiencing the reality overwhelmed him with its fascination.

He was sent off to the famous Farm, CIA's training camp in Virginia, to learn the nuts and bolts of the clandestine intelligence business—the classic elements of what was called the "tradecraft" of running clandestine intelligence operations: how to spot potential agents, assess their access to information, identify motivations that might make them susceptible to recruitment, how to vet and recruit agents; how to run an agent operation, how to meet and debrief agents, keep them motivated, preserve the security of the operation, "letter boxes" or dead drops for messages, the basics of surveillance and counter-surveillance, and how to terminate—retire, take off the payroll, and amicably separate from—an agent after he ceases to be productive. Alex, to his surprise, took to it completely. It was serious, substantive and fascinating work; he was working among intelligent and motivated people, all of whom had an intense interest in overseas life and politics just as he did. And who respected and valued his background. He had found his métier.

After nearly a year of intense training he was ready to report to CIA Headquarters, or Hqs, to begin actual work—on the Soviet desk as he had been promised. He would learn the Hqs side of the bureaucracy before heading out to an overseas post. In any case his target would be Soviet diplomats and KGB officers. His first day in the office he met Maksim, his immediate supervisor. Max, the son of Russian émigrés, came to the US when he was twenty, spoke native Russian, still had an accent, and was driven by a hatred for everything Soviet. To Alex he seemed to carry a thousand years of Russian DNA in every gesture—augmented by operational experience in the field. Alex couldn't believe he was getting paid to hang out with this guy.

"Alex, eh? Aleksandr, it's a good Russian name."

"No, sorry, Greek, my father was a fan of Alexander the Great. And it's a family name."

"Well, it is a great name and it's more Russian than Greek. Only we don't say Aleksandr. Too formal. We don't say Aleks. We say Aleksei, or Alyosha, or even Sasha—five different ways to say the same name. We Russians like to be complicated. I'm going to call you Sasha."

To get a new name is to gain another dimension. Alex wanted to grow into his moniker, and was proud of it, a sign of admission into the group. Other guys in the office picked up on it as well; Alex was the only one who had been given a Russian nickname. From regular proximity to Max Alex hoped to imbibe enough experience to expand into inhabiting the figure of Sasha. "Yeah, we always think of these KGB guys as ten feet tall. But Sasha, my boy, you can always find Russians to work for us," Max told him.

"Nearly everyone has his price. Ivan wants money for a better lifestyle, Sergei needs money for medicine for his son's illness, to get good medical treatment for him, Yuri hates his boss and wants to get back at him. Lev is driven by his balls and wants to afford a mistress and the good nightlife. Konstantin hates the system that killed his father. The offer of money keeps them coming, but what in the hell are you going to do with it in a shit-hole of Soviet Union where all the gold in the world can't buy you toilet paper that doesn't rip your ass? Money keeps some agents motivated, when they know they are building up nest egg out in the West. One day, they hope, they can come out and enjoy. If they weren't under such close surveillance by their own people you could probably recruit half the Soviet diplomats out there.

"But you know what, Sasha? The best fucking recruit you'll ever get is effortless—the walk-in, the guy who wants to work for us, no, who *volunteers* to work for us. The ideological recruitment is as good as it gets, the gold standard. Some guy who hates the fucking system and is willing to work to help undermine it—by working for us. Now *that* guy is motivated. You don't need big bucks, expensive goodies, fancy bank accounts, blonde whores to persuade him. He's already sold, just show him where to sign on the dotted line—and how to keep from getting caught. Getting caught is not smart. You end up with a bullet in the back of the head in some dungeon and your family gets free one-way ticket to some icehouse made of frozen excrement in Siberia."

Max seemed larger than life. Alex felt like a virgin teenager talking to an older boy about what it's like to get laid; Max had been there, done it, possessed the cocky certitude of an experienced hand for whom the mystery of the Soviet-Russian psyche was common coinage. His contempt for Soviets was unbounded.

"But Max," Alex asked, "when you meet these guys, you can't tell them that you think the place they come from is a shit-hole. Surely they're not going to want to hear that from an American, no matter what they think privately."

"You know what, Sasha? That's all Farm bullshit you're talking—how we have to gradually warm up to them, give our cover stories, delicately feel our way into a relationship. We're not kids. We all know the score. Goddam right I tell them the Soviet Union is a shit-hole. They *know* it! They know me, they know I know, I'm an insider to them, part of the dark Russian strain of northern vodka-soaked fucking drunken Slavic race. I still belong, even if my parents fled the bloody place. They know I know the score. We don't need to pretend. None of that kissy-kissy diplomatic cocktail shit, as if we were some kind of equals standing around at the goddam reception respecting each other. They know what I think of their system, I don't even need to tell them. They don't even argue. They've got my calling card. They know what I'm peddling. No sales pitch needed. They can buy or not buy, as they wish. I just let them know I'm there, I know the score and I'm reliable."

But of talent and advice, there was a plentitude. "Tell you what, Alex, it's Friday, I'll take you out to lunch at Appleby Farms—good lunch place nearby, all spooks all the time." François Gratz was another old hand who had worked with Max for years, and he liked Alex's inquiring approach.

"François? Gratz? How'd you get a name like that?" Alex asked.

"Yeah, well, French mother and Austrian father, they split the difference." After munching on the warm homemade bread in the basket, François took on a paternal tone.

"Yeah, we got ourselves quite an office. Max is great and God broke the mold after him. But don't listen to what he says, Sasha. Yeah, he's a goddam ops genius, he can actually get away with what he says and does. He's recruited a lot of Soviets. That's the bottom line. But he's talking about himself. You or me, we couldn't pull it off. We've got to go the old cultivation routine in most cases or we won't get to first base. But remember, we're not trying to persuade them that their system sucks, we're trying to persuade them that we are available, reliable, and trustworthy. That's what they want to know."

"How will they know who I am? That I can be trusted as experienced and reliable?"

"Look, the Sovs all know any American diplomat willing to waste his time with them at a dip reception, much less learn their goddam impossible language to boot, is going to be a spook, with only one thing on his mind. But unless you're a native, with vodka-soaked Slavic instincts as Max says, you can't pull a Max. Enjoy his stories, learn from him, but don't try to play Max out there."

And Max went on to share his casual wisdom with whomever would listen, but he especially liked Alex. "They tell you on the Farm all about loyalty, Sasha, and how to get potential agents to break their loyalty to the system. Let me tell you, as far as Sovs are concerned there's no loyalty. It just depends on how good the system feeds you and strokes you. You can put up with anything if they reward you enough for it. Otherwise, it's a straight calculation for them in their shitty, dull and sometimes dangerous system. How much are they going to risk their life, and for what? If they're KGB they're already elite. Most Soviets do the math and figure it's not worth it, not worth getting caught. But it's not because they're loyal." He paused and seemed to search his memory. "There are some—actually loyal. They are the true patriots perhaps, they will put up with a whole life time of shit and misery and failure because they believe in Russia in the end. Not many of them, but there are a few. Don't count on meeting them."

"Max is basically right on that, Sasha," François said later. You'll mostly meet the whores of the system. But you know, this is an amazing business we're in. Handling a real Soviet agent is a rush. In how many other lines of work you get to sit down and talk with the enemy? The KGB enemy! On a regular basis, drink vodka, share food, laugh, and try to get inside their mind. These evil atheists—who we hear are dedicated to destroying our country and our society. And then you find you actually *like* the bastards! Does things to your mind. Makes other conversations seem humdrum and stale. Once you've been that close, it gets a little harder to just write them off as bad guys. We're probably the only place in town who does that. How many of these other military hotshots in the Pentagon or the security guys have ever met a Soviet, much less revealed their souls over vodka? Might change the world."

Life in Washington—Alex's bottom line: great classical monumental architecture, very grandiose, impressive, official. Very obsessed with itself and the world of policy. Whole town lived, ate, drank and slept with policy. Despite the fact that it was overrun with foreign diplomats, the city still felt provincial, turned in on its own navel, the center of its own rarified universe; it imagined itself doing the most serious work in the world in the most important place in the world. It was hard to resist the excitement of that mentality. But Alex didn't live in Washington, he lived in the CIA. That was why he loved working there.

After a year on the desk, following numerous overseas cases, learning from Max's non-stop commentary on Soviet operations and the human condition, followed by François' corrections to same, the word came through—he was going to be assigned to Latin America. That meant taking a nine-month basic Spanish course as well, so he could get around there, build on it. It was hardly a part of the world he had ever thought about. But he was itching to get out to the field and meet the challenge—and meet some live Soviets. "But don't let it crowd out your Russian," Max warned him. "Russians are from Mars—or maybe more like fucking Pluto—Spanish are from Venus, as they say."

"And one other thing, Alex," the chief of personnel in the Division told him, "you're going out as an NOC—non-official cover or deep cover, as they say. No connection with the American embassy or the State Department, unlike most of our other officers overseas. You'll be working in some major US financial institution, probably a bank that has global offices. You're going to need to start getting integrated into it fairly soon, learn to speak bankish."

When Max heard of Alex's plans he shot him a farewell warning. "Don't let the goddam capitalists corrupt and recruit *you* either," Max warned. "Those bankers, they're in it just for the money. It's only mother CIA will ever really take care of you."

Cover. What did it mean? Concealing the truth? Or just a small part of the truth? Or covering up for something else? For pretending to be somebody else? For dissimulating? In one sense growing up in Pakistan had already led to modest concealment of some aspects of himself. He had avoided identifying himself explicitly as part of a missionary family. He never claimed he was Muslim, but he was happy to pass without openly having to acknowledge he was from a different faith and culture, blue eyes notwithstanding. Same at college. He could initially pass as a typical American, at least in his speech and appearance. He was always guarded about opening up about his childhood in Pakistan. It was unnecessary information that would often only complicate his social acceptance. Now he would adjust to this new role, working as a bank official, while secretly operating as a CIA officer on the side. Or was it the other way around: a CIA officer working as a bank official on the side? He was determined to grow comfortable with this new element of dissimulation that would affect the full dimensions of his life and persona. A slight readjustment of his moral compass.

And the next thing Alex knew he was trying out his new cover story on his own brother. Jack had always scoffed at Alex's plans for an academic career in Russian studies, told him he should get a "real job" where he could make some money. Now Alex had to credibly explain away his sudden change of plans. "Jack, I've been thinking—as much as it pains me to admit my older brother was right—an academic career in Russian studies probably wasn't the way to go. Believe it or not, I've decided to follow your advice—go into international banking. At least it will get me to an overseas branch somewhere fast, which is where I want to be—not sitting around in Washington. And the extra money won't hurt."

Jack had looked at him hard. "Is this for real, little brother? What happened to all the Dostoyevsky Russian-soul shit you were spouting for so long at college? Not even any business school? Just like that, into a bank? Man, that's a lot of big life changes coming awfully fast. A little weird. But still, I knew the good old corrupt capitalist system would eventually get to you too—once you threw off that damn Pakistani dust from your feet."

And with that brief, bantering, dissembling exchange, Alex had realized the first tiny little barrier had now been thrown up, this time between himself and his brother. It came with the turf—the professional necessity of protecting his Agency identity from outsiders. It was a cover story he would prefer to avoid relating, especially to family, or those who were close to him from earlier days. But there it was, and a skeptical Jack had been the first recipient.

Chapter Three

Isabel

Travel is fatal to prejudice, bigotry, and narrow-mindedness.

- Mark Twain

The sea flashed below through a sudden aperture in the clouds, stretching out in an endless silver horizon through the constricted lens of his window seat. Of course, what else would it be but the sea, what else was Chile besides a thin strip of mountains and sea? The loudspeaker on his LAN Chile flight announced their imminent *aterrizaje*, their touchdown in Santiago de Chile.

A terrizaje—what a great word! Spanish was Alex's unexpected discovery in the linguistic cosmos, a tasty treat that had seized his imagination. Struggling to learn a foreign language can be the ultimate in tedium, even torture for many—much as an abstract painter might flinch from a course in accounting. A profoundly humbling experience for all: sudden reduction to the level of a child struggling to articulate wishes in the simplest of words, through a mouth that won't lend itself to the seductive new sounds, and sentences replete with grammatical errors worthy of cave man speech.

But it wasn't torture for Alex. He thrived on them. What he thought would be just a brisk practical course in Spanish for professional purposes with CIA had gone on to be much more; the language had insinuated itself into his creative consciousness.

Arriving in Santiago on his first assignment, it wasn't just the language that was new, of course. Latin America as a continent was truly a New World to him. Compared to the familiarity of Pakistan, this was a mysterious culture whose writers and tales celebrated the fantastical and joyful amidst poverty and violence. So upon arrival he was already psyched up to embrace Chilean life, its *soberbia*, its well-known haughty conservatism, mixed with an earthy zest for life.

He knew there was more beneath the surface than met the eye. "Believe it or not," his language teacher Ernesto had told him, "underneath all our machismo, we Latinos constantly fight psychological insecurity. After all, we're an out-of-the-way niche in the world. Who travels via Latin America on the way to anywhere else? You go to Latin America only to go to Latin America. It is itself, it stands on its own, it is on the way to nowhere, bridge to nothing—a prickly independent corner of the world accessible only to those who choose to go out of their way to savor it."

He spotted the handheld sign in the baggage claim area: Sr. Alex Anders. The American admin officer from First Allied Bank was there to greet him, dutifully inquired about the flight, took one of his bags, and shepherded Alex to a vehicle waiting outside with driver.

"So, first time out with the Bank?"

"Yes," Alex responded. "I'm really happy to be here, I've got a lot to learn on the ground." As they drove into the city the admin officer wandered through his basic arrival briefing, the pedestrian details for newcomers—Alex would be staying in a hotel for a few weeks until he found a suitable apartment, he would ease into the bank routine as he settled in and learned the city, restaurants and services popular with expats, the nice parts of town— "and by the way, you're having dinner with the Bank Manager tomorrow night." Alex tuned out the logistical details as he basked in his excitement about just being here—and as he thought about the more significant task ahead.

"Do you really think I'm ready for this kind of an assignment at this point?" Alex had asked back in Washington. "Yep," Max had said. "You're still a bit of a virgin, but you've been through training school, done well. You're lucky—you're available and qualified just at a time when we desperately need somebody clean out there, ASAP. I have confidence in you. And you speak Russian well enough—although Fyodor speaks good English as well. You won't have to waste your time on a lot of other operational crap. Fyodor is all we care about at this point—the KGB crown jewels in Latin America."

The bank admin officer was pointing out various landmarks of Santiago as they passed, oblivious to Alex's distracted responses.

No officers under flimsy diplomatic cover living in their gilded embassy fishbowls are going to touch him: Fyodor will be handled strictly by a non-official cover officer, was the word from CIA Hqs, anxious to maintain maximum security and protection for this valued asset. As in his earlier tour in Madrid, Fyodor had been handled by a CIA officer also under deep or commercial cover— working out of a large US financial institution similarly willing to provide cover employment to Agency officers on matters involving cases of priority national intelligence interest. And since Alex was clean—no previous operational exposure overseas and no public affiliation with any US embassy, much less with CIA—he was in an ideal position to handle a sensitive case like Fyodor. Working in a bank, he would be free from the scrutiny of local security services an official at the US Embassy would predictably encounter.

In preparation for this case the Agency had arranged for Alex to be integrated into First Allied Bank as a trainee, his Agency connections known only to a tiny handful of bank executives at the very top in New York. And

Alex had also undergone basic introduction to banking—far less engrossing than training in running clandestine intelligence operations, but vital to the credibility of his position at the bank. And now here he was, an Investment Research Officer, with an embossed business card accrediting him to the Bank to prove it. It almost felt real to him. And he would be anointed the next evening at a personal dinner at the Bank Manager's home.

He lay down but slept only fitfully. He felt impelled to leave his internationally generic hotel room as soon as possible, to get outside to taste the real sights, sounds and smells of Santiago. The next morning he came down early to prowl the neighborhood and sample street life. He was relieved to find his Spanish really did work, although the Chileans swallowed their words. He sat in a sidewalk café in a crowded back street and watched his new world go by. The bustle, the vendors, the beggars, the imperious shouts. For all its great charm, Alex had also been fascinated from his readings at how Latino culture also could be touched at the edges with social cruelty, betraying its imperial conquistador origins. Yes, it had been conquered by European Spain, but at the same time this continent had gone on to create a range of food, music, literature, myths, magical realism, foibles and a playfulness that softened the harsher Iberian parentage. In its own way it was Europe too, yes, but also far removed from Europe—sort of European values marinated in unique and distant local tradition and frontier experience. He felt he could thrive here.

He went back to his hotel, took a midday nap and in early evening came down to slide into the back seat of the Bank Manager's car waiting outside and was promptly swept off to Providencia, a posh *barrio* of the city, home to the moneyed class, Chilean and foreign, comfortably isolated from the poorer parts of town.

The manager's apartment building was stylish, although its lobby was modest. The driver pressed the elevator button to send Alex up. Instead of a servant, Grant himself received him at the door and ushered him down the hall into his den, indicating the casual nature of their dinner together. "Linda's out for the evening, so it will be just the two of us," he offered, with what seemed to Alex a certain enforced heartiness. Both of them knew Alex was not just another bank employee, but neither made reference to that fact—a kind of unspoken pact between them. Grant seem compelled to make a lot of small talk, about the countries he had worked in with First Allied, and showed off his life on display on his professional wall with pictures of his kids, various family photos at tourist spots around the world, award ceremonies with handshakes, plaques for loyal and meritorious services rendered. "I gather you've been around a good bit in the world yourself," he added.

"Yes, I grew up in Pakistan. Missionary brat."

"That's rather unusual. I think you'll find Santiago quite different."

Grant seemed unsure about how to discuss their "arrangement". "I know you will have other responsibilities on your mind as well. Your people indicated I shouldn't burden you too heavily with banking affairs so you can have time for…for your other work."

"Thank you, yes, but I still want to pull my weight as much as I can for you as well, Grant. This title—investment research—sounds broad enough to help me get out and around, learn something of the economy of use to the Bank. I don't want to stand out too much." They moved on into a breakfast room where various dishes were set out on the table, requiring no servant's presence.

Alex took advantage of the occasion to move on from the delicate topic of his other duties to something else of interest to him. "How's the political situation? Hasn't there been some easing of Pinochet's dictatorship after so many years?"

"The General? Well, yes, I suppose you could call it a dictatorship, and it certainly has gone on for many years. But I'd be careful about using that term too much around town. There are a lot of people here, especially among the business class that we deal with, who are strong supporters of Pinochet."

"Despite all the oppression and brutality of the early years?"

"Well, a lot of them didn't see it that way. Didn't touch the upper class all that much. They were frankly relieved to see the military coup that overthrew Salvador Allende. They all think Allende was a communist—and he probably was. Your people certainly will know more about that than I do. But communist, socialist, whatever—the elite here saw him as a threat to their interests—what with his socialist policies, reforms, confiscation and redistribution of some lands, too much of a populist appealing directly to the people. And then of course that big no-no, the nationalization of the copper industry. That really upset the foreign—and US—community."

Alex was a little surprised at the semi-positive posture Grant had taken towards the Pinochet regime. "But surely some of President Allende's reforms were called for. I gather that social inequality had been pretty severe over a long period. Feudal land holding, baronial rights, harsh conditions, lack of democracy and all that."

"Well, I don't want to get into a debate on that," Grant said. "But I'd be careful what you say in public. You won't be meeting many people for whom the name Salvador Allende is anything but a bad word. The upper class here is frankly delighted he's gone. And I'd have to say, under General Pinochet, things have gotten much better for US interests in the country, even if he has run a tight ship. The economy stabilized after all the disruptions of Allende's socialist policies. So a lot of people were pleased with the military coup against him, and many are grateful the US backed his fall. Again, your people know more about that than I do, God knows…"

"Sure, yes, and I do know there's still a lot of controversy about it, too, but I don't think we can just…"

"Look, just let me give you one piece of advice, Alex." Grant stared at him fixedly. "What's past is past. Allende was a hard-core radical. You won't be doing the Bank—or yourself—any favors by talking about him."

Point made. Alex would have to negotiate his way carefully through the political thickets of recent history in this country. But he knew the raw facts were nonetheless out there—that Nixon's Secretary of State, Henry Kissinger, had ordered the CIA to work with anti-Allende military forces in 1973—to help strangle the economy and stage the military coup in which populist President Allende had been killed and a pro-US general had taken over.

Grant had steered the conversation back to what the Bank was doing in the country. But Alex was already feeling mildly uncomfortable; he didn't know that much about Chile, but he sensed he maintained a different ideological worldview than Grant. And did that extend to the bank as a whole? He feared he had gotten off on the wrong foot with Grant tonight. But, as Grant said, the past is past, and it didn't serve anyone to talk about it further.

Alex excused himself not long after supper. "Yes, big day tomorrow," Grant said, "your first day at the Bank. I'll do everything I can to be helpful. And I know you'll do your best, to fit in like any other employee."

As the driver took him back to his hotel, Alex reminded himself that the centerpiece of his professional life here was nonetheless Fyodor, the sole reason for his assignment to Santiago. Mastery of his cover story was an essential part of the job. "It will become second nature to you," they had told him during Agency training. "You'll run through your cover story so often that you'll soon get bored with it and actually believe it yourself."

*　　　　　　*　　　　　　*

Fyodor was of course his code name: he had been a Soviet walk-in who volunteered his services to the CIA in Madrid five years earlier. As a KGB officer, Fyodor had known how to employ discreet contacts at diplomatic receptions to let drop word to the CIA Station that he was available. The recruitment of Fyodor had been a major coup for the Agency. Fyodor was rather well placed within his intelligence service and his knowledge of KGB networks in Latin America was extensive. In the first two years he had already provided a great deal of valuable intelligence to his case officer in Madrid.

But what is given with one hand is taken away by the other. While still in Madrid, Fyodor's wife had become involved in an indiscretion with a German businessman—at least that was what was said. From the Soviet security perspective a "German businessman" can himself conceal a multitude of suspicious properties. Indeed the KGB did not take lightly to potentially compromising relationships with any Westerners, even on the part of spouses; thus Fyodor and his wife had been unceremoniously shipped back to Moscow almost overnight. It had been a significant blow for the CIA, particularly because the move had come so abruptly they had no fully established contact plan for trying to meet him or handle him from Moscow—probably too risky from there anyway without a lot of special communications training. They could only wait and hope Fyodor might eventually resurface somewhere in the outside world on the diplomatic circuit again.

And so, three years later, his marriage dissolved, personally chastened, and demoted for his familial indiscretion—Fyodor had showed up one day as a first secretary for economic affairs in the Soviet Embassy in Santiago. Jubilation reigned in the CIA Station, and plans were laid to have a new deep cover officer immediately come out to Santiago to handle him in the most secure way. And so it was that destiny had alighted upon Alex who was clean, spoke Russian and Spanish, and, above all, was immediately available for this urgent assignment.

"You won't be meeting him face-to-face all that often anyway," Alex was told. "Too risky. We're going to set up electronic communications with him so that he can report in without you having to meet face to face—or only infrequently."

"No personal meetings at all with Fyodor down the road?" Alex asked his CIA Station contact when they first met after his arrival in a safe house rented discreetly by the Station. It wouldn't do to have Alex wandering in and out of the American Embassy—ever.

"Of course we can't eliminate personal meetings with him entirely. Despite what Hqs says we've got to be a little more flexible if we want to keep the op going. Arthur, his earlier case officer, strongly emphasizes that psychologically Fyodor needs the personal contact. In fact, he craves it, even if it is risky. An agent like this—you know, ideologically motivated—he needs to be stroked, allowed to pour his heart out periodically to constantly justify in his mind why he decided to take this step—to commit treason."

"It can't be that unusual—I mean, I would think almost any agent in his position might need the human contact and motivation from his case officer, just to maintain his morale."

"Exactly, it's a human need. He probably has many conflicting motives, but he wants to talk about it. He wants to demonstrate to you, but even more to himself, that he is not in it just for the money."

"And he's still not accepting any money, right?"

"Nope, just occasional handouts to pay for his daughter's medical condition back home. Money's not his motivation, as I'm sure you know from his file." Indeed, Alex had read Fyodor's file so many times back at Hqs that he knew it almost by heart.

Reestablishing contact with Fyodor discreetly had now become the Station's—and Alex's—immediate mission. No pre-existing plan was on the books. With all station officers on the lookout for him on the diplomatic circuit, Fyodor was soon enough observed in regular attendance at business lunches at the local Rotary Club. Alex, in his capacity as a bank officer, began to periodically attend as well; from the pictures on file, he was able to spot Fyodor on his second visit. The Rotary Club was a worthy venue for such a calculated move in the clandestine dance. The building stood as a magnificent relic of colonial Spain, over 150 years old, a grand building that prided itself as the biggest Rotary Club in Latin America. The gilded venue seemed entirely appropriate to a smooth initial contact in a classic business and diplomatic venue. In preparation, Alex wandered through many of its grander halls adorned with the revered portraits of forgotten historical Chilean merchants whose vessels had plied the oceans for long decades, carrying fresh produce smothered in ice from Chile's glaciers, to an early California market; scenes from Chilean landscapes, period furniture and glittering accoutrements filled out the elegant reception room.

On the all-important next day, making small talk with assembled Rotarians lined up for the buffet as if he had little more than social chitchat on his mind, Alex was in reality coiled like a snake, waiting for a chance to spot Fyodor, and for an opening to approach him. Fyodor's file photos were engraved on his mind. There was no doubt: flat Slavic face, dirty blond hair thinning dramatically at the top, tall, some fifty years of age, slightly rumpled appearance in a de rigueur ill-fitting Soviet suit, with a congenial but impish look and impetuous personality as noted, sometimes with frustration, by his previous handlers. Of course Fyodor could not know who might step out of a milling commercial crowd at some public meeting to reopen the door to his old clandestine contact with the Agency. But as a professional KGB officer he was sure that moment would come.

There he was. Fyodor stepped back from a buffet table, balancing a plate filled with hors d'oeuvres on one hand, a glass of white wine on the other, looking for a place sit down. For the moment he was out of earshot of the other guests. Alex approached and, using Fyodor's true name, said in Russian, "Konstantin Mikhailovich? I bring you greetings from Arturo in Madrid. He asks how is Larissa's heart." Fyodor lost not a beat, smiled easily and said in English, "Thank you, it's nice to hear from him. Give him my regards. I was wondering when another friend might contact me." And then, in a quieter voice, he said, "let's not speak Russian here. Just let me know how to contact you."

"Wonderful." Alex picked up the diplomatic patter. "It will be nice to talk about old times. Here's my card with my private phone number. Just say you are León. We'll meet the next day in Hotel de Los Angeles, in Barrio Brazil. We'll see each other in the bar off the lobby, four hours and two days earlier than the time we agree upon by phone. I'll give you my room number when I see you there."

"Thank you, I look forward to seeing you." Fyodor, still relaxed, looked around, smiled, shook hands and Alex shuffled off to the buffet again.

The Station was jubilant. Now they waited for Fyodor to make contact.

*　　　　*　　　　*

The Argentinian banker grew more boring with each minute, blindly confident of the fascination that his topic—the role of the Argentinian economy as a stimulus to the Southern Cone markets—would exert on his listener. As Alex stood holding his glass of wine, he looked beyond the banker, nodding as if still listening, while actually taking in a petite young woman with long black hair, dark eyebrows, olive complexion, and aquiline features, long earrings. She was dressed in a Latin American version of a woman's business suit. But Alex was struck that her face could have been from Pakistan as well. Her face was too long to be conventionally beautiful, but she had striking poise and evinced real spirit in her exchanges with the hostess, a blond older women. They seemed to be speaking French. Alex extricated himself from the banker, who was just warming to his monolog, with the excuse that he needed to refill his wine glass and would be right back to hear more. He approached the bottle, priming himself with a question for his hostess about a restaurant in Santiago, and was rewarded with an introduction to the young woman standing beside her.

Isabel Iturbi gave a quick, confident smile, but looked like she was about to move on.

"Pardon my asking, but isn't that a Basque name originally?" Alex said in Spanish as he hurriedly turned to Isabel.

"Yes," she replied in English, stopping momentarily. "As a matter of fact it means 'two fountains.'"

"I have a CD with the pianist Jose Iturbi, are you possibly related to him?"

She studied the young man who appeared to have some knowledge of culture at his command. "Who knows? Maybe distantly. We both come from the same part of the country. My great grandparents were from Basque country, in northern Spain."

"The Basques produce many good artists."

"And we're also the best cooks in Spain, you know," she added with a friendlier smile. "And you are American, judging by your accent in Spanish."

"I had hoped it wasn't that obvious."

"No, I didn't mean to be critical, you speak rather well actually, but you can't really hide being American."

"Hide? I've got nothing to hide, I have to be from somewhere."

They exchanged information about their respective jobs: Isabel worked at the UNESCO office in Santiago, Alex was at the bank.

"You have some French background? Didn't I see you speaking French?" he said.

"No, I am really Chilean. But I spent some years in France with my parents and I was at school there."

"And your English?"

"We all study it in school, from early years. I'm afraid we can't escape it in this world," she smiled. "And now, if you'll excuse me, I need to speak to some visiting French artists here."

"Could I call on you at UNESCO sometime if I get bored with bankers?" He was going for broke.

"Perhaps," she said. And she was off before Alex could get even get her to commit to a phone number. But he would find it. He would follow up, even if it was a more forward move than Chilean society probably approved. The hostess wandered back and helpfully added, "Her father's a prominent artist, you know."

*   *   *

Five days later the call came. "Señor Alex? León here. I have the cost estimates for the printing materials that you are interested in. Shall we meet, say at 8pm on Thursday in my office to discuss it?"

Alex booked a room at Hotel de Los Angeles for the next day; he entered the bar a few minutes before four. Fyodor was already there, seated at the bar; only one other man, older, sat over in a corner looking dreamily at a younger woman. Alex nodded to Fyodor and said, "room 327."

Room 327 was undistinguished, as befitted a hotel whose best days were long past; old, dark, a bit fusty but clean; it had a round marble-topped coffee table and three overstuffed chairs around it. It was in the back side of the hotel, with little noise from the street. Most visiting businessmen in Santiago would prefer a livelier environment. Alex stood by the window looking out at a dreary scene opposite, waiting for Fyodor to arrive.

About seven minutes later there was a knock on the door. Alex bounded over to open it. "*¿Necesita Usted servicio de habitaciones?*" a maid asked, peering into the room. "*No, gracias,* Alex responded and closed the door with irritation. Two minutes later another knock and there was Fyodor, a smile on his face. "*Zdravstvuite,*" Alex greeted him and closed the door behind them.

"Would you like to speak Russian?" Alex said.

"I always like to speak my mother tongue," Fyodor said. "And thank God we have made contact. I had a very bad time in Moscow, I can't tell you, all the psychological tension. I never knew if they knew about my relationship with Arturo in Madrid, especially after they called me home so suddenly. But it turned out to be just my vixen wife, or so they said. Her infidelities with a German, so typical—but you never know with our system, I feared it might be more, might be about me. Thank God, it was not. Nonetheless, the whole time I felt like I was under suspicion and I feared I would never be assigned abroad again. But it really was only about my loving wife. And then …"

"Slow down," Alex gestured, "let's get settled before we go into all those details. Naturally I want to hear them. But at least you are safe, even if Santiago doesn't have the prestige of Madrid. Would you like a drink?"

"I assume you have some vodka? Arturo must have told you I enjoy a bottle of vodka at our meetings. And how is Arturo? Where is he, Washington? I thought they might send him to see me, but I guess they decided against it. Never mind, you are here, Alex, and if he recommends you I am sure we will work very well together."

"Yes, I did bring some vodka, and yes, I knew you enjoyed it, and yes, Arturo even sends the bottle to you with his warmest greetings."

"Thank him and give him my greetings. You and I shall become good friends as well I am sure. We must share life together, after all, in this unpleasant city."

"Unpleasant?"

"Why yes, the Pinochet regime, the security all around, people still uncomfortable in talking about the regime, disappearances unexplained from the old days, lots of secret police, and so on."

"Well, Fyodor, if you'll permit me, isn't that a bit like Moscow?"

"Of course it is, Alex, that's why I don't like it. Did you think that my patriotism for my country leads me to enjoy this type of regime in other places?"

"No... I can understand."

"Indeed, my friend, it makes it that much harder for me to work for your organization with any great pleasure when I see how Washington has supported this Pinochet regime out of self-interest—at the same time that it condemns Moscow."

"Yes, I suppose. But Fyodor, we are getting into heavy topics too soon. I'd like to get to know you, learn about your circumstances, and work out the details of the relationship. We'll have plenty of time to talk about grand politics later on."

"You are right. First, Alex, I need some money to send back to my daughter in Moscow. She suffers from a weak heart, as you probably know, and some extra cash will help her find some better doctors and faster appointments, maybe for an operation. I worry about her all the time." Fyodor poured them both half a glass of vodka into the large hotel drinking glasses, passed one to Alex, clinked them, "*Na zdorovie!*" and took a healthy swig.

Alex took only a sip from his. He had of course read up on Fyodor's daughter and her health condition. "She's ten, eleven now, isn't she?"

"Eleven, a lovely girl, but Moscow winters are hard for her. And, as you know, our wonderful system does not usually allow us to bring our children out with us on assignments. So much for their trust, even in their own intelligence officers. But at least she is with her mother." He took another swig of his vodka. "She is a whore," he observed thoughtfully, "but she is a good mother to her."

"You can send money back to Moscow without raising suspicion?"

"Of course, I have friends in the Embassy. Many of us have little money-making operations, selling beluga caviar, Russian artworks on the side, taking dollars back to Moscow to sell on the black market. No one asks questions. You know our Soviet joke: 'Can you live on your salary? I don't know, I never tried.' And I would guess most of my other colleagues are engaged in other sins, rather than selling secrets to America," he smiled wryly.

"Well, I don't think you are exactly selling secrets," Alex observed. "You have taken very little money from us, only on a few occasions when you have needed it for family reasons."

"You are right my friend, I see Arturo has briefed you properly. No, I am not someone selling out his country for money. I am selling out the regime to the enemy because our rulers are worse than yours. The system is corrupt, harsh—worse, stupid and incompetent. They are destroying our Russia. The sooner it comes to an end, the better." He raised his glass. "To the end of the system, Alex."

"To the end of the system! And I am sure you are helping to bring about that day a little faster."

Fyodor sighed, holding his glass inspectingly. "Yes, it would be nice to think so. I hope so, at least. Sometimes I wonder, though. Power is ugly. It can corrupt. It will corrupt your country too, Alex, mark my words. But you have a better chance of surviving, your system works better, you can at least get rid of your stupid rulers periodically. We are stuck with our tottering and imbecilic Brezhnevs and Chernenkos. Brezhnev was not a bloody Stalin, thank God, but he was stupid. Stupid! An old man leading our country to ruin. You know we have a saying at home: 'Lenin showed us how to govern. Stalin showed us how not to govern. Khrushchev showed us that any fool can govern. And Brezhnev showed us that not every fool can govern.'"

Alex had heard the anecdote before, but laughed appreciatively. "People tell these jokes openly?"

"Of course, Alex, what did you think? Are you so naïve to think that just because Russians have an incompetent dictatorship we cannot discern the truth?"

"No, it's just… I mean, I thought it might be dangerous."

"Well, I wouldn't tell the story at one of our internal party meetings of the KGB, of course not. But at home, among friends, everything is said. Do you know, Alex, why the Soviet sun is so joyful in the morning? Because it knows that by evening it will be in the West. And that's the way it is. We all know the truth." Another swig. "This is where Americans are so naïve, they think we don't know the truth about our situation and that they must lecture us about communism and liberty. Such a bore."

"Maybe we are naïve, but we do want to put an end to this dangerous Cold War, for one thing."

"You know, Alex, I am not working to bring an end to the Cold War. I want to see the collapse of this disgusting system we have. I lost my father to the purges and had a brother who was sent to Siberia…we never heard from him again. I almost couldn't get a job in the system because of him. And I had an uncle who was denounced by his neighbor and sat in prison for twenty years. We have a joke for everything you know. One prisoner asks another, 'How long are you in for?' 'Twenty five years,' he replies. 'For doing what?' 'Nothing.' 'You're lying, you can only get ten years for doing nothing.'"

Alex was unprepared for this flow of political zingers. Even more, he could not keep up with Fyodor, emptying tumbler after tumbler of vodka. Fyodor refilled Alex's glass as well, although Alex felt no compulsion to match him one for one. Still, he could feel his own focus fading while Fyodor showed almost no effect. It seemed to be a session for Fyodor to purge himself of all his pent-up feelings. *It is very important to let the agent talk out all his feelings. You are his confessor, caring and forgiving.*

"We'd better talk a little business," Alex shoved his glass back. "You Russians are better drinkers than we are."

"It is an acquired art. We need it more than you do."

"Fyodor, now look, for your own safety, we can't afford to meet too much in person."

Another knock on the door. Both notably stiffened. Alex thought about ignoring it, but the knock came again. "*¿Quien es?*" Alex called. A woman's voice, "*La camarera.*" "*No! No nos hace falta nada, gracias.*" The sound of footsteps, receding.

"We shouldn't meet at this hotel again," said Alex. "These service people are driving me crazy with their queries."

Fyodor relaxed again. "A bigger hotel would be easier for me, easier to explain why I am there if I am noticed."

"OK, and next time, I wonder if we could start talking about your KGB colleagues here in Santiago? Don't take any risks on any special research, just based on what you know at the moment."

"OK, my friend. I will bring you nice portraits."

"Verbal portraits, right? And Fyodor… We're always especially interested in contacts between the Embassy and the leftist movements here in the country."

Fyodor saluted. And then, in a spirit of maintaining rapport and operational camaraderie, Alex told Fyodor about his background, how he had grown up in Pakistan, studied Russian in university.

"You studied Russian for love!" cheered Fyodor. "I love you! Not in some grubby little CIA language school for spies. You actually appreciate our culture."

"Yes, I do, and that's why I share your desire to change the system, to let the Russian genius come forth, out of prison."

"You are married?"

"No."

"Girlfriend?"

"No, but who knows, maybe I will meet a nice Chilean girl."

"Good for you! I hope to find a nice Chilean girlfriend here myself. The Embassy frowns on it, but if we report the contact and there are no security aspects to it, then these days people usually look the other way. It's the best excuse I have for taking off in the afternoons or evenings to meet you—a little loving on the side. We all need it."

"Next time, let's meet in La Fontana across the street. Give me a call the day before and I'll give you a number for the room, and again, the time will be four hours before what I say on the phone. If you can't make it, just tell me the order has not arrived yet, and we'll meet the following week, same time and place. And soon we'll need to go over to more secure means of communication."

Fyodor took his leave, steady on his feet. Alex, on the other hand, glowing with satisfaction and excitement at his first meeting with a real Soviet agent, reviewed and added to his notes, fell onto the bed and into a deep sleep for hours before leaving the hotel to go back to his own apartment.

*   *   *

Alex provided a detailed rundown of his first meeting with Fyodor when he next met with his controller from the Station, Ted, in the safe house. "The boss is going to love this Alex, kudos to you," Ted cheered. And just before they broke up, Alex asked Ted to run a routine name-trace on Isabel Iturbi and her parents in the station files and back in Washington—standard operating procedure for anyone of possible operational interest. *Remember, never operate in the dark. Always check for information that may already be on file on people you meet of possible interest. You weren't the first person to come to this city or to meet a native. Save yourself a whole lot of time and possible grief by finding out if other people have written down a few things in the past about your new contact.*

"What's the particular interest in them?" Ted asked.

"Nothing special, but her parents are prominent in society, artists, probably left of center, might provide good access into various social circles here."

"Nothing on Isabel," Ted reported back the following week, "but there's a good bit on the parents. Jorge and María. Let's see. According to one card, he was a professor of art at the Academia de Bellas Artes, an active socialist, a suspected communist, very close to the upper circles of former president Allende. Then, another card here, he attended several Cuban and Soviet national day receptions. He was reportedly arrested in 1973 after Allende was overthrown, was in prison for two years, then fled and went into exile in Paris. Sounds just like that whole Neruda crowd. All solidly pink, if not red to this day... even if they've been keeping their heads down now. They could be of possible interest as access to the Soviet community here. Otherwise we know enough about the Chilean communist party here from our liaison with CNI."

"They certainly don't tell you everything, though."

"No, of course not, but they do if there are possible Soviet ties involved. But CNI has always been great at fingernail pulling, so they've got pretty solid info on the Chilean left and their Soviet contacts here. But standard info on internal anti-regime activity, forget about it, they'd never give us shit on that."

*   *   *

Alex had bided his time, until a few weeks later he noted an upcoming artistic reception at UNESCO. And there she was, confidently engaging a group of several men around her. He pushed his way up, and a few minutes later Isabel turned to him and said, "Ah… you're the American?"

"If you insist on that," he said.

"Welcome, but what brings you to our reception?"

"I'd like to learn more about Chilean artists."

"Really? I'm sure you say that to all young women."

"Please, give me some credit. I've always been interested in art."

"You probably wouldn't hear much about Chilean artists in America."

"I grew up in Pakistan."

"Really?" She paused and reconsidered. "That's unusual. Why?"

And Alex briefly told her his story. She seemed to take him a bit more seriously now, aware of perhaps more interesting dimensions than his American banking job might imply.

"If you'd like, perhaps sometime I can take you to our Museo de Bellas Artes, there's a good Chilean collection there."

"I'd be delighted."

The next week, true to her word, they went to the museum. Isabel was charming in her enthusiasms for the exhibition, and they laughed about the pretentiousness of some of the modern paintings. "Sometimes I think the worse it is, the better the critics like it," she said. "My father is modern in his style, but he has color, passion, not just blank space with a few colored bars— like some of these."

"I'd like to see his painting sometime."

"You would have to come to our house. He has been on the black list here and hardly any galleries will show him."

Isabel asked Alex why he sometimes turned his head to the left to look at certain paintings. "Oh, to see better. I lost a lot of my vision in my left eye as a kid—an infection my optometrist father never noticed. Maybe it makes me more inscrutable…"

Over coffee Alex expressed the hope that they could visit some other places the next Saturday.

"Are you trying to 'date me,' as you say in the US?"

"Date you? No, but I'd like to see you."

The next week they met in front of UNESCO. "Alright," she said, "I want to show you my Santiago. We'll start with La Chascona."

"A restaurant? A neighborhood?"

"No, you ignorant gringo, it's Neruda's house. It's almost a shrine, we go there to feel his presence. If you don't know Pablo Neruda, you don't know Chile. My parents were close to Neruda in Paris. He's one of the greatest of all modern poets."

"Come on, of course I know Neruda, everybody knows Neruda, especially after his Nobel Prize, he's the first name you ever hear from Chile."

"But your President Johnson denied him a visa when he was invited to come to the US for a literary conference. We all felt very insulted about that. Fortunately your progressive writers made a big protest and he finally was allowed in. He is very popular in America. Can you imagine, just because he was a communist, his poetry was seen as suspicious there?"

"Well, he was a pretty serious communist. I mean, he did praise Stalin for a long time, and the whole Soviet system. But he finally did get his visa. And that was all years ago. Anyway, I don't need to see the actual house, I don't think."

"Yes, you must see the house. It is a monument to Chilean culture!"

They crossed the bridge over the grungy Mapocho and walked up towards San Cristóbal hill, whose summit was topped with a huge statue of the Virgin, illuminated at night. Alex had visited there shortly after his arrival to admire the view of the city below and the snow-covered mountains in the far distance. Isabel took him around La Chascona. "There was a major clash here between Neruda's wife and the police at the time of Neruda's death. The police wouldn't allow a public funeral procession. So this place is a shrine in Chile. It's one of the three main houses where Neruda worked, and he died right here in 1973, of cancer. For him the true heartbreak was that he had to witness Pinochet's coup against Allende only a few weeks before he died, and saw the crushing of Allende's socialist experiment, and the leader whom he had admired and worked with. Allende had named him his ambassador to Paris. Even in the last week of Neruda's life General Pinochet sent soldiers here to La Chascona and started digging up his garden, looking for weapons they said. A soldier burst into his bedroom and Neruda just looked at him and said, 'There is only one thing of danger to you here... poetry.'"

"Great line. Forever quotable."

"Yes, but then Pinochet tried to ban all speeches at Neruda's funeral. The troops ransacked the house and broke things everywhere. The house was closed to the public because Pinochet was so afraid of the power of Neruda as a symbol of resistance. And even then it was not over. Thousands of people defied the curfew to come to La Chascona for his funeral—the place was filled with police but they could not stop an emotional march to the cemetery when his followers dared speak up against Pinochet and the artists he had murdered. He is now our national myth!"

"It sounds… very emotional and powerful," Alex said. "No doubt, a great poet, even if his politics were pretty leftist."

"Yes, but his poetry and his politics were from the heart, for the people, and not for the ruling class. No one can ever take that away from him. It is only recently that we are able to praise Neruda again and read his works in public. You cannot stop a genius by calling him a communist."

Poetry had never been Alex's thing but he decided to contain his less than enthusiastic feelings in the face of Isabel's passion.

* * *

To Alex's delight, Isabel responded warmly to his attentions and proposals for more weekend walks and talks. They went out dancing one evening and Isabel was astonished that Alex could manage a tango. His Spanish teacher back home had urged him to take a few lessons to help draw him into the spirit. And the spirit was real for him. Alex told Isabel how he had been drawn instantly to the fantastic side of so many Latino novelists, their magical realism —"they sound naïve, yet they're earthy, smart in their view of life, a different way of viewing reality."

"You sound like you read that line on the back cover of some novel, Alex. Don't pretend to be a literary critic. Critics are boring and stuffy. I assume then you have read Gabriel García Márquez?"

"You're testing me again," Alex laughed. "Of course, should I name them? *One Hundred Years of Solitude, Love in the Time of Cholera…*"

"OK, pretty good, you pass."

"But where does this all magical realism come from, I wonder," he asked. "What's the root of it?"

"Mostly our native indigenous cultures, I think. You know, we have a love-hate relationship with them. Kind of a racism. Our elites originally were desperate to prove they possessed strictly 'pure' Spanish blood, so they could look down on the despised and primitive *indígenas*. But all you have to do is to look at the faces of so many of the elites to see their blood isn't so pure after all. We are all *indígenas* in one way or another. And now, here's what your literary critic Isabel would say: 'we have absorbed the vitality and mystery of the soil and the forests from the indigenous peoples.'"

"Impressive. Yes, I can see that in the novels. And it's sad to see how these native cultures were crushed by the *conquistadores*. But, fortunately, they seem to have percolated back up out of the bloody ground again." He raised his index finger to the sky in a melodramatic pose, "to fill the Latin mind with their phantasms, spirits…"

"Oh, you have had too much wine," Isabel burst out. "Now you're trying to be a poet. Bankers can't be poets!"

"Ok, wine helps, but there is something in all this magical stuff. If you ask me, fantasy explains more than realism."

"Have you prepared this speech for me, just to seduce me?"

"No, but some good glasses of wine bring out my romantic streak." And Alex in fact had fallen in love with the place as well. For him these novels were indeed about life on some enchanted continent, far from the stubbornly practical Anglo mentalities of the north. It was a place abounding in contradictions, with wild remnants of medieval Spanish-Arab culture and its codes of honor and haughtiness. Alex talked about the Spanish conquistadores, how they grew out of the Extremadura, the Spanish province that had remained under Arab rule and culture for so long. "It's overwhelming the first time you see all this. Just look at their harsh missionary view of God, and faith, and sacrifice—and all that blood! Look at the suffering Christs everywhere nailed on the cross with blood, the anguish and lean bones and ribs and gaunt haggard face. Where else in Christian art do you see that?"

"You are right. I hadn't thought of that, Alex, but you are right. You don't find that so much in French or Italian crucifixes."

"I'll tell you one more of my little theories on that. Once the *conquistadores* came to the fertile green jungles of Latin America the harsh impact of their home in Extremadura was softened. The softness of indigenous culture civilized them. All these fabled creatures of Latin America were not always as predictably cruel as humans."

"You do love all of this then!" Isabel cried. She stared at Alex in delight, surprised this gringo could match her passion for the spirit of her country.

"Yes, but I have a confession to make." Alex raised his hands and bent over in mock protective posture. "I hate Neruda. Please don't make me read any more of his poetry."

"What? Hate Neruda? How could you, Alex! How can we meet any more?"

"He's heavy, and ideological. Now if you want something more romantic, you should read the poems from where I come, Pakistan, or the Middle East."

"Tell me one."

"*I want you, yet I know that never*
can I embrace you to my heart's content.
You are that clear and bright sky.
I, in this corner of the cage, am a captive bird.
I'm afraid I don't remember the rest, but I can send it to you."

"My God, Alex, you can quote Middle Eastern poetry. That just seems to me to be such a far off exotic place. That's what makes you so different, you know. You have a sense of the world."

"Yup, that's me, man of the world."

The next weekend they drove out to Isla de Maipo for a long lunch in the beautiful setting of the Viña de Martino, one of the renowned local vineyards. As they were well into their second bottle of wine, the poet in Isabel awakened. "Think of where we are Alex, in this little place in our Chile, this little paradise—'fog-bound along our jagged coastline' as Neruda says. Yes, I'm sorry, but it is Neruda. It's unique, this place. It does reflect our jagged soul, our torment right now."

"I never thought of it in quite those terms. Why torment?"

"Really Alex, what kind of a country is this? We refuse to be boxed into some square national container like other countries. We are stretched out—maybe like on a rack—12,000 kilometers, like a diamond ribbon along an entire continent. We are the heart and backbone of Latin America, we are made of mountains and sea, right down to the South Pole. We are the creatures of the Pacific."

"Whoa, you are turning into Neruda yourself. You think the shape of the country really affects it?"

"Of course, don't you see! Our strange shape does not let us think conventionally. We are different, daring. And yes, Neruda is our soul. All the petty clerks and politicians and policemen of the state tried to contain and emasculate him but they could not. Chile's spirit can never be crushed!" She spoke almost impishly.

Alex suddenly saw her as never before. Before he knew it, he impulsively reached for her hand, knocking over her glass of wine. "Sorry, but you know I love you, Isabel!"

"You're getting carried away, Alex. Isn't this a little early?—And my poor wine!"

"I mean it, Isabel, you do something to me. You breathe life and spontaneity into me. That is what I need. It is what I want. I want to be with you."

Isabel did not withdraw. Her hand clasped his and she drew lines between the hairs along the back of his hand with her fingernail. "Yes, *mi amor*. I too love being with you. Let us go somewhere tonight. I want to spend the night with you."

They drove off to a country inn in the vicinity, an old hacienda with charm and character. The proprietor sized up the situation and lit a fire in the great baronial fireplace. Unsure of how quickly to proceed, they sat together and drank more Carmenere and then Alex kissed her. And they started exploring each other. She clearly was far from a virgin.

Later, after a bout of early discovery in a country inn, they lay together looking up at the wood beams illuminated by the flickering fireplace that covered their naked bodies with an orange glow.

"Chile has seduced you," she whispered. "I have softened up your tight Anglo mind…and heart."

"And done other things to me…"

*　　　　　*　　　　　*

Over the following weeks Isabel discovered she truly loved Alex. His blue eyes, his short blond hair, his shy smile, his receptivity, the freshness of his childish sense of wonder which contrasted so wonderfully with the often cynical, world-weary—sometimes even brutalized—sensibilities of Chileans, this sad people who often could no longer dare to be naïve or romantic. Strangely, Alex made Isabel feel more Chilean, he invited her to revel in her own roots as she displayed them to his own eager eyes. In turn, Alex offered her a sense of hope; his Americanness, his boyish yet steadfast optimism that clung to the possibility of creating something better; that one need only act, take the decision, be resolute, just do it, to alleviate the wretchedness around them. Nothing need be "written" or foreordained. "We all have the possibilities in us to change ourselves and our environment," he gushed to her during a discussion. "You know, I'd love to take you to Pakistan one day."

"I'd love to go. I can't imagine how it would be to live there."

All of this in Alex enchanted her; for her he represented the best impulses of America, even if he was not a pure product of America. That was the combination she found fascinating. Someone who could recognize her different world, appreciate it, and bring a new world into her own life as well.

She began to feel she could go on a life voyage with this man, to sail away to a place of greater hope than her dictator-ridden land of fear, shame and oppression.

*   *   *

"Now you must meet Mamá and Papá," she announced, stretching self-consciously.

Alex watched the sheet slide off her breasts and reveal her silken stomach. "Fine, *mi llamita*, but we can talk about that later—after we attend to things here again." He gently laid his head just below her breasts and gazed.

She pushed his head gently back. "No, really Alex, if we are serious I want you to know all about me, to understand our life here. You must know my family."

He raised his head and sensed her seriousness. "OK, I got it. But first things first."

"I'm serious Alex, listen to me for one minute. My parents matter to me."

"OK."

"You didn't feel close to your parents?"

Alex stopped his nuzzling for a minute. "I never could overcome the gulf that was there, especially with my father," he paused and looked up. "I cared about them, but they lived in a different world. They lived in Pakistan but they didn't truly live there. They lived in their own Christian world—in a Muslim land. And they didn't understand me. They were very religious."

"My parents are not. In fact, they are very much against the Church. The Church is in bed with the fascists. You might find it interesting."

"The Church, the bed, or the fascists?"

"No, silly, my parents, meeting them."

"OK. We can talk about it—after one more roll in the hay."

"Roll in the hay? What is that, some American custom?"

"In a manner of speaking. Even if we don't have any hay here."

*   *   *

Alex felt himself drawn ever more deeply to Isabel. Her black hair and flashing eyes, her occasionally tempestuous manner, almost the embodiment of a Latin cliché. She was bright, and her knowledge of the culture of the world, like her comfort within European and especially French circles, sometimes made even him feel like a country bumpkin. Alex certainly had some sense for the international scene, but Pakistan was very different from this. Yet he could feel something of Pakistan in her as well, in her appearance, her self-confident ability to banter.

He also saw how much Latin America was more truly an extension of European rather than American culture. He wasn't used to European culture and it offered a different world perspective, unlike the American. Indeed, it was a point of pride, this Latino sense of cultural superiority over a cruder but powerful gringo neighbor to the north. Isabel enjoyed flaunting it sometimes, to tease him.

Alex was struck too by how much of a living force Pablo Neruda was in Santiago. Isabel already used several of his poems as love letters to Alex on small sheets of handmade paper. And so he wrote back with the first two stanzas of Neruda's Love Sonnet "Morning", adding, "OK, you want Neruda, here is Neruda."

Naked you are simple as one of your hands;
Smooth, earthy, small, transparent, round.
You've moon-lines, apple pathways
Naked you are slender as a naked grain of wheat.
Naked you are blue as a night in Cuba;
You've vines and stars in your hair.
Naked you are spacious and yellow
As summer in a golden church.

Neruda's timeless touch generated intimacy in people he would never even know. Alex began to realize what an impoverished adjective "communist" had been for this man; even if technically correct, even if Neruda's political judgment had been emotionally skewed, it hugely missed the point of this towering figure who moved the nation and the world. He was the cultural lodestar, the frame of Chilean reference, an undeniable power and presence for all except the most hardened right-wingers. He saw how he belonged to all Latin America, and beyond.

*   *   *

Despite his anxieties over close scrutiny from her parents, Alex couldn't put off the meeting any further. Their home, a modest two-story with a hint of Spanish colonial style, stood out from the French architecture that dominated Bellavista, a neighborhood at war between the bohemian and the fashionable. The white stucco of the house contrasted with the surrounding dominant pinkish stone of the French style; its wrought iron balconies were markedly traditional Chilean rather than the imported European style of stone balconies around the windows. Three lone palm trees in front of the house shaded the entrance in the afternoon. A heavy Spanish wooden door compelled its visitors to wield a hefty wrought-iron disk that served as knocker to gain entrance. "I have a key, but I thought you might enjoy it more to be met formally," Isabel said.

Footsteps on a stone floor inside and the door swung open revealing a tall bony figure in simple beige clothing. "*Hola, Aristede, ¿qué tal?*" Isabel greeted him. "*Presento a mi amigo, Alejandro.*" Aristede nodded formally at Alex. "*¿Los padres están?*" Aristede nodded again, confirming the parental presence.

The interior of the house revealed much more space than discernable from the outside. Its cool stone and tiled floor lent it immediate character, augmented by an impressive collection of paintings and artifacts, many folkloric, that adorned the walls and surfaces in the corridors. A slight smell of paint suggested her father was at work in his studio.

They waited a few minutes at the base of a large stone staircase until Doña María descended, the extravagant colors of her clothing with a hint of folk influence camouflaging her thickening body. Alex's eyes were immediately drawn to her large silver Mapuche necklace punctuated by irregular lapis pieces hanging from it, and the heavy earrings also of lapis stones. She smiled formally and held out her hand to Alex, who at first wondered if he was expected to kiss it, but she took his hand in a shake. "Good afternoon, Alex, welcome," she said in English. "*Buenas tardes, Señora, con mucho gusto,*" Alex replied. Undeterred Doña María pressed on in smooth English. "Isabel has told us a lot about you. You seem to have made a good impression. She doesn't always like Americans."

"I'm pleased she has. But maybe it's because I'm not quite typical, I grew up outside the US for much of my life."

"Where was it she said? India?"

"Pakistan."

"And your father was a doctor?"

"Yes, more an eye specialist."

"Well, that is an admirable thing to do, to go and help the poor. I like that."

From around the corner Isabel's father came in, a tall figure, tonsure-like haircut, slightly stooped, but still vigorous. He wore an artist's apron over blue jeans and a thickly woven peasanty shirt. "Papá, this is Alex." He shook Alex's hand firmly, "I am Jorge, you are welcome." Alex was relieved that their unconventional dress softened their formal manner.

They sat on two couches facing each other across a long wrought-iron table set with Chilean tiles. Aristede brought them a tray with French pastries and tea. "Or perhaps you would prefer to try some of our *yerba mate*? It is a herbal tea specialty from Argentina, but we also drink it in our southern region." Before Alex had a chance to answer, she turned and said, "Aristede, bring Señor Alex a pot of *mate*."

Alex began by asking about the many pieces of art on the walls and other objects on display. Doña María fell readily into the role of guide and pointed out paintings from various friends, mostly Chilean.

"This is one painting I'm proud of," said Jorge, "an early work by Ricardo Yrarrázaval, before he became so famous."

"Oh yes," Alex jumped in, "didn't he also do a lot of work in ceramics? I think I've seen his work in the museum." Isabel glanced at Alex approvingly—he had learned something from their museum tours. "Yes, very good, very good," murmured Doña María.

Aristede entered again with a large egg-shaped gourd with silver bands of decoration around it sitting on a silver base that kept it upright; from the top protruded a spoon-like silver tube with a straw at the end. Aristede had filled it up with hot water poured over the mate leaves inside. Fortunately Alex had encountered *mate* pots once before and knew how to handle it without embarrassing himself, sipping the infusion of leaves that offered a grassy taste, considerably more modest in flavor than all the paraphernalia would suggest. Doña María watched him carefully, ready to intervene with instructions but did not. "The leaves are good for you, you can drink a lot without getting too much caffeine," she observed. They chatted about the whole culture of drinking *yerba mate* for some minutes, postponing a more inquisitive period of the conversation that Alex knew was coming.

"And so, Alex," Doña María continued, "what brings you to our Santiago? You are working in finance, Isabel tells us?"

"Yes, I'm responsible for long-range planning at the Bank, looking at investments down the road. It's an interesting job, gets me out around the town."

"Did Isabel say you had studied Russian in university? Isn't that a bit unusual? You know, if you had done that in Santiago you would have been called a communist. You might be in jail now."

"Actually I was interested in the culture, not the politics. I loved Dostoyevsky."

"Yes, yes, good reason no doubt. But how did you pass from Russian to banking, it seems not so logical, yes?"

"Well, you can't make a living from teaching Russian literature, I had to find something more practical. The Bank offered a chance to travel, see more of the world."

"I am sure the American banks are happy to be back in Chile again with Pinochet, after the period of socialism with Allende," Doña María commented drily.

"Yes, but there is no reason why banks can't do business with a socialist government as well."

"Apparently your Dr. Kissinger thought otherwise. It seems he wasn't comfortable with our President Allende."

Alex fell silent for a moment as the dreaded topic arose. Isabel quickly suggested her father show Alex his studio. Jorge got to his feet and took Alex down the hall to the back, passing through stucco-arched columns on the way. Jorge spoke fairly good English, though not as smoothly as his wife. Nonetheless, he too insisted on maintaining the conversation in English, as if it were a prophylactic barrier that protected the home culture from the profanation of linguistic intimacy with an outsider. He was polite, courteous, and, unlike his wife, avoided any political undertones in his remarks with Alex, which were primarily directed toward painting and painters in Latin America.

Isabel and her mother sat in the living room while the two men were gone. "Mamá, you don't need to be so hard on Alex. He's not responsible for what happened here."

"No, but he should know how people here feel about Americans, what we have experienced—yes, still are experiencing."

"He knows, Mamá, he knows. But I'd like you to get along."

"We will, *mi amor*," Doña María patted her hand. "It just needs time. And we have to be realistic about these cultural barriers."

"Culture isn't a barrier between two people, Mamá, it's their personal relationship and feelings that count."

A few minutes later Jorge and Alex returned to the living room and resumed their places.

"I continue to be impressed by everything I see of Chilean and Latin culture," Alex said. "Your artists are very fine. And I've been reading novels as well, to get a feel of the country."

"If you want to understand the real Chile, and not just the European side of it, you need to go to Temuco for Mapuche culture—and to the island of Chiloé," Doña María offered.

"I've heard a lot about Chiloé. I understand it has a very special atmosphere."

"Yes, it is really the soul of Chile. Very green, always misty or rainy, on the sea, it's been isolated from all the rest of the country for a long time. You find real magicians there, beliefs in old myths and legends and superstitions. Our national folklore and folk-arts—a lot of it comes from there."

"I really hope to go soon," Alex said, looking at Isabel.

Doña María continued to dominate the conversation, asking Alex in some detail about growing up in Pakistan.

"So you are more sophisticated, Alex, than many other Americans who seem naïve about the world," she said, balancing her bulk on the edge of the couch. "At least you are aware of other cultures. You can understand why they desire to preserve their own culture and freedom from outside interference." She adjusted her large silver bracelet. "We are happy that we in Chile are so far away, far from most of the power struggles of the world. But," she sighed, "it seems we were not far enough away. Our poor country had to be dragged into these Russian-American struggles. 'When elephants fight it is the grass that gets trampled,' as they say."

Alex nodded but chose to avoid a rejoinder. After a long pause that seemed designed to let Doña Maria's words sink in, they turned to art events in the city, the increasing smog of the atmosphere in Santiago, and the gradual return to Chile of friends from self-exile.

"You seem to enjoy quite a variety of cultures," Doña María said. "Growing up in Pakistan, studying Russian, now Spanish."

"Yes, I feel comfortable abroad, I like the experiences."

"And you are still trying to maintain your Russian too? You have opportunities to meet with some of the Russians here in Santiago?"

Alex shot a glance at Isabel. "Occasionally, not too much. They're not too helpful for my bank I'm afraid."

"If you had been here in the Allende days there were many more of them, to be sure. I think that is what upset Washington so much. We Chileans should have been more careful—it was unwise to upset your President Nixon. We paid dearly for it."

Alex chose to let that remark too pass, for tranquility and Isabel's sake. "Well," he said, "that was almost two decades ago. Hopefully it was just a bad period that we all need to forget now."

"Forget?" Doña María raised her eyebrows archly. "Forget? When we lost our son to the fascists? How can we forget when our parents and our children are buried in unknown places because of the Pinochet terror? When Jorge cannot be treated with dignity in art circles, or ever receive awards that are all controlled by the fascist government? When we still have spies all around us? And so many of the *nouveaux riches* who are sitting high up in power, they are allies of the President? No, Alex, I fear you still have much to learn about what happened."

"Mamá, let's not get into that," Isabel intervened in Spanish.

"No, no," Doña María continued in English, "if Alex is to see our daughter, he must know about our family. That I lost my own son as well in all these events. America has a heavy weight on its conscience from all of this."

Alex felt he could no longer appear simply cowed. "Doña María, look… you know… not everything they say here about the US is true. Nobody doubts that Nixon didn't want Allende as president, and that he put pressure on Chile to get him to abandon his Marxist positions, but there was a lot of opposition to Allende across broad parts of Chilean society. The economy was in bad shape, people were suffering from his policies...."

"You have been talking to too many fascists! What do you expect to hear from the rich in this country, your bankers? The big landowners who sucked the life out of the poor peasants working their land. Allende gave the land back to the poor, so they could farm it themselves. Of course the landowners hated Allende..."

"No, I know that, Doña Maria. But still, everyone says that the economy got terrible, you couldn't find food in the shops..."

"You know why you could not find food in the shops?" Doña Maria's eyes blazed. "Because the US sent millions of dollars to the truck unions down here not to drive their trucks. Of course we had supply problems. The food rotted on the farms, there were no trucks willing to carry food to the cities. It was horrible. And it was deliberate and the fascists helped to make Allende look bad and bring his regime down. That was not all..."

"Mamá, please, we don't need to go into all of that. I don't want another political fight. This country has too much politics, it's destroying everything." Isabel got tears in her eyes, and she glared at Alex as well.

But Doña Maria was on a roll. "This is not just hearsay. Those of us who lived here know all about what Nixon and Kissinger and the US did, how they supported coup makers and were in touch with them. Look at the reports from your own Church Commission investigation in Congress—they admitted that they overthrew our elected leader and put in power a monster who killed and imprisoned thousands of people." Her eyes burned and Alex looked away in silence.

"Mamá! For God's sakes, I wanted this to be a pleasant meeting, not a debate over Allende."

Alex realized he had foolishly allowed himself to be drawn into something that would only hurt Isabel and their relationship. After a long silence the conversation eventually turned in new directions, but the talk was strained, everyone aware that they were simply trying to keep things polite. Alex got Isabel's eye, and they finally stood up to move firmly to the door.

"Mamá, it's getting late, and there's a film we want to see tonight. So I wish you and Papá a good evening."

Both Doña María and Don Jorge worked to recover their graciousness. "Thank you for coming, Alex, Isabel is right, we should let these old issues lie. This was all before your time. You are young and innocent, and not involved in any of it. We hope you will come back again, for a proper Chilean dinner."

"Thank you, Doña María and Don Jorge, with pleasure. This country is very special for me and I wish to know it better."

Aristede showed them to the door. As they stepped out into the early evening air Alex drew a deep breath. Neither of them said anything for several minutes as they walked down to the bridge.

"I guess that didn't go too well."

"Oh, Alex, I warned you. How sensitive all of this is to them—not just to them, to most Chileans. You should just listen and keep your mouth shut. But you went and argued—about something you know nothing about. You weren't here in those days. You didn't experience anything, and you hardly have met a soul who did—except maybe your bankers."

"I'm sorry, Isabel, I really am." And he drew her close to him as they continued over the bridge.

"I just need my head to clear," Isabel said. "Let's let things quiet down for a few days. I'll call you." She gave him a peremptory peck on the cheek and then turned back in the direction of home.

*   *   *

Fyodor was on a roll with a solid flow of intelligence, high quality stuff, details on KGB agents in Chile and all over Latin America. Alex was building a name for himself back in Hqs with his reporting. Fyodor's informal exchanges with Alex, however, did not always move in predictable or desirable directions; since a lot of it represented little more than Fyodor's own personal opinions on world affairs, neither Alex nor the Station bothered to report all of it back to Hqs when any factual intelligence basis was absent. Fyodor was often prickly and unflattering in his views of the Agency and the US. At one session Alex discussed the international situation, inadvertently referring to the need to "confront the Russian threat" in Afghanistan. Fyodor's demeanor changed. "No, Alex," he hissed, "never make that mistake. There is not a 'Russian threat.' You misunderstand me. I do not do this to destroy Russia."

Fyodor, the genial, jaded cynic had now vanished. "I do it to destroy the Soviet Union! It is the Soviet Empire that has turned Russia into a prison for all nations, including Russians. All this bloated, wasting carcass of a system that is ruled by fear and lies just to maintain the empire. The empire and its Caesars must be destroyed. But do not think I am a traitor to my country! I do it *for* Russia."

When Alex noted that remark in his contact report on the meeting, the Chief suggested such material was of local operational interest relating to handling Fyodor, important to note in the file, but not important for Hqs as intelligence. It related to Fyodor's personal quirks and philosophy.

At the following meeting when Alex made some reference to "Washington's requirements" and passed along Hqs' thanks to Fyodor for his contributions, Fyodor unexpectedly snapped back. "Do not flatter yourself, Alex. It is not because America is beautiful and Russia is terrible that I help you. I admire your political freedom. I admire the dynamism of your society. Your system opens the door to expression of national talents. Right now only a strong America can help bring about the collapse of the rotten Soviet system. But you must understand—the power of the USSR is a mirage! I know the American press loves to talk about the Soviet bogeyman, the Soviet superman that the Pentagon and your conservatives work to whip up. You talk about Soviet plans to take over the world, but if you look closely, I think you yourselves are working to take over the world. Well, why not? I suppose, it will be better than Moscow doing it, yes? But why does anyone have to do it?"

Alex bristled at this point. "Look, Fyodor, Washington is not looking to take over the world. It is simply interested in checking Soviet expansionism and in trying to extend the rule of democracy to more states in the world, for a freer world order."

Fyodor stared at him. "Do you really believe that, my friend? How sad! How pathetic! I wonder sometimes why I talk to you and your people. You fall for your own propaganda more than we do in the Soviet Union. You are looking out for your own self-interests just like everyone else, although you try to put a nice democratic face on it. I will grant you, you follow your self-interests more intelligently than we do. But don't pretend it is for democracy or humanity or motherhood or God."

Alex bit his tongue. Fyodor was a valuable agent. If he got into an emotional fight over ideology with him, he might lose the operation and Hqs would be furious. This was not a debating society—to see who was more right. It was a bloody intel operation.

Fyodor steeled his eyes as he swigged down his third vodka. "Let me tell you something else, Alex. One day Russia will be free, and that day may not be so far off. I do not know if I will live to see that day, but when it is free, I will no longer work for you, or help you. You will have served the purpose. Yes, Alex, we will have *used each other*. Russia will gradually restore its greatness. Do not think that we will then run after your system, panting like a dog after a bitch. Your system is better than ours, there is no doubt—right now. But your life in America is also cold. It lacks humanity. Your ideology of free markets is more dangerous than ours. It's all about markets, not human needs. The interests of the banker capitalists represent the supreme value of the country... Do not think that just because Marx said it that it is wrong! You have a system that produces everything, but it borrows on a future in which everyone is in debt. Consume, consume, consume. That is your religion! This is the paradox: Marx invented dialectical materialism, but he was not a materialist. He was an idealist. *You* are the materialists."

Alex was taken aback by such soliloquies which often came right on the heels of a terrific report from Fyodor about Soviet intelligence operations in various parts of Latin America. There was something unnerving about the glaring disconnect—between the secret material only a dedicated and motivated spy could produce on the one hand, and the harsh views of

America on the other, which Fyodor did not conceal even as he turned over his reporting. Indeed, Fyodor had been an ideological recruitment but Alex wondered how deep that recruitment really was. Most of the Station and Hqs assumed that Fyodor was helping America because he believed in the superiority of the American way of life, a desire to be like America. Alex in his contact reports sometimes softened the harshness of Fyodor's comments on America lest too many doubts arise about Fyodor himself. As the Chief commented, "In the end, Fyodor's personal views don't matter one hoot as long as he continues to provide detailed and accurate reports on the KGB." And Fyodor did deliver, over and over again. That was the ultimate litmus test and the only meaningful criterion against which he would be judged.

*   *   *

"Alex," she said early one evening as they lay in the sweet sweat of a late afternoon grappling, "Can I ask you about something?"

"Yes, *mi llamita*, what is it?" he replied with eyes half closed.

"You know Martín who works in your office, in the administrative section of the Bank?"

"Yes." Alex opened his eyes.

"He's a distant cousin of mine. He told me he's wondered a little about you. He says you don't work the same hours as the other officers in the Bank, and that your file is kept in the Director's office and not in the regular personnel section."

"Isabel, I have no goddam idea where they keep the files."

"He says you haven't been through the same training courses for the Bank as most of the others and your accounting procedures seem a little different."

"That's just not true. Where does he get all that stuff?"

"He said he thought maybe you had some special duties here, some other work, and that I should be careful."

"Christ, the usual Chilean conspiracy theories! Your bloody cousin has too active an imagination."

"How come you are always talking to Soviets around here?"

"Look, Isabel, you know I speak Russian. It was my major in goddam university, for chrissake!"

"You don't have to get angry about it, Alex. You just, I don't know, you seem more interested in political issues here than most expats."

"Yeah, well, so what? Yes, I am interested in politics. I've always been interested in politics. I grew up overseas, the politics of different countries interest me."

"Martín joked and said maybe you are some kind of spy."

"Goddam it, Isabel, are you going to listen to shit like that? That's ridiculous." He rose precipitously from bed and started to pull on his clothes.

"I'm sorry, *mi amor*, I just didn't know what to say to Martín."

"Don't say anything to him, he's just another Chilean obsessed with the whole Allende saga. It's crazy."

"So it's not true?"

"No, it's not true." And something registered inside him. *I have crossed a critical line.*

"Well, what about Yevgeni we had dinner with, twice. He always winks at me, and he called you the 'mysterious American' when you were away from the table paying the bill."

"Come on, Isabel, don't you recognize these heavy-handed attempts? These bloody Soviets are the ones who have always filled this city with KGB types. They were thick with Allende. And they're still spreading the old anti-American lies, especially after having lost out after the Pinochet coup."

"Look, Alex, I love you. I want to be with you. I would be happy to join our lives together. But I have to know more about you, I can't marry you with some question mark over our heads. My parents have also told me to be careful about marrying an American, they have a bad record here in this country."

"Come on, you know your parents, Isabel…they're paranoid too."

"Can you blame them? After my father was tortured for two years, and forced to flee from Chile to save his life? And my brother disappeared, maybe forever?"

"I don't blame them. But they're just unthinking when it comes to stories about Americans in Chile. They'll believe anything."

"*Believe* anything?" Her voice flared. "We don't need to believe things happened, we *know* things happened, ugly things." Her voice trembled.

"Isabel, look, this is turning into some kind of an interrogation—let's-blame-the-fucking-gringos day. Let's just drop it."

Isabel dabbed at the corner of her eye with the edge of the sheet. "Alex, this isn't like you, all this coarse talk. How can I drop it? I asked you before about your business meetings at night when you don't tell me much about where you are going. Of course I wonder."

"Alright, goddam it, Isabel, then if you can't trust me… Look, I'm sorry, but this is getting impossible. Maybe we need to stop seeing each other for a while." *Was it coming to this?*

Isabel looked down into her lap and sobbed. "You know that's not what I want, Alex. Don't talk to me like that."

"Maybe this just isn't working. We live in different worlds, we have different responsibilities. Let's let things cool off for a few weeks. Then we'll see."

Isabel got up and got dressed silently. They hugged peremptorily and then she left his apartment, head bowed. Alex sat slumped in his chair, ashamed of himself. *What is this coming to? In the legitimate protection of my status here as an intel officer? How is this going to affect my relationship with Isabel?*

$*$ $*$ $*$

Alex asked for a meeting with the Deputy Station Chief. He felt an urgent need for clarification. In the event, the Chief of Operations Juan Ramírez also came along. Alex was extra cautious now, and double checked for surveillance before arriving at the safe house.

"Look, Juan, as you know, I'm getting involved in some leftist circles. They talk a lot. I'm frankly unsure about some things here. Can I privately just ask, how did all this mess come about with the US in Chile? I mean, what were we up to when we got involved in this overthrow of Allende?"

"Alex, this is above your paygrade—and mine too. Nixon and Kissinger felt threatened in Latin America, and they worried Allende was too close to the Sovs. He nationalized a lot of US companies, especially the big copper companies. If he wasn't a communist then he had communist connections all around him. He openly said he was a Marxist. All that was asking for trouble."

"I know about that. But still, did that call for a coup against him?"

"What do I know? You had to understand the times, the early 1970s. The White House was paranoid about the Soviets. Everything Washington did around the globe was to try to check the communists. All these bleeding US pinstripe diplomats who were trying to report on local politics around the world simply missed the point: the only thing that mattered back home was what the Sovs were doing, and what our response should be. It was a fucking global chessboard. High stakes."

The Deputy Chief of Station chimed in. "Look Alex, it's a rough world out there. The Russkies have been bidding to take over as much of the damn world as they can. They can't do it, of course, they are pretty incompetent when it comes to the grand picture. All they have going for them are weapons and some military training and a very professional intel service. They have been out recruiting up a storm of agents everywhere, and so were we. So I don't think we can get all worked up into a lather that the game got rough and Allende got killed. He probably committed suicide actually, by the time the siege against him really got going and the army was closing in, who knows. That's what Pinochet claimed. Sure, Allende had programs to help the poor, but he couldn't run the country. He was an idealist, not an administrator. And Nixon and Kissinger wanted to make his life a lot tougher, increase his problems for him, to push him out of office a little faster—for everybody's interests."

"Face it, Alex, this is goddam Latin America," the ops chief added. "It's not always a pretty scene. How long do you think any liberal can stay in power down here before the military pulls a coup? All these damn generals and armies, we all know they're linked to the old money, the landowners and the like. Sure, they're a pack of fascists when you get down to it. Hell, some of them were real Nazis who fled to Chile and Argentina and Uruguay after the fall of Hitler. They protect their interests. Guy like Allende comes along, wants to reform this and reform that, how long you think it's going be before somebody yanks out the rug from under him?"

"Yeah, but was it the right decision? I mean, look at the legacy it's left here, what Chileans think about Americans."

"I'm with you. Personally I'm glad the US doesn't quite support all these guys like Pinochet so much anymore. But face it, money has always talked, always will. You can't take on the rich and privileged in any country around here and expect to get away with it. Especially a guy like Allende, praises Stalin, talks non-stop about the goddam workers, that's red flag before the bull. Drove Washington and Congress wild. Now, in an ideal world, I agree, that kind of coup stuff shouldn't be the rule. But you're down in Latin America and that's where this shit happens all the time. You gotta get real. Kissinger told the Agency to help make things complicated for Allende, help out his political opponents who were friendly to the US, help them pull the plug on the guy, and yeah, we did."

Alex left the meeting not any more encouraged. There was in fact more to Doña Maria's account than he had realized. He felt caught, and didn't know which way to turn.

That night Alex twisted and turned in bed, alone, aware of the walls around him, reflecting the lights of passing cars in the street. He felt sick with anxiety about where their relationship was going. He didn't mind passing off cover stories about his work at the Bank to routine contacts—that had become second nature. *When you have a cover story about your life, you must use it frequently, become familiar and comfortable with it, repeat it, let it take on concrete detail inside your own mind. It becomes its own reality, ultimately convincing even to you.* Alex was in fact quite comfortable talking about aspects of his cover job at the Bank that were indeed true, it's just they weren't the full truth about him.

But leave it to some goddam local employee at the Bank to sniff him out, he thought, some stupid asshole of a clerk with time on his hands to notice the subtle differences between him and his colleagues. And for Martín to have the gall to pass along his nasty little suspicions to Isabel; he would confront Martín directly on it, except that might create even more suspicions.

Alex had never directly lied to a direct question from Isabel like that before. Repeating his cover story, yes, but that was automatic, routine, part of the job. It wasn't a violation of trust, it was just a sequestered part of his life. It was almost true. It *felt* true. Hello, I'm Alex Anders and I follow long-range economic trends and the implications for the bank's loans and project planning. That is a *real* function. Banks *are* concerned about long-range economic trends. I can talk about it. I do work in the Bank and that is what people all around me do, and I'm part of it. It's on my calling card that I pass out to everyone, it is *engraved* on the card.

No, it wasn't the cover story thing that bothered him. He had lied directly to Isabel's face now, explicitly denying something important that was true—to the woman he loved and hoped to marry.

A viper had wormed its way into their lives. Was this the end of things, or the beginning? Maybe the Agency was right, maybe he should drop her, reduce the risks. But he could not accept such a cold and calculated act of amputation. He would almost rather sever his ties with the Agency if it came to that. She had touched him in a way no woman had before, she brought to him a vitality and sense of freedom, a joy even, that he could never willingly extinguish.

*   *   *

His next session with his Station contact was not what he wanted to hear. "Alex, you got your balls in a wringer with this Chilean girl. The boss is pissed. He doesn't even want to begin to bring this up with Hqs. Talking of marriage—come on, it's just not realistic. There is no way you can reveal your agency affiliation to her—there's too much to risk. We don't know –even *you* don't know—how she's going to react. This isn't just about you, it's about the security of the whole Fyodor case and your other contacts. If you are going to marry this girl and reveal your Agency affiliation, it can only be after you've left Santiago. You might even have to resign from the outfit entirely if security can't sign off on her. If they do OK her, you'll still have to go with official cover from then on—State Department cover, working out of embassies."

"Come on, Ted, don't give me a hard time. I'm really stuck here. I don't know whether she'll even accept me once she finds out what I do. Yes, I do know her whole family is hostile to the Agency—which is not surprising after all they've been through over the past decade."

"Yeah, and they're communists. If not members of the party, at least closely affiliated or sympathizers. The boss made it clear to me. I'll put it to you straight. If you do decide to continue seeing her then you're going to have to stonewall through all of this with her—total denial. You work for the bank, period. No hint of any other affiliation. And we're not even going to hear about marriage until you're out of Santiago with no more operational ties to it, one way or another. Is that clear?"

"Yes," Alex hissed.

"You know, Alex, if you were really smart you'd find yourself another tootsie with a smaller dossier, or go back to some nice trouble-free American girl. That would save everyone a whole lot of grief—and even risk. Do yourself a favor." He snapped his briefcase shut and left the safe house, leaving Alex seething.

*   *   *

He'd rehearsed his speech many times over—the casual introduction of the topic followed by a low-key explanation. The longer he held off, the worse it would be.

As they lay in bed, passions now drained, Alex sat up against the pillows and pulled Isabel to a sitting position in front of him, with his arms around her. "I need to tell you something…" he began.

Isabel tensed, but decided to lighten the mood. "Let me guess, you're a criminal. You are here incognito, running away from a crime in America," she said, pushing his nose with her finger. "You are a Mafia leader with special instructions for the local Mafiosi here."

"No, come on, Isabel. But I do have some confidential work that I think you should know about by now."

"You're getting too serious. I'm getting frightened. Maybe I don't want to hear this."

"It's not a big thing, but it may help explain a little what I've been doing. You know how I've studied Russian for a long time. After I got here to my first overseas posting, the FBI contacted me and asked for my confidential assistance."

"FBI? What assistance?"

"They are concerned about the many Soviet agents who end up in the US working in various kinds of businesses. The FBI is trying to collect information about them before they ever get there. They asked me if I could spend a little time getting to know some of the Russians here, to write some personality reports on them when I have a chance. But it has to be kept confidential. That's why I haven't been talking about it."

"But is this not some kind of spying? Like the CIA?"

"No, Isabel, nothing so dramatic. Just a few reports on Soviets I meet on the business circuit. But I have to keep it confidential—and now you have to too, really."

"OK, Alex, at least this explains some of your night meetings. I'm still not sure why some of them are at night. But that is not my business. I appreciate that you have told me this. I forgive you. And I promise to keep it a secret. But what would the Russians do if they found out? "

"They would kill me," he said in a deep dramatic voice.

"No," she laughed, "tell me that's not true."

"No, it's not true. But it would mean the end of any help I could give on this. And the Bank would probably be upset that I was getting into other things that was not part of Bank work."

"Well, I don't really like Russians anyway, judging by the ones I have met. And if it wasn't for the Russians maybe Nixon would not have been so hysterical about Allende."

"Maybe not."

"Oh Alex, I'm so glad you told me. I feel much better. I felt there was something secret between us, and I worried about it."

"Well, now you know. So we don't need any more questions."

It was a relief to have opened the door a crack, to help make his private life a whit less mysterious. He had revealed a half-truth to her. But he had still covered up—lied—about the bottom line of his work. A half-truth and a half-lie. Again. But of course he would not have even gone so far as he did with her on inventing the FBI story if he had not decided in his heart that his future was with Isabel.

And yet, despite the relief, he feared the next session with Ted. He had briefly considered telling the Station about his very limited confession to Isabel about "the FBI," but he knew they would be furious with him even for that much; he could be fired for committing a serious breach of security. The raw fact was that he had admitted his involvement in some kind of confidential activity and, worse, to the daughter of an important leftist family in Chile who was anti-American. But what choice did he have? She would eventually have to become witting of his work. In some next posting he would probably be under official Embassy cover— less elaborate and less sensitive, and in a far less sensitive country from Isabel's perspective. Now anyway he would at least have to give Ted some version of what his intentions were towards Isabel, since it directly affected his future and onward assignments.

"You're not serious, Alex. Surely you're not going to try to marry this girl. She's one fat security risk."

"Ted, yes, I am. I am in love with her. This isn't just some casual fling, believe me. I care a whole hell of a lot about her."

"I hear you, but the security people are going to go up the wall. You know she'll have to apply for American citizenship. And pass a detailed security check for the Agency. I don't think she can even get past her own goddam family name before they reject her outright right here in the Station. You'll have to resign your position before the clearance process on her begins. If you're lucky you'll get it back, but only if she passes."

"I know she can pass, Ted. She's not responsible for who her parents are. She's not the one with the leftist contacts. She isn't any more left wing than three quarters of the people in Latin America from what I can see."

"Blood runs thicker than water. This whole damn left-wing thing runs in her genes."

"I don't believe it. And I can break all this to her slowly after we leave," Alex said. "I'll tell her that I'm bored with the banking world and that I've gotten an offer from the State Department. That will get her used to the idea of some official position in the government."

"OK," Ted's voice hardened and his speech was measured, "but do not rush this. Do not even go that far with her now. I'm sure the office will want to know a lot more about her. I can't predict that the boss may not blow his stack and tell you to break off with her, right now, or quit."

*   *   *

It was another reception evening at UNESCO, on a French-Chilean cultural exchange. As she waited beside the crowded bar to get a glass of wine, she noticed a young man with blond hair and Slavic features who nodded to her. She recognized him, but from where? He turned and said, "Good evening, don't you remember me?"

"Yes, but I can't remember from where."

"It was at a reception at the Ministry of Trade. A number of us then went on to dinner together. With Alex, wasn't it?"

Isabel cautiously nodded.

"May I get you a glass of wine from the bar while I'm up there? It's quite crowded."

He struggled to the front of the bar and in a few minutes returned with two glasses of wine.

She vaguely recalled the occasion. Wasn't it some boring dinner she had attended with Alex, with some Soviets and some Germans who were specialists on Chilean economic reform?

"I'm sorry, your name…"

"Maksim, Maksim Golubovski, I'm on assignment here at UNESCO. We may have seen each other in the cafeteria."

They chatted a few minutes about their respective work departments.

"Your friend Alex speaks very good Russian if I recall."

"Yes, he studied Russian literature at university. He's always loved the language."

"What a pity he is here far away from the Soviet Union where he could use it more often."

"Well, it's just a hobby with him now. But he likes to keep it up."

They chatted about life in Santiago, and places to visit around the country.

"Yes, I have traveled around a lot in Chile," he said, "it's a pleasure. I have to admit frankly that with Pinochet the economy has improved. There are more foreign investments, better tourism."

"Surely, for a Russian to say that about Chile is unusual. I thought you were close to Allende," she said, the wine emboldening her.

"You are right, we did support Allende and his Marxist reforms. But we have to be realistic, he made mistakes and his enemies took advantage of them. Our enemies took advantage of it as well. At least Pinochet is stable."

"Yes, if all you want is stability. But the brutality has been repulsive," she allowed herself to say with emotion, especially as they were standing out of earshot of others.

"You don't approve of the regime then?" Maksim raised his eyebrows.

"No, I don't. My brother is dead and my parents suffered a lot and like so many others, we lived in exile for many years."

"Well, I'm sorry to hear that, but you are right, many have suffered from that coup—and the outside intervention." Maksim looked around. "Well, if you will excuse me, Ms…Ms…"

"Iturbi."

"I hope we'll meet again, Ms. Iturbi."

A week later with Alex, Isabel remembered her encounter with Maksim.

"Why didn't you tell me about him?" Alex asked.

"I'm telling you right now."

"Yes, one week later. You don't remember his name?"

"No, it's long, begins with G…like Gorbovski or something."

"Golubovski?"

"Yes, maybe that was it."

"Isabel, I want you to tell me when you meet these people."

"OK, OK, Alex, I'm telling you now. It shouldn't be that big a deal." And she turned back into Alex's kitchen to finish putting the food on the table. Alex decided not to push it for the moment.

The following week Isabel encountered Maksim in the cafeteria again. He was sitting alone and asked her to join him.

"Isn't your father the well-known artist Jorge Iturbi? He's very respected."

"Yes, but he isn't much in the public eye with this regime. They won't give him a chance to show his paintings, because of his politics."

"Oh, I'm sorry to hear that. Maybe he could show them outside the country if he wanted."

"Like where?"

"In Eastern Europe. In Moscow. There is a thirst for Latin American painting there, especially of the more modern style and its folklore images. If you want I could easily look into it for you with the Cultural Attache at our Embassy."

"Thank you, that's kind, but I don't know if my father would be interested."

"Well, that's up to him. I can still look into it and see if there is any interest. I think there is an annual prize for Latin American painters."

And they chatted about various artists. Maksim seemed well informed on the subject. "How did you learn Spanish?" she asked.

"Oh, at the Foreign Language Institute in Moscow. We all had to study English, but I also studied Spanish because I wanted to come to Latin America."

Isabel found Maksim cultivated and surprisingly frank about many things including the deep conservatism of the Soviet leadership towards the arts. "We support arts a lot in the USSR, but I have to admit, they are not always daring, too much ideology, and avant-garde artists are not very popular. But we are learning more after the Stalin period."

That night Alex was busy so Isabel did not go over to his apartment. And the next night as well. When they met the third night Isabel decided she did not want to go through the interrogations of Alex about her second encounter with Maksim.

A week later Alex asked if she had seen Maksim again. To her surprise she found herself saying "no." She didn't want to get involved in Alex's strange obsession with Russians. It was like he was knee-jerk anti-Soviet. Did that mean anti-communist as well? What did he think of her parents then?

When Alex went south to Temuco on bank business for a few days, Maksim met her in the cafeteria. He asked her if she would like to go out for a glass of wine and supper after work. Isabel found herself agreeing.

The supper was pleasant, and they talked more about Chilean arts. Maksim knew a good bit about Chilean writers and mentioned how many of them had been translated into Russian. "That's amazing," Isabel said, "I don't think there is anything translated into English, except for Pablo Neruda."

"Yes, in the USSR we are very interested in promoting world literature, giving writers prominence outside the country. We often publish quality art books on artists of other countries."

"And do you like Chilean music?" she asked.

"Yes, but frankly some of my favorite music is by groups that were in exile, until recently, like Inti-Illimani and Quilapayún." Isabel laughed with pleasure as he described by name a number of songs. "My father knows many of those musicians from when they were in exile together," she said.

"Does your friend Alex like Chilean music?" Maksim inquired.

"Yes but he doesn't always have time to follow up on it. I'm afraid his bank job keeps him busy."

"What does he do at the Bank, anyway?"

"Oh, I don't know exactly, but it keeps him busy many evenings, it has to do with future investment planning, where is the economy going, that sort of thing."

"And that takes him out a lot at night? I'm surprised."

"Yes, he has to attend various business meetings, so we don't always have a chance to do more cultural things together."

"Does he have a background in finance?"

"He actually majored in Russian. Economics was a new field for him when he took the job here."

Maksim then asked about her parents' time outside the country in Paris. He had never been there, he said, but hoped to go. The evening overall was pleasant, and Maksim a polished host. He insisted on paying the bill.

"Your fiancé may be jealous that I took you out for supper."

"I wouldn't quite call him a fiancé, at least yet. Anyway, he's away for a few days, and you and I are just colleagues. But I'll spare him the worry."

"Fine. And I'd like to see your father's work sometime."

And Isabel decided again it would be best not to mention Maksim when Alex got back.

*   *   *

At the next meeting with Ted in the safe house, Alex was surprised to find the deputy chief of Station, Julian, present again as well. Julian asked Alex how he was doing, commented how much everyone liked his work with Fyodor. "His reporting has received a lot of praise back in Hqs, we've really gotten a very good picture of the KGB presence in Chile, and beyond. You've done an excellent job." He paused. "But there was something else I wanted to ask you about, Alex, a personal question, about Isabel. Do you mind?"

Alex sighed. "Frankly I'd like to keep most of my personal life out of this."

"OK, but do you know Maksim Golubovski at UNESCO?"

"Mmm, yes, I've met him at a reception once… I think it was at dinner with him and several embassy types. I think I reported the contact about six months ago."

"And does Isabel know him?"

"Yes, she was along with me when we all met at the reception."

"Has Isabel mentioned that she knows him?"

"Uh, yes… I think she mentioned about a month ago that she had run into him at work."

"Are you aware that she has been seeing him on her own?"

Alex swallowed. "Well, they both work for UNESCO, they are bound to cross each other's path sometime there."

"Are you aware she had dinner with him at La Tosca a week ago?"

"That doesn't sound right. Are you sure?"

"She was seen at La Tosca with him, they were there about two hours."

"Shit! Well, I was away then, down south. Maybe she just forgot to mention it to me. I did tell her I was interested in any contacts she had with Soviets here."

"Golubovski is definite KGB. He studied Spanish at a language school used exclusively by the KGB; he's also served in Cuba."

Alex paled. "What can I say, Julian. I'll ask her about it. I'm sure there is some reasonable explanation—if this is true. She would almost surely have told me, it's just I was away in Temuco around that date I think."

"Well, do ask her about it. And Alex…"

"Yes?"

"I don't know how to say this, but we are quite concerned over Isabel's left-wing connections, mainly through her family. And we like this contact of hers with Golubovski even less. I hope you will think long and hard about this before you decide to continue on with this girl, much less talk about marriage."

"Look, Julian, she's gregarious. She gets around. It's partly her job. She hates politics, she knows what it has done to her father. I've never heard her express left-wing views on much of anything except the Pinochet regime. She has every reason to hate it for what it did to her parents. I don't think this can be turned into some kind of loyalty issue."

"Maybe not. But you had better get to the bottom of this Golubovski thing."

*   *   *

His nerves were on edge—once again he was facing a very delicate conversation with Isabel the following evening. Alex ordered a vodka right away when they met at the restaurant.

"You don't usually drink vodka," she said. "Is something going on? Is work at the Bank bothering you?"

He turned on her. "Isabel, have you been seeing Golubovski at work?"

"Yes. I just ran into him in the cafeteria once or twice for lunch."

"Are you sure that's all?"

"Alex, I will not tolerate this examination, it's like a policeman. Yes, I also met him once for dinner. He invited me to an early supper while you were away. So what? I was going to tell you anyway."

"Goddam it, Isabel, I told you before to tell me any time you have contact with him. Why have you been hiding these meetings from me?"

"I haven't been hiding them, Alex! It's just you have been so...so uptight and tense about all this. It is unpleasant. And it is even more unpleasant now. I didn't feel like telling you anything because all you do is become angry. Maksim is a nice guy, and he is interested in art, not politics. He is refined."

"Isabel, you are very naïve. Look, this sonofabich is probably a Soviet intelligence officer. He is almost certainly trying to use you. What does he ask you about?"

"Alex, whenever you talk about your work you get nasty, you curse, you become a different person. We didn't talk about anything special, I told you. Just artists, writers in Latin America. He is interested in my father's work. He might be able to get him some exhibitions outside the country."

"Oh, like in the Museum of Modern Art in New York, I suppose?"

"Stop being sarcastic, Alex. That's why I didn't want to talk to you about this. It has nothing to do with you. You don't own me."

"Isabel, Isabel, look... I'm sorry, I didn't mean to be offensive. It's just this guy... I'm concerned about what he's doing. Did he ask about me at all?"

"Not much. He was curious about how you learned Russian, that's a perfectly normal question. He wondered about your banking background."

"And what did you tell him?"

"Nothing. Just that this was your first job with a bank."

"Did he ask about what I do?"

"Alex, stop it! No, he just commented that you seem to be a busy man. This is not a big deal."

"Please promise me one thing. That you won't talk to Golubovski any more. This is not a healthy relationship, he's using you."

"And aren't you using me to meet with Soviets as well? I don't like all this phobia about the Soviets, Alex, it reminds me of what Pinochet and his thugs are talking about all the time here—communists, communists, communists! And then prison for all of them!"

"Keep your voice down," Alex said sternly, looking around at nearby tables. "You know that there were many communists, Isabel."

"Yes, many people here were—and some still are—communists. My parents are idealists. They have been close to the party most of their lives. Anybody who thinks and has had hopes for a better future here is likely to have been close to the party, or Allende's United Movement. We all want a future free of the rule of generals. We've lived with it for decades."

"But the communists haven't been better for Chile!"

"Oh, yes? America has not been good for our country either! The whole business of the coup against Allende was a scandal. It was Washington's interference to save your beloved American copper mines. They killed Allende for it! At least the Soviet Union is not trying to take our resources!"

What am I doing, destroying my relationship with this woman I love, with each exchange? He was quiet for a moment and then apologized for his tenseness. "Look, I'm sorry, Isabel, I'm just tired. Maybe we should skip the concert tonight and let things cool down. I'll give you a call at the end of the week."

Isabel looked stricken, but she nodded. "Yes, maybe we should let things cool a bit," she responded.

*   *   *

A breakup with Isabel made every kind of sense. It was becoming an impossible relationship. She was openly raising questions about his life, which spelled real trouble for his work, the security of the agents he was handling, and even put his future professional life into jeopardy. Her parents were prickly, had ties with anti-American circles, clearly did not welcome him even if they tolerated his presence to indulge their daughter.

For Alex this represented a whole new experience—to be disliked, not for who he was personally but for what he represented in the abstract, as an American. And his bosses in the Station were considerably less sentimental about passing judgment on the situation he had created. Worse, while he defended US policies where he could, and he did criticize Chilean flirtation with leftist ideologies, he also understood the Chilean rationale. The views of Isabel's parents were completely understandable, and he might well have shared them in full if he had been in their shoes.

The week went by mechanically; he operated in rote. While the distraction of Isabel's presence had been considerable, the distraction of her absence was even greater. Should he recontact her, hoping the break would now lead her to be more cautious? The management of his relationship with her took on an importance and intensity that much exceeded the management of his relationship with Fyodor. His awareness of the imbalance that emotional issues were producing in him added to a sense of guilt. And indeed, he could expect little change in Isabel: she was a perceptive young woman, how could she stop thinking about his life, what he did and its impact on them both?

The following Sunday morning, as he was sleeping in, the phone rang. "Alex, I can't take this, I miss you. Can we have lunch together this afternoon?" His heart soared, overcoming the complexities that were settling in upon him. A few hours later, he hugged her from behind as she stood in front of the Cava de Dardignac in Bellavista looking for him in the opposite direction. She fell into his arms with an emotion he had not seen in her before, prompting Alex to gently disengage while in such a public place.

"I'm going crazy, Alex. I don't know what I'm doing, and I want you, I want you in my life. We'll manage with my parents in some way. I promise to stay out of politics." All this came gushing out, accumulated, compressed, distilled over a week. The fierceness of her commitment even outstripped his; she was the one who had broken new ground in the relationship and he now found himself trailing at a more cautious pace from behind.

They shared a bottle of their favorite Carmenere, and then another, the warm red liquid healing and restoring their earlier emotions as Isabel went on excitedly about her new teacher in art class. She was determined to devote more time to her painting. And she wanted them to make a trip south now, to Chiloé. The magic of the new venue would help soothe and make up for past misunderstandings. And then they retreated to Alex's apartment to complete the best part of a lovers' quarrel—the passionate reconciliation. Isabel had never been as fierce in bed as that night. "Isabel, I can't call you my *llamita* any more, you have become my *diabolita!*"

"Not devil, Alex, *angelita*."

"Yes, my angel of salvation."

Alex was delighted, and uncertain. The decision to cool things had been rational, but ignored their own emotions. Isabel was becoming life itself for him. But the realities of his work would still not just evaporate away even with their best intentions.

He arranged his schedule and they set off together, to explore Chiloé for a week. "It's the biggest island in South America, except for Tierra del Fuego in the far south, we need time to explore it all." They made the long drive south to Chaitén and the next day took the ferry to Castro on the island of Chiloé itself. The ferry took seven hours, a great deal of it through rain and fog. Isabel was in her element. "In Chiloé you have to learn to live with the rain, you include it in your plans. You celebrate it. Yes, we'll get wet, but it's part of life here. That's what makes Chiloé such a wild and natural place."

She loved the myths and superstitions about the magical and demonic creatures who live there. "These creatures are a reality here. You feel them.

They are part of the living culture and psychology of the islanders." She told him how these myths went back to the early days of the Mapuche Indians and had now blasphemously fused with Catholic beliefs. "Keep an eye out, Alex. If you are lucky you will see Pinkoia somewhere along the rocky beaches, she's naked and incredibly gorgeous, she dances on the beach. That's how she maintains the fertility of the sea and the coast.

"Wow, sounds great!"

"But if you are not so lucky you may run into Fiura. She is short, dangerous, and incredibly ugly, but she has an insatiable appetite for sex that no man can ever fulfill."

"Why do I need Fiura when I have you?" Isabel still was capable of a blush.

For Isabel, Chiloé was the soul of her country. She was thrilled that Alex responded to it. He had found a small book about the mythical figures on the island and how the myths had developed in isolation from the mainland. The Chilotes referred to these entities as *brujos* or sorcerors. Alex was intrigued by the figure of El Trauco, a repugnant gnome who lived in the woods, dressed in natural tree fibres, could kill with one look, and induced erotic thoughts in young virgins. El Trauco's love-making skills were legendary and unsurpassed; no woman drawn to his body could ever expunge the experience from her mind, or find his match among wanting humans. He was well known for being responsible for unwanted pregnancies among young girls who were unable to name the father.

"Maybe I am your Trauco," Alex suggested.

"Are you going to get me pregnant?"

"Hmm. We'll see. But only as long as you can name the father."

Rain pervaded much of their stay, but it only enhanced the wild seacoast that peered out into the Pacific. Each morning as they got up they would see before them the mountains engulfed in mists and clouds that rose and fell, providing fleeting glimpses of the peaks behind. The land made the Chilotes a tough and durable people, linked to the sea, immensely hospitable, and determined to preserve their way of life.

One night at a small inn by the water Isabel insisted that Alex taste the famous Licor de Oro, named for its golden color. "Guess what's in it, apart from alcohol?" Isabel asked before she read the label out to him: milk, alcohol, sugar, cloves, lemons, bitter almonds, vanilla and cinnamon. "This sounds like some love potion brewed up by one of the local *brujas*," Alex commented. "Are you sure this stuff is legal?"

"Well, we'll find out tonight if it works or not, won't we?"

They were alone, gloriously anonymous, far from the rigidities of Santiago society, far from the Bank, from Soviets, from Station liaison officers, from security concerns, from her parents. Isabel had never seen Alex so relaxed.

"That is your real magic upon me, Isabel. You make me more spontaneous, and I love it. You liberate me."

At the same time Isabel found in Alex a naturalness and openness to the world, unencumbered by society, tradition, rules, convention. He seemed so much more integrated in his personality than so many Latino men around her—who inhabited two different worlds: a public life where the exercise of raw power, with their mistresses on the side, coexisted with the carefully cultivated domestic image of decorum and the private life of a good upright family man. "A woman in Latin America has to attract her husband almost as a slut, but then she must become the revered and honored mother of their children. She must be protected from the sexuality of the public world and must ignore her husband's mistresses on the outside," Isabel reported. "Sounds like Pakistan," Alex commented. "And hypocrisy." That annoyed Isabel—partly because he was right. It was part of Alex's inner confidence, his resistance to taboos and barriers. And she taught Alex to stop referring to his own culture as "American." "It's irritating to Chileans, my culture is American too you know, just South American, while yours is North American. You Yanquis don't have a monopoly over the word."

On their last night as they stood at the end of a fishing dock looking out over the inland sea, Isabel hugged him. "I've fallen in love with you, Alex. Your enthusiasm. Your heart. Your mind."

"That's all?" he asked, smiling expectantly.

"Yes, and with that too," she grinned impishly, as she reached down, cupped her hand under his crotch and jiggled its contents.

When they finally returned back to Santiago, Alex was aware he had left behind a magic world that had worked its spell upon them. He knew he wanted Isabel for his wife, problems be damned. And Isabel wanted that as well—but did she know all the problems?

And Isabel could still not be certain about how her parents would react. Nor was he.

*   *   *

When Alex got back to Santiago he found a letter waiting for him, with Pakistani stamps. Majeed! He felt a sense of comfort in opening the envelope, from one of his few unqualifiably old friends in this world—of whom there were none in this Chilean outpost that was growing so complicated.

My dear Alex!

I hope this letter gets to you, you have probably moved since we were last in touch. Hopefully this will be forwarded to you. Where are you now? Some university somewhere perhaps? It has been too long…

Aysha and I are expecting a child in about six months! We are both hoping for a girl—and Zubayda is thrilled that I am not a typical Pakistani father looking for a boy to continue the family name. Well, we'll see, it will be fine either way.

The other big news is that my uncle found me a posting—guess where, with the office of the President! I will be starting next month. It's a big office, and I probably will rarely see President Zia personally, but he is a very determined man, a great patriot, very religious as well as knowledgeable about world affairs. I think he has been good for the country. Although he is a military man, we all expect that he will press for a return to civilian rule after the victory of the anti-Soviet jihad in Afghanistan in the near future.

I think it was my university qualifications in international relations that interested them in me—although my uncle's good ties in high places of course helped as well. It should be an exciting job. I'm not sure yet what it will involve. But it is a great chance to get a good look into Pakistani politics. I will, of course, have to move to Islamabad for the job, but I will likely come back to Lahore on weekends where my wife will stay with my parents and my sister, at least for the time being.

Do drop me a line when you have a chance. Aysha by now has heard so much about you, and Zubayda always sings your praises! And Akmal wants you to come and visit, and continue the tradition of theological debates he started with your father.

Salaams from the entire family!

Your good friend,

Majeed

*　　*　　　　　　*　　　　　　　　　*

My dear Majeed,

Yes, the letter did reach me! How great to hear from you! Yes, too much time has passed, but I've been thinking of you. It was wonderful to get your news, and especially that you will soon be a proud father! Mubarik ho Majeed, yeh bahut achhi khabar hai! And my mother would be sending congratulations too if she had been able to live until the event. She was always asking about you.

You will never guess where I am—in far distant Chile where no one from Pakistan ever comes. But it is a fascinating and beautiful country. You might be surprised to know that I am working for a bank—I'm not sure it's completely my line of work, but I wanted to get back overseas again and see the world, someplace new. And the pay is good.

Even better news is that I too have found a wonderful girl—her name is Isabel. She works for UNESCO and is the daughter of a prominent artistic family. Our wedding plans are still up in the air for the moment, and her parents are of course saddened that she would be leaving the country with me. But she is the right one for sure, and I found her by myself!

I have told Isabel all about my childhood growing up in Lahore and the wonderful Ramazan memories. I have promised Isabel that she will come with me to visit Lahore sometime, and she is eager to do so.

Let's try to stay in touch more regularly. It is really great to hear a voice from the past with such warm memories. My salaams to you, your Mom, Aysha, Akmal, and of course Zubayda.

Alex

*　　*　　　　　　*　　　　　　　　　*

CNI, the latest version of the Chilean security service, previously known as DINA, and DIMA before that under Allende, reported directly to General Pinochet. Yet members of this intelligence organization did some moonlighting on the side, and had found private customers for their product as well, although strictly illegally. Julio Salgado, chief of the surveillance section, ran a discreet but popular business for many different consumers, mostly private and under the table of course. Julio had been sent off to the USSR in the Allende period for intelligence training with the KGB, along with many other Chilean security officers. And as was so often the case, a friendly KGB trainer got to know him well, took him out to the kind of nightspots he missed from home and would never be able to find in Moscow. Soon he had himself a deal: he not only took his upgraded surveillance and intelligence skills back to Santiago, but he occasionally ran surveillance operations against people who were of interest to the Soviet Embassy, or lent to the Soviets certain surveillance reports of other people DIMA was watching for the regime. The work was not demanding and Julio was able to earn triple his salary for his troubles. His Soviet case officer advised him not to throw money around in an extravagant and implausible lifestyle, nor did he: he sent money to his son and daughter who were studying in Spain, and built himself a nice holiday home far away in the Lake District in the south. And he could enjoy some good whiskey at home and a few nice household appliances that made life pleasant, while remaining in his modest suburban apartment. Julio not only benefitted considerably from the arrangement, but he was in his own small way getting his revenge on the system. He had been inspired by Salvador Allende when he was younger and had resented the Pinochet coup that murdered him. "Hide your political feelings in this business, whatever they may be," a grandfatherly senior officer in CNI had advised him one day. "You never know when the new man on horseback will show up and you never want to go down with the changing of the guard." He knew it was sound advice and he followed it.

It wasn't hard to see that trouble was brewing before the actual coup against Allende occurred. When Allende was killed on September 11, 1973— the Chilean 9/11—in the shelling of his official residence at La Moneda, Julio met with his Soviet case officer several times in the confusion that followed, even when the whole Chilean security service was closed for "alterations" until the new system could be put into place. His Soviet case officer advised him that big purges would be coming under the new regime of General Pinochet; he even advised Julio to come to his new bosses with the confession that he had been approached by the KGB in Moscow to work for them, but that he had refused, and had been badly treated while there, and was completely disillusioned by the Soviet system and living standards. The latter two points took little coaching to work up to a convincing story. And his "confession" worked; he was commended for his honesty, warned to be alert for any further approaches to him or his colleagues by communists. For his skills and discretion he was promoted to chief of the surveillance section. Julio was able to report on the many changes inside DIMA, then renamed DINA, and by now again renamed CNI or Centro Nacional de Información—different acronyms, same old ugly work.

Over the years, his KGB case officer was not demanding, only a few reports a month were of any interest to them. He was to report anytime surveillance activity was mounted against any member of the Soviet Embassy in Santiago. This had indeed happened a few times and KGB officers were able to spot such surveillance or to lie low for as long as it lasted. And maybe once every few months Julio was asked to initiate a special surveillance on someone of direct interest to the Soviets, particularly Americans.

At his most recently monthly car meetings with his Soviet case officer, when Julio was picked up on a back street at night and was driven around the city while he was being debriefed, the Soviet asked him to do name traces on an American, one Alexander Anders. Julio later reported back that there was nothing on file about him. The Soviet asked that Julio initiate a discreet surveillance against Anders; Julio decided he could best officially justify initiating the surveillance on the grounds that Anders was possibly in touch with corrupt Chilean bankers in possible currency manipulation.

The head of the Surveillance Division, diplomatic branch, who reported to Julio was another enterprising officer, Antonio Mendoza. Antonio's father was a military officer and had been a classmate of General Pinochet at the military academy; his father had inquired about a role for his son who spoke good English and Antonio had ended up in CNI with a good job and chances of advancement. As cordial relations quickly developed between Washington and the Pinochet regime, they were reflected in the quick establishment of good working relations between CIA and CNI. Antonio was unaccustomed to regular working hours, and found even his own 10 to 4 regimen somewhat irksome and demanding, but he enjoyed the several liaison lunches he would have each month with friendly intelligence officers from the UK, Spanish, French and German Embassies. The wine flowed freely and the restaurants were always excellent. Antonio was helpful in periodically reporting on Soviet and other communist bloc embassy officers. But Julio obviously already had a feel for such processes and had warned Antonio to be on the lookout for efforts to recruit him, particularly from the Americans. And so it happened that at one meeting a CIA officer in regular liaison with CNI suggested to Antonio that he could help tighten the cooperation by reporting informally on certain affairs, for which the Embassy would show its gratitude. "And besides, we're all working for the same cause, we're just making things move faster by going around the bureaucracy."

After six months Julio noted that there was an increased amount of surveillance reports on Soviet Embassy officers coming across his desk from the diplomatic surveillance section. One day he casually asked Antonio about it. "All our liaison contacts keep asking about the Soviets, so I'm trying to be helpful."

"Watch out that they don't end up directing all our surveillance efforts, remember we work for Chile, not the gringos."

"Sure, Julio, but in the end we're all working for the same cause, aren't we? Against the leftist and communist threat?"

Julio bit his tongue and resolved to watch Antonio a little more closely. And Julio reported to his Soviet case officer the fact of stepped-up surveillance activity against Soviet diplomats.

Then one day while Antonio was out for one of his bibulous lunches building rapport with some service, Julio stepped into Antonio's office and looked through the files in his safe on surveillance against Soviets. There were many more than Antonio had told Julio about. Julio began to smell a rat. And there was one new file, on "Fyodor" it turned out, who was photographed going to a hotel into which, one hour earlier, Alex Anders had gone. This had happened on several occasions. The next morning Julio asked Antonio about the file. "Oh yes, that's a new development, I was going to tell you about that." "OK, Antonio, but this is a sensitive one. It involves a Russian and an American, one or both of whom may be intelligence officers. Why are they meeting? We don't know. We need to be very careful with this. I don't want any of this going to the Americans at this point, not until we know more about what's going on. I'm going to take over the file, due to its sensitivity."

Antonio hesitated, then looked away, embarrassed. Julio closed the door. "You're helping them out on the side, aren't you?"

"What do you mean? Who?"

"The gringos."

"No, I would never…"

"Antonio, look at me! The damn gringo has gotten to you, I can tell. How else do you explain all these surveillance reports on Soviets and other communists, beyond what you've told me about?"

"No, Julio, *Te juro,* I swear!"

But as Julio questioned him further on the details, Antonio could no longer hide the truth. He hung his head, trembling and unable to look Julio in the eyes. "Look, I'll stop, I won't do it anymore! Please don't report me."

Julio remained silent for a few minutes, staring at Antonio. "It will stay between us, but only as long as I think you're reporting to me honestly. I know the CIA is a 'friendly' service, but in our business nobody is friendly. I don't want any trouble with the goddam generals at the top either. Beware Antonio, I'll cut your balls off in a second if you screw with me!"

Antonio collapsed into his chair, weeping. "I promise, Julio, I promise."

And a grateful Antonio from then on reported to Julio on every "special meeting" he had with the American. And Julio in turn informed his Soviet case officer of what had been going on. "Here's something you should definitely know about," Julio said, turning over to the Soviet a photocopy of a surveillance report on Alex and Fyodor. The Soviet grew very grave as he read through the file. "Look, Julio, you're to report to no one else about this, especially the Americans. Make sure Antonio doesn't pass it to them, or even be aware of its significance. Got it?" the Soviet demanded. And so it happened that Alex fell under more intensive Chilean surveillance at the order of the Soviet officer. Julio told Antonio of his concerns that Alex was "involved in black-marketeering," so he wanted to know whoever he met with, allied country or no.

And in the course of events, the reports on Alex's meetings with Fyodor ended up on the desk of Colonel Ivan Burin, Minister Councilor of the Soviet Embassy for Security in Santiago.

Once alerted, the Soviet Embassy asked Julio, their main operative in CNI, to look more closely into Alex's activities in Santiago. Four weeks later the Soviet Embassy received a report from Julio.

An American employee of First Allied Bank, one Alexander Anders, was reported by the desk clerk at the Oriente Hotel renting a room #341 on the night of 28 March. Although he took a circuitous route, our surveillance was successful. On the night of 28 March a figure suspected of having engaged in a meeting with Anders at the Hotel Grande was surveilled at 735pm after leaving a meeting and was followed back via an indirect route to the Soviet compound. No detailed observations of the individual could be made except that he seemed to be about 50 years old, tall, between 1.8 and 1.9 meters, dressed in a dark suit, shuffling gait.

A circuit of complex ties had now been completed and documented, linking individuals, embassies, intelligence services, and families. And Ivan Burin, Minister Councilor of the Soviet Embassy and Chief of Security at the Embassy, left a message for Fyodor to report to his office immediately.

Chapter Four

Chilean Closure

Political language ... is designed to make lies sound truthful and murder respectable, and to give an appearance of solidity to pure wind.

- George Orwell

Tell me, Comrade, we hear that you have developed a taste for visiting hotels in the city on your own. What attractions do these places have for you?" Minister Councilor of the Soviet Embassy, Colonel Ivan Burin—known to every single employee inside the Embassy as the KGB Chief of Security—began the conversation in a bantering tone, partly out of deference to Fyodor's own longtime party status. But nobody, not even the Soviet Ambassador himself, outranked Burin on security matters.

Fyodor looked around the room, maintaining an outwardly casual attitude. There was literally almost nothing to see. The room was on the top floor, windowless, with a special electronic access code required to enter. Devoid of human element, it was designed to strip any congeniality from the proceedings as embassy staff came in on command to be vetted, laundered, make their confessions, be chastised, and, if lucky, perhaps then absolved, blessed, and sent off to sin no more. Its wall-to-wall files and dossiers rose insurmountably, inescapably, on all sides, closing off access to all but the doorway out that operated electronically, and only at Burin's touch. Just like the whole fucking system, thought Fyodor.

Fyodor was deeply disturbed when he received word on his summons to report to the office—the Confessional as it was known to Soviet Embassy officers. But Fyodor knew that every member of the Embassy was periodically required to visit the office for confession, and usually did receive absolution for their sins. There was no member of the embassy who had not committed at least some peccadillo against Embassy regulations—relating to illegal financial transactions, black marketeering, contacts with locals, illicit love affairs, drunken behavior on or off the compound, or even some moments when the name of the Communist Party of the Soviet Union or its leadership had been taken in vain in front of others, when everyone was "drunk." Communists were no different than any other human beings, one had to be tolerant and sometimes indulgent towards backsliding; after all, Burin could not arrest the entire Embassy. The confession sessions helped keep things under control, purge the individual of his peccadillos and send him away grateful for the light hand. The Catholics knew a thing or two.

Fyodor did not know how much Burin knew, if anything. This could be the routine confession ceremony. It was always wise to have a few small peccadillos to report in any case, just to avoid suspicion. Fyodor maintained a cool poise. "Yes, Comrade Burin, a few visits to hotels, strictly routine matters. I meet with various trade officers over drinks to update our statistics on the Chilean economy and foreign trade. We drink vodka, and I give you good vulnerability reports on these people. My vulnerability reports are well known for their quality."

"You need hotel rooms for this?"

Need to drop one level deeper in the defense. "Alright Comrade, I will tell you. Yes, what do you expect? You know I have no wife. Of course I must have a love life. I have had a number of rendezvous. Sometimes with prostitutes, but also with a Chilean woman. She has become an intimate friend."

"Have you reported on this intimate friend before?"

"Yes, of course Comrade, do you think I don't know the rules? I submitted the name for checking many months ago. There is no record on her. She is a clerk in a bookshop. We meet for some love in a hotel room when we can. You know how it is."

"And her name?"

"I have reported it before, Comrade." Fyodor sighed at the tediousness of it all. "Eva Gonzales. It is all in my report."

"And you have met no one else in these hotels?"

"Apart from her, only the few business meetings—in the restaurant, not in the rooms—with economic contacts."

"I suppose you have detailed lists of all these meetings with non-Soviet personnel, as is required—who, what, when and where?"

Fyodor looked Burin in the eyes. He still felt in control of the situation. "In most cases, no, Comrade Burin, I confess I have not documented them all. But you know very well that this procedure has not been applied systematically for many years now. If you wish, however, I will begin to follow the letter of the regulations again, as of now."

Burin stared hard, unblinkingly at Fyodor for a few moments. Fyodor held his gaze.

"Alright, Comrade. Be so kind as to maintain 'the letter of the regulations,' as you term them, from now on. Our interview is concluded."

Fyodor took his time, looked around the room, rose confidently, nodded at Burin, and walked towards the door. As he reached for the handle he had to wait before it clicked open, at Burin's gracious touch, denying him even the pretense that he had the ability to leave the room of his own volition.

Once outside, Fyodor drew a deep breath. He had to be careful. He knew that his colleagues were regularly called in for brief security interviews. Infringement of so many of the regulations had become the norm since the Brezhnev period—the whole damn Soviet system was mired in sloppiness now, in a moribund system that seemed near collapse.

He did not think Burin really knew of his meetings with Alex. Nonetheless, he would skip his next meeting with Alex and then review their procedures more closely. Beneath his confidence he now felt his body slip into a delayed sweat. He trembled from the encounter, seethed at the system that degraded the dignity and autonomy of even its most trusted employees. The days of these imperious peasant commissars at the top, with their gold teeth and cunning peasant ways, were numbered—no, they had to be made to be numbered. Russia would not otherwise survive them.

*   *   *

After his Confessional, Fyodor let not one but three meeting schedules go by. Alex was unnerved, wondering what had befallen Fyodor. He did not report to the Station the failed first routinely scheduled meeting. Such things were not unusual. But after Fyodor failed to trigger the second meeting Alex reported the fact to Ted, who reported back the next day that, through one of their penetrations of the CNI, they determined Fyodor was still around, answering his phone and coming and going from his apartment.

What had happened? Had he done something wrong? Alex fretted over it, was again irritable with Isabel and lost interest in going out. "Have I done something wrong," she asked?

"No, no, of course not, my love," he replied, as they finally met for dinner late in the week. "I'm just tired."

"It's more than that, I can see it in your eyes, you seem disturbed."

"Well, I'm having trouble finishing several of the reports for the bank that I'm supposed to be doing and the boss is giving me a hard time. They're a dead bore. I don't know… I sometimes wonder if I am cut out for this business."

"If you ask me," Isabel said, looking directly into his eyes, "I don't think of you as a banker. You couldn't be less of a banker as far as I'm concerned. You have passion for art and creativity, for culture, for politics even. You should think about some other line of work closer to your interests and loves."

"I'm close to my biggest love," he returned, smiling at her and reaching for her hand. Isabel blushed with pleasure and reassurance.

"But really, *mi amor*," she said, "when you leave… when *we* leave Chile, you should think about some other line of work. Maybe a journalist or something, who knows, an art critic, literature professor…"

*   *   *

A few weeks later Fyodor finally signaled for a meeting. Alex sighed a deep breath of relief. Fyodor chose not to tell Alex yet about his summons to

Colonel Ivan Burin's office. It would only upset him, and Washington, and might mean an end to personal meetings. He would find strict electronic communications to be tedious and unrewarding. And after several vodkas, and the passage of some KGB documents to Alex, Fyodor turned to him with a smile. "You know the story about the socialist, the capitalist and the communist who agreed to meet? The socialist was late in arriving. 'Excuse me for being late, I was standing in a queue for sausages.' 'What is a queue?' the capitalist asked. 'And what is a sausage?' the communist asked… This is a funny story, no? But there is a deeper message here as well. Do you understand, Alex? Is this all about sausages? You will not believe me but in the Soviet Union we sometimes have a richer life precisely because of this shit system we have. Our system pushes people together to fight it, to talk about why the system is so bad, to talk about great ideas. We think, because we must if we are to make our society—any society—better. We are obsessed with politics."

"That's a hell of price to pay for some great ideas, and no sausage."

"You don't get the point Alex. Why do you think Russia has produced the greatest literature in the world? In the world! It is precisely because our rulers have always kept us tied up, with a bit in our mouths and with reins over our shoulders. That is the reason we have time and desire to talk about these important aspects of human life. We think about life, Alex, its meaning. All the time! Behind our closed doors we talk about the system, the philosophy of politics, the goals of society—what is important. We are alive, despite our petty little commissars who think about only controls and sausages! When you have too much sausage you think about nothing—except more sausage, better sausage, maybe a bigger refrigerator for more sausages, maybe a bigger house for more of your refrigerators to hold your sausages…. Maybe when you produce less sausage in America you will start writing some great books! And you will please pour me another glass of vodka now."

Alex sighed. He knew the signs, knew it would be another long session, and he had to take notes on it all. In one sense it was all fascinating—and Fyodor was always intellectually exhausting. But Alex no longer passed along to Hqs all of Fyodor's personal observations on the meaning of political life. "Alex," his Station contact had said, "you know nobody back in Washington is going to read all this philosophical shit from Fyodor—a long bunch of boozy observations by a drunk and depressed agent about the two systems. Just stick with the hard KGB docs, the hard intel, that's where you and Fyodor are making your money. Save Dostoyevsky for another day. I know you can't turn him off, but you don't have to write it all up." *Wasn't this exactly what Fyodor was saying?*

"Yes," Fyodor went on, "at least we have the wisdom not to believe our own propaganda—all those lies we tell the world about the glories of our communist system. We know better, we know it's bullshit. But you in

America, you actually *do* believe in the glories of capitalism, even when your working class does not have free medical care, you chase forever after more and more material goods like a dog after its tail, you are eternally unhappy because your television screens tell you what you do not yet have, what you must buy. And why you must be armed to the teeth, and why big business buys your elections. For you, life *is* consumption. Society *is* big business. American spiritual life is empty and depressed. No, Alex, I want an end to the Soviet system and its ideology but, thank you, we will not replace it with your capitalist ideology either."

Alex was shaken after these sessions. Yes, Fyodor delivered as promised. He had lately turned over lists of all Soviet agents in Argentina, and detailed accounts of the underground work of the communist party in several South American countries including Chile. This was rich material. Washington was delighted. Alex received praise, a commendation and a promotion. And he now barely wrote about Fyodor's passing observations on the American scene. It was an article of faith in Washington that Fyodor was an "ideological recruitment." Even within the Agency it was simply a matter of assumption that Soviets knew how much better the American system; everyone knew that all Soviets wanted to be just like America. Only a few who had the experience of handling Soviet agents understood that such an ideological recruitment neither represented a blanket commitment, nor automatically implied a love of the American domestic system or the American vision of a world order. Written reports casting doubt on the ideological purity of these very ideological recruitments might have upset some at the top back home who saw the world in black and white terms.

And Fyodor himself grew strangely more passionate over the months, more productive, sensing that perhaps time was running out on him. He knew Burin might be breathing down his neck. He would deliver what final blows he could to the KGB and its overseas work. But he did not want there to be any doubt about why he did it or about what he wanted for his own Russia in the future—in the eternal Russian quest for a just, upright and moral society.

*   *   *

Alex had spent several sessions with Fyodor in reviewing Cuban activities in Chile. The Soviet Embassy was well informed on Cuban activities in the region and often cooperated with the Cubans to further joint interests. At one point Fyodor brought up a Cuban agent, whom he called Dr. Carlos. It was a long story. Carlos was one of the many young idealists in Chile who believed in the Cuban revolution. Carlos came from the southern regions of Chile and had a lot of Mapuche blood in him. Indeed, he *looked* Indian, always a social hindrance in white-obsessed Chile. His family was typically poor and his village lay far from any school. He'd had to work on the family's plot of land to help produce enough food to eat. At age twelve he was offered a chance to go to school and only then began to learn to read and write. He excelled at his studies and dreamed of becoming a doctor, when someone told him about the possibility of medical training in Cuba. The Cuban government then invited Carlos to an international youth jamboree in Havana where, on the advice of local Cuban sources in Chile, it devoted some attention to Carlos as an ambitious and idealistic boy from aboriginal origins. It eventually offered Carlos a free high school scholarship in Cuba with the option of going on to medical school free of charge—if he joined his local communist party.

Carlos readily agreed, quickly joined the Chilean communist party and left his village to study in Cuba. His family was thrilled at the opportunity for him, but wondered if he would ever come back again. Carlos attended compulsory communist youth meetings in Cuba. He found many of them boring and regimented, too filled with long lectures and speeches about the international proletariat which meant little to him and too much about the Soviet Big Brother, but it seemed a small price to pay for his free education. Cuba was known throughout Latin America for the quality of its medical services due to heavy government focus on both the quantity of medical students and the quality of their education. Most of them eventually returned home, not only in Latin America, but to Africa as well. Opportunities were greatest for those who were poor, ethnic minorities, or of color. Cuba regularly used its large competent medical cadre as part of its own foreign policy tool-kit, sending out teams to disaster areas or to poor undeveloped countries and regions that needed medical services. They also served as eyes and ears for the regime in Havana. Cubans sometimes had access to places that Russians did not.

Carlos did return to Chile, and went back to the Mapuche area where he had grown up, and worked for many years among the poor. While he knew enough about Cuba to realize its claims had elements of propaganda, and that its political freedoms were limited, he was in awe of its medical facilities and believed they represented the best features of the country. If communism could do nothing else than provide medical services to the poor, it was a worthwhile ideology. There were almost no other mechanisms to help aboriginal students study abroad on such a systematic basis. Back in Chile Carlos was asked to maintain discreet ties with Cuba and to help identify potential candidates for medical or other education, and to always speak well of the country. Dr. Carlos became revered as a traveling rural doctor among his people and appreciated for his ability to assist students to go to Cuba. In the course of his medical work he also reported to his periodic Cuban contacts on the conditions of the area, including the political forces at work.

The Soviet Union had become aware of Carlos from their contacts with the Cubans, and he was recommended as someone who could serve as a model for developing a similar Soviet program of medical education for third-world students, to help facilitate the expansion of pro-Soviet attitudes in various places around the country. Unfortunately Carlos believed the USSR was also a colonial country, oppressing the identities of its own minorities, crushing anti-Soviet revolutions in Hungary, Poland and Czechoslovakia, a great power seeking global dominance. His views were partially negative toward the USSR and he did not shrink from saying so in public. The Soviet Embassy pressed the Cuban Embassy to spike such unhelpful views that tarnished the Soviet image, to tell Dr. Carlos to cool it.

This was how Fyodor had become aware of Dr. Carlos. Ill feelings developed in the Soviet Embassy that the Cubans rather enjoyed their image as the only "true revolutionary power" compared to Moscow, whom many Cubans now saw as the defender of the "great power status quo."

Alex reported all this to the Station as part of his regular debriefings of Fyodor. The Station asked that he develop more complete information on Carlos so that the case could be presented on a silver platter to the DNI by the Station as a prize—the uncovering of a Cuban-Soviet agent working to infiltrate minorities in Chile and to propagandize them with communist ideology.

"Why would you bother with a case like this?" Alex asked his Station contact at his routine meeting.

"It's a freebie, a good, easy way to get a few brownie points with the CNI, and pull the Soviet-Cuban chain in this country. I'm sure the Pinochet regime will not view with favor this kind of activity and will bring it to a swift halt."

"But come on, Ted. Why would we want to destroy the life of Dr. Carlos to gain a few brownie points with the Chileans? How dangerous do you think this operation really is to Chilean security, much less American security?"

"Don't worry about it, Alex. It's all grist for the mill. The regime here is out to remove all leftists from public life. That's basically positive. This is small potatoes. Don't sweat it."

"Small potatoes for you maybe, but not for Dr. Carlos or the aboriginal communities down there. Or for the education of other doctors who can serve in the backwoods."

"Communist doctors? Look, doctor or no doctor, this guy is a Cuban agent by any standard. And may be on the way to becoming a Soviet agent. Dr. Carlos should have known what he was getting into. We're reporting this case to the CNI."

"But he has apparently done a lot for the health of those damn Indians in the boonies. That matters a lot more on a human scale than scoring some points off the Cubans. We don't have to like Fidel to believe that perhaps some of the things they do here actually help the Chilean people. Why do we have to expose it, put an end to it?"

"Sorry, Alex, this is above both our pay grades. Cuban agents don't have a future in this country."

"Dammit, Ted, I don't agree. I don't think we should be tracking down every last little Cuban or Soviet agent—if you want to call him that—in some attempt to keep the country pure for US capitalism."

"Point taken. I'll pass your views along. But I doubt anybody is going to go to bat for your Dr. Carlos frankly."

"Shit, Ted. Reporting on Dr. Carlos to this bloody crowd in power here means the end of his medical work, the loss of his services to his community, certain jail and possible torture or even execution. That is not defensible in my view. I'm sorry, I'm not going to ask Fyodor for any more info on this unless someone can make a convincing case to me on the human trade-offs involved."

"Alex, don't be stupid. You can't refuse to collect info. That's not going to help your standing in the Station or your career. Don't fight it. Just do your job on reporting on what Fyodor tells you."

"Well, I object. A lot. This stinks. It's knee-jerk, without any consideration of the people involved. Not everybody or everything has to be a cog in Cold War politics."

"Be smart, Alex. It's not worth falling on your sword for."

"Fine then. Maybe we'll find that Fyodor has nothing more to say about any of this."

The Chief of Operations indeed was not happy with Alex's position. But he chose not to make a major issue of it for now and put the question of whether to pass this information along to the CNI on the back burner. "It's not that big of an issue. But young Alex out there—sounds like he's a bit of a bleeding heart. He should watch out that he isn't perceived as slipping into insubordination."

*　　　　*　　　　*

"You don't think this will come as a surprise to them, then?" Alex sought to reassure himself.

"No, not at all. I told them we have some important news," Isabel replied. "They know our relationship is very serious. Believe me, they don't dislike you. They just have to get used to the idea of 'an American.'" She smiled, and elbowed him gently in the ribs.

Doña María was warm, and embraced Alex before anything was even said. Don Jorge did the same a few minutes later when he appeared, this time dressed in informal attire rather than his painting smock.

"And we understand that you have some news for us?" Doña María coyly asked, never one to shrink from assuming control of the social agenda.

"That's right, Mamá, Papá, we do have news," Isabel beamed triumphantly. "Alex and I have decided to get married! We want your blessing. And we would like the wedding here this summer."

Clearly not surprised at all, both parents embraced both of them again. Doña María patted the seat next to her for Alex to sit down.

"Now first, I hope that you are not going to take our daughter away from us, away from Chile," she earnestly inquired of him.

"Doña María… I… my plans are uncertain. We would like to stay in Santiago as long as possible, but my assignments are not always up to me. But whatever the case, Chile is my second home now and we would expect to come back frequently. I have not begun to see or learn as much of the country as I want, its people, its cultural riches. You have opened the door to all of that for me."

"You see, Alex," Don Jorge warming to the exchange more than normal, "Isabel is our only remaining child, after Gabriel was killed we have no other. It would be very hard to bear to see her leave us for long periods. We will want to see our grandchildren… Of course, a wife must join her husband, we know that. But we would hope you will remain close to us."

"Of course, Papá, how could I not!"

"And we would hope that Alex will truly become our son as well, the son we lost."

"I am honored to do so, Don Jorge."

"And what do you plan to do, remain with the Bank?" Doña María asked.

"Actually I'm not sure. At this point I just don't know if this is really where my heart is. Banking is important, but it is a bit narrow. I don't think I want to spend the rest of my life doing it."

"Ahh," Doña María slapped her hands onto her lap with pleasure. "I am so happy to hear you say that, my son. You know we are artists, we have never been close to the business world, and frankly, do not feel comfortable with its greed. When we first met you we were surprised to hear you are a banker because—well… I will say it—you are worthy of better things."

"Thank you, Doña María, I will take that as a compliment," he smiled wryly.

"Alex is thinking that he would like to become a diplomat!" Isabel interrupted. "I think that would be so much better for him."

"Yes, and closer to my interests and skills in other cultures," Alex said.

"But pity that you could not join the French diplomatic circuit instead of the American," Doña María observed, patting Alex's hand. "The French are more skilled in the way they handle the world."

Alex smiled back, best defense.

"And we hope that you can leave behind any security duties," Doña Maria continued, pointedly.

"Security duties?"

"Oh dear, I suppose I should not have mentioned it. But Isabel explained to us that you have spent some time with Soviet diplomats here as part of some obligation to the FBI."

"I… well… Doña Maria, that is not quite the case." Alex drilled holes at Isabel with his eyes. "I have been visited once by an FBI official for some information since I have met some Soviets, but that is hardly an obligation. Or anything that I will continue."

"Well, that is good. We have had bad experiences with all these security services. I suppose at least your FBI is not throwing people in jail and torturing them in the United States in quite the way our service does here."

"Mamá, enough of politics! I want you to tell Alex more about our artistic experiences in Paris."

Over dinner Don Jorge talked at some length about their time in Paris, the various artists they had known. "We feel Paris to be our second home," he said. "So many Chileans ended up there after the overthrow of Allende and the beginning of Pinochet's fascist rule. Artists, musicians, politicians, diplomats, so many. We met Neruda there, after his daring escape from Chile."

"You don't know what it was like, Alex, in those years, you can't have any idea."

"I know it was very bad in the first year of the coup," Alex said.

"Bad!" snorted Doña María. "That is no word for it! *Infierno*, it was hell. I know you have lived here four years now, but I don't think you appreciate the reality for people like ourselves, the progressive thinkers, the creative people and activists of Chilean society. The fascists of Pinochet have treated us like animals."

"Papá was arrested in the second week after the coup. It was terrible. I told you about that, Alex."

"Yes, I heard about it. I'm terribly sorry, Don Jorge."

"My son, it was a nightmare, a horror, like Nazi Germany," Doña María burst in. "They came to our house in the middle of the night, almost smashed down the door, invaded our bedroom and took Jorge, with nothing but the pajamas he was wearing." Her voice trembled. "And they took him to a concentration camp, far in the south, where it was very cold, very harsh. They were beaten and tortured in the camp, so many died. No one knew where anyone was, if they were alive or dead. Even to inquire was to risk arrest. I had no news of Jorge for over a year. I was sure he was dead. Then someone who had been in the camp brought word that he was alive."

"What did they accuse you of, Don Jorge?"

"What did they accuse any of us for? Communists, we were all communists in their eyes. Communists were like... rats to them..."

"Vermin," Isabel offered.

"Yes, exactly, vermin. To be killed. Any person who worked with the progressive movement, or who was against militarism from earlier years—we were all suspicious in their eyes. And so many of us had joined Allende in the United Front—socialists, artists, reformers, yes, communists too. We wanted freedom from military rule. And, if you will permit me to say, Alex, we wanted freedom from constant US intervention in our country."

"The army said it was defending the nation against evil," Don Jorge continued. "They saw Marxist views on class struggle as very dangerous. The regime wanted to preserve the class system, they said. Of course they did, it always favored the wealthy and the landowners, especially down in the south where they took so much land from the Mapuche Indians."

Alex didn't know quite how to react and could only shake his head at hearing such distasteful information. "That's bad," he said.

"But these people in the DIMA, DINA, CNI—they're all the same, the secret police, the name changes but its criminal behavior does not—they were crazy." Don Jorge had never been so animated. "They said that they whole country was infected by these… vermin."

"You can't know what it was like," Doña María continued, "no national institution was safe; each one had to be 'cleaned out, purified' even places like the churches, schools, trade unions, newspapers. These fascists of Pinochet were afraid of all free thinkers, anywhere. They took so many people away to be tortured or killed or disappeared, for months, years, even forever. And that was when our beloved son Gabriel disappeared…"

"Now, my dear," Don Jorge patted her hand. "At least I myself was relatively lucky, I was not active so much in politics. It was my art they hated, in support of the Allende reforms, the revolution. But the regime did not fear the artists quite as much as the progressive politicians. So after two years they let me out of that concentration camp without a word. 'Now you will remain silent from your filthy words,' they said. But it was terrible. I had many broken bones." He held up the misshapen fingers of his hand.

"Don Jorge was in the hospital for many months," Doña María broke in. "We lived in constant fear. When he got better we arranged to escape from the country. We had passports but we were on a huge blacklist so we could not leave the country without a special permit. And they would never give it to us. But we escaped anyway, over the Andes on horses to Argentina."

"And Alex, I must tell you," she continued, "we heard many stories that the CIA had helped Pinochet by giving him lists of names of communists. If you were on any list you could be killed. Every night during curfew—you know we had curfew for many years? There would be dead bodies on the street in the morning, dogs sniffing them, people just beaten and shot in the night, no police reports or news reports. Nothing. Just 'enemies of the regime.'"

"I surely hope the US was not really involved in giving any names to Pinochet," Alex said. "I'm not sure all of that is true."

"Oh yes, I can tell you, Alex, they were handing over names. I am sure that is what happened to our son. He was a leader in a major demonstration against the CIA."

"But so much of this may be just rumor, from upset people, understandably," Alex said impetuously.

"Rumor!" burst out Doña María. "How can you use that word! Tell rumor to the thousands and thousands of people who died from the DIMA's activities, maybe 25,000. Listen, your own Congress even investigated all this. There was some Commission…"

"Church Commission," Jorge supplied.

"Yes, the Church Commission. The American government itself admitted that it interfered in every single Chilean election through the whole sixties and helped Pinochet come to power in 1973. They spent ten million dollars in bribing people here, to overthrow Allende, to weaken the economy in order to hurt him. This blessed man of peace… who was trying to get rid of fascism and bring justice to the people… a new era to our sad country." Doña María wiped her eyes.

"Mamá, that's enough. We know about this and it's just upsetting to repeat it."

"I'm sorry, Isabelita, but Alex must know about this, what his country did to us, and we are still suffering. I don't blame him, he has nothing to do with what his government does. Pinochet has his powerful supporters and admirers among the capitalists and reactionaries and military. We still fear him and his vicious circles."

"It is still difficult for me to show my art in Chile," Jorge said. "It takes a long time to get rid of blacklists."

"Papá, tell Alex about Quilapayún, how you used to meet with them."

"We had wonderful new musical groups in Chile in the Allende period, we called it *nueva canción*— new songs. We sang about politics, and oppression and justice and human rights. It influenced all Latin American countries. We in Chile, we were the creators of it."

"Right," Alex chimed in, relieved to change the subject, "I have heard their music, I got one of their cassettes. It is wonderful, very creative."

"You know them, then? I am impressed that you would know our Quilapayún. Well, their founder, Victor Jara, you know of him? He was a marvelous songwriter and player. And he was murdered by Pinochet, murdered! Even music was dangerous to this regime. And they sang not only about the crimes and fascism in Chile but also songs about the Spanish Civil War and Vietnam—all the places where people are repressed."

"When we were in Paris," Isabel said, "we used to go and hear them, they came to our house for dinner many times. It was so exciting."

"Yes, and there is Inti-Illimani too. A wonderful group. You must hear them. All based on Chilean folk-music."

Alex had regained a little ground with Doña María and Don Jorge. He knew from experience how people are always delighted when foreigners show some knowledge of their culture. It's a compliment, you have a window into their own heart and soul.

Alex then got Don Jorge to show him some of his latest canvases and he spoke appreciatively of them. It was a relief to escape from the endless and turgid discussion of political memories. But even Don Jorge was not without his lingering passion and went on about his artist friends who had disappeared or whose lives had been ruined. "I regret, my boy, that America always defends the fascists."

Alex could no longer contain his objections and desire for some balance amidst all this passionate leftist rant.

"But, Don Jorge, the Soviet Union did terrible things! Artists can't just look the other way when it's the left that does bad things. Stalin killed millions. He stifled culture. He sent artists and intellectuals to Siberia to die in slave camps. He invaded other countries and kept them under total domination. He destroyed the economy of Russia. It was much worse than Pinochet ever was. You can't overlook that! The US had every reason to oppose the Soviet Union and its totalitarian system—and you should have too if you respect liberal thought."

Don Jorge would have none of it. "Alex, my friend, you are naïve. The excesses of the left may be there. But they are mistakes from the heart, they are from the soul, they possess ideals and vision. Of course they are also human, we know that, and so they are corruptible and can make mistakes."

"But we don't want to live in a world of extremes!" Alex shot back. "The US is trying to be balanced, to maintain democracy to avoid these errors of authoritarian rule—Pinochet or Stalin. The US was the only power to preserve democracy and freedom and moderation during the whole Cold War. You can't just keep attacking Washington as a source of evil. It is not. We try to achieve balance in this dangerous world!"

For the first time Don Jorge showed a flash of anger. "Don't tell me of your North American balance and moderation. How can one be 'moderate' when the goal is the salvation of mankind, of lives, from suffering, hunger and disease? Can we be moderate about justice? No! We must be militant in our demand for justice! Do we really believe that big corporations have the deepest interest of our tortured and troubled poor at heart? No, I would rather err on the side of excess in a good cause than exercise some kind of Anglo-Saxon prudence and worship of the 'workings of the market.' That is without soul, without humanity. I don't want to hear about it." And he turned and walked curtly away.

Christ, I've blown it. This isn't about scoring points, it's about me and Isabel. This isn't going to make it any easier for her, or me.

It had been a grueling evening. Hours later—it felt like days—when Alex and Isabel finally left, he felt immensely relieved. But he immediately turned to her. "Isabel, what were you doing mentioning the FBI to your parents? That is completely confidential, nothing they should know."

"I know, but they kept asking me about why you studied Russian and seem so interested in Soviets here."

"How did they know I'm interested in Soviets? Did you tell them?"

"No…well yes, just a little… but there is a Soviet cultural attaché here who knows Papá, and he mentioned you to him. I guess he knows you know Papá." Alex cringed at the tightening circle.

"Look, Isabel, let's get this straight. Please don't mention anything, *anything* to anyone about this FBI business. It will hurt my reputation, even at the Bank, especially since it was just a favor to them on a few occasions. You've got to be more discreet!" And he realized he was now sucking Isabel into the game.

"I'm sorry, *mi amor*, it's just that my parents have questions. It's not easy for them to be warm to an American, and especially one who might take their daughter away."

"Do you think they really accept me after all of this? I kind of lost my temper with your father." She squeezed his arm as they walked down the street. "Yes, I think for a gringo you have probably passed the test. But they are not happy about it all, I'm afraid."

Alex knew that despite the security implications of his work and status, he could not mention the "FBI" incident with Isabel and her parents to the Station. They would freak, see it fulfilling all their darkest fears about Isabel's influence. It was getting harder to keep all the various balls in the air, who knew what about him, and what his activities were. He felt the pressure rising.

What in fact had drawn him into this line of work? The convoluted identities of being part of a dissembling culture in Pakistan? Had he really ever possibly anticipated all this?

*   *   *

"The boss says to tell you that you need to cut back on the number of personal meetings with Fyodor. It's not good security, and Fyodor doesn't seem very security conscious from all you say."

"Jim, I've told you, meetings for this guy are the central part of his income. It's psychic income. This is where he gets to rationalize what he's doing, convince himself that he's a Russian patriot, doing it for the good of Russia. He wants feedback, he's not going to be satisfied with some flash transmission device once every few weeks sending in documents. I know him. He'll refuse."

"I'm telling you what the boss says. He says this stuff is too good, too precious to lose through the risks of personal meetings."

"OK, OK, I understand, I'll talk to him about it. But no guarantees. I know this guy. We have to keep him motivated. It may be espionage, but the human contact matters."

*   *   *

"And this is what they are demanding of me, Alex?" Fyodor asked. "If you don't mind my saying so, this is so very American: the technological answer to everything, minimize the human element in life, the person-to-person connection."

137

"Look, Fyodor, this isn't about cultural characteristics, you know that, it's about security—your personal safety. Our communication devices are much more secure than these meetings where who knows who might become aware of them."

"What I hear you saying is that it is the raw data you want. The raw lists. Your people seem just like our own little robots in the KGB—you just want some pins to stick in a map somewhere. Now I know…"

"Come on, Fyodor, don't give me a hard time, you know what I'm talking about!"

"Yes, my friend, I know what you are saying. I know very well. I know these agent lists are valuable, of course they are. But our discussions about systems, about the strengths and weaknesses of your system against mine, these are not important? This is the *essence* of the issue! What kind of systems are we trying to produce here, and what is the impact for billions of people? That is what matters in this world, not just agent lists—those are toys, seeing who can get the most toys. Isn't anyone in Washington interested in reflecting on what all of this *means*? Why we should be sitting in this hotel room? Why we have a Cold War? How can we be sure there will never be Cold Wars again? I hope you are making very good notes on all this, because if I have anything to say, *really* of importance, it is this. Agent lists are shit paper—of passing value—they have no civilizational meaning. Who cares in the end!"

"Look, Fyodor, you can write all of your observations down too, include them in the transmission. You know…"

Alex was exhausted by these debates. He knew what Fyodor was saying. He was right in some ways. But Fyodor was also twisting his little knife into him, making him feel guilty, punishing him, punishing the Agency and the American system even while he was giving it invaluable ammunition in this ideological war. He wanted to make Washington squirm for it. Indeed, Alex was unnerved by some of these conversations because he knew there were elements of truth to what Fyodor was saying. But was Washington squirming? They took the agent lists and probably buried all the rest of Fyodor's comments deep into the files upon receipt as little more than the fantasies of a confused, self-rationalizing agent.

Alex and Fyodor did reduce the amount of face-to-face meetings by half. The office was pushing for more. "Tell the CIA to improve their technology so they can just beam a ray into the Soviet Embassy and read the files from outside. That way no human beings will have to be involved ever again. Yes, would not that be the perfect world, Alex, the perfect world for your people? No human involvement? So we just become little machines? I sometimes think that is your ideals…" Alex reeled away, soul sucked dry from these sessions.

*   *   *

He had not been sleeping well. Dank and chilly air came into the bedroom through the slightly opened window. It must have been around three am. Two cars pulled up briskly at the entrance to the apartment. Three men in each car jumped out, leaving the engines still running. Sounds of footsteps moving with determination up the stairs. The door to his apartment crashed and the lights flashed on. Voices in Russian. Footsteps moved swiftly into his bedroom. "Get up, Comrade, you will come with us! Immediately! You will bring nothing!"

Fyodor knew better than to even ask why. He said not a word. He allowed himself to be pulled out of bed, hustled out of his bedroom without protest, out of his apartment, down the stairs, into the cold night air and one of the waiting cars, dressed in nothing more than his underwear, not even slippers on his bare feet. Car doors slammed, and two black cars sped off into the night.

*   *   *

Alex received a signal, signifying an urgent meeting with the Station representative. Ted arrived distraught. "I'm sorry to tell you, Alex, but we have some very bad news. Fyodor seems to have gone, left Santiago. We think he has been arrested."

"Gone? But how do you know he's gone?"

"CNI keeps us up to date on Soviet diplomatic comings and goings. They reported to us this morning that he has been officially removed from the Soviet diplomatic roster and departed the country. It's almost certain they have taken him home, by force."

Alex looked uncomprehendingly at his Station contact. *Damn you, Fyodor! You knew you were playing with fire. You've been compromised. I've compromised you.* Alex felt his guts retch and rushed into the bathroom.

*   *   *

Maksim had been busy. He had asked Isabel to arrange an appointment to meet her father. She told Alex immediately about the request, but did not go to the meeting herself; she knew it would only anger Alex further.

During Maksim's visit, Jorge showed Maksim his canvasses.

"How many of these have been shown in exhibits?" he asked.

"Virtually none in Chile. It has been impossible to show them since Pinochet. The last exhibition I had was a small one in Paris some years ago."

"Would you like me to check with the cultural attaché at our Embassy to see if he has an interest in arranging an exhibition in Moscow next time there is a show of Latin American art?"

"In Moscow? Yes, I'd be grateful," Jorge answered.

"By the way, congratulations that your daughter is engaged. I have met Alex Anders, he seems a talented young man. I hear his Russian is very good."

"Yes, he is interested in many things," Doña María said. "But he seems to have an intense interest in politics, more than I would expect from a banker. He almost never talks about economics."

"Well, Americans are concerned about Chile, they don't want it to go back to Allende times. That's understandable," Maksim said.

"That's just the problem. We had some progressive leadership in this country for the first time with Allende. Then it was all over, when the fascists came," Don Jorge commented.

Doña María's eyes flashed. "Alex may be a good person himself, we like him, but we are angry at his country and I don't believe it is healthy to have so much American presence in the country now. Pinochet welcomed it all, the more Yanquis the merrier."

"Yes, I'm afraid that is the reality," sighed Maksim. "But what can you do, that's the way things go in power politics."

*   *   *

Doña Maria insisted that it be held at the Iglesia de San Francisco, the oldest church in the city. Alex had been hoping for a more modest wedding in a less prominent location that would pass largely unnoticed on the social scene. But the Iglesia de San Francisco, with its magnificent red façade and cloistered interior convent, loaded with artifacts from Chilean colonial history and its marvelous convent museum attached—a wedding at this church made a powerful national and cultural statement. Doña Maria, moreover, had launched herself into the throes of detailed planning of the full traditional religious rituals. "I thought you said you didn't believe in God," Alex asked her at one point in logistical exasperation as Doña Maria raised the profile of the event step by step. "Of course, I don't," she said. "but this isn't about God, it is tradition, magnificent Chilean tradition. And if God did exist, this is the way He would want people to get married! Besides, why should the conservatives and fascists have a monopoly on magnificent weddings? People need to see that leftists enjoy God's grace, too."

"You've got to restrain Doña Maria," Alex pleaded with Isabel.

"She's my mother, I can't. This is more about mothers than it is about brides. And why are you so ill at ease with a big wedding? Are you so shy?" If Isabel didn't understand by now, there was little more Alex could say that wouldn't wreak further damage.

In fact, at least by Santiago standards, the wedding was to be a relatively small affair. It came up in the last few weeks of the Alex's tour in Santiago. And Fyodor was gone, the very reason for Alex's presence in Santiago. Apart from the ceremony in the historic church, to Alex's great relief, Doña Maria was compelled to restrain herself when it came to the reception which mercifully did not fully engage *todo Santiago* and the full range of the country's artistic circles.

However, rather than being a time of joy, the forthcoming wedding imposed mounting strains upon Alex, an event he now contemplated with dread. He could barely conceal these anxieties from Isabel. He felt furthermore guilty that he was suppressing a bride's joy at a key day in her life. A series of events loomed before him over which he had no control. It had all become an exercise in damage control, a desperate effort to placate powerful forces on all sides, every one of which had a stake in the implications of the wedding. Alex found himself running endless scenarios in his mind about how he might handle it.

First there was the confrontation with the Station and Hqs: the Chief of Station had made it clear how strongly displeased they were over Alex's choice to marry Isabel. "First of all, you know you're going to have to resign, outright. That's standard in situations like this—Hqs has got to give some serious thought to whether they still even want you in the Agency at all if your wife is seen as a security risk. In any case, your days as an officer under non-official cover are over. That is already a considerable investment that we are losing. You surely can't believe we'd invest in costly, complex and delicate efforts to place you under some new non-official business cover. And once your wife is witting of your actual Agency affiliation you definitely can't stay under corporate cover."

"The wives of other Agency officers under non-official cover know they're working under cover."

"Right, but not wives whose families are linked to the communist party."

"Look, they're not party members, and I…"

"Alex, get real. These people have been up to their eyeballs in anti-American and pro-communist activity over the years. Their son was a communist and virulently anti-American. You know that and I know that. We'd warned you about this way back. The security people are going to have to take a long hard look at the whole thing."

Alex knew it would be pointless debating the issue. He could only hope his skills were of enough value to the Agency that he would be readmitted into the ranks of officers, this time under routine official cover in the State Department.

"And then this goddam public show at the cathedral! Why can't you guys sneak off somewhere and get married quietly instead of having the whole damn city and its social columns focusing on who you are? You're supposed to be fucking discreet!" Alex wished that the Chief of Station himself had to have it out with Doña Maria and see how he fared.

And then there was Isabel herself. When could he tell her the real story about himself? And how would she react? The Station understandably had forbidden him to tell her about his Agency affiliation until he was out of the country and out from under his bank's cover. But he also had to know if she could handle the transition, the truth about his work. How would she handle it? He had given her the "lite" version of his activities, the FBI story, which never sat terribly well. How would the full story be met? He would delay that until they were back in the US, as Hqs demanded, but he had to test the waters a little more, to determine if she was still roughly comfortable with his plans.

He chose a quiet wine bar in Santiago, feeling the glow of a good meal and the remains of a second bottle of Carmenere sitting on the table. He placed his hand on hers.

"How are you holding up? Your mother is very intense about all of this wedding stuff. I'm exhausted just hearing about it."

"Of course she's intense. I'm her only daughter, her only remaining child, this is a big thing for the family. The key is for her to be happy now. Our happiness is down the road, it doesn't have to come from this ceremony."

"OK, I guess I can hold up. I just wish it was a little quieter…"

"Just let it be as it is, it will be fine. My friends tell me grooms always hate their weddings."

"Well, I certainly wouldn't say hate. But we are kind of secondary to the picture, I feel just like some sort of stud."

"You can be my stud, *mi amor*," and she squeezed his hand.

He smiled with a blush of pleasure. "But how about all these changes? Are you feeling depressed about leaving Chile, leaving your family? Going to the US?"

She studied her wine glass. "I love you, Alex, if that's what you mean."

"I know you do, and I'm very happy about our future together. But I do know this is a sacrifice for you too."

"I always knew I might end up marrying someone from another country and leaving Chile. We are a small country. I just didn't think it would be someone from North America," she smiled coquettishly. "I don't know if I will make a very good *gringa*."

"Don't worry, I don't want you to become a *gringa*," he smiled. "Besides, we'll come back frequently for visits, and your parents will certainly come visit us. Who knows where we will be."

The glow from the fireplace lit their features, complementing the glow of the wine.

"You know how you've always told me you don't think I am a very good banker? Well, I think maybe you're right. I've decided I'm going to resign from the Bank when I get back."

"Well, at least you'll stop being a 'capitalist.' From my parents' point of view that is a huge step in the right direction. Banker is a dirty word for them. It's lucky for you they ever let you in the house in the first place, you know."

"Lucky for you, too."

"But what would you do, after we leave here then?"

How far should he go? He felt manipulative, staging the truth in various guises and performances, dancing around the reality. But this wasn't part of his professional life, it was his wife-to-be. He realized he would have to broach the full story with her, it just had to come gently, bit by bit.

"I don't know… I really like working overseas. There are various jobs in Washington that could take us overseas. I'd been thinking about the State Department."

"A diplomat! I don't know if that's any better than being a banker. It's almost as stuffy. And boring—all that protocol. I've seen more than enough ambassadors in my job, stuffed suits."

"That's the ambassadors maybe. But there are interesting jobs. And it's not boring if we could go to interesting places to live."

"Do I get a voice in where we go?"

"Sure. Where do you want to go?"

She smiled coyly. "Well, Paris is nice."

"Come on, Isabel, that's not very imaginative!" he teased. "Anyway, you've been there, lived there."

"Well, then, maybe Madrid. Or Rome…"

"Yeah, the problem is that for every Rome and Madrid there are also ten Ouagadougous or Daccas. Somebody has to go there too."

"I suppose I could get used to third world fleapits, at least for a few years. As long as we're together. And as long as you promise to keep a good supply of Chilean wine. I can always have my arts while you go off to boring receptions. Just don't expect me to attend them."

"Well, you'd have to attend some of them. How else would you meet the interesting wives of the boring diplomats? And don't forget, I grew up in the third world. Pakistan in those days was pretty isolated. And my parents weren't diplomats drinking cocktails for a living. We were really right out there, in the middle of local life."

"Now that sounds more interesting."

"It was. It's sort of gotten into my blood. I can relate to cultures that are different than my own. I feel a warmth in them. I know how to approach them. I think that's why I'm thinking about the State Department."

"And I'll want a job too. Maybe I can find something through my UN contacts."

"Sure, I'm sure they'd love to have you in UN offices abroad."

"OK, Alex, just promise me you won't turn into a stuffy bore. I don't ever want to be an ambassador's wife, like some trained poodle, with a PhD in cocktail parties and receptions, serving canapés and worrying about who sits next to whom at the dinner table."

"Don't worry." He patted her hand, "I don't think there is any danger they'll make me an ambassador. I promise. No canapés."

So far, so good. But the full truth still hung over their heads like a vast boulder with a fraying cord. He would have to deal with it—before the wedding, regardless of what "policy" dictated.

*   *   *

They went to a small Chinese restaurant Alex liked. It was quiet. And he wanted to talk without wine, it was better that they be sober. He was unsure how to begin a discussion that might have disastrous impact upon all their plans.

"*Mi amor*, you are getting more tense about the wedding. I wish you could relax. All you have to do is show up on time. My family is taking care of the rest of it. Just stay out of my mother's way," she smiled.

"No, the wedding is good. I'm happy about it, even if I'm glad to be spared the details. But I wanted to talk a little more about my work here, what I've been doing apart from the bank work. I know you have been worried about it."

"Yes, the FBI part makes me uncomfortable. But I understand. It's about what the Russians are doing."

"Yes, but it's more than that. I haven't told you quite the full story, but you need to know. It affects our future."

"*Cómo*? She raised her eyebrows. "You are scaring me Alex."

"Isabel, I'm not scaring you, but there is no way to get around this. I have to be frank... I'm a professional intelligence officer. Ever since studying Russian in college I have been working on watching the Soviet Union, reporting on it. It's my main job. The banking work is just a cover for my intelligence work."

"Cover? What do you mean—professional intelligence officer? You've told me about the FBI business, you mean there is more?"

"Yes, I'm really an officer... with the CIA."

Isabel stared at him with uncomprehending eyes. The silence was deafening.

"Alex, no! Tell me you're joking. I can't believe it!"

Alex looked around the restaurant at the nearby tables. "Shhh, Isabel, let's not be noisy. Look, I'm sorry I haven't told you the full story before, but I ..."

"The full story! Alex, how could you have concealed this from me? All this time? What are you telling me?"

"I couldn't tell you, my work is confidential. I didn't want you to worry about this, to have a wrong impression of me."

"Wrong impression. Alex—you've been lying to me! Over and over again. Lying to me, lying to my parents, lying about this whole filthy business. How could you be involved..." Her voice was trembling.

"Look, I've had nothing to do with the whole Allende business, or the Pinochet business. I have nothing to do with Chilean politics, nothing..."

"But you do, if you're with the CIA, they are running this country!"

"Isabel, they're not. I am strictly responsible for watching Soviets and trying to get information about their activities here. Nothing, nothing to do with what happens in Chile."

"I don't care. It's all related. It's all a dirty business. You know the story, what has happened here to everyone. You know what happened to my own parents, my brother, their friends. They lived under one of the most brutal regimes, they have suffered and died because of what your CIA has done! I don't want to hear about it." She pulled out a handkerchief and daubed at her eyes.

"I wanted to tell you earlier, Isabel, but it was never the right time. I knew you would be upset and……

"Upset! The man whom I love, wanted to marry, now tells me he has been lying to me for years and has been assisting one of the ugliest beasts in the world. There is no 'right time' to tell me! It's all wrong! How can I marry you? You think I can accept this?"

She stood up and picked up her purse. In one sickening moment Alex was sure she was going to walk out, but she left her jacket on her chair and headed unsteadily in the direction of the bathrooms.

Christ, I've fucked up! There's no way she is ever going to settle for this. I should have waited till we had left the country, or after the wedding. But I couldn't have sprung it on her then, either. She would feel even more betrayed.

After a few minutes he almost got up to go knock on the door of the ladies room himself to check to see if she was alright, but he held his place. Finally she returned and sat down on the edge of her chair. Her eyes were red. He waited for her to speak.

"Alex, do you know what you have said?" Her voice was now steady, firm, resolute. "Do you really think I can marry you now?"

He looked at her, staring into her eyes. He reached across the table to take her hand; she tried to pull away, but in the end did not. Her lip trembled again.

"Alex, tell me, were you dealing with me on a 'professional basis?' Part of some plan to get close to me, to leftist circles, to check on my parents? To give a report to CIA or DINA or CNI? How can I ever trust you?" Her eyes flared with anger.

"Please, please Isabel, how could you think such a thing! I'd never… I have never mixed my personal life with my professional life. I have been focusing exclusively on Soviets, nothing to do with Chile or Allende or Pinochet or communists or anybody! I'd never do anything to harm you or your family in any way!."

"How can I believe you? You have lied to me for years about what you were doing, and then…then lied to me again with some story about the FBI. And then lies about the State Department. Now it's CIA! How can I believe you? What more is there to tell? That you have killed some people for Pinochet? Or helped torture people? Or just turned them in to the CNI?"

"I didn't lie... not in that sense, Isabel... I just gave you the standard cover story, to keep people from asking questions..."

"Standard cover story! How dare you! Alex, I'm supposed to be your wife. I don't want standard fucking anything!"

Alex flinched. This was the first time he had ever heard her use that word. She glared at him. "I want to know it all—right now! No more stories within stories, no more partial truths. You've covered up the truth too many times."

"I swear, my work never had anything to do with you and me, or your family. I was trying to protect you from all of this. But now we're getting married, you have to know the full story. But my professional life—it doesn't change anything between you and me."

"Have you ever told them about my family?"

"No, not in reports, just when I mentioned that we were thinking of getting married I had to tell them about my meetings with your parents—and what happened there. They had concerns about what subjects might come up."

"You *have* reported on my family to the CIA!"

"Not reports, they weren't the object of investigation, it was just routine, I..."

"Oh, Alex, how naïve can you be. You don't know how much I love you, but... I can't accept this. How could you have been playing me along for so many years? Reporting on my family to the people who helped try to kill my father? Who helped kill my brother? Didn't it ever bother you to be lying to me? How could you do this? And what can I ever tell my parents? You know their sensitivities, their passions. They were unhappy that I'm even thinking of marrying an American. Now you tell me you are a CIA agent... It's like a sick joke."

Alex noticed a couple many tables away who turned to look at them. The place mercifully was not very crowded and light music was playing, but he cringed at the public scene.

"Isabel, please, try keep your voice down, let's not tell this to the whole world."

"But don't you see? That's just it! We have to be sneaking around, hiding this, like criminals, ashamed, living a secret life. I can't do that, Alex, I can't do that for the rest of my life. And what do I tell my parents?"

"For God's sake, Isabel, you don't have to tell them anything. You mustn't tell them. They don't need to know, it would only upset them, and it has nothing to do with us."

"Nothing to do with us? Nothing to do with us! Now you expect me as well to start lying to my own parents about you? About an organization that has changed their lives and the lives of everyone else in this country? To get sucked into all this…this filth!"

Savage instincts of self-preservation rose up in him, instincts to reach out and rescue the only thing that was of value to him anymore. "Please, Isabel, listen to me! I promise, I will drop this whole thing if you want. You are more precious to me than any job. I will quit, I will change my job. I will become a forest ranger, or a college professor, or a garbage collector, whatever, but please don't consider breaking off with me!"

Isabel grew more resolute. "Let's not talk about it any more. Just take me back home. I have to think, I need to think this all over. I'm sorry."

Alex drove her to her parents' home in oppressive silence. It was late so fortunately her parents would have already gone to bed and would not see their daughter in this emotional state. He tried to repeat his promise to change jobs if she would just stay with him. And he begged her not to tell her parents. "I'm not going to talk about it further, Alex." Her voice was cold. "I will call you in a while, after I've had a chance to think it all over. But I cannot lead a life of lies. I don't know where any of this is going now." With a peremptory peck on the cheek, she got out, took the key out of her purse, opened the door to her parents' home. The door closed behind her.

He pounded the steering wheel. Maybe the goddam Station was right, maybe he should never have gotten into this, this horrendous incompatibility that was now destroying him. He had broken his word that he would not break cover with Isabel as long as he was in Santiago. Of course he could not raise the matter with the Station as such. "You have jeopardized your own security and the security of your operations and your agents by breaking your cover to a non-US citizen, a person whose parents are communists and hostile to the US. This is a colossal act of bad judgment." That's what they would say. They might even believe that this was why Fyodor had been compromised and arrested. Was it possible?

But more important was his relationship with Isabel. He could not lose her. She had insinuated herself into his life, his mind, his body, his joy and happiness and purpose. He would make whatever sacrifice needed to keep her. That, above all else, was the priority.

*   *   *

The hours crept by like days and days like weeks. The phone sat on the table, mocking him with a silence for which it was never intended. He did not dare pick it up and call her for fear of pressuring her, further alienating her. Then after five days he received an envelope from her, the very means of communication presaging the contents.

My darling. I do not know what to say to you. I feel broken and torn, like we have suffered some terrible accident. My feelings are numb. My parents are going away to visit relatives in the south, and I am going with them, just to get away and to get some perspective. Know that I love you, but I do not know what I am going to do.

He felt like storming over to her parents' house and extracting her in a passionate gesture, promising to follow her orders, anything. But he knew such a move would not work. Isabel would not be swept off her feet by mere gesture. He had to let her think this through. He had hoped it would not require such a long time.

Would it have made a difference if he had waited until after their wedding? That would have been unconscionable. He needed to have brought it out into the open now. But perhaps not in Chile, in some other foreign, neutral locale where the very word CIA was less raw to the citizens. He felt contaminated, unclean, for the first time in his professional life. Of course other nations conducted intelligence operations, ran agents, worked under cover, sought to influence events abroad. Santiago alone was full of them, from multiple countries. But this was different. This was not geopolitics, this was personal. And few in this country could ever think "intelligence operations" were just about information. It was about lives, power plays, and the entire political order. The operation at the behest of Henry Kissinger to overthrow Allende had gone well beyond collecting secrets. Alex had had no role in those events whatsoever, it was past history. But a whole population here had been on the harsh receiving end of a shadowy international power struggle not of their making. It was living history that had touched and continued to touch people's lives. A population had been wounded by decisions taken far away in a White House playing a geopolitical chess game. Like it or not, he had inherited the stain.

*   *   *

The reality hit him—how he had drifted into the life of Isabel's parents or, more dramatically, how they had entered into his and changed his life. They had dragged a whole historical experience, an agony, a nightmare, now personalized before his eyes. They had explicitly linked their family agony to his own life, to his own country and his own mission. In personally experiencing these events of Chile's past through the eyes of others close to him, he had come to live them himself. It had opened new and possibly unwanted doors, adding dimensions to himself, like a child gradually learning of the peccadillos of his parents or grandparents, the uncovering of some terrible family secret with which he had nothing to do, but that still reached out from the past to touch him, influence him, change him, influence his future course, in ways that he was defenseless against. Had he not been living in his own little shell, in Chile, but not of Chile? Cut off from the true realities of Chile? Yes, maybe it was all just emotional in character, maybe rumor, maybe exaggerated, maybe paranoid—but there were real dead bodies strewn across the land, lives wracked and wrecked by torture and surveillance.

How do you keep the past from touching you? Even when you are innocent, not even present, perhaps not even conceived or born when offenses are committed? Should these burdens be carried by later generations?

Even if you do not choose to carry them, the events influence how others perceive you, your country and its enterprise. Alex could not disassociate himself from this past, much as he wished to. Acknowledging the reality of Isabel, her parents and their experience had become a permanent feature of his own life, his image and his options. It was as if he was awakening to the power of history and foreign events over him, his life formed by previous events about which he was only now just learning.

Learning his own future by learning the past.

*   *   *

My dear Alex,

I can't tell you how sick I feel about what has happened to us. My life has been hell and I have just been turning all these events over and over in my mind. And with my mother pushing me on the wedding plans. It makes me terribly sad, but I have reached a decision— I cannot go ahead. I feel deeply wounded by all that you told me. I know that you say you love me, and I believe that you were not trying to hurt me or my parents, or even to use me. You are a good and decent person, and I'm afraid I can't stop loving you just like that. But what you are doing here, and the people you are working with—it is all too terrible for my country. None of us can forget the past, and even if you had nothing to do with it, I can't overlook it. That you should be in any way at all linked with it is just too painful for me to bear. You will forgive me, and I hope you understand. I simply cannot go ahead with this marriage that is based on lies and such an ugly past, and that will require me to go on lying into the future.

My parents are also shocked at my distress. You know that they were not enthusiastic about me marrying a gringo in general, even if they liked you personally. But worse, I too have now ended up having to tell them a lie—which makes me even more unhappy. How else could I break the wedding plans at the last minute? I have told them that I discovered that you were married before and that the divorce was not yet final, that you are still legally married. I even had to say that it was not clear how and when you might get the divorce. They know I am angry and upset and they are also furious and embarrassed. This lie has not made you look good in their eyes, but I had to say something. Surely you would not want me to tell them the real reasons behind this.

I do not know what more to say, Alex. I have to have time to think about all of this, and it is better if we separate. I cannot say how I will feel in a few months or even a year. I love you, but can't be part of what has happened in Chile and to my brother. I cannot bear to see you again before you leave—it is just too painful.

Please don't try to contact me again before you go. I think it is better if you just leave. If you write to me from the US, I will try to write back, eventually, but not for a while and I do not know where this can go, if anywhere.

With fondness and in great sadness,
Isabel

*   *   *

When his Station contact met with him, Alex was notably subdued.

"OK, you guys in the Station will all be pleased to know that the goddam wedding is off. You can all relax."

"Off? What happened?"

"Too many problems. You've all been telling me about the security issues. In the end, you're right, I can't fight them. The whole wedding was moving towards a very uncomfortable scene. The family is very left-wing. I don't think the marriage would have worked in the end. Too much anti-American feeling."

"Well… I don't know what to say, Alex, but I think you've made the right decision. I know this is personally very painful and upsetting to you. I'm sorry about that."

"Yeah, well, thanks. But that's the real world. The moral is not to get mixed up with foreign women, especially from countries that don't like the US. I'd just like to get the hell out of Santiago now, as soon as possible."

"You're scheduled to leave here next month in any case. Do you want me to try to move the departure date forward?"

"Yes, if you can, in keeping with Station needs."

"Alex, I know this has been difficult for you. The boss is basically very pleased with the work you've done here. You turned in some exceptional work on the Soviet intel net in Latin America. Your contacts in the country have been great, and we hope to follow up on a lot of them. Let me say too—nobody faults you for what happened with Fyodor. It's a damn big loss. But he's been a difficult case all along, he's a very temperamental character, and everybody knows it. Didn't seem to give a shit about his own security. It's not the first time. I'm afraid the poor son-of-a-bitch is probably pushing daisies right now. But your tour has been a good one. I hope this marriage thing doesn't cloud that reality."

"Thanks. Right now I just need to put some distance between myself and Chile."

And weeks thereafter Alex watched the quickly receding coastline of Chile vanish behind him as they entered the clouds, closing off further visual contact with the country. *Visual* contact. But his true contacts with Chile were still buried deep in his heart. He was on his way back to the United States for the first time since first landing in Chile four years earlier. It was no longer the same Chile. He was no longer the same Alex.

Chapter Five

Majeed

There is nothing concealed that will not be revealed, nothing hidden that will not be made known. Everything you have said in the dark will be heard in the daylight; what you have whispered in locked rooms will be proclaimed from the rooftops.

- Luke 12:2-3

If Alex had shared in two cultures, Pakistani and American, Majeed too, was the product of two cultures: the Punjabi heritage of his father and his Pashtun lineage on his mother's side. While his parents' marriage was affectionate and mutually respectful, cultural differences sometimes broke out into arguments over the upbringing of their children. Majeed had been particularly drawn into the web of his mother's cultural and ethnic background during the many memorable summers he had spent in the hills of the Northwest Frontier along the Afghan border—the heartland of Pashtun culture.

As they say, when buffaloes fight, it is the grass that suffers. The borderlands had always been the scene of minor tribal feuds since time immemorial, but whenever international powers forced their way onto the scene, internal violence escalated. Such was the case when the British Empire wandered into three losing wars in Afghanistan starting in the nineteenth century. Such was the case when the Soviet Union invaded Afghanistan in 1979, leading the US to spearhead a joint US-Pakistani anti-Soviet armed jihad to expel Soviet forces. The two superpowers devastated Afghanistan in the process. Pakistan's border areas too, paid full price: local struggles deepened and a massive refugee flow of Afghan Pashtuns fled over the border to live with or near their Pakistani Pashtun relatives.

Akmal had grown concerned over family trips to the border areas. "You can't be serious about taking Majeed and Zubayda to Waziristan this summer! I won't hear of it. The whole area is seething."

"Akmal, hush! You know those problems haven't touched the villages around my family's home at all. There are always some feuds going on. The refugees are far from my family's home. And we have been there every summer, they expect us. The children love it there, seeing their cousins. It's important that they stay in touch with their Frontier roots. Majeed and Zubayda would be heartbroken if they couldn't go. They spend enough of the year here in Lahore as it is."

"It's not about family and customs, wife, it's about safety. I worry about it every year."

"Yes, and you rarely go with us yourself either, so you don't really know the situation. My family will be offended if we fail to go this summer."

Akmal, normally a peaceful man, was intensely irritated at the increasing problems this fractious Pashtun side of the family posed, yet he felt he could only protest so much without seeming to cast insult upon his wife's cultural heritage. He had never felt comfortable in Waziristan on these summer visits, sitting around in a "tribal atmosphere" as he called it, where he felt himself a stranger, accepted only through his marriage to his Pashtun wife, surrounded by people speaking a language he didn't really understand and values he didn't share.

But for Majeed and Zubayda, and Salman too, it was a high point of the year, an exciting break from the urban polish of Lahore. And it was in those summers that Majeed's childhood slipped into the Pashtun world of all his maternal cousins.

*   *   *

As the sun set over the mountains of the North-West Frontier, the magic of the evening fell over the village when the clan would gather. On those childhood occasions Majeed slipped in with his cousins to attend the local *hujra*—the assembly that lay at the very heart of Pashtun village life and culture: when the elders deliberated the urgent issues of the day and celebrated their customs, military exploits, legendary tales of derring-do in struggles against the cunning imperialist *Ingleez*, the local feuds, poetry and music of the Pashtuns. This knowledge made the man. "A Pashtun may pride himself on a PhD from university, but if he doesn't know his own Pashtun culture and traditions, he's considered uneducated," his maternal uncles told him. And the music! The nights where Pashtun poetry and *tappas* were sung before a rapt and cheering audience, accompanied by the brilliant *rebab* whose strings sung in a mournful, rasping, smoky, soul-grabbing voice, along with the harmoniums and the *tambals* whose rhythms were hammered out by hand and stick. The singers, men as well as women, sat on a small raised platform covered with a brilliant red Afghan rug, against a yellow backdrop. The songs poured forth the stories and legends of the Pashtun past, of unrequited love, the sadness of defeat and the glory of victory, betrayal and revenge, unswerving blood loyalty, longing, and religious devotion. Majeed was swept along with the crowd, the rhythms of the Pashtun music constantly shifting, now faster, now slower—and, most tantalizing of all, that savored moment when the music would come to a complete momentary stop in mid-course, an abrupt halt into silence for several seconds, until suddenly the group swung right back up into the rhythm and music, all to the clapping and delight of the audience. The music would drift out into the village night for long hours and sometimes Majeed fell asleep on the pillows on which they sat, only to wake up later on as the music reached another crescendo and met with wild applause. "Yes," his uncle said, "first the heart must be filled to overflowing with the music before it is ready to pour forth from the mouth in song."

It was here that Majeed became aware of the stark and fractious lands of the frontier where Pashtun blood ties extended across the border deep into Afghanistan. "The border does not exist between ourselves and Afghanistan," his uncle told him. "It is an imperial invention of the English—that divided our people in this artificial way. That is the blessing of our autonomy here in the borderland—we are still free to ignore the artificial boundaries of the governments on both sides and to extend our hands and our hearts to our blood clans across the line."

And what are borders? For Majeed's relatives the back roads and foot paths from Pakistan over the border into Afghanistan were so much legal fiction. In Majeed's mind the real border crossing he experienced was the cultural border—between his home in Lahore and the world of his Pashtun cousins in the northwest tribal areas. The Punjabis of Lahore may have been more worldly and sophisticated, yes, but also softer than Pashtuns, too urban, too tinged with cultural intimacy with India just over the border, and lacking the dignity and martial traditions of warriors. Worse, the Punjabis laid claim to running the whole country. Indeed, Majeed's father spoke with pride of the central role Punjabis played in the very formation of the nation.

For Majeed and his siblings the summer trips to the frontier areas were decisive in forming his emotional identity. "Where is your father?" relatives asked him, and he could only mutter something about him being busy. Majeed knew his father never felt comfortable here with them.

Even at home in Lahore, outside the hearing of his father, Majeed's mother helped to regularly school Majeed in his Pashtun past. "We were the warriors of borderlands," his mother reminded him. "We were the only group able to match the military prowess of the Mughals and other invaders of India in those days. The English respected and feared us." Tales of military exploits were as essential as bread; honor was the staff of life.

"Our culture had a code of honor and justice even before Islam," his uncle had told him. "The Pashtunwali, the code of the Pashtuns. We can never forget we are Pashtuns, first, last and always, feared, respected and honored. A Pashtun is your most dedicated and loyal friend—and your most dangerous and feared enemy. The English had powerful guns and large armies but they still feared our courage and determination. They fought us three times in three wars—with overwhelming military force. And praise be to God they were defeated every time. As will all invaders."

His uncles pulled out the old hand-drawn maps. "Look here, Majeed, when we had our Durrani Empire in the 18th century we were a great power! We controlled half of Iran, and all of Pakistan, over into north-east India and parts of Turkestan. We were feared far and wide, and our Empire flourished—a boon for all."

His uncles insisted that Majeed learn to read and write Pashto and assisted him as he struggled to read the classical Pashtun poets. "Our values are embedded in our language. You must learn them if you are to call yourself Pashtun. No one who does not speak Pashto can understand our way of life and who we are. We call even our values *Pashto*—our code is what defines a true Pashtun. Our honor requires us to protect anyone who comes to our doorstep to seek refuge from an enemy. Even if he be an enemy to us we are honor bound to receive him for three days."

When Majeed was alone with his mother, he inquired cautiously: "But what about Father? He isn't Pashtun. Does it count if I am only half Pashtun?"

"Of course it counts. Mother's blood is more important than father's. And your culture is what matters most, that is what makes you a Pashtun. Yes, your father comes from a different tradition, from Punjab. The Muslims of Punjab are not fighters, they are softer than people in the Frontier. They have different strengths, they have more intellectuals, businessmen, they understand politics…And never forget your father is an honorable man—a scholar, a judge, an upright and incorruptible man, a religious man and a good father. He works for peaceful relations among people. That is good. But you, my son, carry Pashtun blood and you must help maintain the tradition as well as your father's."

    *   *   *

"Your mother is very passionate about her roots," his father commented with a sigh when he and Majeed were out in the bazaar together after one of her history lessons in the kitchen. His father always absented himself from those sessions. "Yes, be proud of your Pashtun blood, my son. But never forget that the Pashtuns have rarely been able to rise above their tribalism. United they form a powerful fist against the enemy. But much of the time they quarrel and fight amongst each other more than they fight the outside enemy. They are fractious and unreliable. Their loyalty to the tribe above all is their curse."

"But *Babaji*, we may have tribes, but we also have a glorious tradition of bravery and fighting for the land. My uncles say we are the toughest people in Pakistan."

"Yes, tough. It is wonderful to be loyal and strong and a fighter, but you have to know what you are fighting for. The Pashtun tribes can sometimes be like a pack of dogs—they seem to fight and kill just for the sake of it. The Quran condemns fighting among Muslims."

"But they did unite! To form the Durrani Empire—ruling over Iran and Afghanistan and Pakistan. That was for one hundred years!"

"Yes, it was a great accomplishment, but the Pashtuns rarely unite except against an outside enemy. Don't fall into the trap of tribalism, its narrow vision. In Islam, we do not treat tribes with great respect—they are like small and quarreling packs. Islam teaches us to unite together as Muslims, regardless of our languages and blood ties."

Majeed felt uncomfortable that his father might be undermining the traditions he was learning about. Indeed, what had modern Pakistan to show for itself except repeated defeat at the hands of India? But the Pashtuns could never be defeated! His father was a loving and scholarly man but not practical, he spent too much time with religious books and Sufi holy men—so suggested his mother.

*   *   *

Pashtun, yes, there was no denying the powerful impact of his mother's blood upon him. But when it came to books Majeed was his father's son. His curiosity for learning, his ability to speak articulately and his zest for reading appeared at an early age, clearly marking him for university. Indeed, one of his paternal uncles paid for Majeed to spend a year in the UK at the London School of Oriental and African Studies where he studied Middle East and Islamic politics.

London was an eye-opener—the richness of this huge city made even Lahore seem provincial. The panoply of students from all over the world were his mentors as much as his courses. Students from Latin America introduced him into the concepts of Marxism-Leninism—not as theory but as living ideology, describing the impact of imperialism on their world and the roots of anti-imperial struggle. Majeed was hit by its explanatory power as he read heavily in the literature of post-colonial politics on a global level, far beyond the English in Afghanistan.

If Marxism-Leninism was an awakening, sex was even more. He met Anisa. Her family was from Iran, her father one of the wealthy Iranian exiles who had spirited his money out of the country in the chaotic twilight days of the Shah. She was outspoken, heavily politicized—and liberated. She seemed to adopt serial lovers and Majeed was her male of choice for nearly eight months. He fell intoxicated with her sexuality and her bold lifestyle. She showed contempt for the traditional place of women and her sexuality was partly an expression of that. She flaunted her relationships, and she flirted with Majeed in public in ways that stimulated as well as embarrassed him. In spirit Anisa reminded him of his sister Zubayda, although Zubayda of course was more modest—indeed she had to be cautious in conservative Pakistan, where she could never consider going out with men before marriage. But in the anonymity of London where every student was from somewhere else, Majeed's immersion in Anisa was total and even began to affect his studies. Worse, in its bittersweet way, Anisa treated her lovers to the full power of her privy purse, paying for restaurants and trips to getaways in the countryside. Majeed was thrilled, but also discomfited by her economic hold over him. He felt a bit unmanned, a bit kept, even while in a glorious cage as her lover of choice and whose strictures he could not contemplate abandoning. When her body was not on fire, her intellect was and she dragged Majeed into her world of leftist literature and ideals.

But as Majeed's funding from his uncle began to run out, he had to face the reality of going back to Pakistan. He had flirted with the hope that Anisa might marry him and vouchsafe his future life in England. But Anisa had now cooled on Majeed; marriage was nowhere on her horizon. And so Majeed, sexually wrung out, pockets empty and filled with newer radical ideas, bade farewell to London and returned home to Lahore and its more monastic social scene. He settled for Quaid-i-Azam University in Islamabad, where, after a year contemplating Oriental Literature, he finally turned to the more western discipline of political science. Politics fascinated him and he hoped such a background might stand him in good stead in entering into government service.

Majeed of course never breathed a word to his family about his experiences with Anisa in London, although he did confide in Zubayda, who smiled in approval. Akmal would have disapproved of the relationship and Majeed already felt sharpening political differences with his father. Akmal had pursued a distinguished career as a judge but as he grew older he retreated into Sufi texts and the philosophical-spiritual path; for him this was the surest way to come to terms with the vagaries of human existence. Akmal annotated the page margins in the Islamic classics of the Seera and the Hadeeth—the life path, sayings and doings of the Prophet. And as Pakistani politics grew more radical his anger rose against what he considered gross distortion of his faith for political reasons.

Akmal's gentle manner was often ungenerously interpreted behind his back by his Pashtun in-laws as absence of fire in the belly. While Majeed understood these occasional remarks, he felt they were unfair. He knew his father indeed possessed a fire for justice but one that pointedly did not turn to religious posturing. Akmal's pepper-gray beard, his traditional manner of dress combined with his shuffling gait and intermittent absent-mindedness strengthened the image of a life of scholarship and piety that was not the whole story. Akmal had hoped to instill in Majeed an appreciation for the core of true religious faith and practice, to be repeatedly inspired through the glories of mystical poetry and music in the great Urdu Muslim traditions of the subcontinent; he considered that such cultural traditions rose to far greater heights and moral purpose than the mere vainglory and honor code of the Pashtun warrior.

Akmal rarely failed to fulfill the obligation of praying five times a day. Yet his piety did not lead to rigidity, smugness or intolerance. He possessed an excellent wit, in contrast to the many dour religious figures of the city, which led some of the stricter clerics to doubt Akmal's piety. "Part of the problem with these damn imams and clerics—no sense of humor; as if it was incompatible with Islam!" Those who knew Akmal personally never doubted his piety. His manner was respectful, his way with people was marked by warmth, kindness, graciousness and consideration—qualities he believed had been exemplified in the life of the Prophet as recorded by contemporaries. His piety was inward; he felt no need to constantly invoke religion into his speech and actions as so many others did. He did not criticize the manner or practice of other people unless it intruded upon the rights of others, or strayed too heavily into the political. In his view religion and prayer were essentially private matters, not to be the subject of ostentatious display or debate in public. Still, Majeed was often annoyed that his father's abstract commitment to justice did not translate into discernible practical action.

Majeed still harbored influences of Marxism in his thinking, but he was increasingly fascinated to discover that those ideas weren't all that much at odds with the talk of many of his fundamentalist fellow students. Of course Marx had viewed religion as nothing more than the opiate of the people. But what Marxism-Leninism said about the Western world found many parallels in Islamist analysis of domination of the Muslim world by British and American imperialism.

Akmal had noted a few Marxist turns of phrase that Majeed had begun to use in his political discussions at home and it concerned him; he deeply believed Marxism was an evil in its embrace of atheism and materialism; one had to look no further than Soviet efforts to eradicate all religion from Soviet life. Akmal, and his own father before that, were committed devotees to the Sufi side of Islam—strong spiritualism and the quest for direct knowledge and almost ecstatic experience of God. "You know what angers me most about materialism?" he said to Majeed one day. "It is so sadly impoverished, a cold philosophy that would strip us of the rich poetry and music of Urdu and Persian mystics, one of the key pathways to God."

*   *   *

Majeed had returned home on his last summer from university in Islamabad and was unpacking many of his books and papers in his bedroom. His father wandered in and noted pamphlets on the table. He picked a few of them up to leaf through. Majeed immediately regretted leaving them out; he looked up and indeed found his father frowning.

"What are these books on Islamic politics you have, son?"

"Oh, they were given to me by friends at university. I'm reading them since everyone is talking about them."

"I hope that you are not beginning to consort with many of these young activists in Islamic politics, they are…"

"*Babaji*, I just…"

"No, hear me out please. These people who are trying to drag religion into politics—I reject them. They distort the true meaning of our religion."

"Father, I'm not adopting these views, but I want to know more about them. A lot of my friends are frustrated with the state of this country, they see Islam as an ideal."

"There is much that is wrong in this country, God knows. And we do need wise politics to try to solve these issues. But it is not appropriate to bring religion into them. God is God, the Creator of our world and the Creator of life and Mankind. God is not a politician. He does not form political parties or hold political rallies and elections. Remember that, especially when you talk to these people who sully the name of God and Islam in the interests of their own political agenda."

"Father, I am sorry you don't approve. But you misunderstand these people I am working with, they are serious and pious. They have the interests of the *umma* at heart. They are trying to change the many unacceptable things going on here—the influence of greedy officials, the rich landowners who don't take care of the poor and don't pay their taxes, government officials who kowtow to the Americans. Surely you don't object to those things."

Akmal was taken aback at his son's burst of emotion. "Those are all worthy goals, Majeed. But I object to human beings *acting in the name of God*. That is, in the end, blasphemy."

"We're not doing it in the name of God, but we believe that there are some values in Islam that need to be applied, even in politics."

"We? You include yourself in their number?"

"No… not one of them, but, yes, we meet at university, we talk about these things. And I believe they may be right about bringing at least the values of Islam into politics, to reform the system."

"That is fine, to be influenced by Islamic values. God knows the politicians and parliamentarians could use a little more God and true morality—and reform—in their lives. But when they run around talking about an Islamic state…"

"Why shouldn't we talk about an Islamic state? We are…"

"An Islamic state? Look here, son, do you really know just what you are talking about here?"

Majeed felt increasingly cornered. "An Islamic state, one that honors Islamic values."

"And can you tell me, then, what exactly is an Islamic state? Can you tell me?" His fingers tapped on the table.

"A state whose law acknowledges the Shari'a, one that tries to implement Islamic principles in government, to bring justice to our system."

"Islamic principles in government—whatever that is! What earthly good are these so-called principles unless we first carry God in our own hearts! You cannot reform society until the hearts of *men* are reformed. Otherwise you will just have brutal rule by ignorant or bad people—and all in the name of God." Akmal tossed the book back down on the table.

"I know, Father. But we cannot be timid in our faith. Of course, it is important to pray, and to keep our hearts and minds pure and focused on God—all those things. I accept that. But that's not enough either. No, please, listen to me now for just a second, Father. Our enemies love it when all we do is pray and try to keep our hearts pure. We then present no obstacle, we are passive, neutralized. That is what they call 'American Islam,'—neutered Islam.

"'American Islam'—is that what you call keeping our hearts pure? What does America have to do with this? Islam is Islam, not what America says it is!"

"Look, Father, we want more than praying. We want to change this government. We want to get rid of these leaders who are corrupt, only interested in getting rich, who don't care about the people, these weak politicians who only follow what outsiders tell them. We want people who will reform the system and bring justice to the people!"

"Americans, God, government, justice! My son, these are just words. Politicians love to throw them around while they are looking after their own pockets. And then, sure enough, in the name of justice, a new pack of politicians will throw out the old and take power themselves. Mark my words, they will be just the same. Their personal interests—they are all out for their own self-interest! They are corrupt too. Change must begin inside their hearts first. Otherwise it is all hypocrisy!"

Majeed now felt himself swept into the argument, forced to reveal how committed his own thinking had become, something he had wished originally to conceal. He realized the need for caution with his father and to speak in more measured tones, but he could no longer hide what he had been hearing and learning. "Islam is a total way of life, Father. It is more than just prayer and doing the Hajj. I now see clearly that it means changing what is wrong with our society and our government. I believe these Islamists have more courage than anyone else to bring this change. They care! They want to make Islam strong, Pakistan strong, the Muslim world strong."

His father removed his glasses, closed his eyes tightly and pinched the bridge of his nose. He lowered his voice. "My son, my son, listen… this is the path to corruption. When people get near the altar of power, they become drunk, their minds wander. They begin to think only of extending their power. Of course we need good people to go into politics, there can be no doubt. But I will not go and vote for anyone who tells me that he understands God, or God's message, or knows what God wants and that he will carry it out. Or that he will punish me because I don't want what he wants—because he says he is doing it for God. What do I say in return to him? If he represents God, then how can I argue with God?"

Majeed hesitated. "Father, someone must speak for Islam. These old mullahs sitting around concerned all day with what is forbidden, what is *haram*—whether you should listen to music, or fly a kite, or cover your face, or watch TV, or grow a beard. How can they waste their time thinking about these trivial things when our country is weak, it's falling apart. That is what is truly *haram*!"

His father sighed, gazed down at his slippers. "Majeed," he asked wearily, "do you really feel that these people have God in their hearts? What I hear in their voices is anger, resentment, hatred."

"Yes, they are angry. They should be! God would be angry at the condition of our people and our country."

"Yes, He might be, God should be angry. But what I fear is the *man* who is angry with me. I do not find the light of God in his eyes. God is about compassion, that is one of the first names of God—al-Raheem, the Compassionate. These people you deal with are politicians. Fine, let them tell me what they want to do in economics or politics or in foreign policy. I will listen. They may have some good ideas. But they are blaspheming if they claim they know God's will on every issue."

"What does it mean to believe in God then? What are Islamic values if we do nothing about them in our lives except sit around a pray? Surely, that is hypocrisy."

"Majeed, we *can* believe in Islam, we can believe in God. We should love and fear God. But when someone talks to me about God, I want to see God in their eyes, feel God in their hearts, in their words. When I go to Baba Mian's tomb, my heart opens up. I feel like I have been smiled upon, I have been touched, cleansed, that I am closer to God. Politicians never make me feel that way."

"That's different Father, that's…"

"No, son, it is not different… You know, Majeed, I wish you would come with me some time to the *ziyarat* again and just sit and feel the peace of God that resides there. It can inspire, help you to keep peace and calm in your heart, to feel love towards others and seek good, give you strength even as you deal with the many wrong things in this world."

"OK, Father, but Baba Mian is not of this world any more. He may be a wonderful person, a holy man, but he does not know what is taking place in our universities, or in our government or in the countryside. He can't help in those areas."

Akmal reflected for a moment. "No, Majeed, you are right. He can't help in those areas. But he can help *you* to understand and to work on those problems without being consumed by anger and hatred. Will you come with me on my next visit?"

"Maybe, Father, maybe… I'll see."

"It would be a joy to take you, my son." And Akmal clasped him by his shoulder, trying to soften the conclusion of their argument before he left the room. That was the trouble with his father's generation, Majeed thought. They grew up under English imperialism, they are used to bowing their head to authority. The bloody English had merely replaced their own rule with new Pakistani rulers who would do their bidding, who would keep order and not threaten British interests. Now it was the same with America. His father had grown up in that meek tradition. Saints and holy things were fine, but they were a distraction, an invitation to abandon the earthly struggle. They wouldn't change anything.

And Akmal now seemed to him to be in a permanent state of retreat. Even when Majeed was younger his father was always off in his study reading religious books, writing articles about Islamic history and the companions of the Prophet. In the end *that* was an escape too, typical of the older generation—escape into religion so as not to face the realities around them. How often had his father even come out to spend time with his son? And, as a Punjabi, Akmal had avoided going on the summer visits to the Northwest Frontier—"Pashtun tribal feasts" he called them. He showed no outward courage in dealing with affairs of the world. Even his mother grew impatient with his father's lack of practical interest in the details of running a household. She took care of nearly all family affairs, including financial. "I cannot criticize him. Your father is a good, kind, learned and decent man. He is a good husband and a good father. But he is uncomfortable in this world," she would say. Yes, and that is partly why the world is the way it is, thought Majeed.

*   *   *

Despite Majeed's obvious talents, it was family ties and contacts that mattered. Upon Majeed's graduation, it was his maternal uncle who pulled strings with senior Pashtun military officers he knew to land Majeed a post of responsibility in government.

"Where have you landed, Majeed?" his friends from university asked. His life had seemed to run a strange course. First a Marxist in the UK, now flirting with ideas in political Islam. He had taken the exam for the civil service and had scored well. But after graduation he seemingly dropped out of circulation for six months. Nor did he show up in any of the expected ministries, especially the prestigious Ministry of Foreign Affairs that friends had confidently predicted for him. Then word went around that he had gotten a job with the President's office. He was known to have good political connections through his mother's side of the family. But what job in the President's office? Had he mentioned to somebody he was on the President's staff? Others reported Majeed as saying he was in a liaison office in the Army Chief of Staff's office—a cushy job.

"You've really lucked out, Majeed," cousin Salman told him. "Really, in the Army of Staff's office?"

And now Pakistan was again buffeted by the whirlwind of international politics swirling around it. The Soviet Union gambled everything and sent in the Red Army to support a beleaguered new communist regime in Afghanistan, to keep that country safe for communism. Pakistan thus became a new square on the Cold War chessboard as the US began pumping in massive military and economic support to Pakistan to promote a guerrilla war of mujahideen against the Soviet presence in Afghanistan—an anti-communist jihad.

And within a few years a young Majeed was said to be involved with that effort as an expert on Pashtun politics and occasional private spokesman from the "President's office." He was knowledgeable, articulate, and skilled in addressing foreigners. And he was familiar with the Frontier, a realm of knowledge almost exclusively vouchsafed to Pashtuns who spoke the language and were steeped in its elusive political, social and tribal culture.

This role eventually brought him to the attention of the American Embassy—the nerve center. The US was the key bankroller of the guerrilla war, although it was basically implemented by the Pakistanis. Foreign observers in Islamabad assumed Majeed was actually linked to the powerful and secret ISI, or Pakistani Directorate of Inter-Services Intelligence, the military inner sanctum of Pakistani strategic planning and action—although of course it could never be admitted publicly. As interesting as it was to speculate about Majeed's work, knowledgeable Pakistanis also knew it was always wise to speak with circumspection about ISI; it was well known for its watchful security eye over all of Pakistani society.

His detractors suggested that Majeed was skating on thin ice. Some foreigners claimed he had a roving eye, and there were whispers of a romantic involvement with the wife of a more senior official, surely an ill-founded rumor in Pakistan's conservative social environment. Others noted his occasional presence at various Western dinner parties at foreign embassies; he attended them—those more envious said—because he liked his liquor and flirting with Western women. Unfair, others said: Majeed was the front man to represent many of the views of ISI among foreign diplomats. Yet wasn't he said to have good contacts among the mujahideen? Was something fishy going on here? He seemed to defend the politics of Islam and the mujahideen, but nobody had ever accused Majeed of being a pious Muslim. Was this all just convenient cover?

The anti-Soviet struggle had lasted for nearly a decade, until 1988, the year when Moscow, under the new leadership of Mikhail Gorbachev, recognized that the disastrous Soviet gamble to hold on to Afghanistan was failing, draining the USSR of both blood and treasure. Why had Moscow not learned from history? Russia had become the second great imperial power to taste the bitter gall of disaster in prickly Afghanistan, following on the repeated British military fiascos a century earlier. Within a year Gorbachev made the startling decision to pull the Red Army out, negotiating the barest fig leaf to mask Russian defeat.

While Pakistan watched, the US had achieved its strategic goal: the humiliation and defeat of the Soviet Union in Afghanistan. As the Soviet occupation in Afghanistan wound down, Majeed knew that his own star was rising when one day he was scheduled to accompany his immediate superior, along with the Army Chief of Staff, and President Zia himself, in a military entourage on a major protocol visit to Bahawalpur. The trip was a symbolic milestone in Pakistani and American policy in Afghanistan. The American ambassador to Pakistan was himself conspicuously accompanying General Zia to witness a demonstration of US tank firepower, among the new military toys the Pakistani Army would receive from Washington. But to Majeed's great disappointment, at the very last minute word came down countermanding his prestigious and high-profile trip with the President; instead he was dispatched to the border area to take care of pressing matters relating to a fractious mujahideen group. The American-built Hercules C-130b transport plane in the Pakistani Air Force took off from Bahawalpur on its way back to the capital. Scarcely minutes into the flight it exploded in bright orange against the blue sky, killing all on board including President Zia, the American ambassador, the American military attaché, and the Pakistani Army Chief of Staff.

Aysha heard on the radio about the crash of the plane she believed her husband to be traveling on. Agonizing hours later, after she had begun the horrible and painful process of internalization of his death, she received a call—from what initially seemed a voice from the grave. It was Majeed. Both of them burst into sobs on the telephone line. And for Majeed, it was a profound moment. The door to mortality had just opened a crack, revealing the possibility of death in his line of work.

How does one process a near-death experience? It was more than just the idea of death—something that in the end overtakes us all. No, it was the power of Fate that had suddenly taken on personal meaning. It permeated his mind and he brooded upon it for weeks and months. He now recalled with disturbing clarity the lines from the Quran: *And no soul can die except by Allah's leave—a divine decree with a fixed term!* (3:145)... *Even if you had remained in your homes, those for whom death was decreed would certainly have gone forth to the place of their death.* (3:154). But Majeed had not gone forth to the place of his death. He had been spared. He would never again attempt to calculate risk: indeed, the hour for the very President and the Chief of the Army Staff and the American Ambassador had struck. But Majeed's hour had not.

As the shock and experience of near death slowly receded, Majeed came to feel a new sense of confidence and purpose. Indeed, he found it profoundly reassuring that life or death decisions were *not* in his hands. Fatalism became a liberating force in his life.

Having achieved its strategic victory, the West quickly lost any further interest in Afghanistan and the country soon slid into brutal civil war among contending mujahideen forces vying for power. The heroes of the anti-Soviet struggle now became the predators in a massive struggle for power across

Afghanistan that wreaked more damage upon Kabul than the Soviet presence ever had. Majeed had a ringside seat next to the dismaying spectacle of chaos just over the western border in Afghanistan, a country that was poor and war-wracked but still of vital strategic significance to Pakistan. "Pakistan's Mexico" as one diplomat put it, "that might soon be taken over by enemies." In response, ISI opted to support an obscure bunch of Afghan theological students, or *taliban*, to restore order and peace in the country.

During the Soviet occupation a whole generation of Afghan Pashtuns had grown up in refugee camps on the Pakistani side of the border, hugely swelling the population in border towns like Peshawar, close enough to Majeed's mother's clan. Citizens in the most troubled parts of Afghanistan welcomed the Taliban's rough frontier justice as infinitely preferable to the deadly insecurity and anarchy of warring mujahideen factions that preceded them. Cross-border tribal politics in the Pashtun areas had once again come into their own. And Majeed truly came into his element too with his personal knowledge and experience of those areas.

For Washington, Afghanistan was now out of sight, out of mind. But the deadly mixture of foreign and local jihadis in Afghanistan, many of them once supported by the US, grew in strength, eventually to include the little-known son of a major Saudi contractor, Osama bin Laden.

*   *   *

Majeed revered his older sister. Zubayda's intellect had been clear from a young age and it was matched by a boldness that worried her parents. "I don't see how she will ever get a husband if she has three times more intelligence and energy than most men she'll meet," her mother had said.

"That may be, but she takes after your own mother," Akmal had responded. "Begum Iffat is still writing and talking about feminism and the rights of women. I have a lot of sympathy for many things she says, but by God, she talks my ear off. I'm lucky you don't subject me to all that nonsense," he added with a sly glance.

"Yes, and even my mother found it impossible to live in the North-West Frontier, with all its tribal attitudes. That's why she came to Lahore, to find a place that would tolerate an outspoken woman. And by now you too, dear Akmal, know better than to try to lock me up in the house or out of our business affairs."

"Yes, my dear, I indeed do know better than to do that. But seriously, we have to think about Zubayda. Her intellect is God's gift to her." They recognized she was destined for university education.

"But of course with a university degree she'll be even harder to marry off!" Zubayda's mother said.

"Yes, but maybe she won't want a husband so much at that point. It's her choice," Akmal replied.

"Are you suggesting, my dear husband, that educated women have less use for men?"

"Yourself excepted, my dear."

Zubayda had found a childhood soulmate, Zahida. Zahida too was a bright girl, sharper than her brothers. Fortunately her father, a wealthy Lahori businessman who had studied in the UK, was also progressive enough to appreciate her qualities and agreed to send her to university. Both girls chose to go to university in Islamabad; the family arranged that the two could stay together with Zahida's uncle who had a large house there. Zubayda was attracted to social issues; she decided she wanted to study sociology together with a degree in education. At the university she also found herself drawn to questions of women's rights and ended up joining groups that debated and promoted issues of women's position in society. When back at home in Lahore she often talked about her ideas, sometimes straining even her liberal father's patience. "You are becoming too doctrinaire, my dear Zubayda," he said. "You are as bad as the Islamists—everything has to be a moral struggle, a campaign to overthrow the existing order!"

"Babaji, I hate to say it, because you have always supported me, but you can't understand what it is like to be a woman in this society. These pressures to conform, to be subservient to men. We must change this. I am going to work for female education, that is the only way things will ever change here. Zahida is in full agreement me on this. And Babaji…"

"Yes?"

"We want to go and teach in the Frontier area where the women's situation is the worst. We have had teachers come to talk to us about the situation there, the need is desperate, especially after the Afghan war—children orphaned, refugee camps, few teachers, girls' education is weak. It's the ideal place to start, it's where we can make a difference."

"Zubayda," her father said. "You can't be serious. The Frontier is a rough and dangerous area. It is heavily under the influence of fundamentalists now—if it's not the old mujahideen groups, then it's the Taliban. They will not tolerate women coming in and agitating for female education. That is a crazy mission and, although I don't like the word, I forbid it, for your own safety! Teach in the provinces somewhere, OK, but the Frontier is too dangerous for professional women, especially unmarried."

"But the Frontier is where we are needed. That's where I want to go and work with the refugee girls. We can stay with some of our relatives in Waziristan."

And she proceeded to contact her relatives to try to arrange a place where she and Zahida could stay and teach together. Indeed, her relatives were less than enthusiastic about two unattached females coming to the rural areas to teach on their own, even if they could offer accommodation, protection and oversight.

Majeed did not quite know what to make of all of this. He was proud of his sister, her independence and her accomplishments, and he had always defended her against those who tried to put her in her place or force her to dress in very conservative fashion. Zubayda, by city standards at least, did dress with some modesty; when she was out of the city, she would even wear a hijab, covering her hair and shoulders. But she refused to wear the full-body covering of a burqa. "It is medieval," she said, "looking out at the world through a piece of cloth. It's like being in prison! I would never accept that. Show me in the Quran where it says we have to wear that."

"It's not about the Quran, my Zubayda, it's about custom in those regions. Ask your mother, she's from those tribal places. Personally I agree, it shouldn't be necessary." All her mother would say was, "Like it or not, it is custom. If you want to go there, you need to avoid trouble, you don't want to stand out from everyone else."

So after mounting a campaign with their parents, Zubayda and Zahida went off to her uncle's large house in Miram Shah in North Waziristan where they would share a room. They were thrown together most of the time since they could not easily go out, apart from being escorted by relatives to the local school in a nearby village. Even Zubayda's relatives were uncomfortable when the girls sought to go out to eat in local restaurants together. They were bravely sailing a frail vessel against the waves of tribal custom and needed to rely on each other to maintain their morale in the face of the considerable pressure. Zahida was Zubayda's soulmate, the only person who really understood her. During the winter when the town and their house was permeated with mountain cold they often curled up together in one bed at night to stay warm. Zubayda knew she felt an especial attraction to Zahida, and she was confused by some of the physical feelings she was experiencing. It was deeply comforting to be physically close to Zahida as they slept at night in a close embrace.

One morning her aunt came up the stairs to pass along a message about the school that day. She found the two in bed tightly clenched with their arms around each other. She blanched, but said nothing. But Zubayda knew a line had been crossed and she felt ashamed. And that evening her uncle addressed them with anger in his voice. "You have sinned against God and our ways in practising corrupt ways with Zahida. You have disgraced us and our hospitality! This is unacceptable!"

"Uncle… that is unfair …"

"Silence! We know what we know. You are not my blood daughter, so I will take no action against you. But you and your friend are to depart immediately from my house. I never want to see you again. Be grateful that I do not denounce you to the mullahs."

"We have done nothing, uncle, except share a bed in the cold," Zubayda persisted. "Silence!" roared the uncle. "We will not speak one more word of this abomination. You will pack your clothes and leave in the morning. I will arrange for a car to take you back to Peshawar and on to Lahore."

Although he did not denounce them to the mullahs, Zubayda's distant cousin, Faisal, a religious student a few years older, was visiting. He had long questioned the propriety of the girls coming to the village unaccompanied and teaching females on their own. The uncle told him they were leaving. It was not more than a few minutes before Faisal had pried out the story behind their urgent departure. He was incensed at the idea of an abomination within the family.

Zubayda heard the yelling downstairs and knew immediately it was about them. She lay in bed trembling, not knowing whether she should get dressed and go downstairs to confront the issue and the charges. But she did not have the chance. After an eternity of yelling and the sounds of her aunt weeping, Zubayda heard the voices reach a crescendo and heavy steps coming up the stairs. The door was flung open and Faisal stood there. The moonlight revealed the glint of a knife in his hand as he approached the bed breathing heavily and yelling "Filthy whore! You have disgraced our honor, you have disgraced our hospitality!" Zubayda screamed and saw her life coming to an end. But she fought back, and grabbed his arm with the knife. He was barely able to hold her down as her uncle and aunt came up the stairs behind him yelling. Faisal stayed his hand for a moment, then with a swift movement slashed her cheek in one cut and slit her nostril with another. He stood there panting and looking on as her face ran with blood. He tottered a moment, almost as if drunk with his indignation and exertion. "You are lucky I do not kill you!" he roared, and then threw down the blade and ran out. Her aunt rushed up to Zubayda and used the sheets to stem the flow of blood on her face. Her uncle seemed paralyzed with fear and uncertainty and retreated back down the stairs as Faisal stormed out of the house. Her aunt tried to stanch the slash wounds on her face, weeping. "You must leave as soon as possible, my daughter! You must not even raise the suspicion of violating God's laws!" Zahida too, was in great fear of her own life but since she was not a relative the stain of honor on the family was not the same. At dawn Zubayda and Zahida were bundled into a vehicle, still locked in fear. Only her aunt saw her swiftly off. But as the fear slowly receded with the rural villages of the mountains fading behind them, Zubayda's anger grew. She did not know what her uncle would report back to her father, but the evidence was on her face forever, never to be missed, concealed or denied.

When they eventually arrived back in Lahore, her father met her at the door and embraced her. He put his finger to his lips as Zubayda, sobbing, began to talk. "Don't say anything," he said, "your uncle has called and told me what happened."

"Babaji, it is not like he says, please believe me."

"My daughter, I believe you. I do not know exactly what happened in Miram Shah. All I know is that he has told me you disgraced his hospitality in sinful actions with Zahida."

"Babaji, we did nothing except share a bed in the cold nights. We have committed no sin."

"Only God can know all. But I believe your words. I do not judge you, but you have been grievously punished through the beliefs of others." He spoke in sadness and in tears. "Your mother is bitterly angry because she feels humiliated in front of her family and clan there. She says you have flouted the laws of Pashtunwali and hospitality. Sadly, the truth is what family members will believe it to be. It is not what you did but what you appear to have done. You have flown in the face of known local custom and belief in the Frontier. And that puts you in a terrible position."

And indeed, Zubayda entered a long period of strain with her mother. "I am ashamed for our family, Zubayda. Whatever the true story is, we are ashamed. And ashamed for you. I do not see how you can marry now; what man will accept these scars, and their implications?"

Salman did not fully understand the implications, but he was deeply upset at the meaning of the knife scars running down one side of her face and nose, and he knew Zubayda had in some way shamed the family.

Zubayda and the family told people that she had been in an automobile accident and had flown through the windscreen, that she was lucky to be alive. She did not know what people actually believed, since her scars could also be consistent with sexual sin.

Over time Zubayda was able to find a job as a teacher in a Westernized school in Lahore where her story of the automobile accident was accepted. She enjoyed the teaching and was able to maintain some kind of friendship with her female colleagues. But Zubayda knew enough not to ask her parents to help arrange a suitable marriage, it simply was no longer possible.

Majeed was deeply pained and embarrassed by the whole incident and its aftermath. He grew more upset about it over time as he tried to make sense of it. He avoided any private discussion with Zubayda about the incident until many weeks later. He felt close enough to her to finally ask about the details. She told him exactly what had happened. Majeed paused, shook his head, and was silent for a moment. "But Zubayda," he finally said, "I must ask, do you consider yourself… that your are drawn to women?"

"No, Majeed, I am not a lesbian," she snapped back. But I might as well be, for what man will now have me!"

"You could maybe go abroad and find someone to marry there."

"With this face? No, I have no wish to flee. I will have to accept what is here. God will provide."

The fundamental injustice of the incident increasingly penetrated Majeed's conscience. Justice is justice, but what kind of justice is based on innuendo?

The power and ruthlessness of the Pashtun culture of honor had struck home in a personal way that complicated any admiration he had for it, or his comfort in working with it. In a mixture of compassion and guilt he tried to include Zubayda in some of the social gatherings with his friends and colleagues. She was accepted among some of the university crowd, but there were always questions. In the meantime she sought out organizations where she could work for improvement of the situation of women in the Lahore countryside.

It took Zubayda a long time to come to terms with the whole experience. Her aims had been driven by idealism, social concern, the imperative of educating women in Frontier society. That mission had been reciprocated by terror, brutality, humiliation, and debasement. What seemed to have happened in the eyes of others had not in fact happened. But the truth lay in the perceptions of tribal society; like Caesar's wife, women must be above all suspicion. Zubayda had been brutally punished as a result of harsh perceptions. Her mother was too enmeshed in Frontier cultural values to see things in any other way. For her the "true account" that Zubayda insisted upon was simply irrelevant, unworthy of discussion. Only status and family honor mattered. Akmal supported Zubayda, but she could see how badly he was torn between his love for his daughter and his understanding of the price that such situations inevitably extract in tribal Pakistan. He bitterly regretted he had allowed Zubayda to persuade him to let her go against all his misgivings, to a culture for which he felt scant sympathy. At least Majeed took her side entirely; for him issues of culture and honor in Pashtun society were now no longer theoretical, but deep and personal. He grieved in his heart for Zubayda.

Once she could start to tolerate her red-scarred image staring at her in the mirror, Zubayda began to feel a deep change inside her. She realized she had lost her fear. She translated the horror of the event into a powerful new incentive. Her work became her outlet and vehicle for her values. She vowed that each life of each woman to whom she was able to bring some ease and enlightenment proved that her scars were in fact blessings, impelling her towards ever greater work for the cause. Her scars became her inspiration, her motivation. Indeed they became her liberation.

*   *   *

Alex's departure, and the break-off of their wedding plans at Isabel's own instigation, had proven exceptionally painful to Isabel. Life with her parents became more difficult than ever, particularly as Doña Maria lost no occasion to remind Isabel of their presentiments that Alex had been a poor choice in marriage and to subtly denigrate him whenever possible. Consequently they were eager to press her into new social settings involving the introduction of eligible bachelors—a process she was not ready for. Worse, she had now begun to feel that her horizons in Chile were narrower than she had once believed. Her exposure to Alex had opened doors to new perspectives; she was no longer sure she wanted to make Chile her future, along with a Chilean husband, against the background of a potentially broader world.

Hello Alex my darling,

I know I have not answered your letters for many months. I have been too upset. But I cannot bear this situation any longer.

I feel like my heart has been placed in a deep freeze ever since we parted. I walk around Santiago but it is not the same city. I go places we visited together, but they are now hollow and empty.

Life has also been very difficult with my parents as well. They are very angry at you, even without knowing the true story of course.

I have had little to do over these months than to perform my work at the office mechanically, and think. As I watch politics continue in my own country, now that the monster Pinochet is weakening, I realize that there is no easy right and wrong in this world. Countries behave in harsh and selfish ways with each other, and I fear that will always be so. So I cannot blame you for that. And I know you had nothing to do with anything that happened here.

Alex, I know that whatever your work, you are a good and decent person, and a caring person. You have a broad vision of things that makes me want to see the world with you. I love you. That is what matters most to me. I can't expect to find a perfect world. But I know that I want to be with you. That is where my life is taking me.

So I want to join you and be together again. I have told my parents that you have finally settled the divorce issue. Meanwhile you will do what you have to do in your job. I only ask that you not come back to work in Chile again, for the contradictions are too great here for me to bear.

Can we start again? I can fly to Washington and I am sure I can find a job there. And we can get married, if you are still willing. I miss you terribly and I can't stay separated any longer.

Besos y abrazos fuertes.

Tu llamita,

Isabel

*   *   *

Mi llamita querida,

The best moment of my life! I can't tell you how your letter has transformed my mood, my life, with your news! I really despaired. I know we can make it work! And we will be together for a life adventure, wherever it may take us.

And I agree, I don't think I should go back to Santiago, and I fear your family will be even less happy with our wedding plans this time around. Let's just make it a low key affair here in Washington—maybe a few friends of mine, and then we'll go off and drink some special Chilean wine I found and have our honeymoon in bed for a week right here! How does that sound? I can't wait to see you.

Give my love to Doña Maria and Don Jorge—even if they don't want to hear from me. They are good people, talented and passionate, and angry for good reason for all they have been through. I respect them. It only pains me that they can't think well of me at this point. But at least maybe we can produce a little Chileno for them at some point.

Thank you for this wonderful decision. I can't wait to see you! Our life must begin again! Come soon! Hasta muy pronto!

Abrazos fuertes, cariños y besos .

Alex

*   *   *

Alex was exhilarated. "Sasha, something's wrong, you don't look Slavic anymore, you look happy," Max observed at work. A week later Isabel arrived, and Alex carried her over the threshold of his apartment. "We're not even married yet!" Isabel protested, but she looked joyous. "Take a few days off work if you like," Max offered, "never let it be said that Max stood in the way of true love." And within days of Isabel's arrival in Washington they had gone to a justice of the peace in Virginia to get married. Only Jack was invited down from New York with his wife, their son Roger, now nearly ten, and their daughter Jennifer who was eight.

"Too bad Mom didn't live to see your wedding," Jack said. "Although I think she would have found all this a bit tawdry if you ask me… justice of the peace and all. Sort of like you're sneaking into it. Isabel tells me you were going to have a big church wedding in Chile before you delayed it. I'm not big on church weddings, and certainly not Catholic ones, but that might have been an awesome experience. This here's sort of like Las Vegas."

"Yeah, Las Vegas without the nightlife," Alex replied. "Frankly, I'm delighted at keeping it bare-bones simple." All Isabel got out of the ceremony, apart from a husband, was a free rose from the justice of the peace. But for her it was a wonderful rose. Isabel knew her decision to marry in Washington would hurt her parents, but to go back to Santiago for such an event now could only stir up other issues, traumatic for all.

Perhaps simply demonstrating maternal instincts, perhaps because she wanted to strengthen the bonds between herself and Alex, perhaps also to warm the hearts of her parents, Isabel wanted to quickly become pregnant. But it took longer than she had hoped. Finally, after what seemed an agonizingly long time, they conceived and nine months later their son was born.

"I want to name him Rodrigo," Isabel said.

"How did you choose Rodrigo?"

"Because that was the name of a maternal grandfather of mine in Chile who rebelled against the landowners. He was killed by right-wing vigilante forces, during one of the country's bloody civil struggles."

"Fine, but did you know the name has even more meaning? You must have heard of the great medieval Spanish hero El Cid—his real name was Rodrigo.

171

He fought both with and against the Moors in Spain… I like that, combining Spanish and Muslim culture."

Rodrigo looked more like Isabel than Alex, with dark hair and dark eyes and a nose promising to become aquiline. Isabel spoke Spanish with Rodrigo from the start, encouraged by Alex. He loved languages after all and was thrilled his son would grow up speaking more than one—just like he had. Still, Alex could not help but feel a twinge of isolation from the Spanish dialog between mother and child. Alex's Spanish was good, but hardly native and it was more suited for politics than for raising a child. He spoke English to Rodrigo in the precious few hours of the day that he actually saw him after work. Alex once or twice heard Isabel telling Rodrigo that he was Chilean, reminding Alex of his own cultural insecurities. He opted to stay away from reminding her that Rodrigo was American too, indeed first and foremost since he was born in the US.

Alex was thrilled to have Isabel now sharing his life and Rodrigo's intense little presence indeed did deepen their bonds. With Rodrigo's birth, Doña Maria and Don Jorge increasingly began to agitate for a visit, which Alex dreaded in a way. He even debated even whether to go back with Isabel at all to Santiago. "My love, you must, it's better to face it sooner rather than later," she said. "My parents may not like you, but they will like you even less if you don't go back with me and Rodriguito."

During the long flight south Alex found himself increasingly nervous. In the airport reception hall Doña Maria moved forward with a speed that belied her age and weight to tearfully embrace Isabel, with Don Jorge just behind. They crowded and oohed and aahed over their grandson and took turns holding and rocking him for what seemed like an eternity before finally turning to acknowledge Alex's presence. He was unsure whether it was a deliberate slight or simply the natural priority of events in which he arguably was the least most important member present. When Doña Maria did turn to Alex she embraced him and kissed him on both cheeks as appropriate, but it felt largely pro-forma. And she offered nothing else other than greetings. Don Jorge also embraced Alex, a bit absent-mindedly since his attention too was focused on Isabel. Alex noted his own Spanish had grown slightly rusty for the moment as he had not used it that much, although he of course understood everything that was said.

The formal dinner at home that evening was vivacious with Doña Maria holding the floor, relating with gusto the come-uppances that had been delivered against Pinochet and all his former henchmen in government. She and her husband and the entire range of artists and intellectuals in Chile had been vocally outspoken in condemning the past and now were more than ever basking in the new freedoms of the country. Writers were emerging to describe the Pinochet horrors. In the same spirit even Alex made a toast welcoming "the new freedoms" in Chile. Doña Maria smiled coolly at this gesture, but made no response. Alex sensed the irony she undoubtedly felt at Alex making such comments. The aborted wedding hung in the air, at least in Alex's mind, as a cloud no one wished to acknowledge or address. But he felt he could not allow the issue to fester unspoken indefinitely without tainting the nature of the whole visit.

The moment came soon enough. The next morning Alex came down into the breakfast room while Isabel was still taking care of Rodriguito upstairs. Morning sun was streaming into the dining room, birds were loudly greeting the day in the garden, Doña Maria was renewing her roots with the earth, immersed up to the elbows in some great bread concoction with flour spilled out across the table—full yeasty domesticity signaling that all was right with the world. He and Doña Maria were momentarily, awkwardly alone. "Doña Maria," he said in Spanish, "I wanted to say just a few words about the unfortunate event of the wedding here, I …"

"Say no more, Alex, say no more." Doña Maria waved her hand without looking at him as she arranged her battery of baking tools on the kitchen table. "We understand what happened. We do not need to hear the details. They have already made us sad enough, so the less said about it, the better. Yes, we were made very sad by it, and you broke Isabel's heart. But never mind, we understand what happened and there is nothing more that can be said about it."

"Doña Maria, I just wanted to make sure you knew how unhappy I was myself about the whole situation. My love for Isabel was overwhelming and I could not bear to delay things even though my divorce paperwork had not yet come. I was expecting it at any time. Isabel is the center of my life. I did not want to hurt her for anything in the world."

"Yes? Well, sometimes circumstances force us to hurt the ones we love. But we accept the reality. The important thing is that Isabel is married now, and that is what she wanted. We will accept the situation, even though we as parents never had the opportunity to attend the wedding."

Christ, she really wants her pound of flesh. "I regret too, Doña Maria, that you were not able to be at our wedding in the end. As you know, it was too complicated and costly to come back here for it, especially because of the embarrassment of the cancellation of the first one, but…"

She waved him off, eyes and hands intent upon the pile of dough. "We understand. But you must know that Isabel is our only daughter and her wedding would have been a moment of great joy for Jorge and myself. That was not to be. There is nothing we can do about it. Life has its punishments. But she is now back with us at home, and Rodriguito has come home as well."

Home. "I wish it was for longer, but it is all the time we have. But I promise we will try to come often to visit, and would hope that you could come to visit us."

"Ah, *mi yerno*, we are getting old for travel now. But this is Isabel's and Rodriguito's home, so of course they will be here often." *Not bloody well my home, though.*

Over the next few days the atmosphere eased somewhat. Doña Maria grew less prickly with Alex and he maintained a humble and cautious manner. Isabel told her parents that they might not be living in Washington for much longer, now that Alex was in the State Department as a diplomat.

"Alex, a diplomat. I guess that is better than being a capitalist banker. But you are still working for a government whose actions in this world are viewed with hostility and suspicion. Frankly we had hoped that you might become a professor, or a journalist or something intellectually respectable. But you still seem to be involved in international politics. Not a pretty thing." Doña Maria's heavy jewelry—her huge green turquoise ring on the left hand, a ring in native red stone on the right, and necklaces of native lapis all seemed to lend weight and authority to her pronouncements that took on near regal character. Alex was angered by her constant negative insinuations, but was not in a position to object. One evening in their bedroom when he said something to Isabel about her mother's jabs, tears sprang to Isabel's eyes. "Please, I don't want to discuss this, Alex. This is all very difficult for me. I have basically had to lie to them—because of your lies—in order to spare them from a worse truth. I can do no more."

"But your mother doesn't seem willing to just let it go. I don't know if she even much tolerates my presence."

"Of course Mamá is unhappy, but believe me she too has been careful not to make any direct attacks. She has broken into tears with me about not being present at the wedding. I don't want any more tension in this house than there is already. This is not the way I expected to be dealing with my parents— either as a bride and now as a mother. Please just try to ignore her remarks. And keep in mind how much she has been hurt by what you and I have done."

"I understand, *mi amor*, but it's just... all these references to you now being in your home, and Rodrigo being in his home. Yes, of course it is home, but she seems to be denying any legitimacy of our own home in the US."

"Alex, what can I say? I don't know whether anything will ever change there. Just please don't fight it, for my sake if nothing else."

So Alex put a good face on things. He spent more time with Don Jorge who seemed less interested in scoring points or dwelling on unhappinesses. Indeed he seemed happy to show off his work to Alex, and even took him out to a few galleries to view the latest work among Chilean painters. Don Jorge made no reference to any of the concerns expressed by Doña Maria, but it was evident that he did not deny them. He left it to his wife to say what needed to be said and focused on maintaining courteous and civil relations with Alex. Indeed, there were occasional moments of warmth as he noted

Alex's artistic appreciation of his own work and the work of others. And he appreciated that Alex did not pick up the gauntlet thrown down by his contentious wife.

The issue of Alex's "previous marriage" came up only once again when Doña Maria drew Alex aside as they sat in the garden. Alex dreaded these moments of more "intimate" conversation alone with her and the intensity of her approach. "It is not my place to pry into your past life," she began.

Here we go. She reached out her fleshy forearm to place her hand on Alex's at the table in a moment of signaled intimacy. "But for the sake of our daughter and Rodriguito, Don Jorge and I must ask. Were there any children from your first marriage? Any child who could have claim to your inheritance, or your name? Or who could force himself upon Isabel and Rodriguito?"

Alex hesitated, internally seething at having to contrive further elaborate lies, details and variations onto the original total fabrication about the previous marriage already on the table. "No, Doña Maria, I can assure you there were no children. The marriage was brief, it was ill-considered. I was young, she was young. I have no contact with her at all now, and the marriage, as you know, has ended in legal divorce."

"But is she out of the picture entirely? She will not want to come back and try to take you away from Isabel?"

"No, Doña Maria, I have heard she has subsequently remarried, and will not be part of our life in any way."

Doña Maria paused to gather forces and renew the assault from a different angle. "Does she live near you?"

"No, she has moved to California with her husband and we have no contact. She does not even know my address."

"Where does she live?"

"Oh, I think somewhere in Los Angeles."

"And what is her name?" *Good Christ, it kept coming.*

"Julia," was what he could come up with at the moment.

"Well, at least a good Spanish name. Is she Spanish?"

"No. Her father is German and her mother is Polish."

"Well, that is good, thank God. Because we would not want Isabel to have to meet the other woman, or for Rodrigo to be exposed to her, or to any children she may have."

"I assure you, Doña Maria, there is no chance of that happening. You may rest at ease."

They sat for a few more moments drinking tea. Then, like a cat going back for one final assault on a dying mouse, she still could not leave well enough alone. "You know, Alex, we have a good Chilean friend who is a lawyer in Los Angeles. I wonder if I should write to him, ask him to investigate her, just to find out her status, to ensure that there are no problems with children she may claim are yours."

Alex was dumbfounded. "Doña Maria, thank you, but I don't think that would be necessary. I don't even know the name of the man she married, and I don't even know whether it's in Los Angeles or San Francisco. I think we can safely put the issue to rest."

Doña Maria sat back in further contemplation of what steps might be taken, but her prolonged silence indicated she was seemingly as satisfied by now as she could ever be on the issue. Alex avoided further intimate occasions with her, but had clearly been unprepared to come up with the never-ending ongoing and detailed biographical demands from Doña Maria on "his first marriage."

Doña Maria and Don Jorge kept their social profile low for the two weeks while Isabel and Alex were there and invited no one. It was clear Doña Maria had felt social embarrassment over the aborted wedding. They too had been compelled to concoct for their friends in Santiago their own more innocent version of the sudden collapse of the wedding—allegedly the death throes of Alex's mother in painful cancer at that very time had caused Alex to have to go back to be with her at her deathbed—all suitably dramatic. Operating now within the shells of triple lies, it was a relief when they took a few days on a trip to the countryside, but the grandparents mainly wanted to dote on their grandson and Alex was content to allow Rodriguito to carry the burden of social exchange. Upon their departure Doña Maria was tearful. "Don Jorge and I will not be traveling out of Chile, but you are under a solemn obligation, my son, to make sure that our daughter and grandson are returned to us often. I expect it of you," she said, firmly clutching his arm.

At last on the plane, Isabel stared out blankly at the receding city vanishing into the clouds below them. She sighed. "Perhaps Rodriguito is the only one of us who does not feel some relief at our departure. That makes me sad. It should have been a happy time for me to return with my child to see my parents. There were more shadows than should ever have been." She did not blame him, but Alex felt a moroseness settle in over him on the long flight back. He took her hand in his as they sat in silence in the darkening cabin.

*   *   *

Back in Washington Isabel did not warm to the environment. "This is a cold city," she said one evening over dinner. "No one seems to want to talk about anything but local politics." Alex had made efforts to introduce her to the many cultural attractions of the city from which she drew some enjoyment—"it is more sophisticated than Santiago, I must admit." But she did not like living in a Virginia suburb and she knew no one. Alex's natural orbit of social life was with his colleagues at the Agency and their families, but he did not feel comfortable in inviting them over with the inevitable questions of his time in Chile, and Isabel seemed ill at ease when they were invited to the homes of other Agency colleagues from whom she seemed perpetually on guard, on the lookout for the worst. He could have told her that the friends were with the State Department, but he wanted to put an end to the practice of lying to Isabel. In the event, she seemed to find several of the Agency couples somewhat compatible and interesting, especially since they showed an awareness and comfort with the international scene that she complained she often found lacking in many Americans. One or two spoke good Spanish, which pleased her. Otherwise she reported back to Alex now and then about how she had met yet another American who had no idea where Chile was, or that there even was a country by that name. "They think it is where chili sauce is made, and that it is somewhere in Mexico."

Isabel did discover other Latinos in various embassies and in international organizations and struck up a number of friendships with them; she seemed to find it easier to see them on her own in the daytime rather than involve Alex with them. Alex would always ask her how her day had been, whom she was meeting and where she went with some of her friends, but Isabel for the most part seemed to live a compartmented social life. On weekends she eagerly embraced the chance to spend all her time alone with Alex and Rodrigo, and on taking various day trips to Harper's Ferry or the Shenandoahs or the Eastern Shore, or visiting festivals or museums. On a few occasions when Alex mentioned that they had an invitation on the weekend to go to dinner with some colleagues, "No, *mi amor*, I'm sorry," she replied, "but frankly I would rather spend the precious weekend time together with you than sit at dinner parties talking about politics with people I don't know."

"OK, I understand. But you know when we go overseas there will be many dinner parties and diplomatic affairs. I'm afraid it's part of the professional life. Who knows, you might even find some of the international crowd interesting. And Latinos will be there as well."

"Yes, we'll see, I'm sure it will be fine." Nonetheless Alex felt defensive about his colleagues, his work, and about the world of diplomatic life that surely would come in a year or two. Meanwhile, one security officer noted to Alex at work, "It's good for your wife to have a chance to become more Americanized and feel more at home here. That's why it would be good if she could stay a few more years here in Washington and become more part of the American scene." Alex accepted the statement—in part he agreed with it but in part he was also annoyed. Indeed he did not pass the remark on to Isabel out of fear that she would find it condescending. As it was, Isabel did not inquire about his work at all, maybe feeling she could not, should not, ought not—or simply had no interest in the matter. In turn Alex had little to say about it either, other than the fact he was sitting on the Russian desk and following affairs there. She showed no further curiosity and only commented, "Well, I'm glad it has nothing to do with Chile." He had also noted that she seemed to have lost some of her usual vivacity and playfulness. But he knew also that they could not remain courting lovers their whole lives. She would grow accustomed to his life which would be more adventurous and interesting overseas.

*   *   *

"My God, have you heard? The bloody Indians have now just set off five nuclear bombs—weapons ready to go! *A'udhu bi'llah min al-shaytan al-rajeem.* I take refuge in God from the Devil's works!" Neighbors stopped neighbors in the street, "Run, switch on the TV, tell your family!"

This morning, 11 May 1998 at 0920 India exploded a nuclear....

This was one of those lapidary moments when everyone remembered exactly where they were when it happened, and everyone retold it so many different ways later on, in some voice from our collective memory.

And so we all heard the news, first from the BBC—which we cannot always believe—but then on our own Pakistan TV! We could not wish it away: India had just tested its first nuclear weapon! It came like a death knell to us in Pakistan. The world had accepted India's first nuclear explosion in 1974. Now with these five new explosions we were now only minutes away from annihilation if the Hindus decided to destroy us. And they would want to destroy Pakistan. The Hindu religious party that was in power in India hated Pakistan; the party reveled in its chauvinism. We knew India was determined to threaten the very existence of our country. They started three wars with us and invaded our soil. They supported the breakaway of East Pakistan from West Pakistan in the 1971 war. They were determined to avenge India's weakening hold on Kashmir where the Muslim population was in rebellion against harsh and arrogant Hindu rule.

And now the Indians rubbed our faces in it again with five nuclear explosions across our border! We could feel the effects already—the Indian nuclear radiation seeping into our bodies, permeating our pores. Crossing borders at will, riddling the atmosphere with its deadly radiation, poisoning the cells and bones and flesh of every Muslim Pakistani if we did not now bow down to Hindu power. We faced a grim future and would live in eternal fear, in helplessness. The power and honor of the Pakistani army had now been reduced to an empty shell of its earlier glory. It might still salve the soul of our country, but no longer could protect its body. As India rose in triumph in the light of its growing artificial nuclear sun, power in Asia had just shifted massively, in full public light. Hear, O Pakistan: if you had any doubt, realize that you have been now reduced to a pathetic satellite of Hindu ambition and power. How could you ever hold your head up high again?

And even more humiliating, we knew that it had been a *Muslim* scientist in India, A.P.J. Abdul Kalam, a leading Indian missile engineer, who was the father of the Indian bomb! How could God have permitted this? What message do we draw?

A deep sense of rage, bitterness, and helplessness had descended upon us. God had averted his face from us. Pakistan was now trapped between the nuclear might of four hostile forces—the US, Israel, Russia, and now India. And over three days this week there had been *five* Indian nuclear tests; obviously America had known they were coming but had done nothing serious to stop them! Surely they wanted India to dominate us!

Our throat is filled with gall. And have you heard the latest? Our humiliation knows no end, Washington still warns us against developing any weapon of our own in response to India. America will deny us the right to protect ourselves from Hindu tyranny, openly trumpeted by the Hindu fundamentalists in power in Delhi.

Can we remain naked in the face of this deadly threat upon our very doorstep? Remember what our Prime Minister Zulfikar Ali Bhutto said as far back as 1965— "If India builds the bomb, we will eat grass or leaves, even go hungry, but we will get one of our own. We have no other choice."

*　　　　　*　　　　　*

But... Praise be to God! We learned today—28 May 1998—that God had not averted his face from us. Who could have predicted, who could ever forget this thrilling moment, today, when Pakistani scientists, led by our national genius A. Q. Khan, pressed the button and initiated the same stunning nuclear process at Chagai mountain in Pakistan, invoking the very same power of the sun! Yes, we saw it on our own screens – in front of our eyes; the very earth trembled, Chagai mountain became sheer white powder—and vanished!

Did you hear, brother, that miracles had been observed even during construction at the test site, foretelling this blessed event? What a day—I remember, citizens cheered, people danced in the street, cars stopped and honked their horns in a great national outpouring of relief, joy and pride! Children were handed badges in the shape of a mushroom cloud. All over the country we now plastered posters of our bomb, a Pakistani bomb, our answer to India that we would not be threatened or intimidated! How dare America threaten us to try and stop us from our own national self-defense! It was alright for America to kill hundreds of thousands of innocents to defend their interests. Is it alright for them to dominate the world today with their nuclear arsenal—but God forbid that any other country should have the same right to preserve itself?

No, we were not alone! All over the world Muslims were thrilled to see the first Muslim country emerge and join the nuclear club. We had started on that path back in 1971 just after our terrible defeat by India in a war that tore away Bangladesh from the very body of Pakistan and left us weaker than ever in the face of Hindu domination. And then America imposed sanctions upon us, denying us the right of self-defense and dignity on the international scene. To hell with America! To hell with India! We will stand proud, independent, powerful, Pakistani and Muslim! God has smiled upon us! Praise be to God!

*　　　　　*　　　　　*

The slow, inexorable, unbelievable glide of the flashing silver body of the jetliner against the backdrop of the brilliant blue sky over the city, easing out of the routine flight path and accelerating directly toward New York's towering iconic twin structures—it was a flight into history, changing the world. A watershed in personal lives—where were you when it happened?

Alex had been at work, sitting in a small staff meeting in CIA Hqs that morning when the first reports came in—seemingly about a plane accident. But within a few minutes another officer came in and told them to get to the TV; they packed into the office of the branch chief who was already focused on the screen. They stood silently, mesmerized, horrified at the stately silent spectacle that now included a second plane hurling its tons of metal, passengers and jet fuel high into the second tower. And within less than an hour, millions of tons of buckled concrete and steel, along with hundreds of intertwined bodies, lay on the streets in downtown Manhattan, obscured by an infernal black cloud. Bin Laden's response to the West would fatefully define the new America.

In Islamabad it was late evening. A colleague working late had rushed into Majeed's office, and they joined the global village glued to the television coverage. Once outside the borders of America and across the oceans, the news underwent a transformation quite different from the way it was perceived in the wounded epicenter of American life. Horror, to be sure, was the nearly universal emotion, especially at the most gut-wrenching level with the spectacle of human beings jumping to their deaths to escape the incendiary steel torch. Followed by the awe of watching two massive structures incredibly crumble and gracefully collapse in an almost precision-ordered sinking column of total destruction. "My God, my God," people murmured, long before any political calculus had registered. And then, slowly, hours later with the earliest indications trickling in that it seemed to be the action of Muslim terrorists, the mood shifted. Repressed political instincts and old angers rose above any rational analysis everywhere. A massive *political* event had just taken place whose sheer energy kicked off a panoply of hugely diverse reactions the world over.

-This is an unspeakable act. It should know no limits of punishment.

-Is it really surprising that this attack happened, after the decades of repressed anger in the Middle East?

-What do you expect? The US had it coming, even if those poor people themselves did not.

-Let's hope now Washington will wake up and smell the coffee; this has been fermenting for years.

-I may hate US policies, but there's nothing that justifies that kind of savagery.

-Those arrogant bastards in America finally got their come-uppance.

-It's the goddam Muslims who did this, watch how we will now make them pay dearly for it.

-Our nation calls for revenge. Let's wipe out every last one of those ragheads.
-I'm sure the Israelis must be behind this—they stood to benefit the most.
-All of us are going to pay the price, in the end, for this action.
-I bet you it's a conspiracy by our own government—to seize absolute power.
-Good Muslims could never carry out an act like that, it's against the Quran.

Awe, elation, anxiety, fear, rage, hatred—all of the above—the future of the world was about to change as the American behemoth bestirred itself into action.

Isabel remembered a Chilean friend of the family who worked for an Argentinian company in the South Tower. The black cloud obscured access to almost all information about people who had been in the building. When she later heard Ramón had indeed been in the Tower and was unaccounted for, Isabel called her parents to impart the sad news. Doña Maria reacted as did so much of the outside world: "A terrible event. God have mercy on their souls. I hope this will lead the US to change its ways." And she added, "Are you aware of the bitter irony of this date? Allende was overthrown and murdered by Pinochet and the US on 9/11." Isabel chose not to pass that remark on to Alex.

For most CIA officers and American diplomats in general, reactions were of horror and anger, shock—yet not complete surprise. Anyone who had spent much time in the Middle East could not be ignorant of a long, inexorable mounting backlog of anti-American sentiment across most of the Muslim world—and even beyond. It had to blow somewhere, sometime.

As soon as Alex learned that the Taliban regime in Afghanistan had been indirectly involved in 9/11 through allowing Bin Laden and al-Qaeda on its soil, he knew that Pakistan too would quickly and inevitably be drawn in to the heart of American response. It would be only a matter of time before a call for action would be drawn up, involving the full range of American foreign policy institutions including major tasking for CIA action as well. He cringed: with his Pak background, how could this event not eventually reach out and touch him personally? And within months Afghanistan indeed did lie at the heart of a new American war whose hot breath was already spilling over the border into Pakistan. The American Assistant Secretary of State was widely quoted as demanding full Pakistani cooperation, or else Washington "would bomb them back to the stone age."

History had come full circle: after having abandoned Afghanistan soon after the pullout of the Soviet Army there, the Western presence in Pakistan and Afghanistan now roared back into business in the form of a massive new US military presence inside Afghanistan. Even more challenging, Washington analysts were suddenly forced to painfully grapple with the complexities of political, tribal, and clan links between Pashtun militants fighting the US on the Afghan side, and those on the Pakistani side.

It was an ill wind that blew no one any good; these events facilitated Majeed's steady rise within ISI while maintaining his periodic political contacts with Western and NATO diplomats—still under the cover of the President's Staff. He seemed to grow somewhat sleeker, more confident, more waspish in tongue on occasion, outspoken. Any rumored playboy instincts on his part now now appeared baseless. But his true political orientation was something of a conundrum to those Westerners who had encountered him; Majeed remained elusive, appearing only infrequently on the diplomatic circuit—where he had a tendency to be undiplomatically outspoken.

*   *   *

Majeed had attended occasional receptions at the US Embassy over the years but had not been invited directly by the US ambassador to a dinner there. He was certain the direct invitation was related to planning on Afghanistan. Direct handling of US Afghan policy ran through the intelligence organizations of Washington and Islamabad but grand policy was, nominally, still the purview of the Ambassador, or so the Ambassador liked to think. Majeed checked with his boss General Ramzi about whether he should attend this particular dinner meeting. The General smiled. "Yes, my boy, you should go. And you should speak frankly about all your concerns as you see them. I know you will not try to be diplomatic. You are young, ignorant, naïve and inexperienced and do not understand what you are saying. And we will of course deny everything you say as unauthorized, regrettable and unrepresentative. Let them hear the truth, mull it over in their mouths, and get used to its gall—we will smile and deny. I am sure you will have much to say that is upsetting to our friends. Please do not tell me about it—I condemn it all in advance."

Majeed set off with a sense of empowerment, armed with a license to speak bluntly. Already his lip curled slightly at the sight of various black diplomatic vehicles pulling up into the portico of the US Ambassador's residence. While Majeed hardly lacked polish and education, the stuff of diplomatic evenings had never been his scene. To maintain a provocative image of modesty of position, he often came by taxi rather than chauffeur-driven official car, which confused diplomatic observers further about his real clout. Arriving on his own, he had been subjected to extensive, intensive and offensive security procedures at the entrance, first by Pakistani guards who treated anyone who arrived in anything but a diplomatic vehicle as little more than a day laborer for the ambassador's garden. Diplomatic vehicles were ushered in with lesser scrutiny at the gate but were still handled by American security guards at the door.

The dinner party turned out to be a rather small one. Majeed had met the American ambassador before, but only to shake his hand at some reception. Harrison Spaulding was made for the role—tall, fit, salt-and-pepper hair, impeccably dressed in a dark blue suit, piercing blue eyes that projected the confidence of power. But he was also known for a certain arrogance and bluntness of style. He believed that honesty and directness were admirable American qualities that distinguished American diplomats from the effete styles of other nations' diplomats who were long on finesse and light on substance. Or who were so cautious and circumspect in the way they spoke that they often left doubt about whether they had any actual views, much less intentions. Coming from a family of corporate wealth, Spaulding was rumored to have contributed heavily to the president's campaign, but no one suggested that he was incompetent. Despite being a political appointee, he was not uninformed about Pakistani affairs since he had previously served a stint in Congress on the Foreign Relations Committee, until he had lost his position in the last election. Indeed, he claimed a great interest and fondness for Pakistan, and talked tirelessly about how American and Pakistani interests were at heart one and the same, two horses pulling in tandem—or some other appropriately rural simile. Spaulding's trophy wife was urbane and adventuresome; she expressed a great interest in Pakistani art and had purchased the canvases of many leading artists with which to decorate the residence, and often included local artists in Embassy dinner parties. She was widely liked by Pakistani women with whom she established close ties; she was far less appreciated by the Embassy staff whom she often treated imperiously as befitted the old days of the imperial ambassador rather than the greater egalitarianism of the more modern US Foreign Service.

Majeed had been included in this party since the Political Counselor of the embassy, Jack Devereaux, in consultation with the CIA Chief of Station, had suggested that Majeed was an up-and-coming, if not yet senior person working within ISI circles in the arena of policy and strategy towards the border areas and Afghanistan. He was therefore a person to cultivate and to influence. The Ambassador greeted Majeed at the door, his blue eyes maintaining probing eye contact along with his too-firm handshake—a grip, Majeed noted, somehow associated in American minds with sincerity, but which many other non-Westerners found to signify a less pleasant muscular contest. "Mr. Rehman, it's a pleasure to see you again. I think we met about six months ago at a reception at the German Embassy." Spaulding had been well briefed by his social secretary. "Jack Devereaux tells me we share many common interests in Afghan events."

Majeed smiled noncommittally but made sure to maintain the same firm eye contact with the Ambassador, the first step to making a good impression in American culture. He had learned this in the UK where the American students he had met had all complained the British were limp-wristed and glanced away when introduced, thereby creating a poor impression among Americans. "Thank you for inviting me, Your Excellency." Majeed deliberately chose the more European title rather than employing the American conceit of egalitarianism in the title "Mr. Ambassador."

"And I believe you studied in the UK for one year?"

"You are well informed, Your Excellency. Yes, unfortunately for financial reasons I had to come back, to finish my degree here."

"Well, we always like to see graduates of British institutions here, they're cousins. Similar educations always brings us closer together, you know, shared experiences and outlook."

"Yes, I remember with fondness my time in the UK, thank you. I would say it gave me better appreciation of where Americans are coming from as well, without having necessarily to adopt their views."

The Ambassador eyed him for few seconds, mulling over the slightly ambiguous remark. "Well, Mr. Rehman, please do go in and get yourself some refreshments. I look forward to longer discussion over dinner."

"Thank you, Your Excellency."

Impeccably liveried waiters brought around trays with multiple beverages—alas, as Majeed knew, all non-alcoholic, although he also knew that if he stayed on long enough and in small company with the Ambassador something more bracing might well emerge. He selected a generic cola and passed on into the room. Several other diplomats were standing there defensively holding drinks. Unsurprisingly no women. It seemed to be something of a working dinner. Majeed knew few of those present, but then he did not frequent the ambassadorial circuit. He knew from limited experience that they tended to be one-way affairs—all the diplomats eager to pump him for information, while there was little he wanted to learn from them, nor would they reveal much. Besides, that was the role for Pakistan's official diplomats, not his, to be probing foreign diplomats for information.

He nodded at several of the assembled diplomats and shook hands with them. His name meant little to most of them, and Majeed did not rush to fill them in. He just mentioned his official title as Attaché to the President's staff.

Dinner began fairly quickly, given the more informal and working nature of the evening. Majeed was seated between the ambassadors from the Netherlands and Japanese. The Japanese had served in four cities in South Asia—Delhi, Kabul, Lahore and Islamabad—all, unfortunately for him, happening to contain the linguistically challenging letter "L"; but given his experience he was particularly savvy about South Asia in general. The group at the dinner turned out to represent the countries offering special assistance to Afghanistan, or were part of the NATO effort.

Dinner conversation started with light talk about the unusual heat of the season, as well as fears of flooding further in the north. The British ambassador offered accounts of *shikar* in the old days in the Afghan hills, the hunting expeditions organized for the more daring staff from Delhi in the days of the British Raj—when the Pashtuns themselves were seen as a distinct threat to travelers, lending spice to the hunt. Majeed mischievously quoted an old Pashtun proverb—"First comes one Englishman on *shikar,* then come two and make a map; then comes an army and takes the country. Therefore, it is better to kill the first Englishman." The laughter was contained; the British ambassador flashed a brief smile then looked away, unsure how much hostility was intended.

The army of servants in meticulous traditional outfits, each armed with a dish, made the rounds serving each guest and then receded; it was time to bring substance to the dinner conversation. "Well, with that historical insight, I want to especially welcome Mr. Majeed Rehman here with us tonight," Ambassador Spaulding said. "I am glad the Americans were not traipsing around on those *shikars* in the Pashtun hills at the same time the English were."

"Maybe so," Majeed offered in a lighter spirit, "but the fierceness of our warriors in battle in the Frontier is matched by our tradition of fierce hospitality, as I'm sure some of you have experienced. Nonetheless, history does teach us to beware of foreign mapmakers, as well as scholars, researchers, and even linguists. The agenda often turns out to be less benign down the road."

"Well, I don't know how many linguists and researchers we have here tonight," the German ambassador commented soberly, "but we do have a common interest in trying to bring stability to our poor neighbor to the west."

"Exactly," said Majeed. "But it does depend on what kind of stability you have in mind."

"I think we all know what kind of stability we need."

"And what would that be, Your Excellency?" Majeed countered.

"Well, eliminate terrorist bases there. Bring Afghanistan into the family of democratic nations. A moderate, stable, and pro-Western orientation."

"Stability and an end to terrorism, I think we can comfortably agree. But I'm not sure about the pro-Western orientation," Majeed countered.

Heads at the table turned and the German took up the challenge. "Surely, Mr. Rehman, you would not find a pro-Western orientation undesirable in a neighbor?"

"I might not personally object, but it very much depends on what a 'pro-Western orientation' means. It has served to cover a multitude of sins in the past."

"Would you mind being a little more precise on that, Mr. Rehman?" Ambassador Spaulding said with a new edge in his voice.

Majeed was aware that the conversation was already drifting into some realm of controversy but he experienced impish pleasure at the thought of his license to speak bluntly to Western diplomats. "Too many of them are operating outside of reality," General Ramzi had told Majeed.

"I just mean, Your Excellency, that Western powers over the past century have often had, shall we say, a direct hand in the selection of rulers in much of the rest of the world, not always welcome. And it seems the main criterion for their selection was their commitment to maintain a 'pro-Western orientation,' as you call it. That often simply translated into 'keep the lid on for Western interests.' That is why we experience mixed feelings when we hear the term."

The army of bearers, sensing an opening, strode forward bearing platters without lids, but Ambassador Spaulding waved them off, not wishing to be distracted by hovering waiters in the middle of an important exchange.

"I assume you are referring to the bad old colonial days," he said with a wink to the British ambassador. "I think we can safely assume that those days have passed."

"Well, yes and no."

"Meaning?"

"I mean, while the old colonial armies are gone, new ones are here. And it is not unknown for some of our politicians to scramble to please the Western powers. I wonder if most Afghans, or most Pakistanis for that matter, in the final analysis really place high priority upon maintaining this 'pro-Western orientation' you like to refer to. Indeed many might actually object to the term if it suggests policies not supported by public opinion in this part of the world. Surely our own national interests come first."

"You are not suggesting that Pakistani and American interests are not mutual and shared," Spaulding intervened, warming to a key item of personal belief.

"Well, yes, Excellency, indeed I am. Many of us in this country are not at all sure that our interests are fully shared with America—unless you simply mean motherhood and apple-pie issues, like democracy or peace."

"My dear Mr. Rehman," the French ambassador broke in. "No one is speaking about establishing some kind of neo-colonial regime here. Indeed those days are truly gone. But we have not brought NATO forces to Afghanistan this time to end up creating another regime like the Taliban that brought us the events of 9/11."

"And other jihadi bombings in Europe," the Dutch Ambassador added.

"Yes, we are well aware of that, Your Excellency," Majeed countered. "At the same time we have to be realistic about the nature of forces and emotions that exist here. Some kind of Islamic orientation is the most natural and comfortable for the majority of Pakistanis—and for that matter for most Afghans as well."

"Mr. Rehman, I am uncertain at what you wish to say," the Japanese interceded. "What exactly is 'Islamic orientation?'"

"It means that we are oriented towards the welfare of the Muslim world first and foremost. It means that neither we nor Afghanistan are willing to represent Western, or American interests, as our primary national goal." Majeed looked pointedly at the American Ambassador. "Neither you nor we want to see terrorism planted in Afghanistan or anywhere else. But there are strong conservative Islamic values that exist here, especially in the Pashtun borderlands between Afghanistan and Pakistan. They cannot be excluded, or crushed. And our country values the immense strategic importance of our ties with Afghanistan in the borderlands."

"And what of our programs for the education of girls in Afghanistan?" asked the Dutch ambassador. "Western publics take female education very seriously. We are offended when our aid here to help women is frustrated or opposed by those elements— the Taliban especially—who oppose that kind of education."

"Education for women is very important. I think you can all see the prominent role of women here in Pakistan, including a former female prime minister. Women prime ministers have served in India and Bangladesh as well, for that matter. I am not sure I can recall exactly when we last saw a female president, or even vice-president in Washington, if it comes to that." Spaulding squirmed in his seat. But Majeed plowed ahead. "Certainly schools for girls, there is nothing in Islam that opposes it. But such programs need to be introduced carefully and thoughtfully and not by some one-size-fits-all education program from your countries. Especially at the barrel of a gun. The population's sensitivities must be respected."

"Of course," the Frenchman agreed. "Female education is but a part of the broader program of Western assistance. But we have need of programs across all azimuths of Afghan life."

Servants, programmed to go off on five-minute intervals looked ready to marshal forces for dessert but were waved off again by Ambassador Spaulding. "Please continue, Mr. Rehman."

"Programs are welcome," Majeed said, "as long as they are genuinely dedicated to assisting Afghanistan as Afghans want it. But many are suspicious. They think this kind of aid is really designed to move Afghanistan into some strategic Western camp—a tool as part of a great American struggle against Russia or China, or some Eurasian Great Game. We have all been there before and have no desire to go back."

"Mr. Rehman, I must say, the nature of your remarks suggests a considerable degree of suspicion—I would not want to say hostility—towards American and European strategic plans for stability and moderation in Afghanistan." Ambassador Spaulding had now injected a greater note of emotionality that overshadowed his diplomatic smoothness. "I have spoken often with your Prime Minister, your President, and your Chief of Staff of the Army. I assure you I have not heard this kind of language from them. I assume you speak for yourself here."

"Your Excellency, I…"

"And I am not an 'Excellency,' Mr. Rehman. In my country my title is Mr. Ambassador."

"Alright, Mr. Ambassador. I am not here to represent any particular office in my government. I am only sharing with you my impression of what are very widespread views within my government—and the public. And I hear them often—even if you do not."

A silence reigned.

"Well, let's leave it at that, gentlemen." Ambassador Spaulding folded his napkin. "We can continue on with formulating a Western aid agenda later in the evening. I'm sure Mr. Rehman has better things to do tonight than to hear boring details of these programs."

"It's not that I have better things to do, Mr. Ambassador. I am just interested that you gain some understanding of what are widespread views here, even if many others are too diplomatic to say so. I am not a diplomat. But I think you would all proceed at your peril if you don't keep these realities in the back of your minds."

"Yes, well, I'm sure that you have delivered your message." Ambassador Spaulding arose from the table and extended his hand. "Thank you very much for coming, Mr. Rehman."

Majeed walked out of the bright opulence into the dark warm night, waving off a servant who looked ready to call an official limousine, went out into the street and hailed a taxi.

*   *   *

Majeed's remarks at the ambassador's dinner table were the subject of a discussion at the Embassy staff meeting the next morning.

"For my money he is a self-righteous, self-important little prick with strong anti-American views," the ambassador commented. "I worry that someone like him is working in significant places in this government. Sam," he said, turning to the Chief of Station, "didn't you say he is a significant player within ISI?"

"That's what we've heard, sir. But for that matter, I don't know that his views are all that distant from what many other senior Pak officials think in private. Much of the surface courtesy and talk we get—about how we are all 'allies'—is only skin deep." Sam never shrunk from a chance to deliver "bad news" realities to this ambassador who, while quite intelligent and perceptive, found it hard to fathom foreign resistance to American plans that so clearly were for the benefit of the world.

"Well, I suggest we keep an eye on our Mr. Rehman. I assume, Sam, that your office tries to stay on top of things like this."

"Yes, sir, we do. We are not in any liaison capacity with him, but he sometimes works the diplomatic circuit. I'm sure he will come across our screen again."

"You think he's a fundamentalist?"

"Certainly doesn't look like one."

"You're right, and there was no mention of Islam—well, no, come to think of it he did mention something about the welfare of Muslim countries. But he doesn't have that religious smell about him. And certainly no beard."

188

"He may be more a nationalist than a religious type. It's sometimes hard to tell them apart," the chief of the political section suggested.

"Well, keep an eye on him. I have to say, I think these Paks are two-timing us. They claim they are hostile to these radical Islamists and are supposedly cooperating with us, but they seem to have another game entirely."

"You're right. ISI connections with the radicals run very deep."

"But the question is how much of a 'rogue' organization ISI is."

"Let's put it this way, Mr. Ambassador. It is very convenient to be able to whisper how it may be a 'rogue' organization, hard to control, while it carries out policies Pakistan might want to deny."

"Well, that just makes my gorge rise...." The Ambassador's voice trembled. "After all the aid we give to these bloody people... All we ask is that they help us win this damn Afghan war. This is totally in their own interests as well if they bloody well thought about it for one minute. Who would want a bunch of fundamentalists running around spouting this kind of radical rhetoric? We are offering Pakistan a trusted place at the table. Frankly I think they're just playing games with us. I think the President back in Washington needs to be advised that this Pak leadership is a whole lot less of a team player than Washington would like to think. What do these Paks think we're doing out here, anyway. We're saving their own goddam asses! We're trying to run a war here and get no cooperation. Makes me sick!" And then Ambassador Spaulding fell silent, regretting that he had lost his ambassadorial cool in front of his staff.

*   *   *

"I know you are not eager to visit holy men, my son, but how about Nusrat's *qawwali* concert on Thursday night?" Majeed immediately agreed; even for the secular-minded, a concert by Nusrat Fateh Ali Khan was hard to pass up. The themes of the songs were mostly religious and Sufi in nature—in praise of God, the Prophet Muhammad, and his son-in-law Ali, particularly beloved of the Shi'ites. But there were also many songs of love, and about The Beloved, which could be taken as a reference to God, or to human love and longing. Nusrat's performances, among the great treasures of Pakistani music and beloved in India as well, were invariably packed to the gills. Majeed was not going to miss one.

Akmal set out with Majeed two nights later, profoundly gratified that his son was accompanying him, a healing gesture after their prickly exchanges on religious and political issues. Majeed too felt a special warmth at sharing a cultural occasion with his father. They entered the crowded meeting hall where a stage had been set up, draped with cloths and a green backdrop. The audience was mixed: the majority men, but also many women—some wearing headscarves, many students in scruffy dress, and a few staunchly middle-class figures in suits and ties. "Hardly any Westerners here I notice," Majeed said.

"In the UK there were a lot of Brits who liked Nusrat—although maybe many of them were more hippy."

"Well, maybe in Europe you have to be a hippy to appreciate him," his father said, "but certainly not here."

The ensemble, some twelve people, came out on the platform to wild applause, last of all Nusrat himself, huge and rotund, with a Buddha-like smile accentuated by small, almond-shaped eyes that seemed to disappear into his plump face. His kameez barely concealed his large belly as he settled cross-legged onto his pillow. On Nusrat's left was a musician with a harmonium, an accordion-like box whose wooden back is pulled forward and back by hand, like bellows to keep the air flowing through its trembling reeds. Akmal perceived it as opening and closing the cover of a holy book in tune with the universe. Another musician was tuning his *sarangi*—a bowed stringed instrument whose raw string reverberations pierce the soul. "This is an unusual performance," Akmal whispered, "with some additional instruments. I love the *ney*, that flute-like instrument. Sufi poetry often speaks of how the reed, from which the ney is cut, wails and cries with the human breath, voicing the human yearning for union with God."

The applause fell away and the room quitened as the harmonium began to weave the early melodic lines of the qawwali. As the music firmed up into a clearer melody Nusrat began to intone the words in Urdu, slow, meandering and often repetitive. But the listener sat in anticipation, knowing that a rhythm to the lines lurked not far off; the tablas would soon break in to impose a vibrant beat. The pace began to increase. For each line of poetry Nusrat offered, the members of his ensemble behind him echoed the same line, clapping as well as mirroring Nusrat's words. The beats of the *tabla* sharpened the rhythm and Nusrat warmed to the piece, gesturing more vigorously now, thrusting at the air to emphasize the line. "We are lucky we are sitting so close," Akmal whispered. "I could watch Nusrat's face forever." And as he sang, Nusrat scrunched his eyes tightly at various points in emotion, at other times gave a wide beatific smile, hovering between moods: now angelic, now a crazy, religious, nearly demonic look in his small eyes. Periodically Nusrat's nephew at the other end of the front row would pick up the same melody, and echo it in pure voice without actual words. As the ensemble grew more intense, their emotions and feelings began to fuse as the piece moved towards a crescendo some fifteen minutes later. Nusrat now drifted out and beyond himself as he gesticulated, sometimes wildly, urging on his chorus against the rise and fall of the melody, seeking to bring the audience into an emotional oneness with God. The audience cheered wildly when a particularly long phrase was vigorously and forcefully sung and ended abruptly, with perfect precision, on a given sharp beat of the tabla, only to pause and resume again.

Majeed was moved: it was a joyous occasion, rapturous music. Many from the audience, equally enthused, now approached the musicians to throw rupees at them in a storm of colored bank notes—an ostentatious gesture of piety and thanksgiving to the musicians who had lifted them to new heights of consciousness.

As the concert wore on, various members of the audience began ecstatic dancing in the aisles in harmony with the music. The audience kept demanding more and more, but Nusrat had clearly poured the last drops of his soul into his singing and ultimately fell back exhausted, artistically drained, brow sweating, drawing a close to the evening.

"I feel so moved by this man," his father said as they came out into the warm night air. "To think that there are those who believe this music is *haram*, evil or seductive. We are humans, we have our senses, why shouldn't music help us open the door to God?"

"You are right, Babaji, it is really moving. I thank you for bringing me." And Akmal reflected on how the grace of God, acting through the force of the spiritual music, had helped bring him closer to his son.

*   *   *

"Jim, thanks for stopping by early before our meeting. We need to decide what we're going to say to Alex Anders."

"I don't see why we can't put it to him bluntly. He's not really going to be able to turn us down."

"That's as may be, but I want his solid cooperation on this. I read his file. He's been resistant in the past when it comes to getting involved in Pakistan."

"Yeah, and from what they told me in Latin America Division, he has a very mixed record. Excellent job in handling his Soviet cases, some terrific reporting on the whole KGB structure in Latin America, but in the end he lost his top agent—who was suddenly bundled back to Russia. Never was clear exactly what happened—could have been a mistake by Alex, or the agent, or whatever."

"I'm aware of that. But people on the desk there say they are pleased with his work. Apparently he's something of an individualist, can be a loner, but that's not all bad."

"In Chile he ended up getting involved with some damn girl from a leftist pro-Allende family. The Station warned him off of her, but he went ahead. It was serious enough that he ended up marrying her. Had to be yanked out of his deep cover job as a result."

"Yeah...sex and love trump security almost every time. That may have been poor judgment, at least in his personal life. But no one out there felt they could fault him in his professional work. In any case, we need him now."

"Do you think he's up to it? I don't think he knows enough about the current scene in Pakistan to appreciate how important this whole fundamentalist business is."

"Well, we need him to feel out Rehman at the least—even if he won't be the one to make a recruitment approach himself. I'm concerned he may get righteous on us with this one—not want to compromise himself with old Pak contacts and all that."

A few minutes later Alex, holding a mug of coffee, stuck his head inside the office door. "This is the right office? Good morning, Chief."

"Alex? Good morning, come on in, and thanks for coming by." George Rusher, the Chief of the Middle East Division gestured for Alex to sit down at the small round table. The walls were covered with antique maps of the Middle East and the world, a collection in which Rusher took pride.

"I don't think we've actually met, you were way off in Latin America division for some years," Rusher said. "But dare I say your South Asian past is catching up with you? By the way, this is Jim Nadels, Chief of the Pak Branch. You can see we're switching countries on you pretty drastically."

"Pakistan… Hmmm, why am I not surprised you guys have finally run me to ground—even while I've been hiding out in the Russian division."

"I'm sure no surprise to you. But, yeah, we do want to talk with you about your past years in Pakistan a bit," Rusher said. "Tough place now. Tougher for us to operate in—and the damn country is getting more radicalized by the year. By the way, I was sorry to read in your file that your father had died as a result of trouble out there, quite some years ago. That's tough, can't have left too many good memories."

"Yeah, it was a bit rough. That's why I indicated when I first came on board, some time ago now, I really want to avoid to be assigned out there if I can help it."

"Well, we can talk about that. But in the meantime we may have some shorter-term task in mind."

"Name of Majeed Rehman mean anything to you?" Jim broke his silence.

Alex shifted in his seat. "Sure, he's an old boyhood friend from Lahore, I think he's working in the President's office now."

"More than that, he's playing an active role in liaising between the Paks and the Taliban and jihadis. You in touch with him?"

"Well, yeah, but no—barely… not what you could call a lot. We exchange cards at holiday times, we're still on good terms, but I haven't seen him since my father died."

"Were you aware he's got close ties with the fundamentalists?"

"Majeed? I find that hard to believe. He wasn't particularly religious at all when I knew him."

"Well, he is now. Not clear how much of it is personal conviction, and how much is just his job, in liaison with the muj. The Embassy thinks he's got a hard-on against the US."

Jim broke in. "To get to the point, Alex, we'd like to send you back for a visit, to reestablish personal contact with Majeed Rehman."

Alex looked away out the window for a few moments. "Look, Jim. I'm not sure that I'm the right person for that job. Majeed and I go back a long way, he's a childhood friend. Our families were close. I don't like mixing personal ties with professional ones."

"This could be important. We're not saying that Rehman is a bad guy. But we need a much better feel for what the Paks are up to in Afghanistan. For that matter, Rehman may have drifted over to the opposition."

"Look," Alex broke in. "We, the US, helped the mujahideen fight the Soviet occupation there, right? Together with Pakistan. What's the mystery? You're in touch with Pak intelligence. Why can't you just ask them about what is going on?"

"Come on, Alex, you weren't born yesterday," Jim replied. "Yeah, we've supposedly got close ties with the Paks, but we don't trust them a goddam inch. They've got their own agenda in Afghanistan and it's not ours. They're in touch, hell, they've been in bed for years with a lot of muj groups there that are radical—and hard core anti-American."

"Honestly, I don't think I can just go sashaying over there out of the blue and start asking him a lot of questions about his professional work. I mean, we've almost never had political discussions before, it wouldn't be natural."

"Come on, you mean to say you never talked politics when you were there earlier—even at the time your father got attacked?"

"Sure I did, about the fundamentalist danger to our family, but not politics in general. He'd smell a rat."

Jim leaned forward. "Look, Alex, this is very important. You have unique personal access to this guy who is of major interest to us. OK, I know you feel a friendship with him. We'd just like you to warm up the friendship again, get a feel for him, how he thinks. Attitudes. Sense of where his ideologies lie. That's probably all you'd have to do. We're not suggesting you should try and recruit the guy, for godsakes."

Alex turned as if to appeal to the chief. "George, I'm sorry, I'm just not comfortable with this. I don't even have a good reason to go back."

"We'll help you manufacture a plausible story. Now that you're under official State cover, the cover story for your trip doesn't have to be all that far away from your true mission. Some sort of research trip for the State Department. Hell, you do know Urdu after all, you've got some feel for the country."

Alex's eye wandered over the huge map of the Middle East on the wall, the great blue-green massif of the Himalayas and the Hindu Kush rising starkly around Pakistan. He noted the photos of the chief shaking hands with a former president. "I'm going to have to think this over. Ops are one thing, but I'm just not comfortable with exploiting an old friend. Let me get used to the idea."

"You're not exploiting him, you're assessing him," Rusher said quietly. "You're a professional. You're taking a one-time trip. You don't need to make an intel approach to him. Just size him up. If anybody is ever going to make a pitch to him it wouldn't be you."

"Alex, this is a hell of a lot more important than chasing around a bunch of goddam Soviet diplomats on the cocktail circuit in Latin America." Jim stared at Alex as if he wasn't very bright, letting it sink in. "The Russkis got their ass handed to them on a platter by those muj a decade ago in Afghanistan. That was great for us—back then. But now we need to know a hell of a lot more about the mechanics of what is going on between the Taliban and the Paks. The Paks are holding out on a shitload of stuff they won't talk about with us. There are a lot of very anti-American fundamentalists in the woodwork out there. Rehman may be an important link to them."

Alex sat silently a few minutes, running the situation through his mind. This was exactly what he didn't want. Running ops in a foreign country should have a clinical, professional aspect. But this was his own stomping grounds, his own emotional past that was now becoming grist for the professional mill. Yet, to refuse outright would be professionally very unwise and a bad career move; he hoped he could set limits on what he would do. "Alright," he sighed, "I guess we can work something out. But this is not what I expected to be doing when I came back to Hqs. I'd like to stay in Russian ops."

"Look at it this way, Alex," Rusher said, "there are a lot of Russians still in Pakistan, it's a prime observation post for them. They're still obsessed with what we and the Paks are doing in Afghanistan. It could be a natural place for you in any case." Rusher rose to his feet. "But you don't have to think about that aspect now. Let's focus on the task at hand." He stuck out his hand. "Thanks, Alex, appreciate it. You can work out all the details with Jim on timing, cover story, etc. We look forward to your report."

Alex moved reluctantly toward the door. Jim touched his arm as Alex departed. "Thanks, Alex, I'll be in touch with you shortly." Alex turned and walked off down the long hallway.

Rusher closed the door behind Alex. "What do you think, Jim? Is he up to it?"

"I just don't know. I'm not sure how much steel he's got in him. Depends on how flexible he is."

"I think he'll do well. They said he was a natural case officer in Santiago. We're still a little worried about his wife's outlook. But he fitted in very well into the ops scene there."

"Yeah, well, this ain't Santiago. They play rougher in Pakistan."

"I think he knows that. Let's give the guy a break, OK? And Jim? We better be cautious. Don't show him all the stuff we have in the files about ISI and Rehman right now; I don't want to give him any preconceived notions. Let's just see what he come up with on his own—or if he can even get a damn meeting going."

Chapter Six

Return

Until lions have their historians, tales of the hunt shall always glorify the hunters.
- African proverb

Dear Majeed, how long has it been! I'm sorry not to have stayed in closer touch, but life has not let up. After four years in Chile I finally decided that finance was not really for me. The work just never grabbed my enthusiasm. So when I got back to DC, I got a job with the State Department—they were especially interested in my background in Pakistan.

And I think I had told you I met a wonderful Chilean girl, Isabel. We finally got married in Washington. And, guess what? We have managed to produce our first child, a son, Rodrigo! Life indeed changes with the start of a family.

What about you, Majeed? How did your job work out in the President's office that you told me about?

And guess what? The State Department asked me was if I would be willing to travel out to Pakistan on a short trip and help the embassy do a survey on public attitudes towards US policies in Afghanistan. It sounds interesting, a good way to get back to see all the old places.

So fantastic news! I'll be coming out for a few weeks, probably in November. I'd love to see you again, Majeed, and meet your family. Any chance you'll be around? It's been too long. Let me know!

Your old friend,
Alex

* * *

Dear Alex,

What a great surprise to get all the news about you and your family! And even better to hear that you'll be coming back out here, if only for a short visit. Yes, of course, we would love to see you, you must meet Aysha and the children. I work in Islamabad during the week and have a house there naturally, and I'm pretty busy during most of the week there. But Aysha and the children often stay in Lahore, so I go back to our house there every Thursday nite until Sunday morning. Do you think you could maybe come on the weekend to our family house in Lahore and stay with us then? You can tell us all about your "mission" then. Salaams to Isabel from Aysha and me. We hope to meet her some time too. Looking forward to catching up with you.

Your good friend,
Majeed

*   *   *

You can't enter the same river twice. Alex was no longer an innocent returning to childhood haunts. It wasn't even like his return home on that fateful Christmas holiday. And now he felt mildly cramped by a political mission that he feared would sap the spontaneity and pleasure of rediscovering an old friend and the country of his boyhood.

Not that everything had been simple even then. The innocent solidarity of childhood gets roughed up by the impinging outside world. There had been hints of initial tensions with Majeed even during his last visit as Alex began to view Pakistan with more adult eyes and in the light of his father's experience. And now he was caught up in new coils of complexity, himself a cog within the intricate mechanisms of the US diplomatic presence in Pakistan. By the sound of it, Majeed too was up to his eyeballs in political issues with his work in the President's office, or whatever it was. Alex wondered how much either of them would ever be able to show all their cards to the other. At least the job Alex now claimed in the State Department wasn't that far from the truth—after all, a diplomat was an honest man sent abroad to lie for his country. But how would their youthful friendship be affected by their mutual transitions into professional life?

Isabel reacted with mixed feelings. She knew Alex always wanted to show her Pakistan, and it was far removed from things Chilean. "I'll wait to hear your report on how it all looks, *mi amor*, if we are to consider going there. I'll be fine with Rodriguito while you're gone."

From the air Lahore now sprawled sloppily out in all directions well beyond its old Mughal center. Trapped in a taxi without air-conditioning in the slow moving traffic, Alex found he had lost his tolerance for subcontinental heat. Mile after mile of new environs ticked past with ugly new buildings, commercial centers and generic markets thrown up, masking the city he thought he once knew so well. He struck up a conversation with the cab driver in Urdu and was reassured to see he still felt comfortable in the casual give and take. "You have been in Pakistan a long time, sir," the driver commented. "No, I've been away for a long time, I'm afraid," Alex replied. His anticipation rose as they pulled up to the familiar old compound. Alex got out, modestly overpaid as was expected of him, and rang the bell at the gate. As the gatekeeper opened it, Majeed came bounding out, casually dressed in his *shalwar-kameez*.

"Alex, my God, this is so great, welcome," and the hearty physical embrace, the familiar long hand-holding and the searching of each other's eyes that often made Westerners feel uncomfortable.

"Just the same, Alex, just the same! Few more pounds maybe, but I'd know you in the bazaar a second. How are you?"

"Fine, just fine, Majeed, praise God. And you?"

"Praise God, Alex, we're all well!"

Alex slipped back into the warm litanies of multiple personal queries back and forth about family. "And your father? And your mother? Zubayda? And Salman?"

"Praise God, we're all fine. Come in, Aysha will be happy to meet you."

They entered the old family residence. Apart from a BMW parked in the compound things looked much as they always had, same well-kept garden, green lawn under the old trees, and flowers all around.

"Aysha? Alex is here! Come and say hello!"

A young woman emerged from a side door dressed in a simple sari that lightly covered her hair. She approached Alex shyly but warmly. Alex knew not to extend his hand unless she did, but she seemed familiar with meeting foreign men and extended her own hand cautiously. Alex knew she would not likely be so forward if he himself did not occupy the privileged place of childhood friend in Majeed's life. Aysha called for the children to come out. A girl and a boy, about ten and eleven, came out and stood behind their mother's sari as Majeed beamed. "This is Mian, and here is Fazila… say hello to Alex! I knew him when I was even younger than you two."

Alex knelt down to look at them up close. "*Maashallah*, Majeed, *maashallah*, great kids!"

"Zubayda is out teaching at the moment, but she'll be back in a while and is really looking forward to seeing you. She still lives with us."

"Great, I have wonderful memories of her. She always treated me as if I was a younger brother. Really fetching eyes—and great spirit."

"Well, I'm afraid she's had a bit of a problem. I don't want to go into the whole long story, but the heart of is that she was attacked in Waziristan by some fanatic and her face was slashed. So I'm afraid she has a bad scar on one side of her face."

"My God, Majeed, I'm really sorry. That's terrible! It must be devastating to her."

"Yes, but she's strong, and she's not hiding herself. She's become quite a feminist activist in our male world here… keeping us on our toes." He turned to Aysha and smiled.

"Wow, well I really want to see her."

Majeed took Alex's hand and they walked back into the sitting room. The décor felt different, newer, more Western, punctuated by numerous traditional Pakistani works of art alongside of the accoutrements of Western technology—large television, cordless phone, a computer, a stereo hi-fi set and CD's. They sat in adjoining chairs and beamed at each other.

"My God, Alex, to think of the time that has passed—fourteen, fifteen years? It's wonderful that you are back. But I never thought it would be on business! I mean, this is your home."

"I didn't really expect it either, but once I joined the State Department I knew I had to find an excuse to come right back here. And they sent me out for a few weeks. It's a great opportunity"

"My, my. And a diplomat! I'm not sure I think of you as a diplomat, Alex, too casual, and you don't wear striped pants. And we're not going to be diplomatic either. There's so much to catch up on. Thank you for coming to Lahore—so much better than sitting around in official Islamabad. This is where we all feel at home on weekends."

A servant emerged with two glasses of mango juice and a dish of wrapped candies that he set before them. "Cheers, Alex! I'd offer you a beer, but you know, this is Pakistan. Too bad, but ever since General Zia's morality laws, we've all gotten a bit out of the habit. But not to fear, Alex, later tonight I'm sure we may be able find a little something hidden away for us both, with apologies to General Zia's ghost."

"Majeed, please, God knows I don't want to be the one responsible for compromising your deeply-felt religious values on alcohol," Alex bantered.

"No, no, we have to remain flexible, multicultural. Actually, I'm surprised to hear myself saying it, but I think this ban on alcohol may be a positive social step. The public supports it and the old curse of public drunkenness seems far less present. Not that any of us ever got drunk of course," he said with a wink.

"Of course not, Majeed, perish the thought. Anyway, I'm not complaining."

"Actually, Alex, just an insider tip from a Muslim friend—as a Christian you know you can apply for a permit that will allow you to purchase alcohol here as long as you drink it in your own home and don't sell it. If you want I can vouch for you." Majeed winked.

"Nope, don't need it Majeed, don't need it, thanks. I'm a good Pakistani myself, you know."

"What about your Urdu? Have you kept it up?"

"No, I'm a bit rusty, I'm afraid, but I still understand it well. I've seen an occasional Indian movie in Hindi now and then and that's close enough to keep it up."

"And now, tell me about your family. It's Isabel, isn't it?"

Alex nodded and told Majeed about his time in Santiago, his ultimate marriage to Isabel.

"You said you were in banking there, right?"

"Right, but it was just a way to get abroad, and on a good salary. I'm afraid I wasn't really cut out for banking, though, it's a bit dull. So I quit and because of my international background I was able to get a job at the State Department."

"But isn't being a diplomat a bit dull, too? I don't know if you're the diplomat type. You'll have to prove it… by being very diplomatic with me about all that is going on here," Majeed smiled.

Alex wanted to keep away from professional issues for the time being, and so he turned the conversation to the past, the old days, old haunts, old friends.

Aysha joined them for part of the discussion. "I almost feel like I know you, Alex, Majeed has talked so much about you—all the stories about your boyhood antics at school together."

"Nothing too terrible I hope."

"No, no, quite a part of the old days, when things were more open here. But it must be strange to be meeting again now as adults. I wonder which of you has changed?"

"Certainly it's Majeed. He's put on weight —probably with your cooking."

"I think it suits him, Majeed needed to look a little more serious than the scrawny schoolboy he was," she rejoined

They all sat down to dinner, the familiar rich curries opening floodgates of memories. He was back.

"And, your nephew Salman, how is he? I remember he was keen on going to college in the US. Did he ever make it?"

"He did, he was in California for two years, but then came back. Actually there's been quite a change in him. You remember he had been besotted with things American, but we couldn't afford to pay for more than two years schooling, like what happened with me in London. Your universities are too expensive. Anyhow, he's gotten involved in politics and the romance with American pop culture seems to be over. In fact he seems to be getting fairly nationalist, talking about Kashmir and India all the time."

"Really? That's quite a change. He always seemed so quiet, shy."

"Yes, but not as unusual as you might think these days." Majeed leaned back in his chair. "But tell me, Alex, what's this research you're doing for the State Department? Are you investigating us?"

"In a modest way, but nothing very exciting, I'm afraid. It's just with all the Afghan war stuff going on, the Embassy is doing some public opinion polls on Pakistani public views of US policy since it affects Pakistan so much. They'd like me to help with it for a few weeks."

"Well, you can start right here at the dinner table with us, can't he, Aysha? Fortunately I'm not paid to be a diplomat like you, so I can speak freely, as an old friend. Frankly, I don't think the US gets much credit here with anybody for its past support to the mujahideen in Afghanistan against the Soviets. You are seen as simply pursuing your own national interests, and you find it useful to hire Pakistan on the cheap to do your work for you. I'm sorry if that sounds harsh, but there it is in a nutshell. There now, that's all you need to know. Your report is written!"

"Maybe you've saved the Embassy several weeks of opinion polling and analysis, Majeed. Thank you. That would seem to say it all."

"Don't take offense, Alex, you did ask. You know, I'm afraid Americans always want to be liked, but supporting the mujahideen in Afghanistan against the Soviets in the end was a Muslim responsibility, a Muslim project—we were liberating a Muslim country from Soviet imperialism. So despite all that US money and weapons, there always were suspicions here that we were just pawns in the Soviet-American chess game."

Alex put down his fork. "Surely that's not all of ..."

"Alex, don't get me wrong now, it's good that Washington and Islamabad are cooperating, each for their own reasons, but you Americans shouldn't expect to be loved for it." Majeed's English accent seemed to grow a touch more clipped.

"That's a bit harsh, Majeed. It mattered a great deal that we were working to liberate Afghanistan. It *is* a Muslim country, and we do care. That much should be acknowledged." Alex was uncomfortable at this unanticipated edge in the conversation. And he didn't like the reference to "you Americans." Majeed was categorizing him in a way he had never done before.

"Alex, come on, if it had not been the Soviet Union that was trying to take over Afghanistan but, say, India or even the UK, would Washington have cared much then? Let's be honest, Washington doesn't give a damn about Afghanistan itself, all it cared about was its Cold War with the Soviet Union. Now all it cares about is consolidating a strategic base and beachhead in the heart of Asia, just to keep Russia and China in check. They're conveniently using the Global War on Terror for that. That's the bottom line."

"Come on, we share strong common interests."

"Yes, our interests do happen to coincide at the moment, that's good. But please don't think we should be all grateful. Let's be honest, Pakistan is a bargain buy in the strategic bazaar." Majeed put down his napkin, smiled uneasily, slid his chair back from the table and looked around. "And now, since it's a beautiful evening, I thought we might all go out and get some sweets in Gawalmandi Street. How long has it been since you've had *falooda*?"

"Yes! *Falooda*!" the children cried and their enthusiasm swept away the edgier nature of the conversation in the last few minutes.

"*Falooda*?" Alex asked. "I could die for some. I haven't been to Gawalmandi since I was a kid."

"And here comes Zubayda! I hear her car. I'd hoped she would get back in time to join us."

A moment later a woman walked in wearing a blue hijab that covered most of her hair and and a scarf that swept down around her neck, but slightly pulled over shielding the right side of her face. She walked boldly straight toward Alex and took both of his hands in her hands beaming at him confidently. It was unmistakably Zubayda, the same sparkling inquisitive eyes and engaging smile. The red scar on her right nostril and partly visible down her right cheek was evident, but she was not self-conscious. "Alex, how are you! It's so wonderful to see you again! We often talk about you."

"I'm great Zubayda, but how are *you*?"

"I'm doing well. But I'm sure you've heard from Majeed about my little run-in with a fanatic in the Frontier area. He's left me with quite a souvenir, but it can't be helped. We are all scarred in some respect or other. Tell me, you now have a wife and a little boy? And she's from Peru? How wonderful! I'd like to meet her. What's her name?"

"Isabel, and she's from Chile, and you will meet her, Zubayda. Actually you remind me of her in many ways. You were my childhood sweetheart, even if I was just another bratty little boy to you."

"No, no, Alex, never bratty. But little boy, yes. And now you're grown up—we all are," she said, looking around the room. "Times change. And we take on different tasks. I'm sure Majeed has told you that I've now become a warrior of feminism in Pakistan, thoroughly embarrassing the family in the process."

"Yes," Majeed chimed in, "keeping us all on our toes with modernity."

"You were always a warrior, Zubayda," Alex smiled warmly at her. "Don't ever give up."

"I won't. But the tougher I talk on the local issues here, the more conservative my dress has to become. You see, I now wear hijab, just to show that I am not a rebel about customs, especially since I talk with lots of conservative women about their rights. And you know? I've rather come to like it. Don't you think it becomes me?" she said, twirling around coquettishly.

"Fetching," Alex replied.

"But we can't let fashion talk hold up our expedition, Zubayda," Majeed intervened. "You're just in time, we're all going for *falooda*. You won't say no."

"Majeed, would I say no to *falooda*? Especially with Alex along?"

*　　　　　　*　　　　　　*

They parked nearby. "This is still the children's favorite outing," Majeed said, as they crossed the intersection. The heavy traffic had just been closed off again for the evening on Gawalmandi, creating the wonderful sensation of walking on the once tumultuous vehicle road that was now open just for them. Pedestrians who came for the delicious Lahori specialties quickly moved to take over the whole street. "And it's still open all night too, then?"

"Yes, you know what they say, Lahore never sleeps. And the food is still some of the best in the city. There's a good place. Come children, over here… their *falooda* is excellent."

Gawalmandi was illuminated as if in some permanent Mardi Gras, lights and decorations strung along the streets casting in relief of light and shadow the Mughal architecture—a nighttime fairytale come true. Vendors and food smells wafting down the street, happy crowds drawn in like bees to honey, growing denser by the hour, chairs and tables out on the sidewalk, families everywhere. But as they walked down the street, Alex suddenly had the sense he was being observed by a small man in a brown *shalwar-kameez* wearing thick glasses whom he had noticed several blocks back where they had parked. Maybe a coincidence, he decided. Who would even know he was in Pakistan, much less in Lahore for the weekend. The man took a seat in a café opposite them, smoking a cigarette and drinking tea, periodically looking at a newspaper, casually glancing around. Alex thought about mentioning it to Majeed, but decided it might seem paranoid, smack of intelligence concerns, inappropriate, and he couldn't be certain in any case.

"I want the *falooda kulfi*," Mian cried. "Me too," Fazila echoed as they leaned over the counter and watched the heavenly creations being made— milk and tapioca mixed with sweet fruit syrups, rose water, and, best of all, little bits of colored vermicelli suspended in the drink that often clogged up the straw and made for big sucking sounds. This was the Rolls Royce of all sundaes, as only the subcontinent could deliver it. The colors of the various flavors were lurid, promising every child total fulfillment. "Falooda *kulfi?*" Alex asked Mian. "That sounds new. Isn't it sweet enough without the ice cream?" "No, it's the best in the world," Mian replied.

Putting the man sitting opposite out of his thoughts, Alex went with the spirit of the evening as memories of boyhood delights drove him to go all the way and actually order the lurid pink rose water *falooda*, but without *kulfi*. He couldn't believe how sweet and overwhelming the rose water flavor now was. It was one of those treats perfectly suspended in childhood memory, growing richer with time and absence, and best preserved in memory rather than tested against the reality of adult taste. But sitting here at the table on the sidewalk with Majeed and his family on Gawalmandi, what else could he be possibly drinking if not *falooda?* "I bet I can drink my whole *falooda* without stopping up my straw," Alex leaned over and whispered to Mian. But Mian was equal to the occasion—he had the slurping power to pull the vermicelli pieces through. *I am back—this is Lahore, this is my childhood.* Alex felt a wave of gratefulness to Majeed that washed away the sharpness of their political exchange. The man in brown opposite them was gone.

*   *   *

Zubayda excused herself from the conversation to go to bed. "I've got to go out of town to a women's meeting tomorrow morning early. But I'll definitely see you later, Alex. I want to hear more about what you've been up to." And she left Majeed and Alex alone in the library.

"Now, I warn you, this is only for very special occasions—it's supposed to be banned now, but it's still available if you know where to go—and who better to share it with?" Majeed beamed as he reached behind a row of books in the library and pulled out a bottle of Dimple with a grand flourish. "Don't worry, you're not depriving me, there's more where this comes from."

They drank several fingers in contemplation of the world, the confluence of events that had brought them back to this room in this house.

"And so you're a big man now, Majeed! Working with the President's office! How did you manage that?"

"My own brilliance, my friend, sheer brilliance and talent… Actually one of my uncles had known the President for a long time from the army, and he asked if they would take me on. Sure, it's using inside influence, but you know, that's the way things work here. Anyway, no apologies—I'm good at what I do."

"And what do you do?"

"I help coordinate foreign policy programs for the President, including Afghanistan."

"Really? Sounds interesting. What aspects of coordination?"

"Well, you know, we're cooperating with Washington in Afghanistan, fighting the Taliban there, helping find Osama bin Laden, working with several other countries like Saudi Arabia."

"Yeah, I've heard about the cooperation. That's good. It must be interesting work. But it must be complicated to decide which mujahideen groups are the good guys and which are the bad."

"We have policies to follow."

"Any particular favorite groups?"

"Sure, some groups are more friendly than others. But I don't get into the nuts and bolts, I'm on the policy side. Anyway, let's not talk shop my friend, let's leave it at that."

"Sure, but I think you know there was a lot of respect for the mujahideen in the US at one time—Ronald Reagan even called them, what was it? 'The 'moral equivalent of the founding fathers.' But then with the Taliban violating women's rights and all that…"

"Look Alex, let me be frank. I was thrilled by the exploits of the mujahideen in Afghanistan, taking on the whole Soviet occupying force. They drove the bloody Soviets out of the country by the end. The role of the Pashtuns in that was huge. Yes, I am proud of it. We Pashtuns brought the bloody English to their knees three times in the nineteenth century, and then the Russians. Outsiders should look out." Majeed stood up and pulled off his brown wool vest.

Alex frowned. "Surely you can't have much truck with the Taliban."

"Yes, we can deal quite comfortably with the Taliban if we have to, they're going to be around a long time." Majeed settled back in his chair and put his feet up on an ottoman, careful not to expose the soles of his slippers towards Alex. "But if it comes to that, frankly there aren't that many elements in Afghanistan who are really pro-US—although they'll take your coin. Especially the non-Pashtuns."

"They can't distrust us that much. After all the help we gave them against the Soviets, after all."

Majeed stared at Alex. "Because they see you as a continuation of bloody Western imperialism, that's why. Expanding American power all over the globe, unquestioning support for Israel over the poor Palestinians, supporting reactionary rulers in the Middle East. Buddy-buddy with India. You know the litany."

An old grandfather clock rang the changes of the hour in the next room.

"Do you buy that?"

"Yes and no," Majeed said. "We had a common interest in defeating the Soviet Union and driving the Red Army out of Afghanistan. But in the long run, no, I don't think the US has much respect for the independence of the Third World. You wouldn't have cared one fig about giving us aid here in Pakistan if we hadn't been fighting the Soviets. You certainly wouldn't give a damn about the wretched Afghans if they were located at the end of nowhere."

"Well, I'm not sure that's totally fair." Alex felt the tension rise and sought to cool things down. "So how do you find working with the President?"

"Look, Alex, he's my boss, what do you expect me to say?"

"It's just… I guess I'm a little taken aback at all this Islamization that remained from Zia's time. The ideology that helps produce all these reactionaries—the kind of mentality that beat up my father."

Majeed paused, looking away. "There's no excuse for what happened to your father. You know how horrified we were… still are, at what happened to him. But you should be able to understand, Alex, you know the culture—I hate to say it, but you know your father was playing with fire here. With all due respect, what in hell sense is there in coming to an ancient part of the world to try to steer people away from their millennium-old religion towards a Western religion unrelated to their culture and history? And linked with imperial power? I know he did a lot of good in the clinic for people's eyes, but it's arrogant and pointless to try to change their religion and culture. I'm sorry, but it makes people angry."

Alex studied his snifter for a moment. He felt taken aback at Majeed's vehemence. "I don't think my father was arrogant," he finally said quietly. "Maybe naïve."

"Your country is naïve, Alex. And dominating. Your efforts to stop us from developing a nuclear weapon as well. What kind of friend is that?"

Alex wasn't going to let Majeed plow ahead. "It's just not safe, having all the countries of the world developing their own nuclear bombs."

"Not safe for whom? With the bloody sodding Indians on our doorstep, with their bomb, we didn't have the right to protect ourselves? Think how many times they have invaded us! What right do you have to tell us what is or isn't safe?" Majeed poured himself another snifter. "More?" He lifted the bottle towards Alex.

"Not yet. But a bomb with all these fundamentalists running around? Surely they're not trustworthy. You know that."

"No, I don't trust them, and many of them are extreme. But they also are looking out for the independence of this country—they're nationalists. They won't toady to the US." Majid's eyes glistened. "And you know what? I've got tremendous respect for the power of Islam to stir men's souls—to resist the foreign invader. They fueled the enthusiasm to fight the Soviets in Afghanistan. They're trying to stop a lot of the bloody corruption we have here. You know I'm not all that religious, but there are worse forces in this country than some of the fundamentalists, as you call them." Majeed took a long sip draining the last dregs from his snifter, and pressed on. "I'm afraid you don't seem to have much real feel for what's going on here anymore. Don't fall into the same old clichés, like the other Americans around here."

"Give me a little credit, Majeed."

"No, I'm sorry Alex, but I mean what I say." Majeed appeared slightly flushed and warmed to his theme. "I go to a lot of these bloody diplomatic receptions at your embassy. They all praise my English and my education— they even assume I'm one of them for that reason—the ultimate compliment in their eyes. Look, a bloody wog who can speak our language! Somebody we can deal with. They have no idea how anybody might think differently than they do. They all assume that any educated Pakistani is going to agree with them on the way they see the problem, as well as the made-in-USA solution. It can be goddam insulting—and patronizing. Fortunately I don't have to play up to that, that's not my job. I just smile, and offer occasional undiplomatic barbs."

Alex swirled his scotch around, stood up from his easy chair to change the mood, and began to peruse the photographs on the wall. "Who's this, Majeed? He's a magnificent figure," gesturing at a bearded and turbaned man dressed in robes, eyes darkened with kohl, holding a sword, staring fiercely into the camera.

"Superb, isn't he? That's my maternal great great grandfather, he was a fighter on the northwest frontier, a famous warrior and Pashtun poet. The kind of figure Kipling would have understood."

Alex looked along the wall at other photos. Majeed offered tales and lore. "You know, it's funny, but I've come to feel closer to these figures after having some involvement in Afghan events. I can see the fire of the warrior spirit, its religious beliefs, its dedication to preserving Pashtun independence. I used to think about them as just old tribal types. But they're the ones that have indeed kept Afghanistan independent and still supply much of the backbone here in Pakistan as well."

"Ah, Majeed, I see you're finally reverting to type."

Majeed smiled wryly. "Maybe, Alex, maybe. But I'm exhilarated. I'm finding out who I am through all this bloody process."

Yes, who are you, Majeed? And who am I?

         *   *   *

The next morning Alex woke up and went down to get breakfast where Aysha was setting things out. "Majeed has got to work in his study this morning, and I'm taking the children out. But let's all go to the Red Fort for a picnic in the afternoon. Zubayda should be back before noon."

Alex spent a few hours in the library looking over old books on the North-West Frontier and the days of the British Raj. What a wild and lawless place it had been from the British perspective. In reality, "lawless" meant refusal to acknowledge British rule—the Frontier had plenty of laws governing relations within the tribe, laws and traditions in inter-tribal feuds and settlement of quarrels and differences. Pashtunwali, the complex code of unwritten tradition, was more powerful in many ways than Islam itself.

Zubayda arrived late in the morning, this time with a green hijab and still very fetching. She set about making tea. "Now Alex, dear Alex, tell me about Isabel, and your son—what is his name?"

"Rodrigo, or Rodriguito as we call him." He told Zubayda about his years in Chile, the experience of encountering a new world and culture in Latin America, and how he had come to meet Isabel.

"I've always loved the idea of Latin America," Zubayda said, "although of course I've never been there. It has spirit and color, much more fun than the boring Anglo-Saxons." She laughed. "It seems like Pakistan in many ways, isn't it? I know I would love it."

"It is and it isn't. But a lot of traditional life still exists. And they don't like Yankees there much either, I'm afraid."

"That is your cross to bear, Alex," she said with a sweet smile. "The rewards of being a superpower." And she was up and around the room, talking about her work, her students, and her meetings with women's groups on women's rights. "You don't know how satisfying this is, Alex, to see some real progress in front of my eyes, women who are learning to read for the first time as adults, to think about their condition and develop some aspirations for more education for themselves and their children."

"But don't you find it hard to work in conservative village circles like that? I mean, all these conservative strictures? It's certainly way more conservative now than when I was growing up here."

Zubayda put down a cup of tea in front of Alex, along with a fried vegetable *pakora*. "Yes, you are right, it's less easy. Although the villages are probably no more or less conservative than in the past. But we are working on it. Pakistani women are smart and enterprising, and they know how to get things done via the backdoor. Men can be so dense, so confrontational. Not you of course," she said, touching his shoulder. "As long as you stroke a male's ego, they can't even see what's going on around them. And we *are* changing things." And she spoke with excitement about her travels around the country talking to women and legal specialists. "And you know what, Alex? This scar on my face—it's the best credentials I could have. I bear the scars of narrow-minded ignorant men and their primitive understanding of religion out there. I'm actually proud of it. It's almost become the symbol of who I am."

Alex asked about what had happened. "You don't want to know all the unpleasant details, I was just teaching there and living with another close woman friend. Gossip grew up about us I guess, and before we knew it there were hints that we were lesbians or something. Typical. And a young relative of mine—distant relative—attacked me, allegedly defending 'the family honor.' What a joke! That's a huge part of what this problem is all about—so-called male honor. Even some women are so socialized into this tribal mentality that they have absorbed the honor issue as well—and defend it."

Alex grimaced. "Zubayda, I'm really so sorry to hear about this."

"Well, it happened. Fortunately the story details never got back here to Lahore, although the family knows of course. I actually wish I were a lesbian in some ways, I wouldn't grieve so much—about how my chances of marriage have become about nil now. But," she said, jumping up again, "I'm really immersed in my work and I have extended family all around me, so I'm not unhappy. You shouldn't feel sorry for me...."

"Your spirit is indominable, Zubayda. I've always known that. You're great!"

"Thanks, but that's just the problem, Alex, Pakistani men don't want indominable women!"

*   *   *

When they arrived at the Red Fort, Alex remembered vividly his last visit there, with Majeed, when they had discussed the rising threats against his father and his eye clinic. The powerful Mughal presence saturated the gardens, the huge ensemble of regal buildings, the glowing red sandstone, the fancy crenellations, and the cupolas adorning the top. Pakistan in its cultural essence.

Alex walked with Majeed around the gardens while the children played. The pleasure of the afternoon was only blunted by Alex's concern that he hadn't picked up anything meaty and substantive to report back to Washington. He decided to make one last effort and brought the subject around to the US war in Afghanistan again, and the various anti-US groups.

"Look, Alex, these mujahideen groups, they're like a tool kit. You don't use a hammer for all operations, you have other tools as well. Believe me, they all serve a purpose, even the rough guys. We're not boy scouts here, we're trying to protect our country and we work with whatever works."

"OK, but aren't there risks for Pakistan to be playing with the Taliban over in Afghanistan? I know Pakistan helped them get started, but they might turn on you, and I hardly need to tell you about the large number of sympathizers they have here in Pakistan."

"Yes, of course, we are deeply involved in Afghanistan. Would you rather have a continuing bloody civil war in Afghanistan among all the mujahideen, like after the Soviets left? It was—it is—in our interests to support the Taliban. They're a rough mountain lot, but they brought law and order. It was safe to travel in the country for the first time in six years after they came to power, with their rough and ready mountain justice. What's the matter, Alex, you don't remember the good old American West? Vigilantes, posses, hanging judges and all that?"

"Yeah, but the longtime goals of the Taliban in Afghanistan can hardly be called democratic or moderate—or even friendly."

"Friendly for whom, Alex? They're not there to serve you. They're there to keep Afghanistan quiet and orderly for once, and that is in our interest. It was America that totally abandoned Afghanistan to its fate and to a civil war—you just packed up and moved out after the Soviets left, with scarcely a fare-thee-well. How would you expect them to be friendly?"

"What do you think Pakistan is going to do with them over the longer run?"

"So, I see you're interested in the Taliban now? You know Alex, I suggest we not get into these details, politics will just irritate us both. Let's just enjoy the park. And speaking of external interventions, tell me more about Chile."

The lines had been drawn and Alex knew he had taken a step too far. It was unwise to press his quest on political affairs, even friendship had its limits. They didn't return to politics again the whole day. Alex felt that he had exhausted his welcome, that much of the original cordiality had faded, even as they talked about old times. The next day Majeed had to return by air to Islamabad with the beginning of the workweek, and Alex would have to get back to Islamabad by taxi on his own. They embraced at the compound gate as Alex left.

"It's so great to see you Alex, maybe we will have a chance to meet again soon. Please greet your wife and family for us. We'd love to see them here. And I hope you can meanwhile be of some help to your embassy—on its public opinion poll." Majeed spoke these last three words in a tone of irony. Alex felt subtly diminished, and a little sullied. Worse, he felt he was returning to DC with a fairly empty basket.

*   *   *

Alex was hesitant about how to present his trip report. He did not want to emphasize the wall that Majeed had thrown up by the end of their weekend. Nor did he wish to cast Majeed in a bad light, as anything like an anti-American figure.

"OK, but bottom line, Alex, how hostile do you believe Rehman is to our goals in Pakistan?"

"He's more of a nationalist than I had expected. He's changed a good bit since I knew him, when he was more pro-West."

"And you'd consider him now anti-West?"

"Wary of the West is more accurate, especially of the US. But that doesn't make him anti-American either. He's pro-Pakistan."

"Did he talk much about his work with Pak intelligence?"

"No, of course not, and I didn't feel I could delve into that. I shouldn't have even known anything about it."

"Do you think he's still strongly secularist?"

"Jim, what kind of a case are you trying to make here? The whole damn country is changing, and he's changing with it. Personally he's not all that religious at all, he enjoys his scotch and I haven't seen him go to prayers once. But he is very aware of the power of religious movements in attaining political goals. He sees them as a normal product of Pak society. Even more, I think he accepts them as a valuable asset to the government."

"Alex, you might as well know, we have a lot of other reporting which shows that he is working not in the President's office at all but for ISI. ISI damn well runs Pakistan. Worse, he's directly engaged with the Taliban."

"When I raised the question of working with the Taliban he wouldn't bite, he changed the subject."

"I bet he did. We believe there's a lot more going on there than meets the eye. We didn't want to tell you too much before you left just so you wouldn't go in with any preconceived notions."

"I have the feeling Majeed's just doing his job, and he believes he's helping preserve Pakistan's security from all comers, Russian, or Indian, or American."

"Do you think he is sympathetic to Al-Qaeda?"

"Christ no, Jim, not at all, I got no hint of that. I've told you—I would probably describe him as a secular Islamic fundamentalist."

"That's quite a phrase—whatever in hell it means."

"It means he's not especially religious, but sees how religious groups can serve the nationalist interests of the country."

"Yeah, by working with the bloody-mindedest of them all. Sounds like he's played his cards pretty close to his chest with you—for an 'old friend.'"

"Jim, give me a break! You can't expect me to go back after fifteen years and ride in on our childhood days and get him to spill classified information to me just like that!"

"No, maybe not right off. But bottom line, we're sure he's in bed with the Taliban, and ISI is helping use our money to support them."

"Well, then, go to the Paks and complain."

"We don't have enough of a case. But we do think Rehman might be recruitable."

"Just what leads you to think that?"

"We've had reports, or at least a report, that he's gay—or at least bi."

"Come on Jim, that's a joke, there's not a hint of it. I know the guy. He's happily married, and he had a torrid affair with an Iranian girl in London."

"Not the first time some guy who's supposedly happily married plays the other side of the court too. In good old America by now anything goes, but info like that in Pakistan would not help his career."

"That's incredible, do you have evidence?"

"Yeah, read the file, there is some reporting that he was seen in some gay company."

"If you've got info like that then why wouldn't the Paks be all over him on this? Surely ISI would know him better than we do."

"Can't answer that, Alex, don't know. But he would be a great source inside ISI if we could get him. And his cousin or something, I don't have the name at the moment, maybe Salim, moves in nationalist-religious circles. The family is plugged in with a lot of radicals."

"I can't believe that. He's never been particularly religious. We drank Dimple together, for chrissakes. His father hates fundamentalists."

"So he's more into the politics of it than the religion, who knows?"

"This cousin, name isn't Salman, is it?"

"Yeah, maybe that's it. But anyway, Rehman's high on our list. You may not be the person to make an approach, but we're thinking it over. Anything more you can add to this would help."

"Can I see his file?"

"Sure. But I don't want you to be aware of too much if you're going to be seeing him more. It would be easy to let something slip."

"I'd like to look at it. Frankly I'm not confident it's all accurate."

Jim shrugged. "Be my guest. You know the business, there's always gray areas, bound to be some inaccurate reporting in there as well."

*   *   *

Alex sat down in the file room. Majeed Rehman, coded green for Islamist activism cases. Alex opened the file and began to read. For all his years in the Agency, his readings of hundreds of files, and running numerous operations, this was different. Alex felt like he was inside a friend's bedroom, searching through the bureau drawers and papers on the desk while the friend was out. Majeed wasn't an ops lead, he was a goddam childhood friend. And here he was picking through his dirty laundry.

It's one thing to know someone personally, for a long time, another to get an outsider's perspective of the same person. Characteristics you take as personal quirks suddenly turn out to have a different impact on others. Who was the "real" Majeed? The old friend? Or the other ninety-five percent of people who knew him and might see him in a different light?

Student activist on campus at London University, critical of US policies. Early on a member of a leftist Marxist group; wrote an article supporting Lenin's analysis of the

British empire as example of economic imperialism, use of gun boats and an expansionist foreign policy to establish British hegemony. Was one of the organizers of a demo to protest US cancellation of arms sales to Pakistan. Back in Islamabad was editor of the student paper "The Lighthouse" that carried many anti-US editorials. Alex had never known about a radical activism on Majeed's part as a student. But he hadn't really been in touch with him then. *Became part of the Pak National Student Association, and supported radical speakers on campus. Possible ties with the youth movement of the Jama'at-e-Islami, a fundamentalist political movement with a powerful and sometimes goonish youth wing. Came out vocally in favor of Pakistan's development of a nuclear weapon.* Alex was astonished: this was a different Majeed. Not incompatible with what Alex had seen—Majeed had been critical of US policies in all their talks—but so much of that was par for the course in Pakistan these days.

Rehman's views in an article published in a student newspaper 1983: Our country seems to be divided between two different ways to look at Islam. On the one hand, we see Islam as a way to suffuse meaning, wonder and love into our lives as we contemplate God and his Creation. That's the Sufi way—values of love, devotion, and wonder at the world. On the other hand Islam is also a call to action. It does not contradict nationalism. On the contrary, it breathes greater life and depth into conventional nationalism. Today the mujahideen are the soul of Pashtun national character and resistance. In the end the world will belong to those who act, not to those impotent or paralyzed by meditation or withdrawal into rational intellect. They accomplish nothing… When the nation is threatened, violence is sometimes required to galvanize the masses into clarity of thought.

Someone had penciled in the margins: "Radical stuff. I could see a zealot coming out of all of this. Rehman needs to be watched."

Alex put down the file. *Shit, that means me. That's what they're grooming me for.*

Through this strange optic, Majeed almost began to turn into a different person before his eyes. His old friend was being washed away like a sand castle on the beach by the inexorable approaching tide of politics. *Reportedly seen at a party in Lahore where there were some known homosexual elements and Rehman seemed physically friendly with them.* Alex felt increasingly uncomfortable looking at Majeed through the eyes of his file, rather than the eyes of a friend. Did he believe all these scraps of reporting as presenting the real Majeed? Was any of this informant reporting reliable? Alex was well aware of the possibility of inaccurate, vindictive, or deliberately misleading agent reporting on occasion.

*　　　　　　　*　　　　　　　*

At the office the next day, Majeed asked one of his subordinates to check out the name of Alex Anders in their files, and then to call up the US Embassy's political section with the pretext of inviting Alex along with other Embassy political officers to an upcoming reception. "They said there isn't anybody in the political section by that name," the subordinate reported back. "Thanks, Ahmad," Majeed said, tucking that piece of info away. "Alex, Alex, I wonder how I will be seeing you again?"

Towards the end of the week Majeed flew to Peshawar for his weekly meeting with key Taliban representatives to make arrangements for the latest shipment of weapons and to discuss strategy.

*   *   *

It was some time in coming. Alex sensed Isabel's ever-so slight distancing from him—in shared interests, and the gradual decline of their passion for erotic grappling in their once well-patinaed bed. Some of it was perhaps just the inevitable result of years of familiarity. He also feared some of it had to do with his job in Isabel's mind. With the end of Pinochet's rule in Santiago and the rise of a bolder opposition, more information had come out. What had long been rumor in Chile was now fact and the details of the horrors became common knowledge, appearing in hard documentation. Alex cringed as he read newspaper revelations of Agency cooperation with Pinochet over many of those years. He no longer discussed them with Isabel, but knew she would be reading the same article in *The New York Times*, or in the Chilean press that arrived a week late. And he knew Doña Maria and Don Jorge would be reading them as well.

The Chilean experience didn't sit right with him—looking back over the whole US adventure there that had facilitated Allende's overthrow. The directives of course had come directly not from the CIA, but from the top levels of the US government—the prince of Realpolitik Henry Kissinger, and the President. At the start, every new revelation about the Chilean past in the daily paper led to a small battle between himself and Isabel—battles he didn't even seek. He told her he disapproved of the events entirely, that he had had nothing whatsoever to do with it, that it all came out of the US President's office. It was when Isabel stopped drawing his attentions to these new revelations that he knew strains were growing—there was no longer communication on the issue, perhaps not even any need for communication on it any more.

Isabel was in touch with her parents regularly by phone. Alex knew they often discussed the ongoing revelations, the reemergence of family friends, the horror stories of imprisoned fellow artists. All her parents knew was that Alex had joined the State Department, a sin proximate enough to be considered part of the finely grinding gears of the US policy machine.

Perhaps more worrying to Alex was Gaetano, the Argentinian development economist at the World Bank in Washington. Isabel had met him during her translation work at the Bank. Gaetano had invited both of them for dinner at a trendy new Nuevo Latino place. Gaetano was charming, witty, knew a lot about literature as well as politics, and he and Isabel shared these interests. He and Isabel continued to meet for lunch on numerous occasions, and Alex knew she didn't mention it every time. Alex had no specific reason to think anything was amiss, yet he felt a certain imperceptible drift. Surely if he brought up their lunches it would sound foolish, insecure and jealous, and so he kept his counsel. Isabel still devoted much time to developing interesting activities and programs for little Rodrigo. And they continued to make numerous weekend trips as a family out into the countryside of Virginia, to folk fairs, craft and bluegrass festivals. And Isabel was not inattentive to Alex's occasional quests for intimacy when they were finally alone at night. One weekend he sought out a friend to take Rodriguito for three days so they could go to a rustic lodge in the Blue Ridge Mountains to stoke some fire back into their physical relationship. They enjoyed themselves, but he noted she seemed distracted.

*   *   *

Alex could clearly see pressure building for a long-term assignment to Islamabad. He had argued against it on several occasions, pointing out his discomfort with conducting operations in a place that still felt like home. They held out the plum of being chief of the section on operations against Islamist movements—a major responsibility and a significant promotion.

He shared his misgivings with his old mentor Sawyer. Sawyer Brummel had served several tours in Pakistan and India, knew the area well, spoke Pashto and Urdu and had always taken an interest in Alex and his unique background.

"I understand what you're saying, Alex, but frankly you've got little reason to turn down an assignment like this. From any outsider's point of view, it makes all the sense in the world to send you to a place where you know the culture and the language."

"Yeah, but it just bothers me—to be going back and suddenly having to exploit old contacts."

"Don't think of it as exploiting them. You're not going to be recruiting old friends in any case. You're going to be focusing on the whole extremist Islamist angle. You're the right person for the job. It's an important assignment."

"OK, it is. But the mood of the Agency seems to be changing since 9/11. Seems to have unleashed a lot more closet cowboys out there who don't know and don't care for what makes Afghans and Paks tick. A lot of them seem to be just gung-ho Agency, in it for the action. If we run around, start throwing our weight around, making cold approaches to a lot of Islamic clerics to work for us, it's not going to work, and will just end up pissing off the Paks."

"Totally agree. And so if you don't go, and don't get involved, do you think those policies are going to go away? That they'll be better carried out by the closet cowboys you mention? Come on, you know there is no perfect world out there. You owe it to yourself—and to the Agency, to be the one on the ground there, so that stupid ideas and policies don't prevail."

Alex thought back to Fyodor, who had impressed upon him what a huge and disastrous watershed for Moscow the Afghan invasion had been, contributing directly to the fall of the Soviet Union. The Soviets in their day had plenty of their own commissar cowboys making some very bad decisions in Afghanistan. Yet in Washington it was an article of faith that Afghanistan for the US this time would be different. No conquest, no empire, no permanent bases, just a mission with global support to stop terrorism, to bring democracy and strengthen women's rights.

*   *   *

"So we need to come up with an up-to-date assessment of Majeed Rehman. Anything new to report?" The Station in Islamabad was reviewing key issues at a weekly staff meeting.

"Son of a bitch is pretty anti-American. Just ask the ambassador. Rehman had a blow-up at the residence some months ago, walked out of the dinner, said the Americans were no different than the Brits in trying to take over the world. Said he was tired of the US trying to run his country. He hasn't been back to any official American reception since."

"Yeah, well there's little doubt Rehman is a staffer in ISI. He's a key figure in liaison with the Taliban for them. That makes him a dangerous guy, playing both ends against the middle."

"He's a complicated guy. You know—good education, smart, seemed to be more of a leftist than an Islamist for a long time. I still can't make him out. He doesn't seem religious at all, he's known to enjoy his whisky, yet he hangs out with the religious types and seems to support them. It may be just part of his job. I'm not sure he believes in it."

"What about that report in the file that he might be gay? That would produce an interesting handle."

"We've never had any corroboration of that fact, and the source who said that has reason to dislike him. But yeah, for now we need to keep looking at that angle as well."

"OK, we should learn a lot more shortly when the new branch chief gets out here, Alex Anders next month. He knows Rehman personally from way back."

*   *   *

Alex in the end had found it impossible to turn down the assignment to Islamabad. Everyone advised him it was a significant professional step forward. He was torn between discomfort at returning as a professional to a country he had known as a boy, and fascination for what the country now was, and where it was going. Isabel too was ambivalent, but on a different level. She did want to get out of Washington and go overseas, and Alex had told her she would find the country and its culture fascinating. But she was uncomfortable that his assignment was under the auspices of the CIA. They agreed it would be best if Alex went out to Islamabad early, by a month or two, to find a house, get established and familiarized with things before Isabel and Rodriguito arrived. And so, late one evening as his senses were invaded by the smell of falling autumn leaves, Alex said goodbye to his family, took a taxi out to Dulles Airport for the flight to London, and then on to Islamabad. He would be exchanging one set of sensory perceptions for a very different one.

Two days later, as the car approached the US Embassy in Islamabad, everything signaled significant change. Now he was arriving in Pakistan as an Embassy official. He had barely even known the modern capital of Islamabad. Growing up in Lahore the US Consulate had been far from his world; it barely existed in his family life and circle. But he was now in the capital. His introduction to the Embassy building itself spoke volumes about the world he would inhabit. One entire block away, huge concrete berms extended halfway out into the street, arrayed alternately in a fishbone pattern, forcing any approaching vehicle to maneuver slowly around each one in an undignified creeping slalom up to the gated Embassy entrance. Protocol and diplomatic grandeur of the past had given way to the grimy, impersonal, technical realities of mechanistic security procedures hewed from concrete and steel. It was increasingly of a piece with most US embassies in the world now—hunkered down behind its security carapace whose architectural features proclaimed its feelings of anxiety, suspicion, isolation, siege, warfare.

Pakistani military vehicles were parked around the perimeter and Pak soldiers guarded the gate to the entrance. The once grand-looking Embassy gate was itself permanently closed, chained and barriered, beyond assault even from high-speed truck bombs seeking to ram their way onto the compound. Not an American in sight. An official seal on the gate and the Stars and Stripes flying on the building in the distance was the only hint of the overlordship of this fortress. The driver told Alex to get out of the car by the gate and go to a guardhouse to show his papers. The small door to the guardhouse was actually a caged turnstile, capable of admitting only one person at a time. Once inside the security checkpoint, there was still no sign of Americans. Pakistani security officials on hire to the Embassy constituted the first line of defense to receive all visitors. "Your papers, sir?" one of the guards behind the desk asked. "Your good name, sir?" "Anders, Alex Anders." "Passport, please." Picture check against his face. "Please put your briefcase and all electronic and metal items on the belt." Alex complied, although never without flickers of inward irritation that the world had now, permanently, come to this. As if the source of the overall problem would ever be solved by this. His briefcase and personal items went through the x-ray. A guard passed the magic wand around his body and then nodded to another guard at the door. "Pass, please," the voice said, and Alex was out the other end of the external perimeter security office.

The Embassy building proper was still some distance off. Alex walked along the concrete path that was partly roofed over, shielding it from the sun, for a distance of some fifty yards towards the imposing white stone entrance that constituted the Chancery, the heart of the Embassy compound. He was approaching a medieval fortress, with a huge open field of vision studded with moving robotic cameras from their turrets on the roof, surrounded by an electronic moat. The flag waved prominently in the hot wind. Having passed through enough early security checkpoints successfully, he had qualified to engage in the next round: to face real security procedures conducted by Americans within the building. Cameras were placed at high strategic points along the walkway, following every visitor's move. At his destination he saw a large opaque black glass door marked Visitor's Entrance, the one he would use today until he had been issued appropriate documentation for regular access through the American staff entrance.

Alex was greeted with a gush of cool air, a chilling sensation against his sweaty shirt and skin, heralding a different world, replete with its own controlled environment unrelated to the outside. Several thick panels of smoked plate glass obscured two Marine guards, who represented the first semi-visible Americans in the ten minutes since he had arrived at the Embassy compound. Even in this reception room discrete television cameras in the ceiling quietly turned to leer at the visitor. Alex wondered what the grand console room of television screens must look like, where all entrances to the building could be simultaneously monitored, including each applicant for entry into the Chancery. "Name?" the Marine asked, "and please speak into the microphone—and passport." Alex pushed his diplomatic passport into the drawer under the glass which closed and was pulled through by the Marine to the other side. "I'm a newly assigned officer here," Alex said. "I'm to meet Arthur Swain, in the Political Section." Swain was the deputy chief of the Political Section that provided cover for some of the many Agency officers working within the Embassy. The Marine Guards would figure out soon enough where Alex would really be working and for whom, but that was not a worry. These cover arrangements were more designed to confuse the casually curious outside world. Any serious outsider could fairly quickly figure out the identities of at least a number of Agency officers within the Embassy. "Mr. Swain will be down in a minute, sir," the disembodied voice said through the microphone. "Please have a seat."

Alex sat down and waited for some five minutes until finally one of the heavy hydraulic metal doors hissed open and a short figure in glasses and rolled-up shirtsleeves emerged. "Alex?" he called. "Hi, yes, Arthur?" "Welcome to Islamabad."

"This is about as strong security as I've seen anywhere," Alex said.

"Yeah, it's growing all the time. And believe it or not, all this is already obsolete. We're moving into a huge new compound in a year or two, it's now under construction—they say it's going to cost a cool one billion. For that kind of money it should be *really* ugly and miserable to live in. But that's life. Didn't I see you worked in Santiago at one point? No big security there?"

"No, there was no violence against foreigners, although Americans weren't very popular."

Arthur sighed. "Seems like that's the story everywhere now. But this is the gold standard here. Better get used to it."

"Bet you don't get a whole lot of Pakistani visitors willing to run the gauntlet of all these procedures to come in. It's kind of scary. In Santiago there were regular visitors to the Embassy, and it felt fairly open. That was a while back."

"Not here. Those days are gone. I've come from a tour in Cairo, same story there now. Worst of it is, it may keep the bad guys out, but it keeps everybody else out as well… and it keeps us good guys in. It discourages us from casually going out of the building into town. You get this psychological feel, like we're locked up here on the compound—and for our own safety of course, thank you very much. Most of the time it's just too much hassle to go out. Anyway, Alex, I'll be your nominal superior in the Political Section for cover purposes. You won't actually be sitting in the Political Section with us, but down the hall in one of the Agency suites. But I'm sure you'll be coming to some of our staff meetings every so often since I guess you'll be covering the political scene."

Arthur took Alex up a stone stairway and down the hall to another heavy hydraulic vaulted door and rang the bell; eventually the door swung open like the entrance to a frozen meat locker. "Hi Janice, got one of yours here, new guy. Alex Anders." "Hi, Alex," Janice answered cheerily, "we've been expecting you, come on in. Thanks for bringing him by, Arthur." "Anything for my spook friends," and Arthur waved goodbye.

Janice, the Station's admin officer, took Alex around and introduced him to a number of other officers. "This isn't of course the whole Station," she said, "we've got a lot more people in other sections under military cover, and out of the building elsewhere, but this is our hard-core political reporting section where you'll be."

"So, I'm hard-core now?" Alex smiled.

"Well, you speak good Urdu, don't you? That qualifies."

After seeing his small office, Alex was taken to meet the Chief of Station, Sam Groll. Sam was short, heavy set. He wore a short-sleeved blue safari suit which had gone out of style a decade ago, once a virtual uniform of the old East Asian crowd where he had served. This was Sam's first tour in a Muslim country. People back in Hqs said he was inexperienced in this part of Asia but pointed out he was a quick study and possessed a shrewd political sense. His casual style and ready smile belied a seriousness of purpose. He watched intensely as people spoke, as if making constant assessments. They were joined by Kevin, the Deputy Chief.

"When I was out here in Pakistan on a quick trip about a year ago it was all a different cast. Armand was still the Chief."

"Armand has passed on to his reward—a tour back in Hqs," Sam offered. "Kevin and I are both fairly new here."

"I hear you grew up here in Pack-istan," Kevin said, pointedly using the commonplace American pronunciation. Alex realized his own pronunciation of *Paah-kistahn*—as pronounced by the natives and actually most people in the world except Americans—marked him as on the native side, if not pretentious. He wondered whether he should alter his pronunciation to fit in better.

"Right, I was back on a quick ops trip a year ago to look up an old friend. You may have read about it. I haven't lived here since I was eighteen."

"'A lot of water under the bridge since then. Blood too."

"Yeah, makes me sad, feels like things have deteriorated, and I gather Americans are even less welcome than before. Plus I'm not used to these fortress embassies."

"You'll get used to it soon enough, and maybe welcome it one day. You know about the riots and invasion of the Embassy compound in 1979? The mobs burnt the damn building down, two Embassy officers got killed. Lot of folk out there who do not wish us well," Kevin said as if offering some kind of revelation.

Sam wheeled around in his chair. "So Alex, are you feeling comfortable with running local ops against the Islamists?"

"Yeah, sure, I'm looking forward to the challenge."

"Only because I recall from the file that you had initially expressed some reluctance in returning as an ops officer to the country where you had grown up, had friends."

"It is a change for me, being here in this capacity. In Santiago I was handling Soviet ops, not much on the local scene. And I was under non-official cover so I never went into the Embassy."

"Not too many Soviets left in the world any more," Kevin said. "But there are still Russians around. We're not so interested in them around here any more. It's all about radical Islam now."

"Yeah, I'm sure. There were more than hints of radicals around, even in my last years here as a kid. My father basically died from a beating from a fundamentalist crowd in Lahore."

"We'd heard, sorry about that," Sam said. "But whatever it was like then, it's worse now. And we are expecting you to be at the heart of it, given your fluent Urdu and knowledge of customs. We need somebody good to run operations against the Islamist target."

"I'm happy to work on that. I know it matters. And I do think I understand it. But it's a tough job to start recruiting in their midst."

"I think you'll find the almighty dollar has just as much impact on Muslims as it does on other folks elsewhere," Kevin put in, brandishing the essence of his own operating philosophy. Kevin had served his last tour in Bangladesh where crushing poverty opened doors to anyone flashing easy money in return for services. He had made a whole string of recruitments, including several significant government officials, and his reputation in Hqs had soared. He was now working on being Sam's alter ego in the Station.

"Sure." Alex felt Kevin was challenging him. "You can always find people who will topple for money. But a lot of these guys are hard-core believers. Money won't necessarily turn their heads."

"Well, we'll give it a try anyway," Sam said. "I'm sure they told you at Hqs that we don't have a sufficient handle on these major fundamentalist movements, or their leaders. It matters a lot. They seem to be more and more in league with the Taliban in Afghanistan. We need a good wiring diagram of all these relationships, and of the Pak government ties to them, especially ISI."

"Is the Embassy in much direct contact with any of these leaders themselves? A lot of them are public politicians, you know, they have offices, you can visit them. What's our Political Section doing?"

"Damn Embassy Political Section does a piss-poor job on this," Kevin said. "State Department is skitterish about getting to close to radical figures, the Ambassador's afraid that just consorting with them will lend them greater legitimacy. That's why we need to get some good agents inside their circles."

"So, Alex," Sam continued, "You've got a team of five officers under you. They're relatively young and most don't have a lot of experience in an environment like this. One of them is ex-military. Smart, gung-ho, but needs to learn a lot about operating more discreetly. None of them speak Urdu, but most of the people we're interested in speak some English anyway. You're gonna need to break your troops more into the culture here."

"OK, but a feel for the environment—that takes time."

"You got time. And just to add to it all, I'd like you to try to go back and look up some of your old friends, especially Majeed."

"Yeah, Hqs told me that he was high on your radar."

"We've got big time interest in him. No one can decide what he's up to. He's nominally in the President's office, but he's clearly a significant figure in ISI—and, I might add, in liaison with some of the hard-core Taliban types in the borderlands. Others think he's a fundamentalist himself. So you need to see if you can work your way back into Pakistani society through your old friends."

"Fine. But it's been a long time. And working out of some apartment on the Embassy compound is no great help. I'd like to change that."

"We know. We've arranged for you not to have to live on the compound like the majority of Embassy officers do. A number of us—the Ambassador, Chief Econ and Chief Pol—live off anyway, as well as myself, the head of Cultural Affairs and the AID chief. That should make life easier for you. Course you'll stand out more too, and people will take you for a spook, especially speaking Urdu."

"What does your wife think of living here?" Kevin asked.

"She'll be here in two months, but I know she's game. And I'm sure she'd rather live off compound."

"She's Latino, isn't she? A leftist family?" Kevin persisted.

Alex was uncomfortable that that information was in his personnel file and known to Kevin. He wondered how much else Kevin knew. "Yes," Alex countered, "Chilean, but in Latin America it's not that big a deal to be a leftist. Almost every intellectual and artist is on the left. It comes with the turf."

"Well, I'm sure she'll be happy here. The anti-American environment should be familiar and comforting."

Alex flared. "Look, Kevin, she's…."

"Enough of that, Kevin," the COS broke in. "I think she'll be great in helping mix in Pak society. I welcome it." Kevin smirked.

They discussed Alex's operational focus, in particular in trying to get closer to religious circles, religious movements and the extremists who were close to the Taliban.

"Bin Laden is probably out there somewhere," the Chief waved out the window, "but we're not going to spin our damn wheels turning over every goddam rock to find him. Not sure he even matters that much any more in driving most of the terrorism that's going on in the world. But the Taliban do matter and there are a hell of a lot of them, and of course they help drive events over the border in Afghanistan, and increasingly here too now. I don't need to tell you they can be a dangerous lot."

"It will be interesting," Alex commented.

"And Alex, one more thing," Sam added. "The Ambassador is interested in meeting you. You're the closest thing the Embassy has to an American who really knows Pakistan well, the culture and the language. One or two officers here have had Urdu training, but nobody who speaks it fluently. There is a gal in the Political Section, on her second tour in Islamabad, she's pretty savvy. But do try to keep the Ambassador stroked, happy and off our backs."

"Is he high maintenance?"

"He's an ambassador, 'nuff said. Like most of them, a bit taken with himself. But he's actually pretty good, savvy guy. He's a big political contributor back home. At least he's smart, was in Congress for a while, got some background in the politics of the area, and he's interested in what's going on—that's a lot more than what I hear about some of the other yo-yo political appointees, friends of the President. His instincts aren't all bad, either. He's not happy with the US military mission creep here, leaking in from Afghanistan. Frankly, neither are we. These cowboys ship in and ship out of here in twelve months or less, know nothing when they arrive and whatever little they learn gets lost with the next rotation. A lot of Pentagon big shots want them involved in taking out bad guys inside Pakistan's border area with Afghanistan. Ambassador thinks that would be a big mistake. I happen to think he's not all wrong on that one."

"We're not going to smile our way out of the Afghan war," Kevin said. "I don't know how long we can keep US troops out of combat in Pakistan. It may come to that, given all the refuge the damn Paks give the Taliban along the border."

"Let's get you set up in your office. Until your wife gets here you'll be able to spend a lot of time reading the files. Have Ellen show you around the office. You'll also have a cover office in the Political Section. Not that you'll be sitting in there all that much."

Alex went back to his office to meet the few, mostly junior, officers who would be working for him. They seemed in awe of Alex's reputation as a Pak expert. And he went to the admin office to make arrangements for a house in time for Isabel and Rodrigo's arrival in two months. He was grateful they weren't going to live within the walls of the Embassy compound. That might have been the last claustrophobic straw for Isabel.

*   *   *

After Alex left, Kevin turned to the Chief. They had known each other for a long time from East Asia. Sam valued Kevin's operational shrewdness and insight into people, but his negativity and hard-ass style had markedly slowed his advancement up the ranks. In fact, he was the same age as Sam. Kevin accepted the costs of his anti-social style, and didn't seem to be in a hurry to change.

"Sam, you know what? I'm not sure I'm entirely comfortable with this Anders. I've seen 'em before. He may know a lot about the culture, but I wonder if he'll be effective. We're giving him a lot of responsibility in heading the Islamist ops section."

"What's your problem?"

"That he grew up overseas. That will fuck you up every time. Poor guy like Alex gets dragged all over the world by his parents, living in all kinds of different shit holes. Doesn't know where he belongs."

"OK, point taken, Kevin. That's your grand theory, not necessarily mine. Let's not prejudge him. Frankly I'm damn glad to have someone really grounded in the country who speaks native Urdu."

"Alright, Chief, you da boss. Just saying, you heard it here first." Kevin resolved to keep a close eye on Alex's operating style and management.

*   *   *

Alex slid open his safe drawer and took out the prominent file at the front. Rehman, Majeed. The file had been left with him for his early attention. He'd seen the shorter version at Hqs some months ago. But it felt different here. He and Majeed were located only a few miles away from each other now, living in the same city but separated by massive physical, organizational and ideological walls. The file in a sense represented a closer violation of their friendship. But this was the task at hand. Alex was frankly uncertain how he would handle it.

The top sheet seemed to be a profile summary from six months ago, addressed to the Ambassador:

We have conflicting reporting on Majeed Rehman. Some sources report that he is an Islamic radical, even while maintaining a cover as Westernized and secular. Other sources report that he is a strong nationalist, not particularly religious, who sees the fundamentalists and jihadis as forces that can be useful to the state. He is Pashtun, with good tribal ties. Generally reported as anti-American, whatever his religious views. He may be one of the key figures in ISI in maintaining day-to-day ties with elements of the Taliban—and conceivably even al-Qaeda. We view his role in this situation as negative, particularly since it is behind the scenes. Almost no one in the Embassy has much direct dealings with him any more, unlike in past years. A newly arriving Station officer Alex Anders, however, has longtime personal ties with him and we may be able to get a better handle on him in the near future.

* * *

"Where's Alex? Is he coming to the staff meeting?"

"Naw, he's off with the Ambassador again along with some visiting State Department type."

"The damn Ambassador seems to think Alex works for him."

"He's certainly become the Ambassador's pet," Kevin offered.

"Well, I wouldn't go that far," Sam countered. "Alex didn't ask for it, he just happens to know a lot about the local scene, the Ambassador values that."

"OK, can you ask Lloyd to come in here then? I want at least to get a rundown him on the current status of the Islamist cases."

"Right, boss. Lloyd's here, on his way in."

"Thanks for coming in, Lloyd. Can you give me a quick fill in on the Jupiter case?"

"It's coming along, Chief, but you'll have to ask Alex, he's the one on top of it."

"Aren't you working these cases jointly?"

"Yeah, but you know Alex, he has a lot of contacts he sort of keeps to himself, he doesn't always fill me in on his casual meetings."

"I damn well want you both to be up to snuff on these developments," Sam said. "Things are getting even more serious with increased Pentagon involvement in the intel side. Has Jupiter gone over for training yet in Afghanistan?"

"Don't think so yet, but we're working on trying to get it arranged."

* * *

Surfing through the channels, he stopped for a moment at Fox News in a state of moral high dudgeon over Islam.

"I'm telling you Nick, we can't be soft on this Islamist threat. This is a struggle over fundamental values—our basic struggle for freedom against authoritarianism, Islamo-fascism and intolerance. We can never relax against this enemy who hates our very freedoms. Now I know there are a lot of molly-coddlers out there; they think if we'd made nice with the Ayrabs earlier on, then 9/11 would never have happened. But let me tell you something—these are forces of darkness and obscurantism, hatred arrayed against us. There is no bargaining. And you know what really gets me? They demand tolerance and multiculturalism from us, but then they move right into our societies and start demanding the right to stay apart from us, lead their own separate lives and maintain their own values even if they're hostile to what we believe in. Wear rags on their head and cover up their women. Well, if that's the case they can bloody well go back home.

"And I don't want to hear about these so-called Muslim grievances any more either. That's just apologetics for terrorists. Lots of people have suffered injustice in history. That's what history is all about—winners and losers. But you can't go on nourishing and feeding this resentment forever. You've got to get over it. You don't see other groups that lost out in history going around engaging in mass killing because of what history did to them. Ask me, they've got to get beyond this or they're doomed to imprisonment in their desperate little sand boxes…"

Click.

*   *   *

It must have been the middle of the night. Miryam Popolzai woke up and heard noises outside. Then she saw lights. She, her husband Faisal and their four children had long since gone to bed, but she had slept badly, thinking of all the troubles in the village. And she was frightened. She knew they were up there, circling around, the ghost planes, like the wrath of God, poised to deliver sudden death at any time—on any of the people sleeping below. But this noise sounded like vehicles, stopping outside their house. She did not think Faisal was expecting anybody, and certainly not at this hour. She heard men shouting outside, Pashto, but also a foreign language, maybe English. My God, my God who could this be? May God protect us! Petrified, she roused her husband. "Faisal, Faisal, there are people here, outside the house."

They waited under the covers. Then came a banging on the door, violent smashing. Faisal leapt up and struggled toward the entry way. "Who is it?" he called. "Open up! Security!" someone shouted in Pashto. "We are God-fearing people, we want no trouble," Faisal called, "who are you?" The door burst off its hinges. At least five men shone their lights into the house. A Pakistani man speaking Pashto pushed his way in. Behind him other, bigger, men dressed in camouflaged clothing crowded in, barking a command in English. "They say turn on the lights!" the Pakistani—not in a camouflaged outfit—translated. Faisal reached for the cord to turn on the overhead light. As soon as it came on, one of the foreigners grabbed him and threw him to the floor. Miryam ran into the room, wearing an overcoat to cover herself. She screamed as she saw her husband pinned to the floor. The foreigner, his white skin and blue eyes now evident, barked out in English, "You Faisal Popolzai?" "Faisal Popolzai, yes, yes." "You Taliban?" "No, no Taliban!"

The man said something longer in English. "You are Taliban," the interpreter said, "you were at meeting with Taliban yesterday evening in Miram Shah." Faisal tried to get up, but the foreigner pressed Faisal's cheek down into the floor with his boot, causing Faisal to groan. Miryam shrieked again and another foreigner screamed back at her in English. "You shut up," the interpreter said. "Did you go to meeting yesterday in Miram Shah? Yes or no!" "Yes, I was in Miram Shah, talking to my cousin, but it was not a Taliban group." The foreigner yelled out something else. "The meeting was Taliban, you are lying, you are working with Taliban, they pay you money!" "No, no Taliban. Just business." "What kind of business?" "Farming." "What farming, poppies?" "Yes, poppies, selling our crop." "You are working for Taliban!" the interpreter shouted with prompting from the second foreigner. "No, I am just selling my poppies, I was finding a buyer and getting a price." "Who were the other people at the meeting?" "Other farmers, and my cousin. We are talking about prices and how to get our poppies to market." "You are lying!" the interpreter translated. "By God, this is the truth!" "Are you Faisal Popolzai?" "Yes." "We have information that you are a spy for the Taliban!" "No, I swear it is not true." The foreigner came over and delivered a swift kick to Faisal's ribs. A crack was audible. Faisal screamed, and so did Miryam.

Suddenly out of the back room Faysal's oldest son Ahmad appeared, holding a rifle which he pointed at the intruders. "Leave my father alone. Get out of our house!" he yelled. Before he could even register, the second foreigner lifted his automatic machine gun and pumped a stream of bullets into Ahmad for three long seconds. Ahmad convulsed and fell on the floor, his body streaming blood. Miryam screamed and ran over to him and threw herself on his body, sobbing. The foreigners began yelling. They stormed into the other rooms and found Ubaidullah, trying to pull a gun out of the cupboard. They shot him in the thigh and grabbed him. The foreigners stormed through the house, yanking open all the closets and hanging cupboards, throwing clothes and other items on the floor as they rifled through it looking for weapons. Faisal's two daughters were in their own bedroom and screamed when the men walked in. The men yelled at them, and finally slapped one of them in the face to make her stop screaming, but then left them alone. They ransacked their bureau and threw the drawers on the floor, and poked through the contents, including feminine underclothing. They then went back into the front room and pulled Faisal up from the floor and placed plastic cuffs around his wrists behind his back. He resisted but they hit him in the face and dragged him outside to one of the vehicles. Miryam screamed again, and fell to her knees, wrapping her arms around Faisal's leg. The man struck her with his fist until she let go. The foreigners then searched through the utility buildings around the compound, found a few rifles, threw them in a vehicle and prepared to drive off.

"Where are you taking him?" Miryam screamed. "To the police center, for interrogation" the translator said from the window of the vehicle. "When will he come back?" "When he is innocent."

*   *   *

The intensity and inherent fascination of his daily work in Islamabad filled up most of the void in Alex's life in the two months before the arrival of Isabel and Rodriguito. But he harbored anxieties about Isabel's personal life back in Washington. While his Agency colleagues in Washington occasionally invited her over after Alex left, he knew these were not natural or easy encounters. Isabel's more comfortable friends were from the Latin American community in Washington which constituted a whirlwind social circle all in its own right. And that included Gaetano from the World Bank. Isabel had spoken openly about how she drew real comfort from his friendship—but how far did that friendship go? He preferred not to think about it. Meanwhile Isabel's letters were affectionate and she spoke eagerly of joining Alex.

And their reunion was warm and intimate—a sense of a second honeymoon. The empty house that Alex had been camping in now took on genuine life, activity, sound, and the demands of Rodriguito. Isabel declared she liked the house, and she was gracious and charming when she and Alex were invited to various Embassy officers' homes for dinner. She also used the frequent diplomatic receptions to search out members of the Latino diplomatic community that were present in Islamabad as well. And soon she and Alex were invited to some of those homes. The Latino community in Islamabad, however, despite its warmth, offered little entrée into the circles that were the focus of Alex's operational work. And he had enough social events he needed to attend for professional reasons that he was sometimes reluctant to go to dinners that would not be professionally productive. "Not everything has to have some operational benefit," Isabel sometimes tartly reminded him. Alex noted that she received a few letters from Gaetano. He resisted the impulse to read them, and they quickly vanished.

To Alex's genuine delight, Isabel quickly found the heart of Pakistani life attractive, with its bright colors, emotionalism, bustle, and lively arts. "Thank God they did not acquire the British colonialists' passion for life!" she quipped, and Alex could not disagree. Best of all, soon after meeting them, Isabel quickly fell in with Majeed's family, and particularly Zubayda. Isabel was horrified by Zubayda's story of her disfigurement, and admired her for her passion and commitment. She also quickly noted the conservatism of the country, especially stories of the attitudes of rural and tribal areas towards women. Soon she was drawn into the work that Zubayda was doing, educating women on social, medical and literacy issues to which she could often contribute—in helping teach English, literacy and hygiene issues. She quickly gained insight into that other side of Pakistani life that Alex could not readily enter and condemned women's position in the eyes of the fundamentalists. "How can you stand dealing with many of these religious types?" she asked Alex. "I don't agree with them, but it's my job, Isabel, it's my job."

One day Alex was surprised to find a woman in a sari at the sink when he arrived home. "Isabel, wow. You look terrific!" He embraced her from behind. "You could certainly pass for Pakistani with most people." Isabel was delighted with "her disguise" as she called it. She obviously took pleasure in being able to pass as a part of Pakistani society, at least until she opened her mouth. While some Western women tied to wear a sari on occasion for fun, most lacked the skin coloring and especially the body movements required to pull it off. "Mommy is Pakisani!" Rodriguito would say with delight. And Isabel took to regularly wearing the sari when she went out to work with Pakistani women. It drew less attention to her, made the women feel more at ease, and they were pleased she was willing to wear Pakistani national dress unlike most other foreign women, even though it was locally welcomed. However, among the American community, the story spread that Isabel had "gone native" and she was careful never to wear the sari to Western occasions.

Both Isabel and Alex, while liked among the American community, were also regarded as "a little different," a remark that contained both admiration and a touch of irritation. Isabel, less invested in the community, took it in her stride. And Alex was delighted that Isabel had found an interesting and constructive role in Pakistani life. Rodriguito soon went to international school where his own already-mixed national identity seemed to grow vaguer, even to himself. Zubayda began to be a regular presence at their home, often as she and Isabel came back from a meeting, or had something to discuss. "What is this?" Zubayda asked one time, picking up a small jar in the kitchen. "Curry powder? My dear, you can't cook decent Pakistani food with a jar of curry powder, throw it out!" And she instructed Isabel how each dish required its own unique and particular combination of spices, a teaspoon of this spice and a teaspoon of that. "You wouldn't use one jar marked 'French spices' to put in every French dish, would you? Our curries are creative, each one reflects individual personalities."

Even Alex began to protest at the increase in Pakistani cooking, or Isabel's attempt at it. "I get these dishes all the time in Pakistan now anyway," he complained, "What's happened to the Latino cooking?" He was always delighted to see Zubayda there, and she still maintained, even in front of Isabel, a flirtatious style with Alex, empowered by her knowledge of him from childhood. Isabel did not seem to question it, although one evening after Zubayda had left, she asked if Alex found Zubayda attractive. "Very," he answered, kissing her, "but not as attractive as you."

Since she had taken to wearing a sari, Isabel often found herself treated as Pakistani in public, sometimes ignored, certainly less hassled by men than she was used to in Latino society. But Isabel found herself angered by the demands placed upon the behavior and decorum of women in Pakistan, especially in the conservative rural areas when she traveled out with Zubayda, and she often railed about the fundamentalists she encountered. "I agree, it's bad," Alex responded. "In fact, it's gotten much worse compared to when I was growing up here."

Zubayda showed a deeper acceptance. "I don't like it, but you have to understand where it is coming from," she told Isabel. "These men are angry and frightened; they feel their culture and authority under attack, especially from outside. They are responding by becoming even more defensive and orthodox, as a way of clinging to some kind of identity. We can only change them slowly."

After Isabel came back one evening from one of her day trips into the villages with Zubayda, she told Alex, "In the town we were in today I learned the saddest thing I've seen in Pakistan yet. Many girls are apparently actually raised as boys—up until puberty. They are given boys' names and dress like boys, and mix with boys. You know why? Because the family lacks a male child. The youngest daughter is consciously raised as a boy so she can work in shops, go out in the streets to buy and sell things in the market, and can functionally act as a male in society for the family's benefit. People often know the 'boy' is actually a girl—even teachers in school—but they don't talk about it, because they know the social and economic reasons behind it."

"I've heard about that before. You actually met one of these girls?"

"Yes," Isabel said. "We were talking with one of the mothers who worried her daughter was getting too old to act in public as a boy any more, and they were going to lose a significant part of their income... This is really sad! Zubayda is trying to bring this issue up in many of the villages, and point out what a problem it is—for everyone."

"Zubayda—what incredible courage she has. I hope she doesn't get into further trouble in combatting social issues like this. She's already suffered badly enough from her unconventional behavior."

"Well, I back her fully on this. This is probably the most important mission I can imagine here. We're going to do more."

Alex hesitated. "OK, just please—please try to be careful. You know how volatile these gender issues can be."

"I know, but I'm also not going to be a good Embassy wife on this issue."

Alex and Majeed enjoyed each other's company as the two families continued to intertwine. But when they were alone together a wariness had crept in, a sense that each knew a little bit too much about the other, an awareness of a shadow play going on between them. They often sparred politically, usually without rancor, but they were careful to observe boundaries.

To his surprise, Alex found himself spending more time talking with Majeed's father. Akmal was pleased to see Alex's interest in questions of religious ceremonies in Pakistan, and especially in the visits to the shrines. Majeed was mildly on edge about this, and told Alex "he should leave his father out of all this politics."

"Dammit, Majeed, can't I be genuinely interested in this?" Alex came back. "I've been interested in these ceremonies since I was a boy. Did you forget how we spent Ramazan together one year?"

Majeed smiled, but his chiding about Alex's time spent with his father talking about religion was nonetheless now on the table.

One weekend when Alex and his family were in Lahore with Majeed's family, Akmal asked Alex if he would like to accompany him on a visit to a shrine. Majeed looked at Alex askance, but Alex expressed definite interest. "I don't know how suitable that would be, Babaji," Majeed commented. "The presence of a foreigner at one of these places might send a wrong message."

"If he wears national dress, nobody will know or care," Akmal responded.

Alex had visited a few shrines with Majeed's family as a boy, but had not really understood what it was all about. Now he felt much more engaged, given all his readings about Sufi philosophy and poetry, the heart of the Islamic mystical tradition—and an awareness of how even shrines were becoming issues of political contention.

He told the Station Chief about his planned trip to a local shrine, to get some feel for the tensions between the more mystical and the more fundamentalist sects of the country. The Sufis themselves, after all, were a key target of the Taliban and hard line Deobandi sects. "For chrissakes, be careful," Sam said. "I won't say no, but it makes me nervous. The last thing I need is a story in the Pak press about some fucking CIA officer in Muslim drag penetrating the holy shrines."

*   *   *

Akmal's family lineage traced back to the Sufi traditions of the Punjab and Sind; as a family they had often set out on visits to the *ziyarats* or pilgrimage points and shrines of holy men whose tombs were said to bring healing and enlightenment to visitors. Entire colorful festivals grew up around these shrines at certain times of year when people would flock to them in search of healing and fertility, of boons and blessings from God. These shrines lay at the heart of folk Islam in India and Pakistan—the Barelvi tradition, the largest religious Sunni vehicle in Pakistan—and one of the religious fissures that divided Pakistani society.

As Majeed grew up he gradually became aware that the Barelvi way—the emphasis upon mysticism and shrines and visits with holy men or *pirs* for the transmission of spiritual tradition—was not universally appreciated in

Pakistan. In fact, the followers of the other major school of Sunni Islam in the subcontinent, the Deobandis, though far smaller, were militantly opposed to the Barelvis. The Deobandis, originating from India, were driven by an austere and strict vision that harshly condemned such visitations to shrines or to meeting with *pirs* as rank superstition.

"How can the Deobandis be so opposed to shrines?" Majeed had asked his father when they visited a sacred site. "Shrines are everywhere."

"The Deobandis are fanatics. They are cold, strict, obsessed with legalisms, the law of Islam rather than its spirit. They will tell you that the shrines are a distraction from God, that we take these holy men as objects of worship, instead of worshipping God himself. That, of course, is absurd. It is the saints, the holy men, the mystics who bring us closer to God. The warmth of their hearts gives a hint to us of the warmth of God's heart. But we don't worship them."

"But why are the Deobandi fundamentalists so fanatic about this?"

"They are without joy. Look how they ceaselessly engage in seeking out and condemning the forbidden, what they say is *haram*. But we do not reach God through denouncing what is supposedly forbidden in life. God should be a source of positive acts, of joy, not fear. The Quran says, 'God desires ease for you, and desires not hardship' (2:185). Islam is meant to bring joy and happiness, not suffering. The Quran tells us directly—God does not ask of us what is impossible and difficult to carry out. But these Deobandis, they say that life is nothing but discipline and the banning of evil things. Again, the Quran tells us, 'O you who believe! Make not unlawful the good things Allah has made lawful to you. But commit no excess, for Allah does not like those given to excess'." (4:86-88)

His father's gentleness and faith were powerful symbols in Majeed's mind of how a personal religious life is led. Certainly honor and dignity, spirituality and mysticism were all fine—but how would it fix Pakistan?

Alex had already bought himself a new earth-colored *kameez-shalwar*, the long shirt and baggy pants and the vest of the national dress. The tailor wasn't particularly surprised, Westerners sometimes wore the national outfit when they attended a traditional Pakistani social affair like a wedding, where it was always seen as a sign of respect. He hadn't worn one much except as a boy, but it thrilled him to put it on again. He felt in one sense that he was donning a disguise, to go on a mission. On the other hand he felt he was clothing himself in the culture and tradition he knew well.

Majeed opted not to go. He did not approve Alex accompanying Akmal, given the rising tensions surrounding the shrines. Majeed asked Alex to be careful as his presence with Akmal might provoke troublemakers. "No one says foreigners may not visit these shrines," Akmal said. "Of course I'll be careful," Alex said. "That goes without saying." "Nothing goes without saying these days," Majeed replied.

They took a bus to the shrine, a significant act in itself, sharing a common vehicle to a common destination. Akmal had told Alex about his first pilgrimage to Mecca—the overwhelming power of joining a million members of humanity in a common religious enterprise, all dressed uniformly and humbly in white robes as Hajjis or pilgrims. While there, the individual's drive for autonomy melted into a massive, shared, social and religious experience, at one with everyone else—issues of background, race, language or wealth submerged in a common spiritual expression, tearing down boundaries between individualism and shared humanity.

As it grew dark the bus arrived in town outside the shrine. The evening was soft, swallowing some of the harshness of the day's heat, while the *neem* trees overhead pervaded the air with fragrance and moisture. Tonight would be the special *zikr* and devotional ceremony in celebration of Sufi tradition and the life of the holy man Ghalib Baba. "Here you will see people moved not by anger and resentment, but by love and joy and inspiration at God's love and creation," Akmal said. He knew Majeed was uncomfortable in coming to an occasion like this; he would view it with misgiving, even embarrassment, as if participating in something from the past, an activity of an older generation, not of a young intellectual. None of Majeed's friends ever attended these ceremonies as far as he knew.

Alex stopped along the path. "Why are there police around the compound?"

"Because hard-liners among the Deobandis and extremists have attacked meetings like this before. People have actually been killed."

"Surely they wouldn't kill just innocent worshipers?"

"My boy, a tiny minority might. They seek to impose their will on all of us with their narrow view of Islam."

Near the entrance to the shrine, they saw a bearded man who had been staring at Alex. He came over to them. "*Salaamu aleikum*, brother," he said to Akmal. "Who are you bringing to the ceremonies?" "A friend, from the North," Akmal answered, "and what business is it of yours?" The man scowled and turned away. Alex knew that "from the north" described a variety of mountain minorities, some of whom had very pale skin and blue eyes. Alex drew a sigh of relief. "Who do these people think they are, policing these ceremonies that are the right of all of us?" Akmal said angrily. "It is an offense to God that they should challenge us like that."

They penetrated through a police guard and entered the compound. Alex could hear drums and music in the distance, and as they drew closer, colors in motion flashed in the illumination of the open square. The acrid and cloying smell of *ganja* mixed in with the night air as they passed groups of men in unkempt robes who were sitting on the ground smoking the substance. "*Ganja* at a religious ceremony?" Alex asked. "It is an old tradition in South Asian culture," Akmal replied. "Many Hindus too, believe these substances can be an essential avenue for approaching the divine presence. But the fundamentalists denounce it outright. And I must say, in that case I think they are right; it is not desirable to approach the path to God with one's mind clouded. But, who knows, who am I to judge, maybe they are the clouds of the Divine. That too, is an old theme among some Sufis."

A flurry of sound, color and action now assaulted Alex's eyes as they moved inside through the milling crowds, into the intoxicating presence of religious ecstasy through dance and music. Drums of every sort seemed ubiquitous, many of the dancing devotees carried their own. One old man bore a long barrel-shaped drum that hung from a strap around his shoulders; he held a stick at each end and tapped out a sharp staccato rhythm. In the background other deeper drums darkened and thickened the sound. Some figures whirled in elliptical circles around the arena, their drums swinging outward in centrifugal force at the end of their leather straps. Some dancers held circular tambourines high—a ring of wood covered on one side by a skin amplifying the staccato taps of their fingertips. The number of dancers rose and fell as men wove in and out among themselves in states of near ecstasy, heads bobbing back and forth lost in trance-like motions. A teenage boy in a brown robe suddenly emerged into the center of the group from the side, thrusting his hands now to the right, now to the left in almost classical dance poses, hands outstretched now in supplication, now in prayer, catching the attention of the other dancers with the purity of his movements—spontaneous, unselfconscious and personal. Some other dancers then moved into the center swaying rhythmically, others nearly hopping in frenetic expression. And then, most eye-catching of all, figures in white robes emerged, whirling with arms raised seemingly in tune only with the motion of the universe. A heavy-set bearded man in a white robe passed in front of them, surrounded by four friends who help keep him upright as he twirled and spun, eyes closed, ecstatic, almost oblivious to his surroundings, seemingly not caring if he lost his balance. Beards abounded—some full, others with a stubble of only three days growth, the style reportedly favored by the Prophet and a common sign of piety. Colors ran riot—some figures in brilliant red robes that reached nearly to the ground covering their baggy pants underneath. Others in white or green. Still others in black, yellow, some with colored turbans, others bareheaded. Strings of beads of varying length adorned the neck. As the "whirling dervishes" danced, the rhythmic drumming was pierced by a haunting call of the reeded *ney*. A whirling young man wearing leather sleeves strapped around both calves covered with small bell-like rattles came onto the scene, contributing a rushing, whooshing sound to his motions. Calls of *Allahoo, Allahoo* emerged from the musicians in polyphonic chants of response. Many showed the long hair associated with nearly all holy men in the subcontinent, their locks flailing as their heads rolled to the music.

Faces from all over the Muslim world. Light-skinned Kashmiris of Persian and northern background, slant-eyed Asian influences of Central Asian blood going back to the Mughals, darker skins from India's south, rounded faces from the Punjab, aquiline features with blue and green eyes from the North-West Frontier, all here sharing a common heritage in the process of melding into the One. The participants as well as the watchers drifted out and beyond into a different world. The voice of the main Qawwali singer on a platform against the wall rose and fell and received a response from the other musicians. The crowd periodically shouted out encouragement to the dancers when they executed a particularly satisfying motion and the sense of religious ecstasy took over in what may be trance, maybe hypnotic motion, maybe the mind seized by yearnings for the transformational experience of union with the Divine. The riot of color, sounds, motion and emotion carried well on into the night, summoning people from everywhere to participate in a ritual that surpassed all society, class, status and wealth. They were simply joined in common search for the Beloved—one of the many Sufi names for God.

"This is popular Islam," Akmal whispered in Alex's ear, "every bit as powerful as the message of the mullahs. More powerful than the fatwas of the fundamentalist preachers. All that interests the mullahs is cataloguing and denouncing the many things of life they deem to be forbidden, *haram*. But the joys and ecstasies of Sufism can never be stamped out of Islam and the mullahs know it. It represents people beyond control of the Law and in tune with the deeper call of God in their hearts. We will not let *them* dominate the center of Islam."

Alex was unsure at his own emotions—at first discomfited at this exposure to raw religious emotion and passion. He had felt his hair stand on end with the intensity of the music and the emotions of ecstatic outpouring and communion with the onlookers. This was indeed a far cry from the debates over the political meaning of religious ideas and doctrine. The intellect was distant from this communal form of ecstatic devotion.

For Alex it was all sheer fascination, moments engraved in his mind. The crowd was primarily male in the courtyards of the shrine, but later on he would see street processions of Sufis with women joining in from the sidelines, often swinging their long hair entirely uncovered in a show of religious emotion, certain to inflame the hostility of the fundamentalists who saw it all as an unseemly loss of piety, decorum, a pagan wallowing in religious emotion that unleashed passions not meant to be unleashed.

Before he knew it they had been there for three hours. Akmal was silent as they finally made their way out of the crowds late at night. "I feel touched by God," was all he said. "God says in the Quran, 'I am as close to you as your jugular vein.'" Alex understood.

A young mullah saw Majeed's father emerging from the shrine and swiftly and obtrusively drew abreast of him. He was dressed in a white robe and wore the long untrimmed beard that characterized fundamentalist affiliation. "Brother, assalamu aleikum! You should not be attending this kind of *taghuti* ceremony. This is not Islam!"

"What do you mean, *taghuti*? What are you talking about?"

"This is idolatry—these visiting of tombs of so-called holy men, to attend dancing and music ceremonies that are *haram* in the eyes of the Prophet."

Alex took Akmal by the arm to move him forward. But Akmal did not move, and instead fixed his eyes on the young mullah, challenging him. "And why shouldn't I visit the shrine of this holy man? He is a great deal closer to God than you are with all your bans and *harams*!"

"Old man, the Quran is very clear on this, we should not commit the sin of *shirk*."

"*Shirk*? What does visiting this holy man have to do with *shirk*? I am not taking another God, or finding a partner for God. I am here to simply feel God's love through the words and character of a holy man—a shaykh—and the dancing that expresses that. What polytheism is there here? Tell me!"

"God commands us that there is no God but God. We should not be worshipping or seeking blessings from any other source, not even from the Prophet himself, may God pray for him and keep him."

"I do not worship this Shaykh. But he fills my heart with joy. What do you know of joy, young man, you look like you could use some in your angry life. Don't you know the saying, 'He who has no shaykh has the devil for a shaykh?'"

"That is a typical Sufi corruption of Islam. We don't need shaykhs to tell us what is right and wrong. You should study the Quran and the Hadeeth and decide for yourself what is right and wrong."

"I have studied the Quran, my friend, for more years than you have been alive. I have memorized the entire holy book! Have you? I don't need you to tell me what is right and wrong. Nor is this just about right and wrong, it is also about love, love in our lives, joy at God's creation. I don't think you believe in that very much. Now, if you will excuse me."

"We don't want to see you here any more, old man! We are watching this place of perversion, all these Barelvis who are filled with idolatry and false Islam. We will bring pure Islam."

"I think you will find that we Barelvis are the majority in this country, my young friend. We derive joy and peace from our religion. Sufism was there from the dawn of Islam. It is why our religion is great. It is why our religion has spread so far and wide, because Sufi teachings appealed to the Christians and Jews, and Hindus and others and ultimately brought them to Islam. Your madrasa has obviously taught you to find fault and to ban all that you see. God help *you*, my son."

The mullah scowled at Akmal. Meanwhile, near the entrance, Majeed noticed that a fight had broken out among some young radicals with sticks, and some of the attendees of the dancing emerging from the compound.

"Let's move fast, Akmal, those are probably the bullyboys from Jamaat-e-Islami. Arguing is pointless. We need to get away from here. It wouldn't be good for me to get involved."

"But isn't that what I have been telling you, Alex? This has all become corrupted into politics and intimidation. What do these people have to do with Islam?"

"I agree, but these are roughnecks, it's not the place for philosophical discussion. Let's depart, quickly."

And they moved away from the brightly illuminated compound, through the crowds into the darkened streets around them. As they rode away in the midnight bus, Alex stared out into the darkness. What was happening? This was not the kind of Pakistan he remembered, where Christians were a small but real part of society, where religion had not been politicized. He could feel the cancer of the war just over the border in Afghanistan feeding on the violence and beginning to eat into the body and life of Pakistan itself. Massive forces were at work, combined now with the deadly force of the greatest military power in the history of the world radiating out in all directions from Kabul in a desperate struggle to put down the resistance movement. Yet that very resistance movement in Afghanistan was supported by so many Pashtuns even in Pakistan itself. The hot breath of that conflict had crept across the mountains into the tribal zones of Pakistan and beyond.

What was happening to Pakistan? A country with a glimpse of Paradise itself—the most awe-inspiring scenery in the world, with its magnificent mountains like K-2, Nanga Parbat and Rakaposhi, sacred sentinels to the north. The country was blessed by one of the great Asian rivers—the Indus—that flowed like frothy milk out of the towering glaciers of the Himalayas to spread its bounty and fertility to water the land all the way down to the sea in Karachi. The Panj-ab, the five rivers that flowed through the province. Might not all of this land have stayed together in one great state of India if the British had never come to the Indian subcontinent to divide, conquer and rule? Would Muslims and Hindus not have maintained their own kind of co-existence as they had in the past?

And now, Pakistan seemed obligated to fulfill its Islamic origins, the only other country along with Israel to be founded on religion alone. Defining and protecting its "Islamic identity" had become its desperate mission, its impossible burden. This quest for identity even led some Pakistanis to challenge the "Pakistaniness" of other Pakistanis as to whose religious school was more correct, more orthodox. Sunni or Shi'a? The Barelvi, or the Deobandi sect among the Sunnis? The greater the external pressure across the border from the Afghan agony, the more Pakistan was forced to bend before the gale of ramped-up tribalism, and American demands that it facilitate the unpopular American agenda in the region. Was there a point at which the country could snap? *This is the new Pakistan I'm now in. Where is it going? And where will it take me?*

*   *   *

And within just a few weeks another ugly incident occurred. A spiritual leader, a *gaddi nashin* at a local shrine about three hours away from Lahore—a spiritual successor in a chain of Sufi leaders—was killed just outside its gates. The death sentence, after the fact, was promptly issued by a fundamentalist group: "We had warned this unbeliever repeatedly that he must put an end to these un-Islamic practices of music. Women must not be allowed into the shrines that are dens of passion and iniquity. These dancing ceremonies are not permitted in Islam. He had corrupted the Faith."

The local fundamentalist organization added that it would not be responsible if anything happened to visitors at these ceremonies.

"This is what I am talking about, Majeed!" cried his father, after watching the news on TV. "Look at this violence and murder that these people call for and practice. These Deobandis are a minority, but they are joining the Taliban and taking over—even closing down many of our shrines across the country. People will not accept this!"

"You are right, Father, I agree it is an outrage. But then why don't they do something about it?" asked Majeed. "They could protest if they represent such a big group, take some kind of community action."

"Babaji, you can't just present this all as innocent Barelvis against hard-line Deobandis," Zubayda chimed in. "You know there is more to it. How many of these *pirs* and religious men are supported by rich landlords, even corrupt politicians, who want to keep the peasants and the poor focused on their shrines and away from any political thought or action that would threaten the landlords. Some of these pirs may be holy men, but they are also exploited by the wealthy to preserve the status quo. You've got to be fair about it. That's what some of these Islamists are objecting to."

"She's right," Majeed said. "Furthermore, people don't dare oppose the landlords. So the fundamentalists gain a lot of support when they speak out against them. Who can disagree with them on this? And when our neighbors and clans in Afghanistan are invaded by foreigners—English, then Russians, now Americans—all of whom kill our people, then of course the hard-liners gain sympathy. Who will dare speak out against them under these conditions?"

Akmal fell silent. The proper order of things was undeniably wobbling. What could right it? He slipped out of the dining room to do his prayers and went out alone that evening to a concert of classical singing to relieve his soul of its momentary bitterness.

Chapter Seven

Salman

Nationalism is our form of incest, is our idolatry, is our insanity…Just as love for one individual which excludes the love for others is not love, love for one's country which is not part of one's love for humanity is not love, but idolatrous worship.

- Erich Fromm

Afzal walked into the canteen at the university, grabbed a tray, extended his plate for a serving of goat and potato curry, on top of overcooked basmati rice and some *chapattis,* and sat down at a table by himself. "Hey, you're not going to join us?" yelled a student in jeans at a table nearby. "We're not good enough for you anymore? You can't pray all the time, you know, *yaar.*" Farooq came over with Salman and sat down with Afzal.

"Sorry, Farooq, I didn't notice you. I've just been busy, rethinking some things."

"What's to rethink? We haven't seen you for weeks. God forbid you're not abandoning us."

"No, but I just feel tired, like I'm in a rut. I'm just not sure what I'm doing here at university anymore."

"Same as any of us—who says it's supposed to be fun?"

"Who cares about fun. I'm just on the wrong track, I…"

"Get over it, it's not just you, it's the whole bloody country, if you ask me," Farooq rejoined.

"He's right, we are on the wrong track," Salman said. "We're pathetic—and so what else is new."

"What's all these deep thoughts with you blokes?" said Farooq. "Fix your own lives first, then the country later."

Afzal stirred his chapatti around aimlessly in the remaining curry. "Just look around, things are going to hell all around us—and what do we do? Just sit around and bitch, smoke, drink, look for fun. That's not for me anymore."

"And what's this? Letting your beard grow? You're getting to look like the fundos. Praying won't help."

"I think Afzal's right," Salman said. "The country *is* going to hell. But what do monkeys know of the taste of ginger? We're losing Kashmir. And being humiliated by India and the US. We need more guts, not more prayers and religion."

"Maybe we just need more parties, *yaar!*"

"Come on! I've played around enough in my life, Farooq. We need to get serious."

"Now you're really frightening me. You're starting to talk like bloody President Zia did—please spare us more Islamic values!"

"Well, maybe he wasn't all wrong, did you ever think about that? We are backward and weak—maybe because we've abandoned our principles."

"So are you going to pray your way out of this, huh, Afzal? Let God do it for us?"

Afzal put his spoon down. "Farooq, don't be an idiot! That's just the problem with us. You think if we are religious it means 'Let God do it for us'? No, God isn't going to do it for us, unless we start doing things for ourselves, really understand our religion. Change things. This country is weak, in a mess. And who cares?"

"Afzal, *you* wake up! Those old mullahs, they live in some medieval world. They can't save anything—they can barely keep the fleas out of their beards, head stuck in the Quran the whole time!"

Afzal scowled. "*Achha*, you're right, the old ones don't understand. But there are scores of younger ones in the Islamist movement—they do understand the problem. They don't just study Quran. They may not be mullahs, but they think harder about these questions than any mullah. Or than you or me."

"So don't tell me you're going to join the fundos?"

"No, not join them, but they have something to say and I want to learn more about it."

"Come on, Afzal! Are you really going to abandon us?" Farooq said. "All your old friends from school? I can't believe this is you! You don't come to our parties anymore, you always seem to be off at meetings somewhere. What are you doing with yourself?"

Afzal polished off the last of his rice and got up to get his books together. "Yes, you are right. I am tired of these parties." He looked Farooq in the face. "You can go booze all you want. Only don't blame me when things fall apart. That's why we can't think straight—why the *kaffirs* are taking over the bloody world."

"Serious talk, *yaar*, serious. But I don't think you'll find the fundos much fun either. They're a pretty grim lot, don't seem to smile at much. But it's your lookout."

Afzal looked at his watch and stood up. "Anyway, I've got to get to the library. See you in class later on." Salman went with him.

"Farooq can't do without his parties," Salman said. "You're right. That's the trouble with half our students, it's all party, nobody thinking seriously about things. And these buffoons who are our leaders."

Afzal stopped outside the door and turned to Salman. "You know, all of you have got it wrong in talking about 'the fundos' like this. You don't know what the bloody hell you're talking about. There are some very dedicated nationalist thinkers among them. They truly think about politics—and the nation."

Salman shook his head. "Maybe, but I think the left has a better view of the situation."

"The left? Those tired old has-been communists and Marxists? They're finished, nobody even listens to them. When they took power in Afghanistan what did they end up doing except destroying the country? I'm telling you, Salman, you'll find a lot more good thinking among some of these younger Islamists than in your creaky old Marxists. You should come with me sometime, to one of the meetings. It might open up your eyes, like it did mine."

"Sorry mate, just a lot of prayers? I don't need that."

"No, we do have a brief prayer, if it's prayer time. The rest is discussion, about Pakistan, the world, the imperialists, the state of our country, the corruption, the condition of Muslims. Come this afternoon. Might change your thinking."

*   *   *

They went to the mosque just off campus, new and utilitarian, and down into the activities room in the basement which was always open. It was a large if shabby space, room for prayers, but also fold-up chairs for lectures and meetings. Some fifty people showed up, nearly all students. Some wore blue jeans, open shirts and sunglasses, others wore kameez shalwar, some were bearded, some were not. A scattering of women, all wearing hijab—covering their hair and shoulders. They all awaited the arrival of Nizamuddin, the young preacher who was starting to attract attention with his speeches about the state of affairs in the nation.

Nizamuddin had come from a liberal and Westernized Afghan family in Jalalabad; they had all fled at the time of the Soviet invasion, had lost most of their property and financial holdings, and had been forced to live in the vast refugee camps in the border area of Pakistan. His father had been an electrical engineer who saw no future for his son in Afghanistan and little opportunity in Pakistan growing up in a refugee camp. His father had managed to send Nizamuddin, his eldest son, off to London for university to study engineering. There Nizamuddin had mixed with the large Muslim community and was drawn into much of the intellectual debate and fervor in and around British mosques. He had become radicalized, in part by the racism he encountered in the UK, and partly because he felt he did not truly belong anywhere. Nizamuddin gradually began skipping classes and drifted towards political meetings where they discussed the views of leading Islamist thinkers on the Afghan war and the Muslim predicament in general. He had rejected clumsy efforts by British security services to recruit him as an informant inside Muslim student circles: for that reason he had been unable to get his visa renewed and was forced to leave the UK and go back to Pakistan. His father was furious that Nizamuddin had wasted the opportunity to receive serious technical education in the West. Nizamuddin had become convinced that only local action by Pakistanis and Afghans would ever produce meaningful change. He discovered he had oratorical skills that he believed to be more effective than wielding a slide rule.

There was a bustle at the door and five people entered the hall, all in national clothing. Afzal leaned over to point out Nizamuddin, but Salman didn't need to be told. It was evident—the tallest of the group, thin, lean face, with the trace of a smile, a litheness of body motion, and expression of self-confidence—a figure who commanded attention. His beard was closely cropped, and he had a youthful and direct demeanor and manner. The room immediately quieted as he intoned the usual Quranic invocation of greeting and opening: *Bismillahi 'r-rahman ar-rahim. As-salamu 'alaykum wa rahmat Allah wa barakatuhu.*

"Brothers, it is good to see you all here today. Nothing could be more important than talking about what really matters, the condition of our country and Islam." Nizamuddin's voice seemed at first high, but no less strong and forceful.

"A lot of scholars will tell you that the most important thing in our faith is to come to prayer five times a day. Yes, it is important to pray. It is one of the five pillars of our Faith. And praying helps keep our thoughts on God, *Subhanahu wa ta'aala.*" He paused and looked intently at the audience. "But we can't change things just by praying! We also need to think about action!"

A murmur arose in the room and Nizamuddin paused a few moments to let the thought sink in.

"I do not need to tell you how bad the state of affairs is here in our country. We are surrounded by enemies on all sides—enemies of Pakistan, enemies of Islam! The Hindus want to kill us, to wipe out all traces of our glorious Muslim Mughal Empire that made India what it is today. It was Hindu anti-Islamic campaigns over the last century that forced so many of your families to flee from India. That is why we are here in Pakistan today! To create a true Muslim state." He paused again.

"And we have the Soviet Union, that tried to swallow one of the proudest of Muslim countries, our neighbors in Afghanistan. But thanks to the actions of the glorious mujahideen, the Red Army of atheist Soviets was thrown out of the country after eight years of struggle—a great victory for Islam."

"And then we have the forces of America which are determined to keep Islam weak. The Americans have inherited the mantle of the British empire. And like the British they are learning that Islam is the biggest force of resistance against imperialism. They cannot tame Afghanistan. And as long as they cannot crush Islam, they cannot crush us. That is why they always love to talk about 'moderate Islam.'

"Yes, 'moderate Islam.' Do you know what that is, my brothers?" He paused for response. "Do any of you actually know? I am glad that you do not! It means praying to God, but never raising our voice against injustice. It means remaining pious but never struggling to bring change in our societies and our political system. It means praising God but never standing up to fight against the suffering in the Muslim world. That's what 'moderate Islam' is, and that is what the *kaffirs* want—good, obedient Muslims who spend all their time in prayer and don't give the kaffirs any trouble so that they can run the world for themselves. That is what we call moderate Islam, or 'American Islam' as they call it in Iran."

"Well, by God I am proud that I will never embrace 'moderate Islam'—for it is an invention of the West, to destroy the life blood and vitality of our faith! And I know you will resist them as well. We want to restore the power and force of the true Faith! We reject American Islam, an Islam that has been neutered like a eunuch! Because that is what they want us to be—eunuchs."

Nizamuddin paused and drank a swig from a bottle of water. "Do I need to tell you what's happening to the Palestinians, for example, who have been chased off their own lands and homes by Jews? And who are the Jews? People from Europe who came as colonizers to Palestine and are usurping more Palestinian land every day."

"And do I need to tell you about the brave Chechen people? They have been Muslims for over one thousand years but the Russians are killing them, killing Islam, destroying their lands and homes and mosques and leaving a nation of fatherless children. But the Chechens will never give up their struggle for independence—a struggle that has been going on, not for ten or twenty years, but for more than two hundred years! Sayyid Shamil is one of the great martyrs of the annals of Islam who fought for Muslim independence from Russia over two hundred years ago. What will it take for the Russians to let them go?"

A buzz rose up from the assembled students. Nizamuddin took his time, seemingly savoring the psychological power he was building up in his audience. Salman was astonished. This was not the kind of prayer meeting he had imagined, with people hunched over their Qurans discussing the text. These were issues of daily politics, issues he was concerned about, without even thinking about Islam.

"And maybe you have heard about our Bosnian brothers. They are not even brown men like us, but white Europeans, as white as French or Germans or Swedes. But they are being put in concentration camps and killed. Why? Just because they are Muslim!"

Salman stirred and almost wished the talk to end now because there were so many new ideas here that he wanted time to process them in his mind. But Afzal signaled for him to keep focused.

"My brothers, you all know of the five obligations of every Muslim as set forth in our Holy Quran—all good Muslims practice them: bearing witness to God, making our prayers five times a day, making the Pilgrimage to Mecca, setting aside alms for the poor, fasting at Ramadan. But many Muslims are not aware that there is a sixth obligation—that also falls upon every one of you—and that is the obligation of Jihad!

"We live in a period of great crisis for our Faith. Under these present conditions I must tell you Jihad is now probably the single-most important religious duty of every Muslim. The five duties are designed to keep each Muslim in touch with God, *Subhanahu wa ta'aala*, in his personal life. But the sixth obligation, Jihad, is to preserve the very existence of the umma itself—our worldwide nation of Muslims.

"Is there a Muslim alive who does not know that the entire umma is under threat today from American armies? Our umma is reeling from Western attacks, languishing under the economic power and control of the West. We are drowning in the flood of filth from Western culture that infests our own societies, our television screens, our advertising, our internet and public behavior. We do not even control our public media and entertainment—all of it comes from outside. We must struggle against this corruption of the world. But the West knows that if our youth is infatuated with hi-tech toys and pornography, we will never think about our own pathetic condition."

Nizamuddin took another swig from his bottle—so much more down-to-earth than most speakers who would insist on drinking out of a glass. "The Muslim world has been under attack from the West starting with the Crusaders who slaughtered our populations in the name of Christianity. Our umma has been occupied by imperialist and colonial forces for hundreds of years, controlling our countries, pumping away our oil, overthrowing our leaders and appointing their puppet rulers over us. Many of our rulers in the Muslim world are still puppets of America, and do America's bidding. You know that is true...even in this country!

"This has befallen us because we have abandoned the Way of God! We have abandoned the Way of Islam! Our umma has lost its unity and cohesiveness— its ability to withstand the invader and occupier.

"And how did we lose our unity? We lost our very symbol of political and religious unity—the Muslim Caliphate. It was the Western imperialists who helped destroy the great Muslim Ottoman Empire after World War One and to break it into tiny helpless little Arab states that could be easily controlled. It was Mustafa Kemal Atatürk who destroyed the office of the Caliphate in order to please his Western masters and to ensure that Turkey would be accepted as 'European.' But despite all the elements of their Islamic culture that the Turks surrendered to their Western masters, they have still never been accepted in the West. Still are rejected from the European Union! Why? Because they are Muslim! But think what a crime to our culture Atatürk committed in destroying the Caliphate. Because our umma—which had been led by glorious Caliphs for over one thousand years—now has no political leader. None! No one who can speak for us. The Catholics around the world have a Pope. Who do we have?

"The umma can never be strong until we reestablish the Caliphate—a central voice for Islam. And begin the long and hard task of restoring some kind of unity among us—at least of vision and thought—to the Muslim world. We know this cannot happen overnight. But it must happen and it will happen! Once we again can establish a Caliph to speak for us and inspire us, we can work to restore our power and defend ourselves—and help spread the true word—the true word!—of Islam to the world.

"So know, my brothers, that it is good to pray. But the future of Islam rests on changing things—changing the nature of the Muslim world we live in, changing the politics of Pakistan to ensure that our rulers maintain the march forward towards the law of Islam in all things. Towards strengthening our will to stand up against *kaffir* forces from outside who wish to destroy our culture, our faith, our sovereignty, our power and will to resist. In the meantime consider these ideas and discuss them with your friends. We will talk about them in greater detail in later meetings. Thank you for your attention…"

Nizamuddin let his final words sink in as he fell silent, his presence suddenly diminished as if he had been drained from the passion of his talk. His comrades stood up signaling an end for today. Nizamuddin nodded to several people, shook hands with a few around him, received even two high-fives, then moved cleanly out of the room ahead of the crowd, and got into the back seat of a waiting vehicle.

Salman sat quiet for a few minutes trying to reflect on everything that had just taken place. The Islam he had heard about all his life, including from his late father and his uncle, was always in the context of history and tradition and prayer and righteous living. What Nizamuddin had spoken about here tonight opened the door to an entirely new way of thinking. He brought *relevance* to the meaning of Islamic values, teachings and history in daily life and the state of the country. Salman turned to Afzal. "Thank you, brother, for bringing me. This is not what I had expected. He is an impressive individual. He has made me think."

"I'm glad. We can come again next week," Afzal offered.

Nizamuddin's words echoed in Salman's mind. Salman did not raise them with anyone else, nor tell anyone in his family about his new ideas. He simply let them percolate mentally as he considered their relevance to his situation, to Pakistan's situation. And he knew he would be going to the next meeting.

*   *   *

The next weekend Salman was invited to Sohail's house for a party. Sohail was a distant cousin but they rarely saw each other, even though Sohail was friendly towards him at school. "It's going to be a crazy party, man, you don't want to miss it." Sohail's parents were away in Europe for a month so Sohail had the run of the house, though his parents knew about the party, "As long as I don't have to witness it," his father had said, "and as long as there is still a house standing when we get back, and as long as you do not bring the morals police to our door or besmirch our reputation."

Sohail's father was a successful banker and the style of their house was designed to demonstrate their social standing. It seemed to occupy a whole block, with vast gardens surrounding the house. When Salman arrived by rickshaw—it seemed like he was the only one who did not come in his own car, several official gatekeepers in uniform monitored entry one by one, ensuring only invited guests gained access.

Salman identified himself on the guest list and walked into the compound. He was surprised by its size, lit up with strings of lights. Waves of disco music spilled out onto the lawn. Jacarandas instilled the evening air with decadent perfume. Numerous sports cars were parked inside the compound and a number of young admirers wandered among the vehicles tossing around names –MG, Maserati and Kia—meaningless to him. Salman had never been invited to Sohail's before; he was curious to view the lives of the moneyed elite.

At first Salman didn't recognize anyone—Sohail had said he was inviting a large number of friends from university, as well as his older brother's friends from a stockbroker firm.

Salman already felt that he looked out of place in a crowd like this. He could see he wasn't dressed quite right; he had known enough not to wear a shalwar-kameez but he didn't have in-style Western clothes as those around him here did. It was clear how his upbringing had been conservative compared to Sohail's; this kind of partying and entertainment was not part of his experience.

A servant approached in white livery—"whiskey sir? Or rum and tonic?" Salman was going to ask for some juice, hesitated, and finally took a rum and tonic so as not to be out of place. He recognized his friend Nadeem and walked over to him. Nadeem was holding the remains of a rum and tonic. "So what's going on here?" Salman asked.

"A party, *yaar*, a party! Must have cost a lot just to pay off the police not to bother them."

"Looks like a lot of money here as well," Salman observed.

"And some quite free girls from what I can see." Nadeem nodded his head approvingly toward a group of young women in Western clothing holding drinks and laughing loudly among themselves on the veranda. Salman surveyed the scene, unsure of himself. They watched quietly for a few minutes, uncertain of their next moves; should they plunge into the heart of the throbbing beast inside? Salman felt insecure in the presence of girls who seemed liberated in a different way than his cousin Zubayda.

Another classmate and friend of Nadeem, from a prominent Lahore family, came up to them, eyes out of focus. Salman nodded to him. "Great party, great party," the friend slurred. "Want some ex?" he said, extending his palm with two yellow pills.

"Sure." Nadeem plucked a pill out of his palm and smiled at Salman.

He wondered if he should ask. "Ex?"

"Ecstasy. Where've you been, *yaar*?"

"No, thanks, no. I don't think so right now. Maybe later."

"There's only now, *yaar*," the lolling head observed and moved on.

Near the entrance several young men, drinks in hand, were talking. "London? No, man, we're going to Amsterdam this year. More action. More girls. Anything goes there. Can't stand it here in the summer. It's just a drag. Fucking fundos are killing the place."

"Let's go inside," Nadeem nudged Salman, "some hot numbers in there. You won't see girls like this on campus. Some come here to loosen up, it seems. I saw a girl from one of our classes—always wearing a headscarf, but here she's wearing a silk shalwar-kameez and she's sexy! I wonder if her parents know she's here."

Salman followed Nadeem. The sound from the closed space inside assaulted their ears as they drew near to the entrance. Couples were dancing frenetically and some girls were dancing among themselves. Sohail came up to them in the entry way, wearing a white linen suit and looking very sleek. "Salman! My studious cousin," he called out, and embraced him. "Welcome, you wouldn't want to miss a party like this—*Abbuji* even said he wanted to be away from home when we held it! Get a drink! Go in and dance! Loosen up!"

"Go for it, man," Nadeem said, pushing Salman towards the group of girls. Salman resisted and watched, unprepared, as two of the girls came over to them.

"Don't we know you from some class?" one said to Salman. "I'm Zehra, want to dance?" The sound overpowered her voice and she seemed unsteady on her feet, her pupils dilated.

"Sorry, I don't really know how to dance."

"Come on, I'll show you," and she grabbed him by the hand.

He knew it was a mistake the minute he got out on the dance floor. He felt wooden and uncoordinated. "Come on, just relax," she said. He tried to make his body move in synch with the music, but he felt like a fool, humiliated in front of this elite bunch. She pulled him into a embrace and, as they moved, she murmured into his ear, "loosen up." She hugged him closer and he felt the electricity of her hand down against his crotch, followed by shock at the sense of personal invasiveness, producing a terrifying war of emotions between his body and his mind.

"Sorry, I'm just not up to it tonight," he yelled into her ear, slipped out of her embrace and walked off to the side. She stood blatantly still in the middle of the floor and rolled her eyes at him.

The smoke and the sound reached crescendo and Salman was suffocating. He stumbled toward the front door and out into the yard. A boy was bent over by the wall, vomiting into the grass not far away. Under a tree was another couple in a deep embrace, mouths locked and bodies undulating against each other, naked except for their clothes. He was aroused, jealous, and appalled. Salman felt himself inside a throbbing amoeba from hell, primitive and physical organic functions operating on all sides, sucking everyone and everything into its physical organism in some kind of blind biological drive.

This was alien turf. These people, their clothes, cars, drugs and lifestyle. Thank God his uncle could not see him at this place, surrounded by people he called "the parasites of Lahore." A mindless quest for drunken, lost, vapid, fleeting, crazed, hypnotic, dizzying pleasure. The hot night intensified the emotions, smells, sensations, isolation in this frenetic organism. Why was he finding it hard to wrap his mind around reality, as colors bent before his eyes, the evening odors cresting like waves and the music throbbed.

He heard yelling at the gates to the compound. Many voices, and pounding that sounded like sticks on car roofs. The noise rose and he could see from behind the trees dozens of young men, most bearded, in national clothes pour through the open gate carrying heavy sticks and yelling, "Allahu Akbar." They swarmed onto the compound and began to beat anyone in their path. Girls screamed and there was a general rush towards the entrance hall to the house. But the mob kept on coming, swinging sticks, shouting "whore, whore" to the girls they encountered, and "shame, shame." The partygoers stopped their revelries and began to come out onto the entrance. Vice met virtue in a melee in which virtue was sober and focused while vice was groggy and confused. Students fell to the ground with bloodied faces and heads, crunched into fetal positions trying to shield their heads from the cudgels. Fists were swinging as the self-appointed vice squad headed inside, striking at vases and objects of art, trashing the house as they went. Most of the partygoers by now simply sought to flee the scene and the rioters.

Salman remained huddled behind bushes outside, sheer adrenalin overcoming the intoxicants in his system. He thought of trying to find a few of his friends but he did not dare move into the eye of the storm. He heard sirens in the distance. Keeping a low profile he snuck down to the main gate but was spotted by a bearded youth who dealt a solid blow to his face with a terrible crunch. Searing pain tore across his nose, which burst with red. Salman managed to get out in the confusion and stumbled down the street as police cars passed him, sirens howling and red lights revolving in crazy patterns matching the confusion of his mind.

He was not even sure how he got home. His shirt was soaked in blood from his nose. At least it was late—most of the family probably had already gone to bed. But he couldn't ignore the pain of his nose, surely it was broken, maybe dangerously so. He would have to see a doctor. He could not keep the family out of the incident.

As he opened the gate, he saw another car: his uncle Akmal was just escorting a guest out. There was no way to avoid them.

"Salman, my boy, my God, what has happened to you? What is all the blood?"

Salman burst into tears of humiliation, anguish and delayed shock. "I'm sorry Uncle, I was caught in a riot. I was at a party at Sohail's house. We were attacked by fundos."

"What is all the blood? Have you been cut?"

"No, but I think my nose is broken."

Zubayda came out and went running up to him. "Oh my God, oh my God, what happened? Your face, Salman!"

"Let's get you to hospital before your aunt sees you!" Akmal bundled him into the car to take him to the hospital. He managed to see a doctor quickly for the late hour, and was soon informed that he would have to stay the night. He tried to spare his uncle the worst of the details, but the basic outlines were undeniable. He knew his uncle was shocked, pained, ashamed. But Salman's well-being was his first concern and cross-examination and reckonings could come later. Salman's nose was prodded and moved in extraordinarily painful ways until a hypodermic injection helped suppress the pain. It was clearly broken, the doctor said, and he had to have a splint placed upon it.

Salman's night was tortured by a throbbing pain in his head—both the blow to his nose and the cocktail of party drugs refusing to yield to his need for sleep. He did not dare ask for more drugs to get to sleep. The next morning he awakened feeling as if he had been to hell and back. His mouth tasted foul and his mind was still scattered. The doctor told him that luckily the pieces of bone of the nose were in place and did not require surgery, he could go home. But the mirror horrified him, confirming the realities of the night before: black and purple splotches dominated his face. He looked ghastly. The bruising would not fade for at least a week. He could not skip classes, he had exams coming up. But his face would tell a story and open him to endless queries.

"Can you tell me now, my boy, what exactly happened?" his uncle asked after they brought Salman home. Salman repeated the details of the party, how he had basically stayed out of most of it until the rioters came. "I hope you haven't been doing drugs there, you know that would be very dangerous." Salman, with some guilt, decided not to mention the yellow pill that had been thrust upon him.

"I'm not surprised at a party like this at Khurshid's. He is my second cousin, but I have never liked him. His corruption is well known and his lifestyle is shameful in my view. He has close ties with many senators and ministers, all shady, to protect his business holdings and his monopolies. I don't want you to go to his house any more. Khurshid has his enemies and I'm sure they were the ones who tipped off the religious squads. And Sohail was an idiot if he wasn't aware of the foolishness of having a loud and public party with alcohol in this era of Islamization campaigns."

At the university late the following day, the melee at Sohail's house dominated the talk. Many students had been injured and taken to hospital. A number of people on both sides had been arrested, but the vigilantes were quickly released by the police who sympathized with their religious impulses against the gilded youth of Lahore's elite. Sohail's house had been damaged by the rioters, even as a fire had been quickly extinguished. Before Salman could even think of an alibi, everyone assumed he was one of the party's victims. He stopped trying to deny it.

The Islamist students held an open meeting to discuss the events. They disapproved of violence, they said, but they also felt a distinct obligation to prevent university students—who made up nearly all of the partygoers—from engaging in immoral behavior that was demeaning to them, to the university and to society. The open use of alcohol, drugs, mixed and lewd dancing and a general atmosphere of immorality all contravened the ordinances of General Zia's *Nizam-i-Mustafa* or Order of the Prophet.

The Islamist students would clearly be aware of Salman's attendance at the party. He would be questioned by Afzal: what was he doing there? Indeed, Salman asked himself that same question. He had not even enjoyed the party. Fascinating yes, like watching a python move to the kill, but it was not fun. He had felt unnerved, out of place, threatened by the power of the evening upon his senses, senses that had never been stretched so far before, not even in his year in California. The entire experience had sobered him, even without the riot and his injury. He understood the excitement and lure of the partying, but it brought compelling evidence that that kind of lifestyle was not something he could ever feel comfortable with. Against his better judgment he ran the scene over and over again through his mind, the girl holding him close and massaging his hardness, arousing and disgusting him at the same time. Yes, these temptations were powerful, but they led to loss of control, loss of identity, loss of purpose. They were a mindless escape, a flight from reality and responsibility. They helped sow doubt and weakness in his mind about what was right and what was wrong.

* * *

Two weeks later, Afzal approached Salman again. "I know you were at that party at Sohail's house," he said.

"He's a distant cousin, I didn't feel I could say no."

Afzal's non-response said more than enough. But later he invited Salman to attend the next talk by Nizamuddin. Salman needed little persuasion. He abandoned his jeans for his shalwar-kameez.

Nizamuddin quickly entered the room in the basement of the mosque, dressed in his same white garb. He flashed a small smile to the audience, waited a few moments, and then began in a relatively quiet voice, requiring his listeners to be quiet and attentive.

"My brothers, you enjoy a special time in your lives as university students. You have freedoms and time on your hands that is the envy of most others who must go out daily to earn a living. You have the luxury of studying what you want, to learn what you want, to do what you want. This is a special privilege that God, *subhanahu wa ta'ala,* has given you."

"But when we are young, we do not always understand yet the message that must come to our hearts. We have the freedom, but we also have the responsibility—we must do something with that freedom for our faith, our *iman,* our umma." He paused.

"But I fear many of you waste this privilege which has been given to you. Instead so many brothers use their university years as a time for fun, for play, for distractions that are often not even moral. Yes, it is important to remember the moral principles of Islam and try to fulfill them. You owe that to God and you owe it to yourself. But you have a bigger responsibility to Islam—to help strengthen its future and the future of the umma itself!

"So take stock of yourself. What have you done, what are you doing, what will you do for the umma in this precarious time? Simply taking your classes, studying your books and going to social gatherings and finding ways to enjoy yourselves is not enough. You have the obligation of Jihad! Jihad means making effort, effort for the sake of God, *subhanahu wa ta'ala.* It means carrying the true faith in your own heart, yes, but also carrying it to others.

"I think you know about the time of *jahiliyya,* that period before Islam, before the enlightenment of the Prophet's message. *Jahiliyya* means ignorance, ignorance of Islam. But the great Egyptian Islamist and martyr Sayyid Qutb— *rahimahu Allah*—told us seventy-five years ago that the pre-Islamic time of ignorance, the *jahiliyya,* does not refer only to the period before the Prophet, *salla allahu aleyhi wasallam*—when the message of Islam had not yet come. No, Sayyid Qutb said that *we* live in the times of *jahiliyya,* of ignorance of Islam, even *today.* We say we are Muslims living in the Muslim world. But how many of us are true Muslims? How much do we truly understand Islam? And how many of our so-called Muslim societies are truly Muslim?"

Nizamuddin paused to let his queries sink in.

"In fact our societies are ignorant of the true meaning of the Faith. Brothers, change begins not in the future, not in some other country, but right here and right now. We must seek to create a genuine Islamic state now, here and now. Fortunately, President Zia was on our side on this in the 1980s. He proclaimed the Nizam-i-Mustafa, the introduction of Islamic Laws into our life. But this is not enough. Even he encountered opposition from all sides by those who prefer the comfortable ways that have made us soft, our country soft in the face of our enemies. It is easier to cluck our tongues at what goes on, but to do nothing about it."

Salman looked around. Students were rapt in their attention. This was not like the usual *khutbas* in Friday prayer. He felt thrilled that something new was going on here, something that touched their personal lives. He felt a sense of nervousness about it as well. They were being challenged, to think along new lines that he had never heard in his family. To think for himself about how to bring change, how to take action.

"If you focus your attentions on your own needs and wants and pleasures, you are weakening yourself, and, yes brothers, you are weakening the umma. This is how ruling classes always keep their people under control! Americans are so busy in their shopping malls and their mindless television shows and the lives of their film stars and their pleasures that they give no thought to what happens in the world—and as a result their leaders can do as they please."

"But the umma cannot afford this neglect. We must not be prisoners of our pleasures and distractions. That is the right word—distractions. They distract us from the real things of the world. The true Muslim focuses on the realities of our world, our society, our government and its policies. They must all be brought to the path of Islam, the path of awareness, participation, strength and righteousness!"

"So, my brothers, remember as you leave here and return to your classes—to your years of freedom at the university—remember you also have an obligation. It is not just what is in our hearts and minds that matters, but even more, what we do with our talents to bring change. To save our umma and strengthen Islam!"

"And finally, brothers, let me remind you of what the great Palestinian and Muslim leader Abdallah Azzam said, before he lost his life in the jihad against the Soviets in Afghanistan: 'Muslims can never be defeated by others. We Muslims are not defeated by our enemies, but instead, we are defeated by our own selves.' Think about that." And he stared meaningfully at the assembly.

The room remained silent, even after Nizamuddin signaled the end of his talk, offered a brief blessing, and with his assistants again left the hall without mixing, in a smooth exit. Salman sat for several minutes in silence, astonished, almost trembling. This man had come to speak to him, directly to him today. He had addressed the issues of the party and the riot and its implications. He spoke directly to the turmoil and confusion in his mind. Above all he offered an answer, a way out.

*   *   *

Salman sat in the cafeteria alone, eating a quick snack before his next class, when he was approached by a student. "May I sit down, brother?" he asked. Salman had seen him somewhere but couldn't place him. "My name is Ahmad. I noticed you at Nizamuddin's talk yesterday. Was it your first time? How did you find it?"

Salman mentioned he had been there once before. "He is impressive. He raises important issues that have made me think."

"Good, it is important we hear these messages." And Ahmad went on to talk about Nizamuddin. "Many of us brothers try to meet more regularly to talk about these ideas, to see how we can apply them to our situation here. Would you be interested in coming to some of our discussion meetings?"

"Well, my studies take a certain time," he said defensively.

"We don't need a lot of your time, brother, just your thoughts and attention for one hour a week. If you liked Nizamuddin I think you will find our group stimulating."

Ahmad went on to discuss their group. He seemed open and committed, with an inward seriousness, a maturity missing in many other students. He offered to take Salman to the next meeting.

*   *   *

Zubayda sensed a change in Salman. He avoided looking her in the face, he had taken to scowling occasionally in her presence.

When he came home one evening from classes, he walked by Zubayda in the kitchen on the way to the refrigerator without greeting her. "Salman, what is the matter? Are you angry with me over something? You seem to be avoiding me."

"It is nothing." He continued to look away.

She put down her mixing spoon. "It is something... you don't seem the same. Are you having some problems?"

"No."

"Then why are you avoiding me? Why won't you look at me?"

"You should know," he said, closing the refrigerator door.

"What kind of an answer is that?" she snapped. "Know what?"

"Know about what happened to you in Waziristan."

"Salman! You know what happened to me in Waziristan. There is nothing to hide. It is an old story. How dare you dig this up again!"

"You are behaving in an improper way, Zubayda." Salman looked her hard in the eyes for the first time as he sat down at the kitchen table. "You act in immodest ways."

"What are you talking about? My work with women?"

"You go around all by yourself, and you encourage women to break with tradition, to lose respect for their customs."

Zubayda sat down. "And why are you all of a sudden being so critical of this?"

"It is partly because of women's behavior that this country is losing its morality."

"Salman, I've never heard you talk like this."

"You have the mark of shame on your face. I expected my own family to be pure!" His voice rose as he rose from the table.

"Pure? What kind of nonsense is this? You think I'm not pure? That I'm running around with men?"

"No, not with men."

"I'm a lesbian then? Is that what you are saying? Me and Zahida? Say it!" Zubayda rose from the table.

"I don't know. But some of my friends have asked. I feel ashamed to talk to them about it."

"Well, you must be talking to the fundos if that's what they are saying."

"They're not 'fundos,' they are serious people, they think about the country."

"And I don't think about the country? You think Pakistan will be stronger and better off if its women are ignorant and helpless and locked up at home? What has come over you, Salman? *Babaji* is religious, even conservative. But he has never spoken to me in that way, or opposed the improvement of women."

Salman scowled and picked up his book bag. Zubayda went over to him and held him by both shoulders and looked him in the eye.

"Salman, you are like a brother. You mean a lot to me. I helped bring you up. It is very painful to hear you use this language with me. It doesn't even sound like you. It sounds like you are just parroting words and phrases you have heard from other people." And she hugged him while he stood there stiffly, but not disengaging.

"I'm sorry, Zubayda," he said after a few moments. "I'm feeling confused. I'm trying to work things out in my head."

"But you are in some group now, aren't you? Discussion groups about Islam?"

"Yes."

"Well, it seems to be changing you. You shouldn't have to suddenly rethink who your cousin is all over again. I am who I am, nothing new, nothing different. We've virtually grown up together and there are no secrets. I have not become a different person just because you have been going to meetings. *You* may be a different person, though."

Salman hung his head. "I'm sorry Zubayda. I feel confused. I'm angry about what is going on in this country. We have got to do something about it. ... I'm sorry, I didn't mean to insult you."

Zubayda stepped back and looked at him with a smile. "You know what, Salman? You need a girlfriend."

Salman blushed. "How dare you say that! And what difference would that make, anyway?"

"It will make a difference. You just need to open your life up, find some happiness in things. You can't just stay dark and withdrawn. It's not good for you."

"It's my problem. I'm working some things out in my head. What to do with my future."

"That's good. You should think about it. But don't let some group of people tell you what to do, or what to think. You need to see a lot of different people, a lot of different crowds. Think for yourself."

Salman grunted, picked up his bookbag and went up the stairs. "Good night," he offered.

Later that evening when Majeed got home, Zubayda opened a conversation with him in the kitchen.

"I tried to talk to Salman today, he's not himself."

"I know," Majeed replied. "I think he's hanging around with a lot of Islamists right now."

"He is. But now he's beginning to treat me as if I was some immoral woman. That pains me. I spoke to him about it."

"What did he say?"

"That he's feeling confused, he's concerned about what's wrong with the country, that maybe it's a breakdown of morality. He also suggested that my scars were some sign of immoral behavior."

Majeed sighed. "That's not good at all. And I'm sorry all those old issues have been dredged up again for you. I agree, I'm worried about this too. I've noticed some kind of withdrawal or something, as if he's angry. I'm not sure what to do about it. God knows there are enough Islamists in the university around him. And you know he's interested in politics. ..."

"Politics, OK, but there is more to politics than just Islamists."

"I hate to say it, but at this point I'm afraid many of these Islamists may be the only serious group around doing any thinking or taking any action in politics. The old leftists seem quiet. Most of the rest of the students seem like spoiled playboys. Or don't have any interest in serious political issues."

"Well, I worry when he gets withdrawn like this. It's not healthy. I hope you can keep an eye on him. He softened a bit when I put it to him bluntly, about changes in his manner. I agree, he's confused... And I told him he needed a girlfriend."

"Zubayda, you didn't! I'm sure that really embarrassed him. Anyway, you know how hard it is these days to talk to girls alone."

"Yes, but he can mix more."

"Agreed. But let's not talk about it with Babaji or mother at this point, it will only upset them. I'll try to talk to him."

Five days later Zubayda found a note.

"It's Salman. He's gone, he's left to go the camps." Zubayda met Majeed at the door, holding the note, tears in her eyes. "This was on your desk."

"Dear Majeed. I have left for a month to go for some further education and training in our sacred cause. Do not try to find out where I am, or make inquiries about me—you will only make trouble and danger for me. Please do not tell Babaji and mother or any others that I have gone. I will be safe and will not be going to fight. I am just going to learn. I will be back, inshallah, by the end of the month. May God keep you all.

Wassalaam. Salman

Majeed sank down onto a chair, took off his glasses, and pinched the bridge of his nose.

*   *   *

Salman had boarded the bus for the long ride to his destination in the Frontier. As it finally left the green agricultural plains of the Indus and began to move towards the environs of Peshawar his pulse increased. Here was the heart of the action! This was where mujahideen had rewritten the history of warfare with their sensational sacrifices that enabled them to destroy the atheist empire of the Soviet Union—and was now on the way to vanquishing the world's sole remaining superpower. Both of those powerful states in their imperial arrogance believed they could conquer the lands of Islam one by one.

Peshawar had always been a fabled town, gateway to the Khyber Pass that wound its way directly up into the mountain fastnesses of Afghanistan. Peshawar had long been charming, self-contained, quiet, green, its old British Cantonment area studded with fine old buildings in Mughal Raj style—especially the stunning red sandstone towers of the Islamia College—and the meticulously laid-out streets from the days of the British Raj. The Raj era in Peshawar had lived in quiet splendor, far from the brawling of international politics. It had been touched mainly by the few disastrous British attempts to invade Afghanistan through Peshawar's gateway, only to encounter xenophobic Pashtun tribalism that ate invading empires alive. Now Peshawar's fate had drawn the great powers of the world into this ancient vortex of geopolitical struggle—once Soviets, and now Americans and their NATO fig leaf.

The city had never been designed to accommodate such a logistical inundation of competing powers. Ever since the jihad began in the eighties against the Soviets in Afghanistan the city's quiet and sleepy demeanor had given way to anarchic growth; it was drowning in makeshift buildings and the detritus of Afghan refugees who had literally quadrupled the population. Dusty streets teeming with pedestrians, noisy rickshaws, groaning trucks—the streets sometimes seemed to be made up of fly-by-night vehicle repair centers whose spare parts littered the edge of the road, testimony to the vast increase in vehicles across the burgeoning city, leaving effluvient clouds of blue smoke and begrimed surfaces. Hawkers of fruits and vegetables pushed their colored carts and plied their mangoes, pomegranates, apricots, almonds, plums and quince. And eyes everywhere, endless eyes for hire watching the comings and goings of anyone who might change the balance of forces in the city, in the Frontier region, or across the border in Afghanistan. Kim would not have felt out of place—except for the pollution and the sprawl—had he returned from Kipling's namesake novel to navigate the streets once again as a spy. The exotic intrigues that had fueled British Victorian novels had geometrically increased with more players now than ever before in history—Pakistani Pashtuns, Afghan Pashtuns, Baluch, Punjabis, Sindhis, Americans, Tajiks, Russians, English, Indians, Saudis, Iranians, Arabs, Chechens, Uighurs, even Chinese—anyone who had a stake in the unwinding of the struggle in the plains and mountains of Afghanistan. Violence in the city, marginal only decades ago, now proliferated, reflecting the competing interests of the external players in supporting one brand of violence against another. But the city and its people were the ultimate losers.

Mansoor. That was the name of the person Salman was to contact upon arrival, to let him know where he was staying in Peshawar. "Stay put," Mansoor advised, "and don't walk around the city. Don't talk to people. Someone will eventually be by to pick you up." A day and a half later a tall man with blue eyes wearing a Pashtun wool cap knocked at the door. "From Mansoor," was all he said and gestured to Salman's suitcase. Salman followed him out to a minivan with dark windows. As he got into the car, the driver maintained silence. Salman took the cue. The van rumbled around the new areas of the city overrun with Afghan refugees, winding its way through the impenetrable maze of shoddy new streets that had shrunk the majestic old Cantonment center down to a tiny isolated jewel located somewhere in the center of the swirl of logistical detritus, and grimy workshops and food carts. Salman thought he had known Peshawar from the old days, but lost all orientation and could never have retraced his steps. That was probably also the driver's intent.

The silent driver finally pulled up to a small, run-down two-storey house of tan brick, indistinguishable from all the others—a conspirator's delight. He got out, beckoned for Salman to take his bag and follow him inside. Salman had to bow his head to enter the doorway, went down a hallway, passed several rooms, and came out into a garden courtyard in the back, surrounded by high walls, as were most other buildings, protecting the privacy of each family and its women. Green vegetables grew around the edge of the walls and in a few small plots, presided over by a spindly apricot tree in the corner that seemed to reflect the hard times the city had fallen upon. A pudgy man wearing a Pashtun hat was seated in the garden at a wooden table with several chairs. "Salman?" "Yes." "I'm Mansoor, have a seat." Mansoor beckoned and a boy of about ten brought in a tray with two small rounded glasses of amber tea, each on a small saucer, and a dish of sugar cubes.

"Let's speak in English," Mansoor said. His accent did not seem Pakistani, and its slight crispness suggested an Arab. "I have heard good things about you. We've looked into your background and like what we see. You are educated, but, more important, you seem serious, principled and seeking commitment."

Salman listened in silence, since Mansoor seemed intent on saying what he wanted to say.

"We are doing great work, fulfilling jihad as God wills us, and we will win, God willing. We need everyone we can get. Our numbers are growing and the kaffir cannot stop our attacks against them. Are you ready to join in the struggle, and give your life if needed?"

"Yes," said Salman, without hesitation.

"Good. You will be here in this house for a few days with a few other new arrivals. We will sleep and eat here; there is no reason to leave the house. The streets are filled with agents of every sort. Do not assume that anyone you meet casually, however friendly, is a friend, unless you are told by your trainers that he is. You will need to avoid casual talk, even here, and should try to remain silent except for practical matters. This is in your interest as well. You do not want everyone to know who you are, or where you are from. You should not ask others about themselves either. Some people here may be going to a different training place than you, and none of you should possess much information about the others—for security reasons. Any questions?"

"No, not for now. I assume you will take me on to the camps in a few days?"

"Yes, in a few days, when all the arrangements are made. And another thing—you should choose a name for yourself for use all the time you are in training. Everyone else will have a selected name as well. How do you prefer to be known?"

Salman had anticipated this. "Abu Sayf," he said. "Abu Sayf." He liked the ring of name, which had been his great grandfather's—Sayfeddin, Sword of the Faith. His grandfather would be thrilled at his adopting it for this purpose.

"Alright, Abu Sayf, welcome to Peshawar. God protect you in your mission. You are blessed, we are all blessed, to be undertaking this work for the sake of Islam and the umma."

Salman was shown to a room lit by an overhead bulb, and two charpoy beds. A common toilet was located down the hall. The largest room of the house was off to one side with sparse furnishings; a big oilcloth in the middle on the floor served as an eating place. A shelf of books in English, Arabic, and Urdu, mainly on Islam and politics, offered works of various Islamist thinkers including Sayyid Qutb and Mawdoodi. Salman took a book of Qutb's in English, *Milestones*, and brought it to the garden to read while the light was still good. Towards sunset a thin man with a serious demeanor entered the garden. He nodded at Salman and spoke in English with what sounded like a

Pashtun accent. "I am Abu Marqub," he said, and they shook hands. "We will be together in the same room for a few days I think." A few minutes later they were joined by several other men, nodded to each other, undertook their prayer ablutions in the garden, and went for sunset prayer in the large dining room.

Shortly thereafter they sat down to supper on the floor around the oilcloth cover where several bowls of food sat in the center, surrounded by plates. Bowls of curried chicken and goat, potatoes and chickpeas, rice with tomato sauce, stacks of warm *naan*, bowls of yoghurt—more than enough for all. Everyone nodded to each other but, apart from asking people to pass food, there was little chitchat. Mansoor reminded them again not to discuss their personal circumstances out of concern for their own security.

Salman was struck by the seriousness of the group and proceedings. This was far from the heated student discussions over politics, global struggle and war that had dominated his many past months of life. Those discussions were designed to inform, educate, stimulate, inculcate, persuade, and convince those present about the nature of the challenge they faced and the nature of the solution. This was different. No one here needed persuasion. They were here because they had already reached the point of decision: they knew the time for talk and persuasion had passed, that it was time for action. Despite the few practical words that were spoken, Salman felt already a strong kinship of purpose and commitment. They were all here for one purpose and one purpose only—to learn the skills that would enable them to promote the jihad—the jihad against the imperialists and unbelievers who sought to control, dominate, weaken and destroy the umma and impose Western control over its leadership. Even the discipline of the very silence they observed strongly articulated the message amidst the exchange of intense glances of shared commitment for the task at hand. Yet they could not conceal unspoken elements of anxiety for the unknown ahead. All of them knew they had crossed a threshold; it was possible they would never be coming back.

That evening, however, Mansoor held a small discussion group. He related the lore of the last great jihad against the *Showravi*—the Soviets in Afghanistan—in which he had been a participant. Now history would repeat itself, he said. He told them how the Soviets had recoiled in the face of the faith and bravery of the mujahideen forces. With all their bombers, helicopter gunships and massive weaponry and a hundred thousand soldiers the Soviets had been unable to crush the Muslim spirit of resistance in Afghanistan. The *Showravi* had been atheists, devoid of morals, commitment or drive. Their soldiers were there only because they had been ordered to go there, otherwise they believed in nothing. Their own society was corrupted. The Russians too had been imperialists, oppressing their own Muslim populations in Central Asia and the Caucasus and attempting to stifle Islam.

What made the American imperialists think they were any different at heart? The same fate awaited them. Their society was fat and rich and complacent, it did not want to fight, it could only fight when their great ships and thundering transport aircraft delivered McDonald's and Pizza Huts and television shows to the front lines and airconditioned tents to sleep in. Their soldiers did not even know why they were fighting. This was why their empire too would soon collapse because it believed in nothing except comfort. They talked about freedom even as they delivered weapons of death against the Afghan people. But the power of God's justice and the right would prevail. Mansoor ticked off the most recent successes—the ambushing of a convoy of trucks bringing supplies and fuel to American forces in Kabul, the successful car-bombing of American installations outside Kabul, the ongoing liberation of key villages around the country where the Americans had tried to set up power, the recruitment of hundreds more fighters from around the globe who had answered the call to battle and come to Afghanistan to fight for the umma. The Americans were falling into the same graves where their bones would join Russian bones—and British bones from before them—in unforgiving Afghan soil.

*   *   *

Salman was enthralled at his exposure to the rudiments of jihadi training—basic ideological lectures and discussions, fitness drills and training hikes deep into the hills. Mastery of several types of weapons, and a little bit about the principles of explosives. This was just basic training. The recruits were also being scrutinized and evaluated for their suitability for more advanced training later on, and a determination of which discipline or role each person was most suited for.

In the evening they sat around a small campfire for some further indoctrination talks. This was the first time members of the group had opportunity to hear from fellow trainees, releasing more personal information than they were normally supposed to. And as they worked together, both in training exercise and in doing camp chores, there were moments when one or two of them could talk together in greater privacy.

The training represented a pinnacle in Salman's life experiences: the direct translation of theory and ideas into practical—and radical—action. It gave meaning to his life which had tended to drift during his youth, like a cork bobbing on the sea without apparent location or direction. Yet he was also disturbed at the chilling objectivity and coldness of some of his colleagues. A few had already taken part in local jihadi activities in their own countries and were here for exposure to a more universal form of training and indoctrination. Their countries of origin spanned the globe, although most of them were from the Middle East and South Asia. Salman felt his life now illuminated by an intense leap of passionate flames of belief in this enterprise. But many of the others no longer demonstrated any flames, or external sign of remaining dramatic passion. It was as if the fire in their minds and hearts had been reduced down to the hidden heat of charcoal that betrayed little explicit flames of external emotion, just a sustained elemental intensity of quiet individual determination. And whereas Salman wanted to take direct action to bring change to the system and to strike back against immediate foreign intruders, he was not ready for the extent of sweeping ideological vision that so many of his colleagues seemed to have absorbed.

Abu Rahim, clearly Afghan by accent, spoke out. "True Muslims are very few in this world," he pronounced. "Most of them have sold out to the authorities, to the false preachers who speak against armed struggle. They defend the authorities of the state. They say we kill innocent Muslims. I say that if someone is not a true Muslim, who does not join us in this struggle, he is a *kaffir* and is more worthy of death than a Christian or a Jew. At least the Christian or the Jew has his own religion, they believe in it. But the Muslim who does not actively support Jihad and the armed struggle is not a Muslim. He rejects a key principle of our faith, is a traitor, destroying Islam from within."

"The Shi'a are the worst of all," another man, who seemed to be Punjabi, spoke up. "They are worse than non-Muslims, worse than atheists. They work from inside Islam to destroy it with their innovations, their cults and saints and inventions which dirty the true Islam. All Shi'a deserve death. They follow the path of blasphemy. They are struggling to take over the Muslim world, with Iran behind them. We will never support Iran for that reason."

"We are right to attack these so-called shrines of the Barelvis as well," another said. "They call them Sufi but in reality they are corruptions from the days of the Hindus, tied in to superstition. They are close to the Shi'a. We will close down these shrines. Those whom we kill at the shrines are not innocent people. When we have a true Islamic state, the shrines will all be destroyed."

Salman contemplated these statements and felt confused. The language seemed different than what he had heard from Nizamuddin. The anger of many of these men seemed more focused against other Muslims.

That night he had the recurring nightmare again, bringing back the terrifying late afternoon that killed his parents and his sister when he was eight years old. It was a blood feud, some had said. Others said that his father, a lawyer, had tried to bring an assailant from a rich landowner's family to court on a murder charge. The attack on Salman's family was never thoroughly investigated, the sign of politics and money at work. Salman never truly understood what had been behind the murder, and no one offered much explanation except that his family had been killed by "bad people." Salman now realized that this was a searing fracture point in his psychological makeup, a visceral loathing of clan violence among his own people. War against distant foreigner invaders was one thing, but violence to settle family and clan quarrels...obscene.

* * *

Majeed and Zubayda had remained tense during the weeks of Salman's absence. They did not tell anyone about his departure for the camps. At work Majeed checked intelligence reporting to see if there was any word of Salman's presence, but of course he could not know what *nom de guerre* Salman had used, and he knew too that any inquiries could be dangerous to Salman.

And then late one afternoon the gate opened and Salman came in on foot with a backpack and a beard. He had been gone for four weeks. Both Majeed and Zubayda fell on him in relief. Salman seemed changed: thinner, more determined, more self-confident, more distant and disinclined to talk. He said he was alright, that the experience had been powerful. "I'm still thinking it all through."

"But you are not volunteering to go on any missions, I hope," Majeed inquired.

"No, no missions at this point. But I will probably go back again in a few months for some more training."

"But more training certainly means missions, doesn't it? Salman, I'm very concerned about this. This kind of stuff leads to certain death! Dangerous missions—suicide missions!"

"No, there's no plans of that for now. They want me to help spot other student recruits for training from the university for now."

"Salman," Zubayda broke in, "I implore you, please don't go ahead with this. You will destroy your life."

"I have to explore this. This is where my life is. This is the reality. These are the only people who are willing to take action. They are forcing me to think about the situation we live in. I have to decide how far I go with it."

He went up to bed and slept for almost 24 hours before reappearing. "I don't want to talk about it a lot right now," was all he said, in a distant, but not hostile, response to Majeed's questions.

Majeed was nonetheless anxious to plumb the true nature of Salman's feelings and intentions. A few days later Salman seemed more relaxed and willing to engage in small talk. He, Majeed and Zubayda were sitting in the dining room eating leftover curry scooped up with *chapatti* and talking about the eternal mess in the street with construction, machinery and torn up roadway.

"Well, at least we don't have traffic noise in front," Salman offered in a lighter tone.

"It must take some time to get used to daily life back in the city," Majeed commented. "Can you talk about it at all, Salman? How it was? I just wondered... I mean, do you think this is the right path, for solving our problems here?"

Salman stared at the portrait of an ancestor on the wall. "I don't know. In the end I do think action is essential. Somebody has to do something and not just sit around and give speeches and smile at the Americans and give the country away and bow down to India. The country is still totally corrupt, and there is no progress."

"I agree. But I don't know if guerrilla warfare and terrorism is solving the problem either. It just makes the military crack down more and whips the Americans into a frenzy and it only gets worse. And most of the politicians are too ignorant, or corrupt, or scared to take a strong position, as you say."

Majeed chewed his chapatti without directly looking at Salman.

"Majeed, these are very tough guys. Dedicated. And I support the idea of al-Qaeda one hundred percent. Even if most Muslims reject the idea, Jihad *is* an obligation from God, at least under the conditions Muslims are experiencing today. Their attack on the Twin Towers and the Pentagon was a brilliant operation. America deserved everything it got, a taste of the death and destruction they have been dishing out to the rest of us for decades." Salman was warming to the subject, speaking with an articulation of ideas that Majeed had not seen in him before. "I admire these guys' devotion and commitment. They have thought things through, something they are willing to *die* for. How many people are willing to knowingly die for a cause? That's what makes them so much more powerful than Western soldiers. They have found their destiny and been liberated by it. They have been liberated by their *choice* rather than always calculating in fear of death as they conduct military operations."

"That is powerful, Salman, I agree. But do you see yourself in that position? Ready to die to be free?"

"Or free because you are ready to die?" added Zubayda.

"I don't know. I really admire what these guys are about. But..." his voice trailed off.

"But what?" Majeed gently asked.

"I don't know, the violence against foreigners is one thing, but when it is against other Muslims, that may be something else. I wonder if violence is the only answer to everything. A lot of these people see enemies all around. Hardly any Muslims are good Muslims in their eyes. And so many Muslims get targeted in the process. They are very ready to kill..."

"Did you see any killing?"

"No, no, it was just light training and study. But some of the other recruits talked privately about their experiences—even in their own countries before coming here."

"What other countries?"

"I don't want to get into all of that, I'm not supposed to talk to anyone about it. But there was this one guy from Algeria, for example...." Majeed let Salman take his time.

"I spoke with him when we were alone washing dishes one day. He had a crushed left hand with a few fingers missing. He told me it was from an accident with explosives. We became friendly and when we were alone he told me about his experiences in Algeria, when he was fighting with the Armed Islamic Group. He participated in an attack on a bus going to a town that was held by the Algerian army. Their commander told them that everyone living in that town was now working for the enemy, and were supporting the Army against the Jihad. The Group had to demonstrate their power over the town—and to carry out the vengeance against those who did not stand up for the Islamic revolution. They dressed in Algerian army uniforms and set up a road checkpoint out in the countryside. When the bus came along late at night they forced it to stop. They boarded it and asked to see the passengers' passports. Their leader shouted to them that they were all *kaffir*, tools of the Army, didn't they know the Army couldn't even protect them? He said the people were terrified and begged not to be harmed." Majeed paused, hesitated. "He said... they killed every single person on the bus... women and children as well, most with a bullet in the head. One woman, he said, handed her young son over to one of their team and begged that at least he be spared. But he killed the boy on the spot, before he killed the mother. Those who tried to resist had their throats cut. He said blood ran down the aisles of the bus, that they were covered in it when they had finished. It was like their leader was drunk on the blood, 'We are cleansing Islam,' the leader had shouted and he told them all to shout *Allahu Akbar* with him. This Algerian guy shouted too, but he said he felt sick."

Majeed let some moments pass. "That must have been an awful experience. Even for a hardened jihadi," he said quietly.

Salman looked into his plate as he played with his fork.

"Also, about the Shi'a, I don't think they are right," Salman resumed. "I was disturbed at some of the talk about them. You remember I had two good Shi'a friends in school, Ali and Nadeem. Nadeem was strong and used to defend me from some bullies. He was a very good person and I still respect him. I do not believe that the Shi'a are *kaffir*, or an enemy, in our life here. The ones I know are just as patriotic and just as concerned about the state of the nation as anybody else. And they are serious Muslims."

Salman paused again and Majeed felt it best just to sit quietly.

"Also the attacks against Barelvis. Some of these fundamentalists are too filled with hate. How can I believe that Uncle Akmal, for example, is a threat to Islam? He has always been Barelvi, he understands Islam in his heart, very deeply, even if he does not wish to carry it into politics. He is weak, but he is not the enemy. Some of their remarks I heard... they could have been addressed against Uncle himself—they might have been willing to kill him at a shrine—just because of his ideas."

"You're right, Salman," Majeed said softly. "Those views are extreme—and dangerous."

Salman's eyes teared over and he tried to hide it. "I can't help it, it reminds me of the killing of my parents and my sister. That wasn't about religion, but it was killing, for nothing, for some stupid tribal something!"

Zubayda went over and hugged Salman from behind and let his emotional moment pass in silence.

"Salman, I'm really sorry about all of this," Majeed said. "That's why I say, I don't think you want to be associated with this."

Salman remained silent for a few moments and then recovered. "OK, but that does not mean I don't believe some forceful action must be taken, especially against foreign occupation. I support them one hundred percent in that. But not... not in this war among Muslims. I want to talk about this more when I go back. I understand their anger. But I don't know how can it be directed in the best way. I'm not sure how to follow up. I am going to go back, in about three months."

"But you can't raise your objections, they won't accept that!" Majeed cried. Salman raised his hand to fend off further discussion.

Majeed was dismayed but he did not want to push the argument further now, it might cause Salman to dig in his heels. And over the following weeks he heard more from Salman about his concern over violence being perpetrated against Muslims rather than against the foreigners. Majeed hoped that he might be able to dissuade him from returning.

"I have to go back, Majeed, I am committed. If I quit they will be suspicious. And I believe we must maintain the armed struggle. But we must take our struggle against the state, the police, the soldiers, the Americans—not to the ordinary people. Even Mother, when I was young, I remember when she heard some of this anti-Shi'a talk she didn't even understand it. 'But they are Muslims too, and isn't it wrong in Islam to take human life?' That's all she said."

"She was right, Salman. Once someone starts down the path to killing they will stop at nothing. It gets into your own blood, a blood lust. I need to ask you, do you still identify with these people?"

Salman squirmed under the increasing pressure to define his inchoate feelings. "Yes, some. Their dedication and will is incredible. I saw in some of them a total self-possession and self-control. Their personality had become one with the mission, like a meditation. They almost never smiled. Life and the mission were deadly serious for them, like it was the very purpose of their existence. But I sometimes felt the hearts of many of them, I don't know, they seemed absolutely closed. Not closed, but frozen, untouchable. Most never discussed their personal stories. But with Palestinians and Chechens, for example, God knows what horrors had come into their lives, to their families. I have total sympathy for them."

"But do you want to become like that, I mean, cold, frozen? You haven't experienced having to kill people yourself."

"That's what one of the trainers told me. 'You have not personally experienced such deprivations, and persecution; it has not fused itself to your body and entered your bones.' I objected to that, I said I had thought a lot about these things and believed in them. He just said, 'You are driven by an intellectual perception of the truth of Jihad. But the intellect cannot drive your soul. Your intellect will not support you to go ahead and kill the enemy. Your intellect will fail you under such pressures, Abu Sayf. You also lack the will to obey orders as received.' That's what he said. I didn't know if he was condemning me or what. He said they did not plan to use me for military operations at this point. They want to use my skills to recruit other brothers over to our cause."

"Salman, Salman, I implore you, try to stay out of this. These are dangerous people. You're going to get hurt."

"I can watch out for myself. There are many different types of people there. And I have to know myself. I have to know that I am not a coward. That I am willing to stand up and be counted. That I can take some part in the Jihad for our country against the enemy. I have to go back, Majeed."

*   *   *

The more intelligence reporting the Station received, the more Alex developed deep forebodings about the direction of events in the country and the rising jihadi presence. The only person he could really communicate this to on the Pakistani side was Majeed.

"Pakistan is playing with fire, Majeed, working with these jihadis and Taliban. They don't seem to have any mission except damaging the West now, hitting the US, anywhere and everywhere. This is total nihilism."

Alex was over at Majeed's for another personal late-night session, his head filled with the rising tempers in Washington over the setbacks the US was facing in Afghanistan and the incessant quest to make Pakistan fix their problem. Majeed's private stash of Dimple had loosened their tongues as they sat in the library, the latest bottle courtesy of Alex.

"Frankly, Alex, it saddens me to hear this—from you of all people. You have been reading too many press releases from the White House. Don't you see what's going on here? Of course these people here are angry, they hate the US for your bombings and your air bases and your drones—your desire to keep Pakistan in a weaker position vis-à-vis India. This is not just about some 'jihadi ideolology!'"

"You are talking too much to the hard-core types, Majeed. I'm not sure that that is the view of the average Pakistani here."

"Hard-core types! Look, dammit, my own cousin has been caught up in all of this. He used to be smitten with the American rock lifestyle. Now he himself has gotten radicalized!"

"Salman? OK, a bunch of university students sitting around debating the state of the world, that doesn't..."

"You don't know what in hell you are talking about Alex! For your information, Salman decided to go off for training in the camps. How about that? Damn right, this is striking us in the heart of our own family!"

"Salman did?"

"Yes, Salman did. I shouldn't be telling you this, and I hope you can at least watch out that your maniacs at the other end of the Predators don't target him!"

"Majeed, I'm astonished. I mean, I'm really sorry to hear that. He could get killed... I can't believe that he could buy into all that violence and killing. He seems like a sensitive kid. I remember him when he was up to his eyeballs in American rock, an American wannabe, desperate to go to the States."

"Yes, he was like that once. And now he's not. What's happened? That's what we need to think about. And I'm very worried. Not least because he could get himself killed. But you think this kind of motivation comes from hearing a few speeches and reading a few books? Nonsense, this comes from seeing this reality around us, around the world, month after month, year after year. He's an idealist. This isn't about some theory. He is angry at what he *sees*. There are tens of thousands more out there like him."

"Well, he must be pretty blind not to see how crazy some of these jihadis are. They are killing more of their own people in their struggles than they are killing US troops in Afghanistan."

"You think he doesn't know that? Let me tell you something about Salman. He is a thoughtful kid. He feels outrage from things he thinks are wrong in our country. He is also upset about the bloodshed by jihadis against other Muslims. He has a social conscience. He thinks. He is deeply ambivalent about these jihadis now. That goes for countless people across our society— torn over all this violence and where your Afghan war is pushing us!"

"How can you be so sure?"

"Because he's told me, that's how. He was back from the camps a few weeks ago. He is back at university for the moment, but he has also been searching his soul. He's troubled by this, the seeming willingness of jihadis to kill fellow Muslims in the struggle. We're not all just Muslim automatons on kamikaze autopilot you know!"

*   *   *

Akmal's hearth of faith radiated a warmth that increasingly touched Alex. Alex found himself increasingly drawn to Akmal: his gentleness, his knowledge, thoughtfulness and wisdom. He seemed to represent a religious person who was fully integrated into his faith and the depths of its joys as well as its political and social problems. Akmal too, enjoyed Alex, because Alex showed a genuine appreciation for Pakistani culture in all its manifestations. So one day while Alex was at Majeed's, Akmal suddenly turned to Alex and said, "Let me take you to the Lal Mian Shrine." And Alex accepted the invitation to visit this well-known local shrine. He knew it would help him gain a personal feel for the swirling patterns of religious debate and confrontation in the country.

As they alighted from their taxi and began to walk the remaining distance through a park, Akmal tugged on Alex's elbow. "Let's stop and have a sweet," he suggested. "I would like to chat for a few minutes." They entered the Jameel sweet shop and sat out in the back under the trees, a spot they had almost all to themselves. A slight breeze relieved the worst of the heat, twisting the leaves of a eucalyptus langorously over their heads. After the waiter delivered a plate of *gulab jamun* and *ras malai* swimming in the usual sugar syrup and two sweet cups of *chai*, Akmal studied Alex for a moment. "I have something to tell you. It is a story, something that you should know. Do you remember the attack on the Police Station in Jamilabad some months ago?"

"Yes, Akmal, I do. Wasn't that carried out by some Punjabi group?"

"So it was. But I happen to know one of the young men who was involved."

"You do? My God, how?"

"He is the son of a clerk who works in my law office. I have known the boy for years when he worked as a *chai-wallah*, fetching tea and sweets for the office. The boy—he's now a young man—came to see me about a year or so ago because he knows that I study Islamic texts. I was horrified to learn that he was not looking to study religious texts, however. He was contemplating a suicide mission. And he wanted me to help him justify it."

"In religious terms."

"Yes."

"That's a tough situation. What did you say, if I may ask?"

"I heard him out. He is a very angry young man. He feels humiliated by the situation that the country is in. He is angry at his own position in society. His father is a lowly clerk, has little money and cannot afford to send him to university. He is intelligent but feels that the country is corrupt and failing in its educational commitments to students. And a cousin of his, involved in a guerrilla organization fighting in Kashmir, was killed by Indian police. He blames government here for abandoning the national honor and selling out to America. He wants to take action against our government."

"What did you tell him?"

"I told him that the situation was much more complex than just the Americans and the Indians. That we have many longtime problems of corruption here, a need for reforms in the education system, many other things. I told him an act of violence would not fix any of these things. Well, the short of it is, he was not persuaded. He said that people must take action to end this situation. He believes that the Quran justifies such action in the name of Islam."

Akmal poked at his *gulab jamun*, cut off a piece of the dough and watched the sugar syrup bleed out of it. He then stirred the piece of fried dough around in the syrup, caught up in thought for the moment.

"He begged me not to tell his father. I told him that it would be hard for me to remain silent in the circumstances out of my concern for him and what he might do, in some misguided fashion. And then I told him, first off, that Islam does not justify suicide, for any reason. And second, that if it involved killing innocent civilians it violates all Islamic teachings."

"But he wasn't convinced?"

"No, he was not. We met several times and discussed various surahs in the Quran and several quotes from the sayings of the Prophet. I told him that God does not approve of killing except in self-defense and that if he did what he was thinking of doing that it would be a sin, not a blessing." Akmal sighed. "But he did not wish to hear it. He said it *was* in self-defense, that Americans were in his country and Afghanistan and killing Muslims and that government was impotent. He was intent on finding religious justification for his intentions and wanted my help. I told him I could not—that it was wrong."

Akmal mulled the narration in his mind.

"And, at length, the boy stopped coming to see me. After a few weeks I felt I had no choice but to go to his father. His father had become aware of his son's state of mind and intentions. He told me his son had gone off to meet with a well-known mullah associated with Lashkar al-Tayyiba—you know, the group that calls for guerrilla action against the Indian authorities in Kashmir and attacks against the Pakistani government and the Americans. His father could not stop him." Akmal paused again. "Three months later he got the news that his son had been part of the squad that attacked the police station in Jamilabad. He blew himself up in front of the building, killing the guards and enabling the other attackers to break into the building."

"That's awful, Akmal. I'm sure you feel terrible about it all."

The waiter approached them with more *chai* and Akmal fell silent for the moment. As the waiter retreated, Akmal looked directly at Alex. "I do, Alex, I do. Worse, I feel helpless. I had this young man's life in my hands for several weeks while we talked. But I was not able to dissuade him. When I could not deliver the religious justification he sought, he went off to find someone who would give it to him. And that is what depresses me in all this."

"That you can't dissuade young men from their own interpretation of the Quran?"

"No, that's not all of it. It's like he had settled in his own mind on the action he wanted to take. He only wanted my blessing for it. When I refused to tell him he was right, when I refused to give him that religious blessing, he

266

went to find it elsewhere. It's like he was shopping around. There is always someone who will sell what a buyer is looking for."

Alex sighed. "That is a grim account, Akmal. It supports what I have come to feel over the past few years. That it's not the texts that are sending young men off to die, but rather young men who are angry enough for various reasons to kill and die—and they go out to search for the texts and the interpretations and the mullah—anything—to justify what they have already decided to do."

"You are right, that is indeed the situation."

Before he could think better of it Alex asked, "Could you tell me the name of the young man?"

Akmal looked uncomfortable. "Alex, pardon me, but I would rather not. His father and family have suffered enough and there will be no good for them if the American authorities get interested in them as well."

Alex kicked himself for stepping over a line. "I respect your wishes, Akmal. And I thank you for telling me this story."

They slowly got up to go off to the shrine. "That's what is most on my own mind. We have seen how this cancer is now spreading into our own families. I see it in the thinking and actions of my nephew."

Alex chose not to admit knowledge of Salman's doings, but apparently Akmal had become aware of them, despite Majeed's efforts to cover them up.

"We have never seen anything quite like this before. I would never preach violence, but I must be frank and say that I think external intervention by foreign forces is the last straw for us—only driving our poor country to civil war."

"But you admitted that so many of these problems are old ones."

"Yes, that is true. But somehow we had always managed these problems, in our own way. Now they are out of hand. People now feel they have license and public support to act, especially when violence—and war just over the border—is all around us and foreign countries are trying to direct our policies. I abhor all this violence, Alex, but I have to confess, I also understand it. Worse, I can sometimes sympathize with it, even while I hate it. That is even more disturbing."

They walked on and came to the enclosure of the shrine. Not unexpectedly, numerous men dressed in the typical fundamentalist clothing stood around the entrance publicly denouncing Barelvi practices and visitations to shrines. This was becoming commonplace around the country. They questioned those who sought access to the shrine, there was some shouting and gesticulating.

"You ignorant Barelvis," the man railed, "you come here and kiss the ground and the tomb of holy men and bless your *pirs* and give them money—you think Pakistan will benefit from this? Or the umma? You curse the Deobandis, but we are the educated ones. We are the ones fighting to remove superstition from your minds and hearts. We call on all Muslims to fight against the foreign occupation. You Barelvis will do nothing and change nothing, you only look to God to help you. Well, God will help only those who move in his path as he has directed."

Many in the crowd raised their fists and shouted back. Akmal drew Alex aside. "He is not all wrong you know. The hearts of the Deobandis are filled with anger and not with love. I condemn that. But they are right—there are superstitions among us Sufis and Barelvis. We often spend more time talking about miracles than on concrete issues of our people. And we are slow to raise our voice in politics. And the *pirs* who speak to us of God, they are often supported by the big landowners who don't want change in the system. I despair of how we are going to bring people together."

Akmal turned to face Alex. "I sometimes wonder… if I were seventeen years old, might I not pick up a gun and go and fight? Violence is wrong. But what do we do in the face of injustice and violence here and across the border?"

Alex was shocked to hear Akmal granting some truth to the arguments of the fundamentalists. "Surely you don't believe the Deobandis are really right?"

"Alex, we are tired. Tired of seeing our society flooded with money—Saudi Wahhabi petrodollars and American dollars—all to fight more! Saudi money is helping build Deobandi mosques while the Barelvis struggle to keep their existing mosques in shape. But it has become worse. These Deobandis now seek to intimidate visitors. Yes! I feel intimidated, and at the entrance to my own shrine. And I am afraid, Alex, that it is not wise for you as a foreigner to try to enter the shrine today. I thought it might be more open. But it is being watched. There could be an incident. Let us go back." And they walked back the many blocks to a bus stop.

"I am embarrassed for you and for me," Akmal continued. "But we live in times of stress. In fairness, it is not just the fundamentalists. We find a whole wave of greater religious fervor growing, even among the simpler believers. We hear about crazy beliefs in new magical cures, in legends and in superstitions—even a new wave of miracles."

"Miracles? Like curing?"

"No, miracles of the divine presence. Only last year there was a furor about a footprint of the Prophet—Peace be upon Him. In some small place, villagers discovered the appearance of a huge footprint during Ramazan—the local mullah proclaimed it to be the Prophet's footprint and declared it a miracle, a sign of God's blessing upon the village. Can you believe it? Thousands of people came to visit the spot and they even put up a small shrine around the spot of the footprint in the earth to preserve it. People even believed the soil from the spot might help cure disease. It's crazy! But when people are uneducated, or afraid or troubled, they are gullible for ridiculous events like this. Most mullahs knew the 'footprint' was a sham, but many benefited from declaring it a miracle—even selling access to the spot. But this is it—many people now look to religion *instead of* politics. The old power structure likes that."

"Well, if it makes you feel any better, there are shrines in the West where people have observed milk coming out of the breast of a statue of the Virgin Mary, or shrouds that have the imprint of Jesus' face on it, or real tears flowing from Jesus' face."

A bus rounded the corner and approached their stop. Alex and Akmal climbed on and the bus carried them off, deprived of the blessings they had come for.

*   *   *

It was a vital piece of operational intelligence. In his irritation Majeed had been indiscreet in revealing to Alex what he should not have, and probably regretted saying later on. Salman disillusioned! Alex sensed a major opportunity. He recognized the symptoms in himself—the scent of operational prey, the anticipation of an operational coup moving toward his grasp. The hunting instinct had moved to the fore, akin to his only real hunting experience in his life when his college roommate Kevin had taken him elk hunting at his parents' ranch back in Colorado one vacation. Alex had told Kevin he didn't like the idea of hunting, had never done it, and didn't want to go. But Keven and his father had persisted. The next day all three of them were out in a blind in the woods on a cold and frosted autumn dawn, and Alex was holding a rifle after having been briefed on its use—waiting for an elk to come into the clearing near a pond. They had already drunk a good bit of whiskey "to keep warm," as they waited. It seemed like hours before a big six-point buck did in fact appear. Kevin signaled for Alex to take the shot. When Alex raised the rifle and caught the elk in the scope, a raw, primitive urge coursed through him, the power of life and death in his hands. He could actually kill—yes, possess—this large creature if his shot was skillful. The elk suddenly spooked, looked up, and was ready to bound off. Alex's entire body and mind focused, just on this one thing. Perhaps a call to the latent human hunting instinct over tens of thousands of years—the thrill of the hunt and the kill, when bloodlust took over. He controlled his trembling, took one last sight, and pulled the trigger. The buck staggered, looked around, and dropped heavily to its knees and then fell over on its side. It was a near-perfect shot, blind beginner's luck. Alex had got his buck. As they left the blind to approach the dead animal, Alex's thrill of the kill began to yield to guilt as he surveyed the magnificent creature on the ground, its eyes glazed, no longer of the great woodlands to which it had belonged. It supplied a lot of meat to Kevin's family and neighbors. For Alex it had been a transforming experience, in which the urge to capture prey had overcome moral hesitation.

He now felt the visceral professional instinct kicking in, the possibility of nailing Salman. Salman could provide great insight into a center of jihadi mission planning and operations. Alex knew how hard it was to recruit someone inside one of these organizations; even to come in contact was difficult. But he was in a privileged position, he already knew Salman from years ago, and Salman knew him. There was a chance this could work.

*   *   *

This was his forest and he was now stalking the elk again. The simple tea kiosk was a short way from the entrance to the School of Theological Studies, in a small stand of trees that provided some shade and refuge from the blazing heat of the sun. The school was part of the new International Islamic University of Islamabad. Islamabad's newness lacked the patina of time and tradition that characterized other cities like Lahore, Karachi or Peshawar possessed of great history. Islamabad was orderly to a fault, a touch too organized and meticulously laid out, the product of the architect's drawing board and the city planner's schemes. It lacked the crowds and the anarchic vibrancy of the traditional cities.

But it was still majestic and had its own appeal. Somehow Islamabad's architecture made good on its promise to fuse the modern with Islamic tradition—capturing Mughal greatness even while departing from its designs, especially in the blazing white stone of so many government buildings, that had taken over from the classic red sandstone of the British Raj. The University had preserved something of the reddish-pink brick, the iconic Mughal color of Lahore. Soaring arches dominated the outside, reminiscent of madrasas of old where theological studies had been conducted. And at the center of each building was a delightful courtyard containing a verdant garden, breathing peace and tranquility to the visitor, an oasis in the hottest pre-monsoon days. In the distance shimmered the blue hills and game reserves of Margalla, the hill-stations in the foothills of the Himalayas that provided refuge from the hotter seasons of Islamabad and neighboring Rawalpindi.

This was where he awaited his elk. Alex sat under a tree, imagined himself a student again, perhaps right here at the International University. He would love to be at a place like this, to study Persian, the Sufi poetry of Rumi and Hafez whose lines were endlessly quoted in Muslim literature. Or study the deep resonance and powerful rhythm and formality of classical Arabic, the foundation of Islamic culture and vocabulary.

What had drawn him to all of this? He sorted through the unlikely chain of events that had brought him to this point, here and now in Islamabad, waiting for his target. An odyssey that had started with his parents' feckless quest to help—and convert—the heathen. Had their projects, in the end, been really all that distinct from his own? Even many of his professional colleagues at the Embassy had grown up in the corn-fed innocence of the American Eden, for whom hardship, violence and political agony was the stuff of a thirty-second TV clip covering overseas chaos, or bad guys to be mowed down on an Xbox screen. His colleagues had all been astonished to learn that Christian missionaries had even existed in this day and age in Pakistan, much less as a household to grow up in.

Would not his own present work seem familiar to his father's—a similar, if rather less divine, quest? Perhaps to some in Washington it indeed was a divine quest—the same process of conversion to the ideals of the shining City on the Hill. The mission was deeply internalized, almost unconscious as statesmen spoke of "America the exceptional country." Its range of foreign policy instruments each playing its own role in the grander cause promoted through aid, "security support" to friendly tyrants, or through the gun. To students of the Roman Empire it would sound familiar—the recruiting of talented barbarians into Roman ranks to become loyal footsoldiers in the expansion and administration of Empire. And in CIA the particular path lay through recruitment of select heathens into the ranks of global CIA agents, to further the national cause of a country that saw itself as the hope and future of the world.

Did not that too require some form of religious belief? A faith in the importance, justice and validity of the American global mission? To leave home and come to these places and live under conditions many Americans would shrink from, devoid of the trappings of the good life? Wasn't the very mission of America itself a quest for the Holy Grail, for the future good and wellbeing of all of mankind, "life, liberty and the pursuit of happiness?" How strangely these words of Jefferson rang when seen against the conditions of all of humanity for most of its history; how incredibly presumptuous in their boldness of reach and idealistic vision. Could these words ever ring true in Pakistan as well? Or did Pakistanis, and most of the rest of the world, aspire only to more modest, but no less blessed, attainments of life such as good health, order, family security, life within a community and a religious tradition that offered nurture and solace. A kind of pursuit of happiness of its own, but no less meaningful. And now here he was, poised to interact with Salman—an immediate, specific, small, concrete, finite task that made up a tiny mosaic piece of the American global quest.

It was only a week ago that Alex had first slowly surveilled Salman from his car as he left Majeed's home to go the university by rickshaw; Alex had observed where and when he came and went for classes. Salman had grown a longer beard since Alex had seen him last. An "accidental" meeting, far from Majeed's home, might lead to more engaged talk.

Salman had gotten out of class yesterday in the Faculty of Theology and Islamic Jurisprudence at noon, but he had been accompanied by two friends out to the street where they all piled into a rickshaw. Alex, now standing some distance away, had had no opportunity for an approach. Today at 12:10 Salman still had not emerged. And then he saw him come out, again with a friend in tow. As Alex watched from a distance, he saw the friend then wave to Salman and walk off in the opposite direction, leaving Salman to proceed down toward the main street again.

Alex moved quickly up the path to the Faculty building. He walked toward Salman who had his eyes on the ground, and began to pass him by, then Alex stopped, turned and looked. "Salman, is that you?"

"Yes?" he replied, looking up at Alex, surprised, uncertain for a moment, then recognizing him, and then glancing down again with no particular enthusiasm. "It's you. What do you want?"

"I was just over here to get some course information. A friend of mine in the States is getting a degree in Middle East studies, he was interested in knowing about the University's courses on Islamic civilization."

"Well, you can find material inside the Faculty," he said, turning to go.

"Do you have any recommendations on special departments here that are really worthwhile?"

"No, it depends on your friend's interests," he said tersely, and again turned to go.

"Look Salman, I know you don't think much of the US right now. And you know I work at the Embassy. But don't judge me by that. Frankly I'm pretty disgusted myself with a lot of US policies. They are wreaking havoc in this country—I know that—and I know the US doesn't seem to get it. I have a lot of sympathy with what your generation thinks about things."

"I don't think we have that much to talk about. We wouldn't agree."

"You might be surprised. As time passes I think some of the students here were more right about the situation in Pakistan than I was. And I grew up here. But I failed to see how deep the disillusionment is among younger generations. And our Embassy doesn't see it at all."

"Good. I'm glad you are realizing America's mistakes. But they are still proceeding on. You are still killing people in Afghanistan, and now here."

"We did help to get rid of the Soviet invaders. They would have destroyed Islamic civilization in Afghanistan. Give us that much credit."

"Yes, you got rid of the Soviets. But then you made your own invasion. And you want to get rid of Islam just as much as the Soviets, only in your own way." As they stood there in the hot sun, Alex was vividly aware how thin his intellectual hook-line into Salman was—it was about to snap at any moment.

"Salman, I'm upset you would say that. It's just not true that the US wants to destroy Islam, whatever differences it has with Pakistan."

"You wouldn't understand. Now, excuse me, I need to go to lunch."

"Look Salman, try me. I have struggled a long time to understand this country. It's part of my life. I'm studying Urdu literature right now on my own. I know better than anybody that if the US doesn't begin to grasp some of these realities, we're just headed for more trouble. These bloody US hardliners and flag-wavers, they're running our policies right now. It's part of my job to convince them that they're wrong, convince the military about what the realities really are here."

"They don't want to know, just to conquer."

"Yes, some of them do want to conquer. I hate to say it, but it's true. Look, I'd be really grateful if we could talk some of this over a little more."

"I can't, I'm busy, I need to have lunch before my next class."

"How about having a quick bite with me at least before you go."

"No, Alex, really, it's not... it's not really appropriate."

"What's not appropriate? That we talk about the realities here, how students are thinking? I need the ammunition."

Salman looked trapped. He hesitated. "OK, just some tea for a few minutes."

"I'm hungry too. How about a little better restaurant, where it might be cooler, more comfortable."

"No, there's a little open tea garden a few blocks over."

Alex had to assent. But when he saw the place he knew the highly public venue was far from ideal. Still, he couldn't risk pushing Salman to go to a fancier, less public place. He was lucky to have brought him even this far.

They sat down under the trees at a small rickety wooden table with peeling blue paint around which a few stools were placed. Alex tried to find one less visible from the street. Bare lightbulbs were strung through the trees for evening use. Kebabs, naan and tea were the standard fare.

The waiter appeared to be a student who gave them a surly glance—the Westerner with an obvious local student.

"Are you still living at Majeed's?" Alex asked innocently as he stirred sugar into his glass of dark tea.

"Yes."

"So where do you think you'll go after you finish your studies here? Do you want to be an academic? Or join government service like Majeed?"

"I don't know yet."

"I remember meeting you when you were thinking about going to university in the States. When you were so into rock and we talked about U2 and Metallica? That was around the time when my father was so badly beaten."

Salman softened at the memory. "Yes, I'm sorry that happened. That was bad."

They sat in an uncomfortable silence for a few minutes. "Tell me, Salman, I notice you seem to be more religious than when I knew you many years ago. What do you think is bringing all this youth to Islam?"

"The conditions of course. Look at this country. Look at the wars all around in the region. We're weak and pathetic. Only Islam will strengthen us, give up purpose, give us pride, dignity. Liberate our country."

"Islam can help provide purpose, I agree, but still, it's going to take more than that. Like raising literacy, fighting the power of these bloodsucking landlords in the countryside. I notice the Jamaat-e-Islami, for all its talk about Islam, doesn't even seem willing to take on the landlords, or even criticize the social order."

"They are compromised, like so much else here," Salman flared. "If we have a true Islamic society, landlords won't be able to oppress the poor like they do. That is not social justice."

Alex had opened the door a crack. Salman was at least acknowledging weaknesses in the major Islamist party in the country.

"It sounds like the university may be a little tame for your thinking, then."

"Tame, yes. Most of these professors follow the traditional line. They're not fighters."

"Are you a fighter?"

"Yes. If I can be."

"So what party do you think can bring a real Islamic social agenda here?"

Salman shifted on is seat. "Look, I don't really want to talk about this. Go talk to the party officials, that's your job."

"OK, I know you are pissed off. I don't blame you. At least help me make your case, get some of these realities through to the dunderheads in Washington."

"Washington doesn't want to know the realities."

"Maybe. But what about you? Are you thinking at all of going abroad to study? UK? US?"

Salman looked up. Another student with an Islamic beard was approaching. Alex cursed under his breath. This was exactly what he had hoped to avoid.

"Salaam aleikum, Salman, are you going to class?" he asked in Urdu. He stared at Alex. Alex made no move to greet him or shake hands, and the student remained standing looking him over.

Salman looked nervous. "Yes, just a second, I'll go with you." Salman stood up and collected his book bag.

"Nice to run into you Salman, give my regards to your cousin," Alex said clearly as Salman scarcely nodded to him and went off.

Alex seethed. That was precisely why he hadn't wanted to come to this place. The meeting had barely gotten under way. Salman had had a scarcely concealed hostile attitude, and Alex had had little time to soften him up through personal warmth. He had lost a precious opportunity to explore any follow-up—it wouldn't be easy to contrive another meeting. Worst of all, they had been seen.

*   *   *

When Salman got home late that evening from the University, he saw the light still burning in Majeed's study. He peered around the open door from the darkened dining room and knocked.

"Salman, how are things at the University?"

"OK, Majeed. But it's about something else that I've come to see you."

"Sure, go ahead. Is it about the camps?"

"No, it's that guy, that friend of yours, Alex."

"What about him?"

"Just what is he doing? He's sniffing around me in strange ways. Didn't you tell me he is a CIA officer?"

"No, I didn't say that, but he does work at the US Embassy. Why, what's he been doing?"

"I ran into him at the University today, outside the Faculty building. He stopped me on the path—at first I didn't recognize him. He gave me some story about getting information for a friend on the curriculum. But then he seemed to want to continue the conversation with me and just about dragged me to lunch. Said he wanted to have a better feeling for what students are thinking."

"Yes, he's an intelligence officer. But just keep that to yourself. I'd avoid him, Salman. He probably wants to use you as a source of information, maybe even try to recruit you as an agent. There's nothing good in it for you."

"That's what I thought, and I was uncomfortable in the situation. But he was persistent. But then it got worse—a classmate of mine from the Islamist student group saw me having tea with him, and came up to us. He saw Alex and asked me about him later."

"What did you tell him?"

"I just said he was a friend of yours, that I'd met him in the house here a long time ago. He asked where Alex worked and I said I didn't know, I thought maybe in the US Embassy."

"That's unfortunate, Salman, an unfortunate situation..." The light from the goose neck desk lamp highlighted the shadows around Majeed's face as he looked away for a moment. "All I can recommend is that you avoid him, no matter what, given the present atmosphere."

"I will, I didn't even want to talk to him."

"I'll have a few words with him. He's not all bad—he understands a lot about this country, and he's interested in it, you know, he cares, he speaks Urdu... but he's tied up with that bloody Embassy and that's no good."

"I don't care if he does speak Urdu, he represents the kaffirs and the imperialists. You shouldn't encourage him either."

"Look, Salman, it's complicated. I've known him since we were boys together. But you're right. We can't trust him. And meantime, what are your plans? I hope you aren't still thinking of back to the camps again. It's dangerous."

"I'm helping by taking some more brothers over there for more vetting. We need a lot more people trained up for resistance groups if the damn Americans try to bring the war into our country. I will probably go back with a few possible recruits in a few weeks."

"I thought you said you had some doubts about what they are doing."

"Yes, well, I do in some ways. They can be harsh. And I sometimes worry they are going to lose support from the students if they're too tough on people or encourage killing among Muslims. And sometimes their goals are too extreme—like banning all music and imposing beards. But they are disciplined, they have to be, there are a lot of spies around—like your friend."

"For God's sake be careful, Salman. This is really dangerous stuff."

"Don't worry, I'll stay out of trouble. *Shab ba khair*, Majeed. Goodnight."

And Salman went out of Majeed's study and into the darkened house and up the stairs to his room at the far end of the hall.

*   *   *

Majeed had scarcely waited until a decent hour to call Alex the next morning. "Alex, I need to see you right away." They agreed to meet at the Intercon coffee shop in two hours. Alex had little doubt that it had to do with Salman.

Majeed had chosen a table well over in the corner. As Alex approached he did not even rise to shake his hand, dispensing with all greetings or courtesies. "Do you mind telling me what in hell is going on between you and Salman?"

"Calm down, Majeed. It's nothing. I ran into him at the University. I invited him for a quick tea, that's all."

"Can't you see he doesn't want to have bloody tea with you? What are you trying to do with him?"

"Nothing, Majeed, nothing. I just wanted to talk about what he's up to, how he sees the local situation."

"Listen Alex, don't pull that innocent crap on me. You know damn well you're looking to recruit Salman—or any other kid to get access. This was a pretty crude attempt."

"Look, there was no 'crude attempt.' We barely even talked about politics, we were talking about his courses and things."

"Yeah, and if you hadn't have been interrupted, how far would things have gone? Would you have tried to sign him up?"

"Nobody's trying to sign anybody up, Majeed. Come on! Of course I'm interested in his views, he's close to these Islamist circles."

"I'm really browned off about this. I view this as a personal betrayal. You went after a member of my family because I was indiscreet enough to tell you about what he thinks on all this jihad business. You deliberately exploited our friendship, my confidence, to try to recruit Salman. That is outrageous."

"I have a right to talk to people around town. It's part of my job."

"Not when you're a goddam intelligence officer, you don't! Not when you're approaching my own family, you don't!"

Alex rebooted his mind. The invocation of family ties had touched a chord with him to which he had been professionally insensitive. "OK, I'm sorry Majeed. I won't see him any more."

"Please stay away from him. God knows how much trouble you may have already caused." Majeed rose from the table as the waiter brought the coffees. "And you better decide how far you're willing to compromise yourself in the interests of your bloody 'Global War on Terror.' He turned and walked out the door leaving Alex and the coffee untouched.

Alex sat slumped in his chair as he felt the tide sweep out to sea and there was nothing he could do to stop it. From behind his table the globalized pablum of American hotel lobby elevator music played on, undaunted by local events in pursuit of its soothing one-size-fits-all mission.

That night Alex could not sleep. He kept rerunning the conversation with Majeed through his head. He cringed and felt more keenly the shame of injecting professional work into personal relationships. In the end he really knew better. That was one of the reasons he had objected all along to coming to Pakistan on an ops assignment. Fortunately he hadn't done anything actually untoward with Salman, but Salman sensed his intentions had clearly been operational. And Majeed knew it. Even if Salman could only dimly understand what was going on.

*   *   *

Afzal entered the shack, trembling, where the commander Abu Muntaqim was hunched over the table, his black eyes and beetling eyebrows fixed on a detailed map of the terrain. He looked up as Afzal entered, said nothing and looked back at his work. He sensed Afzal's extreme nervousness. "What is on your mind, brother?" he finally asked.

"I... I don't know what to do, Muntaqim," Afzal stuttered. "I have some information. I don't know what to say."

"Well, if it is important, speak!" the commander answered, still making notations on the map.

"It's about brother Salman. You know I helped recruit him into our group..."

"Well?"

"It's just that... I'm afraid he is in contact with the Americans, maybe with the CIA." He ran his hands down over his face.

The commander looked up. "And what evidence do you have of such a thing?" he barked.

"I can't be certain, but I know that he has met with this CIA officer, through his cousin. Maybe more than once."

"And how do *you* know this so-called CIA officer?"

"He is an old friend of Salman's brother, Majeed Rehman who is working with ISI. Salman himself told me about this officer years ago, his name is Alex—Sikendar—I don't know the family name."

Abu Muntaqim frowned. "That is a very serious accusation, brother Salman, very serious. In fact it is deadly criminal libel if you are wrong. Are you aware of the consequences, in either case, according to our law?"

"Y-yes…yes, Chief, I am." He cast his eyes downward.

"Why are you telling me this if you are not certain?"

"Because I have had this suspicion for some time, I can't keep it to myself. Salman seemed to ask too many questions as I brought him into the movement."

The commander was silent for what seemed like minutes. "Very well, I will open an investigation on this matter. For your sake I can only hope that you are right. If you are raising needless suspicions, blackening the reputation of a serious and committed fighter, that is a crime against our movement and you will pay dearly for it."

"I understand, chief. I would not have come to you if I was not sure, and afraid for what Salman's actions could mean to all of us."

"Return to your tasks, Afzal. I will look into it. Naturally you will say nothing to raise the slightest suspicion on Salman's part. God help you both."

Afzal left the room. Muntaqim was shaken by the charge. He was fond of Salman, he seemed to be one of the more dedicated and intelligent of the young brothers, even if still lacking the guts to carry out a mission, but he knew from experience that would come with time. Surely this story could not be true. But Afzal would not make such a charge lightly. One of their two lives lay in the balance. He heaved a sigh and picked up his field telephone. After a few minutes he got through to his immediate superior. He informed him briefly of the accusation and asked that it be investigated with discretion in Islamabad.

"Please be urgent and diligent in your investigation, Rasheed, I do not want there to be any mistakes about this."

Muntaqim hung up and stared at the wall opposite him. "God help us," he muttered. "How the enemy moves in unexpected and treacherous ways. Do not let this be so."

*   *   *

Salman was angry as he came in.

"Brother Ameen, what's this I hear? Talk about my cousin Majeed, that some of you are declaring him an enemy."

"Sit down, Brother Salman, sit down. What kind of rumors have you been hearing?" They were in a popular student teahouse.

"I've heard that some of you think he's a CIA agent."

Ameen swirled the bottom of his glass of tea around, looking at the few loose leaves swept around in the motion. He stared at Salman for a few moments. "You don't you think that is possible, Salman? Isn't he a good friend of Sikander, the CIA agent?"

"Alex. Yes, of course, Majeed knows him, they grew up together. Alex grew up in Lahore, speaks good Urdu. There's no question he's CIA. He's sneaking around all the time in the Islamist groups, has friends there. He reports to the American Embassy."

"How well do you know him?"

"I've known him ever since he was a kid here, when he made friends with my cousin Majeed. I think he's dangerous. The rest of these CIA idiots don't know much, all they've got is a bag of money to throw around. But Alex, he knows the game. Still, there's no way Majeed is working for him. I'm positive. I know my cousin."

"This kind of person could be a great a danger to us all."

"Yes…. He undoubtedly is a danger, he is active."

"Someone may need to take measures against him."

"He's an Embassy official. It won't be so easy—and it is dangerous. The repercussions could be very serious."

"We have faith in God. Now, are you willing to help? You know where Sikander can be found?"

"I could probably help. He sees my brother Majeed off and on."

"Your cousin is also a danger to us."

"Majeed is with ISI, you know that. He's part of the system. We can't single him out, I don't want to hear about it. He's not a danger."

"But can you help bring Sikander to us?"

"You mean trap him? Bring him somewhere?"

"Yes, or deal with him yourself."

"I can't kill Sikander. I know him too well. He is a friend of my cousin."

Several of the students exchanged glances.

"Can you at least find out more about what he is doing? What he wants? Catch him in that?"

Salman hesitated. "Yes, I suppose I can. I know he wants to talk to me, to get information from me."

"Then contact him, brother, and find out his game."

"I'll see what I can do."

Salman left the meeting deeply fearful. It was one thing to struggle on the battlefield, to fight in a battle or an attack. It was another thing when this struggle took place within his own home situation. Worse, his own cousin might now be in danger. Perhaps the only way he could remove suspicion would be to help entrap Alex somewhere. He should discuss this further with his commander next week when he went back to the camp.

Salman had Alex's Embassy card from the meeting at the teahouse at the University. Nobody was home when he got back and he put in a call to the number on the card. "This is Salman. I would like to meet with you."

Salman was asleep, wrapped in his blankets on the floor in the shack shared with three new brothers who had accompanied him back to the camp. The sky was tinged with red across the horizon with the approaching dawn. Six men approached the door, smashed it open with their boots, and entered—three with guns, three with long knives. The men in their blankets woke up confused in the face of the violent intrusion. One of the men with a Kalashnikov went over to Salman and kicked him in the stomach, brandishing his weapon.

"Get up, traitor!" he bellowed.

Confused, Salman struggled to extricate himself from his blankets and sit up, fending off more blows to his body. "What is this about, for God's sake!" he shouted. Another figure came up behind him, grabbed him around the neck and began to drag him out of the shack, the other sleepers pressing back against the wall in fear. As Salman kicked wildly his feet were grabbed by another figure and a rope wrapped around his legs.

"What is this about?" he screamed again.

The fighters maintained their silence as they dragged him outside and threw him on the ground. They secured his arms behind his back and trussed him with ropes. He was dragged to a chair near the outdoor meeting center in front of a table. "Tell me what is going on!" he screamed.

Other men who had been sleeping in other shacks were called outside to the square, until nearly twenty were present. Salman continued to yell, now filled with terror at the proceedings, asking for explanations. Muntaqim came up to him and slapped his face. "Shut up, you swine."

As the men assembled in the growing morning light Muntaqim surveyed them all in silence. The men glanced around uneasily, themselves uncertain as to what was going on, and why Salman was tied up in the chair.

Muntaqim offered a short prayer. Then he stared fiercely at Salman for a long time. Salman could not hold his glance and began shaking in fear at the roughness of his treatment.

"Do you know why you are here before us?"

"No, no! I have no idea what is going on. Why are you treating me like this?"

"You have no idea why we are treating you like this?" Muntaqim mocked him.

"No, I don't! Please tell me, there must be some terrible mistake!"

"Yes, Salman, there is some terrible mistake. You are a traitor. You are a spy for the CIA."

"Spy? For God's sake no, Muntaqim. I am no spy. I am a *mu'min*, a believer, I am loyal to the cause of the jihad and God, I am an enemy of America and of the CIA!"

"Do not insult us with your lies!" Muntaqim bellowed.

"I'm not lying, for God's sake, I'm not lying! What have you been told? This is all a misunderstanding. Or a slander of the enemy."

"Do not make fools of us, you filthy wretch. We know you are in contact with the CIA officer named Sikendar, Alexander!"

"Alexander? Yes, I have met Alexander, I know him, he is a friend of my cousin, Majeed. He has been to our house. But I despise him, I have insulted him, I have refused to look at him, I have spat on the ground in front of him. Yes, he is a spy, but I am not! I have offered to help have him killed."

"Do not waste our time, Salman, and insult our intelligence. Our brothers have investigated you and your contacts thoroughly. We know who you are. We know you have met with him. We have witnesses. Do not deny it!"

"I do deny it, it is not true, please, listen to me, for God's sake! Let me go! I can explain all this. I have only run into him in my cousin's house. It is my cousin who is in touch with him—not me." His shalwar darkened at the crotch as a patch of wetness spread down his thighs.

The first rays of the morning sun began to reach the hut and the square, touching the assembled fighters, and then illuminating Salman's face. He had to squint in order to see Muntaqim against the sun before him.

Salman's mind raced, accelerated by fear and terror. *This cannot be happening, it is inconceivable that I would be blamed, implicated, in Majeed's doings.*

"The time for explanations are past. There is nothing to explain, Salman. You have dishonored Islam. You have dishonored the umma. You have dishonored our cause and our struggle. And you have dishonored your brothers. You have placed them in danger before the enemy *kuffar*. You are a vile traitor. And now you are to receive your punishment!"

"I swear, Muntaqim, it is not true! I would never do such a thing! Please listen to me, for the love of God!" he screamed.

"Be silent, you treacherous snake. You will never utter another secret again." Muntaqim nodded to one of the fighters who came forward with a pair of pliers. He jammed them in between Salman's tightly-closed lips and teeth, breaking two of them, and roughly forced open Salman's now bleeding mouth. He grabbed Salman's tongue with the pliers. As Salman screamed in pain, the fighter pulled his tongue far out of his mouth, brought up his knife and sliced his tongue off far back in the mouth. It fell as a bloody hunk of gristle to the ground. Salman tried to scream but his throat gurgled in blood and spasms of terror, his eyes rolling.

As Salman's bloody mouth opened in muffled screams, Muntaqim came up behind him, grabbed his hair with his left hand and yanked Salman's head back, exposing his neck and throat. Salman struggled and nearly tipped over the chair. With his right hand Muntaqim brought up the long knife before Salman's face. And then, intoning in a thunderous voice, "Die, traitor!" he plunged the knife deep into Salman's neck and dragged it across as blood spurted from the carotids. Salman's gurgling screams ceased as Muntaqim finally cut through his windpipe, dropped the reddened knife and kicked the chair over face forward. Salman lay on the ground, his body jerking like a chicken as his life ebbed out of his body onto the arid Pashtun soil.

"God is just," were the only further words Muntaqim uttered and he walked back into his office.

*　　　　　*　　　　　*

"We have another report from Horseman, came in last night." The reports officer poked his head into Alex's office. "Looks like more feuding out there in the camps. They claim they've caught one of ours out there and executed him. I left it with COPS."

"Not one of ours, we don't have anyone out there any more. But thanks, I'll check on it."

But then Alex paled, suppressed a thought, but walked up the hall to the Chief of Operations.

"What's this about one of our guys supposedly getting executed out in Karghal Camp? We don't have anyone there now."

"Horseman just sent it in. Apparently some guy who they thought was ours, I was going to ask you about it. Some relative of Majeed Rehman?"

"Shit, no." Alex sickened. "My God, that's probably the kid who I was hoping to develop, name Salman. He's Rehman's cousin."

"We only have the guy's camp pseudonym, Abu Sayf, don't have his real name."

"If it's a relative of Rehman it's got to be Salman." His mind reeled. "My God." Alex sat down heavily on the chair next to the desk, his stomach twisting.

"It's got to be Salman. Shit. I'd met him many years ago when he was a kid grooving out on Western music and gadgets. Went off to California for a couple of years. Since then he turned into a big nationalist, hot on Kashmir, and lately he's become a true believer. He'd been over in the camps last fall. I'd heard recently from Rehman that he was getting disillusioned with it. I managed to arrange an accidental run-in with him at the University, to try to develop him, but he was very cool. I tried to take him to lunch but he insisted on tea in a *chai khana* nearby. And then some bearded buddy of his came over to us and saw us together. I can't believe it. They must have reported it somehow." His head swam at the implications, the massive fuck-up, the moral blindness, to bring it this close to Majeed's family.

"Christ, that's rough. You think that's what it was for sure?"

"God knows. But there's a good chance. Shit, what am I going to tell Rehman?"

"Nothing. We don't know for sure that's the case, and we sure as hell can't let him know we have a source in touch with the camp there."

Alex stared at the floor. "Yeah, I know. But it's gonna hit the fan sooner or later. Rehman's a friend, as well as a valuable contact, even if he isn't recruitable. God knows what he's going to say to me now. Or me to him. Jesus Christ."

He went back to his office and collapsed at his desk. He knew this was a rough business, but this? What should he say to Majeed? Should he wait until Majeed heard it through the grapevine? Or should he find the balls to tell him himself?

*   *   *

For the whole next day Alex's mind was obsessed with the incident, horrified. He couldn't sit on it, that would be sheer cowardice. He had to face his terrible culpability in what had happened. He owed it to Majeed and his family, especially if there was a prayer that their relationship would ever survive. He had to show his concern, his genuine sympathy including assumption of responsibility early on.

"Majeed? I would like to meet with you as soon as possible."

"Is this what I think it's about?" Majeed asked coldly.

"Salman."

Long pause. "What is there to say?" Majeed's voice broke. "You bloody fucking bastard..."

"Majeed, please. '*From God we come, to Him we shall return.*' Let me come over to your house this afternoon after noon prayer. I want to talk with you. My God, I'm incredibly sorry."

"What can you say to change anything? You traitor to our family! What's happened has happened. We don't want to see you any more." The phone clicked off.

Alex penned a note to Majeed and his family, consisting only of the short austere classic Quranic phrase in Arabic designed to offer comfort in hard times: *Fa inna ma' al-'usri yusra*—'Verily, after hardship will come ease.' He added, "Majeed, please forgive me, I don't know what I thought I was doing."

He felt a sickening weight sitting upon his heart, akin to nausea, physically distracting his ability to think about anything else. Alex had known of many operational disasters in the intelligence business; he had been crushed by the news of Fyodor's arrest in Santiago and his forced return to Moscow to likely death. But this was deeply personal, involving a lifelong family friend and cousin. He could rationalize that once Salman had become involved in a jihadi movement who knows what fate he might have found within it. But Alex had clearly helped secure his fatal end.

The separation of personal from professional life was always blurred, one of the constant internal struggles he faced. He knew there was a huge calculated risk in ever trying to recruit anyone to penetrate the guarded circles of jihadis. Outsiders could lose their lives in dangerous intelligence operations into which they had deliberately strayed. But this was a member of a family who meant a lot to Alex personally. Majeed knew the intelligence business, even its occasionally ruthless character—but this was different. There are always boundaries.

Death is death, yet the manner of the death added emotionally to the feeling of devastation. And yet it could come as no surprise—it was rough frontier justice designed to terrify others into obedience, so characteristic of many of these jihadi groups. Would he ever be able to face Majeed and his family again?

Isabel instantly sensed something terrible had occurred to him. He spilled out his story in general terms, although not the details of Salman being observed having tea with him in the tea house. She hugged him for minutes as they stood in the kitchen, and again in bed that night. She said how mortified she was; how tough it had to be on him. He was more than aware of what was going through her mind and he waited defensively for her to offer some broader comment on the nature of his whole enterprise—that in the end there could be no surprises in any of this to her. But she refrained from such comments; perhaps her very restraint made her implied critique all the more pointedly sharp.

*   *   *

Shit, another goddam visitor from Washington demanding my time bright and early in the morning. They seemed to be part of an unquenchable flow of paid consultants who came out to Pakistan for a week to acquire instant expertise, tick off the box and then go back to Washington to talk like field experts and collect fat consulting fees. It took more time putting out the fires that they started in Washington—sending people off half-cocked—than it did to fight the Taliban here. This time it was some Lt. Col. Bruce Culford, or former Lt. Col, now retired, double-dipping, working as a civilian for big bucks in a large consulting firm that worked for the Pentagon. Hqs message had said he was responsible for doing research on the al-Qaeda and Taliban target and was the primary specialist on Islam in his contractor outfit. Wanted to get up to speed on the Station's view of anti-Taliban and anti-al-Qaeda ops. Could Alex please be supportive?

"Name's Culford." A short man with a florid white mustache in his fifties, dressed in civilian clothes that looked more like a civilian uniform, stretched out his hand and then sat down in the chair facing Alex behind his desk. He had a querying expression on his face, seemingly sizing up Alex before opening his mouth. "So, Alex, they tell me you're Mr. Taliban out here. What kind of successes you guys having in penetrating their ranks?"

I don't need to answer to this bastard on this. "Some, Colonel. But it's a tough target. They're very tribal, they're super alert to the presence of outsiders penetrating the system."

Culford moved in closer to the desk. "I don't need to tell you, Alex, as we ramp up Special Forces operations in the Pentagon we need the intel from you guys more urgently than ever. We can follow a lot of these bad guys physically from the skies, but we can't judge the intentions, or even the affiliations. They were supposed to have been wiped out back when we took out the Taliban regime. Now the bastards are back, strong in Afghanistan, getting stronger and more aggressive in their actions in Pakistan all the time."

"No doubt. Ever think that it might be linked to the fact that *we* are getting more aggressive all the time?"

"You're not suggesting that we shouldn't be going after them."

"I'm suggesting that in a war, especially on their home turf, they're going to fight back. We shouldn't be surprised."

"This isn't just about home turf, Alex. They're engaged in an ideological crusade. They are after us, wherever we are. I doubt these fanatics are going to get more gentle if we back off. You have to understand the mentality."

"I think I do know something about the mentality, Col. I've talked to plenty of them over the years. Have you?"

"That's the job we leave up to you. From our side we're concerned about hitting the jihadis with everything we've got. The threat is growing worldwide so it's clear we're not hitting them hard enough. The way we see it, we're going to be fighting these ragheads for two generations or more. It's going to take that long to wipe them out."

"At least that long," Alex admitted. "But doesn't that suggest that the tactics you all are proposing back home may be flawed? They just seem to recruit more support across the region the more forces we bring in."

"Our thinking is evolving. The threat from radical Islam turns out to be much greater than we first thought. We thought we could deal with a lot of these fundamentalist types, as long as they weren't actually pulling triggers or throwing bombs. But it appears we've been wrong. Our study group of specialists has reached the conclusion that almost any strong believer in the Muslim faith is at bottom a would-be fanatic. There's a sea of them out there."

I'm not going to sit here and listen to this bullshit one more time. Alex bit his tongue.

"Our specialists have worked systematically through the Koran," Culford went on. "We've got all the texts and quotes, done the computer analysis. It's very clear that the Koran supports violence and conquest by force. This is deep in Islam and it's not going to change, not until these people realize that they're not going to win—ever. And that we have the power to stop them."

"Look, Colonel, you can't just go by quotations from the Quran. There are some really violent passages in the Old Testament too, like what to do to the enemies of the Israelites. The Bible can be used to justify anything if it you want it to. We need to get away from texts and talk about facts and real people on the ground and their real lives."

"It's not just the Koran," Culford insisted. "It's what they say. The whole idea of Islam is ultimately to take over the world and establish a totalitarian

Caliphate, over all of us, force everyone to become Muslim. These people are dedicated to that end."

Should I even bother to argue with this zealot? "Look, Colonel, I'm sorry, but it's a mistake to assume that all pious Muslims have that goal. You're barking up the wrong tree. At bottom it's really just a small number of radical fanatics. But they feed on a pool of a whole lot of pissed-off people. When they're under the pressure of war and foreign occupation a whole lot more of them are likely to go along with it. Our military presence is the best operational recruitment poster they have."

"Let me tell you something, Alex. I know you've been to school and speak the language, and that's all well and good. But in my view we've been too damn rational about all of this. Just because *we* are moderate, we think everyone else is too. Well, they're not. Hitler wrote *Mein Kampf* and everybody dismissed it out of hand as just wishful thinking, the rantings of a dreamer. Yet it turned out to be the blueprint for taking over all of Europe. He meant every word he wrote. Same with Islam. If we don't take the Koran seriously, we'll be the fools when they come to impose Islam and Shari'a Law on the world—by force."

"Look, Colonel, I've grown up out here, I've had Muslim friends all my life. That's just not the way most of them think. You're projecting irrational fears and end up tarring all Muslims with the same brush. We're never going to win them over with that kind of simplistic approach. Now, if you'll excuse me, I've got..."

"You may have grown up out here, Mr. Anders, but surely you don't expect them to tell you what their long-range plans are, do you? Let me just ask you something—ever hear of *takiya?*"

"Of course, it means dissembling, hiding your true goals."

"You got it. The Koran teaches Muslims *takiya*, to conceal their aims and to lie if it will promote the true faith. You can't believe anything they say, that's naïve. They have their plan—to sweet talk us all about Islam as the religion of peace, until they've infiltrated all of our societies."

"That's too damn paranoid and conspiratorial, Colonel. Muslims are as different among themselves as you and me. And they are reacting to violent conditions here. All people react to violent conditions around them."

Culford stiffened and took a hard look at Alex. "That's precisely where we've been naïve. We've got these academics running around at home now, apologists for Islam, spouting a PC line, talking about how Islam is the religion of peace. Hell, they even got the damn President talking about that after 9/11. That's what Muslims want you to believe. But the history of Islam, if you read it carefully, is a history of violence. There's no peace there."

"Colonel, I'm sorry, that's simplistic. I have indeed read the history of Islam, a great deal of it over many years, probably more than you. All religions have rhetoric of violence, as well as speaking of peace. These people here are reacting to American armies invading their lands. Sure they're violent. Violence begets violence. We didn't have this kind of Muslim violence twenty years ago."

The Colonel stared at him in disbelief. "It's a religion of conquest, Mr. Anders. That's how it spread, from day one, by the sword. Death or conversion. It was a mass terror movement. How else do you think it spread so far so fast? And let me tell you something else. They are pouring into Europe right now, and the gutless Europeans are all wrapped up in their PC games with them. Surprise, surprise, turns out the damn Muslims aren't multicultural, they play for keeps. Don't be naïve. They won't integrate, they're keeping their community locked up tight while they make more and more demands from these countries, to have special rights."

Alex felt his gorge rise, how many times had he been through this. It wasn't part of his job to hand-hold these assholes. He dropped all pretense. "Colonel, that's hysterical and phony-academic bullshit! You guys go on theorizing in a vacuum, but there's hardly one of you that's ever even seen a Muslim up close, ever met one or talked to one. Get real. Go and live in their communities before you spin your fucking theories about how every Muslim nourishes jihad in his heart!. It's thinking like that that's led us into these bloody wars of aggression in the first place."

Culford stared at him for a minute, then stood up and walked out of the office without a word, shaking his head. Alex felt sick with himself for his emotional outbreak—it would surely reach other ears.

Culford sauntered down the hall into the COPS office and sat down. "Whoa! You've got a live one in there, Jack. Seems to me Anders is more Muslim than the goddam Ayatollah hisself. You sure he's OK?"

"Alex is one of our best officers, Bruce. He may get emotional, but he knows the turf, knows Muslims, knows Islam, got a string of recruitments on his rifle that reach the ground. And, by the way, he's generally been right. Other than that, yeah, he's weird—he likes Muslims. Satisfy you?"

         *   *   *

The nights were always worst for Ramzi—the time when the world morphs out of one mode of existence into another, when light vanishes and darkness descends with its own special character. The terror of not knowing which is the true reality, when night invariably seems to overshadow day. And in his village, the rulers of the day were not the rulers of the night.

Night was when the world of the Taliban emerged. They had more or less been there in the village all along, their sympathies known. But they laid low when the rulers of the daylight world, the outsiders, the Pak army, American Special Forces and other intelligence elements strutted their presence. They spun the reality of the day, creating the force fields that pushed villagers in one direction. But the villagers knew that force field would reverse and retreat by nightfall and that new powers and authorities would emerge in the darkness. To try to reconcile in one's head both day and night, light and darkness, the imperious conflicting truths of each side only led to madness, or death. Best to see nothing, say nothing, go along, get along. If only the foreigners would depart at least there would be just one world, one reality, only one set of masters to deal with. Even if harsher, life would be simpler, its particular demands more manageable, even safer.

Right now it was the transient daylight regimen and the Pakistani lieutenant had taken Ramzi into detention for yet another time where he was to supply information on the Taliban of the night. Ramzi had been part of the Taliban movement earlier and was a known element to Pak intelligence. He had agreed to serve as an informer instead of being taken away for a long time. But that choice was exceedingly dangerous.

Empires ebb and flow; scholars in ivied institutions dedicate themselves to a study of the phenomenon. But they didn't have to be a scholar or understand the ebb and flow of empire to know what was going on here. They could smell it, taste it, feel it and see it in the subtly changing rhythms of life around them. Who were the outsiders that showed up, how often, how many, with what equipment, how nervous or how insistent, how confident, how informed, how purposeful? These were the tea leaves that the villagers were good at reading, sensing the subtle way that, what scholars called "the correlation of forces," swirled around them. They had learned over time, from nearly genetically encoded experience, when it was wise to feint to the right, feint to the left, drink tea and break bread with the outsider and for how long, or when to reach for the rifle and cutlass—all keys to preserving life and livelihood. These days the periodic broom of government and foreign forces swept less frequently and less effectively through their lives. The Taliban were not just some outside force; they were a presence in the towns and villages and cities, if not actually as serving officials, at least as sympathizers who let it be known that they were the force of the future, that Ramzi or Ahmad or Jameel or Mahmood or Mumtaz would be fools to allow themselves to be swayed by the transient power of outsiders when life and the final reckoning would always and always be local and swift.

As the balance of forces and confidence shifted, Mullah Bilal's village had decisively shifted over to Taliban rule. He told the townspeople that the time had come for change.

"Oh brothers, the *taghuti* regime in Islamabad is now clear in all its infidel colors. It is openly cooperating with the *Amreekiyun* and the *Ingileez* and other imperialists and kaffirs who seek to control our land and to destroy our Faith. We see corruption all around us! Corruption weakens us, takes our minds away from the Path of God and leaves us only to lust after earthly pleasures designed to distract us. We will have no peace, or peace of mind, until the unbelievers are expelled from our land.

"We see that many of you are still drawn to playing with the Devil's toys. Music and videos are corruption, *haraam*! They will not be tolerated in this town. The purveyors of this corruption will be given twenty-four hours to turn in all these instruments of perdition to us, so that we may burn it in a big bonfire the next night. If you have it in your homes, you will bring it to us, or we will know that you prefer the way of the unbelievers."

"Keep your daughters at home and keep them in their burqa. This is the law of God and we will not tolerate licentiousness of female behavior. Women are the light of our eyes, the preservation of our ways, the mothers of our children and our future and of our faith and our blood. They must remain pure and above reproach in their sacred duty to raise our children as good Muslims.

"Oh Muslims, we have already identified those among you who are working for the American army and the Pakistani army—the same army which has allowed itself to become a tool of the Americans. Do not doubt that we have people inside the army, inside the intelligence, inside the government who report to us. Some of these traitors will meet their fate tomorrow morning in the town square. All adult males are expected to attend and witness this punishment from God! And let this be a lesson to all of you who are hypocrites—those who speak of God and pray while yet serving the infidel state."

Ramzi had been to the barber only last week for a shave. He decided he dare not go out into the street for a week until his beard started to grow back. Meanwhile the barber down the street had closed down, his life threatened if he dared reopen or encourage Muslim men to imitate Western styles instead of going bearded and dressing as the Prophet did—may God pray for him and keep him.

Mullah Bilal might be honest, Ramzi reflected, but he attracted bad followers. The other day three bullyboys in Taliban dress had strutted into a neighboring shop that sold appliances. Among them were digital cameras, cell phones with cameras, and TV sets. After a cursory look around they condemned his shop as purveying corruption and blasphemy. They took a TV set and a camera out to the sidewalk where they ritually smashed them. Then they brought a pickup truck and loaded the condemned merchandise into their truck to take it away and "destroy" it. Ramzi had heard from others how these goods were in fact carted off to the city and sold there. It was a well-known form of extortion. In fact, many real criminals who faced punishment for theft and other offenses were often recruited into the Taliban to carry out the unpleasant duty of imposing discipline in the towns—an unpopular task. They were the worst—coarse men without religion, simply mouthing the words and the slogans while throwing their weight around and exploiting the people with petty extortions. These people had gained strength in the mounting chaos ever since the Pakistani army and the Taliban had begun their confrontations in the Frontier Province.

In the morning blaring loudspeakers mounted on a van moved through town summoning people to the main square—summons not to be ignored. As the townspeople congregated a jeep pulled up in the center of the square. The door opened and a shrouded figure was pushed out, a woman judging by the clothing. A man with his eyes blindfolded was pushed out behind her.

The crowd stiffened with fear, anticipating the brutality of the punishment they were about to witness. A stoning, in all probability. A commander in black stepped forward. They had not seen him in town before. "You are here to witness punishment of those who oppose the laws of God, or who disrespect those of us who are working to bring God's law to the people." He let the words sink in, as feelings of dread grew among the crowd.

"This woman you see before you has been guilty of speaking ill of our movement. She is sympathetic to the government. Such action is treason!" He paused for effect. "But because we are merciful, we will not take her life this time, although she deserves it. She is sentenced to one hundred lashes."

The woman, her face still covered, was brought forward and laid down on a wooden frame with her arms outstretched. Her outer coat was cut off with a knife leaving only a shirt on her upper half. A burly man with a short-handled whip with multiple straps approached. As the sentence was read formally, he raised his hand and delivered a massive blow on the woman's back covered only with the thin layer of cloth. The woman screamed and writhed but was held down. By the twenty-ninth blow she had ceased to scream and lay inert. Her skin running with blood began to appear underneath the cloth. The commander came forward and spoke with the man with the whip. "The punishment and the lashes have been severe. The offender is unconscious. It is not our intent to bring death. I lift the rest of the punishment. But death will be the response if there is any repetition of her crime." Two other men, apparently relatives, came forward and lifted her unconscious body off of the frame and carried her away.

"And now, we have before us Mirza Khan. He has been demanding bribes from the people when they come to him to register official papers on construction of homes or land sales, and government pensions. Mirza Khan has even demanded bribes before forwarding papers to the regional hospital for treatment. Traitors are not only those in touch with the enemy. They are also those who exploit the people, overcharge them for services, or who demand bribes to do the work they are supposed to fulfill for the people. God's order will not tolerate such abuse of the public trust. Such action is treason to our people, our community, our umma. It is men like Mirza Khan who make us weak and destroy our community. He shall be hanged." A truck rolled forward with a small gibbet on the back. A noose hung down. Mirza Khan was dragged forward, blubbering, begging for mercy. He was hoisted up into the truck. A black bag was drawn over his head. He was then pushed off the truck, falling only a few feet before the rope tightened. The fall did not break his neck and he remained dangling and kicking for several minutes before the motions of his body ceased.

"O Muslims, you have seen the justice that is delivered to traitors who do not serve the people. Justice is swift. You may now go to your homes. Remember that we are always here, always watching. Do not allow government agents to take advantage of you. You know they never do anything for you. And you will report all those parasites who demand bribes to do the work they are supposed to do for you as a public service."

Shaken, the crowds gradually dispersed in silence. Mirza Khan had been much disliked, and many in the town thought he had deserved punishment. His punishment came swiftly and was ugly to behold. The lessons were clear; it was unlikely that other officials would be taking bribes in the town for services owed to the people.

*   *   *

They drove up the captivating Swat river valley, where green-grey glacial waters blessed the valley plain, transforming it into a fertile agricultural garden within this mountainous area. Behind soared high peaks of the Himalayan massif. Swat—a legendary venue for Pakistanis yearning for its renowned cool, its landscapes, its fruits, and its treasure-trove of history.

"I haven't been here since I was a kid," Alex explained to his traveling companion, one of his newly arrived officers in Pakistan, who was accompanying Alex on a familiarization trip for two days. "I loved coming here, it was always so great, get away into a cooler climate, swim in the river and eat the honey-sweet fruits that grow all over the valley."

"Yeah, I've read about the area," Enrique said. "Aren't there supposed to be a lot of Buddha statues around here from way back?"

"Absolutely, we'll stop off at Saidu Sharif—a beautiful town—to spend the night. It has a great museum that houses a lot of Buddhas and some ancient Buddhist stupas still in existence too."

While Enrique launched into stories about his travels to Buddhist temples in Thailand, Alex's mind wandered in the hills around them, wondering at the extraordinary nature of this countryside now called Pakistan—the land of the Pure. What was there about it? The religious mysteries of countless faiths over the millennia seemed somehow drawn to the landscape and left their mark, the land littered with traces and footprints of beliefs, cults and rites tucked away in hills, valleys, rocks and caves. Any road in the countryside would eventually lead to a shrine of some sort, sometimes consisting of little more than a sacred spring, where thin strips of cloth tied to branches in the trees marked the spot where prayers were offered, whose origins went back to an early human presence beseeching favors from the Divine. Whitewashed rocks commemorated saints and miracles and sites where humans over millennia had sought boons from a parade of gods, prophets and holy figures who comforted, guided, and succored their visitors. Over time a revered spring or tree would take on sacred qualities as word of its potency spread and the number of visitors grew, leading to the building of a formal shrine next to it to preserve the connections to ancient local spirits. Early pagan, Greek, Zoroastrian, Hindu, Buddhist, Nestorian Christian, Muslim—who knew how far back the powers of the site had been known, acknowledged and commemorated.

Whatever the origin and evolution of a cult and its particular boons and powers might have been, by now it had probably been folded into some kind of Sufi vision and practice. These local rural shrines reflected the common faith of the people of the area and required no official acknowledgment of their importance. Indeed, other places, better trodden, more frequented, had ultimately become sites where later state authorities had decided to establish their mark, to construct the majestic red sandstone Mughal mosques that would last ten thousand years, superb and massive in their construction. But here were the messages of the eternal stones, both humble and exalted. Rivers too bore messages: sacred rivers from sacred sources, like the mighty Indus, coursing down from the frozen caves and retreats of mountain shrines high in the Himalayas, bringing their bounty to those who worked the soil in the low-lying lands of the Indus plain, along with the other Five Rivers, or Panj-ab, that ultimately wended their way down to the rich alluvial flatness of its delta in Sind before its final descent into the Indian Ocean.

As one walked the plains, river valleys, hills and mountains, these stones of the past were scattered like the bones—or eggs—of history and myth across the landscape. What would this or that egg eventually give birth to? People of this land knew the past by its bones, it was part of them, if only shrouded in myth. Here was the confabulation of thousands of years of history into select symbolic stories that contained more spiritual import than historical accuracy. Indeed, Alexander the Great—Sikender or Iskandar as he was known here— in the third century BCE had traversed these lands on the way to conquer Sind and left behind his own mythical legacy known to all. And of course, everybody knew that Sikender was a Muslim—how could he not be?— and that all these ancient ruined mosques and Muslim structures were from his time. Thus did folk religion telescope the entire past and made Sikender part of the Muslim pantheon of saints, living elements of the present, accessible to the common people. The hard-line fundamentalists might rail at the purity of the Faith being sullied through confabulation of random past pagan figures with Islam. But the impulse of the common man, the villager, was to bring together, to synthesize, to find holiness in many places, all of it good—for who could know when a useful blessing, behind a rock or tree, here or there, might be available in an hour of need.

Blessings did not have to come directly from the narrower vision of the clerics and the holders of religious orthodoxy. These Salafis, these Wahhabis, these fundamentalists, these Deobandis knew that the masses, if not kept under watchful vigilance, would drift and slide into a blasphemous pantheism that indeed regularly invested the very rocks and the streams and the mountains with holiness. That was the sin of the Barelvis who allowed the untidiness and universalism of mysticism to detract from the clear and strict laws of the Faith. And the Barelvis, as Akmal had often pointed out, did represent a spirit closer to the country. They also represented the great majority of the population for whom pervasive holiness and mystery, joy and belief transcended the drier legalistic interpretations of the law as monopolized by the clerics and political movements.

"I thought the Taliban were set on destroying the Buddhas." Enrique brought Alex back to the present.

"Yeah, Mullah Omar and his Taliban crowd did do that in Bamyan, over the border in Afghanistan—what an outrage! And now some of the most radical of them are threatening to destroy some of the Buddhas here in Swat valley as well. Muslim governments all over denounced the Taliban for their action in Bamyan, the destruction of those ancient towering Buddhist figures—even the Saudis begged the Taliban not to do it, believe it or not. But some of the Taliban went ahead anyway. That was about as stupid and primitive as these fundamentalists can get. Even the local people were all against it. But, with a war on, they're afraid to speak up."

They continued the drive up along the river valley. "What a jewel of paradise this is. My parents loved to come up in the hot season and stay at the hotel here for a few weeks, it was like going off to another world. But even then I remember that some of these Pashtun towns, like in Dir valley, were known to be very hostile to all outsiders. One time when my brother and I were sitting in the car with my mom, my father was out talking to someone getting directions. Some local kids, hell, they couldn't have been more than six years old, came up and just starting throwing sand and rocks into the car at us. The xenophobia of the Diris is legendary. And that was back in the day. God knows what it's like now."

"Is Swat like that too?"

"No, not at all, Swat was friendly, at least back then. That's the terrible thing. The war in Afghanistan is infecting all these areas, importing tensions, confrontation, polarization. Whole damn area looks like it's moving towards some kind of civil war now. It's a tragedy. It didn't have to be."

They turned a bend in the river and higher snowcapped mountains hove into sight, towering over the green crops in the valley. "The green... so green. So different than the browns you see in most of the rest of the country this time of year. That's why they call this the Switzerland of Pakistan."

"Right, but hasn't this area always been lawless too? I thought the central government never had much control in this tribal frontier belt."

"You're right, you've done your homework—at least no central control. But the area had always been relatively pretty peaceful, apart from some tribal skirmishes from time to time. Local tribal chiefs kept law and order, had their own justice system, and they usually solved tribal disputes as fast as they arose. But now, with the Taliban in Afghanistan coming across the border here to escape US forces there, Washington's putting huge pressure on Islamabad to crack down and impose dominant central order right here. No Pak government has even been able to do it before. It's going to take several generations to change the mentalities, traditions, and autonomous tribal way of life here. From what I can see, the war over there is doing nothing more than afghanizing Pakistan. I'm not sure that Pakistan can survive all this."

They pulled off the road where two little boys were selling apricots in plastic bowls. Alex spoke Urdu to them, but they didn't seem to understand, so Alex picked up a bowl and offered them one hundred rupees. The littlest boy wagged his finger, and put up two fingers. "They're overcharging us, but what the hell, they can use the money. And they know the *Farangis* can afford it. We may be the first people to stop here all day." The boys beamed at the 200 rupees, pocketed it, and generously added an extra handful of apricots into the bowl before they dumped them out and rolled them up in a newspaper cone. "That's always the ultimate insult," Alex laughed. "It's one thing to be overcharged and to accept it, but when they then throw some more in on top free, it's when you know even *they* feel guilty about overcharging you." The apricots were cool, soft, melted in their mouths, and tasted of honey. "Worth every penny if you ask me," Enrique said. "These are the best I've ever had."

They sat out on the veranda of the hotel that evening and watched the sun go down, eating their kebabs and *naan*. "Damn, all I need is a good beer now," Enrique said. "Not here, you don't," Alex replied. "This isn't Islamabad. They take their Islam seriously here, at least in public."

The next morning they picked up Rizwan, the government representative they had been scheduled to meet; an older man with a grizzled beard and a limp, he clambered into the vehicle and directed them to drive out to a village some twenty miles away up a side river valley—pastoral and lush, belying the simmering political tensions. They got out at a small electronic shop in the village where a number of villagers were gathered. He offered them his greetings, hand on his heart. The villagers obviously knew Rizwan, he made all these villages his beat. He reached for a small cigarette pack size item in the shop and proffered it to Alex.

"See this little device? It is an FM radio. Guess how much it costs? Would you believe it, probably just one US dollar. This is why you are losing the war." He shook it in front of Alex's face.

Alex stared at the small device, like a cell phone.

"Everyone here has one of these things. No, it doesn't bring in broadcasts from around the world, but it brings in local transmissions, right from here in the town or nearby villages. It broadcasts local news that the Taliban and the resistance want to spread to the townspeople." Rizwan started a conversation in Pashto with one of the men standing by. The man talked at length, waving his arms, and Rizwan kept nodding.

"He says, 'Every time I turn this radio on, I get nervous,'" Rizwan translated. 'We have broadcasts of the Quran, and everybody likes that, and some news about the world, that's good. And they talk about what has been going on in the town, the news from the fighting in various areas. But then they tell what information they have about the enemy and about who is cooperating with the enemy—with either the Army or the Americans. Then they identify traitors—by name—in our midst. There is no one who doesn't listen in fear to that part of the broadcast, because you cannot know who will be on the list, maybe even your own good name. You don't know who the informers are—either for government or for Taliban. If your neighbor has a grudge, he might just denounce you as a spy. And we all know there are real spies as well."

"That's right," another man added. "I don't think anyone wants to miss the broadcasts, you need to know what they're talking about, what the thinking is."

"My wife listens a lot to these broadcasts. Would you believe it, she tells me that the Mullahs talk about their rights as women in Islam as well, that women have a right to their own property according to Shari'a and that men can't take it away from them."

"Yes, my wife has complained to me about how I dress," the first man said. "Why don't I have a long beard like the Prophet had. She said our son should stop shaving and grow his beard to follow correct Islamic custom."

"Who says that's correct Islamic custom?" Rizwan said. "That's just what a lot of these strict Mullahs say, but the Prophet never said anything about long beards."

"Well, God alone knows. But if everyone is dressing that way, we need to join in. We need solidarity."

Rizwan turned to Alex. "Have you heard about the Sufi broadcasts? From the Barelvi side? Pir Safi Abdullah has been broadcasting messages on these same issues, but speaking for the 'green flags.' He condemns the black flag of the Taliban and their killings. There was fighting between the black flags and the green flags in the village over in Khyber agency a month ago. A lot of people were killed. This isn't just about government or the Americans or the army any more—it's turning into domestic struggle. This is new, we never had this black flag versus green flag fighting."

Alex turned to Enrique. "You see what we're up against? This is a little touch of reality Washington needs to know about. Otherwise we're going to get more delegations trooping on out here telling us how we just need to open up some radio stations and tell all the people about democracy and freedom—then the natives will see the light, revolt against the Taliban and come over the US side."

"And what about the government troops here?" a neighbor broke in. "They have been causing trouble too, shooting in the streets, trying to take over power in the town. We don't want those Punjabis in Islamabad telling us what to do out here. The officials they have sent to us have been corrupt. My neighbor told me that when he went with a complaint about another neighbor letting his animals graze on his land, the government judge wanted a bribe. And then he asked for one from the other party too. And he never did make a decision. At least most of these Taliban mullahs try to get justice. They'll hear the case and then make a judgment quickly. I haven't heard of any taking bribes, as far as I know."

"Maybe not for their own pockets, but I don't think they are always fair. If someone supports the Taliban in their town, they'll get a better deal out of these mullahs than you or I will."

"God spare us, it wasn't like this earlier. We had some peace. This is hell now with all these outsiders—devil take them! Government should clear out, and tell the Americans to get the hell out too, and leave us alone."

"Yes, yes, that's it!" cried Rizwan. "And the Soviet Union and America. It's the bloody outsiders. We could manage these issues on our own, but not when we are a stage for world politics and superpowers."

"My brother was in Afghanistan last year. He was at a meeting when some American officer came in, said he wanted to talk to the elders. He said he wanted to protect them from the Taliban and to help support President Karzai. Told them the Americans would bring peace. And he even gave them money for helping. But you'd be a fool to believe all that. How long do you think that will last?"

"The worst thing are those translators the Americans have, sons of swine. They've sold themselves out to the Americans, come strutting in here like sons of the Sultan, giving orders. Half of them aren't even translating, they're telling us what they want, telling us to watch out or they'll report us to the American officer. They'll be the first to get killed when the Americans leave, they're just dogs of the enemy."

"I'm fed up with all this. No peace anywhere now. God curse them all. Just leave us alone. I'm not going to sign up with any of them."

"That's right brother. Stay out of trouble where you can. Just say yes and smile. One day even this will pass."

"Heard enough?" Alex asked Enrique as they got back in the jeep and started the long drive back to Islamabad. Enrique shook his head in wonder.

"In the end, Enrique, you've got two conflicting fantasies here. The Taliban who think they are the future of Afghanistan, and the American fantasy that the US is going to win the hearts and minds, win the war, and have a firm strategic foothold across Asia."

*   *   *

Over the past year he was just one more added to the ranks—men who had found the easy money. All they had to do was help arrange truckloads of white powder across Pakistan and over the border *into* Afghanistan. It wasn't heroin going the wrong way. It was ammonium nitrate fertilizer, a substance nearly as precious to the jihadis. In Afghanistan it had become the central ingredient in the production of improvised explosive devices—IEDs, or home-made mines that wreaked havoc among American and other foreign forces fighting in Afghanistan. In fact, this perfectly common component of agricultural fertilizer had become the object of a ban by American forces in Afghanistan, but it still made its way into the country starting from the Pakistani port of Karachi, the pulsing gateway for a rich variety of contraband shipments. Every week, large numbers of trucks, usually traveling in conveys, calmly moved the white powder past controls and checkpoints in Pakistan and on to the Afghan border. *Baksheesh* as a system had achieved an art form. Palms were systematically and professionally greased the entire length of the route, reaching up to high places. And why not? Officials were richly rewarded for simply doing nothing, for turning a blind eye as the shipments came through. "The Americans complain, but why should we care? With heroin at least we know it's bad, we are killing our own citizens with it. But why should we weep if the American invaders are being killed by the Afghan resistance with this legal powder? The quicker they leave, the faster things will settle down in our own country."

The trucks trundled along the highways of Pakistan and up into the foothills of the Khyber pass, or across the Spin Boldak pass into Quetta in southern Afghanistan. Farmers could use it for their crops. Deliveries to villages was easy. Eager rural bomb-makers, village chemists, had learned how to mix the fertilizer with just the right amount of diesel fuel to ensure a good explosion. They packed it into ubiquitous clay pipe tubes or clay jugs, blending imperceptibly into the landscape. All it then took was a detonator, common coinage in a country that had already fought twenty five years of guerrilla war against multiple enemies. Hopefully an American convoy would be blown sky high as they hit it. But sometimes, too, a local truck or bus with civilians exploded to smithereens. God moved in mysterious ways.

"Why aren't the people enraged at the Taliban for this?" demanded a US Marine major visiting a headman of a village where bomb makers had been discovered that afternoon. The headman shrugged his shoulders. What was there to say? The villagers regarded the Americans as marauders; their mere presence in the village was observed by seemingly dull eyes that would pass the information on to the mujahideen. As soon as the Americans were gone, there would be a reckoning that night. Who had spoken to the infidel? Who had cooperated? Who had accepted money or some kind of assistance? What did the headman know? The response was often harsh, brutal and persuasive—sometimes terminal. And that was the way it was, and it had been going on for a generation or more. The rationale was simple, too simple for the Major to grasp. Whenever outsiders—British, Russians or Americans, or any other foreigners—marched in, it meant that villagers would soon be dying. Without foreigners here, no villagers would be dying. What more was there to say? Who but a fool or a traitor would choose to deal with transient foreign boots on the ground at the risk of his own life?

*   *   *

Hayya 'ala as-salaat! Hayya 'ala as-salaat! The muezzin called the faithful to noon prayer as Majeed's jeep wended its way through the streets of the bazaar in the main town. His appointment with Mullah Bilal was at "noon," a vague concept suggesting anytime after noon prayer. There was no telling exactly when, or even where, Mullah Bilal would appear. The driver, as instructed, dropped Majeed at the building attached to the mosque administration from where he would be later summoned at the last minute to a location to be determined. The Mullah kept his movements unpredictable so as not to invite a drone with his name on it. It was probably safe in the middle of the town since the Americans tried to avoid extensive civilian casualties if they could, but it was never a sure thing. Were they not driven by the devil himself anyway?

After several cups of tea and biscuits pushed upon him by an earnest attendant in the religious administration building, a different driver appeared at the door. "Majeed Sahib? Please come with me."

The vehicle drove down a long street crowded with various fruit and vegetable pushcarts to another location on the edge of the town where they pulled into a small, well-appointed compound. Several commercial vehicles were parked outside; Majeed suspected it was the home of a merchant. He was ushered into the building, removed his shoes, and went up the stairs to a large carpeted meeting room on the second floor. The servant urged Majeed to seat himself among the cushions against the wall. "The Mullah is on his way," the servant said. Again a possible infinitude of time. Punctuality, a virtue only among the self-important, had now begun to entail security risks as well. Lateness to appointments saved lives. And early ends to meetings saved lives. Majeed took a Quran off the stand to read while waiting. He was pleased to see that he still could understand a great deal of the Arabic. His father had taught him a lot of Quranic Arabic, and he had studied some in school. Often, of course, he already knew what the meaning of many of the Arabic phrases should be, so it wasn't as if he understood all the complex grammar. His father had never seriously required him to memorize the entire Quran, even though his father himself had done so as a child—thus becoming a Hafiz. As Majeed leafed through the pages in the long Sura of the Cow, a line caught his attention: 2:11 *And when the unbelievers are told, "Do not spread corruption on earth," they answer, "We are but improving things!" Oh, verily, it is they, they who are spreading corruption, but they perceive it not.*

He knew the line, but it now it took on new relevance. It was prescient, addressed to the very situation before them, to the US presence in Pakistan; their massive embassy and military presence and mercenary hangers-on, all ostensibly here to set things right, to modernize, to stabilize, to bring security and progress and democracy. *We are but improving things!* But indeed *it is they who are spreading corruption but they perceive it not.* Yes, that was it, *they perceive it not.*

The gap of perception was overwhelming and growing. It might not have been corruption that confronted Majeed in these provincial towns in Waziristan and Orakzai, so much as it was chaos, death, confusion, despair, disorder—now bringing the country to the brink of civil conflict, unleashing the darkest elements of society in response, some of it even dressed in religious garb. What kind of purchase would these religious elements have enjoyed in the pre-war days when the rules of life in the Frontier Province were well understood, well-regulated and power arrangements were established and time-honored? These arrangements had now been shattered and the long-established internal rules of Pakistan's political order were no longer operative. Upstart jihadis had displaced the traditional tribal rulers and *maliks.* The country's delicately balanced order of truces and red lines were in tatters, bringing the country to the edge. Majeed felt his skin crawl at this ancient message from the Quran reaching out to him from a millennium and a half ago to address the present catastrophe. And how many mullahs might be preaching this very text to their followers? *It is they who are spreading corruption but they perceive it not."*

Majeed tried to doze for a few minutes on the cushions, but his mind tortured him with replays of his cousin's death as he perceived it in his mind. He soon heard voices and footsteps on the stairs and Mullah Bilal appeared accompanied by two followers. For all his years proclaimed by his white beard, he bounded into the room with considerable energy. Majeed stood up to embrace him. Courtesies and inquiries were exchanged over some minutes, giving each a chance to ease his way into a discussion Majeed knew would not be easy.

"First, brother Majeed, let me express my sorrow at the death of your cousin Salman. Losing a close relative is a bitter pill, I know he was a brother to you. I cannot say I know all the details of what happened. But sadly Salman seemed to have compromised himself with the Americans in ways that came to the attention of his own camp commander. God have mercy on his soul."

With Bilal's keen eyes upon him, Majeed swallowed back some emotion and remained silent for a few moments before replying. "Brother Bilal, I cannot know for sure what happened with Salman. But I am quite convinced that my cousin did not betray his fellow fighters. He had been in slight contact with the American they call Sikender, but that was because the American—starting with his father—has long been known to our family including Salman. I am confident that he remained loyal and that his blood was shed in vain."

Bilal tapped his fingers on his thigh for a few seconds before responding. "God will judge him. I do not know the truth. But we are in the middle of a war for our survival. We must be constantly alert against traitors and infiltrators from the Americans. This Sikender seems especially dangerous. Traitors from our government as well need to be careful." He stared pointedly at Majeed.

"I know you could not possibly be suggesting that I am a traitor, brother Bilal. One must speak with great caution on these issues."

"I make no accusations. But we observe. Your own relationship with this Sikender makes us very uncomfortable…"

"I have known him since childhood," Majeed interrupted forcefully, staring back intently at Bilal. "His parents knew my parents in Lahore. I learn much about American thinking from talking with him. I have nothing to hide."

"You need not hide anything, but the jackal is known by its pack. I must speak frankly. Your friendship with Sikender is a source of great worry to many of us. You should be careful. Something could happen to him."

"My superiors in ISI are fully aware of my contact with him. He is a useful conduit from which we learn much about American thinking. Indulge me by respecting my own intelligence in knowing how to deal with him."

"That is the problem, my dear Majeed. We cannot know how you deal with him. I may accept every word you say. I may have full confidence in you. We have known each other for several years and you are a key avenue to the generals. But I must warn you that there are many among the faithful, among the fighters, who do not know you and believe that you may have been corrupted by Sikender."

"Brother Bilal, my ears are imperfect instruments. I am sure that you cannot be threatening me."

"Indeed, may God be my witness, I do not threaten you. But I advise you that your actions may be misunderstood by those who are poorly informed and who know you less well than I."

Majeed narrowed his eyes. "I know you will wish me to be frank, as only brothers can be. Forget about Sikender. Your problem is with Islamabad. You must know that several generals in the organization believe that some members of your groups are acting without authority in causing trouble and violence in many of our cities and towns, bombings that not only kill our own soldiers, but our citizens and even our children. This could appear to be a challenge to the state and its leaders—an impression I am sure you do not intend to give."

Bilal stared at him. "We do not challenge the state. We indeed are part of the state. But many of our brothers are impatient. They cannot believe that many top officials of our country seem to be bowing to American power and allowing the nation to be humiliated. Sikender does not wish our blessed country well. He is not an appropriate partner for discussion of our internal problems. The government must pull away from doing America's bidding and humiliating our people. And sending down the ghost planes upon us."

"We will not tolerate humiliation either, brother Bilal. We must all be on guard to avoid its stain upon any of us, from any quarter."

"God is great. We are all in this together." Bilal signaled for his assistant. The discussion had reached its end.

"And now, by your leave…" Majeed said, rising to his feet. They embraced and left separately.

As Majeed looked back, what had transpired? The session had been short but laden. Majeed was concerned that Bilal's message was ultimately more threatening than his own: Bilal had suggested he was not fully in control of forces that could be deadly to Majeed. Their respective positions left little doubt as to where all the players stood. Some tentative red lines had been explored. Could any of them successfully ride the forces at play?

*　　　　　*　　　　　*

Isabel had been horrified when she heard from Alex about Salman's death in the camps. "My God, Alex, I must go and offer Zubayda comfort about her cousin. I know she felt close to him."

"Isabel, I can't tell you how terrible I feel about this. I have already gotten some very harsh words from Majeed, he's bitterly angry. It's going to be difficult for you to talk to Zubayda. She may not even see you. But do try to let them know how upset I feel, that I grieve for them, and ask their apology for whatever I have done to contribute to this."

"I must see her, Alex, you know she is a sister to me."

When Isabel telephoned Zubayda and asked to pay a call of condolences, her response was stiff and unwelcoming. "Come if you must," she finally managed to say.

The house was largely dark with the curtains drawn. Isabel was relieved that no one else appeared to be home, apart from the servants. Akmal had gone to the mosque. Majeed was away at work.

"Zubayda, Zubayda, my God, what can I say? I am so sad for you." Isabel opened her arms to embrace her, a gesture stiffly and briefly reciprocated. Isabel uttered the Islamic invocation about sudden death that she had learned. "This is awful. To lose a family member is a terrible thing. I lost my brother in Chile, for political reasons as well."

Zubayda gave no response and stared at the floor, twisting a handkerchief in her hands. Her eyes were red. Isabel knew silence was best at this point. She took Zubayda's hand and they sat together for long minutes.

"It was a terrible ending" Zubayda finally said. "To be horribly executed—and falsely!"

"I am sure."

"I had begged Salman, so had my father, not to get involved with these jihadis. They are ruthless, they can kill without hesitation. And yes, and we are all paying the penalty for this terrible war next door. But I did not think my own family would be dragged into it…" She turned to Isabel. "And I did not think that your husband would be the one responsible for this tragedy."

"Alex?" Isabel recoiled. "What does Alex have to do with this?"

"You don't know? Alex had spoken with Salman, tried to get him to talk about the training camps and the jihadis. Someone reported on them, that Salman was an American spy."

"My God! I knew Alex knew Salman, had wanted to talk to him, but that Salman was killed for that! I can't believe it happened like that."

"Well, ask your husband. He knows. Nobody is left untouched in this country. Everyone is dragged into this game of death—in one way or another. Either for being too close to the Americans, or enemies of the Americans."

"I don't know what to tell you, Zubayda. I feel devastated. You are a sister to me, I know what you have been through—and with all your work with girls' and women's education—and now this—hit from all sides. Would you like me to stay with you a while?"

"God keep you, Isabel. I know you understand. Your country and ours have been caught in these situations, squeezed by foreign power politics. I appreciate your paying this call. I know you mean it. Let's stay in touch. But I don't want to talk about it anymore right now. And you shouldn't be here when my father or Majeed return." Isabel felt haunted at having to feel shame in front of Zubayda and her family.

When she got home she confronted Alex with the story she had heard from Zubayda.

"Why didn't you tell me about this? That you had been meeting with Salman? That that was why he was killed! I mean, my God, don't you feel any guilt over this?"

"Damn it, yes Isabel, of course I do! I feel sick about what happened. But when you have a situation like this, terrorism across borders hitting the US, of course Washington wants to find out more about who is doing these things. I was hoping Salman could tell me something about these training camps."

"Have you ever thought maybe you are the ones making people turn to violence—in response to all this American violence? My God, look at it! It's just power, power, control, control. That's all I hear. That was the story in Chile, that was the story with my brother—the search for enemies—communist enemies, Islamist enemies they're all the same. I'm sick of this power game!"

"Isabel, listen to me! Maybe it's just my fate in life, that I come from a country that is now a superpower. I didn't make it that way. I didn't choose it. There is always a country in the world that is the most powerful in the world, that throws its weight around. All I can do is try to help understand the situation here, explain the situation, try to get through to the people living in isolation and ignorance back home in Washington. Yes, I do feel it's an important task, to make people see reality, to try to make these miserable situations a little better!"

"Well, you haven't done a very good job in helping or protecting Zubayda's family—you who are supposedly their friend. I don't know how you are able to live with yourself."

Isabel moved towards the kitchen and broke into tears. Alex went over and tried to hug her. She pushed him away at first. Then they stood there in an awkward embrace for some time. "I'm sorry, Alex, for what I said. It's unfair. I know you are a good person. But the situation is not good. I just can't handle it. It is too much like what we all went through back in Chile—only in a different movie. This is truly wearing me down. I don't know how long I can stay living here… in this situation."

I oppose what I see is going on around me, but does it make any difference? What is it doing to me? Who am I becoming in the process? His sleep nearly every night was now broken by the sound of gears in his mind, incessantly grinding, repeatedly rerunning the events leading to Salman's execution. A recurring nightmare that would not leave him alone.

*　　　　　*　　　　　*

The phone rang late that evening. Alex answered.

"Alex? Majeed."

"Majeed!, how are…"

"I don't even know why I'm calling you. But you should know that you are now clearly on the mujahideen screen, especially after the Salman events. You are known, watched, and likely targeted. There are many angry and suspicious people out there. I advise you to act accordingly."

"Majeed, I…"

"That's all I have to say." Alex heard the click on the other end of the line.

Chapter Eight

Higher Policy

Lying to ourselves is more deeply ingrained than lying to others.

- Fyodor Dostoevsky

Ladies and Gentlemen: Let us speak honestly of war. One of its tragedies is well known: sadly, innocent people always die—killed by our enemies, and yes, killed by us too. It has happened in every war in history. And if we take the long view, it is one of the tragedies of the human condition. As much as we would like it, the US is not able to change the dynamics of human interaction down through history, even if we recognize how flawed this struggle is. We are doomed to engage on the same fields of strife as our ancestors have done in order to preserve the values we have fought so hard to achieve in the past. Freedom is always hard fought and can come at a high price. We can never rest, or yield it up.

Nothing would be more gratifying than to welcome the day when force no longer plays a role in determining the course of life on this planet. America, which has offered more of its blood and wealth to keep the world free than has any other nation in history, would be the first to embrace it. Indeed, there are those who urge that we stand outside such global strife and focus on strengthening ourselves at home, that somehow we could thus uphold higher values by foreswearing a military role.

But if we as Americans decide to operate according to a higher standard of morality than the rest of the world, that may be fine—but will anyone else? We become naïve, mere punished bystanders if we stand apart from strategic conflicts, while others wade in to impose their wills. That would represent dereliction of our duties to the American people—to all peoples who seek peace, stability and freedom around the world.

It is the current tragedy of the Pakistani and Afghan peoples to be caught up in this ugly situation after 9/11. But the best we can do now is, first, to identify our most dangerous enemies and eliminate them and, second, to establish a position of permanent and unassailable strength in this region so that no one would ever think of challenging our power again. We need to stand firm here in the heart of Asia as a bulwark against potential aggressive Russian and Chinese moves. And we owe it to all these peoples and countries of the region—of the world—to vanquish those forces of terrorism and anarchy that destabilize the world. We cannot even permit the perception of weakness, for it will only bring comfort to our enemies.

America is obligated by history to stand guard, to project power and influence across the region—to prevent recurrence of dangerous instability that only provides sanctuary to our enemies. It is our solemn obligation to establish peace, stability, democracy, human rights and justice in these and other lands of conflict. That is the American mission. That is what makes us an exceptional nation, and an exceptional people. We are historically dedicated to that cause. It is our heritage. It cannot be otherwise. We will never shirk from the challenge. God bless America! (*Standing applause.*)

*   *   *

Man, I'm telling you this is one shit-hole. Hell on wheels. I had it up to here with this war.

You can't fucking trust no one. All these Hajjis come up, smiling, talking about cooperating and then turn around and pump lead into your gut next night.

Even the goddam little kids. We been handing out candy, being nice to them, sometimes playing ball with them in the street, you know, trying to win over the population—then some little bastard goes off and reports on you and gets you killed. I mean, lying thieving bastards. Just a bunch of sand niggers.

We come in here to save these guys' asses from the Taliban, you know? They was a bunch of crazy killers running the country, these Taliban, locking up all the women in their house, no TV, ass-hole buddies with Osama bin fucking Laden. You'd think these guys would be a little careful, with us trying to help out the country and all. Well OK, Hajjis, we're not here for fun, we don't want to be here. We're just trying to fucking straighten things out, get rid of the terrorists. Yeah, and bring some democracy and all, build schools, help the girls get educated, all that. Bastards don't appreciate shit.

You ask me, we're wasting our time here. Let these fuckers rot if they want, no skin off my ass. Just show us the terrorists. We'll waste 'em and then we're out of here.

Man, I lost six good buddies in this war. Makes me so goddam angry I could scream. We go out on these patrols, you know? You never know who's coming at you, who's a friendly. Ask me, ain't a fucking one of them friendly. We knock on the goddam door, tell them to open up so we can search the place for the terrorists—like they won't even open the goddam door? How in hell are we supposed to know who's in there? Fuckin' A, we shoot down the goddam door, and throw in a smoke grenade on top, just to stop them bastards from trying to fire on us… One time last month we was at this house, my buddy went in, whole damn family cowering in the corner looking at us, hate in their eyes, all shittin' their pants. My buddy looked all around in the house, found one woman hiding in the bedroom all wrapped up in her fucking chadoor. Alright, we're supposed to respect their damn women and all that Islam shit. My buddy turns around and comes back out, turns out that fucking bitch was actually a terrorist in woman's clothes, he comes up behind him and stabs my buddy in the neck with a long knife. Man, he's lying there and bleeding and I just saw red and went and blasted the shit out of the guy with my I-16, nearly cut the guy in half, blood all over. The family starts screaming, and I scream back at them to shut the fuck up. We're trying to get my buddy out of here, but we got firing going on outside the house now and we're trapped inside. I try to stop the blood pouring out of his neck, but I can't stop it, Christ, I can't even take the time cause we got to defend ourselves. I bust out the goddam window to shoot out, and son of a bitch, if another one of them Hajjis behind me doesn't come up with another knife to get me. I ran out the door and sprayed bullets back in, he dropped like a sack of shit, and the rest of the family starts screaming and praying. Man, I really lost it, them bastards coming at me back and front. We just tossed in a frag and took 'em all down. My buddy never made it to camp—goddam Hajjis.

I know that ain't right. I know we're supposed to protect women and children and all that. But what can you do in a war like this? One thing is, Hajjis don't value life like we do. Every one of them itching to die for Allah. How can you fight people like that? We ain't never going to know who's a good guy and who's bad. At least in other wars, you know, you got guys in uniform, like you got some chance of spotting the good guys from the bad—not here. They all look the same, same goddam beards, fucking rags wrapped around their heads, women all covered. Know what? I'm not even sure there are any fucking good guys here. Maybe it's just like the Marines say, 'Waste 'em all, and let Allah sort 'em out.'

How in hell we supposed to bring law and order to these people, bring civilization when they don't even want it. Hell, we trained up a young guy in one of these nearby villages the other month, you know, showed him how to build schools and shit. Brought in some young guys to train 'em up for police. They all swore they wanted to support the government. "Americans good!" they said. You got that one right, Hajji, we're trying to do stuff for you in this god-forsaken place. Next thing we know we come back the next week, the goddam head of the police unit's run off, took all the goddam weapons, and they burned down the fucking school we built. How in hell you deal with people like this?

Me, I had it with this shit. I'm here on my second tour, and you know what? Like I don't see one fucking bit of difference between now and two years ago. Just more dangerous. At least they got some decent camp facilities now, we can score some decent American brews and pizza and chill out for a day or two kickin' it. But man, I'm telling you, this is hell and we ain't never gonna make it no better. Back in DC they got their heads up their ass, goddam politicians come out here on their sick-ass photo op tours, get filled up with a line of bullshit from the top brass here, all these charts and stats about how we're making progress, winning and all. Bunch of goddam eyewash. Fuckin' prez puts on fatigues and boots, comes out and tells us all what a great job we're doing men, we're the finest troops in the world, how the country is proud of us and all, hands out turkeys and shit on fuckin' thanksgiving. Up yours with your goddam turkeys. Thanks a lot guys for thinking about us, how about getting us out of this shit-hole.

You know, I been talking with some of these local guys we been trying to train. Some of them seem friendly enough, usual 'America good' thumbs up shit, some seem sincere. But you can't tell with these damn Muslims, you know Allah tells them in their religion to lie about everything, so you can't trust a fucking thing they say. Only way you win a war like that is just keep picking off any adult that moves. Even the teenagers, they're worse.

Look, I know, this makes me feel like shit. I goddam know I've killed women, even kids at some point. You just get jumpy out there on missions, you know? Anybody makes a sudden move and you let rip.

Me and my buddies been talking about how our number could come up any day here, on any patrol. We think about it. But you know, it's kinda crazy, but what really terrifies the shit out of us isn't even dying from some bullet. It's getting our nuts blown off by some goddam mine. I mean, man, that doesn't never leave my mind. I don't know as I really could live any more if my junk got blown away. A guy in the next unit begged his buddy to put him out of his misery when he took a mine in the balls. What kind of life was left to the poor bastard even if he lives?

And then my mom, she's always on the phone asking me, how you doing son? We're all so proud of you back here. Like I can't tell her shit about what's going down over here. I can't tell her about how I'm afraid of taking a hit in the nuts, or dying. They're asking me all these questions, like telling me what a great job we're doing, saving America and shit—I mean, what can I say? Yeah Mom, it's tough and it's dirty, but we're doing some good here, helping the people, keeping America safe. Well, God bless you son, and all your buddies, she says. Makes me feel bad because people back home don't have a fucking clue what all this is about, it's doing God's work to them.

I been to the padre, you know, wanted to talk out some of this shit with him, like how I know I've killed kids and all, even innocent people when we get too edgy. War is always a dirty business he says, and an offense in God's eyes. Innocent people do get hurt. All you can do is do your very best, son, try to respect life as much as you can, he says. But you're a soldier and we're here to fight for our country. Not every decision is always the right one, but overall we are fighting for what's good and right in this world. Our country believes in God and we're trying to do what is right for as many people in the world as we can. May God protect you, he says. We have to believe in this mission if we're to keep going, to make all this worthwhile and to protect the folks back home from worse.

Well, I hope padre's right about that. I sometimes wonder. Maybe we'd all be a whole lot better off if we just left these miserable bastards rot in their own shit-hole, whole lot less dead people all around.

*   *   *

Neither Akmal's heart nor his mind had been at peace for some time; he needed spiritual retreat and tranquility, spiritual counsel to deal with his distress. His normal meditations and readings at home were not enough to overcome the blow of Salman's death, even if it was something Akmal had seen coming from early on.

The Mian Baradar Shrine lay two hours away by bus from Lahore. Akmal liked going by bus, traveling alone was part of the experience—the beginning of a long personal meditation from the minute he clambered aboard. Despite the hurly-burly of the bus station—the crowds, the hawkers of fruits, cashews, spicy fried snacks, and even the risk of a possibly garrulous seatmate—it was a trip he always savored. Journey meant more than covering mere distance; the mind and the heart were also drawn into new experience. Journey, even travelling alone, implied people—all around, part of the human condition of which he partook. A journey outward always entailed a journey inward as well; the chance to observe his own mind and emotions in new settings. Akmal had not been to visit the Pir since the death of Salman.

Salman's cruel end haunted his mind. It seemed so pointless. What had been the meaning of Salman's life—and death? Was Salman's association with the bloodshed of jihadi struggle a mark of sin in the eyes of God? Indeed, the taking of life flew in the face of all that Akmal had come to believe in his own heart. Was not a horrific end almost the inevitable outcome of combining feeble human understanding of God with the violence of militant certainty?

In the end Akmal had told Alex that he did not hold him responsible for what had happened. He knew the real world: Alex was professionally interested in jihadi activity. And Salman was an adult who had made his own decisions about his life course and associations. Nonetheless, in his heart Akmal could not yet truly forgive Alex for his association with the terrible course of events; indeed it was now painful for Akmal even to see him— doubly painful because Alex over the years had come to be like a son to him too. These events swirled in his mind, keeping pace with passing trees, country lanes, vehicles, animals, houses, people and countryside that swept across his vision from the barred bus window. He needed to put things to rest if he could.

Akmal chatted with a young man who was also going to the Shrine, visibly agitated. The man spoke of his wife's long disease and death, and the problems he had with three small children, keeping a job, and making ends meet. He hoped to find understanding of what life had dealt him, the strength to go on, perhaps a touch of God's boon. "May God lighten your problems," Akmal told him—some psychological peace. To share in human pain was part of the therapy; one is not alone in grief in this world; we all share in the struggle to understand and cope with grief and loss.

He got off the bus with his small bag, and headed slowly towards the shrine complex, measuring his steps with care and trying to remain mindful of his momentary existence, to link every few paces with religious invocation. Now he glimpsed it, in the distance, the striking Persian-Mughal golden dome that crowned the shrine itself, dedicated to the holy man—Hazrat Ishaq Jalilullah Qalandar. The gate was guarded by more police than normal and Akmal reflected on the irony that such sacred precincts should have become the battleground of conflicting religious forces. The shrine compound was nonetheless still busy, filled with many people in a range of daily street clothing as well as religious garb. He headed toward the familiar main tomb complex, approached and peered through the arabesque of silver-colored metal grillwork that separated the tombs within from the outside viewer.

Inside were the tombs of the holy man and his early followers who had been accepted as saints, the first covered with a brilliant crimson silk cloth scattered with flowers and Arabic inscriptions. The tomb next to it was swathed in Islamic green with similar Arabic inscriptions. Each tomb was as long as a human body, almost as if a long mound of sand had been built up over the holy body underneath as at the beach, then covered over by plaster that rose to a long horizontal peak on which the colorful cloths rested. At the top of the tomb was the headpiece, a turban-like shape representing the head. Ishaq Qalandar had been a holy man whose provenance had never been fully known. He had been a wandering mendicant several centuries ago, some said from Iran, some said India, possibly both. He had tended to the ill and the suffering. He had preached brotherhood between Muslims and Hindus. Strict Muslim theologians, of course, had ruled that you can't acknowledge Hindus as People of the Book like you can Christians and Jews—the Hindus didn't even acknowledge one God. But millions of Muslims lived comfortably with the daily Hindu reality around them anyway.

Akmal reflected on how theologians all seemed to be operating on different wavelengths. Indeed they were not all equally in touch with God. Or maybe just with certain faces of God—who after all had ninety-nine names, or differing aspects. Surely judging by their fruits some theologians scarcely seemed in touch with God at all—those zealots and self-seeking agitators who whipped the people up, especially during hard times, into hatred and communal attacks. But Hazrat Ishaq Qalandar had been a man of peace who had encountered the power of several princes and monarchs who had sought him out for his wisdom. Some said in life he had performed a number of miracles. And in death the light emanating from his tomb was said to bring joy, fortune and wisdom to those who consulted him. His tomb sat in the dim interior illumination as if the brilliance of the sun outside would rob the tomb of its own internal glow.

Akmal was hardly alone in the space but his concentration was such that he felt as if he were alone, offering his thoughts for many minutes. He reflected on the lives of many of these holy men, but also on the importance of their final resting place. Their years of lying here in death vastly exceeded their years of life. Surely that suggested that their power in death exerted more force than even during their lives—such was their accumulated power. Visitors still came to seek them out, certain their own lives could be validated in the life and death of the Saint. Surely that's where the power of saints came from: visitors brought them validation, and built up the power of accumulated spirituality for the common good.

The shrine was always busy; crowds congregating, seeking blessing, absorbing the ineffable spirit, each person in his own way. Some did not even seem to delve into the self-reflection urged by the Pir, but more simply sought alms as the most immediate means to alleviate their material burdens. Others were even asleep on the stone floor in midday as life went on around them. Who knew what benefits they drew from their sojourn in the presence for a few hours; it is not for the Muslim to judge the faith of another Muslim.

Akmal had come here once with Majeed and Salman when they were boys, shortly after Salman's parents had been killed. Akmal's eyes teared up now at the memory. *I have come home,* Akmal thought, every time he entered in through the gates of the shrine complex. He would stay at a modest hotel for the pilgrims, share food with them in the fellowship of those seeking some spark, some sacred crumb of the divine that could fortify the body and soul for weeks and months to come amid the turbulence of daily life. He had known the current Pir for over twenty years. The Pir exuded an extraordinary sense of peace. He shunned discussion of daily issues and preferred instead to quietly sense your need, perhaps recite a Sufi tale or a saying relevant to maintaining sanity, love and awareness throughout the hours and days of mundane existence. But Akmal needed extra help in these hours of great trial.

The Pir received him in a small cell with whitewashed walls, the classic picture of a holy figure in Islam seated before a candle. He looked at Akmal expectantly and waited. "Master," Akmal began, "I have lived a long life. I have so many blessings for which to be grateful. But now God has tested me fiercely in recent months. He took my nephew away from me to join jihad, a boy whom we brought up in our own home like a son. He was killed in a most brutal and terrifying way that haunts my soul, especially at night when darkness opens space to the demons and fears in my mind."

"God indeed tests us, brother Akmal. But life, and the world, and the universe that God has created—they contain within it all things, every phenomenon, every event. If we lead long and open lives we are bound to encounter its full range—those things that are harsh, cruel or saddening, as well as those things of great joy and peace."

"My heart is still in pain, Master, even though I strive to reflect on the many benefits I have received."

"Would you rather be a stone? Or a snake or a rat or a camel? That way you would not experience the same tide of emotion as you do as a human being. That is the price that God, may He be exalted, lays upon us as special beings when we are born. Our emotions bring both heights and depths. The greater the pinnacles of joy we are capable of experiencing, the greater is the pain and moments of despair when we encounter the dark side of his full Creation. Do not consider your pain a punishment; it is the reverse face of the coin that has also brought you delight and joy. Above all, do not think to be spared sadness; it is only for a lower creature to be so spared—of both joy and sorrow."

"I do not know how to understand what happened to my nephew, Master. He was a mujahid, fighting *fi sabil Allah*, in the path of God. His heart spoke to him of injustice in the world, of suffering, of the foreign occupation and war around us. He was determined to resist these evil phenomena. He died as a result. Master, my heart tells me that the violence in which he was engaged is wrong. Even if he saw it as the path of God, leading towards a better society, I believe it is wrong."

"Brother Akmal, your heart tells you aright. Violence only begets violence. Furthermore, reflect: no victim of violence is entirely evil or entirely good. An act of violence in return does not settle the score in the eyes of God, it only perpetuates it and spins a wider web of suffering for all."

"But Master, my nephew would tell me that we cannot be passive in the face of wrongdoing and injustice, we must take action to resist it, to bring it to an end."

"Yes, we must always seek to bring wrongdoing and injustice to an end. But we cannot achieve that through exercising more pain and violence. We will only free ourselves from these evils by opening our hearts and the hearts of others. Others must hear the word of God and take them into their heart and carry the message forth."

"That is a long process, Master."

"Do you not think that when God created the World and the Universe it was not a long process? Do you think that His process is now finished, after countless generations? We do what we can as individuals. If we can bring love and understanding and patience and goodwill—even if only for a short time and only to a small circle of people around us whom we encounter in the voyage of life—that is to carry out God's will. That is to lead a blessed and fruitful life."

"If only my nephew's heart had been more open to this message he might be alive today."

"It is God alone who determines when our path has run its course. But that does not mean that we bear no responsibility for that path. Yes, our destiny is written, but we are the ones who reveal to God what we want and how we expect to achieve it. We write our own destiny with our own hands and give it to God and by that means we reveal our own heart. It is God who then determines our final day. That is the basis on which our day of destiny is written."

"So we have a choice even before the face of God?"

"Why would we have prayer, why would we pray if all was simply determined in advance? Why would we strive to lead a righteous life if nothing lay in our own hands?"

"Master, I would like to think that my nephew is not cursed for the blood he may have taken in his membership in jihadi groups that are exercising violence upon others."

"Your nephew has committed evil. But at least his heart has tried to understand God and God's justice, even if only imperfectly. He has not done these acts for personal pleasure or personal gain or personal power. Many others might also kill if they had the chance, but they do not find the occasion. God examines not only their acts, but what is in their hearts. You must believe that your nephew's soul has been touched by God in his meditation upon what is the right, even if he understood it imperfectly. This has more merit than never to have reflected upon it at all."

An assistant came into the room and nodded. "And now you will excuse me, my son. ..."

"Thank you Master, for your words. They help me to understand—and to continue."

"It is nothing, Brother Akmal. Words are plentiful. What matters is to act, to keep the idea of God and God's purpose in your mind at all times. Repeat the *dhikr, 'La ilahu illa 'lla'*—that there is no god but God—in your mind and in your heart throughout the day. That is what keeps God close to us, more than my own poor words can do in a brief chat... Now please prolong your stay in this holy shrine, sitting in silence, and you will feel the message come to your heart without words. But do not forget the constant mention and reminder of God and his purpose throughout the day. It will heal your heart in ways that I can never do."

Akmal kissed the Pir's hand and touched it to his forehead. He went out to the larger area of the shrine that now seemed wholly new; he remained seated in the cool hush as emotions washed through his mind until he was finally able to bring them to a kind of stillness.

That evening as Akmal returned to his lodgings along a back street, a large white car swept up alongside of him. Two men with covered faces leapt out and grabbed him from behind, an elbow around the neck and pulled him backward. *The blade of eternity, it is coming, I can feel it, just as it came for Salman.* A bag was quickly drawn over his face as he was dragged into the car, one man on each side. The car sped off. "Who are you? What do you want?" Akmal cried, only to be treated with silence. Finally the car stopped and he was dragged out of the car and up a flight of stairs and thrown into a room. The door slammed behind him.

"What do you want?" he again cried in fear. "Be silent, old man," was all he was told.

*   *   *

When Akmal had not returned by the next evening, Zubayda grew worried. She called Majeed and asked if he knew anything of their father. "I am sure he would not change his plans without letting us know." Majeed came home at once. Akmal always returned on time from his overnight trip to the shrine. They deliberated in anxiety about how to proceed. And then, near midnight, the phone rang. "That may be Akmal," Zubayda shouted from the other room.

Majeed rushed to pick up the phone. "Yes?" he said, and then paled. "Who are you?" he demanded. "If anything happens to him, you know I am well connected with the security services in this country. You will pay a dear price." He listened for another minute, and jotted down a note. "No, you listen to me…" he said, but the voice had rung off. "Hello, hello?"—after listening for a few moments longer, Majeed hung up.

"They've grabbed Babaji. They threaten to kill him if we don't pay a ransom of eight lakh rupees."

"Who are they?" Zubayda cried.

"I don't know. He seemed to have a Sindhi accent. God forbid they will be taking him to Karachi."

"How can we pay them?" asked Aysha who had just come into the room.

"We can't. That's not even a guarantee that we'd get him back alive."

"What else can we do?"

"I'm going to check through the office. I may be able to come up with some trace."

"But why would they do this to an innocent and religious old man?"

"Who knows with these crazy types. They probably know he's my father. Maybe they hate him because he goes to Barelvi shrines. Maybe they're striking back at the authority of the Pir. Maybe, God forbid, it has something to do with poor Salman. Who knows. But I'm going to try to investigate it through our sources."

Zubayda's lip trembled. "These bastards. These twisted bastards. But what if they kill him if we don't pay?"

"We can't know. They could kill him even if we do pay. Let me look into this. They gave me some crude contact plan about passing some money."

Majeed hugged his wife and sister and left the house again to head to his office despite the late hour, his mind black with anger. His driver had gone home so, taking extra precautions, he drove himself.

*   *   *

Within twenty-four hours Majeed had a better idea of what groups might be operating around the shrine. The fact that their father had been kidnapped and not simply killed outright suggested an almost purely financial motive rather than a political or ideological one. This was not the first time something like that had happened there. Perhaps it was directed against Akmal personally. His father was known in legal circles and perhaps it was simply assumed that he could be a lucrative target.

Majeed's ISI office, in liaison with the police, offered some possible leads as to what gangs it might have been. The word quietly went out to groups in that area that in kidnapping Akmal Rehman, they had bought into a great deal more trouble than they had bargained for. It was suggested the wrath of ISI might descend upon them. And political jihadi groups with representatives in the area were put on notice to locate Akmal Rehman or face bigger trouble.

"It's a long shot," Majeed told his family. "But many times these smaller criminal groups operate in the shadow of the larger jihadi organizations and get under feet, complicating the jihadis' own political relations with the government. It's the only hope we have, that the jihadis don't need these kind of amateur games going on in the middle of their political operations."

And two days later the phone rang at his home in the evening. "They've found him!" Majeed shouted. "He's alive and is going to be released somewhere soon. Let's hope to God he is alright!" Later that night the police called to report they had located Akmal in the streets. He was alive.

When he was brought home at last by the police Akmal felt like he had been returned from another world. He had visited Hell, and had been ready for death, but his faith had told him that he would survive. The family fell upon him with weeping and joy.

What had happened to him? Had he been tested as the Pir had said? And indeed his hour had not yet been written. His heart was overwhelmed by a sense of God's bounty in this dangerous and treacherous world. It was beyond understanding. He knew he would never be deterred from going to the shrine again. But he did not wish to tell his family that at this moment.

*   *   *

"And did you hear what the Minister's reply to all that was? Simply unbelievable. But then one never can get a straight answer out of the Ministry, can one? Maybe we need to draw up another demarche." On it droned, the reception at the Italian Embassy, in full diplomatic bore. Same old faces in the diplomatic penguin parade knocking back scotch, swapping warmed-over diplomatic gossip about the deteriorating situation, none of whom had seen, heard or thought anything original. Nothing in it for Alex to stand around exchanging views with those who knew less than he did. These national day receptions were about as establishment as it got. He craved to break out of polite society and get back into the harsher realities of the real world around him—communists, rebels, leftists, fundamentalists, hustlers, artists, radicals, intel officers. He looked around to find a way to sneak out early.

From the other side of the room a tall figure bearing a drink moved firmly towards him, looking Alex in the eye. Alex did a double take. "It can't be, my God... Is that you, Fyodor?"

"Yes, my friend, it not only can be, it is Fyodor. Are you surprised to see me?" He put his hand on Alex's shoulder.

"Fyodor, I'm stunned. I mean, I wasn't even sure you were still alive!"

"Well, Alex, you can see, I am alive, very much so, but things did get a bit chilly in Moscow for a while. I spent some time as an unwilling guest of the government in tight quarters—five years to be precise—until the whole system came crashing down."

"I never knew what happened to you, Fyodor. I was sick about it. You just disappeared from your embassy and no one knew what had happened. Then we got some information that maybe you were put on secret trial—we were sure you were executed."

"No, no, not quite that bad this time around. I certainly would have been in earlier years. But I also had many connections within the system. I come from a good revolutionary family, you know, they protect their own from the worst outcome when they can.

"But even with a possible charge of spying?"

"You might be surprised to hear it, but I was known to be a very patriotic Russian, even if anti-Soviet. Even some party members have been capable of making that distinction."

"So you're back in the diplomatic business once again? Just like that?"

"No, not fully. I'm just visiting here in Islamabad for a week."

"I thought the Latino world was your beat."

"It is, but business sometimes takes you strange places."

"Oh? So what's your business in Pakistan, then?"

"Why you, Alex, it's you."

*   *   *

Alex placed his gin and tonic glass on a mantelpiece. His head spun and he was at a loss for words. The old relationship had done an abrupt about-face. The old game was over and it seemed a new one had started. He looked around a room still engrossed in its clinking glasses and trivialities.

"Let's go over to the corner, Fyodor."

They sat down in two overstuffed chairs that offered embracing protection from each other. "What do you mean you've come to see me?"

"Aren't you happy to see me, my friend?"

"Why yes, sure, but why would you come to see me? All this way?"

"I've missed you, Alex." Fyodor gave a smile, or was it a touch rehearsed? A note of bitterness in him? A slight mocking? Something more sinister? Or all just part of Alex's own guilt?

"Fyodor, I've missed you too. I mean, I was very worried about what had happened to you. I felt, well, guilty, responsible in a way for what had happened to you, to cause your recall."

"We were both consenting adults Alex. You shouldn't feel guilt. After all, I told you that my goal was to help bring down the Soviet system. And that's what I did. And the system did come down!"

"Well, I'm glad, Fyodor, I'm glad. I don't think either of us expected to see it collapse quite like that, in our lifetimes. But tell me, why did you want to get in touch with me again?"

"We turn to each other in the hour of national need, Alex. You to me, then I to you. But surely this is a long conversation, best left for another quieter place and time."

"Fyodor, I'm not sure what you have in mind, but…"

"Alex, don't worry yourself. I propose nothing out of the ordinary. I would just value a good exchange, an overview on where things stand in the world. We used to have that before, didn't we?"

"Yes, but… that was different…"

"How different? Because I was working for you? And you were paying me in your own way? Because you were in control?"

"It's not about control. It's just… we had a more formal relationship."

"I'm not here about any formal relationship, Alex, just an exchange for old times' sake, my friend. Surely you won't deny me?"

*   *   *

Two nights later, Alex gave the taxi directions to a restaurant in Pindi, the old capital and military cantonment just 15 kilometers down the road from Islamabad, a town vastly more Pakistani in character, where Westerners were less likely to be present. *Why am I coming to this meeting? Should I have reported this contact in advance to the Station?* He was aware of taking a calculated risk in not doing so, conceivably incriminating. It may not be the Soviet Union any more, but he knew Russia was still viewed with great suspicion in Washington, almost as a sacred flame lovingly preserved by the priests and logisticians of the Cold War; operations against Russians had not come to an end, even if now a lower priority. But Alex was curious and, dammit, he had to admit he enjoyed Fyodor's company, the repartee with a thoughtful and insightful individual. He wanted to hear about what had happened to him after he had gone back to the USSR. And what was on his mind now.

Fyodor had selected a Chinese restaurant, Tiger Mountain, a nice touch. Chinese food was reliably good in Pakistan; the close ties between China and Pakistan showed up not only in the weapons business, but also in Chinese restaurateurs. All the clichéd symbols of Chinese culture were on display in this establishment—pictures of the twisted craggy mountains of Guilin, fat smiling Buddhas honoring the rich, Chinese New Year's scrolls wishing ten thousand years of wellbeing, bright red wallpaper, the obligatory dragons with red glass eyes in gold paint entwined around the two pillars at the entrance, round tables with huge lazy-susans in the center, the distinct smell of deep fried duck and soy sauce. Two other tables, both occupied by Chinese, were out of earshot from Alex and Fyodor. The headwaiter was discreet enough to respect their privacy at a table obviously chosen for its privacy. Fyodor ordered. "They don't have any pork dishes, but every other kind of meat is available, all excellent. One area where the Chinese surpass us for sure, in their culinary tradition."

"Isn't it ironic that the two old superpowers should be meeting in the cultural milieu of our mutual rival?" asked Alex.

"It's perfectly appropriate," Fyodor answered, "they're the only country that's left standing now. And besides there's no Chilean restaurant anywhere near here."

They now spoke English, further evidence to Alex that things had changed. That he had used mainly Russian in Santiago had been a symbol, ironically, of his cultural control over Fyodor; he had insisted on it, and Fyodor had been happy to go along. Fyodor's English was always excellent, but what did Fyodor's choice of it mean this time?

"I was told we had to bring our own bottle if we want to get a drink here—as long as we are discreet about it." Fyodor produced a bottle of Stoli from his briefcase, another small sign of the shifting equilibrium, wrapped in multiple newspapers and still very cold. Alex wondered whether the briefcase was wired, but then realized Fyodor himself could be and there was nothing he could do about it. Even to raise the subject would be crude, a sign of vulnerability.

"What was the reaction of your people that I've turned up again?" Fyodor asked.

The question was cunning, and one that Alex left unanswered, providing at least the suggestion that he had not reported the contact, just as Fyodor had suspected he would not.

Fyodor loosened up after a few shots of mother's milk, drunk from teacups the waiter had discreetly brought—without even a teapot. "You know, our KGB moved fast back then, they had me on a plane out of Santiago within six hours of presenting me with evidence of our meetings. I think it was part of a mass surveillance blanketing that DINA had been able to mount, against you primarily. They were able to arrange static surveillance posts sitting on multiple street corners, you never detected it. Nor did I. But I was not surprised. I knew of the capability. We helped train them after all, and we had multiple penetrations still surviving in their service and reporting to us."

Fyodor went on to tell Alex of the harrowing tale of his swift arrest, his isolation in a black hole, probably in Lubyanka, and periodic torture. "They didn't need to torture me much at all. I am a coward. As they say, all they had to do was show me the instruments. I sang like a bird. I have a good memory.

I was able to tell them of every operation I had betrayed. I knew I would die, what difference would it make? Besides, strangely, I did feel a touch of guilt, you know. Not that I was betraying the KGB—I hated it. They knew I hated it. Many of those inside it also hate it but, with all its privileges for the elite, it is not a bad way to live inside the Soviet system. But I did feel guilty about the probable fate of the numerous Chilean agents I had betrayed to you. I don't know what ever happened to them, but they were human beings too, all too human and vulnerable to Soviet cash, and some of them were even committed communists. They are the ones I feel sorry for. They were naïve fools to have believed in our system despite all the evidence to the contrary. But it was easier to believe in it from the distant shores of Chile, far from the Moscow Vatican."

Fyodor was warming to the topic. Alex felt it would be some kind of confession session. "You know, to believe is a wonderful thing, Alex. I never believed in the Soviet system, never. My parents told me not to believe in it. But I think you did believe in your system. At least for a while. I remember our many long conversations. We talked about a lot more than just Soviet agents in Latin America as I recall."

Fyodor pulled the vodka out of his briefcase from under the table again, unwrapped it and poured another half a cup for each of them. The waiter then came by, a Pakistani who mangled the names of the Chinese dishes but assured his customers that the food, though Chinese, was all strictly *halal*.

"Thank God for that," quipped Fyodor. "I wouldn't want to violate God's writ in our meal together. Or are we already doing so with our tea?"

Alex chose to let that one go by. He noticed a new impishness, a new confidence in Fyodor, again reflecting his feeling that he was in charge.

"So tell me, Fyodor, how is your daughter?"

"She is good, thanks. I am grateful to you for the funds that helped get her better private treatment in Moscow. She will never be an Olympic athlete, but she has graduated from the Moscow Conservatory and is a first class cellist. Her health is sound, even if some of her leg muscles are permanently damaged. But she is fully capable of walking. And I know you later got married to a Chilena. How is your wife? Do you have children?"

"Your people have kept good tabs on me. Yes, one son. And ironically, living overseas here with a Chilean mother he's not even fully clear about his identity; he thinks of himself as a Chilean first. But he feels very patriotic about the US too, even though he's scarcely spent time there. Of course he's still too young to know what I really do. Maybe he too will develop some feeling later, for the romanticism of a being in the spy business."

"It's not romantic, Alex, except maybe to a teenager. It cuts too close to the bone."

They were into their third round of Stoli, and Alex knew he should stop. He never could match Fyodor and was seriously out of training in this nominally dry country. And of course he rarely had to drink with his Islamist agents. *Is Fyodor really taking this where I think he is? Is he going to try to recruit me? That would be pretty goddam crude. When will he show his hand?*

"And how did you get back into the KGB? Or whatever they call it these days."

"*Sluzhba Vneshney Razvedki*—the SVR, External Intelligence Service."

"Yeah, whatever. I would have thought your loyalty would be totally suspect."

"You've never worked in a country whose whole system, whole leadership, has been totally suspect and a lie, Alex. It does wonders to your mind. I committed a crime against the Soviet state, indeed—and I was very lucky I wasn't shot. The old system was already breaking down and had lost its zeal. I sat in prison for some precious years. But how many hundreds of thousands of others were there like me, who wanted to change things drastically and put an end to that stupid and cruel system? I did nothing for money. People who knew me knew that. The KGB knew that. I was not alone in my intentions."

"So you were exonerated?"

"Not exonerated, but pardoned, and of course only after the fall of the Soviet system. But I have always been, and remain, a patriotic Russian."

"And they took you back, just like that?"

"They took me back. The entire system had changed. The lies of the old Soviet system were gone. And they needed me. I know a hell of lot about Latin America, my friend, that's of great value to Moscow, especially when starting up a new system."

"And yet you've come back to Pakistan, supposedly to see me, your old friend."

Fyodor stared him in the eyes. "Alex, you know I had to tell them everything I ever did in Santiago, and everything about you, all our conversations. I gave them a full assessment of who and what I think you are—including a vulnerability assessment. They expected nothing less."

Alex bristled. "And so just what the fuck you think I am then, a goddam turncoat?"

"No, please, you're no more a traitor than I was. But you are a person of ideals, you believed in your system. Now, knowing what we know about reactions of so many American diplomats and intelligence officers to the policies of this American administration and its Global War on Terror, it's not hard to guess that you are pretty unhappy."

"I'd have to admit that I am. But that doesn't mean I'm going to become a bloody Russian agent!"

"Alex, please don't speak about us with quite such contempt. We are honorable men too, we love our country. We overthrew our stupid and cruel Soviet tyranny."

"And now what do you have? Paradise?"

"No need for sarcasm, Alex. You should respect what we have been through. The great Soviet empire collapsed, with scarcely a shot fired. This has been a considerable achievement for us. Russia is transformed. It is what even Washington wanted. Yes, I admit, there are elements of the authoritarian approach in Putin. You don't expect a political culture to go from red to green in one decade, do you? All I know is that we live better, eat better, live in a more beautiful city and country, can travel around in and out of the country, can find ways to earn money, and can speak relatively openly among ourselves about our beliefs even if we have to be careful about full public attacks on our dear President. Our newspapers now reflect the real world, contain solid reporting, not like that parody, that imaginary fantasy world of Marxism-Leninism of the Soviet days. We don't live in fear any more. We have options." More libations from the bottle on the floor. "Life is much, much better, Alex. Do you begrudge us that? Now, could it be better still? Improved? Of course, but slowly, slowly. I am very pleased with the huge changes we have made. It will get better yet." Fyodor paused, took another swig. "But meanwhile, what of your country, Alex? Are *you* getting better and better, things improving? More freedom? Better life? Better economy? Greater social responsibility within the capitalist leadership? More national confidence? Are you pleased with the overall direction of things?"

Alex remained silent, tightened his grip on his teacup. "Let's start eating before the food gets cold, Fyodor. Do you know how to use chopsticks?"

"Alas, only the Chinese linguists in KGB school were taught chopsticks. But in Spanish training I learned how to roll an enchilada. I can even wrap a secret message in an enchilada."

"I think you mean in a fortune cookie."

Fyodor's pixie eyes laughed.

Alex spooned some of the lamb and onions onto Fyodor's plate and then his own. They ate in silence for a few minutes, but they were each aware that Fyodor's pregnant question was hanging.

At last Alex took a stab. "I did believe that the US had a superior system. I still believe it is, certainly relative to the Soviet system at least, and probably to your own system even now."

"It was indeed superior, that's why I was willing to work for your service at that time, Alex, to bring down the Soviet Empire. It *was* an 'evil empire' as Reagan said, the Soviet Empire that was destroying even Russia itself. But what about today in America?"

Alex took another portion of the spicy eggplant and stirred it into his rice bowl. He could see how Fyodor cleverly sought to draw him in. But he decided to put his cards on the table, as they had once done as co-conspirators in an earlier period. "Today, at this point, Fyodor, I'd have to say, I have increasing trouble believing that our system is the universal model anymore."

"And why not?"

Alex sighed. "I see the US slipping into its own pattern of building a kind of empire. And it's an empire that I believe is destroying America, as well the lives of people in this part of the world." He looked Fyodor in the face. "I see it close up here in Afghanistan and Pakistan. And it's going on in Iraq. It's ugly, foolish, failing."

Fyodor sat quietly, letting Alex formulate his thoughts.

"I've seen too much. I've watched us slip into war—so casually, so enthusiastically, so assuredly with so much goddam zeal and certainty—even self-righteousness."

"Surely the American people know that."

"No, they don't, that's what really aggravates me. We haven't remotely reached the stage of brainwashing of the Soviet Union, but I'd have to be frank: our press has never been so cowardly in the face of a so-called 'war president.'"

"Ah, my dear Alex, there is another big difference. We always knew in the Soviet Union that our press and television were filled with lies and that reality was far from what we were told. We never believed any of it. But you... your people really do believe that your press and TV are presenting an accurate picture of what is going on in the world. I ask you, isn't that more dangerous? A misinformed public in the world's sole superpower?"

Alex remained silent, in basic acknowledgment. He played with his chopsticks on his plate. He had just poured out some of his deepest fears that he rarely shared in full with anybody—and to a Russian intelligence officer at that.

Fyodor let the admissions sink in. But Alex now realized the implications of what he had said, and reacted viscerally at his own admissions.

"But don't think, Fyodor, that I'm going to turn around and become some goddam Russian agent. You can't recruit me, don't fucking try."

"Alex, such emotion! Have you had too much vodka? Who do you take me for? You can't recruit people who don't want to be recruited, you know that. Recruitment is like seducing a woman."

"Yeah, well, I'm no woman."

"But you suggest that *I* was a woman, or at least dirty enough—lacking principle enough, to accept recruitment from your CIA."

"I didn't say you were dirty. But frankly I couldn't have done what you did."

"That's because your system hasn't quite hit the breaking point yet. Maybe it will, maybe it won't. But you know what? There aren't very many of us in the world who believe that the US is at the top of the heap anymore, except in sheer muscle. And we resent being muscled on our own turf. The Cold War is over Alex," Fyodor's eyes bored in, "yet your leadership is trying to start it all over again, trying to recruit every one of our immediate neighbors—

Georgians, Ukrainians, Kyrgyz, Uzbeks, into some kind of a new NATO, a military alliance whose original purpose was to oppose the Soviet Union. The Cold War ended, we ripped up our ideology, but you came after us like nothing had ever changed, seeking to enlist our neighbors, to foment color revolutions in all of them, stirring up anti-Russian feeling. That's not hard to do in most of those wretched places, you know. Our Soviet policies had been so stupid we had alienated them all. But that's no reason to try to recruit them into your old military bloc again."

"So why did you come to see me then, Fyodor?"

"To be frank, my service wanted to sound you out, hear your thinking in these times. Of course they'd like to recruit you. But I told them I didn't think it would work. Nonetheless they wanted to hear what you had to say."

"Well, you've heard what I have to say. I'm not happy. I think things are getting really bad for us, and that we've lost leadership and direction in the world. But I certainly don't think I want to see Russia run the damn world either, or China!"

"Ah, but isn't that exactly the point Alex? We don't want *anybody* 'running the world.' We want the US to stop trying to do it as well. Those days are past. We have common problems all around the world, terrorism, health, education, climate change—so why are you playing around trying to pick up the little satellite countries around Russia? And try to put missiles in them? And permanent bases in Iraq and Afghanistan? You think we are going to go to war?"

Alex craved some quick antidote to the permeating power of the Stoli. He summoned the indolent waiter and asked for a pot of real tea, strong. The bearded and wizened Taoist Immortals of China peered down upon them from the paintings on the wall, bearers of ancient wisdom. Alex felt there was very little wisdom around them now.

"Look, I agree, these policies toward Russia are pointless. There are still a bunch of old Cold Warriors hanging around. We have them, you have them. They thrive on conflict. And you're right, we do have many more common interests between us now, Russia and America."

"Alex, make this trip worth my while. Tell me how you see the whole terrorist situation here in Pakistan, Afghanistan. Where is it going? What will the US do?"

"I have no idea where some of our crazy policy makers want to go. They may want yet another war, this time against Iran, but I don't think they can pull it off. And they are inadvertently pushing Pakistan to the brink, to force it to solve America's losing situation in Afghanistan." And Alex poured out his frustrations at the way US policies were working, or not working, and his concerns about how they were headed to failure. Fyodor listened carefully, respectfully, posing only a few questions here and there. Finally Alex sighed,

"I think that's enough, that's the way I see it. And these things aren't secrets anyway."

"No, of course they're not secrets—they're better than secrets, they are highly informed personal and professional views and insights into what is going on in Washington today. I never thought for a second you wanted to sign up as an agent for Moscow, why should you? But you know what, Alex? The situation isn't totally different from what it was when you and I talked in Santiago. My information helped Washington understand what Moscow was doing, and why. You were able to take those views into consideration in dealing with our declining power. And your information today—OK, it's not secret, maybe not even information as such, let's say your views—you are helping Moscow understand where Washington is going, how you think it seems headed for failure. It means that there is a chance we can seek to work with the US more closely on many of these other issues we've talked about. Indeed, your policies, your global leadership, *are* failing. And the sooner you all realize that, the easier you will be to work with in the future."

"Maybe."

"You've shown me how many important senior people in your service, and in the military and in the State Department share many of these same views you have expressed. We suspected as much from your press, you know, but you've just helped confirm it with an experienced and thoughtful eye. These policies are bound to change. Otherwise they are suicidal for you in the end. That is the good news for you, and the good news for us as well—that they are bound to change. I am happy to go back to Moscow with this report."

"Fyodor, it's not a report," Alex snapped. "They're my own goddam views."

"Accepted. But it is helpful, and I'm grateful to you. I somehow feel we have restored the balance in our relationship, and that we are now working on trying to prevent the worst abuses of power of *your* country. ...How times change."

"And you can turn off your recorder now."

"Alex, Alex, what do you take me for? Don't you remember my razor-sharp memory? I don't need such cheap intelligence toys."

As they parted to go in separate taxis, Alex spontaneously turned to Fyodor and embraced him emotionally. They stared at each other another moment. "We've been through a lot together, Alex. I wish you and your country luck. I hope maybe I can check in again with you sometime."

As Alex rode home in the taxi, he felt cocooned in a time warp. With all the intensity of Pakistani life around him it had felt strange to revisit the mood and flavor of their intense exchanges of Santiago days. The tables had indeed turned. Through it all, he really liked, he really admired Fyodor. In his heart he knew he would enjoy seeing him again. They shared an instinctive ability to observe and communicate these harsher truths about their respective systems, governments and political blindnesses.

And Alex was disturbed to realize that this dinner would probably remain between himself and Fyodor. More problematically, Fyodor probably knew that too.

*   *   *

"Alex, you must remember Hugh Ellison, says he was with you as a career trainee when you came on board."

Alex sat in the Embassy cafeteria, eating some lamb curry and rice and reading today's issue of *Dawn*. He looked up in surprise when his colleague made the introduction.

"Hello Alex. It's been a long time. Lot of water under the bridge." He pumped Alex's hand enthusiastically.

"Hugh! It has been a long time. What brings you out Pakistan way? Have a seat!"

"I'm on an inspection for the military. You know, I left the Agency about five years back. I'm now working for the Pentagon, looking at coordination procedures between the military and the Agency, see if we can clean up some of the mess."

"Good bit of mess to be cleaned up. You got your work cut out for you."

"So how have you been? It must be hell being back here in Pakistan today after the quiet good old days. Didn't you grow up out here or something?"

"Yeah, missionary brat. Lot of changes since then."

"God knows we need skills like yours. It must sicken you to watch the fundamentalists take over here. Loose nukes all around. We've certainly got some pretty heavy duty problems to turn this country around."

"I don't know about turning it around. The problems run pretty deep."

"Damn right, but you know better than anybody how Islam has run wild out in these parts. It's great to have your skills available here, get inside the local mentality and defeat them from the inside. I've always told the generals, you gotta get inside the mindset, figure out what makes these people so crazy religious, understand what's wrong with their society. We've got a hell of task here. I mean, with all these madrassas and religious education. I'm sure if we could just close down these schools we'd have the Paks on our side in a generation."

"Well, Hugh, the schools can be radical, but there's a lot of grounds for radicalism here apart from that..."

"I know, I know, the whole Islam thing. Goes right back to the foundation of the damn country. Pentagon's been thinking about how we might press the Paks on changing the curriculum of the schools. This anti-Americanism just seems out of control, irrational. Comes straight out of Islam, looking at the West as the Abode of War. If we could change that mentality the Paks would appreciate our strategy out here a lot more. No reason for them to be so fixated on India. It's China that's the real threat, but they don't see it that way here yet. Chinese have pretty well bought them off over the years with all these weapons sales and things. Don't think that hasn't complicated our dealings with the Paks either. But China is the real strategic threat to Asia, we've got to convince the Paks of that, get them to line up these countries out here with us on this issue."

Shit, not this same old line again, Alex thought as he began to tune out the familiar Pentagon armchair strategy and its identification of the true "strategic threat". These guys—experts at identifying threats everywhere. It was a whole industry. What backwater in the world couldn't be suddenly presented as the cockpit of strategic struggle, vital to American interests? Somalia, Georgia, Yemen, Chechnya, or in the old days Granada, Panama, Nicaragua. Anything to justify keeping up the guard, the eternal vigilance, the high military budgets, the weapons development and acquisitions, the war games of coming conflicts that often ended up as self-fulfilling prophesies. Stoking insecurity and fear at home.

"So how about it?"

Alex struggled back to the present. "Sorry, Hugh, was thinking about something else for a moment. How about what?"

"The Chinese. We're looking for some ideas on how to drive a wedge between them and the Paks. Any ideas on how to do that? Maybe try to pressure some of the top Pak brass to cut back on their arms purchases from China? Prejudice them against the quality of those arms? Any way we could sabotage the Chinese weapons—make the Paks think they're no good? Prove how anti-Muslim the Chinese are? How China is taking over Asia?"

"It wouldn't be that easy, Hugh. For one thing, is the US willing to replace China as the source of Pak arms? I don't think so. We won't sell them half of what they want, for security reasons, and we're trying to prevent them from ever using them against India—who they see as their biggest strategic threat. And frankly, you know what? The Paks don't trust us. Know what they call the Chinese? 'All-weather friends.' That's a slap at us because they know we're not. We've been fair-weather friends at best. After they got the bomb we slapped an arms embargo on them for years. The Pak Army hasn't forgotten that. There's not much trust there. And looking at the record, I'd have to say with good reason."

Hugh glanced at his watch. "Well, OK, Alex, I've got a meeting in a few minutes with the Ambassador. But it's great talking, and I'll get back to you. We need people like you who can get inside this culture here, help turn it around. Keep up the good work. See you."

And Hugh was off, in the unshakeable certainty of his mission–to be shared with others equally certain of the way the world works—according to the Washington bible.

*   *   *

Kevin, the Deputy, stuck his head into Alex's office in the middle of the afternoon. "Hey, Mr. Muslim, guess what? You're going to have a little competition now," he said with some glee. "New officer been assigned to us out here—he's Muslim, the real McCoy, Punjabi background, grew up as a teenager in the States, speaks fluent Urdu. Should give you a run for your money."

Alex was fed up with Kevin's grating manner—and he regularly chucked it back in Kevin's face. "That's great, Kevin. Then that'll make two of us out here who know what's really going on."

Alex was happy at the news, a potential fellow comrade-in-arms who would see things the same way, provide backup in the debates, share outlooks. So when Moe Tanner arrived two months later, Alex immediately invited him home for dinner to show hospitality and get to know him. They sat out in the back garden where they wouldn't have to worry about possible listening devices in the house. The Paks were known to be good at bugging select foreign residences.

"Moe Tanner? That name's got me puzzled."

"Well, it was originally Mohammad. But nobody calls me that, and hardly anybody even realizes what Moe is short for. It's weird, it's also short for Moses, and a lot of people think I'm Jewish. And Tanner, well, my Dad officially changed our name from Tanvir after 9/11. So at least I don't stick out like a sore thumb."

Moe was of slight, tennis-player build, had light coffee-colored skin, could have been from any number of places in the Mediterranean or Latin America.

"So when did your family get to the States?"

"Oh, when I was around eight. We're from Punjab originally."

"So you speak Punjabi?"

"Yeah, we spoke it at home all the time. I know it's not very different but I need to get my Urdu up to snuff, and written Punjabi. I never got educated in it or used it for professional work. So I'm going to have to buckle down and start reading newspapers and such. Maybe you can help me, I hear you're fluent in Urdu."

"Be happy to if I can. It's great having you here, Moe. It's a struggle sometimes to get local realities across to people in the Embassy. You're the first native Pakistani officer we've had in the Station—if you'll permit me to call you that."

"Well, it's funny, ever since being in the States I've always tried to avoid being viewed as Pakistani, always wanted to be accepted as American. And didn't want to be seen as Muslim. Now here, my selling point with the Agency is that hey, I'm Muslim, and 'native' Pakistani. So, yeah, I guess I'm 'Pakistani.'"

"And your wife, she's Pakistani, too?" Isabel inquired.

"No, no, she's American—strictly German-Irish. That makes us kind of a typical American family by now I guess. She'll be out here in a few months, she's finishing her degree work at UCLA. And we're fairly recently married so no kids yet."

"I guess you've found it difficult at times being Muslim in the US these days. I mean after 9/11 and all that?"

"Not too much I guess. But there's very little about our lives that makes us Muslim in any case. We don't go to the mosque, and we have avoided socializing within the Muslim community. We fit in to the US pretty good. Most of my Dad's friends are from the bank he works for. In high school I hung out with pretty much everybody, and not with the few Muslims there were."

"Well, that was smart," Alex said. "As long as you haven't felt discriminated. Any relatives here in Pakistan?"

"Yeah, some uncles on my Dad's side in Multan, but I wasn't sure whether I should contact them, it might just complicate things for me—and them. They don't know I'm here even and certainly wouldn't recognize my name right off."

Alex and Isabel found Moe sympathetic, a little like a lost puppy. He tried painfully hard to be accepted. They invited him over for casual family supper regularly until his wife arrived. In the office, however, Alex was getting concerned that Moe's reporting from agents he was now handling in the Pak military and in fundamentalist political parties seemed to be gentler compared to the reporting from their previous case officer. The kinds of attitudes and language towards the US that these agents had reported from inside their own circles earlier now seemed to be toned down, even if most of the factual substance was still there.

"Moe, you're off to a good start here in the two cases you're handling," Alex said after the first month. "You seem to be getting along fine with the agents. But I did sort of wonder, the sharper views and remarks about the US, well, they seem a little softer now as you report them, compared to your predecessor."

"Really? Well, maybe. I just felt I should take it easy in reporting stuff that's too critical of the US. It may piss off the customers and make Washington nervous. And some of the Pak views, they can sometimes be pretty prejudiced as well."

"Look, Moe, let me tell you something. We report and analyze what we hear, period. If Washington likes the insights, that's great. If it pisses off policy makers then that's just tough shit. It's our job to report what we hear from sources that we believe to be reliable. And both of the sources you are running *are* reliable, they have a track record. So really, don't pull any punches on what they say and how they think. Let the chips fall where they may. Tell it like it is, including their attitudes."

Moe fell silent. Then he said, "OK, but how is it going to reflect on me if I'm the source of anti-American reports?"

"It doesn't reflect on you, Moe, you're reporting what your sources are telling you, what they are hearing about views in the military towards the US. You're just a conveyor belt—an important one—hopefully with an eye to keeping these agents honest and accurate."

Moe shifted in his seat and put his glass down. "Alex, I'm still a little uncomfortable about some of this. You have to understand, I'm technically Muslim. I know I'm under special scrutiny and…"

"Come on, Moe, you're not…"

Moe raised his hand to cut Alex off. "Alex, be real. I'm Muslim and you're not. Of course I'm going to be under special scrutiny. All Muslims are, even in the US government. I may not think of myself as Muslim—hell, look at my name! And no, I never go to a mosque. And my family, we eat pork when it is served to us, all to keep from attracting attention. We all drink. People in the Agency treat us fine, but I can feel it lurking in the background—everybody is wondering about our loyalties in all of this—at least in the back of their minds. Nothing is said, of course. Don't you remember that US Army officer who was Muslim? Guy that one day shot up a lot of his colleagues on some US base? People remember that sort of thing. If I send in a lot of reporting with angry, anti-US language, some people are bound to wonder about me. They may not say it, but some of them will think it."

"Moe, you're a professional. You wouldn't have this job if you weren't, if we didn't have confidence in you. Really, don't worry about it."

"That's OK for you, Alex. I know how critical you are of stuff going on in US policies—you say it right out in Embassy meetings. But I can't afford to do that, and on my first tour. OK, reporting is one thing, but I can't afford to speak critically of US policies here in Pakistan, given who I am. Think about it."

Alex paused, pained yet familiar with the perspective; he had no ready answer. He knew what was sometimes said about him for being born in Pakistan and speaking fluent Urdu. But at least he was "American" in the eyes of his colleagues. Moe was liked, respected, a good guy, and would probably become a good officer. There wasn't much prejudice in the system that Alex could discern. But what Moe was talking about wasn't outright prejudice or discrimination. It was that corrosive quality of unspoken, lurking cultural suspicion in the minds of others, the insinuating, subconscious elements of uncertainty about Moe's own identity and loyalties—a black snake that could never be completely killed.

"OK, I hear what you're saying," Alex said at last. "But I'm sure you'll be fine if you just do your job as you're supposed to. That means not skewing the reporting—in any direction."

Alex's conversation with Moe came to mind a month later when an old friend, Doug Fury, arrived in town. All Doug knew was that Alex worked at the Embassy, he didn't know anything about Alex's Agency affiliation, nor should he have known. Alex had known him when they were at college together, when Doug was majoring in Middle East studies. Doug went on to become an academic and had come to Islamabad for some conference on South Asian studies. Alex invited him over for supper, happy to have a break from the usual Pakistan-centered discussions. Over beer and old times they talked about what Doug had been up to in his academic career at UCLA since then.

"You know," he sighed, "times have changed in our field since 9/11."

"Tell me about it," Alex replied. "We're up to our eyeballs in it here."

"No, I mean even back home. It's not the same, dealing with Muslims any more. Just one typical case in point. You know, I had this friend Nasir. He was from Pakistan originally but had gotten a grant to go to the US to study, and he ended up marrying an American girl. And no, he wasn't just after her passport, it was a real love match. I learned lots from him about how young Pakistanis in particular were thinking about the US. Nasir was a good friend, personal friend, and used to come around and see us, we shared a lot of things about our personal lives and problems. He wrote some good stuff, trying to make Americans aware of thinking in the Muslim world, their grievances and all.

"But after 9/11 this all changed, and fairly rapidly. I think this was true for most Muslims in the US. The President had painted everything in black and white—a struggle against good and evil and all that. I mean, all of a sudden we had this massive new goddam internal security program and all Muslims were under the microscope. And you know, it was amazing—I never heard Nasir say another negative word about the US after that. He even grew uncomfortable when I would bring up my own critiques of American policy, you know, support for dictators around the Middle East, lack of balance on the Palestinian business, all that. Nasir just clammed up. He didn't want to talk about it any more. His biting newspaper analyses about Middle East policy disappeared. No more, zip...."

"Well, the President did say you are either with us or against us."

"Right. And I guess Nasir got the message, like many Muslims. He had a choice, and he made it, he ended up joining the choir. No more thoughtful writing—he adopted the good ol' standard mainstream American critique of what was wrong with the Middle East, wrong with Arabs, wrong with Islam—not with US policy. Really sad. He began to avoid me after years of friendship because my criticisms were growing sharper in the face of the whole Global War on Terror. It made Nasir uncomfortable. He didn't want to be associated with them—or with me. Too uncomfortable, too risky."

Alex shook his head in sympathy and took another swig of beer. "Is it surprising? Muslims hauled off planes because someone sitting beside them got spooked when they saw them reading Arabic. Muslims seeking to pray in public places. Expression of any sympathy for Palestinians. Pulled over by cops on a DWM—'Driving while Muslim.' A lot of Muslim friends have told me about that."

"I'm not surprised. And let me tell you, it's gotten even rougher since then. All around LA, Muslim friends of mine, a lot of them were called in by the FBI. They got leaned on to work as informants within their own communities. Their mosques were infiltrated. Christ, agents provocateurs on the FBI payroll might sidle up to you and make some harsh comments about US policies just to see how you'd react. And if you looked like you were pissed off with things, then they suggested taking stronger action, maybe exploding some bombs or something, to see how far they could push you. I mean, trying to actually talk people into terrorist acts, for God's sake."

"Yeah, that's rough, especially since a lot of these poor bastards fled from countries like Iraq and Egypt—where the security services were really all over them 24/7 there. But still, you know, I got to admit, the FBI has one hell of a challenge and I don't envy them. All it takes is one bad guy in these communities to pull off some terrorist crap, and then the Bureau's on the chopping block for why they didn't see it coming. It's goddam mission impossible in the end. You can't have one hundred percent security, but that's what the public demands."

"It's more like the fucking politicians who demand it one hundred percent—they're always grandstanding about how any breach of security is unacceptable, crucify the guy in the system who missed the signals. It's really hard for the Muslim communities out there now. They're afraid they'll be all held responsible if one soul out of a six-million community goes on a rampage. They're really getting jumpy." Doug squinted up at the sun. "You know, I speak Arabic, I've always enjoyed using it at Arab grocers, you know, shawarma or falafel stands around the US, chatting up the owners, asking about where they're from and I how I've been there and all. Shit, you just can't do that anymore, Muslims don't want anyone to speak Arabic to them, man. They get all spooked, even if you just tell them you like shawarma or Umm Kalthoum songs or whatever. They're all on guard. Who is this guy speaking Arabic? Maybe he's some goddam FBI agent trying to compromise me."

"Yup. I used to have great discussions with Muslim cab drivers in the US about the politics of their old homelands, or on current affairs and problems. Not any more. Lead shield's come down and we're all just happy campers now, not a thing wrong in the world. Kind of makes you wonder how a country trying to be a leader of the world can operate, you know, when the immigrants from those Muslim regions are now dedicated to see nothing, hear nothing, know nothing—just maintain a goddam happy face."

"Yup," Doug said, "Just like Mom used to say—don't talk to strangers."

Alex thought of Moe.

*   *   *

"Yeah, OK, Alex, but why in hell is he taking *you*?"

"I don't know, Sam. You ask him. What can I say, the Ambassador sort of likes me, he thinks I have some insight into the system—Pak mentality and all that. And I speak Urdu, just in case Jahangir lapses into Urdu, which he sometimes does—just to score a nationalist point."

"OK, Alex, but it's damn awkward, it cuts across our liaison arrangements. Hqs will not be happy having Mr. Goddam Striped-pants Ambassador going off for talks with a Pak intel chief and taking one of our officers with him. I suppose it helps that you're there—at least we're not being blindsided."

"Maybe that's one reason he wants me to go along. It might really be crowding you on your own turf if he insisted on going with *you*."

Every Embassy section was jealous of its own turf; in seeking a direct appointment with a top level of Pak intelligence, the Ambassador was technically breaking the rules—except that the Ambassador was also nominally Chief of Mission—if that counted for much anymore in the gradual militarization and Pentagonization of foreign policy. Still, not only was the Chief of Station nervous about Agency turf being trampled, the chief of the Embassy Political Section was even more unhappy. Why was *he* being excluded from an obvious political meeting involving the Ambassador while an Agency officer was going along?

The Ambassador's car, *de rigueur* stars and stripes flying, pulled into the portico of Pakistani Army Hqs. Pakistani duty officers, guardians of the grand old traditions of British pomp and ceremony—never to be confused with power—sprang into action, snapping exaggerated salutes that would have been self-satirizing except for the seriousness with which Pakistan maintained the tradition. The Ambassador did his best to strike a civilian version of a smart salute in return; Alex opted not even to try. Inside they were waved on through right past any security check. *Good old Paks*, Alex thought, *still innocent enough to permit seniority to take priority over security—none of that demeaning egalitarianism for them.* They were shown towards a small elevator, but the Ambassador opted instead to ostentatiously spring up the huge staircase that fanned out onto the ground floor, a relic from when the building served more ceremonial purposes. Pudgier aides were forced to puff up the stairs trying to keep pace. This indeed was not the official Hqs of ISI at all, but the General's working office in a military compound. The invitation to meet at the less elegant working office was actually an honor, a sign of acknowledgment that the meeting would be of substance and not simply *protocolaire*.

Did ISI really even exist? That was the question many outsiders and journalists often posed in their casual examination of Pakistani politics. Indeed the Pakistani government itself played down the existence of this powerful intelligence organization. Over the years its capabilities had grown increasingly indispensable to successive Pakistani presidents who found themselves forced to cede ever greater power to this organization in its control of many internal events within the country as well as to gather information about external enemies. Indeed, the government found it useful to occasionally drop hints that the ISI was only a small organization within the military, sometimes described as a bit of a rogue in undertaking actions not always approved by the government. The convenient myth of deniability had largely crumbled in the 1980s as the CIA truly clambered into bed with ISI and other elements of the Pakistani government during the anti-Soviet jihad in Afghanistan, when real Agency station chiefs held regular and substantive policy meetings with the real chiefs of ISI. But, in the nature of intelligence organizations, not all is what you see; the ISI had decidedly developed an additional powerful domestic agenda that lay at the heart of Pakistani political and strategic action. Pakistani prime ministers could still suggest in a moment of whispered faux intimacy to a foreign diplomat that ISI often "exceeded its brief." Washington had slowly learned to know better, but the diplomatic fiction remained useful.

Fictions can be two-sided. Successive US and Pakistani diplomats regularly intoned their belief in the "shared strategic goals" between Pakistan and the United States. While that belief was privately questioned among most foreign observers, it was an article of faith to large numbers of official Americans. Why should the Pakistanis *not* share American goals? Were not those US goals broadly and intelligently conceived, vital building blocks in the universal interests of most of the world? Designed to create a global order based on stability and freedom, facilitated by the benign actions of American power and diplomacy? US power helped make the world free. How could Pakistan, if it was truly an ally and a friend, want anything other than what America wanted?

The Ambassador was not an unintelligent man. He had worked with business partners from India. He had a feel for international politics and was quick to think in terms of alternative scenarios, or the long-term implications of policies he might recommend. He too assumed, however, that while the interests of businessmen might differ, countries who were "friends" should not diverge in their core interests. It was his mission to straighten out any misunderstandings, to demonstrate to Washington that Pakistan, for all its occasional aberrations and worrisome drifts "off the reservation," was essentially "on message" when it came to cooperating with Washington. American diplomats in Islamabad lived in fear of Congressional scrutiny of Pak-US relations, where any hint of genuine strategic differences could produce Congressional calls to pressure Pakistan and make life very difficult for the State Department.

The Ambassador strode purposefully down the hall, aware that personal carriage always created a certain impression of resolve, certain that hard political realism on both sides could impose agreement upon the deliberations of rational men. But General Jahangir was of a different stripe: he had the reputation of a powerful and prickly individual with a clear and unwavering view of Pakistan's strategic interests. He was also known for his powers of persuasion in imposing such views on a series of often feckless and shallow prime ministers and presidents of Pakistan; presidents could mouth the necessary diplomatic words, but the Holy Grail of Pakistan's geopolitical reality resided within ISI and would not brook compromise by mere self-serving politicians. Pakistan's true interests might occasionally be diplomatically clouded, fogged, concealed, dissembled, even denied perhaps— but never compromised.

On the other hand, General Jahangir also had a longstanding reputation of bluntness where his predecessors had often preferred to soothe over differences. A Pashtun himself, tribal affairs ran in his blood, their complexities incorporated into his own psyche. There were few within senior levels of Pakistani leadership with such an instinctive feel for the politics of the North-West Frontier and its cross-border realities. General Jahangir was a soldier's soldier, still crisp in bearing despite his graying hair and deepening lines on his face that revealed him to be well past retirement age.

General Jahangir was also known for his contempt for diplomatic niceties. When the Ambassador was escorted into his office, he was seated with a telephone to his ear and pointedly did not stand or end the conversation for well over a minute while the Ambassador and Alex were seated in their chairs waiting. The Ambassador may well have taken umbrage at the apparent slight to his own personage, but Alex sensed that the General was simply unimpressed by diplomatic gravitas and felt comfortable in finishing a necessary call, which had seemed substantive enough, from what Alex had heard from the Urdu conversation at this end, relating to the movement of certain military units. The General then hung up and turned to the Ambassador who had to rise again from his seat and shake the General's extended hand in an informal manner while the General indicated that he should retake his seat. Alex gave his own name as the General shook his hand and peered at him probingly.

The office was huge and strangely spare. The high double doors were padded with leather. Several couches ran along the wall, a massive Pakistani clone of an Afghan rug on the floor, with a large round teakwood coffee table covered by a huge hammered brass tray with Mughal design. The tan walls looked like they had not been painted for years. Several fans rotated lazily in the ceiling, although a few air-conditioner units sat quietly humming in the windows. The General had a few antique flintlocks on his wall, several carved wooden regimental insignias, and numerous pictures of himself and other officers at various locations around the country, as well as pictures of him receiving various high personages from the Pakistani government over the years—enough to establish who he was, but not enough to suggest boastfulness. Tea was brought in swiftly along with a plate of sweets. The Ambassador and Alex sat in front of the General's desk who had clearly decided to preside over the meeting by not suggesting that they all move to the chairs around the coffee table.

"Thank you for receiving me today," the Ambassador began. It was lost on neither Alex nor the General that the Ambassador had not even bothered to include Alex in a royal "we," leaving perhaps the suggestion Alex was a mere note-taker. Or that he was not significant to the exchange. But Alex pointedly did not take notes, to signal to all that he was not simply a spear-carrier. Although he did not acknowledge it, General Jahangir knew of Alex through his own sources. He was perhaps even disappointed that the usual nostrums he might palm off onto most ambassadors could come under greater scrutiny with Alex present. General Jahangir strikingly had included no aide of his own at the meeting.

Jahangir lost no time in living up to his reputation. In pointed absence of opening rituals, the General turned to the Ambassador: "I understand that some members of your US Congress are querying our country's commitment to the war in Afghanistan. Why would they have that impression, Your Excellency?" Jahangir disregarded the strained American insistence on the plain, egalitarian "Mr. Ambassador."

The Ambassador seemed thrown off his stride by the blunt opening gambit in which he was essentially being asked to explain why his side seemed to have failed to transmit reality to Washington. "Well, General, let me first say that the President personally asked me to extend his greetings, and to express his appreciation for all that you are doing in Pakistan to help the coalition's war effort in Afghanistan." Jahangir nodded briefly to the predictable diplomatic pablum and elected to save his reply for later while the Ambassadorwas now forced to plunge on forward without the expected badinage of niceties. "As for our Congress, well, surely you know that we're a democracy and…"

"We are not, Your Excellency?"

The Ambassador was taken aback at the speed with which the meeting had already turned into a sparring match. "No, General, I didn't say that. I was simply pointing out that neither the President nor the State Dept can control what duly elected representatives of our people have to say on things in Congress. Pakistan's experience with democracy must have familiarized you too, with that same phenomenon." Nice volley.

"But it would seem then, Excellency, that someone has not been doing his job back in Washington in adequately informing members of your Congress about events out here."

The Ambassador chose to let that one fly by. "General, I can't take personal responsibility for how certain congressmen choose to inform themselves about events in the world."

"Indeed, Excellency, but ignorance does complicate our relations. And when loose talk about Pakistan flies around in Washington, it may appear only on page ten in your American newspapers, but I can assure you it will make headlines in ours. It angers the public and greatly complicates our jobs—for all of us."

"Indeed it does, General. That is why…"

"I am concerned, Excellency, that people who are supposed to be intelligent and informed in Washington do not understand our situation here. I fear people there lack adequate grasp—or even interest—in our problems."

The Ambassador shifted in his seat. "We appreciate very much what Pakistan has already done in our common cause and common interests—and what you undoubtedly will be doing in the future." Having passed along the niceties, the Ambassador decided the time had come to move onto the offensive himself. "Nonetheless, there are certain problems that also complicate our cooperation, General, and that frankly hinder the efforts of the coalition forces in Afghanistan."

"You speak for the coalition, Excellency?"

"No, I'm not in Kabul nor in charge of the war, but…"

"I think it might be realistic, in discussing any problems we have, to dispense with the word 'coalition.' Frankly we view it as an absurd proposition. This is an American project, driven by the US, primarily financed and manned by the US, and directed and controlled by the US. It is not a 'coalition' view of the war that prevails, but an American one. I did not think I needed to include the German or the French or Dutch ambassadors into our meeting today to help reach any conclusions. Let's speak honestly. We are talking about American interests here, and whatever NATO camouflage is placed upon it only obfuscates our understanding of the problems."

Even Alex was surprised at Jahangir's willingness to ride roughshod over established diplomatic practices. This certainly was no meeting at the polished Pakistani Foreign Office. The Ambassador clearly perceived that more challenging ground-rules were at play.

"General, we believe the symbolism of NATO involvement in the Afghan war is of major importance, and it suggests indeed that more than just American interests are involved, but…"

The General intervened. "Our diplomats report that there is scarcely a single NATO country out there that believes in this war, except, of course, for the British. And the British are, as we both know…shall we say, unhesitatingly loyal to Washington."

Jahangir let a brief moment of silence pass and the Ambassador did not seem to wish to rise to this particular challenge so he moved forward. "But we are not here to debate that question, Your Excellency. What we are really doing now is frankly discussing basic American and Pakistani interests."

General Jahangir permitted a smile to flit across his lips in appreciation for the move away from diplomatic-speak and to escalate the challenge. "Now, Excellency, you have been authorized by your President, as you say, to deliver certain messages here. I, for my part, must say I have not been authorized by our government to say anything at all on their behalf. Indeed, I am speaking not even on behalf of ISI." He let the message sink in. "I am speaking as someone who has a lot of experience in dealing with your government, particularly your intelligence services—but not only the intelligence services. I have been around a long time, Your Excellency, and I have learned a lot. In my view there is very little benefit in pretending; that simply wastes our time and insults the intelligence of both of us. Now, let us get down to business. What are the main grievances that your government directs towards our work together? From Congress, the State Dept, or the CIA."

"Alright, General, let's indeed put cards on the table. First, we appreciate what you are…"

"Please, let's not waste time. Let us focus on the things you do not appreciate."

This pace and sharpness of exchange exceeded the Ambassador's diplomatic experience. "Very well, what we do not appreciate, then. Despite your help in identifying, capturing and turning over to us selected and important members of al-Qaeda, we believe that you are complicating—even helping defeat—our task in Afghanistan through your contacts, and support to elements of the Taliban inside Pakistan. These elements are important sources of support to the Afghan Taliban in Afghanistan—including even to al-Qaeda—and greatly hinders the prosecution of the war by the coalition."

The General smiled at the ambassador's continued, nearly reflexive use of the term coalition. "We have received demarches from your government before," the General said, "identifying some of these contacts between us and certain Taliban elements on our side of the border. I will not waste your time or insult your intelligence by denying these things. Please understand I am speaking strictly at the personal level and I will publicly deny that these are official views or that I have even said them. But at least my humble personal views may help clarify to you why this government does some of the things that it does."

"I appreciate your frankness, General."

"Now, why do you think that we are in contact with key Taliban elements in the border areas?"

"That is a good question. That is for you, not me, to say."

"You are an intelligent man, surely you might have some ideas."

The Ambassador paused, again struck by Jahangir's ability to maneuver him into difficult situations. "I would have to say that… I think this policy of

Pakistan is... erroneous, if that is what you are really doing. These Taliban elements make it harder for us to fight the war in Afghanistan, and it creates problems for the Afghan government itself. And, if you will permit me, I believe you are naïve in not understanding that these very Taliban inside Pakistan itself are a danger to your own government and your own national security."

At last, the Ambassador's starting to show some balls, Alex thought.

Jahangir stared at the Ambassador. Had he drawn blood? "Your Excellency, do you really think we do not understand the damage some elements of the Pakistani Taliban have already done to our internal security? Do you think we are blind? Think for a moment, why do you think we would pursue—tolerate—such policies?"

"I suppose you believe that in the end you can control these forces, and use them as pawns in your effort to dominate the politics of Afghanistan in the future." The Ambassador was getting the hang of the volleying.

"Yes, Your Excellency, perhaps a bit oversimplified, but what you suggest is basically correct. These Taliban forces are nothing new. The North-West Frontier and tribal areas have always been dominated by tribes, crazy men, holy men, religious warriors, fanatics, tribal leaders who rise and fall preaching religion and their tribal codes. They can indeed be a nuisance but they can never be ignored."

"Nuisance!" snorted the Ambassador. "More like a serious threat—to have these jihadi ideas being propounded among tribal elements that are all predisposed to carry religious banners."

"And yet, Your Excellency, I can never recall your own government ever voicing concerns about such tribal elements during the struggle against the Soviet army in Afghanistan. You were happy then to incite them, organize them, arm them with weapons and intelligence, provide them with sensitive advanced anti-aircraft weaponry, mass-distribute their messages of jihad around the Muslim world, and send them off against the Soviet enemy to fight imperialism and atheism. Now your country seems to have changed its tune—even though it is the same Afghans, doing the same thing... I repeat, the same people, doing the same thing."

"I admit, General, that we both took advantage of their fanaticism at the time. It was a worthy cause in helping defeat the Soviet Union. In retrospect some of that may have gone too far."

"But you can't have it both ways, Excellency. We perceived their natural 'fanatic character,' as you call it, to be useful then. So why shouldn't we in Pakistan still find it so today? Yes, to be blunt, we Pakistanis need these same religious elements again, to shore up our interests in Afghanistan."

"That is playing with fire, General."

"For you, yes. For us, no. Certainly we have some periodic problems from the more uncontrolled and fanatic of these elements. But most of them we

337

can control, have controlled, and will control. Now, let's be frank. You and your 'coalition' are not destined to remain long in Afghanistan. The struggle is hard, you are not winning, you lack the staying power, you have no guts for it, your publics will tire, the costs are rising, and you will soon go home discouraged. But we in Pakistan are there until the Day of Judgment."

"You misunderstand, General…"

Jahangir waved off the Ambassador's intervention. "Please let me continue. Now, the consequences of this reality are very clear. We simply will not sign on to a desperate and failing American strategy that seeks reckless short-term advantage against our long term interests. We will not allow Afghanistan to fall under the control of the enemies of Pakistan. These so-called Taliban in the end will be responsive to the greatest needs of our country. You may not appreciate that, Excellency, living as you do bordered by neutered countries like Mexico and Canada. But for us it is quite riveting to live next to the Indian Goliath on our eastern border that seeks to destroy us. In our thin, narrow-waisted country we cannot therefore tolerate an anti-Pakistan force on our western border as well. If you were in our shoes, Your Excellency, would you do otherwise? If China was on your northern border, how would you view your position in Mexico?"

"I can only speak to our own interests in a real world, General."

"Fair enough, but I am speaking for mine. Let's stop pretending that our interests are congruent. You are desperate, you are looking for a way out of a conflict that is failing, you are losing and that will make your country look weak. But that is your problem, you chose to go into Afghanistan. But that conflict that you now pursue so feverishly is simply not in our interest. More important, it is tearing our own country apart. We will do what we need to do to preserve our own interests, not yours. If you were in our situation you would do nothing less. Indeed, right now you are looking out only for your own transient American interests—except you like to maintain the fiction that these interests are 'universal and shared.' They are not."

The Ambassador flushed and stiffened, and Alex knew the warning signs. "General, let me remind you that you are talking to the emissary of a superpower. We bear primary responsibility for maintenance of the international order. I will not be lectured to, or condescended to, by a regional power that is not pulling its weight on an issue of global significance—the need to eliminate the forces of international terrorism."

I didn't know the guy had it in him, but he's trying to pull rank now…

"I am well aware of your superpower status as you call it, whose future, by the way, seems far less certain in the years ahead by the looks of it. Surely you need to think realistically. What does it actually mean when you cannot control even one of the weakest, poorest, and most pathetic countries in the world like Afghanistan? That has no real army, no navy, no air force, no industry, no economy, no ethnic homogeneity, and no coherent national government? I assume you must know your history—of the fate of earlier global superpowers in Afghanistan." Jahangir waved the irate Ambassador off. "Now, Excellency, we are willing to cooperate with you in helping stabilize that country, but we will not place at risk our own country to help you salvage a losing strategy over the border. This is not a disagreement, Your Excellency, it is a frank statement. What you want and what we want are not congruent. And our first task is to protect our own vital national interests—indeed our independent existence—even if they seem to be of relatively little consequence to you in your efforts to protect your shredded honor in Afghanistan."

"I hardly need remind you, General, that we are not just talking about strategic preferences. There is a little matter of some three billion dollars a year that Congress has granted to your country, to assist you in working with us. I am sure you would not want to see that aid threatened—as will surely happen if Congress is displeased with your level of cooperation."

"Excellency, I am sure you do not mean to convey the notion that you are threatening me. Let me ask you, this three billion a year, do you give it out of the generosity of the American heart? Or is there a specific value in it for you on which you put a price tag? How much of us do you think you can buy with that sum? What do you think you have already bought with three billion? To the extent that such a sum weakens our pursuit of our national interest, it is a bad deal for us. We might in the end be better off without it rather than forced to demonstrate our gratitude while damaging our deeper interests and losing our own honor."

"This is not about honor, General. We are attempting to find and strike a bargain of mutual interest."

"Thank you. We know our interests; we will adhere to them and will not be deterred from them. I would hope that your superiors in Washington will think wisely and carefully about this before attempting to bludgeon us to meet your needs." Jahangir stood up without a smile. "Now, if you will permit me Excellency, I have another appointment. I am confident you will treat all these remarks as strictly off the record."

The Ambassador was down the stairs, out the door and into his limousine before the full import of the meeting had settled in upon him. The flag on the limousine recommenced its insouciant gay flutter as they drove away from the General's office, belying the Ambassador's anger. He shook his head. "That's the bluntest damn conversation I've ever had in my entire diplomatic career. In fact, it was goddam insulting. I could raise hell over this meeting if it had not been off the record. So what was your take on it?"

"Well, we knew the General has a reputation for being direct, and there it was. But he was even blunter than I expected, yeah maybe bordering on the insulting. But we've heard views like these repeatedly from our own sources—

this is the way most of the elite really think here. You just don't hear them saying it to our face much."

"Arrogant son-of-a-bitch. But I suppose you're right," the Ambassador sighed, staring out the window. "Our isolation from reality back home, it is so overwhelming—it's the isolation that comes with power. So in the end I suppose it's better to get these cards on the table."

"Yeah, and frankly it may help to try to get our diplomats to stop mouthing stuff like 'common interests.' The General is right on that, in my view."

"Goddam, boy, whose side you working on anyway?" the Ambassador deadpanned.

"Just reporting the news, sir, that's all. That's what they pay me for."

Before they reached the Embassy, the Ambassador turned to Alex. "We will keep the contents of this meeting to ourselves for the moment. I'm going to have to figure out how to get these views across to Washington—very gently, and over time, so they don't choke on it."

*   *   *

Alex was delighted to hear that the Chief of the South Asian Division, his old boss and mentor at Hqs, Sawyer Brummel, would be coming out for a visit to the region, the first visitor from official Washington whom Alex could welcome with enthusiasm.

Alex had immediately liked Sawyer, an old South Asia hand at the Agency, a soft-spoken southerner who ended up being an early mentor to Alex. Sawyer himself had spent years working with Pashtun tribes and was one of the rare officers who spoke the language well and was steeped in Pashtun culture and lore; he often joked that coming from the American south had perfectly equipped him to understand the Pashtun tribal mentality, with their long-standing family feuds and culture of honor. Sawyer in turn had been delighted to find someone like Alex who spoke Urdu fluently and knew Pakistani culture, so he had taken a special interest in Alex's future.

"Sorry, lunch has to be down in the Embassy cafeteria, Alex, but I've got a busy schedule this afternoon—tedious admin sessions with the COS on budgeting—things that take the fun out of the job. Should be a word to the wise about the hazards of getting promoted beyond one's levels of organizational interest. But I did want a chance to chat with you a bit." And like explorers who constituted a private club of two, dedicated to reminiscing about a distant region they had mutually experienced, they understood each other's instinctive attraction to the pleasures of Afghanistan and Pakistan, a fondness not always shared by others. And now that Alex had been working at the Station in Islamabad for two years he felt a strong need to discuss some of his misgivings about the job, and US policies.

"Alex, you may already have noticed, how different operations are here in the South Asian division than it was when you were working Soviet operations. Nobody ever broke a moral sweat running operations against

Soviets. Maybe not easy to operate against the USSR, OK, but the Soviets were the unquestioned enemy in everyone's eyes. No real moral ambiguities involved and everybody was on board. That makes things comfortable."

"It's interesting, you know," Alex commented, "that's what Soviets called us too, *glavniy vrag*—the main enemy."

"Right, but as you know, here we're dealing with countries that are not the enemy. In fact, they are places we're trying to deal with on a fairly friendly basis, sometimes as partners and allies. And there isn't much policy unity at home on them either. Partisans and lobbies up the gazoo, leftists and rightists, partisans of the diplomatic or the military approach, people who want to sell arms, or want us on their side against *their* enemies. That complicates life."

"Yeah, I've noticed actually."

Sawyer smiled, nodded to a passing acquaintance at the next table, and put down his white plastic soup spoon next to his styrofoam bowl. "And I gather you're already feeling some contradictions between the realities out here and the policies being set back home."

"I think I had already felt some of those contradictions when I was in Chile, looking back at the role of the US government in the coup against Allende."

"Yup, that was certainly one of the less pleasant acts of policy by the White House in that era. I'm not sure we ever really learned anything from that whole episode, either. But somehow most of us continue on in our work anyway—not as cynics, but because we do believe in something, in something better."

"Sawyer, I hope there is something better. Frankly, from what I saw of it, all that stuff in Santiago had very unpleasant consequences."

"Yep. And these days I frankly don't know how much better off Afghanistan is either, when you look at the mess there today."

"OK, Sawyer, you say you believe in something better, but how do you maintain that when sometimes things seem to be getting worse?"

"Well, it may be a cop-out, but I do believe that our deepest duty is to get the reporting right, our biggest obligation. CIA doesn't make policy, and it shouldn't—it's not our job. But if I've done my goddam best at getting a clear picture of the problem to the policy makers, I've done at least all I can do on my side. That's all you can hope for. You can't be responsible for the acts of every foolish politician that ever gets into high office."

"So you think there is a kind of values behind what we do? Not just blind serving of the national interest, whatever that is?"

"Alex, I couldn't do what I did if I didn't believe that. Yes, we do break the laws of other countries when we recruit spies there. So do most big countries around the world. But to most of the practitioners in the Agency, it's not so much immoral, it's more amoral—in an amoral world. But we do it for the country, because we believe in the country, not blindly, but we believe in it."

"Right," Alex paused, "you know I couldn't help being struck, that very first day when I went in the main entrance of Hqs building to report to work there, I saw that huge seal on the floor—'And the truth shall make you free.'"

"That's right, right out of the Bible. Kind of lays a heavy load on us, doesn't it?" Sawyer said, smiling. "But there's something more going on here. Frankly, I don't really know that the truth always does make us free—and certainly not necessarily happy. I don't know whether espionage in the end always serves its practitioners either. The truth, the reality as you learn it overseas, isn't always the pretty picture folks conjure up in their comfortable life back home. To people back there, the US are the good guys, the rational guys, up against the irrational dangerous crazies, the good fight for democracy and all that. That's what our TV assures us every day. But that's unfortunate, because it isn't always the case, and is way oversimplified. Now you and I, we can't do what we do just because we believe our country is on the side of justice and truth, that we're the best. Every country probably thinks that about itself."

"If it isn't for the country, then what is it for?"

Sawyer smiled and looked out the windows onto the broad green lawns of the Embassy compound. "Eating a quick bowl of chili for lunch in the Embassy cafeteria is not probably the ideal venue for a discussion of grand truths. But if you ask me, at least *my* goal, *my* truth that keeps me going in that crazy town of Washington is the search for truth—or reality, or whatever you want to call it—as it exists overseas. The search for that reality, as best as we can objectively identify it, has got to be *our* professional truth, our moral code—if we have any here at all. You're paid to report what you hear, to submit what you think is an accurate picture of what's going on out there. You can't shrink from what the impact of that information might be, where it'll take the country. A lot of it may be bad news. It may not make our country look good, much less please the President, or the Pentagon. It may even increase our understanding of why the other guy does what he does— thereby jarring our certainties even more. But if that's where the reporting and analysis takes you, then that's your patriotic duty to report it, as best you see it. If we have a moral compass, that's it. At least get the story right, chips fall where they may." Sawyer glanced out the windows again, pushed back his chair, and stood up. "OK, 'nuff said for one working day. Next time we should do this over a beer somewhere, if you can still get one in this country. I'll tell you some stories about my time in the Pashtun hill country."

*   *   *

The wheels of Pakistani history had ground him up and spat him out— twice damaged. First Homaid came from a poor background of Mohajirs, immigrants from India who lost everything they had when they fled from India to the southern port city of Karachi in Pakistan at the time of the infamous *Hindustan ki Taqseem*, the British-engineered Partition of India in

1948. Like millions of other Mohajirs from India they had fled for their lives, fearful of Hindu mob reckoning against Muslims during the population exchange—all Muslims to Pakistan, all Hindus to India—that sparked so much fear-induced killing among Hindus, Sikhs and Muslims. Iconic images were branded into the memory—of trains pulling into stations over the border with every soul on board slaughtered.

Homaid's family itself had not arrived in Karachi from India unscathed either: his father's younger brother Yunis had horrifyingly slipped from his mother's hands on the roof of the lurching train one night. The child was remembered on family occasions thereafter as the family martyr, proof of the human cost of the migration. Yet they had to acknowledge their relative good fortune: they had lost only one family member, and the family's women had been spared rape or worse. Homaid's father traced his family's earliest roots back to the Pashtun tribal borderlands of Pakistan. After they had migrated to India they had long since lost their knowledge of Pashto in favor of the Urdu spoken by most Muslims in northern India—but they had never fully forgotten their original Pashtun identity. Communities never did forget—never were allowed to forget—their identities in the rich and colorful salad of diverse ethnic, religious and linguistic elements of the subcontinent. To forget was to face the loneliness—and dangers—of belonging to no one.

Homaid's grandfather had been a tailor, a skill not to be despised: his occupational skills were the one priceless possession the family owned; it traveled with them and could not be taken away from them along the blood-soaked paths of migration routes. So Homaid's own father in turn had inherited the same professional lifeline to survival, growing up learning the art from his father in the swarming Mohajir quarters of Karachi.

The family had also believed in the idea of the creation of a Pakistan, the "Land of the Pure," because it was a place of refuge, a new homeland, for Indian Muslims. But because they were newcomers in the new state of Pakistan they would be forever thereafter be referred to as Mohajir or "immigrants," distinguishing them from the "native" Punjabis and Sindhis around them. Indeed, the Mohajirs had soon found it essential to look out for their own rights through establishing a political party of their own, dedicated to representing and protecting the community.

In that sense, Homaid was never able to quite feel himself a "native" Pakistani; he remained an outsider except in his own community's circles. And even though Homaid's own family had been Pashtuns generations ago, with the fading of their original language they did not fit into the quite different social milieu of Karachi Pashtuns either. But Homaid still wondered about the family's earliest origins and his Pashtun roots. He mentioned his background once to a Pashtun friend at his workplace, but his friend simply nodded in reaction to a piece of information that was not particularly relevant to anything, barely worthy of passing mention, rooted in the distant past of an unstable world. Still, for Homaid, that Pashtun past stuck in the back of his mind and burned like a small flame in his evanescent identity.

Of tailors there were many in Karachi. And besides, with the shifting fortunes of the country, the growth of smuggling through Karachi's port seemed to offer easier money. Homaid's father ended up exchanging his tailor's yardstick for a more promising job of truck driver. His family and his relatives and his new employers were eventually able to get enough cash for him to buy a major share in a truck that had seen better days, with the promise that he could become a small link in a long chain of an active smuggling network that ran the length and breadth of the country. Sitting up in the cab of his brilliantly painted red truck adorned with palm trees, Koranic names and invocations, floral arabesques, and scenes of cool and welcoming oases, Homaid's father felt king of his world.

The run was lucrative indeed—but also dangerous. To succeed required familiarity—a sixth sense—for the complex and shifting rules of competing criminal turfs, their complex power relationships, rival gangs, patterns of police greed, and the necessary payoffs to what seemed to be a long list of people all along the route with their palms outstretched. This required a constantly updated knowledge of all the customs officials, police, and competing gang interests and extortionists—every one of whom sought a piece of his action and who controlled constantly shifting portions of the long stretch from the port of Karachi on up northwards and then over the Afghan border to Kabul or Kandahar. It was a high stakes gamble: if you crossed the wrong people you ended up dead. But unless you crossed with silver every one of the necessary outstretched palms, you could also end up without profit to show for having risked these long hauls with sensitive cargo. After two years of turning his family's fortunes around with a greatly augmented income, one day Homaid's father's judgment lapsed, just once, and he crossed the wrong people on a hash route. He ended up slumped over the steering wheel in his cab, a bullet in his head, discovered at first light at a truck stop outside of Jalalabad, his precious stash missing. Indeed, an unremarkable event in the smuggling business. But no less tragic to Homaid's family.

What was Homaid to do? His father's gamble and cruel end were hardly encouraging. He had accompanied his father on a few runs—though not, providentially, on the final one. Still he felt he had a nimbler mind than his father who had never quite broken free of the inflexible measurements of the tailor's workshop, who had lacked the touch to play at a gambler's game of confidence and bluff that called for alternating moments of prudence, bravado, silence, humility and retreat.

Despite his mother's and his sisters' importunings, and plumped with the confidence of youth, Homaid assumed his father's late-found profession with the help of friends who assured him he could work under the protection of one of the mujahideen groups that ran hash and fertilizer routes. The major mujahideen groups actually provided a kind of insurance policy against some of the more local petty crime along the road. Homaid impressed those in the world of smuggling as a savvy and obliging kid; and over time found himself actually recruited into the support mechanism for one of the many jihadi groups linked with the Taliban. His contacts with Pashtuns in the border area grew and, partly out of practical need, partly out of interest tied to his roots, Homaid began to pick up Pashto. He lacked any contemporary tribal connections that would help him fall into a specific tribal group in the Frontier area, but his "honorary" Pashtun status was a help—all Pashtuns knew of the distinguished history of the Rohilla Pashtun community of India who had played a significant military role in the campaigns of the Mughal dynasty going back to the 18th century. Not bad for a kid out of the poorer neighborhoods of Karachi, and Homaid made the most of it. Indeed, he painted "Rohilla Express" over the cab of his father's truck, now his, in the hope it might also serve as amulet to ward off a murderer's bullet.

Homaid liked the money, but he also wanted to deepen his Pashtun warrior identity and to go where the real action was: he asked for military training—to go and fight in Afghanistan. But his Mohajir background was held against him by the Pashtun and their Frontier-dominated inner leadership. Furthermore he didn't project the right image: pudgy, a watery smile, eyes that didn't hold a stare, and soiled clothes, Homaid did not come across as a natural fighter. But he persisted in his quest to change his life. He started getting some physical exercise, lost some weight, took some classes at a friend's martial arts studio. Finally he was taken seriously by one of the Pashtun sub-commanders who decided to give him some brief guerrilla training in Waziristan. But Homaid stupidly blew it, he was expelled for smoking hash outside the camp. A more zealous commander might have executed him on the spot as an example to others. But his original recruiter spoke up on his behalf, pointing out his potential logistic usefulness to the organization. Homaid was grateful for the reprieve. But he still resented the watchful eyes upon him—it felt like the old familiar story of discrimination as he repeatedly tried to find a place among the mujahideen fighters. He swore he would give up the hash habit and after much investigation was finally admitted back onto the old logistics route, with a promise of perhaps some basic field training down the road.

Homaid had a cousin in Karachi, Mushtaq, who had joined one of the bullyboy squads in the violent urban politics of the Mohajir Movement. Mushtaq had attended one year of accounting classes before dropping out and being taken on as an assistant in a small photography business. His involvement in the Mohajir Movement had attracted the attention of a spotter for the CIA and Mushtaq had eventually been recruited as a source on the Mohajir politics of Karachi and its violent underbelly. With the book of Mushtaq's life now open to his Agency handler, Mushtaq eventually came to identify his cousin Homaid as someone active with the Taliban group. Over time Mushtaq also provided details about how Homaid had been constantly denied access to the inner circle of fighters; Homaid and Mushtaq both believed his ill-luck was due to discrimination against Homaid's lack of local Pashtun tribal ties. When other aspiring fighters who seemed to possess fewer skills than him were accepted into training, Homaid had grown angry and resentful.

The Station gathered enough information on Homaid that he became a strong target for potential recruitment, with access to the smuggling routes and jihadi Taliban groups. Mushtaq had described Homaid as adventuristic, but harboring resentments against the Taliban leadership that could be turned into a source of motivation to work against them. Mushtaq's Agency case officer in Karachi arranged to meet Homaid indirectly and, after a few sessions and significant financial incentive, was able to recruit him. Homaid was quickly turned over to Alex since he had greater expertise in handling the complexities of such cases.

Homaid still found himself torn. On the one hand, he had been drawn towards the romanticism and commitment of the Taliban struggle; he saw himself a part of it, a budding revolutionary figure. He was engaged in genuine action, moving to redress the wrongs that had been visited upon Muslims by both Hindus and Westerners. He found new identity in being part of this grander struggle. On the other hand, he was angry at the slights he had encountered over the years from Pashtuns while he served them with his trucking run. Within the circles of the Taliban he had learned about the grander geopolitical struggle taking place in his country, how the US had helped feed the Pashtun in the war against the Soviet Army in Afghanistan and had then left them high and dry after the Soviets had pulled out. Now the US was back again, but this time as enemies of the Taliban and their Pashtun supporters.

He had come to hate the US as a symbol of dominance, and he heard the tales around him of this relentless trigger-happy occupying force in Afghanistan. Yet here was the US now coming to *him*, recognizing his personal importance, demonstrating it in the salary they offered him, appreciating his influential role in the key issues of the day. Furthermore, Alex as his case officer truly *understood* him, appreciated his potential, his broad political knowledge of the situation. Alex was able to talk at length about Homaid's family background, their place in Indian society under the Mughals—he *knew*. Homaid was now a human being appreciated in his full dimension. He gained from Alex a broader understanding of many of the forces at work in the Frontier region, which he was able to use to his own advantage and project a more intelligent exterior. While Homaid was often treated as an outsider by his own people, bolstered now with the respect, counsel and support of Alex, he knew in his heart that he had in a way become more powerful than they were, that armed with his new contact in the

Agency he could even break his oppressors if he wished. Such was the importance his new situation, his new sense of individualism, took on in his mind.

With his new duties as a reporting source to Alex, Homaid seemed seized with new zeal to succeed, to show Alex *and* to show the jihadi circles. He no longer haggled over every penny in his provision of contraband goods to the jihadists. He developed increased political knowledge of the internal struggles within Taliban factions so that he could speak more confidently, choose sides more wisely and with greater insight. And Alex seemed different than most Americans; he spoke Urdu, he knew what was going on in the country, he even had sympathy for it. "Trust me," Alex said, "I agree with a great deal of your criticisms of American stupidity and the wrong direction we are taking. Don't think I don't say these things myself within the system. I have reporting channels into Washington that have influence. We need to educate these people in power in the US who seem to know nothing and often make stupid decisions. You can help me make the case for smarter policies and for an end to these unjust assaults in the name of the Global War on Terrorism. We can work together on this."

Supplied with this rationale, Homaid believed in the importance of his role. And Alex too believed every word of what he said every time he talked with Homaid. If a case officer did not believe the story he was living with his agent, it would show. A good officer *did* believe the story, with passion and sincerity, at least while they were together in an operational situation—and because the story always did contain meaningful elements of truth. Indeed, nearly all narratives contained elements of truth—but whose? Even Alex's critique of Washington's policies was genuine, at least in part, despite his acceptance of the grander scheme of things and of the importance of broader US strategic goals. Besides, it was only the small mind that could not believe several contradictory things at one time. Were they not different faces of the truth which both contradicted and coexisted and together made up the whole?

Yet who was fooling whom? There is something subversive about the role of the case officer. Alex, when he was with Homaid, believed in what he said in order to reinforce Homaid's emotional commitment and sense of cooperation. This narrative nonetheless did have a serious place in Alex's heart. And when Alex was back inside the Station, like many of his colleagues, he understood that one had to accept the realities of certain short-sighted policies from Washington that were beyond his control, while continually working to try to change them with fact-based arguments and reporting. Yes, even some of his own immediate superiors might well have shared many of those views and misgivings.

But in the solitude of the wee hours, the folly of many of these policies that Washington was blindly pursuing across the region took on greater salience in Alex's own mind. Indeed, Washington seemed to be patently exacerbating the situation, even on a daily basis, a process he witnessed before his own eyes. And in writing up his reports from his meetings with Homaid and other sources, Alex took pleasure in exercising the license that a good agent always bestowed upon his case officer: to report unpalatable truths to superiors based on reliable sourcing—often hard, irrefutable evidence, indicators that many of the policies were not working, that the Taliban command had contempt for American competence, had full confidence that time was on their side, and would act accordingly. These reports from field agents were in fact accurate and insightful, and represented privileged reporting that would reach high places in Washington. Unpalatable or not, such reporting could not be refuted back home—only ignored, or rationalized away. Not only did such definitive information demand to be read, but once stamped "Secret" because of its clandestine sourcing, it was afforded greater credibility and clout than Alex's own informed but personal views would ever have possessed in Washington.

Homaid's improved attitude and show of seriousness gradually impressed his commanders. One day he was summoned by the unit commander Abu Muqtada and told that he should prepare himself for a month in camp in explosives training. Flush with his accomplishment, Homaid sent a message to Alex to trigger a meeting in Peshawar. Like a father at the graduation of his own child, Alex delighted in Homaid's progress that he himself had helped craft, and for the extra clout that the success of this operation provided Alex himself within the Station.

*   *   *

The Salman events had all but shattered Alex's relationship with Majeed and his family. Months of silence followed, softened only by occasional visits between Isabel and Zubayda who appeared to be picking up after the mess of their men's professional lives, as well as serving as custodians of the tenuous contact between families. There was surprisingly much less rancor between the two women over Salman's death—did they not both share an intuitive awareness of the complementary political drives that lay behind the events that had led to his harsh death? Out of their diverse backgrounds they shared an unspoken repugnance for the way politics in all its forms were destroying lives.

At the least they shared a desire to get on with the transformation of Pakistani society through empowering women. They also shared an intuitive certitude that ultimately they, and not the men around them, bore the more important task of the future on their shoulders. Zubayda also loved spending time with Rodriguito. "He seems a very serious little boy," Zubayda noted one time, "I don't see him laughing a lot." Isabel nodded, but did not comment; she feared a certain coolness was creeping into her relationship with Alex that could be affecting the home atmosphere. Alex's work demands were considerable, and he could not talk about them in much detail. Even more, Isabel felt a growth of latent anger in him—even if mainly job related.

"What is on your mind, *mi amor?*" she asked him one night in bed after they had made love, almost as a desperate obligation to demonstrate that the relationship was still alive.

"Nothing really… just work, I suppose." He knew that did not sum up the multiple inchoate feelings in his mind.

"You haven't been sleeping well. I can feel it at night."

Alex sighed, nodded.

"It is not about us?"

"No, no, really not." He rolled over and put his arm around her again. "I know I've been hard to live with. I just feel sometimes like I'm engaged in a fruitless task here, like working on a slowly sinking ship."

"What can you do about it? Is it Sam, Kevin?"

Alex laughed. "No, I wish it was. I can live with them. It's bigger than the office, it just feels like everything is crazy—only maybe it's me that's crazy."

They were silent a few more minutes but neither ready to fall asleep. "I went over to see Zubayda again today," Isabel offered.

"Oh, how is she?"

"She's well, still lively and very engaged in her women's groups in the countryside. She wants me to get more involved with her on that."

Alex was silent again, reflecting. "That's good, you should get out of the house and this guilded diplomatic cage. Does the Salman thing come up between you?"

"No, she hasn't spoken about it in so many words. But I can see she has been very shocked, that's why she's plunged so much more into her work."

"Do they still blame me?"

Isabel hesitated. "Yes, in some ways, but not completely. She told me that Salman had been heading in the wrong direction for some time, turning more to radical Islamist ideology. The camp business terrified her; one way or another she knew it would destroy him. That all preceded you. But…"

"But what?"

"She and Majeed do believe you helped set off the immediate events that led to his death, just by being seen with Salman. But Majeed as well knew Salman was playing with fire, that it was a matter of time."

"I still feel agonized about it all. It haunts me at night sometimes. I don't know how I let myself view Salman as an operational target—except that he was in a very significant place."

Isabel remained quiet and let Alex talk.

"Majeed and Zubayda mean so much to me, from childhood. They are family. This has been a terrible thing. I don't know how I can forgive myself. Or whether they will ever forgive me." Alex found his voice trembling. "And I fear what is happening in our lives too. I love you, and don't want to lose you, Isabel." He turned to embrace her again with tears in his eyes.

And Isabel raised the issue when she next saw Zubayda. "I know it can't bring Salman back, and I know there is no excuse for what happened. But you and Majeed should both know—Alex is mortified and suffering very much from the event."

Zubayda's eyes filled up, and she took Isabel's hands silently in hers.

*   *   *

Akmal finally decided to take the step. "I think we should invite Alex and Isabel and Rodrigo over on Friday afternoon. Silence and distance will not heal. We all are in need of healing." All of them recognized the hunger to restore the profound friendships that had existed across many levels for so long. Mian's eleventh birthday celebration was a good occasion on which to invite Rodrigo and his parents.

The affair was deliberately kept short and dominated by the children's party, but it gave Alex a chance to return to Majeed's household. He embraced Majeed warmly and Majeed returned it. Zubayda was emotional in greeting Alex, all of them craving to overcome the domination of the incident in their minds. The animation of the children's party provided a lot of lubricating small talk and catching up that was healing and gratifying in itself. Both Majeed and Alex took pictures of the children and planned to exchange them. And slowly, over the next weeks and months, the tradition of periodic Friday family get-togethers began to creep back into existence. Both Majeed and Alex were ever more aware of the intricate ties that formed their relationship. Childhood friendship and deep personal affection had been augmented by the complexity of adulthood: shared professional interests, a national and professional rivalry, a sense of the pain that Pakistan had inflicted on both their families over time. Their special relationship transcended the bounds of their professional discipline, with an intimacy rarely achieved in relationships established in adult life.

On a pleasant fall morning as the summer heat was beginning to yield its hold on the city, Alex's family were present for another Friday lunch. Their meal was interrupted by a call for Majeed who then asked to be excused. "I've got to go to a meeting locally. Bloody office! What nerve, they dare call it today, on Friday, after prayers."

"Must be important, Majeed," Alex laughed. "Or you must be important!"

"Yes, well, don't ever forget it!"

"I hope Akmal will permit me to have tea with him later anyway," Alex said.

Akmal was aging. He had been out for Friday prayers and had just gotten back after seeing friends. His hair had grown whiter, possibly as a result of the kidnapping incident which had heightened his intimations of mortality. If he had slowed down a little physically, his mind was still sharp. The death of Salman had hit him in multiple dimensions. Akmal was not fully aware of the exact precipitating character of Alex's role in Salman's death. "I think it is best not to tell him," Zubayda advised Alex.

"I hope I may still enjoy the pleasure of your company, Akmal. I know you have been through some very hard times. And I feel deeply the weight of tragedy about Salman. I am so sorry."

"Thank you, Alex. We are humans, thus we experience suffering—the opposite face of joy. It cannot be avoided But come, sit down with me. We must not allow Salman's death to poison the other important relationships we have in life. You are welcome."

They sat down in the garden in the back under the trees, a soft breeze rustling the leaves.

"And what aspects of the human condition are you writing about these days, Akmal?"

"There is always more than enough to write about. I'm not sure why I still study these insoluble, unanswerable issues of God and man's condition. But there it is. We cannot escape them."

"Well, maybe the insoluble and unanswerable may be the only issues really worth pondering."

Akmal nodded. "I feel the weight of the past upon me more than ever before. You know, we have a saying in Urdu—maybe you've heard it: *Kal ke do pehlu hain: Ek jo beet gaya aur ek jo aanewala hai.*"

"The two faces of tomorrow?"

"Exactly. Isn't it remarkable that in Urdu we have the same word—*kal*—for both yesterday and tomorrow? This saying means: '*Kal* has two sides: One that has gone by and one that is to come.' In other words, our past is our future."

"Sounds like fate, karma."

"Exactly. And it feels like Pakistan is always involved in something intractable and insoluble, unable to shake its past. The soul must seek some relief from the driving power of the past. But since you ask, yes, at the moment I'm doing research on Sufi pirs in the Mughal dynasty. It is truly fascinating. You may know in those days these Sufi holy men were often very outspoken to the Emperor, to any authority. A strange kind of intimacy existed between them in one sense. A *pir*, even an impoverished one, often would express the bluntest truth to the emperor, things no one else would dare tell him. Of course, the emperor could have the *pir* killed on a whim at any point; while he feared the unvarnished honesty of these penniless holy men, he also knew they might offer the only honest opinion he would ever hear."

"Any good stories?"

"Well, Zubayda has always liked the story of the King and the Dervish under the tree. It seems one time a mighty King was on a trip to Samarkand and was passing with his impressive retinue through an oasis. All along the way people ran out of their houses and bowed deeply to the King, chanted his praises and offered him food and drink. As they came to the end of the oasis there in the sand sat a Dervish dressed in a ragged woolen cloak, deep in meditation. As the King and his retinue passed by, the Dervish barely looked up to acknowledge the King's presence. The King, angered at his insolence, ordered one of his retainers to drag the Dervish before him. 'I know about you dervishes,' the King said. 'You are dirty and insolent and dressed in rags, the lowest of the low. How can you fail to acknowledge my presence as the mighty King over all these lands?'

'Oh Emperor,' the dervish replied. 'If you want homage and glorification, you have come to the wrong man. You will receive such homage only from those who want something from you. Since I seek nothing from you, I pay you no heed!'

'How can you want nothing from me?' demanded the Emperor.

'Kings are created only for the protection and wellbeing of their subjects,' the Dervish replied. 'So that is the service *you* must offer *me*. We subjects were not created for service to the King, and so I offer you none.'"

Alex smiled. "I like that. I wonder how many emperors were willing to accept remarks like that. No wonder the Sufis were suspect."

"Yes, many were. The emperors always had doubts about whether the Sufis, even the ones in the court—were truly dedicated to the emperor, or were perhaps attached to a higher power."

"Meaning God?"

"Yes, but not just God. It means a perception of a higher cause. The Emperor may be a great man, a powerful man, but still he rules in his own interest, and in the interest of the kingdom at the moment—as he sees it. That for him is the highest value. But for the Sufi it is not the highest value. The Sufi looks to the values of human kind, of eternity, of God."

"But nonetheless some Sufis did work in the service of the Emperor, right?"

"Yes, some did. But most of them realized the contradiction—to either be true to higher values, or true to the Emperor's interests."

"So how did they manage?"

"Well, unenlightened Emperors banished them, but the more enlightened rulers valued their message—or liked them for the religious prestige they brought. We have rulers in Pakistan today who fall into that category— religion is mainly a show to help consolidate their power in the eyes of the people. But the people are not usually fooled. There is always a contradiction."

"Tell me, Akmal, does a ruler's advisor face a contradiction if the emperor is not all bad, but makes mistakes, and if the advisor has values of his own?"

"Most men who are honest and upright, who work in the service of the emperor and the state—they generally must believe in the emperor's cause.

They have experienced the anarchy that comes from warfare and chaos and so they seek to bring order to the state and society. But their loyalty is to the good state—not to the ruler himself.

"Well, what is wrong with that, from a Sufi point of view?"

"The problem is that the state cannot always be noble and enlightened. Its officials can frequently be corrupt, in some way. Or even stupid and wrong-headed. Or blind to reality. It is hard to be an official of the emperor's state and not be corrupted. How far do you go along with it to try to improve it, and how much are you obliged to break with its wrong actions? We see that in Pakistan every day."

"So you worry mostly about corruption then?"

"No, by no means. The ordinary corrupt man poses very little real danger. He simply helps himself to things, is out for himself—at a petty level. We all see him for what he is. And he usually knows full well in his own heart that he is corrupt and a sinner in the eyes of God. On the other hand it is the ones who actually *believe* in a cause, like the power of their state, or the power of their idea—they are the ones who can be truly dangerous. They are dedicated not to personal self-gain, but to the imposition of a grand idea. They are even willing to do terrible things in the name of the grand idea."

Alex wanted to hear where Akmal was going with this. "Like what?"

"Like imposing Islamic Law on everyone in accordance with the ruler's own interpretation. That is why I am so opposed to these followers of political Islam. Salman died because of it. Even Majeed has been influenced by them in part. In the name of one idea, some ideal, they become willing to break other ideals, like protecting humanity…"

"Yes, Akmal," Alex reacted enthusiastically, "I agree! Protecting the people, protecting life should rank as number one priority. We have in the West, you know, the doctor's Hippocratic oath—'above all to do no harm.'"

"Absolutely. Protecting humanity is the ruler's most fundamental and sacred obligation of all. But these people often spill blood in the name of 'protecting humanity,' or serving the world. They may spill more blood than they save in the process. Look at us right here, the zealous are willing to shed the blood of the Barelvi sect and destroy our Sufi shrines in the name of this harsh religious vision."

Alex pushed the thought further. "Tell me, Akmal, where else do you see this occurring?"

Akmal laughed. "Almost everywhere. It is the human condition. I think you know. Do you not remember the Soviet communists in Afghanistan? They were going to bring in the light of the future, progress for humanity. They were willing to kill hundreds of thousands of Afghans to do it. And…"

"And…?" Alex felt something more was coming.

"Well, I should not say this, but this conviction among leaders that they possess the truth even affects your country."

"Which truth?" Alex asked anxiously.

"That they are bringing democracy and human rights and order and freedom and free markets. This can also be a narcotic."

"You don't believe in those values?"

"Of course I believe that those ideas can have value. But not when they are delivered with a gun. Or when they are a cover, even unconsciously, to promote the power and dominance of your own state. I'm afraid these so-called values can just be a nice word, a euphemism, for the projection of power. As we saw with our emperors and their causes."

"But in the US we do believe in democracy and human rights."

"Yes, indeed, when it is convenient. But not when it is inconvenient."

Chile, Allende, Pinochet coursed through Alex's mind ...

"But you asked about the Sufi commitment," Akmal continued. The true Sufi will oppose even the emperor in order to serve the cause of justice. So the state is really only comfortable with people who do not ask questions."

Alex stirred. "Akmal, surely employees of the state must believe somewhat in what their state is doing, or else..."

"Look, my boy. It is simple. The values of the state and the ruler can *never* represent the highest values of humanity. They only represent the interests of those in power—which may be more, or less, enlightened. And those in power always, always, believe that their values and interests are good for all mankind."

"Come on, Akmal, isn't that is a bit cynical?"

"No, not cynical. Wise. The Sufi must always have doubts in the face of power—doubt about motivations and real goals. Doubt about the ruler himself, who always wants to see himself as acting in the name of justice and the good."

"But a democratic state does engage in self-examination or criticism."

"Not really, Alex. That is the hard truth. No state can basically tolerate fundamental doubt about itself or its mission. Especially in times of crisis or war."

Alex fell silent. "Thank you, Akmal. Like a good Sufi, you like to stir up doubt."

"Yes. But too much doubt is exhausting. It is time for my nap." Akmal rose up and waved his hand.

Alex sat for a few moments alone in thought about their conversation and gave a small smile. He too then got up and went out to the front garden to watch Rodrigo and Mian laugh and play. Isabel was busy in an intense conversation with Zubayda about their next women's meeting. The afternoon was cooling under the trees. Refreshing breezes came down from the mountains, perhaps even from distant peaks in the Himalayas. He sometimes felt astonished that he lived here, had grown up here, in the heart of Asia. The region offered him a sense of comfort that he could not explain. He felt he could sit here forever in reflection. But how productive was mere reflection? It perhaps inevitably carried consequences. He felt forces building inside himself.

*　　　　　*　　　　　*

Kevin, the Deputy Chief of Station, called Moe in for his first periodic work proficiency review. Moe came in with his coffee cup, and sat down on the edge of his chair in front of Kevin's desk. Kevin leaned back in his swivel chair, feet up on the desk between them. "Moe, bottom line, we like what you're doing. Your handling of the cases have been good, you write them up well. You've produced some good intel. Sounds like you're getting more comfortable with agent handling."

"Good, I'm glad you're pleased. I wasn't sure at the start how it was all going."

"What do you mean?"

"Well, Alex felt maybe I wasn't fully reporting everything from the personal remarks from some of these sources."

"Were you being honest?"

"Sure, I thought I was. I didn't include every last little negative personal comment they made on the US and its policies, but…"

"Did Alex want you to emphasize the negative?"

"Well, no, just to include it in full detail every time, even if it was just the agent's personal opinion."

"The agent's personal opinion isn't always relevant to the report. The report is about the facts."

"That's right. That's sort of the way I felt."

"Let me tell you something, Moe. Alex is a good officer and all that. He knows a lot about Pakistan. But sometimes he goes out of his way to stress the negative in a lot of his reporting—and in his personal comments. That's OK, everyone is entitled to his own opinion. But between you and me, I think he's too sympathetic to this country—it could affect his objectivity. I'd be sorry to see that happen to you. You're too smart to let that happen. Even though he's a good officer, he may not be the best model for you to follow."

"I didn't want to say it Kevin, I mean, he's been really helpful to me, but I've had an impression that, well, I've discussed it with him. But yeah, I do think he's too tolerant when he looks at a lot of stuff these crazy Paks are doing."

"You really think they're crazy, Moe?"

"Yes, I do, a lot of them. It's been sort of a shock for me. Like our family back home, for example—we'd totally gotten away from all this endless talk about bad-mouthing India, supporting Islam, paranoid about outsiders—all that. That's what we love about being in the US—the chance to be ourselves and not have to be playing up Pakistan all the time. I can see this country is fucked-up in a lot of ways, that causes a lot of problems."

Kevin leaned back in his chair, twirling a pencil in his fingers, and looking at Moe. "You know, Moe, you're right. I'm glad you do see things clearly and that you don't let your own background get in the way."

"I may look Pak, but I'm American. That's the way I see things."

"Good, Moe, keep up the good work. And don't worry about what Alex told you. He's got his own little love affair going with the country here. You don't need that. There's nothing in it for you."

"Thanks, Kevin, I hear you."

*   *   *

The jeep climbed up the last of the khaki-colored rocky passes and began to lumber down into the narrow strip of green below. The sun was still high in the sky. The smell of dust from the road mixed with that of lingering straw on the fields below, and an unidentifiable combination of trees, crops, animals and flowers told him it was Musa Khel, Majeed's tribal home and the residence of many of his relatives, some of whom he had not seen in years. It was a less propitious time, however, to come here in view of events of the past year.

He anticipated the traditional welcome in his mind's eye: the drums and dancers would come out to greet him back home. The sheep would be brought in from the fields and tethered outside the kitchen waiting to be sacrificed for the evening's celebration; after all, how often was it possible to welcome back the clan member who had attained a high place in government? For them, Majeed's position was money in the bank, potential protection from official depredation, a representation in the councils of power where the clan perhaps could have a voice.

The village seemed not to be suffering. New four-wheel drive Toyotas stood in front of several compounds, a few small shops—provisions, canned goods, hardware items, a music stall with cassettes and CDs, a sewing and materials shop, an ironmonger—all open and at first glance adequately stocked. Majeed entered the large walled compound that comprised several stone buildings. Children rushed out shouting in greeting; soon thereafter his uncle hobbled out of the house on his cane. Majeed bent over and kissed his hand. His uncle embraced Majeed and kissed him on both cheeks, while Majeed held both his uncle's hands and shook them, and they gazed into each others' eyes, exchanging the litanies and wishes of well-being, how is it, health, yes, thanks be to God, all are well, yes, good fortune, things are going well, praise God, you are welcome, the children are well, God preserve them, the guest is sacred, thanks be to God, God preserve you too. Majeed brought out a finely worked antique pistol as a gift for his uncle, some fine woven Kashmiri material for his aunt, and a number of smaller mechanical toys for the children.

They sat down in the men's reception room, on brightly woven rugs and pillows, leaning against the walls. Tea in small glasses quickly arrived, steeped in more sugar than usual in honor of Majeed's visit. Younger relatives entered, came up to kiss Majeed's hand, and sat down quietly at further remove from Majeed and his uncle.

"And how are things, Uncle?" Majeed had posed the question twenty times in ritual exchange, but conversation was nearing the point when such queries actually began to be taken seriously.

"Praise God. We are surviving, despite the attacks."

"Attacks?" Majeed knew where the conversation was heading.

"The ghost planes, the planes with no pilots. The spawn of the Devil. They are spreading fear."

"What is happening, Uncle?" Majeed wanted to hear it in his uncle's own words.

"The government cannot protect us any more from these attacks by the Americans. They are killing our people, and everyone is terrified. Even the children are afraid to go to sleep because they know the 'black plane' might come in the night. They strike us at random. No one is safe."

"Are the Arab and Uzbek fighters still in the neighborhood?"

"The outsiders? No, most of them are gone. May God preserve them, but keep them away from here. They are brave fighters but they have their own cause and we don't want them here with us, they only stir up trouble for us and bring in the ghost planes. They don't understand us, our way of life and politics. They are too fanatic. They are not interested in Pakistani politics, or the welfare of the villages, they only want to talk about jihad in the world. But we have jihad right here, in trying to remove America from our region, and keeping government soldiers out of our villages!"

Majeed looked out across the narrow green valley, its rushing waters, fruit trees, houses and gardens—idyllic. He remembered scrambling up the rocks with his cousins as a child during visits to his mother's side of the family; they sometimes laughed at his Pashto before he got more serious about it. His uncle had taken him out to teach him to shoot, something his father knew nothing about and wasn't keen for Majeed to take up either. A family warmth, a love of poetry, combined with austerity of tradition, so different than the more relaxed, urban, and indulgent Punjabi ways. His cousins used to call him a "softie", coming from the Punjab. Tribal law had always reigned here; his uncle, the local *malik* remained the supreme political and social authority among the people. This place was a jewel of autonomy, one of many large portions of this North-West Frontier that for the government remained indigestible pieces of political turf they could not yet truly control. It was officially called FATA, the Federally Administered Tribal Areas, a system of local autonomy that went back to British days and beyond. No one had ever mastered these tribal groupings for long and not much had changed. The locals were fiercely loyal to their own clans and tribes and fought efforts at centralized government control, especially from what they saw as grasping government authorities in Islamabad. Indeed, God help the zealous representative from the central government who might seek to impose his will on the region. Or who sought to change the structure of an elaborate and interlocking complex of rules, traditions, customs and laws developed over long centuries across the region. The exact chemistry of local tribal interrelationships and balances were impenetrable to all but a local resident.

"Nephew, your people in ISI, in Islamabad, are destroying us. You permit the ghost planes to send down like rain these missiles upon us. Nobody knows how or why what villages and houses among us will be attacked."

"Uncle, you know they are hunting for Taliban, you know how the Americans are obsessed with the Taliban."

"Taliban? Of course there are Taliban in our midst! What can we do about it? Who is not Taliban, at least in part? Over in Kabul the Pashtuns will soon regain their power after having been evicted by the US. Here we Pashtuns are protecting our local autonomy."

Majeed listened quietly and then said, "The Americans blame the Taliban in Kabul for hosting Bin Laden. They will not let Taliban come to power in Afghanistan again."

"Yes, we blame their Taliban leader there too, that fool Mullah Omar who protected the Arab jihadis in Afghanistan, like Bin Laden. The Arabs abused Afghan hospitality and brought down the wrath of the Americans on all our heads!"

"And they want Bin Laden's head."

"Let them take Bin Laden's head! I myself would offer it on a platter with saffron rice, pomegranate seeds, and jasmine blossoms if I could. They are foreigners—that whole al-Qaeda group. They are brave, but they are also reckless and hence dangerous. But the Taliban are different, they are from among us, from us Pashtuns on both sides of the border. You know that many from our own clan have joined them. We cannot separate ourselves from them, even when we disagree. Their cause is our cause, even when they are heavy-handed, arbitrary, even brutal. I may think their understanding of Islam is primitive, simple, uneducated. But they are mostly sincere and above all they wish to get rid of the foreign occupation in Afghanistan. Even if we object to their methods, we cannot quarrel with their political goal. And they have the power."

"Everyone wants to get rid of the foreign occupation over the border, Uncle. It is a stone around our necks. But the presence of these Arabs and other foreign jihadis here makes it harder to tell the Americans to go home."

"We do not welcome the outsiders. Actually here it has been the Chechens from Russia who are the fiercest. God is witness, they have suffered terribly from the *taghuti* Russians, and they are good Muslims, sincere people, good fighters. But they are a danger for us, they attract the ghost planes. We finally asked them to depart from our villages."

"If you want to get rid of the Americans, Uncle, you must do it yourselves. The presence of the Chechens, Uzbeks, Arabs and other foreigners delays the departure of the Americans and give them an excuse to attack this area."

His uncle signaled to the boy lingering in the background to bring more tea. "That is true, nephew, God alone knows, but at the same time many say the Americans are building huge bases, they want to stay in Afghanistan and Pakistan forever, to fight the Chinese and fight the Russians. And they want to keep Islam weak. They expect us to take their orders."

"The Americans are indeed afraid of the power of Islam," Majeed responded. "I know that from Americans myself. But my hope is that they will now see they cannot prevail here, they cannot dominate us, it is costing them too much blood, too much money. We know they will go eventually. If we can at least remove the foreign mujahideen then the Americans can save face, and say they have accomplished their mission, won their war. Then they may go home at last." Majeed shifted his position on the pillows, his legs no longer used to long sessions of sitting cross-legged.

"The Americans may or may not leave, nephew. Their ambitions seem without limit. But we will fight forever until they depart our lands. We have our honor to defend. Otherwise we are like sheep tethered to our homes during Ramazan, waiting for the knife to drop from the sky onto our necks. You must tell your chiefs in Islamabad, they must stop these American rockets upon our villages. If they cannot protect us we will all join arms with the Taliban to overthrow the corrupt politicians in Islamabad. Tell that to your masters in the city, nephew!"

"Uncle, it is not that simple. You know that the Taliban have become far bloodier now, they are supporting suicide bombings in Islamabad and Peshawar, innocent people are being killed. Women, children. You go to Peshawar often, you know about this. The government cannot tolerate this defiance and violence from them."

The boy brought in a silver tray hanging from a ring with more glasses of tea upon it. Majeed could already smell the lamb cooking outside for their lunch. Another small boy came up and sat down next to Majeed sliding under his arm looking for a hug. "And who is this young *mujahid*, Uncle, who wants to take part in our discussion?"

"That is Mahmood, your cousin's youngest."

"*Maashallah*," Majeed stroked Mahmood's hair as the boy nestled in closer. "May God keep him."

His uncle resumed. "We had an understanding for years with the government to leave us alone, to grant us the funds needed for basic things, but to leave the local governing to us. It has been that way for hundreds of years. Now you have changed the rules. You are sending in the Army, stupid young Punjabi soldiers who do not understand the language here or what is going on—they are scared and sometimes they just shoot. Sometimes there are American advisors with them. You may be trying to keep the Americans happy. But you will never be able to make the Taliban stop their operations."

"The Americans are putting big pressure on us, Uncle, to stop our Taliban from crossing over into Afghanistan."

"The way to stop the violence is to tell the Americans and the other *farenghis* to go home. This kind of invasion by troops from Islamabad is turning all our youth against you. I warn you, they will fight you forever to regain their honor and their independence here. We have contempt for the government, it simply licks the American boot that marches across the face of the Muslim world."

The arguments were familiar by now. What else could Majeed say except to remind the local villagers at least to keep out foreigner jihadis. He knew that for the local people to take on the Taliban as a force was nearly impossible. The Taliban were from among their own families. The Taliban in part represented Pashtun political power, especially in Afghanistan.

"But let us now eat," his uncle said, struggling to his feet. He and Majeed linked arms and went off to the festive lunch where he joined the other men sitting around the dishes on the floor. Feasts were more than food; feasting stimulated the juices of conciliation and lubricates the wheels of understanding that might have previously been clogged with discord. His uncle stood over the several metal *karhais* placed in front of them. He picked up a loaf of flat bread and ritually tore off pieces by hand to offer to each of those around him in a symbol of hospitality and participation as they began to dip into the steaming dishes before them.

Majeed spent two days in the village and visited several other surrounding villages. He went out into the fields so well known to him. The air was sweet, the lifeline of water flowed, a green band between the bare hills, and the earth was bountiful. He sat with his aunts, several of whom wept about their fears for the children. He heard the villagers talk about the economic situation and the impact of the war across the border. When Majeed finally left, he felt he had a better grip on the local situation to report back to Islamabad. Yet he knew the situation was volatile, and that things could reach the breaking point in which the whole tribal region could rise in rebellion, against even the Pakistani army itself. The tensions produced by the war across the Afghan border could for the first time actually threaten the unity of the entire Pakistani nation. Especially when outsiders sought to force Islamabad to abandon its light-handed pattern of relations with the autonomous tribes and clans. To force a change in that overnight could indeed bring brother upon brother that no government in Islamabad could survive.

*   *   *

The team had arrived the day before. "This is an important one, guys," the Station Chief had warned his top few officers. "Make sure you're there. They're here from the Pentagon to discuss some freshly minted hotshot ideas about new covert action ops against the Taliban… Alright, eye-rolling is not an option. We need to hear them out and decide what we need to do. If nothing else, to keep these guys from pushing us into some half-ass plan and embarrassing Uncle Sam big time."

The Pentagon team walked into the secure conference room where all high-security meetings were held. The team consisted of two military officers, one a full bird, Colonel Rasmussen, and his deputy, a Lt. Colonel Ginelli, accompanied by two civilians. They were part of an interagency operations group in Washington that combined both CIA as well as Defense Intelligence Agency, or DIA, and Army special operations forces. They were joined by the COS, deputy COS, COPS, Alex, a younger woman case officer who did research on religious groups, and a specialist in psyops, or psychological operations.

Colonel Rasmussen cut an imposing figure—and he knew it—with erect posture, lean body, a jutting chin, and piercing green eyes. He had learned early on that exercising command—at any level—was the key to promotion. He had consistently volunteered for the lowliest of duties throughout his career as long as he could be in command of the unit. As a later graduate of an MA program in political science at Michigan, however, he had grown interested in the more strategic aspects of military service and had later found himself drifting into intelligence—not always a career path conducive to fast promotion. As a longtime combat officer, however, he was determined that intelligence involve "more than just contemplating your goddam navel," as he put it. "Intelligence ain't worth shit if it's not actionable," was his regular exhortation to his people. He believed too that earthy expressions were a quick way to intimidate egghead civilians within the halls of intelligence. He had become known as a hard charger, restless, and determined to implement bold ideas based on the application of intelligence information, and with an eye always honed to his superiors. Colonel Rasmussen rose to his feet address the group, as small as it was.

"Gentlemen, thank you for coming. I know you're all busy men —and pardon me—I see a woman sitting among you as well—we always try promote involvement of women in our work. As you all know, the President is concerned that we are not being creative enough in taking on the enemy in Afghanistan. The task is indeed tough. But as he has also said, there is no alternative to victory." He let the words sink in, as a kind of revelation.

Alex shifted uncomfortably. *Here we go again, policy leading the intelligence, and not the way other way around. What is all this victory crap? Victory by fiat? To prevent intelligence reporting from sounding defeatist? In the end we're going to be lucky to get out from this place with our asses intact.*

"Now, ladies and gentlemen, if we are to succeed, a key tool will be in the area of psyops against the enemy. At this point in time we have brought together in Washington a group of experts on Islam and on Afghanistan and

Pakistan from within our respective agencies and commands back in CONUS, back home. State-of-the-art expertise, if you will. No country has ever had such broad and in-depth knowledge of a country as we have accumulated on Afghanistan and Pakistan today, thanks to computerized data and modeling and some very smart folk. We have produced a briefing on what we believe is a creative proposition for you—the product of many months of analysis back home." The Colonel paused for dramatic effect and then flashed some slides onto the screen.

Shit, here we go, PowerPoint. The ultimate eyewash program. The Pentagon loves it. How to present a lot of information within a rigid framework of assumptions that will keep the discussion from ever getting outside the box. You tell me it's in PowerPoint, I'll tell you the gist of the argument.

With a confident smile, the Colonel turned to the COS. "The plan is fundamentally designed to create splits and divisions among the Islamist sects that will damage the Taliban. We think we have identified some basic fault lines, if you will, within the culture that might be ripe for exploitation. But we need to shop the plan around with some of you area experts here, give it a scrubbing, and then see what we can do about implementing it. And before I start, gentlemen, I hope you will appreciate how politically sensitive these findings are in this part of the world."

Alex exchanged glances with the COS. They'd both been here before with these Washington whiz kids and visionaries who annually reinvent the wheel as gospel—soon to be imposed and endowed as "doctrine." *This guy is talking with certitude of someone who has just taken Sociology 101 of Pakistan and Afghanistan. God save us from these instant experts, grasping around for buttons to push, any buttons, to extricate themselves from the foreign quagmires of their own creation.*

"I think some of you may be aware that Islam out here in Pakistan is basically divided into two rival groups, the Barlevi..."

"Barelvi," Alex corrected.

"Right, yes, Barelvi sect—you've heard of them then—and the ultra fundamentalist Deobandi sect. These two groups have been at each other's throats for centuries. No warm Islamic brotherhood out *here*, if you will. Your Barlev... Barelvi group is basically comfortable with the US; they believe in keeping religion out of politics and keeping Allah firmly inside the box of their own personal lives. Now back home we see these people as basically the good guys. That is the kind of Islam that we like, that will maintain stability, stay out of politics, marginalize the fanatics. The ones we want to support, if you will. Now, your Deobandis are hard-liners, like your average Taliban or al-Qaeda types that are trying to impose Shari'a and a Caliphate and employ violence. That's the basic split." The Colonel looked around for a moment, expectantly.

"Roger, now for the heart of the ops plan." The slide flashed up on the screen, this one marked *Top Secret*. "Objective number one: to sow dissension between Barelvi and Deobandi Muslims. Which will have the following effects: First, promote disputes among religious groups in order to discredit overall Islamic politics in the eyes of Pakistanis. Second, use the Barelvis, who are a majority in Pakistan, to discredit the Deobandis in the public eye. Third, this kind of quarrelling will weaken the overall credibility of Islam among Pakistanis as a whole and weaken the appeal of al-Qaeda. While it is in our interests to discredit all of these Islamist groups, we don't mind strengthening the Barelvis as long as they stay on Uncle Sam's side."

"So bottom line, folks: our top priority is to recruit Barelvis who will dedicate themselves to hard-core armed attacks against the Deobandis and what they stand for. In short, keep them at each other's throats instead of ours."

"Colonel," Alex spoke up, "I'm sorry to interrupt, but you should know that these hostilities are already out there in full force, they're happening." The COS shot a warning glance at Alex. "They have been killing each other for many years. The Deobandi radicals have been attacking and destroying Sufi shrines of the Barelvi and threatening the religious leaders of these communities. And the Barelvis aren't just passively taking this. The pirs, or Sufi leaders, are usually connected with top feudal families in the country—who have a direct interest in protecting their followers."

"Well, there will be more hostility against the hard-liners if we can stimulate a Barelvi pushback."

"And how do you propose to do that?"

"We need to recruit Barelvi activists and strengthen their campaign against the radicals. Provide them with weapons if need be for defense of their shrines. The public will switch into negative mode vis-à-vis the Taliban and al-Qaeda types if their traditional shrines are seen at risk. We need to get the clerics ginned up, as it were, to speak out on the subject. We propose to fabricate some anti-Barlevi—anti-Barelvi—posters and writings as if they were from the Deobandis that will stir them up and cause them to more violently oppose the Deobandis."

"With all due respect again, Colonel, many of these conflicts are already bloody. I can't imagine a worse disaster for the Barelvi than if they are exposed as having ties—especially involving arms—to the US government. The Pak government will go wild. And it provides the kiss of death for the Barelvis. It just proves what the Deobandis have been saying all along, that the Barelvis are tools of the old order—associated with foreign occupation troops in Afghanistan now and spilling over into Pakistan. It vindicates Deobandi arguments that the Barelvis are betraying true Islam and that they need to be swept away."

Colonel Rassmussen frowned. "I hardly think it is appropriate, sir, to describe US forces in the area as 'foreign occupation troops.' We are not occupying Afghanistan, we are there to liberate them from the Taliban and al-Qaeda, to destroy the jihadi militants and to establish democratic rule."

Alex found himself tasting blood, irresistibly drawn forward to the attack in the face of such thinking. *If ever a little knowledge was a dangerous thing...* "That's as may be, Colonel, but in the eyes of a great deal of the population in Afghanistan and Pakistan the US presence does amount to a foreign occupation. The Taliban have been very successful in presenting it as such. But my main point here is that deliberately exacerbating existing tensions is not a smart idea. Pakistan needs less turmoil, not more. The country is already being torn apart in dangerous ways. And they can fight their own battles internally. It is not going to help anyone to have a foreign power taking sides and pumping up more violence in an internal religious competition. If the Sufis end up supporting the US in Pakistan, they too will become utterly discredited in the eyes of most Pakistanis—and we will have handed the fundamentalists victory on a platter. On top of that, it is a mistake to assume that the Barelvi are pro-American. Precious few people in this country are pro-American..."

"Goddam right," the Colonel broke in, "and that's why we've got to turn this whole show around here. Make them understand and appreciate what we are doing, the sacrifices the US is making to keep this area stable—how we are working for Pakistan's true interests."

Warming to the topic, the Colonel swung around to face Alex full bore. "Mr..."

"Anders."

"Mr. Anders, I'm afraid the kind of thinking you represent—just letting things run on as they are—is one of the reasons we are not having the kind of success that we need. We can't sit on our hands and wait to see which way the forces of history are going to blow. We are here to take action." He rapped his laser pointer on the table and looked around. "The Commander-in-Chief wants results, gentlemen. We had hoped that the Station might be in a position to participate or take the lead in this vital operation. We're not just talking about what you folks are doing in Pakistan, we're talking the future of the American strategic posture across Central Asia, with implications for the rising Chinese threat against American interests." The Colonel's voice grew more clipped.

The COS turned to the group. "I don't think this is the place to have a debate about grand strategy. We're here to listen. I think we'd all be best advised to sit and hear the Colonel out. We all have our ideas and we can discuss it later in the Station and decide what best role we can take in supporting this proposal."

"Thank you, Sam. Right on, folks, yes, this is just a proposal, you don't need to put your John Hancocks on anything yet. But I do suggest you listen up close because this is the direction in which the Chief Steering Group for covert action is inclined to move. This will soon be working US military doctrine for covert warfare. We cannot sit here passively and watch the whole place turn to shit, if you will pardon my French. We owe it to the people of Pakistan as well their government to set this country on the right path. None of us here wants to be accused of having lost Pakistan on our watch."

Alex seethed as the presentation blundered on, but he had said his piece and his chief clearly signaled he wanted no more.

"Now, we would ask the Station to inventory your assets and see if you have any existing sources close to religious circles that might serve in this role." Sam again exchanged glances with Alex, aware of his ties to these circles.

"OK, Colonel," Sam rose to his feet, "thanks, this has been a stimulating presentation. I see your group back in Washington has been doing some serious thinking on all of this. We'll have to review our own assets and see in what ways we might be able to help out. As Alex indicated, some of this might be controversial, but we are team players and want to support the broader mission as much as possible—and of course support the Commander-in-Chief. We have a good idea what you are looking for; we'll discuss it among our officers and get back to you soon. Thank you so much for coming."

The COS turned, shook the Colonel's hand who looked startled at the abruptness of the end of the briefing. He marshalled his papers and then followed the others out of the conference room.

Well down the hall Sam turned to Alex. "Goddam it, Anders, I don't need any more challenges like that to top visiting brass. You're going to land us in fucking trouble at home and damage your own reputation."

"Sam, I'm sorry, I shouldn't have been so outspoken maybe, but this is out of control. These guys are just churning out dangerous half-assed ideas in some desperate bid to turn this losing situation around. Find anybody they can use to kill somebody else. You know this proposal is crazy, and irresponsible. It stinks."

"I know it and you know it. And we have time-honored bureaucratic techniques for dealing with such things: halfhearted and slow responses, posing more questions, study committees, just letting it all slowly die. We don't win by fucking confrontations with Hqs and Pentagon brass in the field. Is that clear?"

"Yessir, clear as a bell."

*   *   *

Alex continued to see Majeed on regular intervals, usually on a personal basis, although he reported much of the conversation's political content to the Station. These insights were considered useful input. Majeed of course knew that what he was saying would be passed along, but there were few real secrets to be kept. The more the Americans understood the realities, the better. For that matter, Alex's views were reported back to Majeed's boss in ISI. Both of them knew their exchanges contained personal elements but also reflected certain informal views of their respective offices.

After getting back from the Frontier villages, Majeed felt frustrated, trapped in a no-win situation between US, Pakistani, and Frontier population concerns; he expressed his anger as he addressed Alex at the end of a supper in Majeed's home one evening. They had withdrawn into Majeed's library.

"Dammit, Alex, it's one thing to try to get rid of Bin Laden and the foreign jihadis. But your bloody embassy is now at war with the Pashtuns!"

"That's not really true, Majeed. It's just that so many Pashtun seem to support the Taliban. Washington is scared that the Taliban will come back to power and welcome al-Qaeda again."

"That is just plain stupid. If you had any decent intelligence you would know that the Taliban never really liked Bin Laden. He was here years before the Taliban came. They inherited him as part of the package when they took over the country. And yes, he helped out the Taliban in the early days to extend their control over the country. But even the head of the Taliban government, Mullah Omar—he never bought into all this international jihad business. He even wanted to get al-Qaeda out of the country. He knew it was costing him. He was ready to make a deal. But your president couldn't wait, no, you could taste the blood in your mouths, you wanted war!"

"Do you really think the US would just roll over and forget about 9/11? After three thousand dead, seen all over the world live on TV? Of course there would be a military response!"

"But you didn't have to have a war to get Bin Laden's head. If you had been patient, if you hadn't issued these insulting high-pressure ultimatums to the Taliban government, believe me, you might well have gotten his head soon enough. The whole Muslim world was pressing on the Taliban to do that. They knew Bin Laden was dragging them into a disastrous confrontation with the US. Bin Laden violated the terms of hospitality that allowed him stay in Afghanistan. Mullah Omar would have found a way to give him over,—he needed more time to lay the groundwork. But the insulting nature of the ultimatums guaranteed he wouldn't do it. And your president didn't want it any other way, he wanted his little war."

"Look, Majeed, I'm not going to argue this, it's all water over the dam. The fact is that Washington still wants Bin Laden's head, and all the rest of his organization. It doesn't want to see the Taliban come back to power. And now that your own Pashtuns in Pakistan have joined the game, it's getting really dangerous."

"What do you expect? We are blood brothers, we are kinsmen, we have ties over long centuries. There is no real border here, except in the minds of literal-minded Westerners who love to draw lines on maps and divide up the world just as you please."

"The fact remains that if Taliban inside Pakistan are helping out the Taliban in Afghanistan, then you're going to get smacked. Washington is convinced that the whole Taliban movement is now spreading into Pakistan, and it is determined to stop it."

"Stop it? What a fantasy! How?"

"By forcing the Pak army to enter into the Frontier zone and take the Taliban out."

"Take the Taliban out? You think the Pak army can do it? Will do it? Just like that? It's a fantasy, a political impossibility—hell, a military impossibility!"

"Look, I know that. But Washington doesn't believe it. It's desperate, it wants you to save its ass in Afghanistan. And it's going to squeeze you like a boa constrictor until you do it."

"You're trying to make us solve your own stupid mistakes in Afghanistan by pushing the problem onto us."

"Well, it does involve you. Pashtun tribesmen and Taliban are running back and forth across the border all the time."

"We live here, god dammit, Alex. Of course we cross these borders! They are meaningless, these lines the British drew. You're idiots if you think you can stop cross-border activity, among cousins!"

"I know you can't stop it. But I'm warning you, Washington is going to try. They are going to try very hard. And they are going to fire Predators onto your territory and try to assassinate any Pashtun leader that looks like he is cooperating with the Taliban. And God help the ISI if they are playing around in this, supporting the Taliban in Pakistan."

"God help the ISI? What in hell do you expect them to do, Alex? Do you think the ISI works for your president? Or for the CIA? Or to protect American interests in this country? It is designed to protect Pakistani interests. Pak-is-ta-ni interests, got it?"

"OK, so tell me, what are Pakistani interests?"

"Come on, Alex, you're not stupid. We need a friendly regime in Kabul. That needs to be a Pashtun regime. And we can't afford to alienate Pashtuns in Pakistan either. I'm bloody one of them."

"I'm just reminding you, you're courting real trouble. Some elements of the US are really trigger-happy, and you're likely to get more Predators on your doorstep. In fact, Majeed, you'd better be pretty damn careful yourself when you're out there in the border areas. I'm concerned."

"So. I need to be careful in my own country. Warning received. Thank you very much."

*   *   *

Alex was on edge. He knew Majeed was in touch with Abdul Haqq, a key Taliban commander in North Waziristan. Majeed had implied as much and that it involved very complex efforts of the ISI to control the situation there, maintain working ties and even some degree of control over groups like Abdul Haqq's. Islamabad had no virtually no choice but to work with these organizations, try to steer them rather than engage in a confrontation nobody would win. Majeed had told Alex that he was leaving this very afternoon from Peshawar and on to Waziristan for a major meeting that night. Alex was well aware that Abdul Haqq was high on the American kill list and that he was subject to drone surveillance. He warned Majeed of the risk in general terms. "So I should abandon my job because it is dangerous? Dangerous thanks to your people?"

Yet Alex knew that for Majeed to meet with Abdul Haqq was to expose himself to possible retribution from the sky. Who knew whether US satellites had been able to trace Abdul Haqq to the specific location where Majeed was headed? And that they might try to take him out during their meeting, unaware that Majeed was there? Or perhaps they didn't care that Majeed might be there—didn't "dallying with the enemy" have its price?

The jeep from Peshawar had lurched its way into the darkness for hours along mountain roads. Majeed had dozed for part of it, and in any case knew nothing himself of the maze of back roads they had taken. He only knew they were somewhere in Haqqani territory in North Waziristan. Majeed was not immune to Alex's warning, and his stomach churned as they approached his destination. Was some eye in the sky already looking down on him? The meeting was to be in some isolated village where Abdul Haqq had chosen to stop off for a few hours for this meeting. He kept on the move in any case, to avoid the ever-present threat of drones. No meeting with Abdul Haqq would ever be in predictable locations.

The driver gave a signal and Majeed climbed out of the jeep and quickly entered a small non-descript compound, glancing upwards to the skies, as if it would do any good. He could see from the inside how much of an interim office the place was—in the musical chairs these commanders were playing to avoid identification with any one location. The room had a little light inside, a makeshift office. The desk had a few papers on it, and a laptop sat on a wooden floor made from irregular wide planks that sagged at various points across the room. The walls were unfinished, painted a sickly green in some places. A single mujahideen poster hung at an angle. Numerous rickety wooden chairs were placed in front of the desk and in the back of the room were a few old rugs and cushions for more informal discussion. Two electric bulbs hung from the ceiling and several Coleman lanterns, as yet unlit, sat along the edge of the floor. The office was separate from a house to which it was attached but could be entered only from the outside. A chequered black-and-white Arab kaffiyeh also hung from the back of a coat hook, possibly left by a passing fighter as an incentive, now representing a universal symbol of resistance. Abdul Haqq sat at the chair, his black beard contrasting with his white Pashtun cap, his face half in shadow. He was a small, wiry man, but the slight figure nonetheless suggested a coiled energy inside that had brought Abdul Haqq to the forefront of Taliban commanders.

"What do you have to say for yourself, Majeed?"

The voice came suddenly at him out of the shadows and the question was harshly abrupt—even hostile, lacking the most elementary nod to traditional exchange of greetings and courtesies. After a long pause Abdul Haqq abandoned his staged theatrical opening, stepped forward out of the dark, laughed and embraced Majeed, easing the tension and yielding to the ritual exchange of pleasantries.

"But since you ask me, Majeed, yes, I must say in frankness, I am not happy. Surely you know why?"

"I assume you mean the increased presence of Army troops, and the skirmishes with them."

"By God, what can be on the minds of your generals back there? Don't they know they are losing the support of the population here? What kind of a game is this that you send in your troops into our areas of control?"

"We are concerned about rising violence in the country, Brother Haqq. If the generals in command are breaking the old rules, so are you, in extending the war into the cities, car bombings, attacking the civilian front and army centers themselves. How long do you think ISI will accept that?"

"How long do you think we will take invasions of our space by these... these Punjabis and Sindhis and their corrupt government of thieves in Islamabad who obey the Americans? They are the ones who are seeking to put pressure on us. Of course we respond."

"The attacks and bombings from your side are opening very dangerous doors, Brother Haqq. It creates the impression that the whole country is under siege, that the central government is weak, and that things are getting out of control. The Americans are very concerned."

"Fuck their mothers' cunts, Majeed! They do not run our country! They must not be allowed to run our country. Why are the generals in ISI permitting this foreign pressure to be placed on us? This region will explode! Go back and tell them. We've tried to reason with them on this before."

"Yes, the Americans are placing major pressures on us," Majeed replied. "We cannot ignore them, or things might get worse. But the Americans are not in control. We are. We will conduct a few formal military operations in this area just to show that we have the capability and that the government is in control. We do not intend to remove autonomous power from the region. But you must show some understanding for the dilemma we are in. You must curtail your attacks on government and civilian targets. Do not worsen the problem for us in Islamabad."

Abdul Haqq lowered his head and glowered at Majeed, his pupils at the top of his eyes casting a deliberately menacing look. He made no comment, and allowed Majeed to sit mired in the tense silence. He then continued in a markedly quiet voice.

"You, my friend, must understand our situation here. We cannot, we will not accept these invasions of the army, their crude tactics. I do not care if they are essentially designed to 'impress the Americans' as you say. They also make our forces of resistance look weak and impotent in the face of Islamabad's troops. God willing, we will only respond out of self-defense. You can pass that message along to your superiors."

"We must reach an understanding, Brother Haqq. Conflict and fighting does none of us any good. It only strengthens outsiders who can then play us off."

"Then allow the situation to return to normal. As God is my witness, we have no desire to attack the government of Pakistan. Our enemies are the Americans, the kaffirs, the so-called NATO clique, and their puppet government in Kabul that is designed to keep the Pashtuns out of power. The government is the one that has opened the conflict with us. Let us focus on ridding our lands—first Afghanistan and now here—of this stench of the occupiers."

"We are concerned that the US will push us still harder. The situation is tense even in other parts of the country, not just in the tribal zones. It is causing a breakdown of authority."

"Then you must resist them. Who do you think represents the long-term force in this country?"

"Nobody represents the long term…"

"That is a lie! It is our brave mujahideen fighting in the path of God who will carry the day—not the generals, not the fat government officials with their perfumed hands, not the crusader Americans, not those who fawn in front of Western power. You know it, and Islamabad knows it. So why these games?"

Majeed remained silent as part of his mind inadvertently sailed back up into the black skies, each passing minute here with Abdul Haqq perhaps straining his luck; he wondered whether he would ever even know what had hit him.

"For that matter, Brother Majeed, haven't you ever thought about working with the forces of the future? If you could offer us regular insights into the thinking of the generals and their plans, we would be very grateful." Abdul Haqq opened his hands in a expansive gesture and smiled. "We would express our appreciation."

"If you are asking me what I think you are asking me, the answer is no."

"It is a natural question among friends. We trust each other in the end. The offer is always open. Someday those that chose to work with us early on will benefit greatly in the new regime."

"Sorry, Abdul Haqq. We do not need to discuss your generous offers now."

"As you wish," Abdul Haqq continued. "In any case, do not forget what happened to the Soviets when they invaded Afghan lands. They were defeated through the will of the God acting through the people. Pakistani Pashtuns, Afghan Pashtuns and other Afghans, foreign mujahideen—all fought in that brave war. We will do it again. This is our home. They are the invaders. Never forget."

"Brother Haqq, I hear your point. I think we all agree that the power of our religion and our Islamic civilization will emerge victorious. But we must all be very cautious now. Understand our position. Carry on your jihad against the foreign forces. But I warn you, do not humiliate our government. You are only giving ammunition to the Americans to accuse us of weakness, to take measures into their own hands. It should be no secret to you that the Americans want to get their hands on our nuclear weapons. When you attack the government, you make that prospect more likely."

"Then Islamabad must be more sensitive to our needs. The pathetic puppet government in Kabul is not long for this world. Time is on our side. We do not need to negotiate what is already ours, or what will fall in our lap."

"But you would be willing to facilitate talks in Kabul, with Afghan Taliban forces."

"They can do as they like."

"They listen to you, Abdul Haqq. You can influence them."

Abdul Haqq tightened some loose ends of his turban. "We are not opposed to discussions in Kabul. It might spare us from further fighting among us. Such fights among brothers is not good in God's eyes."

"Then that is an important message for me to take back to Islamabad. We very much want you to persuade your Afghan brothers to sit down in Kabul and talk. You have interests in that settlement as well. The generals will stay off your back if you are willing to help work such an agreement out, in consultation with us. This must be a settlement to Pakistan's tastes. It cannot be imposed by the Americans. Pakistan will always be the older brother in this. Neither of us can rely on the Americans. You can only rely on us."

"I do not say no. We need to build some trust between us. We will then consider opening many doors in Kabul."

Majeed nodded in satisfaction. He felt he had just achieved a major concession from Abdul Haqq, who could be an invaluable centerpiece in bringing about a permanent arrangement of forces in a new Kabul government that would include a strong Taliban role.

Abdul Haqq placed his hand over his heart. Each had said his due, and had understood the other. They shared a common need to engineer an eventual end to the devastating war in Afghanistan on terms favorable to Islamabad, and to the Pashtuns on both sides.

Majeed left the meeting partly exhilarated, but also with a sense of foreboding. He felt caught between massive forces, all operating on their own independent trajectories that admitted of little compromise. His exchange with Abdul Haqq was one of the toughest Majeed ever had with a major mujahideen commander. But would Washington now drive Pakistan over the brink in the demand for relief from its own compounded errors in

Afghanistan? Would it ever permit Pakistan to reach its own long-term settlement in Afghanistan that included a major Taliban role? It was a role that only a leader like Abdul Haqq was superbly qualified to do.

The men embraced in the night air in front of Majeed's vehicle. Majeed climbed in and the driver set off in the long drive back as Abdul Haqq went back into the house. The black planes had not visited them that night, but safety could never be assured until Majeed's car was back in Peshawar.

About fifteen minutes down the road there was a huge orange flash in the distance behind them and as Majeed turned to look back. It was followed by a noise like thunder rolling in the mountains.

*   *   *

Max parks his car in the parking lot and walks toward the entrance of a massive, sprawling single story edifice—a military big box. He can already feel the day's incipient heat in the air, waiting to be released in its full fiery intensity. The parched brown desert hills of California loom only some miles away. He remembers he forgot to turn on the outside sprinkler that morning and will have to call Cindy to do it after she gets back from taking the kids to school. It's Presidents Day, only half day of school due to the ceremonies in the afternoon. Max removes his badge with its neck chain from his pocket, inserts it into the turnstile machine and punches in his code. The turnstile admits him into the building. Others around him are doing the same, some in uniform, many in civilian clothes. He walks down an endless, featureless, cavernous but brightly lit corridor with closed gray doors on all sides bearing cryptic military designations on a card by each door. Early post-9/11 federal security architecture. At the end of the corridor he comes to the last door on the left marked Remote Operations, bends over a silver box by the door and punches in a five-digit code. A buzzer rings and he pushes open the door. A colleague is right behind him. Max greets him by name but does not let him enter with him, nor does his colleague expect him to; the door slams shut behind Max. His colleague waits to punch in his own code.

Inside Max negotiates his way among multiple identical desk carrels, all equipped with complex consoles resembling flight training devices. He sets down the essential working elements for his morning stint—his cup of coffee, black, and a jumbo chocolate-covered donut with sprinkles; he takes off the lid and takes a sip of the sweet liquid. He feels tired this morning—stayed up too late watching football on television. Maybe he should have brought an additional sugar-glazed donut to get him through the morning—but he is fighting a losing battle with weight. He sits down in his executive-model rolling four-way adjustable armchair in front of his own console and punches in another code to activate the computer.

"Morning Max." A voice from the neighboring carrel.

"Morning, Kurt. Gonna be another hot one out there."

"Yeah, wife's already taken off with the kids for the weekend up in the mountains, but I may not get to go this week."

"Anything new?"

"Bird's up, but target clearance didn't come in during the night yet. Maybe this morning. Happy hunting." Kurt rises from his seat to signal the end of his night shift, while Max's screen lights up, gradually revealing a large map marked into sectors. A few sips of coffee. A few pushes on the keyboard and a black joystick bring up a series of still images showing multiple houses in a village, each surrounded by mud or cinder block walls. He stares at them, trying to make sense of the images on the screen, zeroes in on one image and gradually guides a camera mounted on an aircraft half a world away to the site of another compound, still distant. As the pictures become clearer and closer, Max eliminates some compounds from his area of interest and moves on to others as the bird moves south for closer shots in that zone. He pauses, checks a map and sheafs through a clipboard of incoming messages, turns back to the screen and eventually zooms in on a specific locale and watches. He can see a few individuals walking around, some carrying something that looks like ammunition. There are over a dozen pickup trucks, one with something that could resemble an automatic weapon mounted on the back. The figures are almost surely all men. Max scrolls through the images in search of a compound that should be marked by the proximity of an electronic tag emitting a signal, highlighting that compound among the others. The many men in the image are busy, engaged in loading several of the trucks. But the light in distant Pakistan is fading and soon there will be no daylight pictures available any more, only infrared. As the light fades, he now notices the presence of a number of women and children arriving at the compound in a van. They move into a smaller building just behind the main building, complicating the targeting. The acquisition pictures are good, but the bird cannot linger in the area too closely without eventually alerting the targets. After consultation with Washington center he guides the bird back to its base on the Pakistani border where it will refuel and await mission clearance for re-targeting. He has many hours to submit the paperwork for a strike before dawn breaks in Pakistan, to communicate with the local command, and settle on a firm target. Many hours later, after a quick Big Mac and double chipotle fries at the concession in the food court, he returns to watch dawn break at the far end of the world. The compound begins to fall into sharp relief.

Max flew pilot missions in Iraq before he was assigned to seven-week Predator training at Creech in Nevada and quickly thereafter was posted to a remote base in southern California. The fighter pilot environment was familiar to him, with its rush of adrenalin from flying close support missions and the camaraderie of the sessions with fellow pilots for the debrief after each mission. The Predator is a different story. He finds it strangely dislocating to be fighting a war—killing people and destroying materiel—all from eight thousand miles away. There is stress in his work here as well, but it's silent and without personal risk; he shares that tension only with his sensor operator in the next booth, Steve. With the new technology, they have vivid visuals into the target area, they can often clearly distinguish single individuals, men from women and children even though their individual faces are not fully distinct. Max's job is trickier: he has to pilot the Predator remotely, often through thorny conditions of heat, wind and dust over barren landscapes, all the while maintaining contact with a range of different satellite connections. His years of pilot training actually serve him in good stead in this new mission. For Steve, this is all new.

Steve is only 20, fresh out of Creech on his first operational tour. Unlike Max's generation, Steve admits that all those years playing Nintendo games in high school were his most important academic preparation for this job. But killing bad guys on game screens doesn't have quite the same rush as doing it live and real time. OK! They now have clearance on the target. Max guides the Predator towards the target location, some half hour away. As the bird approaches, Max says, "Over to you." Steve is the one who locks in on the target. He is now ready. He waits, and then releases the missile. It is silent to Max and Steve, but emitting a hiss to anyone nearby in the region. He guides the missile on into the target via laser. For Max the sense of unreality continues. In a fighter aircraft you roared on past the target after releasing the ordinance; never really getting a close view of the damage delivered unless you could double back, often risky. But with the Predator you can usually linger after an attack to get a clear—and graphic—photographic record of what the missile has done, both to people and structures. Steve says he still finds waves of adrenalin washing over him as he guides the missile in to a direct hit. It's like hunting big game. It is a rush, combined with a sense of ambivalence that he—he alone—is about to kill something big, far, far away. A momentary white flash on the screen obscures everything. In the distant Afghan compound he knows something has happened, something fearful and deadly. He also knows that the dark splotches, now lying on the ground and coming into greater resolution, are people—often many people and probably now all dead people. But they are also almost surely all enemy, all al-Qaeda—or Taliban, not much difference. That's what the intel reports indicated. But he prefers not to think about it very much—something in his heart tells him that they cannot all of them be all al-Qaeda all the time. There have in fact been several occasions where families of the fighters had also been present. But hey, if you run with the wolves you get hurt. And it isn't all his choice—after all, the decision was made by other specialists, the target was believed to be high value and worth the dozen or so other lives who may not have themselves been all bad guys but who chose poor company. Too bad, but this is war.

Most of the time this line of reasoning worked well enough. But as he went home at night to his quarters he sometimes thought about those people, the ones he had just killed—killed not in a visceral defensive reflex to an imminent attack upon his own person, but by a careful professional decision based on the best intelligence they had. These people were all very far away, faceless, very often even nameless but fitting computerized targeting profiles. But what did he expect—what did they expect—war was war, sometimes murky. Still, it was eerie, it was all so easy, yes, just like his Nintendo when he was growing up and blasting bad guys on his screen. Now they were real bad guys. Yet it felt a bit more unsettling as well. He knew from later reporting that many times there had been errors—not his, he was just carrying out the mission to fire on the target. But the targeting turned out a number of times to be wrong. Then later on they got word about some of the taggers in the field who were tagging houses and compounds and clans that they had a personal or family grudge against. Some of the taggers were in it maybe just for the money, tagging anybody they could claim were known bad guys, collecting on a bounty.

No, the system isn't perfect. He finds that after a few months the thrill of the successfully executed laser-fired missile on target begins to wane and he always wonders who the people on the ground might really have been, what kind of lives they led, families they had. But this particular day on the battlefield is over, their eight-hour combat shift successfully executed. They've made their kills for the day. Max and Steve turn the consoles over to their reliefs and step out into the cooling evening desert air, horizon still tinged with pink as if some distant firefight raged on the horizon. Steve is off to his quarters to catch a few z's, maybe grab a beer with some friends, or supper at the club. Max is on his way home, to his wife and kids, have dinner; just another day on the job. It's all just been on on a screen after all--at least here in California. But it had been live in Afghanistan, alive in Afghanistan. There were now real bodies on the ground to show for it. Bad guys. Pretty surely. A fair number down already, but way more to go out there. It's going to be a long slog as their commander said. You can't change a hostile civilization like that overnight.

Chapter Nine

Clarity

Wake me up, God; ignite my passion, fill me with outrage. Remind me that I am responsible for Your world. Don't allow me to stand idly by. Inspire me to act. Teach me to believe I can repair some corner of the world.

- Rabbi Naomi Levy

Alex, this is great, Hqs is creaming its jeans over the Homaid op. It's a real coup for the Station to get close in to this Waziri bunch. But now they want to move the op beyond the intelligence reporting stage. They want to see if Homaid can get up close to some of the commander types."

Alex was wary at the COS's compliment that seemed to precede a bad idea. "I don't want to push this too fast, Sam. Sure, Homaid's been much more successful in getting into the camps and meeting some of the commanders than we had hoped, but there is no way they are going to let him into the inner councils of their own planning. He's not a tribal, he doesn't have the years of field training to take a commander's position. He's still a newcomer."

"They're not thinking about hard-core inside reporting. They want him to get closer personally, provide targeting info for drone attacks. We can take some of these key commanders out permanently with a Predator if we know what actual locales they work out of."

"Jesus, Sam, you know what a half-ass track record we have in bombing the Taliban or suspected al-Qaeda in the past? I mean, think about it, how many times have they hit some goddam wedding party or blown up a house with whole families in it? What's our success rate in the end? One out of three killed is a bad guy? Why do you think they hate us out there? Can you imagine how the US public would feel if our police—much less foreign troops—were killing two innocents for every criminal killed?"

"Look, they're getting better at targeting the Predators. And frankly they've built up the tracking infrastructure and bureaucracy at home big time. Whatever you may think, when you have a toy, it gets used. What is critical is to get real-time intelligence on the specific locations where a commander is staying, even if it's just overnight. Homaid is the best potential tagger we have in Waziristan at the moment. Kills are more valuable than intel at this point."

"How many times do you think he could do it before he's suspected? All it takes is suspicion and they'll execute him on the spot."

"Agreed. But we've got to try. See if you can arrange some way for him to help out on logistics for some of the commanders like Jalal al-Haq, get closer to their operations centers, enough to spot where they're staying. All he has to do is make the electronic tag, the drones will pick it up. Then it's all over." Sam closed the file.

Alex stared at him. "I don't know if I can persuade him to do it, Sam. It's one thing to report on what's going on in some of the camps, but accessory to assassination's another. I don't think he's ready to go there, at least not yet."

"OK, Alex, let me put the cards on the table. You've done the hard part, the part you're great at. You've turned this guy into a solid recruiting source, groomed him, and shoehorned him in to the periphery of some of the higher commanders. You've won real kudos. But we've decided—it's not even my decision, it's coming from Hqs—you should turn Homaid over to another officer at this point, let him run it for this purpose. It's a fairly routine op by now and doesn't require the special skills on intel reporting and political structure that you've got. I'd rather have you out there spotting and recruiting again, getting a feel for the scene—that's something hardly any of our other case officers can do as well. So I'm recommending we turn Homaid over to Art from now on, let him run the case. Do you think Homaid's ready for a handover?"

Shit, they were taking the case away from him. A handover—always painful. A bit like leaving your five-year-old at kindergarten on her first day. It's a time of transition, when the case—the budding agent that you've nurtured with your own style and set of skills—is turned over to someone else. However good the new officer may be at picking up the case, you know he won't be the same, won't show the exact same sensitivities as you. He's not you. The relationship that began with a genuine personal connection between the recruiting officer and the agent now becomes more professional, regularized—pretty much all business. Yet the step always has to be taken. The principle has been established—the guy is a paid agent. Now it's time to act like the formal business relationship it is, less schmoozing and more professional cooperation for an understood salary, deliverables, and benefits.

Alex knew Homaid was a good case, he had educated him, trained him, molded him, directed him, cajoled him through initial periods of self-doubt as he taught him about how to approach the senior commanders, how to be useful, how to elicit information. But if the case was going to be directed at targeting assessments for assassination, it wouldn't be any more the classic intelligence operation that it had been. Furthermore, he knew Homaid could never really penetrate into the heart of these groups, and Hqs knew it, and that was why they wanted him as a spotter and tagger for jihadi commander locations in the Frontier villages. It would take some of the burden off Alex, mean less trips to Peshawar, give him a little more time at home.

"OK," he sighed. "I'll turn him over to Art; I'll see if we can do it for the next meeting in Peshawar."

         *   *   *

The phone by his bedside rang. Alex opened one eye to look at the alarm—2am. It must be the damn duty officer in the Embassy, no rest for the weary. He picked up the phone.

"Hello, Alex?" The voice was hesitant. "It's me, Jack."

"Jack! Is everything OK?" His brother would not be making a courtesy call at this hour.

"Negative. I'm afraid we've gotten some very bad news. About Roger." His voice broke. "He's dead, Alex, he's dead."

"Oh Christ no, Jack! Roger? In Iraq?"

"Yes, in Fallujah. He was out on patrol and… he was picked off by a sniper. He was killed instantly."

"Jack, that's terrible! My God, I don't know what to say! I'm so sorry, Jack, I am so sorry!"

"Roll of the dice. You go to war, people die. What else can I say?"

"How long had he been there? Six months?"

"Seven months. He was so young, Alex, so young. Not even twenty yet." Jack's voice broke down.

"Jack, please accept my deepest condolences to you and Kathy. I know Isabel will be horrified. This is so terrible."

"Do you think… do you think you might be able to come back for the funeral, Alex? I know it's a lot to ask, and you're busy as hell, and it's far away and all, but it would mean a lot to us."

"Jack, absolutely I want to. Let me know when I need to be there. I'll try to clear the decks to make it back. It's a bad time here, but I'll make it work. I'll be there, for a few days at least."

"Thanks, Alex. It would really mean a lot to us… My God, we somehow never really thought this could happen."

         *   *   *

Airplanes were hardly designed with meditation in mind. He could tune out with onboard whiskey, or watch films whose lite content perfectly matched the tiny screen in front of him, or suffer through the thousandth travel story from the non-stop talker in the seat next to him; otherwise the mind was the only other resource for diversion. Meditation, reflection, mind running on, it was all a blur, even as he tried to sleep as the interminable hours crept by. It was a long haul back to the US.

Although operational events were moving fast, the Station had clearly recognized this as a personal emergency for Alex, especially in light of the war-related death. Alex would loved to have taken Isabel along, as comfort and as partial buffer from the rawer emotional scenes that were yet to come, but with Rodrigo and all the additional cost it had not been feasible. Isabel had received the news about Roger with great dismay. She hugged Alex and they stayed in a long embrace as she took it in. "And poor Kathy, what a terrible loss for her. I just can't help believing what madness this is, all of it. Why was Roger there, Alex, why?" Alex knew this discussion would be a rehearsal of those yet to come with Jack and Kathy in New York, and he didn't want to have to preview it all with Isabel. "What can I say, Isabel? He said he wanted to serve his country—that's it."

"And all I can say," she commented grimly, "is that I will never allow Rodriguito to be sent to a senseless war like that. Or like this one here. I will take him away to Chile first."

Alex nodded in broad affirmation. It came boiling up from the depths of many long discussions. She had never really grown comfortable with life in Islamabad. Yes, she was at ease in its society, she had found many simpatico friends, including Latinos. She was very close to Zubayda and had found many interests in the local culture working on social and women's projects with her.

"It's the environment, Alex, the environment I can't handle. The unspoken backdrop to everything is war—senseless war for empty goals. How can we pretend to maintain a sparkling social life in the midst of this destruction?" She no longer made references to Alex's work, but the reproach—personal and political—was no less real, and sweeping.

Jack was exceptionally touched that Alex had flown the distance to offer support and comfort. "You don't know what this means to me," he said, as he, Alex and Kathy all hugged each other at JFK. "I couldn't tell him not to sign up, not to go," he said, tearing up. "He felt our country was challenged, it was something positive that he could do. We felt it seemed to provide some positive direction in his life that otherwise had been kind of drifting on the fringes."

Jack had kept Alex abreast of the ongoing saga with Roger—his unfocussed odyssey through teenage years and tangle with drugs. Bright kid but unmotivated, a high school dropout. And then, he suddenly decided that the Army was what he needed. Newly inspired with a sense of purpose instilled by his dedicated recruiting sergeant, a Navajo from New Mexico for whom the military had become family, Roger sat down to study and finish his Certificate of General Education on his own and had been accepted into the Army. He wanted to go to combat. And then Fallujah.

"He knew people could die there," Jack said, "but he never felt somehow that he would die. He told us he felt fulfillment, of being engaged in something real. He was working with real people, trying to solve real problems. We never felt we should dissuade him—it just seemed like maybe it was the right vehicle—for finding himself. His letters and calls back from Iraq were enthusiastic, he felt he was doing the right thing."

Alex smiled in sympathetic understanding. "What can I say, Jack? It's really important that he felt he was doing the right thing, that he wasn't drifting any longer, could make choices. Maybe that's all any of us can ever do."

"I don't even know he particularly believed in the war itself. It was his commitment to people around him, his buddies in combat, that was real. That's what he always talked about. And we've gotten some marvelous emails from his platoon mates, telling us how Roger helped build up a strong team spirit, got them through some tough spots out on patrol and all. You know," and Jack's voice broke again as he paused, "he apparently did not even have to have died. He went into a walled-in orchard to check it out before the rest went in; he had volunteered for the job. His luck just ran out."

Alex was moved at the simplicity and discipline that attended the military funeral, in itself a personal affirmation. It put Roger's life in a context, as the centerpiece of a classic and long-exercised ceremony, a ritual of life and death, that suggested meaning and purpose behind it all. Roger was not alone but had been a vital part of a larger human unit striving together. Jack and Kathy accepted the flag from the coffin and kissed it, drew huge personal comfort from it—more as a symbol of intimacy with Roger and his sacrifice than as a statement of policy support.

Late that night after the funeral, Jack and Alex went into the brown leathered library in Jack's upscale New York suburban house and sat back in deeply upholstered leather chairs over a bottle of whiskey. Jack began to unwind.

"I never asked them exactly how he died, you know? The details. They said it was a sniper. But I think maybe it was a mine. We were not allowed to view the body. Maybe we don't really need to know more."

"The details probably only provide more pain, Jack. You just want to know he died without suffering, as they told you, that's the most important thing."

Jack studied his whiskey glass. "Yeah, if you can believe it…"

"Why wouldn't you?"

"Because I don't think they want parents and friends to hear the gory details. They want to give the impression of quick closure. It is easier on everyone. Helps lessen brooding over the what might-have-beens. Lends dignity."

Alex reflected a moment. "Yeah, dignity and purpose. I think that's really important."

"Purpose?" Jack asked.

"That his life and death was part of a larger canvas of national meaning and participation. It's probably important to believe that."

"Alex, I wish I could say I believe that. We heard those words from the Army officers who visited us. That he had played a part in a significant war, an important national struggle. That he hadn't died in vain." He hesitated.

"So you don't think that?"

"I hate to say it but no, I'm not sure I believe that. I think he may well have died in vain, and all the other poor bastards out there as well in this stupid war that's only going down the tubes."

Alex felt in an awkward position. He wanted to help console his brother by sharing the national myths of meaning and purpose at a searing moment like this. Yet, not to his surprise, Jack's instinctive cynicism still lay not far beneath the surface. But Alex did not want to say those things himself. This was Jack's son.

"I don't know, Jack, when do people in war ever die for a 'good cause' or 'die in vain?' No death can be good in one sense. And anyway, we can't talk about death in general terms. There is only particular, specific death, of this person or that person at this time and place. It's hard to say whether my death or anybody's death in war is 'in vain'."

"Alex, I can't help it. I'm afraid I just don't buy it. That's what's crushing me." He put his empty glass down on the table. "I'm afraid I believe that Roger did die in vain. I think maybe most people in wars die in vain. I never thought I would say that, but the feeling has been growing on me. Even as Roger started talking about joining up. I just didn't think it would happen."

"But Jack, you've generally supported US policies over the years. This has to be bigger than Roger."

"Of course it's bigger than Roger! I'm just more aware of it now. I'm afraid the bullshit factor looms higher in my mind. It just seems like governments always want to sell the public on their overseas wars, especially one the politicians wanted."

Alex studied Jack's face that showed lines of weariness and accumulated grief. "I didn't want to be the one to say that Jack... You know Mom's uncle Jimmy, the one who died in the Spanish civil war? In my view he died in vain. Some feckless fucking failing effort to overthrow Franco. But it's hard to bring ourselves to say that. It's too cruel."

Jack flung out his arm out in an impatient, whiskey-laden gesture of disgust. "Yes, it's cruel. But we goddam well have to say it. That's how we get into these things, because we're all kissing ass at the altar of our brave troops, the finest troops in the world, in the great cause for this and that. And when these wars turn to shit, then we get this line thrown at us 'that they shall not have died in vain.' Nobody dares stand up and admit it—'yes, we fucked up, it was a mistake, and yes, your wretched sons died in vain.' What lily-livered politician would ever say that?" He glared at Alex.

Should he agree? Alex did agree, and saw this in spades in Afghanistan and Pakistan. But he didn't want to have to be the one to force this bitter pill down his brother's throat. Jack always had such a cool and calculating eye for the hard truths of this world. Some called him surly, but he wasn't. It was just his low bullshit threshold. Humor and cynicism had long formed his shields against the pain of existence. He preferred not to have to go there in his mind.

Yet, for himself, Alex knew he could never go the cynicism route. He felt driven to explore these issues, to look for some truth, something to believe in somewhere, some ideal, however unconventional, some way to break the deadly patterns of mindless and incessant military interventions as a national way of life.

"I know it's painful. But you do know I do agree with you, Jack. I see that in my own daily life, in the spillover of the whole Afghan morass into Pakistan. If politicians can never admit mistakes, never admit that wars were a mistake, then we're going to keep on marching down that same damn path every time."

"Goddam right! And that means we're forever fucked to repeat it all, mouth the same bullshit every time, wave the old red, white, and blue so people can't see what's in front of them. Keep up the good old arms sales, good for the economy... You know Alex, I never thought I would find myself saying stuff like this, some damn lefty line about merchants of death. But shit, it's true! It's clear! All our goddam corporations are happy with this system, they back it all up. Long live the empire! Golden goose that lays the fucking golden eggs...."

The next morning both of them felt like they had been through the wars—the pain of the funeral coupled with their own exploration of truth-in-whiskey the night before. Alex was struck by the deepened level of Jack's cynicism. It was not limited to the tragic loss of his son alone. He spoke bitterly about his job at the investment bank as well.

"I used to think that I was working in a field of brilliant financial minds. But all these buyouts and mergers and hostile takeovers and stuff that is going on—it is basically highway robbery. People lose their jobs, real value is stripped out of good corporations to be plundered by the stockholders for short-term gain—it's a fucking scandal. I used to have great admiration for American capitalism when I was in business school. It all seemed so modern and rational and clever—especially after seeing Pakistan. But I don't see it now. These people aren't creating value, they're manipulating paper that produces nothing except short-term speculative profits. They're up to their eyeballs in corruption. The shit that they're selling out there now, these derivatives and stuff. Yeah, I'm making money. But it stinks. And there's going to be a big cost in the end."

"I'm surprised to hear you say that, Jack. I just don't know enough about such deals to comment one way or another. But I didn't think it was that blatant."

"Oh, it is, little brother, it is. If it wasn't so high level, so pervasive, you'd call it crime. But instead we just call it 'high finance.' One day the heads will roll."

Alex had a creeping sense that his brother's world and his own—professionally poles apart—were beginning to converge in some sense. A gradual recognition about the Emperor's new clothes, pervasive in both their lives and professions in different ways.

"Oh, don't think I'm going to blow the whistle. I'm not. I don't have a whistle to blow and I'm not involved in anything close enough to do anything about it. I probably don't have the guts. But it's all around me. Fuck it, I'm making mine, as they say. I've got a good income, a nice house, a good life." He faltered, and then burst into sobs again, belying his bravado. Alex stood up and embraced him.

"Don't talk to Kathy about any of this," Jack urged him later. "It would be cruel to talk in front of her about deaths in vain. And I don't want her to get ginned up about the banking world. She's far outside of it anyhow. A psychologist doesn't watch the bank ledger, just the mentalities behind it. She's suspicious enough of much of this Wall Street crowd in any case."

Two days later Alex was back on the plane for the long journey home.

"How was it?" Isabel asked as she hugged him at the airport.

"Rough," Alex replied. "In the end we were mourning for something more than just poor Roger."

*   *   *

"You knew they were going to try to kill Abdul Haqq! You led me into a trap, you bastard!"

"Majeed, please. I warned you not to go! I told you Abdul Haqq was high on the kill list! That it was extremely dangerous to go."

Majeed had called Alex to come over to the house. From his voice on the phone, Alex knew he was distraught.

"And how convenient it would have been if they had killed me there, along with Abdul Haqq. The two conspirators, meeting their justly deserved punishment at the hands of the avenging American Predator!"

"Majeed, I had no idea they were planning a strike soon. I have nothing to do with these targetings whatsoever. I doubt they even knew you would be there. They track these guys all the time, looking for an opportunity. There may be people out there reporting on Abdul Haqq's movements for all I know!"

"But you don't know, of course, do you Alex. How convenient!"

Majeed had been shaken by his near-brush with death. Miraculously, as it later turned out, Abdul Haqq had not died. Distrustful of Majeed, and those following Majeed, Abdul Haqq had departed immediately after Majeed himself for another location. Indeed word was sent that he had suspicions that Majeed was trying to have him killed by luring him to this place for a Predator strike.

"You clumsy fools! Your operators are just out there happily pushing buttons on TV screens while serious people here are engaged in some very delicate negotiations. Of course we don't want Abdul Haqq dead—he is key to our efforts to gradually bring the Taliban under some kind of control and to play a role in negotiations in Afghanistan. Don't your people get it? Or maybe they don't want to! Maybe you've learned a few lessons out of the Israeli playbook—keep killing off any serious interlocutors until all you have is outright rejectionists with whom no deal is ever possible!"

The ISI command was furious. Abdul Haqq was one of the key commanders over whom they had some purchase, and whose support they would need over the longer run for any kind of future settlement. Now Abdul Haqq believed that ISI itself might have conspired in the attack. It would take a long time to persuade him otherwise, and meantime Abdul Haqq would likely turn more harshly against the Pakistani government and would refuse cooperation or coordination with ISI or even honor ISI's minimal requests and red lines. And it had nearly cost the life of Majeed as well. Alex was unsure how much could remain of his relationship with Majeed, already stressed to the core.

*   *   *

Alex had raised hell in the Station over the near-assassination of Majeed. "Look Alex, calm down," the COS had said, "you know we don't plan these missions. It's all out of California or Nevada or someplace." Sam concurred that it had been a bad call from a political point of view and promised to raise the issue with Hqs. "I agree, it's a goddam contradiction. But as a military target Abdul Haqq was obviously important and that took precedence over political considerations."

"OK, but that's just the goddam trouble with this whole US operation, Sam. Military needs seem to be driving it all. You can't put the military in charge of what supposed to be a political process. They're trained and paid to kill bad guys, not negotiate with them!"

Now the topic of Majeed had come up again, in a different context: Majeed had suggested that Alex accompany him on a visit to North Waziristan, to the areas of Predator strikes, to get a feel for attitudes there. It was obvious he wanted to influence Alex and US perceptions, but it was also a rare opportunity to get into these areas and see it firsthand. Alex sat in Kevin's office, along with the COS.

"Look, Alex," Kevin pointedly swirled around in his chair. "You've been dicking around with this guy, for how many years now? You're in a virtually declared liaison relationship with him. He knows who you are in this town. Nobody knows him better, so why don't you do the hard part now and pop the question to him? A trip like this could be an ideal occasion."

"We've been over this before, Kevin. I know how he thinks. I'm telling you he's not recruitable."

"That's the old can't-recruit-a-friend bullshit. He may be a friend. That makes it easier, and safer, to approach him, not harder."

"It's not that he's a friend. I'm telling you he's not the type to accept a recruitment pitch. He believes in his country and its mission, whatever else."

"Yeah, well, nobody's that lily-white that you can't find something that will sway them. Have you thought about all the possible vulnerabilities? Girlfriends? Boyfriends? Didn't we have some report that he hung out with some gays at university?"

"I think that's bullshit, Kevin. I have never seen the least hint that he's gay. He's got a wife he loves, and is a family man."

"Wouldn't be the first time you see that in a closet gay."

"In the absence of any shred of evidence I goddam well am not going to go down that crazy route of assumption."

"What about money?"

"He's doing well enough. I don't see any longing for toys and goodies in which money would make a big difference. He likes his scotch. He's got a good supply. He doesn't even drive a fancy car."

"Isn't there anything he could do with some extra money?" the COS broke in. "He doesn't have to be corrupt. On the contrary, maybe there's stuff he could do with extra money to help his family, his kids, his extended family, the ones out in the boonies?"

"He might want to help out his cousins and all that, but not enough to tumble to work for us. I'm telling you, he's got his pride and his principles. I know him."

"What about the old line about 'helping smooth understanding between our two services if we can speak frankly?' That angle sometimes appeals to more idealistic types," Sam suggested.

"Don't think so. Shit, we're already talking pretty honestly between us, more than his service would want, I suspect. You know I'm getting some useful stuff out of him, attitudes on policies—you see it. I don't want to wreck that. He's already invited me to go on this trip to the border with him. We already have quite an 'irregular' relationship, as they like to say in training. Sometimes that's as good as it gets."

"Bottom line, Alex, we're under pressure from Hqs to make some progress on the ISI target. Majeed is the best damn lead we've got. I can't tell them that we're not going to make the effort to nail down a recruitment by someone with total knowledge of him and total access to him."

"So what do you want me to do then, goddammit? Cold-pitch him?"

"Cold pitch!" Kevin scoffed. "It's the longest damn developmental stage I've ever seen, like thirty years? All we're talking here is just an effort to formalize the approach. What's he going to do, report you to his bosses? I don't think so."

"Alex, frankly, if you don't make the approach then we're going to have to have somebody else do it," Sam said. "Maybe bring in an officer from outside so nobody in the Station here gets burnt. But we can't let this opportunity go untested."

Alex offered no response.

"So what is it, Alex? Yeah or nay?" Kevin demanded.

"Alright, goddam it, but I'm going to do it my way. I'm not going to twist his arm, but I'll let him know the offer is there."

"OK, but don't make it so halfhearted and unconvincing that it doesn't register: I-know-you-don't-want-to-do-this-but-I-have-to-ask-anyway bullshit. He's got to be convinced that you're convinced. Talk to him about the standoff between Pakistan and the US. How it's in the interests of both of us to have a clearer understanding of where we're coming from. That the miscommunications are already massive. That the stakes are too high on both sides for us to run the risk of misunderstanding between the two countries. Offer to put aside money so his kids can go to college in the US down the road. Whatever it takes. You know the routine."

And indeed, their meetings and exchanges were slipping well out of the professional and into the personal, out of the correct and into the "irregular." Their friendship was too old for them each not to have an interest in the other's personal life and welfare. They knew what each of them was doing professionally, without making it explicit. But now Alex was required to make it crystal clear. Alex waited until the Friday family dinner was over, the day before they were to leave for North Waziristan. They had withdrawn into the study and Majeed had drawn out the Dimple from behind the books.

"Majeed, there's something I've got to talk to you about. I'm going to have to be frank."

"Frank? You worry me Alex, you mean we haven't been frank all along?"

"OK, maybe explicit is the better word. You're right, we are always pretty frank."

"So what's on your mind?"

"The relationship between our services."

"Oh, we are talking about services now? I thought we were just interested political professionals who enjoyed sharing views with each other, as they say."

"Come on, Majeed, you know what I'm talking about. We both see the rising tensions between our countries. Different geopolitical views even. I am certain Washington doesn't grasp the dynamic, and I don't think Islamabad gets it all either."

"So what are you proposing? Wait, don't tell me. You need my help."

"Help, yes. We need someone who can tell us the whole story, the real nature of the tensions, where we're failing to communicate, honest recognition of where maybe our interests don't coincide and what we can do about it."

"Isn't that what we have been talking about all along?"

"Look, Majeed, don't give me a hard time. Yes, I'm under instructions. I have to say that so at least you will know who is talking. Washington has immense respect for your knowledge and political savvy. They would love to have you as a confidential source on the personalities and background on the decisions your service makes. It might make dealings between the two countries more transparent, maybe easier, more beneficial in the long run."

"Are you doing what I think you are doing, Alex Anders? Are you trying to goddam recruit me as a spy?"

"No, not as a spy, but to see what the prospects are for a confidential relationship with our service. For mutual benefit."

"Goddam it, Alex!" Majeed slammed down his glass. "I wondered whether it would ever someday come to this. I can't believe it! You're trying to fucking recruit me. You bastard." Alex cringed at the coarse words he rarely heard from Majeed's mouth.

"I told you I was operating under instructions."

"After all that has happened, Salman, the Predator attack on my meeting with Abdul Haqq—I can hardly believe this. Who do you think I am? Some goddam pathetic agent material?" Majeed glared at him.

"Majeed, I'm sorry. You know how these things work. All I can say is I'm authorized to offer you any help you might need in return."

Majeed raised his hand. "Alex, don't say one more goddam word. I never heard this, it didn't happen. Go back to your little spy agency and deliver my carefully considered response: 'Fuck you.'"

"I never doubted for one second that that's what you'd say." Alex smiled, almost in relief. "I'm trying to keep a lot of cowboys under control here, Majeed, that's all I can say. You may not believe it, but you're lucky it's me in here with you and not some gung-ho true believer."

"You're damn lucky it's me in here with *you* and not some patriotic-minded Pak military officer. With a ham-fisted recruitment approach like that, he would have had you out of this country so fast you wouldn't have known what hit you… And you know what? Listen to me! We see enough of your gung-go true believers tromping around this country, and in Afghanistan. Half of them are out of control. Do you realize how many of your mercenaries are currently charging around our country, snooping, shooting people up, taking photographs, hiring agents and forming little goon squads?" Majeed stopped to recover his composure for a moment. "But yes, I know the game. It's still a fucking outrage that your people would be that crude about approaching me. Anyway, let's put all that aside. Whiskey was talking and I didn't hear anything."

"OK, and I will report back that you were not flattered by the offer."

"Just one more thing. I'm not taking you off to North Waziristan if there is ever a hint again of any such recruitment talk."

"OK, Majeed. I'm sorry. I fully understand. And I do want to go with you on the trip."

Alex paused, took another sip of Dimple. "Heard the latest *qawwali* disc from Nusrat's nephew, Rahat?"

"Now you're talking."

*   *   *

The SUV with its local driver left the main highway to turn onto a back mountain road that would take them into North Waziristan. The invitation hadn't been purely spontaneous from Majeed. ISI had thought it would be desirable for a US intelligence official see the situation for himself. It was one thing for American officials to read the military reports in clinical and sterilized—dehumanized—language of "collateral damage" reports, or even to see the high altitude photography of the target area struck by the drones. If the tagger had gotten his information right and identified the right building at the right time, and if drone surveillance had accurately identified it from great distance, then one or more jihadists would probably have died in the execution of the US mission. But accurate identification was by no means certain and the margin for error was considerable. The Embassy had to see the consequences for itself, and understand its political implications. In the end, because of his close ties with Majeed, Alex had been selected to go; the Chief of the Embassy Political Section had timidly begged off as a family man near the end of his Islamabad tour; he knew the risks of the Frontier.

Even Alex had initially hesitated considerably before agreeing to this trip, even to verify what he knew to be the often inaccurate targeting of the Predators. Worse, he knew about the erroneous, sometimes even deliberately false information fed by taggers into the targeting mechanism that would result in the deaths of many civilian non-combatants. In the end he stifled his many concerns; it was imperative at least to witness firsthand the situation in this dangerous province and personally take its psychological pulse.

Alex sat in the back with Majeed, tense about the scenes he was going to witness. Furthermore, he could have no confidence that some damn hothead on the other end of a drone camera might decide to target their vehicle, despite the fact that the trip was known to the Embassy. Death lurked invisibly in the sky—all the time and potentially for anybody.

This time they were going to the village of Yusef Khel, which neighbored the village where Majeed had often spent summer months of his youth with his relatives. He had gotten a call the week before from his cousin that there had been a major strike in Yusef Khel, destroying three compounds and leaving nineteen dead. His cousin Amar claimed that all the dead were innocents, mostly women and children, while the men were away at a meeting in another compound. Supposedly none of the men were part of the Taliban or active insurgents, although they bitterly opposed US policies that had forced the Pakistani military into clumsy intervention in the area. By now they were all sympathetic to the Taliban if forced to choose between the US and the Taliban resistance. And here in this area these days, who wasn't?

"We will only be speaking Pashto. But I'll translate. I'll say that you represent one of the NGOs here concerned with reconstruction. You don't have to say much, just listen. Obviously there should be no hint that you are American—the emotions might get out of hand. I'll say you're Dutch."

As dusk descended they were not far from their destination. Alex felt he was under God's—or Death's—microscope, a malevolent eye that wielded powers of life and death, linked to a distant and incomprehensible, erratic, and unknowable bureaucratic brain halfway around the globe.

As they drew into the village, there was no sign as yet of destroyed compounds in the falling darkness. The driver stopped to inquire about the headman's compound and was directed onward. Soon they came to a larger compound with a solidly constructed large two-storey building behind its wall. The gate opened and they were waved in. The malik of the village, Toryalai Khan, came out to greet them, dressed as if back from battle with a bandolier of ammunition wrapped around his trunk. His beard was gray, his lips narrow, eyes piercing, with a wan smile. He welcomed Majeed, kissed him on the cheeks, and then shook hands distractedly with Alex paying scant attention to who he was—it was enough that he was there under Majeed's protection. Alex offered some courtesies in Urdu which were acknowledged by Toryalai with a silent nod of the head, but received no formal response.

Toryalai took them inside where they sat on pillows arranged against the wall; the obligatory dark hot sweet tea was brought out, a particularly welcome refreshment after the long ride. A plate of chapattis were also set down along with some honey and white cheese. But Toryalai did not dwell long on formal courtesies in addressing Majeed. "Your mother will be very upset at the deaths of several people here. Tell her Gulbano and Husay from the clan died here three days ago along with their eight children. As well as some visitors from another village brought here by God's fate to meet their end. Praise God, we cannot discern his purposes." Toryalai's eyes teared over, and he did not hide it.

"What have we done that they should kill us in our homes—and at night like this? Our families live in fear, there is nowhere they can go where it is safe. The Americans are cowards, hiding behind their technology, living in their air-conditioned camps—they do not dare to confront us as warriors. God curse the enemy, for we have done nothing wrong. And God curse the government in Islamabad that does not protect us from this slaughter."

Majeed translated much of what was said; most of the exchanges in Pashto Alex did not really get, although he caught numerous words here and there in common with Urdu relating to funerals, compensation, destruction, burial, fear, Islamic invocations. Majeed could only listen to the sadness and anger welling out of Toryalai; he felt inadequate to make any long responses other than to cast his eyes down, shake his head periodically in sadness, disbelief and sympathy.

After nearly two hours, during which chicken karhai and bread was brought for them to share from the common pot, Toryalai took them to a guest room furnished with four charpoys, bed frames with a net of knotted cords across them to support a thin mattress. It seemed almost suicidal to be sleeping here in a compound with known connections to the Taliban. But both Majeed and Alex were tired and fell asleep quickly, although Alex at least remained mindful that the avenging exterminator was prowling the dark skies above and musing over its next move. Hopefully word had been passed to drone Hqs of their official visit here. But had word gotten through? There seemed to be a sense of malevolence, of an animal ferocity that invested the technology and gave it a semi-human form. Alex did not have time to ponder these uncertainties of fate for long before sleep took him too, even with the awareness that something more than sleep might take him without his knowledge.

The next morning, after chapattis with apricots, cheese, yoghurt and hot tea, Toryalai led them outside. It was a refreshingly cool morning so far, and the brown hills stretched out, relieved by swathes of green fields and fruit trees mixed among them. They walked past some eight compounds before they arrived at the scene. As they walked with the headman down the street, they collected a crowd along the way. The villagers sensed their visit was related to the devastation and the dead. Majeed did not want to advertise his presence since elements of his extended family in the next village were well known. Among the growing entourage came many children, then women, many already calling out in tears about their losses. Sounds of keening and mourning began as the villagers realized that outsiders were there on some kind of inspection.

"Look at what has been done to us!" shrieked one woman. Alex had to ask Majeed what the women were saying initially, but it was quickly clear that extensive translation was not required, the grief patent and unhidden. The names of the children were frequently mentioned, as well as their ages, chanted repeatedly—for the boys, "O Raheem, O Baryal, O Mir Wais!" And for the girls, "O Balbala, O Husay!" Alex experienced a sense of oppressiveness and wished he could squeeze into the ruins and not have to witness—and share—even indirect responsibility for this public grief.

They came up the hill and approached the compounds where the three devastated houses were visible. A massive hole had been blown in one wall and the back wall shattered beyond recognition. Household goods lay scattered, flung onto the ground obscenely exposing the intimacies of family life—tables, chairs, pots, clothing, underwear, rugs, pictures, dark stains of blood on the ground. A group of men appeared outside the shattered compound. Toryalai told Majeed that they were the husbands and relatives of the dead women and children. Majeed nodded to them. The men's faces were dark, their eyes reddened and bitter. They stared blackly at Alex and said nothing. No one made any effort to introduce anyone. Their wives and female relatives had said it all with the appropriate emotions. Alex found the men's sullen silence more unnerving than the women's keening and weeping with their voluble accounts of events several nights ago. "What have we done, what have we done to deserve this?" was their constant refrain. Alex felt helpless and could say nothing except to repeat the universal Koranic phrase of consolation upon death, *Verily we are from God, and to Him we shall return.*

Alex frequently caught the word *badal* in the women's conversation—vengeance. Such deaths had radicalized the village and vengeance was not an idle threat, it was a certitude, indeed a moral obligation to protect the honor of the families. Only how and upon whom vengeance would be visited was not yet clear. Alex was deeply uncomfortable in this setting, as a Westerner, much less as an American; he knew that to be German, French, English, Canadian or American mattered little, they were all in a way equally complicit, it was all part of the same historic cabal of Western powers of invasion, superiority and destruction in the eyes of these people. The villagers knew their history even if the Western invaders did not—once again kaffirs were intervening in the tribal territories, oblivious of past catastrophes of British, Russian, and other expeditionary forces into the area, each time insulated by the same arrogant certitude that their mission was this time "different." If it were not for his alleged UN status and protection of Toryalai, Alex felt he might have been personally at risk himself.

A little girl aged five dressed in an embroidered green dress with tiny sewn-in silver reflectors came up to Alex and took his hand without self-consciousness. She had a torn doll in one hand and was crying, pointing to the compound and repeating "Tofan, Tofan!"

Majeed spoke to her, then told Alex, "Tofan is her little brother, he is gone."

The little girl continued to pull on Alex's hand. "What is she saying?"

"Help us, help us," Majeed said.

Majeed had been right. This visit had put a human face on it all.

The women led Majeed and Alex first to the *kabristan* where villagers were buried and showed them the recent graves of piled-up dirt. Some said nineteen dead, others said twenty-four. Keening began again and Alex could not be sure what the direct relationship of the living was to the dead. The village felt the loss as a unit. He could feel the weight of the tragedy in the women's faces who all spoke at once about what had happened, wiping their tears with their kerchiefs. "It was after midnight," Majeed told Alex. "They had finished a festive dinner with their visitors. Their husbands had gone to a village meeting in another house. The only men killed in the strike were a few teenagers, several old men, and children who had stayed in these compounds and had not gone to the meeting."

"Do we know what the meeting was about? Anything to do with the Taliban?" Alex asked.

"The villagers say it was related to a recent case of murder between families; the meeting was meant to achieve a reconciliation between them, and there was a solemn ceremony."

Alex was struck by the ease of expression the women used in the village in talking with all the men, acting with far greater freedom than in Punjabi villages where women's place was more publicly conservative.

After a walk through the shattered compounds, Toryalai took them back to his own home and the women and children dropped away. Majeed told Toryalai of his terrible grief at these events and assured him that he would try to ensure compensation for what had happened. *"Inshallah,"* was Toryalai's terse, unconvinced response. He repeated that the villagers could not live like this in constant terror. No one was safe. Many of these families had sons who indeed had gone off to fight with the Taliban to liberate the country from foreign occupation. Events like this only deepened their resolve. More sons would assuredly go from the village now. No, by no means did they all approve of the Taliban, but who else had the power to drive out the hated kaffirs who only brought death and destruction?

As they drove away late in the afternoon they exchanged few words. Alex was well aware that Majeed had made a strong point, indirectly. He was grateful Majeed didn't feel he had to spell it out. What was there left to say?

But there was more to say, more had to be said. Alex desperately sought to process the emotional power of what he had seen. It was nothing he had not known intellectually from before, but never with the sense of personal impact; it simply could no longer all be intellectualized. Alex felt smitten with system overload, a crisis of how to square new awareness on the ground with a carefully fabricated political balancing act that was becoming increasingly difficult to maintain in the face of realities.

*   *   *

Men, ladies, it's a great privilege for me to be out here in Afghanistan with you all today. I don't want to take your time with a lot of speechifying, we all know it's Turkey day and I know how much you all want to get in there for a well-earned Thanksgiving dinner. But I just want to make sure you know how important it is, what y'all are doing. And how much we appreciate it. As Commander in Chief I sleep better at night knowing you are working to keep our country and our way of life safe from fanatics who would destroy it.

You are the finest troops in the world—the best motivated, the best disciplined, the most courageous, most professional, most determined, the best armed and the best trained ever. I am proud of you. Your families are proud of you. And your neighbors and fellow countrymen all know what an important sacrifice you are making out here.

This is no picnic. But it is a vital part of our security. What you are doing here today will make us safer tomorrow. We are fighting them here so we do not have to fight them on the shores of our own great nation. Because we *will* defeat the enemy and eliminate the evil-doers. They cannot stand up against the truth and what is right.

America is a beacon to the world. We are winning this war, and they are losing, and they know it.

We Americans don't know the words defeat or surrender. The enemy must never doubt our resolve, and you are the first proof of that. American leadership must never be challenged. We pray that these global threats to our nation will not require us to stay here for a long time. But we will do what it takes for America to emerge triumphant and victorious in restoring a world order. Your bravery and skills are what is making this possible. We all owe you. God bless you all, and God bless America.

*   *   *

Alex and Majeed had stopped off at the unoccupied country retreat of a relative of Majeed's the next evening to rest before continuing the long drive back to Islamabad the next day. With no one else there they sat on the furnished veranda around a table snacking on the basket of food that had been thrust upon them as they left by Toryalai's wife in Yusef Khel. They had said very little so far about the experiences of the day before, as if letting it process. "I was mindful enough to bring along a little something else for us as well," Majeed smiled as he pulled a small flask out of his suitcase. They found a few glasses and sat on the veranda looking out on the fields and mountains in the distance. Majeed finally asked Alex how he planned to report on the trip to the Embassy.

"I'll tell them what I saw. But frankly, I don't know how much difference it really makes to them. It's only one eyewitness account of what is already known in general terms."

"But surely the massacre of twenty or so people like that might give pause, cause a rethink. Can't you get that across? Speak out for what is patently wrong?"

Alex suddenly turned defensive—unable to reign in mixed feelings of guilt he'd been having all day. He knew his position was untenable, but emotionally he was not going to be driven into a humiliating admission at this point.

"Majeed, look. I'll report what I can report. But I can't challenge every damn policy of our government across the board every day. That's not what government service is all about."

Majeed felt his own emotional reactions flaring. "Who are you, Alex? We've been talking about Pakistan here, Pakistani lives—now you're trying to defend policies of your government that you clearly don't really seem to believe in. Who are you? Tell me, what do you represent?"

"Don't push me Majeed," he said in a tired voice. "I do what I can do. I don't have to agree with all the policies that are being implemented. I can't take everybody on."

"Well, you know what, Alex? In the main I *do* support what our government is trying to do, in terms of protecting the country. It's very clear to me that Pakistan is at a life-or-death juncture. We've got the bloody Indians, like some giant standing on our eastern border, with their massive territory, powerful army, expansionist instincts—and yes, frankly, better run as a country in many ways than we are. They were also lucky. They inherited the traditions and the governing infrastructure of India at Partition. What did we get? The unruly hinterlands of the empire, unruly tribes, the borderlands, always in turmoil and lacking decent governance or democratic practice. Hardly a meaningful city in the whole subcontinent was left to us in the lot, except thank God for Lahore, our only prize. We know damn well India would like to put an end to us as an independent country some day—bring us back into the boundaries of a greater India. India may have a great future ahead of itself. But we're not having it."

"Come on, Majeed, nobody is pushing you to surrender to India! Don't give me that Pak fantasy. That's not Washington policy."

"No? Well it looks like it. You wanted to stop our getting the bomb, keep us weak and defenseless vis-à-vis India—and the US. And just what is it about our getting the bomb that has you all so upset? We're not worthy? We're not white? We're Muslim? We're going to use it on the US? Or on your beloved Israel?"

"That's not it, you know that. It's just that when there are a lot of nuclear weapons floating around, somebody might end up using one."

"Yeah, like you did when you killed 10,000 civilians in Hiroshima and Nagasaki."

"That was to end the war faster, it was better for everybody. It saved lives!"

"Yes, American lives. I wonder how the Japanese felt about how great it was. You know, Alex, the main reason you don't want us to have a bomb is because you want to maintain your own power around the globe. The more countries that have the bomb, the harder it is for you to maintain that dominance."

"Given the politics here, nuclear weapons are frankly dangerous. Suppose some crazy fundamentalist—they're all around here—should get his hands on the bomb, he might use the damn thing!"

"Oh? There haven't been crazy leaders before with nuclear weapons? What about Stalin—he butchered twenty million of his own people on ideological grounds and wanted to take over all of Europe. Did he use the bomb against you in forty years of Cold War? And what about Mao in China? He killed twenty to thirty million of his own people in crazy ideological schemes, Great Leap Forward, the Great Cultural Revolution and all. He said China could even *afford* to lose a hundred million people in a war with the US and still come out ahead. Did he even come close to using it? And crazy Kim Il Song in North Korea? Big talk, but even they haven't seriously thought about using it. So I don't think it's all that likely that Pakistan or India will use it either. But damned if we'll allow India to hold their bloody bomb over our heads when we have no deterrent! That *is* suicide for us!"

"Washington is still worried about a nuclear war here."

"And why should it be scared of a nuclear war? More than we are? More than Russia and China should be scared of it? They're right on our doorstep after all, where the nuclear cloud will go. What's the big deal with Washington? I'll tell you what, it wants to dominate—everything. No rival power centers. Call all the shots on the international scene."

"Majeed, calm down, nobody in Washington says that! You're exaggerating!"

"No? Maybe not in so many words. But what do you think 'asserting American leadership' is all about? It's a nice word for dominance."

"A lot of states in the world welcome having some kind of US leadership."

"Yeah? Tell me, Alex, can you imagining the US welcoming so-called global leadership by any other nation? Even co-partnership? With France? Brits? Russians? Chinese? Indians? Who? Come on Alex, face it. Washington wants a free hand in everything. I'm sorry, but no one else wants it that way. That's the best argument of all for us having the bomb—you'll have to deal with us more as equals!"

"Look, Majeed, I know the US could deal more sensitively with other countries, including Pakistan. I know that. We can be overweening. We do need to change our attitude and we're…"

"Attitude! This isn't just about attitude. I happen to know that the US is trying to figure out just exactly where all the bombs are stored. We know you have plans to seize those weapons, you've talked about it in your bloody Congress, your think-tank studies."

"Majeed, please, this is getting paranoid! We're hardly perfect, but we're trying to keep things on a steady keel. That's in everybody's interest."

"How convenient. Your steady keel. Nobody else rock the American boat! What's good for America is good for everybody. Well, I'm sorry, it isn't."

"Look, Majeed, I'm only…"

"You know what Alex? In the end, you're helping everyone else find their identity in all of this—and they're finding it in opposition to *you*. I have discovered who I am. I'm a Pashtun, I'm a Pakistani. I am a Muslim. I am an Asian. In the end with all this Global War on Terror crap, I am gradually being driven to feel I am now a *Muslim* first. I never thought I would say that. It is now my Muslim identity that is starting to matter the most in this struggle with Washington. I am fighting to defend my own country and culture. But who are you? Who are you? You're fighting for a goddam empire!"

"Majeed, I'm not, that's not my ideal. I'm an intelligence officer. We're just trying to keep people back home informed. I…"

"Alex, wake up! You're working to keep the imperial system going, whether you want to or not! That's your function. You're serving America—the homeland, where your parents were born! Bottom line is you're defending an overseas empire, and letting your own young men die for it, and killing others! Is that what you believe in?" Majeed paused, and let the level of voice drop. "Think about what has happened to you. Have you been brainwashed? Don't you remember how we grew up together, played together, fasted together during Ramazan…"

"Of course I do, Majeed! You know that is a part of me!"

"Well, then, what has happened? You act like you don't understand this country any more, like you're standing behind some glass shield and manipulating radioactive instruments by remote control in some laboratory. None of this mess needed to have happened if you hadn't come barging into this country with your goddam soldiers and mercenaries and weapons and started throwing your weight around! People hate you here, your pressures, manipulations, demands, your damn relentless push for what it is you want in this world. Never mind that we don't want it! Never mind that it damages our country, our interests, our people, spills our blood, breaks apart our society. No, America doesn't care about that, it's all about what the empire needs at the moment. Well, we don't want the empire. And I can't believe that you, you seem to have sold yourself out to this system! Don't you see it? Understand it? It's right in front of your face! You, above all! How many others are in the US embassy that understand the thinking and the way this country works like you do? You should be the one speaking out on this—not going along!"

"Dammit, Majeed, I'm not going along! I do speak out. All the fucking time. How much influence do you think one person can have on this system? It works on its own, it's on autopilot! Nobody I know ever talks about empire or how to maintain it, we're just thinking about getting our own daily reporting jobs done, trying to understand what's really going on, trying to get an accurate reflection to people back home. Almost everybody I know is trying to be objective, balanced as much as they can. We don't sit around the Embassy and have meetings and talk about empire all day."

"That's as may be, Alex, but…"

"Wait, hear me out, Majeed! You've dumped a lot of shit on me over the past few minutes. You know what? It's your country that's more screwed up here! At least we have a pretense of objectivity in the Embassy. I talk to your goddam mullahs and mujahideen—do you think they sit around and go in for a lot of introspection? Objective analysis? They are totally wedded to their cause, their prejudices, they aren't worried about what others think. They don't know zilch about the world, but do they have any doubts? No! No doubts, no discussion, no trying to balance! They just act, and they goddam well spill blood too in the process, if need be, without any thought. They're absolutely convinced they're right and that those who oppose them are the enemy! They are turning against the US in a knee-jerk fashion now, whipping up feeling against us. You think that's balanced?"

"Alex! They... are... in... their... *own... country!* Their own country! They act to defend their own country and situation as best they can. That doesn't take complex philosophy or a PhD in international relations. People defend their own country and their own society against the invader. Of course they're sure of themselves, even if so many of them are ignorant or brutal. There's nothing to debate. But look at you, and your own damn troops and soldiers and mercenaries and agents and bases and snack bars and mini-America's built behind walls all over the world—and God knows what else. They're ten thousand miles from home, in some place most of them never heard of before. They're trying to control others that they don't even understand the language or the culture or the mentality. That's the difference! That's why you claim to try to be 'objective'—you're scheming on how to run *other* people and *their* countries! I daresay if you had an army of damn Chinese or Pakistanis or Zulus patrolling in your own country, firing off missiles to kill selected Americans they don't like, breaking down doors and houses and killing people—you think the American people would agonize very long about what to do? For God's sake, can't you see the difference? Can't you put yourself in other peoples' shoes? Don't Americans understand the meaning of dignity and self-respect in others? Or are you so wrapped up in empire now that you think that's the way of the world?"

The long pause that followed left little doubt. Majeed had just made the final volley of the match, he had slammed the ball irretrievably into Alex's court, a shot that Alex could never hope to return. The game was over.

After several moments of silence, Majeed ended with a near whisper: "Alex, you have helped shed others' blood on this soil, directly or indirectly, as well as the blood of your own countrymen. You are locked into its destiny that you have helped make. And I can plainly see that that is extracting its own personal price on you. I feel sad for you."

Something shifted in Alex's head as he felt a moment of clarity. Majeed had raised the same questions that had been eating away at Alex's consciousness for some time. Those fateful words kept echoing in his mind: *They are in their own country.* He realized how long he had been trapped in a cross-fire of competing ideas—opposing ideologies and worldviews—with fierce partisans standing behind the barricades on each side blazing away, bullets flying. Where could he take cover? He had no answer for Majeed. He could trot out some official rationale, the daily pablum at the Embassy, the operating instructions of the day, the Washington directives written by mindless bureaucrats as PR handouts for the world, substitutes for thinking, secret plans by Pentagon think tanks on how best to manipulate Pakistan. And he knew he did not believe any of it.

Alex fell silent, numbed. He felt his eyes lose their focus, he let the arabesque patterns on the red Afghan carpet merge and separate in his vision as everything swam together in one orgy of shifting shapes. The patterns and arabesques might differ here and there, but they were all blood-red, the entire galaxy of the rug was red, intense red. Alex lifted his whiskey glass against his forehead and drew in the coolness of the ice. Time stood still. He felt no need to respond. Nor did Majeed.

*　　　　　　*　　　　　　*

Isabel woke up to one more day of her increasing discomposure with life in the diplomatic circle of Islamabad. Too many people professionally trained to speak cautiously, never to reveal their hearts. The rules of diplomatic intercourse for the world had been written centuries ago by the masters of *sangfroid,* the British. Isabel craved to savor something real, and Zubayda was now her lifeline. She found herself asking to accompany Zubayda more and more on trips to neighborhoods and the countryside, to meetings about women's rights and activism. She felt privileged she had met a number of poorer Pakistani women who still could speak English well enough to communicate with her, tell her of their hardships, of the male violence that took place in the villages and male dominance over their lives. "Their stories are absolutely real, my sister," Zubayda told Isabel. "We are cursed with this mindset across the whole Indian subcontinent. The Hindus sadly are no better, they traditionally required wives to leap onto the funeral pyre to be consumed with their dead husbands. Over there and here you can read about brides having kerosene thrown on them, being burned to death in the kitchen by their mothers-in-law who don't like them. I tell you, we're in a bloody mess. But at least we are working on it, we're slowly bringing awareness."

"Zubayda, it's not just here, I know. Even in Latin America women's position may be slightly better, but we have always had honor killings in the villages, and the cult of virginity. And *macho, machismo*—they're Spanish words!"

So Isabel spent more and more time with Zubayda on these day trips, often getting home late in the evening to find Alex fretting about her whereabouts. "Look, Zubayda's a good friend," he said, "I'm glad you two are close, but you also have a household here, Rodriguito can't just stay with the servants after he gets home. And I would hope sometimes you would be able to come out with me in the evenings. There are some interesting people around. And it makes me feel bad if you're absent a lot. Even the Ambassador has inquired if you weren't feeling well."

"Alex, I'm sorry, but you know how meaningless… empty this diplomatic life is to me. What are these people accomplishing? Being diplomatic about things when the world is going to hell around us? These are things that should not be spoken of diplomatically, but bluntly, and with passion. I know you are busy, engaged in understanding Islamic politics, I can see that matters, but so much of this is empty society. Maybe they just need a good revolution! I just can't waste my time on social gatherings like this anymore."

Alex saw how Isabel was gradually growing more radicalized as a result of her activities with women's groups, and reverting to her more classic Latino leftist views and interpretations of events. It wasn't just about women: part of it seemed to be in reaction to her negative feelings about the war in Afghanistan, the tensions in Pakistan, and to Alex's job.

"You know, Alex, I've only realized how universal all of this is, this oppression of the peasants by rich landlords, the wealthy classes running everything," she said. "This reminds me so much of what Chile was like, before Allende came to power with his reforms. People accused him of being a communist, but he was right! He tried to change the order. That has to happen here too, and it can't come via the mullahs. You need a real revolution. We are teaching these women about women's movements and peasant movements in Latin America, to open their eyes. But I don't expect the US cares about reform of people's lives—it's all power politics." She seemed to goad him.

Eventually it got back to the US Embassy that Alex's wife was professing revolutionary views in women's groups, which was upsetting to many of the big landowning families who could not believe this was coming out of the wife of an American diplomat. "Alex, look, tell your wife to tone her language down." Sam took Alex aside one day. "The Ambassador has asked me about this, he really likes you and Isabel, but this is embarrassing for us, and we don't need more radicalism in this country. We're getting quite enough of it with the Islamist radicals."

"They're just chic radicals, Sam," Kevin had said to Sam earlier, "that's what this couple is—Alex and Isabel, chic radicals!"

Alex had to pass along the Embassy's concerns to Isabel and she did not take it well. "This is getting to sound like Santiago in the good old days of Pinochet," she said bitterly. "We can't have any revolutionary talk about change around here, it might upset the American boat." Alex understood the Ambassador's concern about her as the wife of an Embassy employee, but he also agreed with Isabel—this was a kind of gutless caution that dominated Embassy life.

Alex had delivered a full report to the Embassy about his trip out to Yusef Khel to view the damage. Few at the staff meeting expressed much surprise at the details of what had happened. Indeed, it was regrettable, but this was war; hopefully the methods could be further refined to avoid more errors like this but there were lethal enemies out there, still looking to kill Americans. Many militants were being eliminated. The Ambassador had listened to the discussion in silence. He then spoke up. "I, for one, want to congratulate Alex on the thoroughness of his report. More than that, for the strength of conveying the atmospherics. We all see various numbers on casualties, among militants and among civilians, but this report brought home to me the feelings on the ground out in the Frontier that Washington must be aware of. I'm forwarding it on with a strong recommendation that people read it in detail— to get a sense of the political problems that we face with these drone casualties. This can severely impact our broader policies." And after the meeting, the Ambassador drew Alex aside. "This report is helpful to me, Alex. And just between us, you won't be surprised to know that I'm having a considerable struggle with the Pentagon over this matter. They seem still convinced that military means are the most efficacious way to prevail. I think they are wrong, but I have to be artful in how I argue this. I appreciate your help, and your sensitivity to the scene."

Alex told Isabel with some emotion about what he had seen, but did not want to push it too far with her either. She already had strong feelings about the entire conflict. The emotionalism of the scene in Yusef Khel would only upset her and further entrench her in her thinking.

"Maybe you need a break, Isabel," he said one night as they got ready for bed. "Do you think you'd like to go back to Chile, at least for a few weeks, with Rodriguito? You know your parents would love it. And I know things are hard on you here. I'm sorry about it." And he hugged her.

She brightened up. "Yes, maybe, Alex, maybe I should. In one way I hate to leave, as if I were fleeing something. And I don't like leaving you here either, *mi amor.* I worry about you, and these conditions. If I go, I wish you could come too." They agreed that in the next month or so they would arrange for Isabel to fly back to Santiago for some leave.

Two days later he was off to Peshawar near the border area, for his turnover meeting with Homaid. Isabel was nervous as usual about him going on each occasion. She tried not to say much about it, it was his job, he knew the risks, what could she say that would change anything, except to make him more nervous? And there were the regular TV reports about incidents in Peshawar.

Her sense of restlessness was not improving but rather increasing the longer she was exposed to the tortured Pakistani environment—its political tensions, growing anti-Americanism, the aridity of the diplomatic circuit, the clannish and isolated American Embassy crowd, the occasional violence in the city and surrounding countryside. Fine, she had grown accustomed to headscarves and conservative clothing, but the sight of women with their faces completely enshrouded in black burqas had begun to repel her, these creatures struck her as non-people. She and Zubayda often tried to persuade women to at least reconsider the necessity of such face cover, and stressed the lack of any religious requirement for such attire. But the women had told her that they knew it was not a religious requirement, but a social requirement, that their husbands or brothers or even sons felt it necessary and helped perpetuate it. To fight it was an anti-social act. Isabel felt as if these women had chosen to seek refuge behind dark veils from the pain and ugliness of the world around them. And she had come to understand that the phenomenon was more than just suppression of women— Zubayda had explained that it also implied a statement against pro-Western moneyed elites in Pakistan. Isabel had been to a number of Pakistani women's gatherings with Zubayda where some of the enshrouded figures would come into the house at an all-women's gathering and remove their burqas to reveal an attractively dressed woman who was no shrinking violet when it came to expressing their opinions. On one occasion one of them had even criticized the "so-called freedom of women" in the West which she described as dominated by market exploitation of sex. Isabel felt this view was exaggerated, but not without foundation.

Furthermore, Isabel was hardly a stranger to violence, she had grown up with it, seen her relatives tortured, imprisoned and disappeared; they had suffered in the face of the unending strut of bemedalled uniformed dictators who had imported, or replicated—with swagger stick and gloves and highbrowed military cap—all the pomposity and full pageantry of Mussolini's fascism or Franco's Spain. She wondered if this was not simply a rule of life for humanity, the default situation which arose all over the world when politics were conducted through violence, either by terrorists, or by military weapons—or underdeveloped men.

But the emotionalism and tensions inside Pakistan were a few notches higher than in Chile. Violence here was brown, earthy, local and lethal; it was democratic—anyone could play terrorist. Such violence seemed to envelop them all now, a kind of inescapable and pervasive cottage industry. Latin fascism was so much simpler, it was top-down. It didn't have tribal elements lurking behind it. Sure, she knew how many of the big families of Chile were themselves clans in their own way. But the violence there was exercised mostly by the regime against its enemies, it usually did not entail the whole nation at war with itself. Perhaps most important, it rarely involved Latino governments fighting against foreign invaders any more—a key reason their struggles lacked a religious component: everyone was of the same religion.

Sensing her unhappiness, Alex had actually grown more attentive to Isabel. He made greater efforts to decline social invitations of a *protocolaire* nature, and to take time to do things as a family on days off. As he grew older Rodriguito too was getting more responsive to picnic trips to castles and forts in the area that excited him. Isabel appreciated Alex's new efforts and she did draw greater sustenance from family time together. Nonetheless, in Alex's eyes it did not altogether bring back the spark that had once so intrigued and attracted him from the old days; Isabel seemed to be under a slight pall of depression. Rodriguito, and her work with Zubayda made up her main daily emotional sustenance, although Rodriguito did go now to an international elementary school leaving Isabel time for her own activities.

Still, apart from Zubayda, Isabel felt she had little other really meaningful and substantive companionship, leaving her feeling essentially alone and vulnerable. Isabel realized how much she missed Latino culture, the crispness of Spanish speech surrounding her, the pleasure of expressing herself in her language of childhood, in a society that seemed to possess greater freedoms even within its often rigidly masculine structure. There were few Latino embassies in town to provide that milieu. She did like Miranda Rivera, the wife of the Argentinian ambassador, who had similarly suffered exile with her family from Buenos Aires during the Peronist dictatorship in her childhood years. But Miranda seemed over time to have contracted the ambassadorial disease of her husband, and most ambassadors—an insufferable sense of self-importance. Whose head is not turned when you are referred to all day long as "Excellency?" Isabel liked much more the down-to-earth UN representative, the Guillens, from Colombia.

With Alex away in Peshawar, Isabel decided to call up Sandra Guillen and found that she was indeed free for lunch. Isabel went out to her car at noon and was vexed to find it had a flat tire. She tried to find the gatekeeper to fix it, but he was gone. Of course, it was Friday, everyone would be off at noon prayer and the weekend. There was no spare tire in the trunk even if she had had the time to try to change it herself. She thought about taking a tuk-tuk but there weren't any in sight at this time on a Friday either. She considered going back in and calling Sandra to ask that she come over to pick her up. Instead, she reluctantly decided she would take Alex's jeep; she didn't like the car, it was uncomfortable and dusty. She clambered in, sat down, and turned the ignition switch.

The jeep leapt three feet off the ground, sending parts flying in all directions as a ball of flames arose from the hulk, searing all the flowers and shrubs the gardener had carefully planted along the whitewashed wall of the compound, now splattered with oily black and traces of red. The sound of the impact echoed for blocks and then receded into silence until the first people in the street cautiously made their way in through the compound's twisted gate that had been torn off its hinges to expose the flaming wreckage.

*   *   *

It was only late in the day that the call finally reached Alex in Peshawar from Jim Perth, the duty officer at the Embassy. "Alex, I'm terribly sorry, I don't know what to say. We have some very bad news—about your wife…" Alex knew what it was before he even heard the duty officer out. She had been so vulnerable in even being associated with him; his own vehicle was such a logical target. A cold fury swept through him as he listened, numbed to the message, to the well-meaning, pained, sympathetic but official voice on the other end. "So, if there's anything we can do right at this moment, please let us know. We have taken your boy to the home of the econ officer where he's friends with his son I believe, and they said they are happy to take care of

402

him as long as is necessary and to help out in any way they can… I'm afraid it's too late now for the flight back from Peshawar. Do you want us to send a car from the Embassy to bring you back to Islamabad late tonight? If it's not too late? Again, we all send our deepest…" Alex no longer heard the words. Tears, emotions were not even on the horizon yet, only the blunt devastating slam of a body blow that suspended nearly all other senses of his consciousness. He declined the offer of a car and said he would take the early morning flight back as scheduled. He lay down on his bed in the hotel and stared at the ceiling. In the background Peshawar's taxi horns, calls to prayer and smell of roasting kebabs receded to another level of his consciousness. Santiago came rushing back, the sweetness of their many rendezvous, their magic trip to Chiloé. His struggles to bring Isabel around to an acceptance of his life, his job, to his *Americanness*. An Americanness in him that she clearly felt and appreciated, even if it was not always recognized by some other Americans for whom Alex was always "a bit different." It was also Isabel's association with official Americanness that had finally dragged even her into its deadly embrace on this distant stage—as an indirect but no less real victim.

As the first wave of silent grief passed over him, his thoughts broadened— a desire to strike out. How could he avenge her? Who or what should be the object of his vengeance? Myriad bearded faces flashed through his mind. By now there were multiple groups and suspects who could be involved. Obviously he and his car had been the direct target, not her. It could be a disgruntled agent, a local Taliban group, al-Qaeda sympathizers, all kinds of people who wanted the US out, wanted to punish the US and its occupation. Maybe he was just a random Embassy officer like any other whom fate had selected as a local target. He was one of a smaller group who lived outside the Embassy compound. He could even suspect radical forces within the labyrinthine structures of the Pakistani military itself. Or someone from the Afghan side. Or someone who had fingered him in the Salman incident. Or some kind of generalized vengeance for the drone attacks. The whole situation seemed escalating without end, insane.

Over time the litanies, the repeated verities of the respective causes of everyone in the country, tasted like chalk in his mouth. For Christ's sake, couldn't anyone see this wave of madness that had been unleashed? The theories, the geopolitical calculations, the bloodless posturings of the think tanks for whom this was all a fascinating game of political science, sophisticated moves on distant geopolitical board games, chessboards all quite devoid of human element, no trace of a human story, human lives and deaths anywhere.

And which narrative was it to be anyway? In twenty or thirty years, the names, the family sufferings on all sides would be forgotten, it would be the geopolitical calculations that would be remembered, written about, sagely assessed for failure or success. The human stories—the book of names and lives—were never known, never part of the calculation, except for an occasional journalist's human-interest story to serve as fodder for some pro- or anti-war group.

Which was the real narrative? The daily lives twisted, uprooted, destroyed, the souls maimed? Or the grand view of the historians and the professors of military and diplomatic science? Of mission accomplished. Of terrorists brought down. Of policies successfully imposed. Of countries forced to bow before power. And of diplomats often little more than preening, intelligent, informed errand boys responding to the requirements of the White House and its ancillary agencies. For God's sake, where was the perspective of all these follies? Instead it was just thousands of little pieces of a huge mechanism, each piece innocent of the grand structure of which they made up a part. The best way to remain sane was to live within the confines and rationality of your own little piece of the mechanism. It was disturbing, even unhealthy for the mind to think big. And for Alex right now, to think big was to think of Rodriguito, his last lifeline to real life, to protect him at least from this madness.

Alex decided he would go through with making the ops meeting to turn over Homaid—now less than two hours away. It was a key agent turnover and it would be the last time he would have to come to Peshawar for a while. It would bring closure to that particular case for him. And the meeting served to distract him from the black beast lying upon his mind and heart whose presence he still could scarcely comprehend. He turned over Homaid as quickly as he could to the new case officer and said nothing to either of them about what had happened; he then left the two of them together to gain familiarity with each other. He went back to his room in the hotel and lay down. At last tears broke through and he shook convulsively for long minutes. He could not even identify each distinct element in his swirling emotions—pain, agony, rage, fury, frustration, guilt, helplessness, isolation— ultimately tailing off into an exhausted awareness that this was the way it was, and the way it would be. He could not even immediately personalize it against an enemy out there. They were all enemies, one to another, all conducting shortsighted missions in the interests of some broader cause over which neither he nor they nor anyone had any control. He was but one solitary, troubled, convulsed figure among thousands and thousands, lying on his bed, apart from all the others in their separate agonies as part of the grander game. What was the Hippocratic oath? "Above all do no harm." How simpleminded a political philosophy that was! And how unerringly clear in its vision of the basic foundation of all human relations.

Could anyone act and do no harm? Possibly. If you were a farmer tilling your land out there in some field you could be relatively innocent of the more vicious human political game around you. But the higher you rose in the system—any system—the more your actions had consequences upon others, intended, unintended, but nonetheless inevitable and predictable. Alex was still just a modest player with only a small piece of responsibility, on a small but particularly violent stage in this world. He could, he even did, change small events, affected people's lives—and deaths. In this jungle of a world, was it better to be caught up, passionately engaged? Or to simply opt out, to accept the carnage as a given in human life and attribute no grander meaning to it? His most important human task now was to get back on his scheduled morning flight to Islamabad and Rodriguito, his flesh-and-blood direct human connection to life.

*　　　　　　　*　　　　　　　*

It took him two days before he could face it. He had to let Doña Maria and Don Jorge know of the death of their daughter and last remaining child. They did not use email and he did not want to have to manage such a formidably emotional scene by phone in a foreign language, so he sent a cablegram—reverting to a technology of another era, another mentality, and one also traditionally associated with tidings of death.

Dear Doña Maria and Don Jorge,

I have the terrible pain to have to tell you that Isabel is dead. She was killed by a bomb placed in our car while I was away. I do not know who committed this act, but there is a near civil war taking place here and many foreigners are targeted. I am shattered and heartbroken. She was worried about my safety as I traveled around Pakistan, but we did not think the danger could extend to her.

Rodriguito, thanks be to God, is safe and well, but he is of course devastated. I spend as much time with him as I can, and he spends most of the day with some good friends of ours in the Embassy who have a son the same age. Please know I will give the highest priority to taking care of him and always keeping the memory of his mother alive to him.

And for you, of course, Doña Maria and Don Jorge, I know the blow is equally terrible as you lose your daughter. I don't know what to say to you except that she was the light of my life, the best thing that ever happened to me. I adored her and I do not know yet how I will go on living life without her. Her optimism, her joy, her enthusiasm, her artistic abilities, her wonderful appreciation of other cultures made my own life a joy.

We will have a small funeral here in Islamabad for Isabel on 27 November. I know it is almost surely too long a way for you to come, but I would of course be honored if you could attend.

We have the painful question of her burial as well. Due to the terrible nature of her death, we have already had to cremate the remains. But I think she would want her ashes to be buried in Santiago. Pakistan is not our home, although I grew up here. I will not be spending the rest of my life here either. And we have no real place to call home in the US. So I would like to see her rest in Santiago close to you. I assume this would be your wishes also. I will bring her ashes back personally to you in Santiago very soon.

Again, please accept my condolences to you. When we came to Islamabad obviously we could not have known this would happen, but Isabel did not want to shrink from the realities of political violence anywhere. And we all share in our terrible and sad loss of our beautiful Isabel.

Con cariños y abrazos fuertes en la tristeza,
Alex

*   *   *

Caro Alex,

Don Jorge and I were shocked and horrified to hear the terrible news about our beautiful and beloved daughter Isabel. This is a monstrous thing. I do not know how we can go on living without her, she was the light of our life and our treasure. She filled our days, even when she was far from us. Her long phone calls with us were a constant joy without which we have no life.

I must speak plainly. We are deeply upset with you for this terrible event. We have no choice but to hold you responsible. You know that we have always been angry about the politics of the United States—first of all in our own Chile. I know you are not personally responsible for what happened in Chile, but you have been associated with US government and its policies. And now it is the same in Pakistan, another place with a terrible American war where you took our beloved daughter. And now she too is dead, in this environment of killing that seems to surround everything the US touches. She is another innocent victim of ugly politics. We were afraid when she married you, and we did not want you to take her away. And now she is gone forever.

Don Jorge and I are too old to travel to Pakistan—it is far away, it is alien, and it is dangerous. So I am pained to say we cannot be present at Isabel's funeral in Islamabad. We will ask the Chilean Ambassador to attend with a flag for her casket. As for her remains, we definitely want to have them here with us. This is Isabel's place, her home and her country. This is where she belongs for all time, and where she will rest eventually with us as well. You must bring her remains back here immediately.

We are also deeply concerned about our precious and sole grandson Rodriguito. Pakistan is not a place for him to live without a mother. It is dangerous and you do not have time for him. We do not want him in the care of people outside the family. We want Rodriguito to come home to Chile to live here where he has grandparents and cousins—family and home. He is our sole remaining flesh and blood. You are always welcome to visit him, but you cannot take proper care of him, especially while you are alone in Pakistan. He is our last precious link we have to our beloved Isabel.

With respects,
Doña Maria and Don Jorge

*   *   *

Dear Doña Maria and Don Jorge,

Thank you for your message. I am sorry that you will not be able to come to Isabel's funeral here, but I completely understand. Perhaps you can have a memorial service later in Santiago. I want personally to bring her remains back to Santiago very soon.

I am pained, too, that you partly hold me responsible for Isabel's death. I do feel guilt myself in this respect, but Isabel never hesitated to share my life, even in potentially dangerous places. Fate moves in strange ways, and there is nothing certain in anyone's life. But still, this guilt will never fully leave me. I want you to know that.

As for Rodrigo, I cannot give him up, he is my own son, he is dear to me, and represents the soul of Isabel in my life. But you are right, it is not a good place for him in Pakistan right now with the memories of his mother's death and the violence here. Ordinarily I might insist that he perhaps go and stay with my brother in the US. But he has not been part of my brother's family and does not even know his cousins there very well.

Therefore of course I am ready to take Rodrigo back to Santiago for the remaining year of my tour in Islamabad. Certainly Isabel would have wanted him to stay with his grandparents and cousins for a while in Santiago, to deepen his roots in Chile, and to improve his Spanish. But I must insist that I have the freedom to take him back with me when my time in Pakistan is finished. He should be with his own father when the conditions are safe. In the meantime I am grateful to you both for receiving my son and your grandson for this period where he can be far away from this tragedy.

Again my deepest condolences in our joint loss.

Cariños y abrazos,

Su yerno,

Alex

*   *   *

Majeed heard about Isabel's death through intelligence channels before he even heard from Alex. He was stunned. And tragedy can help wash away accumulated bitterness. Blood had literally come repeatedly between Alex and himself, first in Lahore decades before when Alex's father had been beaten nearly to death. And then Salman's death. And now Isabel. Death—politically-driven death—had thrice crippled, and linked, both families in tragedy. He left word for Alex to contact him as soon as he got back to Islamabad. "Alex, what can I say? *We are from God and to Him we shall return.* This is terrible. We feel devastated. Isabel was a wonderful person. And Zubayda is bereft. Please come to our Lahore house on Friday with Rodrigo for dinner with our family."

Alex's guilt over Salman had joined the growing pool of blood of ongoing family tragedy. He desperately wanted to spend time now with Majeed and his family more than with any other company. Majeed understood him, understood the dimensions of the issues, the intertwining of the personal, the intellectual, the political and the professional—twisted strands that could not in real life be separated.

As Majeed opened the door to them he saw the slight figure of Rodrigo behind Alex and swept him up first into his arms. Tears came at once to Alex's eyes and he too then fell forward into Majeed's embrace. Zubayda too came to the door and then embraced first Rodrigo, then Alex, now more than ever members of the family. Aysha and Majeed's children came in and saw Rodrigo holding his father's hand. "Would you like to come and play with us?" they asked, but Rodrigo hung back and clung to his father. "Later perhaps," Alex suggested.

They went in the family salon to sit on pillows on the floor against the wall, the comforting, traditional Eastern nest of intimacy. Majeed inquired about the practical aspects of Alex's life, care of Rodrigo, whether Alex had time off from work, softening the ground before turning to the burning nodule of pain in Alex's heart. "What can we do to help you, Alex? You know this is your home, it has always been your home."

"God keep you, Majeed..." He was silent a moment trying to recover his composure in the flow of tears. "Do you know, Majeed, this is the first time I have really cried in front of anyone else since the day she died? It is really a sign of what your family means to me, that you soften my heart and help my emotions to flow." He paused again and Majeed carefully held his silence, himself swallowing back emotions, and allowing Alex to manage his thoughts.

"It happened, Majeed, it finally happened. How could it have been otherwise? I brought first your family, and now my family into this tragic situation, how could I believe they would not be touched by it too? None of us are spared the pain and loss that this situation... that we are delivering upon each other."

"God is great. He is our sole consolation. Only through Him can we ever hope to understand these things."

"Understand? I think we can see what is happening. We are all caught up in it and we all become victims, like some Greek tragedy —everybody knows where things are going but we are helpless to stop it."

"Yes, it is bigger than us. But that does not mean that we should stop trying to change it. We owe it to ourselves and our dead family members..." They lapsed into moments of silence. Majeed then gently asked, "So what do you plan to do now?"

"I don't know, Majeed. I need time to think. I have to work out something for Rodrigo for a start."

"We will take him into our house here. He is one of us."

"Thanks, Majeed, but I just don't think that will work. This is still a risky environment—and the one in which his mother died. I think I need to take him back to his grandparents in Chile, far from this bloodshed, from the blood of his own mother on his own doorstep."

"As you wish, my dear Alex. But the offer is there. Do you not think you will feel even more alone if he is not here with you?"

"Look, I have to be realistic. I'm sure this will not be the only attempt against me. It just comes with the job. I can't leave Rodrigo exposed to that. It would just be selfish, irresponsible to try to keep him here with me."

"Do you blame yourself for this, Alex? Because you shouldn't."

"I do and I don't. We all walked into this with our eyes open, at least myself and Isabel. Maybe I shouldn't have brought her. If I feel guilt, it is a deeper one."

"Deeper?"

"I am not an innocent. There is no way I can be. This whole enterprise we are engaged in, this whole struggle, it just feels empty and pointless. No one is winning and more people are dying. If you are 'naïve' you see the death all around you and see it as fundamentally pointless, and you fight against it. But if you are really 'sophisticated' then you shut out the human face of all of this, you close your eyes to it and try to believe that it must all be viewed on some kind of so-called 'strategic level,' filled with political meaning, devoid of human content. That may be the most naïve view of all."

"Well, let's go out in the garden. The cook has some delicious food for us all. Some good food and fresh air can start to heal our souls."

"Thanks, Majeed, you don't know how much it means to me to be here..." his voice quavered.

Majeed threw his arm around Alex's neck as they walked out to the spacious back garden shaded by fruit trees, where Rodrigo was already kicking the ball around with his friends.

After they had eaten Alex felt restless, as if called. "Do you mind if I just go out, and maybe walk around a bit by myself, Majeed? I haven't spent any time in Lahore in a while. A few old haunts." And he went out into this city of his childhood, and walked for half an hour through the streets, finally ending up at his old home. He stood in front and gazed at it behind its walls. Some parts of it had been painted a different color, but it was the same house, the same smells of the neighborhood, spared the voracious pace of change on the bigger commercial streets some blocks away. He almost thought of ringing the bell, of asking to go in to see what had once been his world and his life, but decided against it. It would not be the same, and he preferred to remember it as it had been. He had been innocent of so much in those days—of his emerging sexuality, of Isabel, of the professional seduction of his work, of the agonizing complexities of a political and social scene he could not yet be aware of. He meandered slowly around several more blocks until he arrived at where his father's eye-clinic had once been. A sign in green lettering now proclaimed Siddiqui Chemist. There was no trace of the violence that had transpired here, that had gutted his father's clinic, that had ultimately taken his father's life and transformed their family's existence. Yes, he had been exposed to that terrible blood, the blood of his own father, even then. But he had not seen it in its full context at that time.

Alex wandered for another hour, past old haunts, some unchanged and others transformed beyond recognition—a simile for the country. And he finally landed back on Majeed's doorstep. "We were worried about you, Alex," Zubayda cried.

"I'm OK," he smiled. "Don't worry, I'm fine, just revisiting something of the past." And he realized this house was the heart of emotional existence now, as Rodriguito came running up and hugged him.

*   *   *

"Take off, Alex, please, you deserve some time away and with your son. Don't worry about your cases, we can handle them."

Bureaucracies are huge impersonal machines, institutionally run without much human impulse. But on the ground locally they are still administered by real people who can still interact with real human responses. Even though political events were piling up, Sam was attentive to helping Alex through his time of trauma and grief. There was no question, Alex should go with Rodrigo back to Santiago with Isabel's remains as soon as possible.

Her remains. A gruesome reality, but the only appropriate term. The explosion had left no identifiable body, only random parts and pieces that Alex mercifully never had to identify. No one else had been killed in the blast so whatever fragments were found surely had been part of the body he had adored. Only the chief medical officer at the military unit that took care of casualties had raised this issue with him, as required. Such remains as there were recoverable were cremated. Shortly thereafter Alex received a small box of ashes. He arranged for a flight back to Santiago on his sad mission with Rodrigo.

Rodrigo had only been told that his mother had been in a terrible car accident and had been killed. Rodrigo wept bitterly over his mother's loss. He knew what death was, as much as a seven-year old could. He had picked up from adult conversation, however, that it was not just a car accident, but an explosion. "Why did Mommy's car explode, Daddy?"

"We don't know, but there are many bad people here fighting in Pakistan and they are driving around with explosives in cars."

"But why would they want to kill her?" His lip trembled.

"They didn't want to kill her, son, but when there is fighting many innocent people get hurt." A paradigm for the country.

That was another reason why it would be best for Rodrigo to leave Islamabad, so as not to be exposed to stories, theories and idle speculation from his contemporaries about what had happened. Inevitably some in the Embassy would speak indiscreetly at home in front of their own children about the incident, and who was with CIA and who was not—none of that would be healthy for Rodrigo to hear.

Rodrigo had asked too about his mother's ashes. Alex told him that it was very common now for people to be cremated, "turned into ashes."

"But why turn them into ashes? Doesn't it hurt them?"

"Rodriguito, my son—no, once a person is dead, their body doesn't feel anything any more. It is just an empty shell. But their spirit and soul remains in the world."

"Is Mommy's spirit in the box?"

"Not just in a box, no. Her spirit is everywhere, inside us as well."

A pause. "Can I hold the box for a while?"

"Do you really want to?"

Rodrigo solemnly nodded and took the box that contained a dark blue urn.

"We're going to take the box back to Santiago to *abuelita* and *abuelito*."

"Why are we taking it there?"

"Because that's where Mommy was born and grew up and where all the rest of her family is. We will put her ashes in the cemetery there with the rest of her family."

"Why can't we keep the box ourselves at home?"

"Because… because we all come from the earth, and are made of earth. So we put the remains back into the earth." And yet on the longest leg of the flight, from Dubai to São Paulo, and then on to Santiago, Rodrigo did not sleep for a long time. He did not want to watch the film, but just sat quietly, seemingly in thought. At one point, as Alex had just begun to doze off, Rodrigo turned to him. "Daddy, do you think Mommy might ever come back?"

"No, Rodriguito, I am afraid she won't be able to come back. That's what happens when people die. And when animals die too, like your hamster last year."

Rodrigo stirred the ice in his drink with his finger as he took in the information. Adults can conjure evasively among themselves in theoretical concepts and metaphysics. It is the small child that forces us to define our theology and beliefs with concrete precision. There is no diluting or postponing these pressing and earthy questions that spring from a child's desire to understand impinging reality. However mixed Alex's personal religious views were, he could not escape specificity when his son worried about the fate, condition, and destiny of his own mother. Alex had always found close parallels between the Muslim formulation of condolence—"For we are from God and to God we shall return" and the Christian "ashes to ashes, dust to dust." Both touched the same eternal abiding elements of existence, fused into a greater order, however one chose to call it.

"But where do they go when they are dead?"

"No one knows, Rodriguito. Some people think they go to heaven to be with God, other people think they return to earth, to be with Nature again."

"What do you think?"

"I can't be sure," Alex replied, ruffling Rodrigo's hair. "But we are all made of material and minerals out of the ground, out of Nature. That's why some people say Mother Nature. And we surely go back to Nature when we die. I think God is Nature too. And some people think the person's soul lasts long after their body."

"Do you think Mommy's soul is here?"

"Yes, Guito, I do. As long as we think about her and remember her, her soul is always alive and here with us. And you grew in her tummy, so she is part of you and you are part of her. So you will always be part of her, always close, through your own body and mind."

"Oh," Rodrigo said, and returned to pensively stirring his drink. The reality of death dawns slowly, evolves, changes, never disappears. Rodrigo was in the early stages of processing these existential facts. "But I want her…"

During the layover in São Paulo, Rodrigo announced that he didn't want to stay in Santiago, that he wanted to stay with Alex in Islamabad.

"I know, buddy, but you'll be happier in Santiago. I'll be working so much in Islamabad that I won't be able to see you that much. And here you have your *abuelos* and your cousins and they all love you. And King is there too, he'll lick your face when he sees you." King, the huge white Grand Pyrenee that belonged to Don Jorge's brother, had always entranced Rodrigo, even as King had once stood taller than Rodrigo himself.

"When will you come back here again, Daddy?"

"I don't know, soon I hope, by the time school ends for you here."

"That's a long time."

"Not so long. You'll see, you'll have a good time and time will pass quickly."

"And where will we go after you come and get me?"

"I don't know yet, son, somewhere nice, maybe back in the States."

They were both exhausted by the time they arrived in Santiago, up over twenty four hours. Sleep had mercifully spared Rodrigo from too much dark musing, for at least part of the three legs of the flight. Alex had remained in the toils of wracking thoughts—about Isabel, his responsibility in the whole affair, his role in driving Isabel into unhappiness and despondency in Islamabad, about Rodrigo's welfare, his own agent operations and mistakes, the threat to his own life, the gradual destruction and devastation before his very eyes of a country that had once been his life. In which he too played an instrumental role.

*   *   *

Santiago was more poignant than ever for Alex. This city, its cafés and sidewalks and parks all were laden with memories of Isabel. Santiago *was* Isabel. The smell of the city, its traffic fumes mixed with the trees and flowers—all triggered an avalanche of memories, now bittersweet with Isabel gone. Given the late hour, Doña Maria and Don Jorge had not come to the airport, but had sent a driver. But what would he say to them? How would they react to him? Her telegram had not been warm towards him, and she had offered him no sympathy or condolence for his own loss in the tragedy. She met them at the door, deep bags under her eyes, dressed in a white peasant sweater and her pendulous earrings. She bent down immediately to embrace Rodrigo in her arms as she wept, rocking back and forth, "*Mi niño, mi niño,*" as she held him. Rodrigo, who had borne up solemnly for the long flight, now began to cry as well in her arms. Don Jorge approached from behind and looked at his wife and his grandson both, and called out to Rodrigo. He too made no gesture of recognition as yet to Alex. Then finally Doña Maria stood up and came over to Alex and gave him an embrace, followed by Don Jorge. "Welcome to your home," she said in English, in what seemed to be an act of pointed exclusion from the bosom of the Spanish language that they perhaps no longer wished to share with him, as if excluding him from their emotional orbit.

There was not a lot of talk, it was late, and Alex and Rodrigo were shown to their guest room.

*   *   *

The next morning Doña Maria focused all her attention on Rodrigo, speaking Spanish, spoiling him with little treats.

"Your mama was a wonderful person, Rodrigo, an angel. We must never forget her. She is up in heaven watching you right now."

"Really?"

"Yes, and you must remember to think of her in your prayers and tell her what you are doing."

Was she subtly working to undermine him altogether, Alex wondered? He was disturbed that he might turn into a non-person in Rodrigo's eyes if he did not keep close touch with him, even from afar.

"I thank you, Doña Maria, for taking Rodrigo for this period while I finish my work in Pakistan. You are right, it is not a healthy place for him right now."

"And obviously not a healthy place to take anyone," she replied. "This did not have to be."

"No, it didn't have to be, but bad things happen to lots of people all the time in this world. Isabel had been fascinated by Pakistan, and she was not unhappy there."

"But you had no business taking your family to these… American wars. They are a curse to the world. We know enough about that here."

"Doña Maria, I don't want to get into an argument with you about all these past issues, in Chile, or other places. This is the way the world has worked for a very long time, for better or for worse. If Chile had great power and great global responsibility, it might be involved in these crisis areas as well."

"Wise men do not take their countries to wars across the globe. There is no honor in this US empire. But you are right, we cannot bring Isabel back. Now, let's talk about Rodriguito. I think it is best for him to stay here in Chile. He is half-Chilean, and we will get him a Chilean passport. This is a healthier place for him to grow up in, more stable, and he has a large family here. My brother is happy to adopt him into the family."

"Doña Maria, there is no talking about any 'adoption.' Rodrigo is my son and I am not giving him to anyone for adoption, or to take over my role. He will stay here until I finish my assignment in Pakistan, maybe for six more months. After that I will come and take him with me, probably back to

America… I mean, to the United States. I promise you that we will come and visit often, but he cannot grow up in Chile without me."

"Don't you think you have already proven what kind of a father and husband you are in taking them to this war?"

"I resent that accusation, Doña Maria! I loved Isabel deeply and we shared in our decisions about what to do. Diplomats work all over the world—including Chilean diplomats in Pakistan—and sometimes yes, it is in dangerous places. For everyone."

"Well, maybe adults can make those decisions, but children cannot. They must be protected. Rodriguito will be safe here, and loved."

He bit his tongue. But as she took Rodrigo off to lunch, he knew he could not afford to break with Doña Maria. He would only be the loser. He needed her assistance.

Don Jorge stayed aloof from the struggles. He was courteous to Alex but did not have much to say, as usual. His eyes teared up one time as Alex talked about their lives as a family in Pakistan together, the many happy moments. Don Jorge had been hurt too many times by politics to wish to engage in polemics; he accepted the bitter and unjust nature of the international order as a given, that it was a ruthless game of power in which "the people" were always the loser. His certitude was only slightly shaken by the fact that the old ideological caricature of the ugly American had now taken on a more complex and concrete face in the form of Alex. He did not wish to argue with Alex. Unlike his wife, Don Jorge had no desire to score political points in what was a game far beyond the control and understanding of any of them. Alex might even be a good man at heart, with decent instincts. But the ugly nature of the global system was only more deeply etched into his heart through all of this: even good people could be caught up into the system, to serve what were ultimately evil purposes, even if they did not personally choose to do evil. Indeed, some of them even talked as if they truly believed they were doing good.

Rodrigo cried at night alone with Alex that he did not want his father to leave him to go back to Islamabad, but he was not crying about staying in Santiago. He received more warm attention from more people in the spirit of an extended family than he ever could in Islamabad. He was quickly seduced by *abuelita* and her attentions and treats from the kitchen, and by *abuelito* Don Jorge who took him into his studio and showed him around and then coached him through doing his first oil painting—of a dog, or so Rodrigo said. "Perhaps a dog in the style of late Picasso," Don Jorge suggested. And the trip to visit his cousins, where he would be living, was highly successful, in part because of King, and because of his three other cousins who were thrilled Rodrigo was coming to stay. At the end of five days Alex felt Rodrigo's anxieties lifting, even though he still did not want his father to go.

Alex took several walks alone through the streets of Santiago, visiting old haunts that he and Isabel and frequented: the park where they had first kissed, the restaurant where he had first invited her to dinner, his old apartment where they had spent their early passionate nights together. With the decompression of Santiago and away from Pakistan, the reality of her death had only now begun to sink in and he found his eyes tearing over with regularity. He sat in the park by the river and watched the world go by. The city still had great power over him and he felt it was notably more relaxed as the terrors of the Pinochet period had further retreated. And his Spanish, a language that had always warmed his heart—it had been "their" language—began to come back more strongly. He could not separate Isabel from the city, and now her ashes would be interred here in a ceremony for when he next came back, as he had agreed with Doña Maria and Don Jorge.

"I will come back to see you at Easter, *mi hijo.*" He knelt down to embrace his son as the day of his departure arrived. "And I will call you often. And your *abuelos* and your cousins will all take care of you. Be a good boy, and have fun. I want to hear all your news." Rodrigo blinked back tears, but seemed to accept his departure. Even Doña Maria had softened her reserve and acidity; she and Alex had seemingly reached tacit agreement to be civil with each other. Discussion of Alex's "first marriage" mercifully seemed to have faded. He promised to send Isabel's things back to her parents. "Take care of yourself… in that place," Doña Maria said as she gave Alex a warmer *abrazo* this time. "Rodriguito must not lose a father as well." And he was off, with twenty-eight hours of travel now facing him on the long way back—ample time to brood over everything that lay behind him and, even more, what lay ahead of him. He had done right to bring Rodrigo to Santiago, but where was his own future heading and when would he return to take his son back again? And how easy would that extraction be, given Doña Maria's strong views on the matter—and her physical control of Rodrigo?

And back in Pakistan, above all, where was this dangerous course of events heading?

*　　　*　　　*

Among the various expressions and notes of condolence that he had received, Alex was a little surprised that he heard almost nothing from Moe about Isabel's death. Moe had been over frequently to their house in the early days, and Isabel had liked him and received him warmly. Yet Moe had increasingly avoided him in the past months and had said nothing yet to Alex about Isabel. Moe seemed uncomfortable, or even angry about something. He had grown close to Kevin, which did not count in Moe's favor in Alex's eyes. Maybe Kevin had influenced Moe against Alex. But this was all politically tedious and not worth thinking about. He was disappointed, however, because he had thought he and Moe would have a close relationship as a result of shared Pakistani background. It never happened.

*   *   *

"Alex, you're the expert on the local scene, I want you to go over and represent the Station at the military briefing this morning. They've got in a team of Pentagon anthropologists—some "Human Terrain Team" or something they call it—designed to win hearts and minds, yadada yada, the usual. They want our best area expert to contribute to the program. And Alex, for chrissakes don't get into a fucking fight with them. Just make nice, we don't need them on our backs too. We just have to be seen to be with the program, mildly helpful, even if it's minimal."

The briefing room at Military Hqs was full, mostly uniformed officers, some civilians, the podium was on the stage, the usual briefing maps of Afghanistan, PowerPoint slides, laser pointers. *Technology trumping reality, as usual.* A team of three men in civilian clothes sat on the dais and were introduced as the first component of the Human Terrain Teams that would be deployed to the theater. Colonel Billings, Chief of the local US Joint Forces Command's Intelligence Directorate, or J-2, opened the meeting.

"We're here today to discuss some interesting new approaches to the Global War on Terror. As you know, our Directorate's mission focuses on implementing continuous improvements in information technology to ensure the interoperability and integration of our intelligence systems—it's all designed to enhance our war-fighting capabilities, as well as to develop information systems and network requirements. We provide oversight for developing doctrine, modeling and simulation systems and tactics, techniques and procedures used to drive realistic training and exercises. Now this requirement for rapid response to threats and targets mandates the integration of both intelligence and operations and, at the same time, the development of new doctrine, organizations, processes, and training to support emergent operational intelligence needs. Indeed, we're here today to look at new approaches to the problems our command faces in prosecuting the war in Afghanistan and its corollary impact on Pakistan.

Who could understand this crap? What a wall of impenetrable, meaningless organizational bullshit, obscuring and obfuscating the disastrous human and political reality of it all.

"As you know, our success in Afghanistan can never rest purely on military competence alone. We must win over the hearts and minds of the population if we and they are to create the kind of political order that we believe is required to ensure lasting regional security and secure our national interests and preeminence of our leadership in the region. We frankly need to do a much better job at understanding the way the local population is thinking if we are to bring them over to our way of thinking and to support our strategic goals in the region. To this end we are inaugurating an exciting new field approach—known as Human Terrain teams—designed to integrate the skills of anthropologists and social scientists to better pursue our policies and our military strategies to defeat the enemy."

Alex felt his eyes glaze over as Pentagon-babble poured out of the mouth of the briefer on autopilot. *Where in hell did they find these people—native speakers, it seemed, of Pentagonese. Were they capable of speaking English? Or was that the point, to keep it immaculately removed from all common sense and rationality?* Alex knew he would never even try to speak their language; by its very vocabulary it was an exercise in obfuscating and distorting reality. He was overwhelmed with a sense of déjà vu as the briefer boldly waded ever deeper into the material on the American agenda for changing and remaking the regional order in the American design. He looked around the room at the collection of bright-eyed and bushy-tailed young people who seemed to find something new in the discussion, even as the empty words and phrases wafted past his own partial consciousness into ever deeper thickets of military-speak.

"Sharpening knowledge-based engagement with the enemy... the Organization of Cultural Materials schema to which we contribute our research results in enriching our existing database of cultural practices and social systems... cross-cultural analysis that enables us to get closer to explaining causation in the development of attitudes among local populations... implementation of social control of the human landscape that can be achieved by the recording of, and then manipulation of key variables in these environments... ethnographic and ethnological toolkits... newly established tactical overwatch reach-back links at the Ft. Leavenworth Reachback Research Center ..."

My God, who could think this up? A surge of impatient anger and bile rose into his throat as he sat witness to this feckless and empty exercise upon which so much money, energy, attention—and eventually human lives—were being lavished. The impenetrable phrases of cold social technology spewed out like frozen bits devoid of any human element or emotion—part of a giant Orwellian exercise of euphemisms that ensured no one would ever have to come to terms with reality. Except for the goddam grunt out on patrol where real bullets and IED's spilled real human blood and guts—far from the pseudoscientific sanitized laboratory words of the high priests of the strategic conflict. And far from the realities that had hit his own wife. Alex tuned out, and drifted into his own ongoing mental swirl. By question time he had had enough, and a deep anger arose within him, demanding release. He should not, he had promised Sam, but he could not restrain himself—he raised his hand.

"Colonel, I thank you for your briefing. I am amazed at all this technology, science, databases, integrative analyses, anthropological matrices and the like, brought to bear seemingly to answer one simple question you pose—why don't the Afghans and Paks get with our program? Now, I may be simpleminded, but it strikes me that an elementary reading of the history of

Afghanistan—admittedly a low-tech approach and without the benefit of computers—makes it abundantly clear that the Afghans hate foreign invaders. In fact, they kill them. What kind of research and social science is needed to verify that fact? Do we actually believe that a bunch of American PhD's and graduates of Army War Colleges and teenage military recruits with a Pashto phrasebook will be able to decipher the keys to what is the most heavily tribalized of all societies in the world—and deeply xenophobic to boot? As long as there are foreign boots on the ground, Afghans will fight. If your Human Terrain Terms work long enough and hard enough to overcome their advanced degrees and just sit down and listen to what real people on the ground have to say, then the team just may eventually be able to move beyond the sociological eyewash and reach the obvious conclusion—they hate our war, they hate our presence and they want us out. I wonder how elegantly that can be expressed in military and social science terms, and whether this concept will ever penetrate the skulls of the planners."

Momentarily at a loss after these direct but aggressive words, like bullets penetrating through the linguistic force field of Pentagonese, dangerous, blunt, without euphemism, the briefer sought to recover, and launched into something about advances in social science and anthropological techniques that would enable more sophisticated analyses to lend backup to war-fighting and win over the population. Many in the audience were turning around in their seats to look at the individual who had thrown down the blunt challenge. Alex regretted that he had not just excused himself from the meeting. But no, he had to go and open his goddam mouth.

He drove back to the Station in dark anger and sense of frustration at the enormity of the institutions created to infinitely perpetuate a folly like this. Would *any* intelligence reporting ever be listened to back home—even when it was spot on the mark—if it didn't serve the agenda of the White House and the various war parties? He vowed never to go to one of these briefings again.

*   *   *

Art poked his head into Alex's office. "Welcome back. I hope the trip to Santiago went OK with your son. I can't tell you how sorry we are."

"Thanks, Art. This is just no place for a kid. I'm afraid it wasn't any place for his mother either." His voice betrayed a quaver.

"Well, if there's anything we can do, like have you over for some decent meals once in a while, Doris and I would love to do it."

"Thanks, Art, I really appreciate it. So what's on your mind?"

"I just wanted to talk a bit about Homaid. His first week he really pulled off a coup. He was able to tag Abdul Jaafar's compound and the drones got him and his close lieutenants together in the one house. We've been after that guy for several years."

"That's great Art. I'm not sure I have a lot of confidence in these Predator ops run by cowboys back in Arizona, but if we can pinpoint the exact locations of high-value targets, that's a lot cleaner."

"Yeah, he did well on that. But since then things have gone downhill. A few weeks ago he tagged another compound. Said a lot of Arabs were staying there. So they sent in a Predator and blew the place to hell. Turns out a pile of non-combatants were there, and we're not even sure that they were any bad guys at all. He swears he was told they were Arabs on training missions."

"How do we know who they were?"

"Well, we don't. And then he tagged another building quite quickly. That turned out to be a false identification as well. Killed a lot more civilians. He claims it was all based on good information. But as I query him, I'm not sure I trust him. He seems to be scattering these tags like candies. We can't afford that."

"That sounds bad. But I don't have any experience with him on this either. You remember we were developing him as an information source initially, and then Hqs decided that he should become a tagger, a higher priority."

"The reality is we don't know how much we can trust him anymore. The Taliban of course routinely claim that all these drone deaths are civilian. But this time the damn UN is getting involved in looking into it and it doesn't look like it was Arabs or Uzbeks or even Taliban as Homaid claimed. Our military command in Afghanistan is pissed about it too, since it makes them look bad in President Karzai's office when civilians are killed. And when the Afghan president speaks out against it, it really makes the military look bad."

"I know, we've been through that before. Shit, Art, we've ended up bombing a hell of a lot of targets over the years that turned out not to be combatants. Remember that bloody wedding party?"

"Yeah, wasn't that some agent getting revenge against another clan—sicking the damn US military on them? Bad stuff. Anyway, Homaid's signaled for a meeting on Friday in Peshawar, assuming he can make it out."

"That doesn't sound great, Art. I have no idea about how he operates there in North Waziristan. He supposedly has relatives there who should know something of the lay of the land. But you're right, misidentifications like that really cost the whole damn mission. Hard to know how responsible he is on this kind of stuff."

"Ok, Alex, just wanted to update you on the op. I may have some other questions for you later on this. We really want to get him to focus on Abu Ismail right now. We've missed him before. He's high on our list now and it's clear he is in contact with ISI. If we can get Abu Ismail, it should warn off ISI pretty clearly."

I'm gone for less than one freaking month and the whole damn operation has been militarized. Abu Ismail was one of the names Majeed had mentioned as a key person he was in contact with.

419

It was late in the evening but Alex put in a call to Majeed's private phone. When Majeed picked up, Alex spoke without identifying himself.

"Majeed, you must not go to South Waziristan this week. If you do, you'll likely get killed."

"What are you telling me? What do you know?"

"There is information on your doings; people know that you are scheduled to go to Waziristan to meet Abu Ismail. He is on the list, and there are already people out there spotting his house for a direct drone attack. Don't go."

"What are you saying? How can I believe you?"

"Would I make this up? All of the drone operations are being stepped up. Washington is convinced this is the best way to kill off the top leaders. But the targeting is crazy, unreliable. I know you may warn Abu Ismail off in any case, I can't do anything about that. But you should not go there yourself and get involved." And Alex clicked off.

*   *   *

Karl was the first to bring it up, at the staff meeting.

"My South Waziristan guy tells me there are Americans operating around there in jeeps. They have guns and have been trying to recruit sources of information there. Why are we sending guys in there to run around in broad daylight?"

"What guys?" the COPS asked. "Who are you talking about?"

"These guys, Americans supposedly, they're not Agency guys. Are they military? They're not wearing uniforms."

"What are they doing?"

"They're going around with a Pashto translator, and making fairly crude intel approaches to people in the villages, throwing around money. It's got the villagers terrified because now the Taliban supporters will accuse them of being spies for the US, even if they're not. At least one guy has been shot by the Taliban after he was approached by these Americans."

"This is the first I've heard about this," the COS said. "They certainly aren't our guys. They may be related to special forces ops. But they should be coordinating with us, at least in general terms. Shit, this can screw up our own ops in the area and tighten up Taliban control."

"So what can we do?"

"I'll check it out with Hqs, see if they know. Not that they'll tell us. Too damn many gunslingers running around out there."

In fact, Sam was not able to get a clear picture of what was going on. Hqs response said some kind of "hip-pocket" or "private" ops were being run out of the Pentagon, collecting information on the local situation. The Station should report any info on the subject but not interfere.

And so, over the next several months, more reporting did come in from field agents, especially now in North Waziristan. A group of Americans dressed in fatigues but without insignias had been seen in Miram Shah holding meetings with people. Some people were offered money for reporting but were too scared to accept, and feared it was some kind of provocation. It made the Station's own assets more nervous about collecting their intelligence in the area if they might be associated with these Americans. At liaison meetings the ISI threatened to arrest Americans out in the area unless the Station specifically told ISI where they were and what they were doing.

"This is crazy," Karl said. "My guy says pale faces almost never show up in Miram Shah. If they do, they are usually Chechens or Kashmiris or someone, but not European. But these guys were supposedly speaking American English. Looks like goddam bounty hunters. My guy wouldn't believe me that they weren't CIA types. Can you imagine how it's turning this place upside down now?"

"Well, they're not with us." Sam said. "Please continue reporting anything more you hear on this. This is goddam amateur hour. Friends back home tip me off that there are supposedly mercenary elements running private operations for the Pentagon. At least one of them is run by some old retired CIA guy, kind of a Captain America type living out his fantasies. Just what we need."

"Christ, that's the limit," said Karl. This goddam war—slimeball parade."

Moe spoke up. "I agree mercenaries aren't the way to go. But it's going to take a lot more firepower out there in the boonies before the Taliban start to back off. The drones are scaring them. And they're not going to change their thinking any other way. We're gonna have to play rough, whatever it takes."

Our Moe here is getting pretty hard-line, thought Kevin. *Interesting…*

Alex had had enough. "Look, it's obvious! This isn't an anti-terrorism campaign we're fighting, by now we're fighting a goddam insurgency against a foreign presence. The only way this is going to settle down is when foreign occupying forces are out of Afghanistan."

"I hear what you say, Alex," the COS said. "I can't even say you're wrong. Fact is, this is not our decision to make. All we can do is report the facts as we see them on the ground."

"But the damn reports aren't registering back home. It's like nobody listens to any of them. Who is looking at the big picture?"

Kevin swung around to address Alex. "Remember who *we* are, my friend. We're not out here to protect goddam Pakistan, whatever your happy childhood memories from here may be. We're here to represent American interests."

"That's a goddam cheap shot, Kevin, and you know it!" Alex shot back. "I care one hell of a lot about US interests, that's why I'm upset. We're fucking up this country and fucking up the US as well as we go from war to war. The world used to look up to America—now they think we're a bunch of fucking trigger-happy cowboys wading deeper and deeper into the swamp."

Kevin rolled his eyes at the COS. "That's enough of this!" the COS snapped. "We're not having any challenges to anybody's loyalty here! Kevin, you're out of line. And Alex, if you're looking for a soapbox to talk about America in the world, go somewhere else. This isn't a goddam pulpit, or the State Department. Now let's get back to our tasks at hand, what we're being paid to do here."

*   *   *

The COS asked Alex to be sure to attend the top-secret meeting early that afternoon with Major General Francis Maerkl, a two-star who had arrived from the office of the Director of National Intelligence in Washington, the pinnacle of the US intelligence hierarchy. When Alex, the COS and the Chief of Operations arrived, the classified briefing room in the Embassy contained only a few select individuals. The Ambassador and the senior US Military Attaché, Brigadier General Howard Decker, were already present. Alex was included since the Ambassador wanted more in-depth political knowledge on Pakistan available at the meeting, despite Alex's propensity for speaking out sharply to top visitors. General Maerkl's face was lean, weathered, a lanky runner's body, receding silver hair in a buzz cut, ascetic blue eyes, a slightly bent nose, overall projecting a crisp and confident manner.

"Gentlemen, I think you know the subject at hand—a very sensitive issue—the Pak nuclear weapon program. I hardly need remind you how it affects American interests in the region directly. At DNI we want to ensure that the elements of this multi-country Pak nuke working group are all singing from the same page. It wouldn't be an exaggeration to suggest that Pak nukes are probably more important, yes, certainly more dangerous than al-Qaeda itself. They are capable of involving the whole region in a nuclear war—certainly India, maybe even including China. The ownership and possession of nuclear weapons may be gravitating downwards into increasingly less responsible hands as the technology spreads. It is hardly inconceivable that one of these governments might end up actually using one in the face of an existential threat."

This guy doesn't seem to have heard of World War II.

"In Washington in the past we have primarily worked to determine the whats: what weapons does Pakistan have and what kind are they. But we are increasingly concerned now about what Pak nuke doctrine might consist of—what are the red lines for their usage? India seems to be the only plausible target for Pak nukes. In reality they also threaten our allies Israel and Turkey. But we need to know more. Where exactly are they all stored? What are the command and control protocols that govern their usage? How secure are they? How easily could fundamentalists get their hands on them? And how much sympathy for fundamentalists exist among top Pak military ranks?"

"General," the Ambassador spoke up. "I have it on the highest authority, from the president of the country himself and several top officers, who have personally assured me that Pakistan anticipates no first use of their nukes in any confrontation with India."

"Mr. Ambassador, I am gratified to hear that. It represents an encouraging and important statement. But with all due respect, we cannot take even the president of Pakistan at his word. The use of Pak nukes is not primarily his decision. The top ranks of the military are likely to be the ultimate determinants. And their use is probably highly situation-specific that can't be predicted in advance with much confidence, especially in a combat scenario.

"But more to the point, since we are in the room with intelligence collectors and specialists on this country, we need to consider how much any of the high military command here might have sympathy for Islamic ideas that could influence their actions, conditions, and targeting of these weapons."

The COS decided it was time to establish a presence in the discussion. "General, one of my key operations officer here, Alex Anders, is perhaps the closest to these Islamist circles of anyone in this Embassy. I'd like him to address the question."

Alex looked around the room. He knew that few shared his views on the issue. He also knew that few of them had any firsthand knowledge of the issue.

"General, first of all, if you will permit, I'm not sure the best way to pose the question is whether any of the top generals have 'sympathy for Islamic ideas,' as you put it. You can take it for granted that most of them do, to one degree or another."

"That's as may be," the Military Attaché spoke up. He was a recent arrival at the Embassy. "But I know many of these generals are known to quite happily put down a whiskey or two at the old officers club on occasion," he chuckled. General Maerkl smiled.

"Yes, a whiskey or two," Alex continued. "But don't let that mislead you. That's part of the old Indian officer tradition going back a hundred years to British days. We are talking about supposed sympathies with Islamic ideas, as you put it. Remember, these officers are all Muslims, some more sincere believers than others. But whatever their personal piety, patriotism here *includes* Islam. Don't forget this country was founded on Islam. That is what distinguishes it from India, and why there even is a Pakistan at all—a homeland for Muslim Indians."

"We all know the history, Alex. Let's get on with the question," the COS interjected, fearing Alex might digress on the Pak mystique.

"No, no, that's an important point," the General said, "I'd like to hear a little more on that."

"I don't want to get into a long spiel on this, but they are Muslims. They observe Islamic culture and religious practices by and large. Most of them will fast at Ramazan. OK, maybe they'll take a drink once in a while with Westerners, but alcohol is one thing. Their Pakistani Muslim identity is another. You can't separate Islam out from patriotism. That's what makes them Paks and not Indians."

"So how far do their sympathies with Islam lie, then?"

Alex wasn't sure how much further to delve into it in this meeting, with a General who clearly was unfamiliar with the nature of Pakistan. "I'm saying that most generals will have sympathy with most international Muslim issues, like Palestine, or the Chechens, and the Kashmiris of course. And they are extremely prickly about their own country, their religion, their sovereignty, and any hint of foreign domination over it. That's where their Islam is a kind of nationalism. Islam is about the common glue that holds this multi-ethnic state together."

"You're not suggesting that they think we are dominating Pakistan?"

"From their point of view, we are. We control military sales, we provide the military aid, we tell them what we want them to do when it comes to the Afghan war, or the War on Terror. And they know we tried to stop their nuclear program in its tracks once in the past. And then we slapped sanctions on them after they tested one, and then cut off delivery of needed strategic fighters that they had already paid for. The bomb, frankly, is a source of great pride to most Pakistanis, a sign of achieving membership in the elite nuclear club. Not to mention the ability to deter India."

"I'd have to concur on that General, as painful as it is to realize," the Ambassador spoke up. "I've heard some pretty blunt talk from senior officers about their national interests and national sovereignty, which they don't necessarily see America sharing."

"So General," Alex continued, "I'd have to say they are lukewarm at best on the War on Terror. They see it as an American exercise to extend power and control into Asia. And they believe a lot of the homegrown terror in Pakistan or at the borders with Afghanistan is provoked in part due to what they see as misguided policies of the US. Finally, as you know, they are quite ready to use Islamist militias against India as a weapon in the struggle over Muslim Kashmir. "

"OK, Alex, we don't need to get into that whole discussion." The COS looked impatient. "We're talking about collecting intelligence on the military controls and whereabouts of the nukes. And I'm afraid, General, with one major exception, our handle on this issue is not as great as it should be. It is a very difficult collection target."

The Milatt, General Decker, raised his hand. "And what of the role of India? I mean, India has the biggest stake of all in what the Paks are doing with their nukes. I believe we should share our intel with the Indians on the precise location and nature of Pak nuclear weapons. If there was a war, the Pak nukes would need to be taken out fast—just to prevent a nuclear exchange. We share a lot of common interests on this with the Indians."

"I don't know as we are that committed to India to take decisive sides in a future conflict," the Ambassador said. "It's my task here to make sure the Paks believe we are committed to their security. They can't even think we are tipping towards India."

"But Mr. Ambassador, the fact is that we are," General Decker turned to face the Ambassador. "We at least need to be frank with each other here in this room. I served four years in Delhi and I know how tight our relationship is with the Indian military establishment. It has to be that way. The Paks are frankly not all that reliable, and are paranoid about India. They could do something foolish if the temperature rises high enough. And God knows they can't win any war with India. Meanwhile, we are trying to get the Paks to look at the rising Chinese threat, with whom they are far too buddy-buddy. So I don't think there is much question about who our real ally is in all of this."

General Maerkl furrowed his brow. "This is not a briefing about international geopolitics. We are talking about intel collection on Pakistan—as authorized at the highest level from the Director of National Intelligence. But yes, I think we have to say that American interests lie far closer to India. We share common antipathy to China. We've weaned India away successfully from its long ties over decades with Russia. We want to keep India on our side against Russia. It is vital to our ability to manage the power relationships of East Asia."

Alex squirmed. "Why is it our duty to manage—as you call it—power relationships in East Asia? We can't run East Asia. The interests of the key Asian powers are vastly greater than our own in this region. I'm not sure how wise it is to be constantly intervening actively in everything that goes on here, especially when we don't have a particularly stellar track record or even a full understanding."

"Mr… Anders is it? We are getting into issues above our pay grade. We are not here to debate American grand strategy. We are concerned with getting a handle on Pak nukes, identifying them and ensuring they do not remain outside our ultimate ability to control them, including through seizure, or other means of neutralization."

The COS shot a glance at Alex to cool it.

The meeting went on for one hour. "Gentlemen," General Maerkl looked at his watch, "I believe it's now clear that the Agency takes the lead on collecting the intelligence and helping develop the plan to facilitate the eventual seizure of these weapons, when the time comes, probably working with US Special Forces."

"And when does the time come?" Alex asked.

"When exactly is highly classified. Specific circumstances will dictate, and I won't go into details. But basically when any government comes to power in Pakistan in which we have no confidence, one which assumes an overtly anti-American posture, or in which we feel the Islamists are gaining too much voice, or in which we feel Islamists are gaining in the country, or if we have no confidence in the military's ability to protect its nukes."

"General, frankly I can't call any of those contingencies as unlikely, given the increasingly negative views towards the US presence here with each passing year."

General Maerkl chose not to respond to Alex's remark. "Back in Washington this is a priority right up there with neutralizing al-Qaeda and top Taliban commanders. Intelligence must be precise and ongoing on their location and access, to facilitate our eventual military operation to take control of them, without any hitches. We may be talking about something that is only a matter of time—fairly short time. We need to be ready to move. Your Station's work is at the heart of this plan," the General offered, looking at the COS. "Your source within the nuclear establishment is the only significant insight we have from human intelligence about the program and the location of these weapons and how to get to them. I would like to discuss further how to target and direct that asset for our needs in Washington for maximum speed in taking control of Pak nukes."

"Please be aware, General," the COS quickly broke in, "that this source is on extremely close hold, strictly on a need-to-know basis. Not everyone in here is even cleared on the operation." The Milatt looked down at the floor. "We don't discuss it and it must not become common knowledge, even within the intel community, that this asset exists. His compromise would be catastrophic. He is irreplaceable."

"Point taken. But at some point we will need to have some exchange on future directions to be given to this source. Special Forces are actively engaged in planning for early seizure of these weapons; that will be very difficult without the extremely precise knowledge of what they will encounter in the process that your source can provide."

"That's fine, but I want no further discussion of that source at this meeting."

"Thank you, gentlemen," General Maerkl said. "I think you should know, in the strictest confidence, that many elements within our government and Congress are urging that we take preemptive control of these weapons right now and destroy them, long before they fall into the hands of the Taliban or any possible war with India. That decision has not yet been officially taken, but we believe it is imminent and we seek expansion of the intelligence assets necessary to pave the way to this action.

"I should add that back in the Pentagon we view the state of Pakistan in the most negative terms. Put frankly, gentlemen, this is a failed state. It is a risk to the world. It is hostile to the US and it is hostile to Israel. As long as it remains a rogue state unwilling to follow the US lead, its independence of action remains a threat to all. We must not shirk in our global responsibilities."

A surge of impatience and frustration tore through Alex. "Whatever the planning may be in Washington, let me say for the record here that I would view such an operation, such an action, as catastrophic. I'm not sure you realize, General, what kind of explosive reaction would take place in this country. Pakistan would be solidly united against us and we could expect massive violence against the American presence across this country. We are talking about tampering with the crown jewels of national sovereignty and pride. We will intensify Muslim passions against us on a lasting basis. It will solidify anti-American action not just in Pakistan but across the region like almost nothing else. It will empower the most radical of forces. I cannot stress enough what a dangerous step that would be."

Maerkl looked studiedly at Alex for a moment. "I appreciate your concerns. You may well speak for some of the nationalist elements in Pakistan. But we cannot allow local reactions to sway us in this decision. American control of Pakistani nukes has to be our top national priority. Indeed, we speak for the concerns of most people in the world. Frankly we have little reason to any longer trust Pakistani authorities to exercise responsible authority over these issues. It is an American obligation to world security and stability to ensure we are in charge."

The COS drew the meeting to a close. After seeing the General back to the Intercon, Alex and Sam sat down at a corner table for a quick bite alone after the meeting. Sam stared Alex in the eye. "You went too far at that meeting, Alex, again. You know more about Pakistani thinking and motivations than anybody. But you can't take on the whole goddam policy establishment in Washington through haranguing their spear-carriers when they come out here. You're building up quite a negative reputation back home."

"Sam, he's not a spear-carrier—he's a goddam two-star; he's got a huge voice in handling the whole damn Pak nuke account. Didn't you see how far that conversation went?"

"You were the one who pushed it to greater limits than it was supposed to go. Our job here is to find out where the damn things are and how to get at them. It's the job of others to decide to take them out, or seize them, or whatever."

"Look, Sam, for chrissakes, that's the story of all these goddam Washington disasters over the past decades. Nobody lower down in the ranks thinks about the implications of all these series of little orders and tasks that we carry out, that in the end amount to a huge decision of massive importance. The ship is already launched. All we do is sit around and stoke the coal and polish the brass and oil up the engines. Somebody's got to speak up about this."

"Get this straight, Anders. I already regret asking you along to address these issues. You are out of your depth. Our office is not going to speak up about this. We have been asked to collect intelligence. Period. That's our job.

I'm not going to challenge orders that are not illegal, they're not even unreasonable in my view. And another thing. You are not cleared for the intel from the reporting source on the Pak nuke issue. You didn't hear it. It wasn't supposed to come up at the meeting and you will forget what you heard."

"I understand. But I'm talking about this whole damn mission."

"Look, Alex, you're tired, you've suffered a great personal loss, and you're discouraged. No, no, hear me out! Of course you are. You've paid a terrible price—with the loss of Isabel, sending your son away. I don't blame you for feeling angry, even bitter. But you've got to stay aware of the strongly personal subjective element in your thinking."

"Sam, dammit, I appreciate your concern for me, and my situation. But I'm also not going to let others write off my views as all a reaction to Isabel's death. I know this country. I've been here for longer than most others in this embassy. I can see where things are going. The country is being pushed over the brink by our policies. Give me some credit that my thoughts might be something more than just subjective meltdown."

Sam fell silent. "It's mango season," he finally said, surveying the menu. "Let's go for the Mango Blowout for dessert."

"Yeah, right, Pakistan's answer to crisis, Mango Blowout."

"Beats nuclear blowout by a shitload."

*   *   *

He knew his hosts were being kind. Alex, you need get out, not sit at home and brood. Let's include him in more social affairs. Alex now had even less stomach for Embassy social affairs that lacked professional operational purpose. It was one thing to stand around having drinks or sitting down to dinner with someone you hoped to learn something from, or get close to—that had the whiff of the chase, the professional focus, or even just the desire to get close and enter another person's world, discover new horizons. But small talk over an evening solely with other members of the American community was a chore. He was talked out; chitchat with people he knew only casually and had no need to know was physically and mentally tiring.

Tonight was no exception. Jasper had kindly included him at a dinner. But as Alex saw the guest list heavy with American bankers and Embassy economic officers—Christ, what did he have to say to them, nice people, but of no professional interest to him and he didn't want to be forced into the small talk, the lowest common denominators: four people at each card table, force-marched through various polite conversational gambits, struggling to create some common element of interest for the chat over generic diplomatic food. God knows they were well meaning: he remembered the Urdu phrase— God take care of them, but keep them away from me.

Standing around at buffets was different; being on your feet could be tiring but at least an escape route was always at hand—you could excuse yourself from entrapment with a bore to get some more wine or roast beef. Alex had long since acquired the skills of professional international dinnerpartymanship; maneuver, boldness and timing were everything. Critical and swift decisions about whom to intercept as a conversational partner when plunging into the buffet line and, if necessary, strategically waiting around for an interesting interlocutor to sit down at a table before joining him and before someone else took the spot. Once seated, too late, *les jeux son fait*, and there is little pulling out of the game, you're stuck in the boat with the same crowd for better or for worse for the next hour or so.

Tonight I'm just not in the mood for it. No sympathy, no warmth, no gentleness, no cheery voices seeking to distract me from the pain, make me laugh, feel good, distract my mind. I don't want it. He actually craved the revitalizing character of bluntness of exchange—tough, searing, penetrating, challenging, uncompromising looks at this bullshit world we are all operating in, the why's of it all, what are we living through out here, and let's call a spade a spade and not rearrange deck chairs on the Titanic. Let's get to the heart of the fucking matter here and now with honesty in full frontal mode. Yet here tonight was a crowd that would not provide the substantive sharp debate he needed. Indeed, he was considerably off his dinnerpartymanship game tonight; he ended up forced to sit at a table with a new young econ officer, his wife, and a visiting AID representative from Washington—a very bad hand indeed.

Once all were duly seated, the switch was flipped on to begin predictable conversation, the discussion tape loop set for the next hour with no relief in sight—unless the Economic Counselor's residence were to mercifully catch fire. "And I hear that you actually grew up in Pakistan, Alex?" the wife said. "That must have been fascinating." Here we go, off on the usual gambits; but surely in his present state of mind they would not expect him to mount the stage and perform his standard routine of recounting his childhood to fascinated new parties. "Wasn't it difficult to live here in those years? I mean, you were in Lahore where there was no Embassy and not much of an American presence at the time. You must have quite felt isolated. Did you find Pakistanis friendlier in those days? I must say, I don't find them terribly welcoming now. What does it feel like to be back here now as a professional, working, after seeing it through a child's eyes?"

Perfectly reasonable, numbing stupefying questions. As he sought to fob off these queries with pro-forma replies he could see what a bore and tight-mouthed party-pooper he was in the eyes of his fellow card-tablers; his mind was distracted, drifting back to his house with the shattered twisted gate not yet fully fixed, thoughts of Isabel, and what Rodriguito was doing halfway around the world. He even failed to hear a few of the questions put to him.

"...And we're so sorry to hear of your wife's tragic accident. What a terrible thing! Do let us know if there is anything we can do to help out. I understand your son has gone off to live with your wife's parents for a while. Oh, really, in Chile. So far away. Does he speak Spanish?"

They seemed to give him a break as dinner interlocutor; was he naturally surly, or simply wounded and in pain? The AID visitor from Washington picked up the slack and inquired about local living conditions. "Yes, and then we've been having trouble getting security clearances for our servants as well, especially if they are new. It's hard enough to find reliable help anyway, and now there's all that checking to be done to ensure they are politically clean. It is difficult to entertain properly now when you can't rely on a firm staff."

Don't leave him out, alone, to brood. "And what is your favorite place to visit in Pakistan, Alex? You must know the country quite well."

The questions swirled around his head like tireless flies; he should simply play a prerecorded message that would cover all their sincere queries and interests. At the same time he hated being cynical about it. They were all, all well-meaning, decent people who wanted to help. He had actually learned that the one way sometimes to avoid a truly stupefying evening was to relentlessly pursue everyone's favorite subject—themselves, their lives and pasts. At least it was new, sometimes interesting in the perspectives he encountered. He feared he even approached these sessions as an anthropologist or social psychologist might, studying the subject before him, building profiles, plumbing attitudes and their cultural roots. *And how goddam unsympathetic and condescending I am!*

"...And it is worrisome how the security situation has deteriorated. At the very least it means we can't get out on trips at the weekend like we used to. Our Canadian neighbors say they still go out with their children for picnics. I suppose they have less to fear."

"I remember when we were back in West Africa, in the bad years. That was even more worrying, and the violence seemed more generalized. You never knew when you might be attacked."

"And did you spend much time in Chile yourself, Alex? Is that where you met your wife?"

"...I've heard cooks are the hardest of all to find, and now with all the military arriving—they seem to be paying better than average wages so there are less cooks available for diplomatic homes."

"And you know, it's hard to get them to cook decent Western food. It's usually tasteless English cooking that they've learned, or else Pakistani dishes. We all enjoy a Pakistani dish now and then, of course, but we're looking for cooks who have a broader range."

"And you speak the language! How wonderful to have picked it up like that. We got to know our way around a bit in Spanish in Lima, but I must say we have found our initial lessons in Urdu a bit difficult. They have such a strange way of positioning their tongue as they speak."

"Yes, and the alphabet is so strange."

Yes, the powerful weight of Urdu words absorbed in childhood. Each one was a vehicle laden with experience and associations carrying memories of youth, richly freighted. But for someone new to a language that special taste of a word in the mouth, its implications, rich associations, connotations and double meanings was almost unattainable. For the newcomer, newly learned words were hollow shells, waiting to be filled with bits of meaning and experience that came only over long periods of time. But Urdu spoke to Alex from its depths in which he had been steeped in childhood. Yes, he loved Spanish, he could function professionally in it, but the deeper emotional and psychological roots of its words and their linked associations were beyond his reach, short of spending most of the rest of his life in Chile. And except for the emotional content that Isabel had helped breathe into it for him. Isabel...

"Yes, it does have some strange sounds. But you'll be able to manage quite well in the bazaar if you work at it for a little while."

Hadn't Urdu even compromised the integrity of his English mind? Urdu was an independent mental and cultural system that lay secretly behind the English firewall of his brain, containing a whole separate world of a distinct cultural life, never evident to anyone who knew only his English façade. It represented an alternative cultural persona, a personal treasure to anyone who had truly absorbed another foreign language. Did Alex owe them full disclosure on this? He felt pressure building in his heart that he could only relieve by excusing himself from the company. He did excuse himself, seeking desperate release from the clinging toils of kindness around him, using the pretext that he wanted to call his son in Santiago.

"He does seem to be an intense man. Certainly understandable after what happened to his wife. And to have grown up here! What a cruel thing to happen to him upon coming back. Did you know her at all? And what of his poor son?... He does seem to be a bit withdrawn. Maybe we should invite him out more often..."

*   *   *

Alex remained haunted by the revelation he had gained at the meeting with General Maerkl. He had been dimly aware of the existence of a developing source in the Station on Pak nuke issues, he'd picked up intimations of it. He also knew the existence of the case had been placed on close hold several years ago, even within the Station. This was standard operating procedure in sensitive cases, to limit awareness of them, even within the Station, to the narrowest list of strict need-to-know. Even Alex had no real need to know about US planning on nuclear seizure. But now it sounded like hard-liners back in Washington were serious about moving to take control of the weapons. He could not imagine what kind of fantasyland they were living in if they did not realize the incalculable repercussions such an action would create. Yet he was ever more aware how many policy makers and pundits indeed did seem to be living within their own fantasy-world—reflecting a national tone set by Fox TV and domestic politics that operated utterly independently of the reality of world events, that permeated the attitudes of much of the nation, the shrill politicized voices on the Hill, the pressures of the Israel lobby, and the general paranoia about Muslim terrorists perceived to be running wild in Pakistan and about to threaten the Homeland. And indeed there *were* some terrorists—lethal ones—out there. He knew as well or better than most.

The issue festered in his mind and he couldn't let it go. It seemed like the ultimate recipe for American catastrophe in Pakistan, and the region. That night, after working late in the office, he decided to probe more deeply. He went to an old file of Cactus, a former agent in the Pak military. He found what he was looking for. A short paragraph buried in a contact report from the former agent in the late seventies. "There is a young man at UCLA studying nuclear physics, from Sind. He is probably headed for a career in the nuclear organization. You might want to look him over. He is angry at the Pak government for ruining his father's business in a corrupt power play by Punjabis." There was little other information, but this tidbit clearly had been the genesis of the later operation. And Alex recalled now that he had heard mention of some asset in Kahuta, a key Pakistani nuclear installation—again before all aspects of the case had been put on special hold.

This was insane, he thought. Would they actually try to do this? Seize control of the weapons? Yet an intelligence source like this presumably could lead them to the very doorstep, identify the exact location of the moment, the way to gain access to them, and turn over the keys. This was no fiction.

*   *   *

It had been another night of restless, relentless introspection. But towards the first rays of dawn, he knew. He also realized it wasn't a single decisive moment, but the result of an evolving process. Throughout his professional career he had taken the basic rationality of the Washington system for granted. Warts, foolishnesses, ignorance, mistakes, sure. But he never thought to challenge the fundamental premise of the entire course of what the US was doing abroad, a system in which the Agency represented the primary eyes and ears, even if the military was the primary action arm. But the steady accumulation of a long series of events were proving overwhelming. Familiar landscapes had suddenly begun to take on a different appearance. It was like looking at a negative of a film—the picture was identical in all details, only reality was reversed.

He had never felt quite so complete in his isolation.

Alex remembered a good Canadian friend who once took him aside after some political debate at a dinner party. "Let me tell you something, Alex. For all your criticisms of the US, you're right out of the typical American mold, if you allow me to say it. It's been my experience that lots of Americans are deeply idealistic about their country. You guys are true believers about your nation, propelled by idealism, visionary hopes for a perfectible future. It's all rah-rah enthusiasm and patriotism… until suddenly one day the veil falls and you perceive the warts, the inconsistencies and the hypocrisies and the cruelties and the follies of your policies. And then the disillusionment sets in, you feel jilted, cheated, get angry about the unrequited ideals, unfulfilled hopes and you rebel against them, you're pissed off the scales fall from your eyes. And then—you turn on the country. Policies aren't just simply erroneous, stupid, or failing, but you see them as a *betrayal* of the country itself. It's always this love or hate." At the time Alex nodded, "Interesting theory, Ken. I'll think about it," and sauntered off. But lying in bed that night he was haunted by the observation. Was that the process whereby faith was broken? Whereby ideological recruitment by another became possible? That was Fyodor. That was his great uncle Alex who went to fight in Spain.

He recently read a stunning phrase in one of the novels of Graham Greene: "Treason is an act of love." It was a desperate response to the country you have loved but that had failed you, jilted you, and could not be supported any more.

Alex had been tormented by all of this. But now he could see it clearly. Americans actually believed that their vision of the global order was grounded in objectivity, embodying universal principles for the benefit of all. How could anyone ever rationally oppose such goals? You'd have to be ignorant, perverse, or evil to object to Washington's plans. Yeah, we love democracy, but not if they elect the wrong guys. We love human rights, but don't get too critical of friendly dictators. That double standard explained so much of foreign anger. Foreign resistance to US policies, particularly when it drew the blood of the engineers of empire, was quickly classified as radical, hostile, "rogue," dangerous, anti-American—a "challenge" to America that had to be crushed. Otherwise, how could thoughtful people of goodwill reject what was essentially an American public service to the globe? A free good, taken on by the US at burdensome cost and unremunerated, acting in the name of common welfare?

Alex had a friend—a political scientist at Berkeley—who used to complain about all those countries sitting around out there who benefited from the American global mission *without even contributing to it*—"free riders"—that was the political science jargon he used. But what if the ride was ruinously expensive, or if they didn't want to be riders to that destination at all? In the days of the British Empire it was called "White Man's Burden." Or the elegant French *"mission civilisatrice."* The parallels were now painfully, crushingly obvious to him and the revelation tortured his sleep.

When morning dawned Alex got up blearily; he wondered at his own sanity. Each daily event now propelled him with accelerating speed in a new direction inside his own mind. How could two people witness the same event and perceive it so differently? Wasn't that the way humans had advanced through history—by gradually coming to acknowledge elements of ever broadening common humanity and common interests? Did it all have to end with victor and vanquished?

He thought back to Akmal. "If you have ever grasped the idea of common humanity and common human interests, you can't ever go back. You are doomed to frustration at why others around you cannot quite see the new horizons. What does it really mean 'My country right or wrong, but my country?' What is 'my country?' Is it not perhaps my tribe?"

He was now well down the slippery slope. He couldn't simply turn these thoughts off, pretend they had never entered his head. Once the switch flipped, once you'd made the psychological transition, you couldn't go back. It was like trying to regain your virginity. It was a glimpse of a new reality. You had to move on to the consequences of the new vantage point, regardless. You were condemned to live in the loneliness of your new vision.

A new path beckoned, even if it led to isolation. But at least you would have kept faith with yourself. At least you wouldn't die cynical. At least you'd have tried to alter the course of tragic evolution on autopilot.

Should he act? Could he act? He was just a small cog in a massive machine that was slouching toward disaster—the destruction of Pakistan and all of US interests in it.

And yet, the Station in Islamabad was not a vast machine. Within that microcosm he occupied a large role, large enough to have impact on the machine as it ground forward. He could not change the world, he could not change the system, but he could affect the cogs in this one small part...

What was it one of those existentialists had said? Whatever happens, whatever fate dishes out to us, we still always have choices. Maybe worse choices or better choices, but still choices—choices to change things, however modestly, at least in your own plane of existence. You couldn't change the world, but at least you could bear responsibility, bear witness for your little portion of the great skein. There were values that had to be preserved, American values he believed in.

That thought now spoke to him, now channeled his thoughts with new clarity. And opened the door to action.

Chapter Ten

Reckoning

The end of our exploring will be to arrive at where we started, and to know the place for the first time.

- T.S. Eliot

The diffuse strands of past and present snapped together, fusing into a moment of crystallized reality. Action could now only point in one unswerving direction. Right now.

Alex walked out of his house, opened the gate and closed it decisively behind him. He walked three blocks to a small food market that had an outside pay phone.

"Majeed, I'm sorry, it's late, but I've got to meet you someplace. It's urgent."

"Alex, surely not tonight, it's late, it's past ten pm. I'm sure it can hold till morning."

"Look, Majeed, this really matters. I've got some important things to say. Please take my word for it."

"What is so urgent it can't wait?"

"Trust me, Majeed. Please meet me."

Long pause. "Alright, in one hour, at my aunt's home. Come by cab and then on foot."

As Alex hung up, the dimensions of it all began to sink in. He had just set into motion a series of events that would quickly follow their own course—indeed, would soon become irreversible. And Majeed wanted him to take precautions in going to their meeting. Did Majeed sense something in Alex's determination? Or did he know something special about surveillance on him? Alex got out of the cab a few blocks from his destination and walked the rest of the way irregularly through empty backstreets. He passed various large homes looming on the right and left. From one came the sound of Western pop music pouring out into the night air as if in defiant cultural contradiction to the cultural surroundings. From others came the ghostly flickerings of TV screens portraying histrionic fictional dramas of the subcontinent. Life continued as usual for other people. As he walked, time seemed to stretch out in front of him, as if it took him hours to reach his destination. He felt calm, resolved.

The gate was open and he knocked lightly on the front door rather than ringing the bell. Majeed opened and they walked silently down the corridor. "My aunt is away, but we have a distant cousin staying here upstairs. She won't disturb us."

They had dispensed with all the usual greetings and rituals—instinctively acknowledging that this was not a social call. Alex had indeed declared it urgent. Surely he was not going to launch another clumsy recruitment approach, but who knew what his instructions were. They entered the dining room to sit at the table rather than in the formal living room or pillowed area in the corner. Majeed did not turn on the chandelier over the table; the lights on the mantelpiece created a softer light, casting shadows on the opposite wall. No tea, no Dimple.

Majeed did open even this encounter on a personal note. "We think about Isabel often, Alex, may God have mercy upon her soul. I hope you are coping with her loss. And we hope Rodrigo is alright. We all feel for you deeply. I'm sure you must be really missing her… "

Alex nodded, dispensing with personal exchange.

"What's on your mind, Alex? What can I do for you?"

How many conversations had Alex had with Majeed over the years? After the intimacy of boyhood they had moved in divergent directions. Since Alex's return to Pakistan they had shared, sparred, sympathized, fought, debated, exhibited anger, and conspired on a thousand issues. Indeed they had come to play roles as actors on the stage of mutual national tragedy. Personal tragedy too had marked even more deeply their individual lives. What concatenation of events had brought them together at this particular moment, in this house, at this hour?

"Majeed, I know you are angry about the approach I was instructed to make to you a while back. You have every right to be."

"Alex, we've been over that ground. If you are here to rehash that conversation, you are wasting your breath and my time."

"No, Majeed, that's not it at all. I want you to know that things have now reached a critical turning point… in terms of what Washington and our Embassy are doing here in Pakistan. I feel I've reached the end of my rope. So much of what is going on now seems to be moving on its own trajectory, blindly, ignorantly, stupidly, dangerously, sometimes even unwittingly. I can't see any sign that anybody is really thinking about this heavily-laden ship that keeps plunging on ahead into the gathering storm. I just feel things are… on clear collision course. It is obvious to me at least that this ratcheting up of American force cannot work. It is bringing Pakistan to the breaking point as well."

"Yes, Alex, we have known that for some time, we've talked about it. And I think you are letting your own country off lightly. It is ignorant, but not 'unwitting.' It is all quite willful and part of a long-term American agenda. Surely we are not here to debate that at this hour."

"I'm afraid that blood will rise, and that the US is going to find itself in even worse situation, pushing the situation to the brink."

"Agreed. But what do you have to say that is new," and he glanced at his watch, "at eleven at night?"

Alex looked down at the parquet pattern on the floor for a few moments, collecting his thoughts. Endless little pieces of wood stacked in contrary and arbitrary directions against each other. He looked up directly into Majeed's eyes. "I have some vital information to give you. About some operations the US is conducting here in the country. Operations that are dangerous and wrong. Furthermore, it could be dangerous to you personally."

"Your Embassy bears little love for me, that's been true a long time."

"Yes, but now that you are traveling more often to North Waziristan you need to know that almost any contact there with Taliban figures is potentially lethal to you."

"I learned that some days ago, in a meeting with Abdul Haqq. We both were within minutes of being killed."

"That could happen again. They would have no hesitation to kill you along with him if you happen to be in the way. In fact, some believe it might even send a message to ISI about American seriousness of purpose."

"That would be foolish indeed. Not because of my life, but because many of these commanders, like Abdul Haqq, are vital figures through which we attempt to monitor and control Taliban action. He might be a key future leader of Afghanistan—who could bring the Taliban to the peace table. This could be ultimately valuable to your country too. It doesn't pay, you know, to kill off all your potential future partners in negotiation."

"Washington doesn't care about that. All they know is that he has contacts with major Taliban operations in Afghanistan and with al-Qaeda. That's more than enough reason to kill him if they can. They are working seriously on it."

Majeed shifted uneasily on his seat. "How will a drone know I am there with him, or even where I am?"

"Because we have spotters who are able to electronically identify houses for drone attacks. You must already have some idea of this. We have one agent in the Miram Shah area already. All he has to do is electronically tag the house to be targeted, that's all it takes."

Majeed took this in for a few moments. "And who is going to do the tagging?"

"We have several agents. But in North Waziristan we have one individual at the moment... specifically looking to target Abdul Haqq. He has some periodic access to Abdul Haqq for provision of guns, fertilizer and the like. I should say, Majeed, I strongly oppose these US measures. They are crude, a blunt instrument. You know better than I how many innocent civilians have been killed and their survivors radicalized."

"And?..." Majeed asked softly.

Alex took a deep breath. "And I have decided to try to stop them."

"What? Do I hear you correctly?" Majeed took off his glasses to stare Alex directly in the face. "You propose to block your own Embassy's operations?"

"Yes." Alex could hear the ticking of clock, inexpressibly loud, in the next room. Majeed seemed suddenly to listen with new intensity. There were noises of people in the street outside the compound, as if in some kind of altercation. Then the voices subsided. Majeed turned to Alex again.

"And how do you propose to stop them, then?"

"By identifying the spotters."

"You are prepared to do that?"

"Yes."

"By revealing their identities to us?"

"Yes."

Majeed took a deep breath. "I hope you know what you are doing. Can I even trust you on this? Why should you do this? This is an act of disloyalty. Or worse."

"I am aware of that. But we both know how dangerous, how brutal and crude so many of these attacks have been. Wedding parties, families in their homes and neighboring homes killed."

Majeed put his glasses back on. "Of course I know, but your people seem to believe in these operations, they're the magic bullet to save their skins in Afghanistan."

"They are part of a greater tragedy, for all of us. You've told me for some time about how it is polarizing politics in the Frontier and destroying relations between the populace and the security organizations. Destroying future political options. We must force a rethink. We are headed for a mindless catastrophe."

"You would do that?"

"Yes."

Majeed stared at Alex and sighed. "Alright then. Are you really prepared to identify the person tagging these locations in Waziristan?"

This was the moment. Alex's agent whom he had personally cultivated, trained, educated, brought along, groomed—he was now delivering up. "Yes. His name is... Homaid, Homaid Nasiri. He is a Pashtun truck driver."

"And he is known to some of the commanders?"

"Yes, he is close to Abdul Haqq."

"And you realize what will happen to this Homaid as a result of this information?"

Alex glanced away momentarily and then met Majeed's eyes firmly. "Yes," he said quietly.

Majeed shook his head in disbelief. He scraped with his fingernail at a piece of food that had dried onto the table surface. "Very well Alex, I appreciate the information. As you know, I am in touch with Abdul Haqq as part of my job. I'd just as soon not be around him when the drones strike. Furthermore, I don't want *him* to be anywhere near where a drone strikes either."

Alex turned to look Majeed straight in the eye again. "I wanted very much to make sure that you were not hurt. We go back a long way, Majeed." His voice wavered slightly. "But this is not just about personal friendship. I think this whole course of American policy is plunging off a cliff, costing more American lives, and money—even moral standing in the world. The policies are not just wrong, they are failing. And they are destroying the fabric of Pakistan as well. I can do only so much as one individual to stop it, but I must try."

"Well, thank you for this information—and the warning."

Alex raised his hand. "There is more. Much more. The nukes. This is building into a huge crisis, soon. You should know that we also have an agent who is very close to the military end of your nuclear weapons. He is an important element in US efforts to track the shifting location of these weapons.

"Alex, do you..."

Alex held up his hand again. "Wait, listen. Detailed active plans are underway to seize them under a variety of scenarios. I think that such action may take place in the not too distant future."

Majeed stared and shook his head. "I think you know, Alex, that any US attempt to seize our nuclear weapons would result in... well, I'd call it an uprising against America here. An explosion. The impact would be incalculable. The strains are already immense. Everyone already thinks the worst of you. But to try to seize our nuclear weapons would result in a bloodbath against all Americans. Our relations would be irrevocably destroyed. We would quickly reconstitute our nuclear capability down the road and you would be our primary enemy. And every fevered Islamist in the country will be out for your blood, here and abroad, across the Muslim world, perceiving that America had destroyed 'the Islamic bomb.'"

Alex nodded. "I know that. The mere existence of this agent—this is an extremely sensitive operation—incites the hard-liners back in Washington to develop operations to seize the nukes, soon. They believe they are on top of the situation, that they can get away with it. They are ignorant of, maybe they don't even care, about the repercussions."

"So I am compelled to ask—do you know who this agent is?"

Alex had been ready for this moment, the supreme moment. "It is very close hold. I don't know his actual name. But I can give you information to identify him fairly easily. He was at some point a graduate student in physics at UCLA. He is a Colonel in the Army and is responsible for nuclear scientific security at the Khan Research Laboratories at Kahuta. I believe he is also in close liaison with Sarghoda Air Base."

"This is extremely important—extremely serious information, Alex. What can I say? Obviously I'm astonished… and very grateful. And of course very disturbed. I don't quite fully know what has brought you to this point—to this very clear major change of heart. I guess in a way I'm not totally surprised. But for you… you know of course what a major personal step this is for you to take. What potential cost. So how can I protect *you* now if we act on this information? I don't want to drag your name into it."

"You can say that you received the information in an anonymous message on your phone from an unknown Pakistani source. The information will test out. Just cover my trail."

"And what will you do now?"

"I don't know. Frankly, I think it is possible that if you take action the information may be traced back to me in any case. But I have made my decision and I will face the consequences."

"Alex, I don't know what to say. You are very foolish. And you are very brave and honorable. You are driven by strong moral principles. Our governments are not. It is hard to combine moral principles and moral discrimination in these situations."

"That is one of the reasons I have decided to take this step. It has been brewing in my mind for some time—as I watch the stupidity, and the ignorant ambition around me, day in day out at the Embassy. And in the people coming from Washington even more so. So many of them are cowboys. Not all of them, but most. Or wallowing in the feeding trough. Unfortunately the cowboys and adventurers are gaining strength, their voices seem to dominate, in pressing ever more for operations that violate all legal and intelligent norms."

"As the Taliban often do as well."

"As the Taliban often do as well. But I don't have a voice over the Taliban's operations. You do. And as you point out, this is their country, not America's."

"Alex, look, we are attempting to keep the lid on, keep the Frontier from exploding, maintain some paramilitary capability there which inevitably is based on certain radical groups. We need them but we are also determined not to let them get out of hand. It is a dangerous game as well. I fear for some of the leaders within our own organization. Yes, they are strategic thinkers, consider themselves strong patriots, but they can sometimes also be blind and take equally foolish actions, especially when it comes to facing India in Kashmir."

"Right, Majeed, I know." Alex clasped his palms over his eyes. "And frankly, right now I'm exhausted. Drained." Alex rose from the table, staggering momentarily. "I've said what I have to say. These actions speak for themselves."

"Alright, my friend. *Khoda Hafez*. God keep you." Majeed embraced Alex tightly and held him for many seconds. "*Inshallah*, we will certainly see each other again. We are all enmeshed in personal—and national—tragedy."

Majeed opened the backdoor for Alex and he stepped out into the black night, enveloped now entirely in the warm and humid Pakistani air. He paused, and then decided he wanted to walk the long way all the way back home.

*　　　　　*　　　　　*

Two days later Majeed signaled to Alex that he needed to have a discreet meeting and gave him an address of a friend. Alex parked several blocks away and, checking for surveillance, walked to the designated gate. He knocked and was immediately let in by Majeed who led him straight into a drawing room at the back. On the way he stopped and said, "Alex, I'd like you to meet someone, an old friend, General Keshwari. He asked to meet you, and I'll leave you alone. I've arranged this meeting entirely at his request."

"What do you mean, 'alone'? Is this something confidential that you shouldn't be present for?"

"The General wanted it that way, if you don't mind."

"And who is the General?"

"I'll let him explain." Majeed led him into the salon, made the introduction in formal and brief terms, and took his leave. General Keshwari seemed to be in his seventies, filled out the easy chair in which he was seated, and only made a perfunctory effort to raise his bulk when shaking hands with Alex. His eyebrows were florid silver, highlighting piercing blue eyes—Kashmiri or mountain blood. He lacked the spit and polish of so many Pakistani officers, suggesting he had not served in traditional military capacities. He was dressed in civilian clothes, and possessed a casual, almost avuncular style.

"Alex!" He smiled warmly. "If I may call you that. I feel I have known you for a long time."

"General," Alex nodded, on guard.

"First, let me immediately offer my condolences on the tragic death of your wife. It is so cruel that innocent civilians continue to die in this conflict."

"Thank you."

"I've heard a lot of fine things about you, from Majeed and many others."

"And what might that be, General? And in what context?"

"In the context of your work in Pakistan, your understanding of our country."

"And what do you do, General?"

"I'm an old man. Let's just say that I serve from time to time as a special advisor to the General Staff."

"And your interest?"

"I'd like to talk to you about the situation we all find ourselves in here."

"Yes, we all are indeed in a 'situation,' and not a good one."

"I know you speak almost native Urdu, and know our country very well, from childhood. We view you as a friend of Pakistan."

"Thank you, General. Friend maybe. I very much feel part of this country's life. It has been with me for much of my life. But that doesn't always apply to politics."

"We know that you share our intense discomfort at our present situation. In a country where our government has always had a good feel for internal dynamics, for the first time we feel we might be losing it. The pressures are intense and not least from your country."

"I'm well aware of that, General, and I share your concern. I have spoken out about this in our own Embassy circles. But the problem is far bigger than the Embassy, it goes back to Washington. And to the mistakes of your own leadership as well."

"Yes, well, we agree we have a problem. The Frontier zones, as you well know, are now very restive. We find it hard to meet all the requirements that our American friends are currently levying upon us. The Frontier is a special place, and not easily grasped by outsiders. Impatient outsiders who are in a hurry to get the Afghanistan burden off their back. Perhaps that grand old imperialist Rudyard Kipling understood it best of any Westerner."

Alex smiled wryly. "And seemingly we have not learned a lot from him. People don't read novels nowadays in government, they read intelligence reports."

"Pity. Intelligence reports are like a recipe for a good curry. You can read the ingredients, but you can't really imagine the flavor unless you make it, by yourself."

"Point taken. But you didn't invite me here to talk about curry I'm sure."

"No, you are right. We can get to the point. We are frankly in somewhat desperate straits now, and find Washington to be the biggest problem we face—even more dangerous and destabilizing than the Taliban or other radical groups in the Frontier. We have had long decades of experience handling the Frontier, but not at handling an irate and cornered Washington."

"And?…" This could now be heading only in one direction.

"So we seek your assistance in advising us on how best to proceed. We believe you understand the nature of the problem well, you understand us. We hoped you might be able to keep us informed on current trends of thinking so we can better meet US demands."

"General, let's not play games. You are asking me to be a spy."

"No, not a spy, but yes, a consultant, to offer us informed advice on what is going on, what we can expect, and even recommendations on how best to meet US demands."

"General, I'm sorry, but that is simply out of the question." His flash of irritation grew. "Do you take me for a fool, General? That's the oldest recruitment pitch in the book, to become a 'consultant'."

"Please do not take offense. I mean no disrespect. But we had hoped you might have some sympathy for our problems, and might find it in the interests of both of our countries to try to handle things better. We know you care."

"General, I do care, but I am frankly offended by this approach. I am open in my discussions in this country with Pakistanis. I don't need to provide 'confidential' information."

"But permit me to note that you do deal in 'confidential information.' Not to put too fine a point on it, but of course we are well aware of your own extensive 'confidential' contacts here among our own Pakistani citizens. We have been monitoring many of them. Some more narrow-minded Pakistani authorities might consider what you have been doing to constitute illegal activity in our country."

"General, why don't we end this conversation now. If you have charges to make against me, make them. If you are interested in my views on issues, you have only to ask, in a less compromising environment. If you are thinking of really insulting me, then I suppose you will now suggest you can 'compensate me for my time'."

"No, Alex, we would not do that. We know you are a man of integrity. But we are also honest in admitting we need help. Real help. We are in trouble. That is why we turned to you. I'm sorry if we have offended you in any way."

"No, General, I will not be offended if we end this now. But anything further and I would be compelled to report a highly irregular approach to me, which neither of us would like. You are crossing a boundary. For all I know this session is being recorded, by you. Or by me as well. And so, with your permission, I wish to take my leave. I understand your predicaments. I will try to deal with them as best I can in my own way, as the situation permits. Good luck, and good evening, General." Alex turned and walked out of the room. The General offered no further words. Majeed was not present as Alex left the house, steaming. *Majeed, I suppose this is only payback. What our organizations do.*

*   *   *

"Next item: Alex—his jihadi and Taliban operations. OK, I don't mind saying, I'm a little uncomfortable about the way some of this is going. He can go off half-cocked, without guidance, and do stuff on his own. Ask me, we need to put a tighter leash on him." Kevin, the Deputy COS and never a fan of Alex, delivered himself of his strong opinion. He was briefing Morris, the newly arrived Chief of Station who was replacing Sam. Morris was heavyset, dressed in too tight a suit only emphasizing a pudgy image that caused those who met him to quickly size him up as soft or effete—at their own peril. His bulk distracted from his dark, penetrating eyes and a style that varied between casual and authoritarian but was quick to perceive the central issue at hand. He had only been in Islamabad a few days. He was new to South Asia, but had a background in Latin America where he had acquired a reputation as a strong leader in working with, and against, local guerrilla forces, depending upon Washington's politics *du jour*. Undermining existing leaders in Latin America had been a central part of the US foreign policy tool kit under a whole series of US presidents going back more than a century.

"So can you fill me in a bit on what his section does?"

"Morris, this guy is special, an unusual case," Miguel, the Chief of Operations spoke up. "He grew up in this country, he's got a good feel for what makes it tick. Knows the language. Got contacts. But you're right, I don't think anybody has ever gotten a solid feel for what makes him really tick. He can be a loose cannon at times. But nobody's got access like him. You got to put up with some of his individuality if you want the good stuff."

"But is he with the program, with the policy? He seems to defend a lot of these religious types, some of whom look pretty hard core to me. I mean, Taliban types. He gives me the impression his own political views on the local scene can be more radical than Pak moderates I've met so far."

"OK, Morris, but with all due respect, you haven't been out here all that long. The whole spectrum is different. There *are* no fucking moderates from a US perspective. It's all relative. And it's a receding horizon. Christ, we would have called the Jamaat-e-Islami radical ten, twenty years ago but now they're virtually mainstream, almost working with us compared to the rest. And take the JUI, they're…"

"What's the JUI again?"

"Jamaat-i-Ulama-i-Islami. The Association of Muslim Clergy. Ulama means the clergy. They're linked more closely to the radical clergy than the JI, the Jamaat-e-Islami, is. And we've come to think of *them* as moderate now."

"Oh, yeah, I remember reading up on them. But they do seem quite anti-American."

"Morris, again, it's all relative. There's probably not a pro-American politician left in the country today—unless it's some toady who wants our money and backing for a passport to the presidency of the country. Or somebody like Benazir Bhutto who wants to ride in on US shoulders and stay in power that way. You can only do that so long before you get chucked out of the system."

"So what has been the formula then, for approaching a hard-core target like this—recruiting among these radical and anti-American circles. Sounds tough."

"It's not easy. It's hard just getting to meet these types face to face, much less think about recruitment. That's where Alex has done a damn good job. He knows what the real score is here, who counts as sufficiently 'moderate'— people we might be able to deal with—as opposed to the hard-core Bin Laden types. He knows a lot of people here, and how they think." The Ops Chief was getting in his statement of respect and support for Alex before Kevin could completely poison the well.

"Yeah," Kevin said, "what was that they used to say twenty years ago: the definition of an Iranian moderate? An Iranian who has run out of bullets." Morris smiled weakly. "So what's Hqs thinking on this now?" He turned again to look at Miguel.

"We're in a tough spot, under a lot of pressure. This has drifted some way beyond classic intel gathering operations of the past. Now we're instructed to get the goods on the hard-core types—and pass it on to the military, Special Ops, and let them take 'em out. Too many years have passed since 9/11 and there are still a lot of jihadis left out there."

"OK, so have we been pushing to get human assets in closer to these guys? Or have you been working more technical ops?"

"If we can get people in close, that's great," said Miguel. "Alex is good at directing agents against these targets. But yeah, Alex is sometime hard to fully control. He has had a mixed career in the past—getting out ahead of orders."

"You know what?" Kevin broke in to trot out his standard theory. "I'm basically not sure I trust these guys that have grown up native in these places. They often end up seeing the situation from the eyes of the locals."

"Well, frankly, that's not all bad in a lot of ways," Miguel countered. "How many of our corn-fed blue-eyed Americans are going to come out here and get a feel for a culture like this? You gotta gain some empathy so you can think like them. Alex is a pretty rare—and valuable—bird."

"Fine. But in the end, what's the line between empathy and fucking sympathy?" Kevin persisted.

"Look, Morris, you know this is an old debate," Miguel spoke up. "There's no winning it. Sure, the more cultural insight you get, the more you understand the culture, the language, the people—hell, the more you might actually get to *like* the damn place and understand it better. But you can't have fucking virgins assigned out here who believe all the bullshit propaganda coming out of the politicians in Washington and still be effective at the job. How far you think you'd get in recruiting some of these Pak and Afghan types if you preached the White House line on freedom and democracy and human rights and the axis of evil? The White House itself may not even really believe it. Out here people would think you were a liar—or an idiot. Are you going to go out there and tell them they're evil? That they've got to sign up with us or we'll waste 'em? I mean Jesus, Morris, think back to Latin America! We both know the place. Back in the day how many Yankee-lovers could you find there? Except for the goddam billionaires—they of course loved the dictators and the US because we kept their billions safe from the masses. And the US loved them for keeping the lid on and protecting US businesses."

"OK, Miguel, I remember. But this seems way more serious out here. These people seem steeped in their religion, eating it and breathing it. From what I've read so far they'll support anybody who says 'Allahu Akbar' and leads the charge against the US... We've got a job to do here, identify the bad guys and pinpoint their whereabouts so Special Forces can get them. I don't need a whole lot of political finesse to get the basic players straight. But tell me more about our liaison with ISI," Morris asked.

"ISI?" Kevin butted in. "They're the worst of the fucking lot. They are in bed with half the crazies of the world out here. They've lied, and run circles around us here ever since the start of the war against the Soviets in 1979. They insisted that every ounce of aid we sent in go through them, they parceled it out to their own guys, like Hekmatyar, who seemed busier trying to kill his rivals among the muj than he was at killing Soviets. But he was ISI's boy, could do no wrong. And we got squeezed out of the decision on the ground about who got what."

"I know," Miguel sighed, "but I don't see we got any choice but to work with them. They're in touch with every single group out there in the field. They know this country cold. They're in thick with tribal politics in the Frontier. We figure they may even be in with the fringes of al-Qaeda. There's no way we're going to get closer to the Taliban or al-Qaeda than ISI is."

"What kind of allies do you call them then, if they're in that close with the people who are shooting at us?"

"Because in the end, Morris, you and I are going to pack up our stuff one day and go home. The Paks are here till the end of time and they're not going to risk their future by having a hostile regime in Kabul while they've got the Indian Goliath breathing down their ass on the other border. The Paks will move heaven and earth to have a voice over the Taliban because one day they and their ilk are going to be in power again in Afghanistan. And there's not a damn thing you or me or the goddam prayzident of the US can do about it."

The meeting came to an end, but within a week the new COS stopped in on his Ops Chief.

"Miguel, apropos our talk the other day on Alex, I am a little disturbed at some of the negative policy comments I hear he has been making to visiting brass out here."

"Morris, there's no doubt Alex can be quick off the handle," Miguel offered. "And way too outspoken when he should keep his mouth shut in front of visiting brass. But who isn't disillusioned? You know Washington's made a goddam mess out of this whole scene, it's going from bad to worse. You think we should be some kind of cheering section for the White House and Pentagon? You know that's not our damn mission—thank God. We're supposed to tell it like we see it. Leave policy-making to the striped-pants brigade at State. And by the way, you might ask the Ambassador what he thinks of Alex. He has tremendous respect for him, asks his opinion a lot of the time."

"All well and good. But the Ambassador doesn't pay our salaries. Do you think Alex's negativity comes from the impact of the death of his wife and all?"

"He's a damn good officer, Morris. He knows the country and the people and the mentality. What more can I say? We don't have many officers like him who do."

"No, but when outsiders from Washington come through he's got to give lip-service to the policies, at least outside Station walls."

Miguel persisted. "You know, Morris, this intel business, it's a curious thing in my experience. Most people who don't know anything about it might assume that your average CIA ops officers are just a bunch of flag-waving cowboys. Yet when I think back, our outfit used to attract a whole lot of people who grew up overseas in one capacity or another. Military brats, or, in Alex's case, a missionary brat. Sometimes diplomats' kids. They made incredible intel officers, because they knew instinctively, from childhood, that there's more than one way in this world to live and think."

"So what are you getting at?"

"Just that what I see in Alex is what I've seen before in other guys like him. Kind of rebels—angry. Just sticking it to Washington can be a predictable pattern in them—when they don't see any sign that people back home are listening to facts on the ground."

"Too bad, but that's all we can do," Morris rejoined. "That's our job, not to give Washington a report card on how they're doing."

$$* \qquad * \qquad *$$

It happened the very next day. "Morris, some really bad info this morning." Kevin, breathing heavily, pushed his way into the Chief's office and closed the door behind him. "We've lost Mojo at the nuke installation…"

"What do you mean, lost?"

"He's missed his last two meetings with his case officer, his signaling apparatus has gone dead, and we've now gotten word that he has been arrested for espionage. He has apparently admitted to the Paks that he was working for us."

"Shit, don't tell me!" The Chief pulled his feet off the desk, put down a document and bolted upright in his chair. "Do we know what happened?"

"No, we don't know what happened yet, but we're working on it. Maybe he got sloppy, or unlucky. Maybe they've been onto him for some time but we didn't know it—maybe they moved now as we start developing an ops plan against the nukes. Or—could even be some kind of leak."

"Jesus, that case is our bread and butter! Just about justifies all our salaries out here. That's the one case Washington really cares about."

"Yeah, it's a goddam disaster. We can't remotely replace him."

"Christ! Hqs is absolutely going to hit the fucking roof. Even the goddam White House—they've had a special interest in this case all along. And that damn General Maerkl will be all over us on this one—it's the end of their planning on pinpointing and grabbing the nukes."

"The Paks are sure to move them to a new location again and impose new protocols—even the info we already have is going to be useless. And the Paks are now alert to any more penetration attempts by us."

"Don't we have anyone else positioned within the nuclear establishment that can pinpoint these weapons and give us the access codes?"

"Nothing close, only Ivy, but he's small potatoes, just in the admin office, doesn't have access to anything really useful to us in planning the operation."

"OK, Kevin, we obviously need a full-bore counterintel review of the case ASAP. We've got to try to solve this ourselves here quickly before Hqs gets ideas of sending out some team to turn the whole damn Station upside down. That would really be miserable."

"OK, will do."

"You think the leak could have come from Washington? You've got all those Special Ops guys straining at the leash to go in and confiscate those nukes. We don't know how tight a hold Maerkl has kept on this info in his shop. I hear he talked out of turn when he was out here, in front of several non-cleared people."

"It could be Washington. But I have a few other ideas, right here in the Station…"

"In the Station? That case is on close, close hold. There's a tiny handful of us cleared for this case here. It's special channel reporting. The leak can't come from us!"

"Yeah, but frankly I'm suspicious… about our friend Alex. He was at a meeting with Maerkl. So was the Milatt, also uncleared."

"Alright, that's an even more serious supposition. Let's start our CI investigation on a nominally routine basis, but focus on Alex and the Milatt. Otherwise let's not say or do anything till we have a better handle. Christ, this is the pits."

Morris stood up, sighed, went over to the windows and stood looking out at the green hills in the distance, shaking his head. He had just lost the crown jewels. Early on his watch.

*   *   *

Alex felt sick about the process he had unleashed with Majeed. Not about what he had done—he had no second thoughts about that. He had been clearly moving towards such an act for a long time as his thinking crystallized. The anxiety came from the waiting. There was no other way to view it—it was a deliberate act of sabotage with immense consequences. But he could easily imagine war if the US attempted to seize Pakistan's nuclear facilities and weapons. The country would explode. There were some crazy fire-breathers back home that wanted to carry the war into yet another Muslim country in this relentless Hundred Year War against Islam. One hundred years of potential recruits for the Taliban and al-Qaeda across the region...

He knew that after Majeed had received the info it would only be days, hours, before the Paks wrapped up Mojo inside the nuclear installation at Kahuta. They could not tolerate for one second having a CIA agent inside their most sensitive installation. Alex knew too that the Station would launch an extensive investigation to find out how the information leaked. It was only a matter of time.

He knew the game. Engaging in espionage—secretly passing classified information to an unauthorized foreign intelligence organization—was a game filled with sudden death. You placed your entire fate into the hands of the recipient of the information. So many of the infamous American spies in history working for the KGB had been exposed in just that way—it wasn't due to any professional mistakes on their part. Often, it was just that someone inside the KGB was reporting to the CIA; that source then found out that the KGB had acquired a new mole inside the CIA and soon reported that information back to CIA. And so it was that a CIA source inside the Pakistani government became aware of the spectacular information Majeed had received from Alex—about a CIA spy within the Pakistani nuclear establishment. And he reported it to his CIA contact. And although Majeed never revealed Alex's name, it took only minimal analysis before it became clear to the CIA Station who the source of that information was.

The COS and his deputy put together the pieces of the puzzle, without letting anyone else in the Station—especially Alex—know that they had lost Mojo, or that Mojo had ever existed. The evidence pointed all in one direction. "Christ, I knew it was going to be Alex!" Kevin seemed to tingle with repressed delight, his theories and prejudices fully borne out.

"Morris, our source in the military reports they got some a secret report from an American source who revealed Mojo's name as our agent. Alex was probably aware of the beginnings of the Mojo case from the agent who spotted Mojo for us in the first place. The case was put into special channels thereafter, but it was too late. Alex maybe was able to figure it out. Furthermore, the info probably almost certainly came to ISI via Majeed Rehman. We know he's in close with Alex."

"Jesus! That son of a bitch!"

"There's more. SIS got further information about our tagger in North Waziristan—who has now been killed."

"Goddam it all to hell!"

"I told you, Morris, you can't trust these guys who go native on you. Classic. You should hear what Moe has to say about him."

"Just what does Moe have to say about him?"

"That Alex is more Pakistani than the Paks. That he feels uncomfortable when he hears how Alex is always highly critical of US policies. He doesn't like having dealing with Alex, because he feels he's putting him into a difficult situation, making him feel disloyal."

"Fair enough, but Moe isn't Chief of Station here, I am. And second, Moe doesn't know shit about policy and I do. So I don't want to hear his prissy concerns about Alex, they're not relevant. Above all, I want no further discussion of this until we have clearer information. This info is not to leave this office. I don't want Alex or anyone to know what has happened. If Alex is the source of all of this, he probably knows the Paks would take fast action. We're not going to charge Alex—or anybody—until we have firm and reliable information. This is now a criminal issue. It's going to cost us dearly here whatever happens. We've got to handle this by the book."

"Alright, Chief, I get it."

"And second, Kevin, I expect you to behave professionally on this as well. I know you don't like Anders, you've been open about it in the past. And regrettably you've been right in some of your suspicions. But we're going to require careful evidence that goes beyond your hunches and theories on guys who get too close to foreign cultures."

"I hear you." The DCOS suppressed a smile.

*   *   *

Two days later the COS's secretary looked into Alex's office as he sat reading a fundamentalist Urdu newspaper. "Boss wants to see you in the secure room right away, Alex."

His gut twisted. His bowels turned to water. *Shit, that's it, they're onto me. It had to come.* What should he do? He felt ill, stood up, went out into the corridor, and made a rush to the men's room to relieve his heaving stomach tensions. While he was on the toilet, his guts pouring out their tale, he could hear voices in the corridor outside, "Shit, where is he? Has he snuck out?" The bathroom door then swung open. "Anders? Anders? You in here?" It was Kevin's voice. "Yes, I'm in here. I'll be out in a moment." Kevin remained right in the men's room, standing just outside Alex's stall. When Alex eventually flushed the toilet and emerged from the stall, Kevin's face showed it all. Alex took his time washing his hands, then walked unsteadily down the hall with Kevin behind him towards the secure room, the stark and dreary space in which his fate would be written. In the hallway outside were two armed military police. Their presence removed all doubt about the issue at hand.

As he entered he saw there were three people at the table. The COS, the Chief of Ops, and the Embassy security officer, with Kevin coming in behind him. "Close the door," the Chief's voice called out harshly. Kevin pulled tight the double doors.

"Alex, I'm not going to play any games. I'll put it straight to you. We have lost Mojo, our source in Kahuta. He was blown to ISI. We now know the info came to ISI via Majeed Rehman. We have solid reason to believe that you were the person who revealed this information. What do you have to say for yourself?"

Alex looked away, but only for a moment. His moment of panic had now passed. The moment of truth was here and he was ready. He looked up at the Chief, held his gaze firmly for a few seconds. Then he said in a voice that amazingly did not tremble, "Yes, Morris, that is correct. I did pass the information to Majeed Rehman."

The Chief paused, astonished at his forthrightness, and looked knowingly at the other officers in the room.

"I assume then, you know the magnitude of what you have done? This was the single-most important asset we have in the Station, vital to Washington's nuclear planning vis-à-vis Pakistan."

"I am aware of that."

Morris paused, waiting to hear further elaboration. "Well, goddam it, is that all you have to say for yourself?"

"I am sorry. I really am sorry. Not because I blew the case, but because it had come to this…"

"Just what do you mean? Come to what?" barked the Chief.

"I mean that the whole situation here is getting dangerously out of hand. We are in the process of destroying Pakistan, possibly moving to war with it. If we seize the nukes there will be an unbelievable bloodbath here against Americans. This is all…"

Morris broke in. "What gives you the right, you self-righteous little prick, to take such a decision into your own hands? Who do you think you are?"

"I don't have the right, Morris." Alex looked him in the eye. "But I believed I had the obligation—I still believe I have the obligation, to attempt to stop this madness that is unfolding in front of us. You know about these planning groups in Washington waiting to seize the Pak nukes. An insane operation by people cut off from local reality. And no one is speaking out against it. There are no rational voices at work anywhere in government on any of this entire Afghan-Pak-nuclear catastrophe."

"So you do not deny it?"

"No. I told you, I do not deny it."

"Are you aware this is a criminal act? That this could amount to treason?"

"Yes. I know that."

"That's all you have to say?"

"I did what I believe I had to do. I know you will do what you believe you have to do."

"Alex, I am placing you under immediate military detention. The military will not know the reason, but you will be incarcerated. Someone from Hqs will come out to interrogate you on the full particulars of the case—what you did, when you did it, with whom, and how."

"I expected as much. I will cooperate. I have nothing to hide."

"You don't even seem upset, you bastard!" Kevin threw in.

"I knew this was coming. I'm not upset that it has happened. But I *am* upset about the general situation here in the country, and where it is taking us all."

"That kind of defense won't cut any ice with anyone. You have violated security regulations, worse, broken the law. You're finished. Thank God at least your kid has gone back to Chile."

Rodriguito. Alex remained silent.

"Do you really believe that what you have done is justifiable?" the Chief of Ops asked in a quieter tone.

"Yes, Miguel, I do. You know I have been unhappy about nearly everything that is going on for a long time here. It's feckless, failing and creating ever greater damage. I know some people in this Embassy happen to share that view. But somebody had to step forward and try to do something to stop a catastrophic decision from being taken. That's why I decided to do what I did."

"Well, we're not here to argue this with you," Morris said. "What kind of compensation did you get from ISI for this information?"

"Morris, not one penny. I am not working for ISI. They have done nothing for me. I passed along this information as a onetime thing. Strictly at my own volition. They have no handle on me, even though they wanted one."

"Wanted one? You mean they approached you… to recruit you?"

"Yes, but only days after I had passed the information via Majeed."

"And what did you say?"

"I turned them down flat."

"Why the sudden scruples?" Kevin smirked.

"They're not sudden scruples, dammit!" Alex's first flash of real emotion. "Don't you understand? I'm not working for the Paks. I passed along only that piece of information that I believe will prevent terrible mistakes from being made by cowboys back in Washington."

"Did you pass along any other vital information?"

"Yes, I also blew Homaid's identity. That boy had begun to stick his tags anywhere just to get money. He was a murderer of many innocent civilians. I have seen the wreckage myself. You know that too."

"You know Homaid will die now, he may even be dead already."

"Yes, I know. But he has huge blood on his hands. He was a useful source on the Taliban when I was handling the case. It was Washington and the military that pushed him into the job of tagger. You know I wasn't happy about that. Of course he got corrupted, got greedy in the process."

"Anyone else whose lives you have readily dispensed with as judge, jury and executioner?"

"No, that's it."

"You are sure?"

"Yes. I am sure."

"Well, you are in a world of trouble, Alex. I despise you for what you have done. I hope you pay a serious penalty. We may disagree with our government's policies, but none of us have the right to take matters into our own hands."

"That's the problem, Morris, nobody does."

"That's enough. This is over."

The security officer stood up. He opened the big double door and escorted Alex out of the room by the elbow, walked down the corridor and turned him over to the two military police. Nickel-plated cuffs flashed and clicked onto his wrists. They escorted Alex down the long hall, down the stairs and out the back door to a waiting military van with driver. An additional Marine Guard accompanied them into the van. He knew Alex, but said nothing. As the van moved out, Alex looked back through the window at the Embassy, gates closing behind them, gradually vanishing from sight. He was now bereft of friend or ally. *Rodriguito, where are you?*

*   *   *

An interrogator and inquisitor was quickly named. Hqs sent out Patrick Ryan, a senior officer who had retired a year earlier, to investigate Alex's case. Ryan was one of the few remaining members of an entire early generation of CIA officers in which Irish Catholics were strongly represented. The Cold War was their generation's defining experience—an era of moral and theological struggle around the globe. Ryan's CV was studded with operational tasks around the world, capped late in his career with responsibility for the Agency's most arcane of all intelligence activities—counterintelligence. Indeed, the art of counterintelligence turned the entire intelligence game on its head.

For the majority of CIA officers, including Ryan, the central mission had always been clandestine collection and analysis of strategic intelligence. Mutual trust and cooperation made up the professional glue among officers, the source of *esprit de corps*, camaraderie, and collegial success. But to the high priests of counterintelligence the game was very different. *No one* in the Agency was assumed to be above suspicion—anyone could be subverted by the enemy. In a profession already marked by a realism about the human condition, the counterintelligence specialist viewed everything and everybody with a dispassionate and beady eye in which nothing was ever as it seemed. Who could know whether your most trusted colleague working alongside you in intelligence might himself actually be the enemy, secretly working to subvert the organization for the KGB?

Nor could this foundation of suspicion be attributed to simple paranoia. Like so many other officers of his generation, Ryan had been shattered in his early professional years by a stunning, indeed inconceivable, revelation: that in the early years of the Cold War the Agency's fledgling counterintelligence branch itself had been penetrated by the KGB from day one. As incredible as it seemed, Britain's supreme counterintelligence specialist, Kim Philby—had been sent to Washington to work with the CIA to help train its first officers in the art of counterintelligence; only years later he himself was to be unmasked as a Soviet agent. The Holy of Holies had thus been penetrated at the outset by the enemy. Penetration was the right word—suggesting a physical violation, a rape of the integrity of the security process. The Philby story had sent a chill down the spine of the counterintelligence world, in which reality seemed to outrun fiction; paranoia now justifiably knew no bounds.

And so Ryan, years later and now retired, flew out to Islamabad, tasked with investigating the case of Alex Anders in detail and to thoroughly document his devastating betrayal of the preeminent intelligence operation of Islamabad Station.

Ryan had his doubts about Alex Anders from the start. He thought Alex smacked of the intellectual, the cultural cosmopolitan to whom treason came more easily, just like the polished and glib Oxbridge Philby. Working with an assistant, Ryan conducted a detailed interrogation of Alex that lasted four months, working in shifts often lasting up to twelve hours a day, partly designed to wear Alex down, trip him up. Everything was to be put on the table from Alex's first induction into the Agency—any and all elements of his life that might contain grounds for suspicion. The exact nature of Alex's relationship with Fyodor in Santiago, his relationship with Majeed and every single contact he had ever had with him or any other Pakistani intelligence officials—all was examined repeatedly in exhausting detail; indeed the very intensity brought Alex close to losing his mind in the relentless grilling, plowing the same material over and over again for possible anomalies. Nonetheless, Alex made every effort to cooperate with Ryan and his assistant. He had initially chosen not to reveal, however, his more recent recontact with Fyodor in Islamabad, mainly out of concern that his failure to report that meeting at the time could now be interpreted as damning to his case. A polygrapher was also brought in to "box" Alex—Agency jargon for a lie detector. The technician reported that it looked like Alex had been telling the truth: he had accepted no money or any other compensation at any time, he had no formal relationship with ISI, his act had been a one-time event, and based on personal ideological grounds. Alex had explained in full his own ideological odyssey and policy objections to what he thought were ruinous, failing and unethical US policies in Afghanistan and Pakistan.

But Alex's case turned sharply worse when during a polygraph session with Ryan in attendance, the operator asked routinely whether Alex had ever had any contact with other intelligence organizations apart from the Fyodor operation in Santiago. Alex replied, "no."

"I am getting indications of deception on that response. I repeat the question: apart from Fyodor in Santiago, have you had contacts with any other foreign intelligence agency?"

Alex could no longer conceal the incident.

"Yes. I had a meeting one year ago with a Russian intelligence officer."

Ryan nearly leapt out of his seat, on it like a terrier. They had now reached pay dirt—he knew it! There was a Soviet angle to the case after all!

"What? A Russian?" The polygrapher's cool professional style fell by the wayside; he turned off the stylus that had already jumped across the graph paper on the machine and turned the interrogation back over to Ryan.

"Explain."

"It was Fyodor, whom you know about. The Soviet who had been an agent of mine in Chile a decade ago. After the fall of the USSR he was rehabilitated. He came out here to see me."

"And why did he come out here to see you?"

"He said he wanted to talk about the local situation and to solicit my personal views."

"And what did you tell him?"

"I told him nothing that I wouldn't tell anyone else—about what I personally think on these issues."

"You seem quite ready to share these negative impressions with the world. That's all he wanted?"

"No, he hoped I might now be willing to work as a Russian agent."

"And what did you say?"

"I told him I had no intention of doing so, I told him to bugger off."

"Why did you say that?"

"Because I'm not a spy, goddam it! I wouldn't work for the Russians or anybody else."

"What did he say in response?"

"He said he wasn't surprised, he didn't expect me to agree, but he was required to ask."

"Did he offer you any gifts? Money?"

"No, only more vodka than I cared to drink at the dinner."

"No other promised benefits…"

"No!"

"Did you report this to the Station?"

Alex hesitated. "No… I didn't."

"You did not? Really? You are surely aware you are legally required to report all such approaches, from any intelligence organization."

"Yes."

"Then why didn't you?"

"I frankly felt it wouldn't look good. I had drawn enough negative feelings in the Station in expressing my views on the political scene here, it would just undercut me, serve as ammo to those who don't like me and my views."

"Well, you're damn right. It certainly doesn't make you look good, on top of everything else. Have you had any further contact from Fyodor?"

"No."

"Any messages, communications, other Russians?"

"No."

"Did they provide you with any means of communicating with them? Addresses? Cut-outs? Electronic communications?"

"No! There was nothing like that. It was a one-time thing."

"Did he say he would see you again?"

"No, not particularly."

"Why do you think he came out to see *you* specifically?"

"Because, as I said, we had known each other extremely well, we'd had many long talks about politics, he wanted to know how I felt about the world—now that both the USSR and the US situation had changed so much."

"Were you happy to meet with him?"

"Look, he had been my agent, alright? It was an intense relationship. I had to have good rapport with him to get the maximum out of him. We spent many hundreds of hours together in Santiago."

"Did you like him?"

"If you're asking whether we enjoyed each other's company, the answer is yes. He was an interesting, complex, intense man, intelligent, with a lot to say. A sense of humor."

"Did he try to persuade you his system is better?"

"No, he always acknowledged that the Soviet and Russian systems were worse."

"Do you agree with him on that? Or do you like aspects of the Soviet system?"

"Look, goddam it, I don't think the US is without faults. We talked about that on occasion, but he never tried to persuade me that his system was better."

"Do you still believe that the US system has many faults?"

"Do *you* believe it does not?"

"I'm asking asked the questions, Anders!"

"Every system has its faults. I'm American and I believe in my country, but I also believe it has its faults, serious ones now, that need correcting. And our foreign policy is a disaster. We're not living in some Paradise, you know, they don't exist in this world. And stop trying to incriminate me."

"I think you've done a good enough job of that on your own."

Ryan spent weeks going over the details of the Fyodor case again and again and the circumstances of his renewed contact in Islamabad. He seemed convinced that the Russians were behind Alex's exposure of Mojo, the Pakistani agent in the nuclear lab.

"Did you tell Fyodor about Mojo?"

"No, I did not."

"Yet you told the Pakistanis."

"I told Majeed, yes."

"If you were willing to tell a half-ass intel service like the ISI about Mojo, what compunctions could you have about telling a Russian intelligence officer?"

"Because I was not interested in helping the Russians, I was interested in ending the Mojo case because of its dangerous implications."

"Doesn't it help the Russians that you exposed the Mojo case to the Pakistanis?"

"Not directly. Or only in the sense that it weakens US capabilities in intervening in the nuclear complex."

"Did Fyodor tell you to tell the ISI?"

"No, Fyodor knew nothing about my contacts with ISI!"

Ryan seemed incredulous that Alex was willing to betray the CIA's top case in Islamabad to the ISI without any Russian connection. But he could find no linkage and in the end Alex tested clean on the box in verifying his account with Fyodor and his relationship with Majeed. But Alex's original instincts had been right, his second contact with Fyodor in Islamabad had indeed made his case look even messier; he gave every impression of being a loose cannon, out of control, making his own rules. And it opened up still longer investigations about his handling of Fyodor in Chile. More questions, repeated questions, more details, more search for inconsistency. Ryan was often mocking, belittling, sometimes treating Alex like some kind of an outsider, a weirdo. And Alex was kept under incarceration and round-the-clock observation throughout the whole course of the interrogation, month after month. For the first time in his life, Alex could see how people in prison could contemplate suicide. Only his concern for Rodrigo kept him centered in his desire to see this through to the end, to face his penalty and see if there was any life left for him at the other end of the process—and a likely long jail term if no death penalty. The ultimate irony, he realized, was that in the course of a long incarceration his American son would probably be turned into a full-fledged Chilean, with no knowledge of his father or America as he grew up.

After four months the intensity of the interrogation eased somewhat, punctuated with down days when there were no questions and no polygraph. Then one morning Ryan came in. "Alright, Anders, it's over."

"What do you mean?"

"I mean the investigation is over. Washington is now processing all the information and has no further questions at this time. My job is finished. I'm leaving for Washington tomorrow. You will remain here in custody until a decision has been reached about your prosecution."

"How long might that be?"

"As long as it takes… and you better get used to these conditions, this is likely going to be your life for a long time to come."

Alex felt despair creeping over him. Limbo was worse than interrogation. This indeed well might be the conditions of his life for years to come, some prison cell somewhere. Could he have ever imagined during his childhood in Lahore that many decades later he would be languishing in a prison cell in Pakistan only a few hundred kilometers away from his childhood home?

Ryan packed up a few extra papers in a briefcase, and then turned to go. Alex wondered how they might part after these unpleasant months together. Just before Ryan opened the cell door, he turned around again.

"Anders, I'm going to tell it to you straight. I've heard all your arguments about all your views and concerns over the past four months. I have prepared a full damage assessment on what you have done. In the end that is my sole function: I'm here to get the facts of the case and report them back. I have no legal authority over you whatsoever; it will be up to Hqs to decide the disposition of your case; perhaps more accurately, up to the Department of Justice. That's my official role. But I'm also going to give you a little bit of my own personal judgment about you and this whole case, off the record. Because I feel it needs to be said.

"Frankly, Anders, I don't like you. I don't like you one goddam bit. I believe you are childish and spoiled—immature and self-centered—to believe that you possess the understanding to make critical judgments about US policies in Pakistan, Afghanistan, and in the conflicts we are engaged in. *You* are out of touch with the real world. A psychiatrist would say you have delusions of grandeur. You are arrogant, so fucking taken with yourself as to believe you have the right to pass judgment on—much less sabotage—sensitive Agency operations that directly affect vital US interests.

"I've seen kids like you before come into this Agency. Missionary family, wants to do good in this world, believes the Agency can help bring the truth of the world to ignorant and narrow policy makers. That's all bullshit—so spare me your moral sermons.

"You're one of that crowd. You think you're different, but you're not. You're totally typical. Cocky because you've grown up overseas. Or maybe been to some goddam Ivy League school or wherever, never had to get your hands dirty working for a weekly paycheck, or delivering newspapers, or dragging bricks up a ladder, or unloading boxes off a tractor trailer, or flipping hamburgers. You don't even really know what life is like, at least life back home. You're a white boy, you've been treated like an elite your whole life by all those little brown men out there, servants all over the place, bowing and scraping, yes, Sahib, no, Sahib. I've been there, I've seen it.

"OK, so you speak a foreign language, that's great. But you know, when you speak the language you've got spook written all over you. And anybody we're going to want to recruit in most cases knows English, even these terrorists with their technical training—it's usually in English. So don't put on airs about being able to speak a language. In the end it doesn't mean a damn thing if you've got shit judgment. And you've got shit judgment."

Alex sat there, staring at Ryan, listening to his speech. He was too tired to even try to respond, he had long understood Ryan's deep antipathy to him. The gulf was unbridgeable.

"You know what? You're more foreign than American in the end. Great at understanding Tutsis but not a damn clue about Americans. Idealistic about the kind of role the US should be playing in the world. Want to fix the world, make things right. Carry the white man's burden. Bleeding heart about how foreigners think, but not a lot of concern about Joe Sixpack's thinking back home. All kinds of talk about how we need to understand the goddam Pashtuns in their tribal ways, but not a kind word for your own countrymen. Total double standard. In the end I've got to wonder who you're working for, the Russians, the Chileans, the Pakistanis? Or maybe the Rwandans, the Vietnamese or other losers? It couldn't be the US government, could it?

"It's a rough world out there. Some people just hate us because we've got wealth and power and can call the shots. Or they are just envious wannabees. And you know what? Some people out there want to kill us, they've got a laundry list a mile long of grievances that you will never, ever be able to satisfy, Mr. Bleeding Heart. Even the damn Europeans, they talk a good line about the need to maintain values and cultural understanding, holding negotiations, avoiding force—but in the end they're just like everybody else, in it for themselves. Do you think the goddam French would run a better world than the US? That they'd have any more scruples and values and would run a kinder and gentler world? Or would they be looking to their own bottom line, *la gloire de la France*, and all that bullshit?

"Or the Chinese? Gimme a break. Five thousand years of civilization and they're as cold and calculating as a snake. They watch, they observe, they ponder, they do what they think they can do—without any scruples, morals, or values. For them, values are only somebody else's handicap, there just to help the Chinese win the game. That's their weapon to make the US stand down right now, because they don't have enough military power yet. I tell you I wouldn't ever want to be down and out in Shanghai: the Chinese would step over your fucking dying body without a concern. If you're not kin, you're nobody, you're shit. And the Japanese are no better. They're all so civilized with their high-tech toys right now, but how long ago was it that they were raping girls and disemboweling civilians on the streets of Nanking? Bayoneting all the survivors on Corregidor? Yet we're supposed to eat humble pie and tiptoe around in guilt because we dropped the A-bomb on them to stop the war, but the damn Japanese half a century later still won't even admit in their textbooks that they started the whole bloody war in Asia. They just look at you with cold, hard, calculating bottom-line eyes.

"So you know what, Alex Anders? It helps to have a little global perspective, something they maybe didn't teach you in your fancy-ass college courses. Now, would I like to see a more moral world? Sure, but I'm not going to be talked into some liberal guilt trip about how the US is the worst outfit out there ever, just because of all our power. I'd like to see how many of those complaining about US power would choose to turn the world over to someone else. To the French? To the bloody pompous English who ran a racist empire for centuries and won't talk to you if you didn't go to Oxbridge and talk the King's English? To the morose drunken Russians, for God's sake? Don't bet on it. People may bitch but they know they've probably got as good a deal as it's ever going to get in this cruel world, as they all sit under the American umbrella to get out of the hot sun. Hell, these people only stop badmouthing the US long enough to fill out a visa application and haul their asses down to the US Embassy to stand in line to emigrate to America. How's that for voting with your feet?

"So no sir, I'm not going to get all clutched up about how unpopular we may be around the world. I don't see anybody else willing to try to stop the world from getting even worse. Sure, we've made a lot mistakes from time to time. Do we get pushy, throw our weight around, get all moralistic on occasion? You bet. And we get trigger happy too, after getting shot at long enough. But in the end we're the only people willing to stay the course, try to bring some order to that mess out there. Because, mark my words, it is one goddam mess. It's a dark, dog-eat-dog world, kill or be killed, take care of yourself and your own first. It's never going to be any different, no matter how many little UNs you set up. Strength is what will keep people on the straight and narrow.

"You think the Finns or the Canadians are ready to take a lot of casualties, spend their national blood and treasure in an effort to keep things together? Don't bet on it, they're happy to leave all the dirty work to somebody else so they can keep their consciences clean, and enjoy the good life, worry about the social issues of their own little towns and not have to worry about the shit accumulating elsewhere in the world. Keep their principles, keep their hands clean, let the US do it, and then feel more righteous than thou about how the Yanks are screwing it up, being too violent, don't understand the culture, using too much force, intervening too much. Nice work if you can get it."

Alex, as numbed as he was by Ryan's last unexpected departure tirade, was beginning to feel his own fury rise. "Listen, Patrick…"

"Wait one minute Mr. Anders. I'm not fucking done.. Now let's get specific. You got a lot going for you. You're smart, you're savvy, and yeah, you do know a thing or two about how all these third-world types think. And you do know the language. Some people may even like you. But in the end, I'm just not sure where your heart is. I don't think *you* know either. You think you're American, think you're giving the best advice you can, that you're approaching it in the best way to win respect among your little rag-head friends, but in the end you're not going to get the job done. Too fastidious, not sure on whose side you really are in the end.

"If it were up to me, I would prefer to recruit officers into our Agency who have not been exposed to life abroad until adulthood, individuals whose cultural exposure to foreign countries is limited. People who are unlikely to get too up-close and personal to a foreign culture so as to identify with it. Those kind of people can keep their priorities straight. Not these damn chameleons like yourself."

This is outrageous. How much more of this shit and abuse do I have to take before Ryan feels good about his world?

But Ryan was on a roll. "They tell me you've got a lot of cultural sensitivity for how this system works here in Pakistan. Well, if you ask me, cultural sensitivity is way overrated. Sometimes we just need people to go out there who are going to level with Paks or whoever it is, no bullshit, and leave the stark choice in front of them, no sugar coat. We're not looking to charm the pants off them, we're looking to scare the hell out of these guys so they'll shut down their own damn killing machine. This isn't optional. It's not sensitivity training. It's hitting the mule over the head with a two-by-four to get his damn attention. That's our damn job. Not to improve US-Pak fucking relations, we'll leave that to the striped pants at Foggy Bottom. We're here to stop the killing. Whatever it takes.

"Now, some officers like you don't want to get your own hands dirty, don't want to have to get down in the mud in this ugly conflict, take out a few really bad guys. Think all the dirty work should be up to the damn military. That shows how much you know about the military. You really think you want to leave a job like this up to a bunch of eighteen-year old kids, half of them zonked out, their brains in their balls, wheeling around in tanks or APVs with submachine guns in their laps, hopped up on heavy metal in their earphones, looking for something to kill? Freshly trained from killing enemies on their Game Boys? Jumpy, trigger-happy, homesick for East Jesus Wyoming, scared of the wogs all around them, don't even have a scorecard to know the good guys from the bad? We all know what that leads to.

"So get this straight. If we intelligence officers can't get this problem nailed down and protect American security, the next thing you know the goddam President is going to kiss us off and turn to the goddam military to fix the problem. We know all about that, we've seen it. The reason we're entrusted with this goddam mission is because it takes a little adult supervision, some smarts, a lot of knowledge and some restraint. I'm happy to take out a few bad eggs in these societies if there's any chance that it's going to take the air out of the terrorist tires. Surgical incisions, that's what it's got to be. Not sending some goddam army in there to shoot up the place and guarantee enough recruits for al-Qaeda for another generation.

"So I may sound tough to you, Alex Anders. I may sound cynical, bitter and uncaring. But I tell you, I shiver in my boots when I think about what the other option is going to be if this Agency can't get out there and find these bastards—the key ones—and kill them, one by one, till there aren't enough volunteers to run their suicide missions anymore, till young volunteers figure it just isn't worth the game anymore. And yes, we grab their nukes so they stand there fucking naked and can't threaten anybody.

"You don't want to kill people? That's your call. But somebody's got to do it, and do it right and do it with precision, or it's going to be the goddam US army on steroids wasting them all. Is that what you want? Our troops with body armor and good old Fort Bragg sensitivity training? Joining hands with the born-again armchair strategists back home in touch with God? And national leaders grooving on America's sacred mission? With a finger on the button, ready to nuke a Muslim for Jesus? Or some crazy Congressman who wants to nuke the whole fucking Muslim world to make the world a better place for Christianity? How do you like that option, Mr. Anders? Huh? Does that make your skin crawl a bit more? If you, who know the area, know the people, know the problem, know the culture—if you're not the one to make the hard choices, pull the trigger when needed in hard-core cases, then who is it going be, huh? You decide. ...."

Ryan stopped, drained. It was more sustained emotion than he had ever displayed in the interrogation. He had taken his gloves off for the first time in speaking beyond the particulars to offer his personal views of the Alex and the world. He stared hard at Alex. "Now, do you have anything to say for yourself?"

Alex looked him in the eye for some seconds. "Patrick, clearly you have enjoyed your rant at me. And you know what? I don't disagree with a lot of what you say—especially why serious trained professionals should handle security questions rather than the military. But it goes deeper. You also speak the language of power—national power. A vision of suspicion, enemies and eternal vigilance. It's people like you that keep this dinosaur of a system going. With that kind of dog-eat-dog defensive mentality the world would never have learned a thing over the last ten thousand years—no aspiration for a better world, greater rule of law, or respect for anything that is different than us. You and I have really have nothing to say to each other. And no, I don't have one thing more to say that I haven't already said—many times over, to many people."

Ryan's face hardened. "Well, goddam it, I'll be glad to have you out of my sight. I hope they throw the fucking book at you."

*　　　　　　　*　　　　　　　*

Life in the Embassy had changed very little. Embassy staffers had learned that Alex Anders had suffered a nervous breakdown from overwork and tension following his wife's death and had left the country for indefinite recuperation. With Alex's departure Kevin appointed Moe to be the resident Pakistan expert in the Station. Only two people in the Station knew the truth: the COS and his deputy. Because of the gravity of the incident, the Embassy security officer was briefed in general terms about the compromise of unspecified classified information.

Hqs instructed that Ambassador Spaulding be fully briefed on the event. He listened in grim silence to the COS' briefing. He asked no questions. At the end he stood up and walked over to the windows and looked out over the hills in silence for a few moments. He then turned. "Morris, this is a most unfortunate—even tragic—incident. I've known Alex Anders as long as he has been at this Station. I want to tell you I think he is one of the most brilliant officers I have ever seen in this Embassy. We were lucky to have him. I immensely benefited from his knowledge, his insights, and, yes, his unflinching intellectual honesty.

"I'll just say one thing inside the confines of this office. There is no way I can condone what he did. No doubt serious damage has been done to our intelligence interests. But I want nonetheless to state my admiration for him as a brave and principled American. Frankly, things have come to a pretty pass in our government when we find distinguished officers like Alex driven to such pain and distraction as a result of watching the mess our policies are producing. There are deep disconnects here between what is going on and how things are perceived at home. Drone policies are a mess, deeply complex, and skating on the thinnest of moral, legal and practical ice. This incident reflects on all of us. We need more voices of conscience, not fewer, in our system. It shouldn't have had to come to this. When you have an opportunity please forward to him my warmest personal regards and best wishes." Morris left the Ambassador's office taken aback and in deep discomfiture. He did not pass along the Ambassador's comments to anyone else.

Majeed of course had received no word from Alex since the night he had introduced Alex to the ISI general. He began to make a few discreet inquiries at the US Embassy via channels there, only to hear of Alex's breakdown and departure for a long rest. Majeed knew enough to realize that that was not the real story. And then ISI received an intelligence report that Alex was in US custody in a brig in Rawalpindi undergoing interrogation.

Majeed was smitten by the news. This was yet one more event in the tangled, warm, harsh, brotherly, competitive, intensely personal, sometimes brutal, relationship he had maintained with Alex; their professional obligations had cruelly imposed searing events upon each other and both had suffered. Both had lost dear ones as victims to the broader struggle within the country. And the conditions that brought this vicious struggle about had not changed.

Majeed did not know what to do. There was no one he could call who could tell him the full story. There was no way he could reach, much less help, Alex. He did not even know how long Alex would remain in Pakistan. *Alex, Alex, didn't we know something like this was bound to happen when you brought me that incendiary information that night? You took yet one more step that involved many more victims, including yourself. You identified two people who were betraying our country. And whether you wished to or not, you helped condemn them to death for their sins. And now you could face the same.* He could not keep such an event to himself; he soon spilled out at least some of the story to Zubayda who broke down into tears. "Harley, Salman, Isabel, Alex, Rodrigo—where does this all end?"

Majeed nodded. "And that's just within our two families."

*   *   *

With the interrogation over, Alex sat for six more weeks in his cell, time on his hands, time for reflection. He had one hour a day outside his prison room to pace the walled-in yard like some kind of tiger looking longingly up at the hills in the distance, a Pakistan that was no longer in reach. In his mind, he kept reviewing the details of the interminable interrogation. And he still was burning at the condescending and offensive personal remarks Ryan had leveled at him at his departure; he ran endless possible speeches of refutation through his mind. Like Ryan's revealing remark about "Most of our agents speak English anyway." Ryan of course didn't speak a foreign language himself, except "enough to get around in Germany and Vietnam." But it was about something vastly more important than mere communication. One language was not as good as another. Languages weren't neutral vehicles. It was about the mental change of gears that language learning inevitably entailed. *It meant you chose to cross over the bridge to the person on the other side, not wait for them to come to you. Yes, everything Ryan had said was just a brilliant rationalization of the status quo—defense of an unchanging world that would never get any better as long as that kind of mentality prevailed.*

Sometimes Alex would wake up in his cell and smell the night air, still unmistakably Pakistani with its whiff of acrid burning in the countryside, the smell of curry from nearby tenements in the breeze, the honking of horns, the distant passing of busses blaring their Bollywood music to the world, the cries of street vendors afar. Yet at other moments in the night Alex's confidence would sag and he would lacerate himself: maybe Ryan had nailed him exactly for who he was. There were two distinct worlds here. In Ryan's world, inside the bubble of his organizational and professional perspective, he had indeed described Alex precisely. But in Alex's own world he was not who Ryan said he was. Alex still had the strength of his own convictions, the ability and necessity to see beyond the daily strife, to perceive a grander, dismaying, dysfunctional reality. But whatever Alex might think of himself, the bottom line was that the world he lived in was irrevocably Ryan's world; he could not change that. He would always have to pay at least lip-service to it. Ryan could not and never would live in Alex's world. He could not even rationally conceive of it, except as a twisted perversion. Nor would he ever move the US one inch towards policy enlightenment.

They brought him some books, the US press, all short on information about current events in Pakistan. He had plenty of time to reflect—and sweat—about his future.

Then, after nearly two months more of deliberation and angry debate back home, Washington reached a decision. A high-ranking ops officer was selected to come out to Islamabad to deal with the case; this time, to Alex's delight, it was his old mentor and long-time South Asian hand Sawyer Brummel. With the investigation and interrogation over, Sawyer's close personal ties to Alex were seen as a plus in helping move the case towards some kind of workable resolution.

Sawyer knew the terrain well; legendary as a seasoned field officer—"they don't make them that way anymore"—he was now a top operations officer in the Agency. After arriving in Islamabad and consulting with the Station, Sawyer was driven out in a military jeep to the isolated US military prison compound in Rawalpindi that was used as a holding pen for select, important, but non-violent non-threatening prisoners undergoing interrogation. The newness of the facility was captured in its starkness; it did not even have the softening affect of old growth trees around it that characterized so much of the landscape of Pindi. The sky was gray, diminishing somewhat the intensity of the heat of the day, a climate well familiar to Sawyer. The chain-link gates swung open and the US guard snapped a salute to the military driver after seeing their papers. They drove on in towards a large one-story building whose entrance was protected by two more armed Marine guards. Sawyer entered the building alone, showed his pass, and asked to be escorted to Alex's cell. Instead he was taken far down the hall to a windowless room with some basic furniture, table, chairs, kitchenette and bathroom. After taking a seat, Sawyer waited for Alex to be brought in. After some minutes he wondered if there were any problems. Then he heard footsteps and Alex walked into the room, accompanied by two armed guards. His face immediately registered utter delight at seeing Sawyer—the warmest moment Alex had experienced in a year. Sawyer rose, and Alex moved to hug him, but a guard restrained him momentarily. Surprisingly, Alex was not handcuffed. He was clearly under the control of the guards but he was not treated with any perceptible roughness or hostility.

Sawyer shook Alex's hand warmly as befitted an old friend. "It's really good to see you again, Alex… although I must admit I am pained that these should be the circumstances." Alex then hugged Sawyer emotionally and wiped away tears from his eyes. Sawyer smiled at him sympathetically. "We've got a lot to talk about, Alex. And I'm happy to say I have the authority to change the venue of our talks. I have asked permission to take you out of here and go somewhere where we can speak freely and at length for a day or two. Nobody is afraid that you are going to bolt for the hills. I was thinking we could go up to Murree for a day or two where we can walk and talk and be alone. Besides, it would be nice to escape the heat down here in Pindi. OK with you?"

Alex was still overwhelmed with emotion. Sawyer had been nearly a father figure to him, and he understood Alex well. And he was the first sympathetic person to talk to him in six months. "Do you have any word on how the case is going to be handled?" Alex asked. Sawyer raised his hand, averting the question. "There's a lot of ground to be covered before we get to that." As Alex left the facility, taking only an overnight bag and accompanied now only by Sawyer, he felt buoyed, as if taking his first breath in months. The gates opened and allowed the two of them in Sawyer's car to emerge into the outside world. Alex felt he was emerging not just from prison, but from the tortured labyrinth of his own mind. Looking at the familiar Pakistani scene around him he felt like a blind man who could now see—at least with his one good eye.

On the drive up to Murree, Sawyer asked Alex about his family, catching up on the past. "I trust your son is alright?"

"Rodrigo's with Isabel's family in Santiago. I'm very worried about him, and have almost no news from there, about how he is. Of course he was terribly shocked by what happened to his mother." Alex teared up again. "And I have heard very little about him from my in-laws there; they of course know nothing of my situation. I just don't know what is going to happen to him—and so much depends on how my situation comes out."

They wound up into the green hill station and arrived in Murree in the middle of the afternoon. Sawyer swung off quickly to the Cecil Hotel, a magnificent old institution from Raj days when half of the British in the Rawalpindi Cantonment took refuge in the forested highlands for summer relief. "I haven't been here for how many years, maybe ten?" Sawyer mused. "This place is probably less comfortable, less 'mod cons' as the British say, than many of the newer places, but to me it still reeks of the Raj and my own early days of skullduggery in Pakistan. Besides, the gardens and walks are worth the price of admission alone. We can do a lot of walking. I'm sure you haven't been doing much of that."

They strolled around the expansive gardens admiring the views below and then sat down at a table with white tablecloth under the trees and ordered two cooling fruit-yoghurt *lassis*. With Sawyer Alex felt completely at ease for the first time in a long time; he represented the first person he did not have to be on guard against. But Sawyer had so far said nothing about the circumstances of his case. The longer the time Sawyer took to get to the heart of the matter, the more nervous Alex became.

"It's nice to be back," Sawyer noted. "I haven't had good *lassi* like this for a long time. The ones at McDonald's don't quite do it." He quietly surveyed the scene as Alex remained silent, waiting for the opening. Sawyer finally turned to him. "Look, Alex, I hardly need tell you, you are in a shitload of trouble. This is a very grave matter. The question now is, how are we going to get you out of this?"

"I know it's bad. I'm making no excuses. I did what I believed I had to do."

"What you have done can essentially be considered treason. I'm sure you realize that?"

"Yes. I suppose you can call it treason… from one point of view."

"One point of view! For crissakes, Alex, what other point of view is there when you pass highly classified information along to a foreign power with the deliberate intention of burning the agents involved, leading to their arrest and probable execution? Destroying the most important intel asset our government has in the country? When you deliberately sabotage high-level decisions taken by the top levels of our government in the prosecution of this war? What do you call that, 'creative dissent'?"

Alex initially cringed at these words coming out of his mentor's mouth. "Sawyer, no. But I acted out of the conviction that this war in Afghanistan is wrong, US policies are wrong—and they're dangerous. Plans to seize the nukes are insane. And although it might sound quaint, I think these policies are immoral as well. How many people have died, civilians? Hundreds of thousands on both sides of the borders. And to top it all, the policies are failing."

"That's as may be, but it's not your call. I'm going to tell it to you straight, Alex. You know perfectly well these are not our decisions to make. Whatever feelings we have, we've got to defer to the Director of Central Intelligence and the President. They alone possess the authority to make these decisions."

"So we should all be good Germans, then."

"Goddam it, Alex, don't give me that self-serving smug shit! I expected more out of you at this point! There's no comparison whatsoever. I'm here to try to help you. These are policies legally determined and vetted by a congressional oversight committee. We can't have every officer out here a little president or DCI on his own, passing judgments about what he will and won't do."

"Just how good do you think that congressional oversight is, Sawyer? It's a rubber stamp. The US press carries hardly any of the real details on the ground, of what's really going on."

Sawyer's face stiffened. "Get this straight, Alex Anders. I'm not here to argue with you about policy. Drop it! Neither of us are going to change that. I don't even know how changeable it is. I might even agree with you in a large number of respects—far more than you think. What we're here for is to discuss the consequences of your explicit violation of the law on secrecy and national security. Technically this is treason—an old-fashioned word, not invoked much any more, but no less meaningful for all that. Under certain circumstances it could even invoke the death penalty. I'm not saying it will here… but it's that serious."

Alex looked around him, the branches of the trees waving overhead, occasional shafts of sun rays shining down upon the table and the impeccably English tea service in front of them from an old imperial world long gone, even as a new form of one was coming into being. Yet he still could not quite believe he was out here, in the free air, sitting in a Pakistani hill station, with a trusted mentor. The world had moved on while he was incarcerated. He wasn't even sure where things stood anymore. He was silent.

"I want to get on with the real matter at hand, OK? Now, let's review the bidding. Here is where Washington is coming from at this point. From all the interrogation reports we believe you had no economic motive, no personal greed or personal interest behind what you did. You haven't been paid or received any benefits from any source to do what you did. Your polygraph indicates you have not been recruited by anyone, and that you are not serving as the agent of a foreign state or organization, although you stupidly and unnecessarily concealed your meeting with a Soviet—Russian—intel officer. So far so good. But the fact remains you have passed a foreign government, the Pakistanis, highly sensitive information that deliberately sabotaged high-level national operations."

Alex nodded.

"But we also have to take into account your own grievous personal loss of your wife so recently in all of this. That was no doubt a huge emotional body-blow—an act of terrorism against your own family. You have our condolences and our sympathy. We know how hard this can be. It can warp your judgment temporarily."

"Sawyer, that event may only have been the straw that broke the camel's back. My views have been building for a long time over this whole situation."

"Alex, will you let us fucking try to help you out here? Without demolishing virtually the sole argument in your defense—mental aberration? What you have done is unacceptable, damaging, illegal and criminal."

"I know."

"For what it's worth I'd have to admit that I share much of your basic assessment of the political situation. But I'm not ready to go public on that, at least at this point, much less act on it. But you, you stepped over a huge red line, a white-hot one—"

"Sawyer, I…"

Sawyer waved him to silence. "You crossed a powerful red line. Now look, most of us in this game, we're realists. Any intelligent observer of foreign policy knows that red lines are quite movable things. Public consensus shifts.

Rah-rah patriotism over a war at the beginning can quickly sag as realities come home. What I couldn't say about the war yesterday, I can maybe begin to say today, but only privately. Tomorrow maybe even say it publicly. Then the liberal press starts out airing unmentionable thoughts about the conflict, the unlikelihood of victory, even as the mainstream holds steady in its convictions in favor of the war in all its received wisdom. But over time more and more mainstream figures start to change their views, change sides, join the crowd. And suddenly it becomes a sensation when Senator X or Congressman Y or General Z start saying the same thing, something honest—that they think the war is a mistake. Now, what they say is hardly new or original. Indeed, they're latecomers. But the sensational news is that those figures, mainstream figures, finally come to acknowledge the very same thing, in public that many others of us have been saying for some time."

"Right, and that's why I'm saying these things now, regardless of when others are going to say them."

"Alex, look, the difference between treason or wisdom isn't so much a ringing matter of conscience and truth at all; it's often just a matter of timing. You have spoken out extremely prematurely—a sin, until others catch up to your judgment, which they probably will eventually—but even then, that's not what this is about. We're not here to discuss the timing of your views. Or even your views at all. This wasn't just about thoughts. You acted. You sabotaged, you betrayed agent confidences. Lives were lost."

"Goddam it, Sawyer, so were other lives, Pakistani lives, Afghan lives, even American lives. Those lives should matter at least a little."

"The US President is not constitutionally charged with protecting Afghan or Pak lives. You know that. He's charged with protecting American lives and welfare. That's not going to change."

"Yeah, but even American lives and the welfare of our nation do suffer from stupid policies. What in hell do we think 9/11 was all about in the minds of the perpetrators."

"Alex, for God's sake, let's stay on track. I'm here to try to fix one hell of a mess, and I'm not sure how. We need to keep these events outside the realm of criminal investigation, for everybody's sake."

Alex sobered. "Thanks, Sawyer. I know. I appreciate that."

"Now, lucky for you, a charge of treason is a tall order these days, a bit quaint, something of a dead letter in the law. But you could well qualify for prosecution on grounds of espionage or conspiracy. But either of those two charges require proof of longer-term and formal cooperation—recruitment—by the enemy as an agent to supply classified information. That doesn't seem to apply here. This is more a kind of one-time thing. It was voluntary. There was no personal gain. It would seem to be a kind of 'espionage in the third degree,' one might call it."

"Third degree?"

"Like third-degree murder, committed in a fit of anger or emotion due to specific situations. The fact that your wife was killed in a terrorist act aimed at you... No, wait a minute, I'm not done. A fair number of people in Hqs and the Justice Department believe you deserve something pretty harsh. Old Patrick Ryan really has it in for you, as you may have surmised."

"Yes, Patrick generously shared his opinion of me, in full, before he left."

"In any case some kind of punishment has to be served. The only question is what kind. And it's not just about you, or justice. We're also talking about the interests of the Agency and the US government. The last thing we need is to put you on trial in a case that embarrasses the Agency and the Embassy, our relations with Pakistan and with ISI, involving a sensitive US intelligence penetration of the Pak nuclear holy of holies. Sensational information of that sort could cause a violent reaction inside the country here. A trial would open doors to deep public scrutiny of US policy as part of your defense. Even a closed trial would leak. Nobody wants that. And even more so when an officer has had a pretty distinguished career of service like you have. Your opinions in a trial could be quite damaging."

Alex nodded, looking slightly heartened. "So where does that leave us then?"

"Bottom line, we want to try to settle all of this via administrative and not legal channels. Of course, you'll be immediately fired for cause. If we're lucky it will be categorized as exercise of extremely poor judgment, lack of professionalism, and gross negligence in the handling of classified material. We will make a plea that your thinking had been deranged by Isabel's murder."

"Thanks, Sawyer, but you and I know that it..."

"Do you want me to try to keep you out of a long prison term, or not? Have you even thought about your son? Stop this foolish posturing! Do you think you can make a more powerful statement by going to prison? And leaving your son forever in Chile? Face it Alex, your principled opposition to these wars, it won't even make the back page of *The Washington Post.*"

Alex heaved a sigh. "Yeah, OK, Rodrigo is probably the biggest reason why I am willing to go quietly on this."

"Even then, there will be some tough administrative penalties. You can probably guess. First, obviously your days as an Agency officer are over. Your employment was terminated upon your arrest. You're never going back into the Station or Hqs again."

"I figured as much."

"Second, your pension savings and all other benefits are gone, you lose all that has been accumulated over the years. Think of it as a huge fine. And third, you are disbarred from ever getting clearance again for any US government job."

Alex swallowed. "Yes, I understand that."

"You accept?"

"Yes, I accept."

"Good, now, let's take a walk and enjoy the setting." They wandered through the gardens and out into the wooded trails with views out over the countryside below. For Alex it was almost surreal that Sawyer at this point showed intense interest in learning the details about the latest overall political situation in Pakistan, and in soliciting Alex's opinions. Indeed, Sawyer did seem to share most of Alex's assessment of the way things were going in both Afghanistan and Pakistan. Even more importantly, he acknowledged that a small but significant group held these views privately back in the Agency, a group that was always seeking small openings to promote these thoughts with policy makers whenever possible.

"We're paid to deliver intelligence assessments. And they can be as bleak as we want—as long as they are based on evidence. Solid, reliable evidence."

"I know that, that's why I've been so upset at watching this parade of know-nothings from Washington filing into the Embassy here trying to get us to make a lousy case or run a stupid operation they had already decided on."

"You're right, that's a bad scene. But we have to resist those pressures. That's how the Agency gets its tit in the wringer every time—when some ambitious Director decides to exploit his access to the President to make policy suggestions, especially when they turn out wrong. Then he's just joined the crowd of failures."

They spent the night in the Cecil, its cavernous wood paneled rooms unchanged since the days of the British Raj. Sawyer felt back in his element. "Damn it, Alex, I do love this country. But it has really fucked itself up, and with a whole lot of help from us…"

Alex spent a restless night in his oak-paneled quarters with its huge high ceilings, the closest thing to air-conditioning from a British century ago. The ghosts of the room were still there. He was just the latest Westerner naively exercising a kind of troubled colonial power in these lands. This building, this compound, this hill station had probably witnessed similar debates over failing policy and morality and pointless deaths going back a long way. And then relief, huge relief surged over him—that he would not be sitting in a prison for the rest of his life. That he would soon be free to leave, to be with his son, pick up the pieces. That mattered a lot.

The next morning as they sat down, Sawyer looked dubiously upon a colonial breakfast of cold overcooked eggs, cold toast sitting in wire racks, bready sausages, lumpy porridge. "I've got to hand it to these cooks. The Raj tradition of British cooking is still alive, more British than the Brits, lovingly preserving the finest details of terrible British breakfasts. All things equal I'd have rather had the Pakistani breakfast. I'd love an *idli*, but at a place like this they'd rather die than serve a native dish. Go figure."

"I must say I'm really happy with any breakfast that isn't courtesy of the Rawalpindi brig. I'm enjoying myself out on my little liberty. And it's thanks to you, Sawyer. You've done a lot for me. I haven't really changed my mind about things, but I do see it in bigger perspective. I mainly want to put all this past me, get on with my life. You have helped hugely to make that possible. Let someone else carry on the struggle."

"Someone else will undoubtedly carry on the struggle. Because you are right in what you perceive about all this madness. But dammit Alex, *you're* the one who's created trouble for yourself—by essentially buying into this stuff about 'American exceptionalism'—that doctrine you keep attacking. *You're* the one that thinks America should live up to its great values, that it's so exceptional it shouldn't screw up, can't be wrong. Why not? Why shouldn't we fuck up? Are we better than anybody else that we're immune to fucking things up?"

"Yeah, but I do believe there were exceptional values behind the vision of our country. I felt that even as I grew up here in Pakistan. My parents kept telling me about them. I felt them when I was in college, reading American history. We have to have some ideals, not just be a bunch of cynics."

"Ahh, my lad, sadly, high vision brings high disillusionment—I see that in you."

"You know what makes me feel really badly? I've damaged the Agency in particular, its own proper intel-gathering function. In the end, somehow it isn't even the Agency I feel disillusioned by. I can put up with the small compromises with truth and transparency, that's part of our work—the cover stories, the illegal operations of espionage. No, it's the big show—the whole US government and all its hangers-on, mercenary bottom-feeders, consultants and all—all off on this crazy binge."

Sawyer nodded as he contemplated the oil still exuding from his cold egg. "You know, Alex, what our tragedy is? That our great power has magnified all our bad qualities. We're so damn powerful that no one can really check us or stop us any more, make us pause for thought. Or protect us from our worst instincts. You know those elephants you see at work around the subcontinent here? We're like an elephant. We do what we want, and no other creature dares get in our way. But now that we've gotten to be the world's sole superpower for a decade or two, it's clear that we can be just as bad and stupid as the rest of them. And yes, you're right, our power has even corrupted the intelligence process. That's our only contact with reality. And that is everything that you and I signed up for."

"And so we should just give up the struggle? Nothing is ever going to change?"

"Ah, actually it *is* changing, whether we like it or not. Already. Look around. We're losing our position as number one, we're all beginning to see that now. We don't have the power to do whatever we want anymore, to call the shots. Other countries don't listen to us as much anymore, they go their own way. And we can't afford these wars anymore, while other countries are gaining in strength, China owns our economy and we're going to have to share the world a bit more, like it or not. And I hate to say it—and I hope the walls don't have ears here—but I'm glad."

"You? Glad?"

"Yah. Think about it. We supposedly believe in separation of powers in our own government. And Microsoft may be a great company but no one wants it to have a monopoly of power in the IT market. Monopoly of power isn't healthy anywhere, you need checks and balances, even in the international system. That's where our world is headed now. It may be painful for us, but in the end it's good, even for us. Share the damn burden. That's why I'm upbeat in the middle of all these goddam foreign policy disasters." Sawyer rolled his napkin up into the napkin ring and pushed back his chair. "OK now, Alex, speech over, back to the real world. We need to get some papers signed, get you packed and onto a plane and back to your son."

Alex thought for a moment. "Thanks, Sawyer, I hadn't thought about it quite that way before. I suppose there is some kind of message of optimism, in what has seemed to me to be a pretty dark American voyage. God knows I want to be back with Rodriguito—before they turn him into some damn llama-herder in the Andes."

And so, in a sober mood, after getting back to the facility in Rawalpindi, Alex was officially released from detention. Sawyer stood by with the paperwork. Alex was ordered to sign papers, acknowledging his permanent dismissal from the Agency, loss of pension and all benefits and governmental security clearances, vowing to sever any and all contacts with Pakistani government officials and to leave the country forthwith, at his own expense, and accepting all the other conditions of his terminated employment. His long saga was coming to a close. He realized how very, very lucky he was.

*   *   *

Alex's absence from the Embassy was barely noted any more. The story about his nervous breakdown seemed eminently plausible to all but to the tiny handful of people who knew. The prohibition of any further contact by Alex with Pakistani authorities made impossible any final meeting with Majeed and his family. He nonetheless penned a letter that he would mail from outside the country.

Dear Majeed,

I assume you have learned by now that the last six months have been very difficult for me. Not surprisingly, people were extremely displeased by my actions and I will no longer be working for the government any longer. I regret too that I have had to leave Pakistan on very short notice. As much as I wanted to say farewell to you, to Akmal, to Aysha and to Zubayda and your children—none of that will be possible under the circumstances.

You know that you have been like a brother to me over many long years. Your fate and mine have been intimately connected as we have shared so many incidents—painful and tragic as well as joyous ones—in Pakistan. This country is a part of me. I believe I understand it. But these are not useful attributes for foreign officials. The tension between who I am and what I know on the one hand, and the need for professional "objectivity" has been too much. You may be in the same dilemma. But we both know each other's views on all this already. We have both been toiling in our own garden, while well aware there are other gardens around as well.

I am leaving for Chile to be with Rodrigo for the next few months. I would like to come back to Pakistan at some point down the road however, especially to see you and your family. I would very much like to see Zubayda. She has been on my mind constantly as I think about her wonderful qualities, her many benevolent activities, and her cruel experience in the Frontier. She is a remarkable, brave, intelligent and caring woman. You know that Isabel was very fond of her. I can remember back to the time she treated me as a little brother. So would you tell her that I would like to write to her if she will grant me permission to do so?

You should know that I am thinking about a new career—something that poor Isabel had always urged me to do. Perhaps journalism in South Asia would be close to my heart— this beautiful, sad, haunted and tortured region that is in my blood.

Please look out for yourself, try to survive the challenges thrown at you every day by these terrible conditions… and try not to upset the US Embassy too much, it's not healthy. My salaams to everyone.

Your close friend,

Alex

*　　　　　　　　　*　　　　　　　　　*

The plane lifted off, leaving behind the green oasis of Islamabad contending with a massive browns of the encroaching Pakistani landscape. A wave of alternative emotions swept over him—an indescribable mixture of relief, sadness, exhilaration, ruefulness, anger, bitterness, and hope. His ordeal of the last year, of the last six months, had been overwhelming; it might require a lifetime for his psyche to absorb and process it in all its complexities.

Looking out the plane window, he began to look back, way back, almost as if upon a previous life. What might he have changed? Certainly not the big things. Not the power and unstoppable trajectory of Washington—deeply mired in the physics of imperial momentum. Not the durable emotional stubbornness of Pakistan, its endless existential fears, divisions, its flirtation and fascination with unbounded religious fanaticism and its tortured geopolitical calculations. All of which had been made worse by the outside world. Nor could he change the broader international order in its surly yielding to US *force majeure*. Nor the psychology of armies, or tribes, or the calculus of honor, arrogance, or dignity. He couldn't change the narrowness of vision, or ignorance of foreign realities that afflicted most states.

But in his own personal life, might he have done things differently? *Did I have to have fought the system—at this huge personal cost to myself and those I loved— Isabel, Rodrigo—even Doña Maria and Don Jorge? Was it my own personal arrogance that brought me to this, the sense that I saw the need for higher values when those around me did not? Should I have resisted, fought back? Did I need to have broken the law myself, personally, even if sovereign states break the law as a way of life? After all, I could have just quit, and be done with it.* These multiple decision points had formed the building blocks of his life—with unpredictable, even fateful consequences.

No, *bas*, that was enough. He could no longer stand it, constantly rerunning this game of what-might-have-been through his own mind. It was an exercise in futility. How much of who he was, what he was, what he did, came out of an accumulation of a lifetime of events, many totally beyond his control—a form of Karma? His boyhood in Pakistan, his parents' feckless mission, the fatal beating of his father at the end of it all, his own attraction to foreign cultures and a desire to welcome them into his life; his decision to join and remain associated with the Agency, an organization ostensibly dedicated to discerning overseas reality, regardless of the unpalatability of its message to power. Each one of these events or decisions continued to make great sense to him, even in retrospect. His life in a sense, had been "written" from far, far back.

Many long hours and airports later, after fitful but restorative sleep, Alex finally found himself peering out over the Andes once again in the approach over Chilean territory into Santiago—one of the many fateful way stations he had traversed in his life. This was where the complex professional web of compromise had started to be spun, where he had met Isabel and where his personal life began to rub up against the realities of his professional life. Now he was back yet again, having left Isabel's very life behind in Pakistan, to where he had insisted on taking her—*my unintentional cherished offering to the country of my own childhood. Doña Maria could never grasp the disconnect between her prejudices and my real life and final decisions.*

As he came out of the customs area in Santiago, Rodriguito spotted him first. "Daddy!" He came rushing forward. "You've come home!" *Home?* As he swept Rodriguito up in his arms he knew he would be mulling over the meaning of that cry for some time to come. There would be some painful words with Doña Maria and Don Jorge as he negotiated Rodrigo's eventual departure with him from Chile over the next month.

As he sat under a tree on a hill in Santiago the next day looking out over the distant Andes with Rodriguito at his side he knew he had no choice. He would come to terms with a drastically scaled-down vision of what he wanted or hoped for out of his country—with a diminished but no less real affection and awe for its own spectacular national version of both greatness of spirit, immensity of folly, and implacability of drive. Now slowly being reduced, it seemed, to a story more appropriately brought to us on the big screen in Hollywood.

Maybe there was a more comforting and forgiving thought here: maybe it was wrong to think of America especially as posing an exceptional problem, or as exceptionally erroneous in its actions. Maybe in witnessing the follies he had observed in his life he was only a witness to just one narrow and specific chapter of the collective human condition in general. This was what happened with great power. Yes, overwhelming power dressed up in the particular vestitures of one particular dominant country and culture in each era. Different peoples were imperial in their own different ways. Maybe some better at it than others. "Better" in that maybe they killed less people, or had left behind something of greater value, despite the damage inflicted upon their colonial subjects. Some empires clearly had been worse than others. What mattered, though, was that his saga had been *his* reality, here and now. He could not react against the collective human condition, only the specific. And that was why he had acted in the way he felt he must at a specific time and in a specific place—his unique moment of destiny.

"Daddy, *abuelita* says that I'm Chilean, not American. Is that true?"

"No, Rodriguito. You are partly Chilean, because your dear mother was. But you are also American, because of me."

"But you were born in Pakistan. Are you really American?"

"Yes, Rodriguito, I really am. And you are too."

Acknowledgments and Thanks

This novel is not autobiographical; it is entirely a work of fiction. All its characters are fictional and are not meant to represent anyone. Kissinger, Zia ul-Haq, Allende and Pinochet are the only real statesmen referred to. Many of the background events and attitudes do, however, reflect substantial elements of US, Chilean, Pakistani and Afghan political and cultural realities.

I owe a special debt of thanks for their particularly close reads, detailed textual comments and valuable criticism of the manuscript to George Fowler, Meredith Fuller, and Faith Fuller.

Further notable thanks for their comments and ideas on the book: Mark Perry, Richard Sale, Russell Brant, Jim Haefele, Kenneth Dekleva, Kay Thompson, Larry Thompson, Nadeem Kazmi, VG Fuller, and Gordon Smith.

In gratitude for their kind words of praise for the book: Mark Perry, Milt Bearden and Anatol Lieven.

And in appreciation to Margreet Dietz who edited the manuscript, made important substantive recommendations in the process, and who formatted the book and cover for publication.

I'm grateful to so many others as well for their thoughts, support and encouragement over the course of this adventure in writing my first novel.

And I am personally grateful for the time I have been able to spend in association with so many different aspects of the people and cultures of Afghanistan and Pakistan—two countries whom modern history has dealt particularly difficult hands, who deserve better, and who possess the spirit to rise again to the occasion.

Made in the USA
Middletown, DE
11 January 2016